Looking Forward

and

Second
Time Around

Marcia Willett

headline

LOOKING FORWARD first published in Great Britain in 1998
by HEADLINE BOOK PUBLISHING

SECOND TIME AROUND first published in Great Britain in 1997
by HEADLINE BOOK PUBLISHING

First published in this omnibus edition in 2005
by HEADLINE BOOK PUBLISHING

A HEADLINE paperback

10 9 8 7 6 5 4 3 2 1

ISBN 0 7553 2665 2

Typeset in Times by Avon DataSet Ltd,
Bidford-on-Avon, Warwickshire

Printed and bound in Great Britain by
Clays Ltd, St Ives plc

Headline's policy is to use papers that are natural, renewable and
recyclable products and made from wood grown in sustainable
forests. The logging and manufacturing processes are expected to
conform to the environmental regulations of the country of origin.

HEADLINE BOOK PUBLISHING
A division of Hodder Headline
338 Euston Road
London NW1 3BH

www.headline.co.uk
www.hodderheadline.com

Looking Forward

The Chadwick Family Chronicles
The Early Years

To John and Grace
and the members of the
Avonwick branch of the
Mothers' Union

THE CHADWICK FAMILY

Edward Chadwick (1788-1881)
married 1847
Elizabeth Courtney (1826-1887)

Four other children

James Chadwick (1848-1916)
married 1886
Charlotte Bridges (1867-1897)

Theodore (1897-)
Theo

Bertram Chadwick (1891-1916)
married 1914
Frederica Stanbury (1894-)
Freddy

Three children
died in infancy

John (1916-1945)
married 1943
Prudence Clarke (1923-)
Prue

Peter Chadwick (1916-1957)
married 1940
Alison Pickford (1918-1957)

Henry (1943-)
Hal

Katharine (1943-)
Kit

James (1944-1957)

Felicia (1946-)
Fliss

Sam (1952-)
Mole

Susanna (1955-)
Sooz

Book One
Summer 1957

———

Chapter One

The three children stood together, waiting. Other passengers had disappeared homeward and the tiny branch-line station drowsed peacefully in the June sunshine; the big bright faces of the hollyhocks nodding against the tarred fence; roses and honeysuckle growing together in a scented tangle by the booking office; milk churns waiting for collection. The station master leaned from his door at full stretch, the telephone receiver still in his hand, watching the small group. The eldest, a girl of ten, was clearly exhausted, her pale pointed face pinched with silent endurance. She was skinny, her gingham dress was creased and limp, and damp wisps escaped from the two plaits of thick fair hair. Her grey eyes were fixed with desperate intensity on the station master as he waved his free hand at her cheerfully. His cap, pushed far to the back of his head, looked as if it might tumble off at any moment.

'Left 'arf'n'ower ago,' he shouted encouragingly. 'Trouble with the car, I shouldn't wonder.'

The girl swallowed audibly, her arm tightening around the boy who was holding a fold of her skirt, and nodded back at the station master, who disappeared

3

inside his office. His voice could be heard, discreetly lowered, talking volubly. The boy looked up at his sister and she smiled at him, loosening her hold on him a little.

'Grandmother will be here soon,' she told him. 'You heard, didn't you, Mole? You heard what he said? "Trouble with the car." She'll be here any minute.'

The boy stared toward the entrance. His grubby Aertex shirt had worked loose from the grey flannel shorts and his eyes were frightened. She bent to him again, guessing his thoughts.

'Only trouble with the car,' she repeated. 'Not . . . Only trouble. Like a puncture. Nothing else, Mole. Truly.'

The small girl, who had been clinging to her other hand, let go suddenly and subsided on to the platform. She lay down amongst the luggage and crooned to herself, holding her dolly high above her as though offering it towards the swallows that dived and wheeled in the blue air.

'Oh, Susanna,' sighed her sister helplessly. 'You'll get filthy.'

She wiped her freed sticky hand on her skirt and looked about her. Near the office the porter was checking over some parcels piled on a trolley. She watched him as he whistled quietly to himself, turning the labels with stubby fingers. Pasted on the wall above his head the Ovaltine girl smiled eternally, clasping her golden sheaves of corn, swinging her basket with its tin of Ovaltine which repeated the picture, so that her smile grew smaller and smaller . . . A car was approaching, chugging over the level crossing and round the corner, and the station master was hurrying out, craning to see who was arriving. His cry of greeting was so full of relief that the girl instinctively began mustering her small group.

'Get up, Sooz. Get up! Quick. Grandmother's here. Come on, Mole. Take hold of this. Get *up*, Susanna!'

The sound of the voice, which had been talking breathlessly outside, was coming closer and the three children, clinging together, stared at the elderly woman who hurried out on to the platform and stopped short with an involuntary gesture of compassion and grief. Freddy Chadwick looked at her three grandchildren and her throat constricted.

'My darlings,' she said. 'Forgive me. The stupid woman was supposed to make sure you stayed put at Totnes, not send you on to Staverton. And then I was driving too fast and went into the ditch. Muddles all round. And at such a time. Forgive me.'

She had driven like a maniac through the deep narrow lanes; the tall grasses and the white flowers of the umbellifer brushing the car's sides and dislodging bees, which fell in through her open window. She brushed them aside distractedly. All the grief and horror of the last few days had been finally concentrated into this one vital intention: that she must be there to meet the train. The family had been united in agreeing that it would be better to collect the children from the station and take them straight home to The Keep. This meeting must surely be fraught with emotion; therefore the shorter the time spent publicly together, before all four of them could relax privately, so much the better. Freddy felt that this was right but feared that to put off her responsibility, even for a matter of a few hours, must be a cowardly decision. Yet the thought of attempting to deal with three shocked, frightened children on a long train journey was a horrifying one. How could they postpone their shared grief for so extended a period? Yet how could she possibly consider the prospect of displaying their vulnerability to the curious gaze of strangers? Everything had happened so quickly. The children, dazed by the abrupt dislocation of their lives, were bearing up – but it was expected that they would break down once they were united with their grandmother. Racked with indecision Freddy had allowed herself to be persuaded that this meeting should be postponed but she was determined to be there waiting for them at the station, to hurry them home to safety. She had not allowed for a last-minute confusion in London. The children's adult companion had been suddenly taken ill, and a well-meaning passenger, travelling down to Plymouth, recruited in her stead at the last moment.

Her thoughts hurrying ahead of her, Freddy had taken a bend too fast, lost control of the car, and put the two nearside wheels into the ditch. Almost weeping with frustration, glancing continually at her wristwatch, she had tried to back the car on to the lane. It was a farmer and his wife, driving home from Newton Abbot market, who finally rescued her but, when she arrived at Totnes, she discovered that her children had been sent on the branch line to Staverton. The woman in charge of them had consulted with the station master, who was convinced that there was some mistake. Mrs Chadwick, he told her, always travelled to and from Staverton, changing at Totnes, and was probably waiting there now. The children were hurried on to the train, which was just leaving, and the guard told to put them off at Staverton station. Freddy was both furious and anxious.

'I should have gone to London to meet them,' she told herself over and over as she fled back towards Staverton. 'I knew I should. I shouldn't have risked it.'

At least her anxiety briefly blotted out the continual inward vision of her beloved son, with his wife and eldest boy, murdered by Mau Mau. The shocking news had been too terrible to take in at first; too terrible to comprehend. Now her husband and both her twin boys were dead; all victims of war and violence. Darling Bertie, returning to the war in 1916 after a brief respite at home, had died at Jutland a few days later; their son – dear, kind, amusing John – torpedoed on a convoy in the second war; and now Peter – restless, charming, clever Peter – attacked and murdered. If only he had been content to settle down after the war; taken an interest in the china clay business which had supported the family for over a hundred years . . .

Freddy groaned aloud as she drove the car onwards, thinking of the three bewildered children waiting at Staverton. She had never seen the twenty-two-month-old Susanna, who had been born in Kenya, and Sam – whom the family had named Mole because of his propensity to crawl and hide under rugs, chairs, tables – had been barely a year old when Peter and Alison had left England. Felicia, usually called Fliss, had been a quiet child of seven, deeply attached to her elder brother, Jamie . . .

Freddy wrenched the wheel violently as a tractor

lumbered out of a field gateway ahead of her and, trembling a little, she pulled in at the side of the lane for a moment to blow her nose and calm herself. Jamie had been tall and blond, just like Peter; outgoing, capable, loving. He had been sent back to school in England but, although he spent most half terms and exeats at The Keep with his grandmother, for this fateful half term he had flown back to Kenya. He should have been at school in England, but having been in contact with a friend with measles had to remain at home until the quarantine period was over. Darling Jamie, how joyfully he had written to tell her the good news that he was able to stay at home for an extra three weeks. Now he was dead; buried with his parents in the African earth . . .

Briefly, Freddy dropped her head in her hands. How was she to manage her own grief and loss whilst sustaining these children? At the thought of them she set the car in motion and plunged on. She jolted over the bridge which spanned the river, over the level crossing and, turning left, she parked hastily beside the gate and hurried on to the platform.

They stood together in a pool of sunlight. Fliss kept her arm protectively around Mole, whilst Susanna stared with round brown eyes at this tall old woman who seemed strangely familiar. After those first few words of explanation there was a moment of silence.

Freddy thought: How can I? How can I possibly deal with these three children? Self-pity and terror and love strove together in her breast. I can't! she cried silently. I am too *old*.

Fliss thought: She looks like Daddy. I mustn't cry.

How shall I tell her about Mole?

Mole thought: She is *safe*.

Susanna gazed up at the tall figure, her doll clutched to the smocking on her chest. She was conscious of a connection, of a sensation of security.

'Hello, Grandmother,' said Fliss wearily but politely. 'This is Susanna. I expect you remember Mole.'

'He has grown a good deal since I last saw him.' The child's courage had the effect of reactivating Freddy's own confidence. 'And so have you. So this is Susanna.'

'She's very tired,' warned Fliss as Freddy lifted Susanna into her arms. 'We all are . . .'

Her voice faltered and she bent to pick up a small bag, which she handed to Mole. Freddy saw that, though he took it obediently, he did not release his hold on his sister's skirt. He was watching Freddy warily, hopefully . . .

Freddy settled the unprotesting Susanna comfortably on her arm and picked up the larger case. 'Come,' she said gently. 'Let's go home to tea.'

In the early 1840s, Edward Chadwick returned to England having spent a quarter of a century generating a considerable fortune in the Far East. It took him barely a week to realise that he had little in common with London society and that an inactive life would see him into an early grave. Following a consultation with his banker, Hoare, he investigated a number of possible investments and determined on one: to become a major shareholder and director in a company being formed to acquire a large tract of land in

Devon from which to extract the china clay which lay below the surface.

Once this decision was taken, his next step was to find a house that suited his sense of importance whilst appealing to his romantic core. He was unsuccessful. He did, however, find and purchase the ruins of an old hill fort between the moors and the sea and, by using the stones still lying about the site, he had built a castellated tower of three storeys which he named The Keep.

Soon he was able to convince himself that he lived in a property of ancient lineage. He used his wealth – and considerable charm – to buy himself a well-born wife, half his age, but his formidable energies were, in the main, channelled into ensuring the success of the china clay workings so that, before his death, his fortune had doubled and redoubled.

His male descendants, whilst maintaining a presence in the company, had made careers within the Royal Navy – but they continued to preserve and modernise The Keep. It was odd but quite delightful. The wings, two storeys high and set back a little on each side of the original house, had been added by a later generation. High stone walls had been built to form a courtyard, which was entered from beneath the overarching roof which linked the two small cottages of the gatehouse. Old-fashioned roses and wisteria climbed the courtyard walls and the newer wings but the austere grey stone of the tower itself remained unadorned. The Keep and the courtyard faced south, whilst to the west stretched the garden, bounded by orchards. To the north and east, however, the ground fell sharply away; rough grassy slopes descending to the river which came tumbling down from the high moors. From bubbling issues the cold peaty waters raced through narrow rocky beds, down into the quiet, rich farmlands; moving more slowly then, the river surged onward into the broad reaches of the estuary where it mingled with the salt water of the sea.

Freddy drove into the courtyard, bumping across the granite paving stones and carefully skirting the central square of grass. She backed the Morris Oxford into the garage, which was built into the gatehouse, and climbed out. The three children sat together in the back, refusing – even for this short journey – to be separated, and she opened the door, hauling Susanna out and setting her down on her short sturdy legs. Mole scrambled after her, staring about him, observing the castle-like building across the courtyard, the height of the surrounding walls and the comforting thickness of the tall wooden doors in the gatehouse. He hoped that they would be closed and, as if she had read his thoughts, Freddy went to swing together the heavy oak barriers.

Mole took a deep breath; he thought: We are *inside*! – and looked with relief at Fliss.

She was struggling with their small quantity of luggage – all the large possessions were coming by Carter Paterson – and he went to help her, pulling at her arm and pointing towards the gates. She knew at once what he was feeling.

'We're quite safe here, Mole,' she said in a low voice. 'I told you so, didn't I? Quite safe here at The Keep with Grandmother.'

Freddy was laughing at Susanna, who was running on the turf, throwing herself down on the sun-warmed grass and rolling about, enjoying the freedom after the days of restriction on aeroplane and trains and in hotel rooms.

'No escape now,' she told her cheerfully. 'You're in! You can't come to any harm. You can't get out.'

'And no one,' said Fliss, 'can get *in*.'

Freddy looked at her, aware of a kind of urgent intensity, as if Fliss were passing some kind of message.

'True,' she agreed, realising at once how important it was that the children should have absolute security so that their terror might abate. 'But you are completely safe here, you know. Only friends come to The Keep. And we have Ellen and Fox to look after us. You remember Ellen and Fox, Fliss?'

'Oh yes.' The pucker of anxiety between Fliss's brows vanished and she smiled. 'Oh yes, I do. Ellen and Fox,' she repeated, as though it were a magic formula. 'For a minute I'd forgotten them.'

'Well, don't let them hear you say that,' said Freddy as the small party collected their belongings. 'They're eager to see you again. Come along. They'll be in the kitchen making tea.'

As they trudged towards the front door Fliss felt her anxieties return. It was becoming increasingly important that she should speak to her grandmother alone so that she could explain. She had to tell her what happened on that dreadful day when she had heard Cookie screaming in the kitchen and she had run in to see the policeman shaking Cookie, shouting at her, telling her to be quiet. Suddenly he had slapped her stingingly across the cheek and she had gasped and gulped and relapsed into silence. It was at this point that Fliss had seen Mole cowering, ashen-faced beneath the table, a witness to the policeman's shocking revelations.

Even now Fliss did not know exactly what Mole had heard. From that moment Mole had been dumb; locked into his own silence. It was too late to concoct a story for the children. The policeman assumed that the small cowering boy would repeat the appalling news which he, shocked by the violence of the scene, had related so incautiously to the cook. Cursing himself, the policeman did the best he could – which was bad enough – but Fliss was spared the harrowing details which Mole had heard as he crouched beneath the kitchen table. Since that moment, Mole had refused to let Fliss out of his sight – and, if possible, out of his grasp.

How to find a moment alone, so as to explain? Fliss felt weighed down with responsibility and anxiety as she struggled with her own grief and loneliness.

'You are the eldest now,' a well-meaning woman had said. She was their mother's friend and had cared for them until they were able to fly out. 'You must be a little mother to your brother and sister.'

Fliss had remained silent, staring at her, whilst Mole burrowed into the chair beside her. 'But I am *not* a mother,' she longed to say, 'not even a little one. And I can't be the eldest. Jamie is the eldest. Because he is dead it doesn't change anything. You can't just become the eldest because someone dies . . .'

At the thought of Jamie, so much in charge, organising them all, comforting, capable, her big brother,

Fliss's lips shook and tears filled her eyes. She had clutched Mole and wept into his dark hair as he lay passively against her, still too shocked even to cry.

'Come now.' The woman was clearly disappointed by Fliss's lack of control. 'You must set the little ones a good example. Here's a handkerchief. One good blow now. That's a good girl.'

She had blown her nose obediently and smoothed at Mole's hair, hugging him, hoping that she was being motherly, but the tears were still there, running down the back of her throat. Now, here at The Keep, she hoped that some of her burden might pass to her grandmother; but first she had to be told . . .

Fliss sighed heavily and, holding tightly to Mole's hand, she followed Freddy up the steps and into the hall.

Chapter Two

The Keep had been built for comfort, each generation adding its own variations on the theme. Left alone to bring up her twin boys between the wars, Freddy had drifted into rather a reclusive existence. She was a Hampshire girl and Bertie had died before he could introduce her into local society – such as it was in this very rural and fairly isolated place. Many of his contemporaries had died in the war and very few of them had been married. So it was that The Keep became a small world of its own and Freddy gradually converted the house to her own convenience. She loved it: the high rooms and spaciousness; the enclosed courtyard; the startling views; the huge granite fireplace at the far end of the hall; her little upstairs sitting room which overlooked the courtyard; the big airy bedroom with windows to both south and east so that she could wake to the early morning sunshine.

Freddy's variations on the comfort theme had been to install more bathrooms and modernise the kitchen. She had turned Bertie's dressing room into a bathroom for herself. Her excuse for a second bathroom on the first floor was that she disliked sharing with her daughter-in-law Prue when she came to stay. Freddy hated talcum powder scattered over the linoleum, stockings draped over the clotheshorse and the lingering scent which Prue used so extravagantly. As they grew up, the boys had continued to use the nursery quarters on the second floor so Freddy had become accustomed to having the bathroom for her own exclusive use. She was surprised at how much she resented sharing with Prue, surprised and guilty, so that finally she'd consulted her brother-in-law, Theo Chadwick. Theo was six years younger than Bertie and it was he who had nicknamed the young Frederica 'Freddy', he who had comforted her when she found herself a widow, pregnant with the twins, the owner of The Keep and a major shareholder in a business about which she knew nothing. He had taken Holy Orders and until recently had been a naval chaplain.

'Do you *need* an excuse to put in another bathroom?' Theo had asked, puzzled. It was unlike Freddy to consult him in such matters. 'Why shouldn't you have your own bathroom?'

'It seems so self-indulgent,' explained Freddy. 'There's a perfectly good bathroom already, and Prue and the twins don't come down that often.'

'Perhaps they'll come down more often if they don't have to share a bathroom,' suggested Theo slyly.

Freddy frowned a little at this, saw Theo's grin and glared at him. 'You are a wretch, Theo. Now I feel even more guilty.'

'I notice that you never felt guilty when poor old Ellen had to pant up and down the stairs with hot water,' observed Theo. 'Where have all these finer feelings sprung from, I wonder.'

'I don't know why I bother to tell you my problems,' grumbled Freddy – and immediately remembered those early years when she had seemed to do nothing but weep on his shoulder. She burst out laughing. 'Oh, go away,' she said. 'I shall have my bathroom and glory in it!'

Now, as Freddy stood in her little sitting room staring out over the courtyard, it was Theo to whom her thoughts turned. Would Theo know how to deal with a small boy, struck dumb by tragedy? It had been whilst Ellen was bathing him earlier that Fliss had been able to tell Freddy about his silence; how he had been under the table when the policeman arrived and had not spoken since. Freddy had been shocked, quickly guessing what the unwary policeman might have revealed to the cook. Imagining those details were, after all, part of her own mental agony; what must Mole be suffering? She had warned Ellen and they had stared at each other in desperation, wondering how to deal with this new problem. It explained why Fliss had insisted that she and Mole must share a room, that he must be able to see and touch her, and why she had been so relieved when she saw that this was exactly how the nursery was arranged.

Long shadows lay across the grass and she could hear the swifts as they raced, screaming, high above in the still warmth of the evening air. The scent of roses drifted in at her open window and a thrush was singing in the orchard. These familiar joys calmed her but fear was not far below the surface of her thoughts. The prospect was daunting enough without this added complication.

Freddy turned away from the window and contemplated her room. It was to this private sanctuary that she had carried her favourite pieces, allowing herself to buy occasional luxuries to enhance it. She had rejected the heavy Victorian furniture, chosen by earlier Chadwicks, for the delicate furniture of a more elegant age – but she was not a purist. She chose things because she loved them and her love seemed to weld everything into a delightful pattern. The room was all of a piece. Here was the bow-fronted bureau with the shallow drawers; a tall glass-fronted bookcase, full of her favourite reading; a small inlaid table bearing a bowl of roses; two deep comfortable modern armchairs. A corner cupboard held a few precious pieces of china and glass; a wireless, tuned to the Third Programme for concerts and recitals, stood on a stool near her chair. There were several Widgerys hanging on the pale walls – Freddy loved his moorland paintings best – and the heavy moss-green curtains reflected the colours woven into the thick Axminster rugs.

A measure of peace soothed the nervous clamour in her mind and she breathed more deeply. She remembered that she had been thinking of Theo . . . he had asked her to telephone so as to report the children's safe arrival. Irritation sprang readily into her heart. He should have been here to support her. Instead, he was closeted away in his few rooms in the Southsea flat which looked out on the Channel, writing his damned book, *Ethics of War*. Despite herself, Freddy smiled a little.

'Are there any ethics in war?' she'd asked him. 'I think war is terribly unethical. Why don't you do something useful if you're going to retire?'

'How do you define useful?' he'd asked politely – and she'd been stuck for an answer. Or rather, she'd been unable to speak what was in her mind, which was: 'If you're going to retire then come down to The Keep and just be here. Keep me company and make me laugh.'

Awareness of her selfishness kept her silent. She knew that Theo would not impinge on her privacy or interfere with the running of The Keep; knew that she wanted him there for those moments of intolerable loneliness, to cheer her through her depression. Across the years they had shared a strange companionship. After Bertie had died, Freddy had argued and Theo had listened whilst she expounded her reasons for being unable to believe in God and, when he refused to be drawn or to be cast down, she had demanded explanations that she *could* believe. In her unhappiness and loss after John's death she had railed against Theo's steadfast beliefs and insisted that he justify them. Theo had resisted; he'd shaken his head, knowing that now was not the time for one of their theological discussions. Nevertheless, she was comforted by his presence. The mere sight of Theo, with his thick dark flopping hair and brown eyes, had the effect of relaxing her. It was as if some weight of loss or pain or fear was shifted to him so that he could bear it for her.

Now, Freddy felt a faint hopefulness at the idea of sharing this new problem with him. Shutting the sitting-room door quietly behind her, she went downstairs to the study.

★ ★ ★

In the nursery, the children were asleep. The midsummer evening was still light behind the drawn curtains and Ellen moved quietly, folding clothes, picking up towels, examining garments taken from the cases. Ellen: a background figure, a spectator; a Martha, tireless in her mistress's service. Her pride – when she was elected to look after Miss Frederica, to go with her as her maid when she married – was a kind of exultation, but it was pride tempered by a keen sense of humour. This humour informed all Ellen's work and gave her strength. When young she'd had all the qualities required by those who serve. She was colourless and unremarkable to look at, yet a close observer might have seen the quirk about the mouth, the straight uncompromising glance that stripped away pretensions, the firm set to the jaw. She was always neat and clean, her brown hair smooth, her pinafores starched and spotless. Light on her feet, quick to anticipate, she loved Freddy – and those whom Freddy loved – and counted herself lucky to be able to spend her life at The Keep.

In the years after the Great War she and Freddy had drawn close together, sharing the duties of bringing up the boys and running the household with the help of Fox. Fox had been a young gun-layer, serving under Bertie when he was promoted to assistant gunnery officer in 1915. After the war Fox had found his way to The Keep to tell Bertie's family the truth about the courage and gallantry of Lieutenant Chadwick's last battle. A bond formed at once between the young Fox and the officer's widow with her twin babies. He left her for only as long as it took to collect his belongings from a Plymouth boarding house, and had spent the rest of his life looking after The Keep.

Ellen liked Fox. The war had matured him beyond his twenty-six years and he was reserved but diligent and conscientious. For a while she had considered whether she might fall in love with him. It seemed perfectly reasonable, even fitting, yet somehow she could never raise *quite* enough enthusiasm to bridge the final gap of his reserve. Anyway, she enjoyed her independence, the freedom to say what she pleased to him without the guilt which the married state seemed to endow along with all the worldly goods. She would watch him covertly, noticing the thrust of his jaw, the broad deft fingers, his legs stretched out negligently as he sat drinking tea with her in the kitchen. Often, she had imagined them together in more intimate circumstances but these fantasies, though they might speed her breath a little and give an odd glow deep in her abdomen, were not enough to make her pursue him.

She turned back to the nursing of Freddy's babies, sensing that this was where her fulfilment was rooted. As the years passed she sometimes wondered if she had sacrificed her own happiness but these thoughts were fleeting. She and Fox knew far greater contentment together than had their passions been engaged. She adored the twins – and her strictness and sharp discipline were the measure of her love for them. Those whom Ellen loved she chastened and the twins – and occasionally Freddy if necessary – were chastened rigorously. There were no favourites in Ellen's nursery and so the twins grew up confident and happy. They were loved – yet given strict boundaries; cherished – yet punished if they transgressed those rules by which society, even nursery society, must live. Sooner or later they must conform to that society which supported them and the earlier they realised it, so much the better for them and the greater their freedoms within it.

Now the boys were dead. John's children, the twins Henry and Katharine – Hal and Kit – came often to The Keep and Ellen watched over them, fed them up, listened to their griefs. She was sad each time they left but realised that she was getting too old now to be more than cook and housekeeper – jobs she had taken on gradually as staff became difficult to keep out here in the countryside. So she and Freddy and Fox had settled into their quiet domesticity, enlivened by visits from Prue and the twins or Theo.

Then suddenly this dreadful news had come, to destroy their hard-won peace and acceptance of loss, to disrupt their gentle journey into old age. Ellen had held Freddy whilst she cried, her own tears sliding down her cheeks and dropping gently on Freddy's faded fair hair, but there had been little time to grieve. The children were to be sent straight home to their grandmother in England and Freddy, with Ellen and Fox, plunged into a whirlwind of preparation. Anything to keep their minds from the horror . . .

Ellen pulled the curtains a little closer and turned to look down into the big cot at the sleeping Susanna. Her limbs, heavy in sleep, were disposed negligently; a starfish hand rested on her Viyella-covered chest and her dolly leaned against the bars. Gently, Ellen covered the sleeping child with the sheet and moved quietly away. She paused at the other bedroom door. Silence; yet something drew Ellen into the room.

Fliss was sleeping the sleep of the exhausted but, even in slumber, her brow was furrowed. Ellen watched her thoughtfully. She knew of Fliss's adoration for her elder brother and she guessed at the child's misery, wondering how she might help her to come to terms with it . . . There was a slight movement in the gloom behind her. Ellen turned to look at Mole, tucked into the other white-painted, narrow iron bed, and experienced a faint shock. He was sitting up, watching her, eyes large and frightened. She moved quickly towards him, sitting down halfway up the bed so that he had to curl his legs back, and, after a quick look across at Fliss, he stared up at Ellen.

'She's fast asleep,' she whispered. 'See? Don't wake her.'

He shook his head obediently, but he looked unhappy and she adjusted his pillow and pushed back his dark hair – Theo's hair – from the smooth childish brow.

Mole, worn out earlier, had fallen instantly asleep, spiralling into the now familiar nightmare vision. The policeman's words had created a dreadful moving picture in Mole's head; words, punctuated by wretching gasps, which echoed relentlessly in his ears. '. . . And they were hiding in the trees, just waiting, still and dark as shadows until the car came out of the sunlight into the shade. Oh my Christ! The blood was everywhere. They had machetes, axes, sticks . . . They dragged the Chadwicks out of the car and just beat and chopped them down. The boy's shirt was soaked with blood . . . They'd smashed his head to pulp and nearly severed it from his body . . .' At this point

Cookie had started screaming and Fliss had appeared in the kitchen doorway . . .

Mole woke suddenly to see Ellen standing by his sister's bed. For one terrible moment he had forgotten where he was but the terror passed as Ellen sat down beside him. She continued to sit silently with him, brooding whilst he watched her, until slowly an idea came to her.

'Come,' she said quietly, turning back the bedclothes and taking his hand. 'Come with me and I'll show you something.'

He hesitated, looking hopefully across to Fliss, but Ellen shook her head firmly.

'We mustn't wake her,' she whispered. 'The poor lamb's exhausted. Come along. You'll be quite safe with me.'

He went with her unwillingly, chin on shoulder, longing for Fliss to disturb, but inside Ellen's little room he momentarily forgot everything but the sight of a puppy, lying in a large dog basket with its mother. Mole crouched beside them, tentatively reaching out to touch the small warm body. The large, rusty-coloured bitch raised her head and stared steadily at Mole for a few seconds before falling back with a groan. The puppy stirred and yawned, the pink mouth wide, and struggled up. It staggered out of the basket, tail wagging, and climbed on to Mole's knees.

'Fun, isn't he?' whispered Ellen. 'Eight weeks old. The others have gone but we're keeping this one. He hasn't been very well so I've been minding him up here at nights for a bit. He's right as rain now. I'm going to heat some milk for him. You shall have some, too.'

Entranced, Mole played with the puppy, who drank his milk greedily and presently went away and was busy on some newspaper near the door. He came running back to Mole, hurling himself against him and worrying Mole's pyjama sleeve, shaking it, his teeth gripping it firmly. For a brief moment Mole smiled. He looked up at Ellen – a normal happy little boy – and she felt a great surge of relief as she smiled back at him.

'He's a terror,' she whispered – and decided to break a lifetime's rule. 'Like to take him back to bed with you?'

Mole gazed at her disbelievingly and she nodded at his unspoken question.

'Why not? Come on. I'll tuck you up.'

They snuggled together in the narrow bed, the puppy content to settle down in Mole's warmth.

'No noise now,' she warned him. 'You'll frighten him. He's only a baby. You must look after him so that he isn't frightened. Can you do that?'

Mole nodded. Yes, he could do that. Ellen smiled and bent to kiss him.

'Sleep, then,' she said – and went away.

Mole raised his head cautiously and stared across at the hump that was Fliss. He longed to show her the puppy but he neither wished to incur Ellen's wrath nor have the puppy removed. The puppy slumbered peacefully and Mole stroked him gently, his thoughts confused but his tension receding, until presently he, too, slept.

Chapter Three

Theo Chadwick leaned on the railing watching the ferry which plied between Portsmouth and the Isle of Wight. The tide was rolling gently in, quietly but ineluctably obliterating the sandcastles that appeared by the dozen on any sunny Sunday afternoon in early June. The sunset was slowly dying out of the sky and the island rose up, indigo blue, sharp-angled as a cut-out, against its paler background; remote yet anchored for ever in the deep waters of the English Channel. As thundery clouds, blackly purple but gold-edged, began to roll in from the west, only its lights defined the ferry as it chugged towards Ryde. It was a cheerful note on the swelling surface of the darkening sea and Theo watched it for some time before pushing himself off the rails and turning his steps back towards the town. Soon the holiday-makers would be overrunning the place; arriving by the train-load, filling the boarding houses, staggering down to the beach loaded with rugs and bathing costumes and picnics, their children carrying buckets and spades as well as the coloured windmills and flags with which they would adorn their sandcastles. He had already decided that he would escape to

Devon, to the peace and quiet of The Keep.

He had made this decision before the ghastly news had arrived from Kenya but Freddy had begged him not to change his plans. She assured him that he would not be in the way; on the contrary, she had said rather desperately, she *needed* him more than ever. Theo, who had never been able to judge whether he was an asset or a liability, had assured her that he would certainly come as soon as the children had settled in. Then had come the telephone call telling him that young Sam – Mole, the family called him – had been struck dumb. Out of Freddy's confused torrent of words, which had included car accidents, the children's foolish travelling companion and other minor dramas, had come this terrible news. Only too clearly could Theo visualise the scene: the policeman rendered voluble by shock; the hysterical cook; and Mole – hidden beneath the table. What horrors had he heard?

Theo climbed the narrow stairs to his rooms, in the upper half of a converted house, leased to him by friends, an elderly ex-naval commander and his wife. It was a pleasant enough place, with a good-sized bedroom and a big sitting room with a gas fire, and a bow window which looked out to sea. There was a dressing room which overlooked the back garden, a very small kitchen and an adequate bathroom. Theo worked in the dressing room; he had quickly learned that a distracting view leads to a disappointing output of work.

He went into the kitchen, lit the ring on the gas stove, filled the blackened kettle and stood it over the flames. He was indifferent to the faint smell of mice and the ineradicable stains on the wooden draining board, just as he was indifferent to what he ate and drank when he was alone. At present he was thinking about Mole, remembering the many different reactions to terror, shock and violence that he, Theo, had witnessed during the war. At least Mole was very young. One could only hope that, with love and security, the horror might fade. Or might the damage go much deeper than that?

Theo reached for his old brown teapot and made tea, his thoughts now with Freddy. How brave she had been; with what courage she had faced the blows dealt her.

'Why me?' she had cried to him – and he had been unable to answer her.

Theo contemplated an unknowable, unseeable, unimaginable God; spiritually he had moved beyond the need of symbols to a contemplative worship which filled him with a kind of trembling bliss and he watched helplessly as Freddy raged, pouring her scorn out upon a God-figure whom she rendered small and selfish, capricious and mean-spirited. He had tried to help her. As the years passed, he talked of free will and of the transforming power of love; of the foolishness of attempting to 'understand' God. He quoted from Job – '*Where wast thou when I laid the foundations of the earth?*' – and tried to show her the Mystery in terms of scientific rules laid down; inexorable, unchangeable. Freddy, however, saw things in only personal terms and all he could really do for her was to continue to love her.

He carried his cup and saucer into the sitting room and sat in the bow window, looking out across the

Channel, watching the first few drops of rain pitting the smooth oily surface of the water. Presently he would find his train timetable and check the trains to the West Country. He might break his journey in Bristol to see Prue. Theo sipped his tea thoughtfully, wondering if Prue knew about Mole. Quite unlikely, he thought. Freddy's mind would certainly not be on Prue. It was sad but fairly normal, he supposed, that Freddy and Prue should be perpetually locked in misunderstandings. Each felt she had the monopoly in grieving when it came to John.

'I was his *mother*!' Freddy had cried. 'He was mine long before he was hers.'

'I was his *wife*!' raged Prue. 'A wife means more to a man than his mother.'

Theo had attempted to mediate.

'Of course you would take *her* part,' snapped Freddy. 'She's young and pretty. Men are so susceptible. Naturally, I hoped for loyalty . . .'

'I guessed you'd be on *her* side,' sniffed Prue, accusingly. 'Trust the Chadwicks to stick together.'

'You are a Chadwick now,' Theo had pointed out calmly. 'Your children are Chadwicks.'

Prue snorted. 'I don't know how Freddy expects me to cope on that measly allowance. It's never the same from one year to the next . . .'

Theo had tried, yet again, to make Prue understand the principles of a dividend being paid from the number of shares which would have been John's portion had he lived. Freddy didn't trust Prue with the shares – and had said so to Theo – but the amount was a reasonable one considering that Freddy paid the school fees for Hal and Kit and helped out in many other small ways.

Theo finished his tea and placed his cup and saucer on the round oak table where he ate most of his meals, there in the window, looking out to sea. He would go down to Devon and see what could be done and, meanwhile, he would telephone Prue and arrange to see her on the way.

Hal answered the telephone. 'Hello, Uncle Theo,' he said cheerfully. 'How are you? . . . We're all fine . . . No, Mother's not here, I'm afraid. Shall I take a message?'

Theo explained that he was hoping to cadge a bed for the night sometime during the next week on his way west.

'Lucky you,' said Hal feelingly. 'I wish we could go down. It's ages till the summer holidays.'

Theo made sympathetic noises and asked after Kit.

'She's all right,' he said. There was a tiny pause and, when he spoke, Hal's voice had changed. 'Are they all right down there?' he asked awkwardly. 'What a terrible thing to happen. Grandmother telephoned to say that they'd arrived safely . . .' His voice trailed off.

Theo assured him that the children were settling in, sent his love to Prue and Kit, and hung up. He would check on the train times and speak to Prue tomorrow.

'Who was it?' asked Kit, who was fiddling with the tuning dial on the radiogram. '*Palm Court*'s finished. What shall we do now?'

'It was Uncle Theo.' Hal looked thoughtful. 'He's going down to The Keep.'

Kit wandered away from the cabinet and flung

herself on to the sofa. 'Lucky him. I wish we were going, although it probably won't be the same with all those kids there.'

'Oh come on.' Hal looked uncomfortable. 'It was a pretty filthy thing to happen.'

'It's no worse than Daddy being killed in the war,' said Kit defensively. 'Torpedoed. Blown up or drowned. What's worse than that? We didn't get all this fuss.'

'We still had a mother,' pointed out Hal reasonably. 'Anyway, we were just babies. We wouldn't remember. And it *was* twelve years ago.'

Kit shrugged. She was jealous of her position at The Keep and suspected that her nose would be put well out of joint with the arrival of Fliss and the others. Secretly she was horrified at what had happened to Uncle Peter and Aunt Alison and to her cousin Jamie. After the telephone call, Prue had wept and Kit had cried with her. Unlike Freddy, who had managed to maintain the traditional role despite Bertie's death, Prue had treated the growing twins more as friends than as her children. They shared her hopes and woes, just as she shared theirs, and they were a happy if unconventional little group. Prue was not strong on discipline – 'She hasn't any idea how to discipline herself, let alone Hal and Kit,' Freddy had said crossly on more than one occasion – and the twins often traded on her good nature; but they adored their easy-going, slightly scatty mother and always took her side.

Kit swung her legs round so that they stuck up the back of the sofa and hung her head upside down over the seat. Her hair touched the carpet and she made a face at her brother, crossing her eyes and waggling her tongue at him. Hal sighed with relief. He knew that Kit's brief sulk was over and she was her usual sunny self again. These strange new moods seemed to threaten the even tenor of their relationship and they puzzled him. The twins were not alike. Hal resembled his father and grandmother; he was tall and fair, elegant and well co-ordinated. His sister looked like a smaller, younger edition of Prue. Her ashy brown hair was silky and her eyes were smoky blue. Her odd moods puzzled her, too, and she was glad to have Hal at hand. It was as if she tested herself against him, practising attitudes and ideas before presenting them to the rest of the world. Anyway, it was rather nice to have a brother whom all her school friends adored. They were both going away to school this autumn; Hal to Clifton College; Kit to Badminton School. Both of them felt excited but apprehensive . . .

'I know.' She suddenly swung herself upright and slithered off the sofa. 'Let's play Monopoly. I'll have the boot and you can have the car. Pudge and Binker can have the hat and the iron.'

Long ago they had invented these two other friends to join them in their games. No one, not even the twins, knew quite who or what these characters were; even their names were not constant but grew and changed and diminished according to the twins' mood, and, although they had begun to grow out of such childlike imaginings, they had not yet abandoned them altogether.

Hal followed her across the narrow hall into the dining room. Kit went to the sideboard and searched for the Monopoly set while Hal pulled out the heavy oak chairs. He was still thinking about his cousins at The Keep and Kit's earlier reaction. He guessed at her fears but did not know quite how to allay them, suspecting that this sudden urge to play the once-favourite game was Kit's way of seeking security. It was a particular kind of security that was missing from their lives in Bristol but he knew that she found it at The Keep and was afraid of losing it.

She was setting out the board now, humming to herself, and Hal relaxed. The mood had passed and his spirits began to rise. He felt quite certain that when they went down for the holiday her fears would be laid to rest and he gave a sigh of relief. Kit smiled at him, sensing his concern, feeling happier again now.

'Highest number starts,' she said. 'I'll throw for Pudgie,' and she reached for the dice.

'I must get back, darling,' said Prue. She drew the large square crocodile-skin bag on to her knee and felt for her compact and lipstick. The man sitting opposite watched tolerantly as she stared at herself in the small mirror, painting her lips with concentration, examining her face critically, pulling at a curl. She gave him a quick smile as she snapped the compact shut, dropping it with the lipstick into the capacious handbag, and he leaned forward and covered her hand with his.

'Must you go?'

His voice was coaxing but she shook her head. 'I told you it was just a quickie tonight. The twins are on their own.'

'They're not babies,' he said. His voice was hardly less affectionate but he removed his hand and sat back in his chair.

'I know that.' Prue looked anxious. 'Don't get upset, Tony. It's just that we've been out rather a lot this week and we agreed that we'd take things slowly, didn't we? Remember?'

'I must have been mad.' He swallowed down his whisky and seemed to regain his good humour. 'So when shall I see you?'

'Phone me.' Prue was on her feet and he knew that he had lost her; that all her thoughts were with her children now. 'It's half-past ten,' she was saying, peering at the ridiculously tiny gold wristwatch, winding the long chiffon scarf around her throat. 'I said ten at the latest. You said you'd remind me . . .'

'Have a heart, sweetie.' He was laughing at her as he opened his cigarette case. 'I'm hardly going to be the one to break it up, am I? I don't see you nearly enough as it is.'

'You promised,' she began edgily – and then began to laugh with him. 'You're hopeless.'

'And so are you,' he said softly, the touch on her arm and his complicit look reminding her of some earlier intimacy. 'Thank God!'

She coloured, pressing her lips tightly together in an attempt to hide her delight, the love she felt for him. She shook off his hand and turned to pick up her jacket, heart bumping, regaining her composure. He lit his cigarette, smiling to himself, lifted his hand to the bartender and followed her between the tables towards the door. The trio on the dais at the back of the smoky room was playing softly – 'My Funny

Valentine', one of Prue's current favourites – and she glanced back wistfully.

On the pavement she shivered, clutching her thin jacket about her shoulders, hoping that he would kiss her before he drove her home. Tony slipped his arm about her, holding her against his side as they walked slowly towards his car. He wanted to marry her – for all sorts of reasons – and her caution was beginning to irk him. He concentrated his thoughts on the essential factors, those small but interesting slices of information she let slip, such as the mention of a flourishing family business, the description of the old castle down in Devon, the dividends on which she lived so comfortably . . . His arm tightened about her and she looked up at him with an expression which few adult males could misunderstand.

As he kissed her she trembled with weakness and longing. It had been twelve years since Johnny died and although there had been one or two little affairs – and any number of flirtations – Tony was different. Experience had taught her not to be too free with her favours. The trouble was that men expected a widow to be sophisticated about these things, ready for a bit of fun, and had no patience with virginal airs and graces. The presence of the twins had saved her from many indiscretions, for Prue was a true Friday's child – loving and giving – and found it difficult to with-hold those favours. Yet when it came to marriage with Tony she was oddly reluctant. Some tiny remnant of self-preservation held her back from the final commit-ment. Or perhaps it was the fear of Freddy's reaction when she presented him at The Keep. Prue could imagine the curl of Freddy's lip, the comparing of

Tony with Johnny, the questions, the embarrassment of her own desire.

Her hold on Tony loosened and he released her reluctantly. They drove in silence, both smoking thoughtfully, and her quick kiss when he arrived outside the charming Victorian mews house was almost perfunctory. He leaned across as she looked in at him through the passenger's window.

'I'll telephone you,' he said, concerned now that he was no longer obviously in control.

'You do that.' She kept her voice low, glancing at the upper windows of the house. 'Good night, Tony.'

'Good night, darling Prue.' His voice was soft and he blew her a kiss. 'It's been a wonderful evening.'

She nodded, returned his gesture almost shyly, and ran up the front steps, feeling in her bag for the key.

Kit heard her come in. She'd wanted to wait up but Hal had bullied her to bed and she'd finally given in on the condition that she could read for as long as she was able to keep her eyes open. Having finished *Veronica at the Wells* she had lain for some while imagining herself studying at Sadler's Wells School, dancing Odette-Odile on the stage at Covent Garden, performing the thirty-two *fouettés* to gasps of amazement and thunderous applause. A few weeks before, she had passed her Grade Five RAD ballet examination with Highly Commended and she was having one of her 'I'm going to be a ballet dancer' phases. She reread all her Lorna Hill books, and then borrowed from the Central Library anything else she could find whose main character was a young girl who became an overnight success in the world of dance. Her

family had learned not to take her too seriously
during these phases. Tomorrow she might pick up one
of her Noel Streatfeilds and have a tremendous urge
to be an ice-skating champion or a tennis star. On the
other hand, she might become absorbed in an Arthur
Ransome and demand sailing lessons and holidays in
the Lake District or on the Norfolk Broads. Even Kit
herself was beginning to take her sudden passions
with a degree of caution.

She rolled on to her side and began to think about
her cousins at The Keep. She couldn't remember Mole
– she liked the fact that he was called Mole – and had
never seen the baby, Susanna, but she could remember playing with Fliss and Jamie. Fliss was a quiet,
rather shy little girl but Jamie was very like Hal – they
could almost have been twins – and there had always
been a certain constraint between the two boys. She
didn't want to think about Jamie so she wondered
what Mrs Pooter would think of her cousins and
whether they would, like she herself, climb into the
huge dog basket which had belonged to her grandfather's great mastiff, Caesar. Kit liked to lie in the dog
basket with Mrs Pooter, feeling her furry warmth,
snuffing up the lovely doggy smell . . . and now there
was a puppy.

She gave a sigh of drowsy happiness, jerking
suddenly awake as she heard the car stop outside,
listening until she heard her mother's key in the lock
and the door close quietly behind her. Kit knew that
she would make herself a cup of coffee, pottering a
little, and she wondered whether she might slip
downstairs and talk to her. It was fun to do that,
sipping at her mother's coffee, both talking in

whispers. Kit yawned and decided that she was too comfortable and, instead, began to imagine the new puppy and what she might call it. Puppies were such fun . . . When Prue came creeping up the stairs, Kit was fast asleep.

Chapter Four

By the time the children had been with them a week, life at The Keep had undergone a complete change. Poor Ellen was up and down the two flights of stairs between kitchen and nursery a dozen times a day and Freddy's peaceful hours of reading, gardening and playing the piano were ruthlessly cut short and continually interrupted.

'It's a question of routine,' insisted Ellen, running from her vegetable peeling to rescue the forgotten rice pudding in the oven.

'We just need to be better organised,' muttered a distracted Freddy as she hurried to pick up Susanna, who had tumbled into the herbaceous border, whilst the puppy ran off gleefully with Mole's teddy.

'Can't be expected to think of everything at once,' said Fox soothingly, taking over from a harassed Ellen at the mangle in the wash house. 'The baker's just arrived and wants to know if you need extra.'

'We're getting too old for this, Ellen,' sighed Freddy, toiling upstairs with an armful of linen and small garments and meeting Ellen coming down with the laden tea tray. 'Perhaps we need someone to help us.'

'It's twenty years since we had children in the

nursery,' said Ellen, who had no intention of allowing strangers into her domain. 'It's bound to take time to get used to it again.'

'And it doesn't help that Mole won't speak.' Freddy looked hopefully at Ellen. 'No sign of anything this afternoon?'

Ellen shook her head. 'It's early days, Madam. He's very highly strung. Over-imaginative. It'll take time.'

'The puppy helps.' Freddy took a firmer grasp on her load. 'Oh well, Ellen. On we go. But I think we shall have to give in and get extra help. Don't forget that Mrs Blakiston is coming for drinks.'

Ellen went into the kitchen and put the tray on the long refectory table with its odd assortment of kitchen chairs. The puppy, now allowed to be a fully fledged member of the family, was curled up on the rug by the Aga, whilst his mother snored in her enormous basket. At the corner of the table sat Fox, drinking tea, a basket of vegetables, washed clean under the tap in the scullery, at his elbow. Ellen looked at him consideringly, ideas forming and reforming in her busy head, aware that Fox was rather enjoying himself. He had unearthed Peter's kite and had taken the silent Mole out on to the slopes behind The Keep to show him how to fly it. Fliss had come too, of course. Mole was still unhappy unless she was somewhere at hand – within sight and touch – but he had forgotten her for a few magic moments as the kite soared up into the blue air and bobbed high above him. Fox had let him hold the string and showed him how to make the kite swoop and glide. There was a stiff south-westerly blowing and the enchanted Mole had forgotten the dark terrors which had inhabited his mind for so long. He'd stood, balanced against the wind, the string clutched tight in his fist, his eyes fixed on the wide-shouldered kite with its long fluttering tail.

Fox had watched him, privately overjoyed. In the child he could see Bertie again, dark-haired, dark-eyed, the same intent expression and sensitive mobile mouth. Bertie's sons had been the image of their mother, whom Fox adored, but here was a Chadwick back at The Keep again – and Fox felt all the challenge of restoring Mole to the happy careless paths of childhood. Watching him with the kite, he'd realised that it was in these ways that the boy's mind would heal, not in brooding over him and consulting with doctors.

Ellen had agreed with him and now, as she piled the empty dishes into the deep porcelain sink, she wondered how to make best use of him.

'Madam's worried,' she said casually, her back to him, as she ran the water. 'Thinks we're all getting too old to manage.'

Fox studied Ellen's back view. The once slender waist had thickened and the smooth brown hair had plenty of grey in it but her ankles were still pretty and she was surprisingly light and quick on her narrow feet.

'Perhaps we are,' he suggested provocatively. He enjoyed a bit of a sparring match with Ellen from time to time. 'Not as young as we were.'

'Don't need to be an egghead to work that out,' she said tartly. 'And speak for yourself. I've noticed it takes you a bit longer to mow the lawns than it used to, now you mention it.'

Behind her back, he grinned appreciatively. It was true, too. Trust Ellen not to miss a trick. He sighed heavily.

''Tis all right for you youngsters,' he said. 'You've certainly kept your figure, maid. Must be dashing up and down those stairs . . .'

'Not so much dashing these days,' she said, mollified by the compliment, though she didn't believe a word of it. 'Crawling more like. Madam's talking about getting in extra help.'

The burden of three small children would come hardest on Ellen, he knew that, so Fox hesitated a little before he spoke.

'And how do you feel about that, then?'

'Don't want strangers here, do we?'

She didn't look at him, head bent, elbows busy, and Fox pushed his chair back from the table, cocking an ankle on his corduroy-clad knee, feeling in his waistcoat pocket for his crumpled packet of Woodbines.

'Did she have anyone in mind?' There was no disrespect in the use of the 'she'. Freddy was the mainspring of their lives, her wishes paramount, and they loved her too much to be jealous of each other in her service.

'Shouldn't think so. Difficult to get anyone out here regular. They'd have to live in.'

She turned to look at him as she reached for the teacloth, needing to see that the full import of her words had sunk in. Fox scraped his blunt calloused fingers thoughtfully round his jaw.

'Wouldn't want that, would we?' He spoke tentatively, still attempting to read her thoughts. 'Must fall heavy on you, though.'

'That Susanna's a handful.' She leaned against the rail of the cream-coloured Aga, quite serious now. 'And it's a big old place to keep clean . . .'

'Anything I can do to help,' he offered, 'you've only to say the word.'

'So long as we know where we are.' She nodded at him. 'I might call on you a bit. Needn't tell Madam.'

There were steps on the stairs outside the door in the back hall and Fliss entered, followed closely by Mole.

'There's a storm blowing up,' said Fliss, standing just inside the door. 'The wind's howling and howling. I've told Mole it's only the wind.'

She looked beseechingly at Fox, who rose at once to the occasion.

'And so 'tis,' he said. 'Blows terrible hard round The Keep but it's a wonderful sound when you get used to it and you know you're safe inside and nothing nor nobody can get to you.'

'That Susanna hasn't woken, I hope,' said Ellen, putting the cushion from the rocker into the big Windsor chair at the end of the table beside Fox and whisking Mole on top of it. 'Nothing wakes her, it seems.'

'No, she's fast asleep,' Fliss assured her, wriggling on to another chair. 'Grandmother came to say good night and she told us to come down to see you. Mrs Blakiston's just arrived, she says.'

'Time for a game before bed,' said Fox, ruffling Mole's hair. 'Why shouldn't we have the dominoes out, Ellen?'

Their eyes met over the child's head and she nodded, abandoning the hope of accomplishing some of the thousand small tasks which awaited her. As Ellen went to the built-in dresser, bearing its delicate survivors from long-forgotten dinner services, Fliss gave a sigh of relief. These were the best times; when she could relax knowing that others were sharing her responsibility. She looked at the sleeping dogs, the geraniums on the deep windowsill, the soft gleam of china – rich reds, dark blues and gold leaf – on the dresser shelves. Patchwork curtains matched the cushions on the window seat and the rocking chair; the rag rugs on the slate-flagged floor, though faded, were thick. Beyond the two windows, the hill sloped away so steeply that the kitchen seemed to be poised high up in the air. One evening, kneeling on the window seat, Fliss had watched the birds circling below her as she stared out over a huge sweep of neat multi-coloured fields and rounded bosomy hills which unfolded, distance upon distance, into a misty blue infinity where the sun was setting in showers of gold.

'I like it in here,' she said now, contentedly, watching Ellen take the lid off the domino box. 'It's always so warm.'

Coming from Kenya the children felt the cold of an English June keenly. Even the hottest day seemed barely warm and they shivered when the cool mists rolled up over The Keep or the winds blew over the high moors from the west, driving what looked like solid curtains of rain across the hill. As soon as the trunks arrived, Ellen had bundled them into their winter jerseys, summer or not. Now, as she watched Fliss's face, another idea occurred to her.

'Of course it would save my old legs a bit if we had a few of our meals down here in the kitchen,' she said as she tipped the dominoes on to the table. 'Warmer, too. Nothing against it, is there?'

'No reason as far as I can see.' Fox turned the oblongs of ivory carefully. He smiled at Mole. 'Like that, would you? Like to have your meals down here with that old puppy?'

Mole nodded, watching Fox's fingers as they turned the dominoes. He missed his mother's warmth and his father's strength, and he missed his big brave shining brother. It had always seemed to Mole that Jamie shone; his skin was brown and shiny, his fair hair was bright as sunshine; his face glowed with life and health. He was afraid of nothing; not of the animals that prowled at night outside the compound; nor of snakes in the long dry grass; nor of black faces nor the sinister rhythm of the drums. He was invincible, immortal – yet he had died. Once again the scene formed behind Mole's eyes and he heard the words – 'the boy's shirt was soaked in blood. They'd smashed his head to pulp . . .' At once it seemed that Mole's own head was filled with the blood, his throat closed with a muscular spasm, lest he should choke on it. Now the picture seemed always there in his mind; Jamie covered with blood . . .

Mole gave a tiny gasp and put his head down on his folded arms. Fox's fingers were stilled, Ellen stretched a hand towards him but, quick as light, Fliss was off her chair and down with the puppy.

'Look,' she cried, 'he's waking up.' She lugged him up in her arms. 'Look, Mole. He's looking for you.' She dumped him on Mole's lap. 'We've got to think of a name for him. Grandmother told me that we can choose. What shall we call him, Mole?' Her chatter had distracted him, as she had intended it should, and she turned to Ellen while Mole struggled with the sleepy puppy. 'Why do you call her Mrs Pooter?' She crouched down beside the bitch who opened one eye but remained quite still.

'It was your cousin Kit called her that when she was a puppy just like this one,' said Ellen, her eyes still on Mole. He looked calmer again. The puppy was licking his face enthusiastically. 'Said it was in a book. A Mr Pooter, she said and she just liked the sound of it. Great one for names, is Kit. So she became Mrs Pooter. Dear oh dear, she was a terror.'

'That's true,' agreed Fox, who had started to shuffle the dominoes. 'Ate up one of my gumboots, she did. Couldn't leave her for a minute. Come on, now, we're all ready to start.'

'You'll have to help Mole,' warned Fliss, scrambling back into her chair. 'He can't count properly yet. We've just—'

She bit her lip, turning over her dominoes and standing them in a semi-circle so that no one else could see them. She had been about to say, 'We've just started to teach him' and suddenly remembered that they were all gone – Mummy and Daddy and Jamie. Just now and then it seemed that she had dreamed it all and this was simply a holiday. The door would open and the three of them would come bursting in . . . She swallowed hard and tried to focus on her dominoes.

'I'll start us all off,' Fox was saying cheerfully. 'Nice double three, now. Who's got a three to carry on? Let's have a look, young Mole. I think that puppy wants to play, too . . .'

The moment passed and Ellen realised that she'd been holding her breath, watching the desolation on the child's face. They both needed to grieve, she felt sure of it. Grieving was a natural, healing process, denied as yet to both of them. She realised she was holding up the game and quickly put down a domino.

'There,' she said. 'Who's got that double two, then? Could anyone manage a nice Sharps toffee while they're looking?'

'So how are you coping, Freddy?' Julia Blakiston sipped appreciatively at her gin and bitters and glanced up at Freddy, who was still busy at the drinks tray.

'I'm not at all certain that I *am* coping,' answered Freddy frankly.

She sat down beside Julia on the sofa and raised her glass to her, smiling with real affection at the short, stocky, rough-haired woman who worked so hard for the needy and sick. They had been friends for thirty years, meeting at a charity event and feeling an immediate rapport. Julia had also lost her husband in the Great War but she had no children – they had been married only a few weeks – and she had dealt with her grief and loneliness by harnessing her no-longer-required love to charitable works. They were both independent, intelligent women, determined to make the best of what was left to them; they liked each other enormously; each respecting the other's abilities, each accepting the differences between them.

'I had completely forgotten how tiring young children are,' said Freddy, tucking one leg up beneath her. 'And *I* have Ellen and Fox. How some of these young mothers manage with half a dozen children I simply cannot imagine.'

'I think it is especially hard,' said Julia thoughtfully, 'when one is dealing with one's own grief at the same time. How heavy the burden seems each morning. The heart is weighed down with misery and one's energy seems non-existent. It is good to be able to be busy. It distracts the mind and keeps one struggling on but,' she shook her head, 'goodness, it is exhausting. No one ever tells us just how exhausting grieving is.'

Freddy looked at her gratefully. 'That is quite true,' she admitted. 'I have to contain my own grief each morning before I start. It was such a terrible thing. So senseless, so violent. It doesn't bear thinking about. Yet I think about it. My mind won't leave it alone. It probes like a tongue at a particularly painful tooth. I think of their terror, you know. I see them travelling along in the car – probably singing; they often sang in the car – and then the ambush. Death coming suddenly out of a bright day. What were their thoughts? How much did they suffer before they finally died?'

Julia stared into her friend's anguished face. 'We can only hope that it was quick. But what comfort is that? Sometimes there are no answers. There is only the pain. We both know that, Freddy. We have to use the pain. You've done it before.'

'Oh, yes,' said Freddy. 'I've done it before. So have you. But how does that help the dead?'

'We can't help the dead. Our concern is with the living . . . When is Theo coming?'

'Soon. Yes, Theo will be a comfort – although I never quite know why.'

Julia laughed a little. 'Theo simply *is*,' she said.

'He's one of those rare souls who make us feel better simply by being in the same room with us. There is something stable, something unchanging about him.'

'Which is odd given that he is totally impractical. Quite useless at anything of a really important nature.'

Julia felt a sense of relief as she heard the faint irritation in Freddy's voice. She knew how much Freddy resented admitting that Theo sustained her emotionally and spiritually, resented his unshakeable belief in something she could not share. The note of irritation indicated that Freddy had regained her self-control, that the moment of anguish had passed – for the present.

'So tell me when you can come over for lunch. Or come to tea and bring the children. We could picnic in the summerhouse by the pond. Yes?'

'Yes,' said Freddy. 'Bless you, Julia. That would be something to take us out of ourselves. Let me fetch my diary.'

Prue strolled down Park Street thinking about Tony. She knew that she must make a decision about him, about their future, but her mind shied away from it. She simply couldn't judge how the twins might react to a man living with them. They were used to boyfriends coming and going but this was rather different.

But I'm only thirty-four, thought Prue rebelliously. I'm not that old. Why shouldn't I get married again?

She knew that the answer to this question was really summed up in one word: Freddy. If she had been proposing to marry a man with decent prospects, something solid behind him, reliable and hard-working, then she knew that Freddy would not object. The trouble was that Tony was none of these things. He tended to be evasive about his war record – Prue had heard him say different things to different people – and he had no job at all at present. Nor did he have his own place. He rented a small, poky flat in Park Row and never seemed to have too much cash to splash about. His explanations were very plausible. His parents were dead and his home in London had been bombed in one of the raids whilst he'd been abroad. He had lost everything. As for his wartime service, when she challenged him about his inconsistencies he told her that he had been in the Secret Service and he was unable to talk about his exploits.

All this seemed quite reasonable – and very romantic – to Prue but something warned her that Freddy might not be so easily satisfied. After all, the war had been over for more than ten years, quite long enough for Tony to have settled down and found himself a job. He had hinted to her that he was still in the pay of his wartime masters but, if that were true, why was he usually so hard up?

Prue paused to stare at the shoes in Meek's shop window. It was difficult to quiz Tony too closely. It made her look so materialistic and, as he had once implied, she had enough for both of them to manage on at a pinch whilst he got himself sorted out. Of course, he thought that she owned the little Victorian mews house in Old Clifton – and so she did. Freddy had bought it when Hal had won the scholarship to Clifton College and she had given it to Prue and the twins – but Prue continued to look upon it as if it were loaned to her and she hadn't yet explained this

to Tony. Would Freddy be happy for Tony to share it
with them?

She turned her back on the shoes and crossed the
road, strolling across College Green until she came to
an empty bench. She sat down, gazing at the cathedral, thinking about Tony. Her stomach lurched over
when she thought about him kissing her, touching
her . . . She dug into her handbag for a cigarette and
inhaled deeply, feeling the sun on her face, watching
the trees. She knew that she must give in or lose him –
but supposing Freddy took away the house or
stopped her allowance? Surely she would expect Tony
to provide for himself and Prue? She'd probably
continue to look after the twins, put the shares into a
trust for them, but still . . .

Prue ground out her cigarette and glanced at her
watch. She was meeting a girlfriend for lunch at the
Royal Hotel. Meanwhile there was time for a quick
browse and a chat in the dress shop across the Green.

Chapter Five

Theo, leaning from the open window as the train steamed into Temple Meads, saw Prue long before she saw him. He smiled at the sight of the slim, alert little figure gazing eagerly towards the wrong part of the train. As usual she looked smart and modern, each detail of her outfit chosen carefully. The neat bodice of her blue summer frock was gathered at the waist with a wide tight belt; the full gathered skirt had two big patch pockets and fell almost to her ankles. She wore white strappy high-heeled sandals, clutched a small white bag under her arm and a blue and white confection of feathers was perched on the newly permed hair. Watching her, Theo wondered why she had the shining ashy fair hair tortured into unnatural curls – although she no longer dyed it – and why she covered her wide pretty mouth with glistening red lipstick. The train slowed and stopped, panting and steaming alongside the platform, whilst porters swung back the doors and waiting passengers crowded forward. Theo stepped off, dodged a porter hurrying forward with a trolley, and approached Prue with a shout.

She turned, hearing his call above the clatter and

the whistle of steam, and a smile of pleasure and relief lit her face.

'I thought you weren't on it,' she said, standing on tiptoe to hug his spare frame. 'How are you? Too thin as usual. Oh well, Ellen will feed you up.'

She chattered on, hanging tightly to his arm until they were outside and heading for the taxi rank. He nodded, studying her, listening to her, until she sank back on to the car seat and turned to look at him properly.

He smiled at her. 'So . . . Kit is well and has passed her dancing exam with Highly Commended and Hal is playing cricket for the school and both of them are looking forward to the holidays. But how are you, Prue?'

She gave a little shrug, fiddling in her bag, and Theo bent – as he always did – to glance through the window at the elegant spire of St Mary Redcliffe Church, looking back at it as the taxi trundled on. He turned to her again, touching her lightly on the arm, eyebrows raised as he waited for her answer.

'Oh, you know. Just the same.' She turned her head to puff the smoke sideways but her eyes were watching him, flicking away and back again.

Theo thought: She is trying to decide whether or not to tell me a confidence.

'I've been wondering whether to go away for a week in August,' said Prue, as the taxi turned up Park Street, 'when the twins come down to The Keep. I could join them a little later on. I can't see that Freddy would mind. What do you think?'

Theo guessed that this was only a small part of something which was important to her and realised that she did not want to discuss it in detail in the taxi.

'I can't imagine why you shouldn't,' he said. 'Have you had an invitation from a friend or do you just need to have some time alone?'

Prue put her hand over his where it lay between them on the seat. 'Darling Theo,' she said warmly, 'you are one of the few people I know who would understand about needing to be alone.'

She leaned forward to direct the driver to Waterloo Street. Theo dealt with the fare money and his small case while Prue went ahead and unlocked the front door. She was waiting for him in the hall, hat discarded.

'You're in Hal's room, as usual,' she said. 'He's on the camp bed in with Kit. They're not too old to share! Lunch will be ready when you come down.'

It was white fish – bought fresh that morning from Macfisheries – in a creamy sauce with tiny new potatoes and sweet garden peas. Theo ate with a rare hunger, surprised as he always was when he remembered that Prue was a very good cook. It was because she was so decorative, he supposed, and such fun to be with that one never imagined her being practical. She grinned down at him as she put fresh strawberries on the table with home-made shortbread and double cream.

'Don't complain about it not being clotted,' she warned him. 'You're not in Devon yet. Just be glad rationing is over.'

'I wouldn't dream of complaining about anything so delicious,' he told her – but he saw that she had relaxed whilst they had been eating and he was mentally preparing himself to listen to her latest problem.

From the beginning he had been the buffer between Prue and Freddy and he wished that they could each accept the other's differences and become friends. He wondered if he were simply a naïve old bachelor and that it was more realistic to accept that Freddy and Prue were as unmixable as oil and water – but he continued to hope. He poured his coffee black and sat back to wait.

Prue, sitting opposite, poured some of the cream into her coffee and watched it swirl thickly into the black liquid. How to begin? She glanced up and saw him watching her and her heart was suddenly caught with a little thump of love for him. Dear Theo! How often he had sat, just so, watching and waiting, with a kind of tender patience on his face.

'I do love you, Theo,' she said – and blushed scarlet.

'And I love you, too, dear Prue,' he said, undisturbed. 'So what is it that you are going to tell me?'

Prue sighed, shook her head at her own foolishness and relaxed. She had known all along that she would confide in Theo, so why all the silly fuss?

'I'm in love,' she said baldly.

Theo raised his cup and sipped meditatively. If this were all then there should be no problem. Prue had been in love a dozen times since her beloved Johnny had died. Theo's view was that she was unconsciously searching for a replacement; Freddy's view was less complimentary.

'It's not like that,' said Prue acutely, well aware of Theo's thoughts and correctly interpreting his silence. 'It's different this time. I really love him, Theo.'

'Does he love you?' asked Theo.

'He's asked me to marry him,' replied Prue, almost

defiantly. She swallowed her coffee and set the tiny cup back in its saucer, reaching for her cigarettes.

'That doesn't really answer my question,' said Theo thoughtfully.

Prue frowned at him. 'He'd hardly ask me to marry him otherwise, would he?' she asked indignantly. 'Of course he loves me!'

'That's splendid, then,' said Theo imperturbably, refilling Prue's and then his own cup. 'So what's the problem?'

The indignation died out of Prue's face and she tapped her cigarette nervously against the rim of the ashtray. 'It's telling Freddy,' she said obscurely.

Theo gave an inward sigh. He guessed at once that the prospective suitor was not what Freddy would dub 'suitable' and he felt the first twinges of real anxiety.

'Why should Freddy object?' he asked. 'If you love each other . . .?'

The question remained hanging in the air and Prue lifted her chin and looked at him squarely.

'Tony hasn't got a job,' she said, 'and his background is a bit murky. It doesn't matter a bit to me but it will to Freddy.'

'If he hasn't a job, then how does he survive?' asked Theo, his heart sinking. 'Does he have a private income?'

'No,' said Prue almost sulkily. 'He lost his house and everything in the war. A direct hit. His parents are dead. He says he was with the Secret Service in the war which is why he can't talk about the things he did. Perhaps that's what makes it so difficult for him to get a job.'

'So how does he survive?' asked Theo again. He

was really interested and it showed. Prue stopped feeling defensive and propped her elbows on the table, inhaling on her cigarette.

'I don't know,' she said, turning her head to blow the smoke away from the table. 'Sometimes he has a windfall and then he's very generous but I don't know where it comes from. I don't like to ask.'

'Perhaps you should,' suggested Theo gently. 'I can see that Freddy might be unhappy if she thought that he intended to be living off you.'

'Why should it matter?' cried Prue, stabbing her half-smoked cigarette into the ashtray. 'If it were the other way round it wouldn't matter a bit. Everyone would expect me to live off Tony's money.'

'That's quite true,' agreed Theo, 'but unfortunately society isn't yet so advanced for it to be the done thing for a healthy young man to live off his wife.'

'The "done thing",' scoffed Prue. 'Honestly, Theo, you sound just like Freddy!'

'Very likely,' said Theo ruefully, 'but you know that it is exactly what she will say, Prue, and, unfortunately for you, Freddy holds the purse strings. If it were *your* money, if *you* had earned it or inherited it, then that would be very different. As it is, Freddy has the right to ask a few questions.'

Prue stared at him. 'That's a bit below the belt, isn't it? No one would be talking about the money if Johnny were still alive.'

'If John were still alive,' pointed out Theo, 'we wouldn't be having this conversation.'

'Oh, Theo.' Prue slumped down on her folded arms. 'It's not fair. I love him. It's really serious this time. What shall I do?'

'May I meet him?' asked Theo. 'At least I shall be able to make my own decision about him. If you want my advice the least I should do is to make Tony's acquaintance.'

'I'd like you to,' she said at once. 'I just know you'll get on. He's really nice, Theo.'

'Well then.' He smiled at her. 'Let's postpone any judgements until we've met each other. What about some more of that delicious coffee?'

'I'll go and make some fresh.'

She went out, her heels tapping on the wood-block floor, skirt swirling, and Theo shut his eyes for a moment. Living so much alone, he always needed a little time to adjust to his family and he could see quite clearly that there were going to be ructions. He thought of Freddy at The Keep with the children, imagining her reaction to Prue's bombshell, and began to prepare himself mentally for action.

'And is it Tony that you're going away with in August?' he asked, when Prue reappeared.

'No,' answered Prue surprisingly. 'It isn't. You were right the first time, Theo. I need time to think. Tony's around quite a bit at the moment, especially in the day, and I just want to be by myself. Think things out. You know?'

'Certainly, I know.' Theo watched the coffee pouring thickly, inkily, into the fragile white cup. 'It sounds a splendid idea to me.'

'Well, that's a relief.' She grinned at him. 'You'll back me up then? With Freddy?'

'I shall be more than happy to convince her that you need a break,' agreed Theo cautiously.

'That will do for a start.' She poured her own

coffee. 'You'll like Tony, I know you will, Theo. He's had a rough time.'

'So have you,' said Theo gently. 'You've managed splendidly. We all agree on that, you know.'

Prue was taken aback. It was rare for the family to acknowledge that things had been difficult for her and she was more accustomed to defending her position than accepting praise. Theo raised his cup to her in a little gesture of homage and deftly turned the conversation into other channels. Enough had been said for the moment and he had no wish to be drawn further until he had met Tony.

Freddy stood in the garden room arranging roses in a cut-glass bowl. She had converted the ground floor of the west wing into a garden room where she did the flowers and kept her gardening gloves and tools. French doors opened out into the gardens on the west side and here Freddy spent a good deal of time. Today she worked at a big deal table, snipping and plucking at the yellow blooms whilst the children pottered about her. Fox had plumbed in a cold-water tap and small sink and had built shelves to hold vases and bowls and all the paraphernalia that went with Freddy's gardening. Here stood reference books and yellowing newspaper cuttings, held together with paperclips; spools of garden twine lay beside half-used seed packets, whose tops were tightly folded down lest any tiny precious seed should escape. There were jars with scribbled labels and several trays of seedlings, basking on the south-facing window ledge in the sun.

Serious potting-up was done by Fox in the large

greenhouse in the kitchen garden but there was a satisfyingly warm pungent earthy smell in the garden room which Freddy loved. On the whitewashed wall several old coats hung from wooden pegs, beneath which stood a row of gumboots and overshoes, and an old straw hat lay on the faded cushion of one of the wicker chairs. A trug held muddy gloves, a pair of secateurs and a small trowel and fork. Just outside the door that opened into the courtyard, a bee droned lazily amongst the big tubs of geraniums and the puppy stared at it curiously, dodging back quickly as it bumbled heavily towards him. He danced about, growling and feinting, pretending to play with it, but when it flew towards him he ran in to the safety of the garden.

Fliss, curled up in one of the chairs, laughed at his antics – and then stopped abruptly.

She thought: I am *laughing*. Mummy and Daddy and Jamie are *dead* and I am laughing. How *can* I laugh when they are dead? How wicked I must be.

This had happened several times now. Susanna laughed a lot, of course, but she had no idea what had happened in Kenya. And within the first few weeks she seemed to have forgotten that she'd ever had parents and another brother, and had settled in happily with Grandmother and Ellen and Fox. No one could blame Susanna for being herself; she was too young to know any different.

Fliss looked at Mole, who was sitting beneath Freddy's table. He had caught several leaves and petals which had fluttered down and was playing with them, smoothing them and smelling them, content and quiet. The puppy had found him there and was fossicking about now under the table, and Mole was suffering himself to be licked and climbed over. Fliss watched him. Of course, Mole had never been noisily cheerful, like Susanna, or positive and outgoing, like Jamie; he had always been of a quiet, passive disposition, not even anxious and over-sensitive as she, Fliss, was.

Things had changed so much. Once it had been the Big Ones: Jamie and Fliss – and the Littles: Mole and Susanna. Now the three of them were simply 'the children' and her special status – along with Jamie's comradeship – had vanished. Jamie had always included Fliss in his plans and she had been an excellent first lieutenant: obedient, watchful, prepared, adoring. He had calmed her anxieties, laughed away her fears, taken the decisions. Now she had the responsibilities of her siblings without Jamie's common sense and readiness to take over. She wasn't prepared for this responsibility and had no aptitude for it; it brought her anxious nature to the surface.

If only Mole would speak. Several times she had thought that he was on the verge and she had encouraged him desperately – but each time he had shaken his head, near to tears, and she hadn't the heart to be angry with him. It was as if his throat had closed up – yet how could it? He ate and drank, so his throat must be able to open. Fliss thought about it, brow furrowed. It was as if he gagged on words . . . Susanna, who was sitting on the floor beside Mrs Pooter, decorating her with plucked daisy heads, gave a loud yell as Mrs Pooter stood up suddenly and shook herself. The flowers flew everywhere and Susanna shrieked with frustrated creativity – and then laughed with delight as the daisies settled on her hair and in her lap. Fliss sighed enviously. How like Susanna that her tragedies should become pleasures.

Freddy glanced across at her, wiping her hands against her green hessian apron. She was exhausted, not just by the relentless physical demands of three small children but also by her inability *really* to help them. It was so frustrating to be witness to Mole's dumbness, to feel the helpless flutterings of Fliss's fear and anxiety. Only with Susanna was there any kind of real naturalness. Freddy was by nature autocratic; she liked to feel herself in control. She had brought up her twins with confidence, despite her loneliness and youth, and had grown used to having the last word and taking responsibility for her decisions. It was she who had insisted that Fox should teach her to drive when the Great War was over. He was perfectly happy to continue to act as chauffeur, almost shocked that she wanted to be independent to such a degree. She had shown a ready aptitude, however, and was soon skimming through the narrow lanes in the little coupé, taking the boys for picnics and, later, to the station at Staverton to see them off to school. Without this unusual freedom it would have been almost impossible to have made such a close friend of Julia, who lived on the edge of the moor beyond Ashburton and had a car of her own. They were both lucky – and they knew it. In those days in rural Devon, cars were rare enough; women drivers were almost unknown. Even now, twelve years after the war, cars were still a luxury and wives and mothers planned their social lives around the local transport.

Freddy relished her independence and grew even stronger as the years passed. She never dithered or panicked – or never openly. She often discussed problems with Julia – and certainly listened to her suggestions – but she was rarely to be influenced once her own views had been formed. The twins had remained under her control almost until war had been declared, although the Navy was already weakening that control. After the outbreak of war, things had happened too quickly for Freddy to find her bearings in a rapidly changing world. She had absolutely approved of the quiet, practical Alison, judging her to be an excellent wife for Peter; a proper foil for his brilliance and charm. Prudence had been quite another proposition. Freddy had looked askance upon the bright – too bright – curls and the red mouth; the fashionable clothes and easy manner. Yet John loved her, loved her to distraction, and Freddy forbore to show her disapproval. She realised that the time had come to let her boys go. Even this decision she made with confidence and, having made it, implemented it with a brave generosity. She never imagined that she would be left with only one daughter-in-law and with the total responsibility of three of her five grandchildren . . .

She noted Fliss's confusion, heard the small sigh, and braced herself.

'Shall we go out into the garden?' she suggested, untying the strings and pulling the apron off over her head. 'Who would like a turn on the swing? Come on, Mrs Pooter. Out you go.'

She helped Susanna to her feet and peered under the table for Mole. Fliss slid off the chair and followed them out into the sunshine. Susanna ran forward on the grass and the puppy galumphed with her, ears streaming, dashing to and fro, until presently they became entangled and rolled over and over together, Susanna's cries of delight mingling with the puppy's high staccato barks. Fliss glanced at Freddy, anxious lest Susanna might be hurt but Freddy was watching the scene with enjoyment and Fliss relaxed and looked at Mole. With a tremendous shock she saw that he was laughing, laughing so much that he shook – but absolutely silently. If he had been weeping it could not have been less shocking and Fliss felt utterly confused.

She thought: Mole is *laughing*. He knows that they are all dead but he is *laughing*. Does that mean that it is all right to laugh?

Freddy had hurried to sort out the tangle and Mole was running after her, grabbing the puppy as he bounded towards him and falling and rolling with him in his turn. Fliss felt as if some huge weight was lifting gently from her heart. If Mole could laugh, might he not also be able to speak? If only he would talk to her again so that there was someone to share with, to remember with, she would feel less lonely. Grandmother and Ellen and Fox were so kind and so safe – but they were also so *old*. She yearned for the companionship of the days gone by, fearing that it would never return.

Mole had reached the swing, hanging from the lowest branch of the huge oak, and had scrambled on, clutching at the ropes. He waved to her, his face still beaming, and she raced across the lawn towards him. It seemed that it was all right to laugh sometimes, even to be happy. She seized the wooden seat and began to push him, higher and higher, while Freddy laughed and Susanna clapped her hands and Mole flew to and fro in the dappled shade beneath the oak tree.

Chapter Six

Fox let himself out of the gatehouse cottage and paused to light a cigarette. The metalled drive stretched away for half a mile, lapped by fields on either side, before it reached the lane, but Fox turned to his left, passing along the path beside the high stone wall until he came to the green door which opened into the small kitchen courtyard where the washing line was stretched, screened from the lawn by a high thicket of rhododendrons. His hand on the latch, Fox turned to glance down the steep hill. Here Mrs Pooter enjoyed an early morning walk, frightening the rabbits, alerting the grazing sheep and generally being tiresome, which is what she liked best. Mrs Pooter's ancestry was uncertain: Border collie, certainly, of the large and woolly kind, crossed with retriever or maybe spaniel. It was impossible to decide. Fox had brought her to The Keep as a fluffy puppy, saved from a litter which was about to be drowned by a neighbouring farmer.

Freddy's beloved cairn, Kips, had recently died and Fox had hoped that the puppy might help to lessen her grief. He'd said that it was for Ellen, to keep her company, and Freddy had pretended to believe this fiction and the puppy had stayed with Ellen and Fox, rarely straying into the front of the house. Freddy had insisted that no dog could replace Kips; nevertheless she'd loved to watch the puppy's antics and often took her for walks as she grew older so that, in the end, she was simply Mrs Pooter and belonged to them all. She grew to be a large bitch, rusty coloured, with flopping ears and a wily look in her dark brown eyes. She was greedy, cunning and ungrateful, and even now no one quite knew how she had got herself in whelp. After years of never straying she had suddenly escaped from The Keep, returning many hours later with a look of complacency on her hairy face. Later, suspecting the worst, Freddy had summoned the vet, who examined Mrs Pooter and confirmed Freddy's suspicions. When he had gone the three of them had stood staring down at the unrepentant Mrs Pooter.

'I do hope,' Freddy had said, distressed, 'that she hasn't been back to the farm. Wouldn't that be incest?'

'Not in dogs, Madam,' Fox had replied at once. 'It's not the same at all. They don't work like we do.'

Freddy had looked at the self-satisfied Mrs Pooter, lying content and lazy in her bed by the Aga.

'I wouldn't be too sure of that,' she'd said drily.

Fox had found good homes for the two bitches – suspiciously black and white – but it had been a unanimous decision to keep the rusty-coloured dog puppy for themselves. He still had no name. They were all hoping that this might be the thing that would spur Mole into speech. They all talked about names, making suggestions, rejecting them, trying others, whilst all the time praying that Mole might be inspired to make a contribution. So far, each time he had been asked if he liked this name or that, he had merely shaken his head – but they kept hoping.

This morning, Mrs Pooter and the puppy were already out in the yard. The puppy was far too young yet for serious walks; playing in the yard and garden was more than enough exercise for him. Mrs Pooter, however, was ready for her outing, looking forward to a bit of mayhem amongst any straying livestock and hoping for an opportunity to terrorise the rabbit population. She was fully recovered from the tiresome maternal feelings which had taken her by surprise. Motherhood was behind her now and she could settle back into her more familiar and less inhibiting habits.

Fox, gently but firmly, put the puppy inside the back door, took his stick under his arm and he and Mrs Pooter passed out through the green door on to the hillside. It was a still, grey morning and the distant hills rose mysteriously from the mist that flowed quietly over the valley. He might have been looking out across a sea from which islands reared up, insubstantial and remote. There was an echoing silence broken by the harsh cry of a crow and the mournful bleating of a sheep.

He followed the well-worn sheep paths that crossed and recrossed the slopes, his eyes searching for the familiar landmarks: the slab of granite where he often sat and smoked a cigarette; the patch of gorse which overhung the path; the hawthorn tree. Mrs Pooter, nose to ground, ran ahead. Her back view looked busy and alert and Fox wasn't surprised when a rabbit suddenly broke cover and she tore after it in hot pursuit. She never did any real harm and he was content to stroll on quietly, knowing that she would return in her own good time.

His head was busy, however, sorting and resorting the events of the past few days. Fox cherished his independence, glad that his quarters were slightly removed from The Keep itself. Devoted though he was to Freddy, fond as he was of Ellen, he needed to be separate, to go apart. In the early days, his adoration for Freddy had been the mainspring of his life. It was, however, the adoration of servant for mistress and it seemed to him that she was as unreachable, as unattainable, as an angel. He was uplifted by his passion but, as the months lengthened into years, something more physically satisfying became necessary. He guessed at the thoughts in Ellen's mind, realised the suitability, the *neatness* of such a solution, but knew that it would not work. Their mutual affection was too lukewarm for marriage and he cared too much for both women to risk a rupture in the harmony that existed at The Keep. They functioned better separately, united by a disinterested love which was not hampered or confused by messy physical desires.

Isolated as The Keep was, the nearest villages a two- or three-mile walk away, there was little opportunity to build any kind of social life. Nevertheless, one evening at The Sea Trout in Staverton Fox had met a young woman, widowed by the war, struggling to make ends meet. She was renting a tiny cottage in the village and they were hardly friends before they were lovers. She was a farmer's daughter and presently she returned to her family and their farm in North Devon and the young Fox was alone again – though not for too long. This time the woman was older than he was, unhappily married to a lout who blacked her eye and raped her when he was drunk. Fox brought her a measure of tenderness, a gentleness that she had long since forgotten, and gave her back some self-respect. This relationship lasted some years and, when she died suddenly, he was sad. His melancholy stayed with him for some while until he met a widow who ran a bed and breakfast establishment in Totnes – by now he was the proud owner of a bicycle and thus had widened his horizons – and with her he maintained a comfortable relationship which had gently dwindled into an easy and undemanding friendship.

Now, he was too preoccupied by the arrival of the three children to have time for his own affairs. As he wandered on the hill his thoughts were with the silent Mole, his mind worrying at the problem, attempting to see some way through to a solution. Perhaps the newly arrived Theo might have some ideas . . . He heard Mrs Pooter barking excitedly somewhere in the spinney of beech and oak below him, and he glanced at his watch, surprised to see for how long he had been wrapped in his private thoughts.

There was a faint glow now towards the east, a soft diffusion of light which warmed the cool grey of the cloudy vapour. A gentle breeze, arising from nowhere, shredded the mist so that it parted and reformed, allowing glimpses of shapes and familiar vistas. Mrs Pooter appeared suddenly beside him, tail wagging, and he dropped a hand to her moisture-covered head.

'Old bitch,' he said affectionately. 'Home then? Time for breakfast?'

She seemed to understand him, setting off at once the way they had come. He paused to light a cigarette, cupping the match with his hand, and began the climb, following her back to The Keep.

'We have another drama looming,' said Freddy as Ellen placed early morning tea beside her bed. 'Theo tells me that Prue is thinking of marrying again.'

It was a while now since Freddy had dropped the formalities of the earlier years. She knew that she could relax with Ellen, talk to her openly, even gossip with her, knowing that Ellen would never take advantage. Ellen and Fox, trained to the old ways, still referred to Prue as Mrs John in public and to her face; privately, on their own together, they were less formal. They appreciated Freddy's informality and would never have done anything which might have made her regret it. She knew how lucky she was. Without the support and love of Ellen and Fox she would have been very lonely and she knew that she would never be able to replace them. It was a luxury to unburden herself to Ellen, to chat with the ease of familiarity with Fox.

'Fancy,' said Ellen, now, non-committally. She stood back, waiting for more information which might indicate how she should react.

Freddy hauled herself up against the pillows and reached for the cup. 'Theo's trying to be reasonable about it,' she said irritably. 'So annoying, that soothing rational tone he uses when he wants to reconcile me to his way of thinking. Prue introduced him to this Tony, apparently.'

'Did she indeed?' Ellen was surprised. Prue must be

serious indeed if matters had gone so far. 'And what does Mr Theo think about him?'

'Theo says he is very charming.' Freddy began to laugh. 'Why are people surprised when confidence tricksters and rakes are charming? Surely it's part of the job?'

'Is that what he is?' asked Ellen, shocked. 'Surely not.'

'Theo is being tactful and cautious.' Freddy sipped gratefully at her tea. 'But I can see through him. The young man is out of work and has no prospects so far as we can tell. He is also well educated and charming and very good-looking. So there you have it.'

'What can Mrs John be thinking of?' asked Ellen. 'How would he look after her?'

'Precisely my question. It appears that Prue is going to be supporting *him*.'

Ellen clicked her tongue against her teeth and looked disapproving. Freddy sighed.

'Quite. But Prue is in love with him, it seems. And he with her.'

'Well . . .' Ellen hesitated. 'And is Mr Theo in favour of it, then?'

'Not quite. But he is in sympathy with Prue whose feelings for this man, according to Theo, are very real. He's hoping we won't antagonise her so that she does something foolish.'

'Perhaps he's more in love with her money,' said Ellen bluntly.

'Those are my thoughts, too,' said Freddy. 'Of course he might be genuinely in love with her.'

'But how can we be sure?' Ellen sounded anxious. She was very fond of Prue and felt that Freddy was often rather too tough on her. 'We wouldn't want her to be hurt.'

Freddy sighed. 'Of course we wouldn't,' she said impatiently, 'but why couldn't it be someone sensible? Or is that too much to ask? Well, we'll see what happens when he discovers that Prue's allowance will be reduced if she remarries.'

'That sounds hard, Madam.' Ellen frowned a little. 'How will she manage? What about the twins?'

'The twins will be looked after,' said Freddy firmly, 'but there is no reason why we should support a fit young man who is perfectly capable of work. Prue won't starve, don't worry, but this might show him in his true colours.'

'I see trouble ahead,' said Ellen gloomily.

'So do I,' agreed Freddy. 'As if we haven't enough on our plates at the moment. She'll be down with the twins in a few weeks' time so we'll be able to talk it over properly. Theo's staying on for a bit to help us through.'

'Thank the Lord for that,' said Ellen, with more sincerity than tact.

Freddy grinned. 'Don't you trust me to be subtle, Ellen?' she asked mischievously. 'Surely you don't think I might be tactless and upset our poor Prue's finer feelings?'

Ellen breathed heavily through her nose as she picked up Freddy's cup and saucer. 'Mr Theo keeps us all on the straight and narrow,' she said repressively. 'And I must be getting on with the children's breakfast.'

Freddy watched her go, still smiling to herself. She felt certain that once Prue's young man realised that he wasn't getting a free meal ticket for life then he would probably back off. From what Theo had told her, she guessed that his professed love for Prue contained a large portion of self-interest. She was not so certain about Prue. Freddy's smile faded. Deep down she was genuinely fond of Prue, although often irritated by her, and she did not want her hurt. Perhaps the whole thing was a passing fad and a few weeks at The Keep might restore her sense of balance.

Pushing back the bedclothes, Freddy sat on the edge of the bed, deep in thought. It would be sensible to talk it through carefully with Theo. The last thing anyone wanted was a pair of star-crossed lovers on their hands . . . Freddy groaned. She had been up late, talking with him and she was tired, worried about Mole, her whole life turned upside down, and now there was Prue and her problems. Freddy's heart was heavy and she felt lacking in energy and the ability to cope. She was reminded of her conversation with Julia, telling her that she had forgotten how exhausting young children could be, and remembering what Julia had said about grieving.

She thought: I am sixty-two. Ellen is sixty. Fox is sixty-five. Such an *old* household for very young children.

She continued to sit, brooding. She had an idea which she knew Ellen would resist strenuously but which she wanted to discuss with Theo. Her thoughts ranged to and fro – school for Fliss, Mole's continuing dumbness, Susanna, Prue – until she became confused and almost desperate. Life was becoming altogether too complicated for her. She took a deep breath, stretched, picked up her dressing gown and went to have her bath.

The children were eating their breakfast in the kitchen. Fox and Ellen had theirs together early, before the household was awake, but Fox generally appeared for a cup of tea at the children's breakfast time. A highchair had been found for Susanna, and Mole was perched on a cushion so as to be able to deal competently with his egg. Mrs Pooter kept a weather eye for occasional accidents whilst the puppy, exhausted by earlier foragings in the garden, slept by the Aga. '*In* we go,' said Ellen, popping an eggy finger into Susanna's open mouth. '*Good* girl, then. Now, one more for Ellen.'

Susanna crowed eggily and beat on the little tray with her fist, leaning out to look down at Mrs Pooter, who had come closer, hoping for a mislaid crust or a carelessly dropped porridgey spoon. Fliss ate slowly, carefully removing the dribbles of yoke which spilled out over the shell, dipping her soldiers gently into her egg. She glanced at Mole from time to time, lest he should be having difficulty, but he was dealing very well with his breakfast and she gave herself up to enjoyment. She only truly relaxed when Ellen and Fox were present and the kitchen was fast becoming her haven of peace and safety.

The cold damp weather, which had rolled in soon after their arrival, had given way to brighter, warmer days. The early morning mist had vanished and the sun was shining. As she drank her milk, Fliss was aware of a kind of excitement that she had not experienced for many weeks. It was an anticipatory, fluttery feeling in her stomach which seemed to make her breakfast difficult to swallow. Today, she and Mole were going to try out their new bicycles. Of course, they were not really new: Fliss's two-wheeler had belonged to Kit when she was younger – younger even than Fliss, for Fliss was tiny for her age and the bicycle was now too small for the leggy Kit. Mole's tricycle had belonged to his father and had a lid to the shiny 'boot' between its two back wheels, in which Mole could put his treasures.

Fox had brought these bicycles out of the store-room which flanked the gatehouse to the right of the gate and had promised to clean them up and oil the necessary parts, ready for today, and Fliss looked up hopefully when he appeared at the kitchen door. He gave her a little wink before going to the Aga to pick up the teapot where Ellen left it stewing for him. Fliss put down her mug and looked at Mole. Fox had allowed him to pedal the tricycle along the paved path of the courtyard and Mole's feet had gone round and round like pistons as he crouched over the handlebars. Fliss and Fox had laughed at the sight of him and he had been very reluctant to climb off. Fox had showed him the patches of rust, and explained how oiling it would make the pedals go faster, and then Fliss had had an experimental wobble on Kit's little Raleigh . . .

As Mole swallowed the last of his toast and drained his milk, his eyes were fixed on Fox. In his mind's eye he saw the tricycle, blue and shining, with the little hatch in the back which he could open. He wanted to speak, to ask if it was ready for him, out in the courtyard, but his silence had become such a habit that it was as if it had become impossible to form words; the more he thought about it, the more difficult it became. He swallowed and swallowed, tension rising in him, his throat dry, and Fliss, watching him, grew frightened.

She thought: He is trying to speak but he can't. Something is stopping him. Supposing he never speaks again?

'Mole,' she said desperately. 'Mole, don't!'

Ellen looked at them, distracted from holding Susanna's mug to her mouth, alerted by the fright in Fliss's voice. 'What's wrong?' she asked sharply.

'It's Mole,' cried Fliss, near to tears. 'He's trying to speak. I *know* he is. And he can't. Oh, *why* can't he?'

They all looked at Mole, who stared back, his throat working, eyes round with terror. It was Fox who stepped forward, swinging Mole up from his chair, holding him tightly.

'Course he can speak,' he said contemptuously. 'Course he can. Got rusty, that's what 'tis. Only to be expected. Like the old bikes. Haven't been used for a while so they needed to be oiled up, didn't they? Same with young Mole. Open up. Let's have a look.'

Mole obediently opened his mouth and Fox peered in.

'Nothing wrong there,' he said cheerfully. 'All in working order. It'll come back, given time.'

He waggled Mole's tongue, chuckling, and both Mole and Fliss felt the tension running out of them. If Fox could laugh about it then it must be all right. In due course, Mole would speak again. He just needed oiling up.

'Quite right,' Ellen was saying, wiping Susanna's

mouth and sticky hands. 'Can't speak, indeed. Whatever next, I wonder. Worst thing to do is to get worked up about it. Don't try too hard and it'll come natural.'

Fliss thought she might collapse with relief and she clasped her trembling hands tightly together, trying to smile. It had been horrid to see Mole, swallowing and swallowing, his face so strained . . .

'So who be coming to ride bikes, then?' asked Fox, setting Mole gently on his feet. 'Out there waiting in the courtyard, they be. Anyone interested?'

Fliss scrambled down, the fluttery excitement returning, and she and Mole raced out of the door. Ellen and Fox exchanged a speaking look before he followed them, leaving Ellen with Susanna and the dogs and the task of clearing up the breakfast with the company of *Housewives' Choice*.

Chapter Seven

Theo's quarters were on the top floor of the east wing. He liked to be tucked away, up high, looking down into the valley and out across the great sweep of countryside. He would be seduced from his daily round, drawn to his study or bedroom window, to watch the clouds tumbling across the great reaches of the heavens as the gales roared from the west; the scarlet and gold banners streaming before an east wind blowing out of a bright dawn; a thin new-minted moon hanging in the eggshell green of the evening sky. The constantly changing scene entranced him, drawing him back time after time, distracting him from his work. Previously, it hadn't mattered too much – there had been no really serious work from which to be distracted – but Chapter Four of *Ethics of War*, entitled 'Minimum Force', lay neglected on his desk as he idled upon the window seat.

His quarters were not extensive: two large rooms and a bathroom. The larger room was his bedroom, looking north and east, and here he always kept spare sets of clothes so as to be able to travel light. This room adjoined his study, with a window facing east whilst the other looked over the courtyard. Both rooms were furnished with an almost ascetic economy. He felt uneasy when he was weighted down with belongings, fastened to the earth with unnecessary encumbrances. Books he loved; books – and cricket. No ornaments or photographs decorated the chest in his bedroom and the cream-painted walls were bare. His study was always tidy; papers stacked neatly; pencils and pens kept tidily in an earthenware jar on the old battered leather-topped desk.

Theo uncurled himself from the window seat and wandered back to his desk. He stood for some moments staring down at his small clear writing on the page – but he was not really seeing it. He was thinking about the conversation regarding Prue which he had had with Freddy a few days before. She had been remarkably restrained. Apart from observing that Prudence was quite staggeringly the wrong name for her daughter-in-law, she had listened to him quietly and agreed to make an effort not to antagonise her when she brought the twins down for the holidays. He had told her that Prue would be going away for a week on her own – and here Freddy had raised her eyebrows cynically – but he had emphasised that Prue *would* be alone, that she wanted time to *think*. At this unusual suggestion Freddy had exhibited certain emotions, which she made an effort to control when Theo looked at her severely, but still she had held her peace. Theo was deeply grateful – if surprised. It wasn't like Freddy to mince her words or hide her feelings. He wondered if it might be the advent of the children which was having a softening effect on her. Or it might be that she was simply so exhausted that she had no strength left with which to argue. Whatever it was, Theo was too relieved to question it.

Voices floated up through the open window which looked on to the courtyard and Theo strolled across the room, his footsteps muffled by the Chinese rugs which Freddy had laid on the oak-stained floorboards: he wouldn't have noticed if the floors had remained bare. Below him, Susanna, in a poppy-red sunsuit and a floppy linen hat, was being given a ride on Fliss's bicycle. Freddy held the small wriggling body firmly in place on the saddle whilst Fliss wheeled her slowly round the rectangle of grass. Mole led the procession on his tricycle, looking backwards at regular intervals to make certain that the others were keeping up. Susanna's bright little face was turned up to Freddy, who bent over her, encouraging her, whilst Fliss pushed manfully with her load, grasping the handlebars tightly.

The sun had shone fitfully all day but it was very warm; close and thundery, with an airlessness which was oppressive. Fliss and Mole were in grey shorts and Aertex shirts of buttercup yellow and there were sandshoes on their bare feet. Mole's skin – like Susanna's – was already a warm dark gypsy brown but Fliss, being so fair, had tanned to a golden honey colour. Freddy was her usual weatherbeaten self. Hours of gardening and walking Mrs Pooter kept her permanently exposed to wind and sun so that her bare arms, emerging from the short-sleeved blouse which was coming adrift from her tweed skirt, were as brown as Mole's, despite the fairness of her hair and skin.

Theo, watching her, recalled the young Freddy who had come as a bride to The Keep. How striking she'd been; long-legged, graceful, her blonde hair piled up on the small well-shaped head, her grey eyes clear and untroubled. Bertie had been so ridiculously proud. He had barely been able to take his eyes from her, this daughter of his captain whom he had met at a ball. He had no mother to greet her. Their mother had died at Theo's birth after a succession of miscarriages and stillbirths. She had carried Theo to full term and had died giving him birth – and Theo had never quite been able to forgive himself for causing her death. Their father had been almost as much in love with Freddy as Bertie was, but he had died within a few months of their marriage and a year later Bertie had followed him. It seemed impossible to believe that all this had happened more than forty years ago.

Looking down, Theo remembered how he and Bertie had played there in the courtyard and how, later, the twins, Peter and John, had ridden round and round, just as Peter's children were riding now. He remembered Prue with John, home on a few days' leave from the war, holding Hal and Kit whilst Freddy took photographs, and Peter and Alison with their small brood, setting out from The Keep for Kenya with such tremendous enthusiasm . . .

The scent of the Albertine, which clothed the wall beneath his window, drifted in and he leaned out to breathe it in, turning a rose to inhale its delicate perfume. The movement attracted Mole's attention and he stopped pedalling to stare up at him. The others turned, too, and Freddy waved.

'Teatime,' she called. 'Come on down, Theo. I need reinforcements. Ellen is still in Totnes with Fox and we're all dying of thirst.'

Susanna crowed to him, waving her chubby fists as Freddy lifted her from the saddle, and Fliss smiled. She liked Theo. He wasn't the same as the other adults she knew and she liked the way he treated her as though she were grown up.

'Come down,' she called suddenly, abandoning her usual reserve. 'Come and have tea with us. Please.'

He bowed to her from the window and they waited, watching the door from which he would emerge into the courtyard. He went straight to Fliss and she saw that he had plucked a dark pink bud, which he gravely tucked in the buttonhole of her shirt so that she could smell it if she dropped her chin just a little. The others watched as she smiled at him and took his hand – and they all went in to tea together.

'You do agree with me, don't you?' Freddy asked Theo some days later. 'Now you've had a chance to weigh the evidence? We need someone to look after Susanna. It's simply too much for Ellen.'

'Ellen doesn't think so,' replied Theo thoughtfully.

They were sitting in the breakfast room after dinner, Theo was nursing a brandy and Freddy knew that they would remain undisturbed now and were free to talk. The breakfast room was a high square room, one of its windows looking east so that it was at its best in the morning. Freddy had never liked the dining room and, when the twins had gone away to school, she had taken to eating all her own meals in the breakfast room; all her meals except tea. Tea, by tradition, was eaten in the hall. During the winter a log fire burned in the huge granite fireplace; in the summer the big front door, and the windows to each side of it, were left open to the courtyard.

Freddy and Theo were sitting at an oval drop-leaf oak table, placed by the window. She had rejected the heavy mahogany dining-room furniture, which seemed rather portentous for a woman living so much alone, and had furnished this more intimate room with smaller pieces. The sideboard was actually the lower half of an oak dresser and the chairs, with their graceful curved backs, had tapestry seats embroidered by the first Mrs Chadwick to live at The Keep. On the walls were some delightful watercolours, painted by a Chadwick who had served in South Africa, and those delicate paintings of seascapes and mountains of the Cape lent an odd, exotic touch to this quiet and very English room.

Freddy pushed back her chair a little so as to stretch her long legs. She was well aware of Ellen's resistance to her idea but hoped to have Theo on her side.

'It's not simply the work,' she said. 'We're such an old household for three young children. Susanna isn't yet two. I know that she has Mole and Fliss but there's a whole generation missing. Do you see what I mean? Their parents' age group is wiped out. I can't think that this is right for them. The balance is all wrong.'

Theo had been temporarily distracted from the immediate problems at The Keep by the Test Match at Lord's. He and Fox gravitated at regular intervals to Ellen's wireless, which sat on the dresser in the kitchen. They huddled together to listen to the commentary, alternately groaning and cheering like schoolboys until Ellen had lost patience with them and turned them out. Fox had gone to disinter the twins' old stumps, cricket bat and an ancient tennis ball whilst Theo had gone to find Mole. The three of them had met up on the small side lawn where they'd indulged in an impromptu and very noisy game, watched by a fascinated Fliss.

Now, Theo was remembering how Mole had laughed – that strange internal silent laughter – to see Fox running to and fro like a madman whilst the ball had gone flying up over the rhododendron bushes and Fliss, infected by their enthusiasm, had raced after it with Mole at her heels. Later, they had allowed her to bat . . .

'I think you might be right,' he said. 'They need people to teach them games and how to play.'

'Exactly,' cried Freddy eagerly. 'You see my point? Fox and Ellen are wonderful but they simply haven't the energy. And it's more than that. We're old-fashioned. I'm well aware of that. We live a very secluded life here. It's important that the children are kept up to date.'

'The *whole* balance is important,' said Theo slowly. 'The elderly have their place in family life. Traditions, experience—'

'Of course they do,' said Freddy impatiently. She could barely allow Theo to finish a sentence, so anxious was she to hurry on, to carry her point. 'I quite see that. But they have more than enough of us here. Four of us. It's the middle generation that is completely missing.'

'Mmm.' Theo was nodding, agreeing with her. 'Of course, there's Prue . . .'

'Prue!' exclaimed Freddy dismissively. 'Anyway, she's not here, is she? She doesn't come nearly often enough to be of help.'

This was quite true and Theo had no intention of pressing it. He gazed out into the light summer evening, remembering Mole's creditable performance with the bat. No doubt Peter or Jamie had already given him some simple training. Perhaps he might grow up to be a cricketer . . .

'Well, she doesn't,' said Freddy defensively, mistaking Theo's silence for criticism. 'We need someone here all the time.'

'I'm sure you're right.'

Theo smiled at her and, suddenly, Freddy really saw him properly for the first time since he had arrived. She had been so preoccupied, so busy, that she hadn't noticed that there were new grey streaks in his hair, that he looked older . . . Panic tickled under her ribs, her heart jumping with an odd fear. Theo simply must not grow old. He had always been Bertie's younger brother, to be teased or mothered; it was inconceivable to think of Theo as an old man – or to think of life without him. Julia was right: just being near him soothed her terrors.

She thought: He is fifty-nine. That's not old. How would I manage without Theo?

'Don't leave us,' she said to him. 'Don't go back to Southsea. Stay with us here. I *need* you, Theo.'

'Not nearly as much as you imagine, my dear Freddy.' He was laughing away those terrors. 'I don't think I'm quite ready yet to settle permanently at The Keep.'

'That's because you're utterly selfish,' she grumbled.

'You talk about God and religion but all you think about is yourself.'

'I very rarely talk about God or religion,' he protested mildly, still laughing. 'And I think your idea of a young nanny to deal with Susanna and help out with the others is a much better idea than installing yet another old codger at The Keep.'

'We're *not* old codgers, at least—' Freddy saw the illogicality of her reasoning and began to laugh. 'But you won't go just yet, will you?'

'Not just yet,' he agreed. 'I shall wait to see Prue and the twins arrive, anyway.'

'Yes, of course.' Freddy sighed and shook her head. 'It's going to be a very full house. Poor Ellen.'

'The twins will muck in,' said Theo comfortingly. 'We all will. And it will be good for the little ones to see their cousins.'

'If only Mole could overcome this terrible dumbness.' She had said it a thousand times. 'Occasionally I think he's on the edge of it but he never quite makes it.'

'He will. I'm quite certain of it. One day something momentous will happen and he will forget himself long enough for his tongue to be unlocked again.'

Freddy looked at him curiously. 'You mean it needs some kind of crisis?'

'I . . . think so,' said Theo slowly. 'I think he needs to be shocked out of his terrible preoccupation. It *must* happen sooner or later.'

Freddy was silent, thinking of her own loss and grief. She had very little time to dwell on it but it was there in her mind. Theo watched her, knowing what was coming.

'How can you believe in God?' she burst out. 'How *can* you, when things like this happen?'

'These were men's actions, Freddy, not God's. God tries to draw us to Him by love. It is we who reject Him, preferring violence and greed and hate. We have free will to choose.'

She shook her head, blinking away tears. 'Ellen will be putting the coffee in the drawing room. Let's have a stroll outside before the light goes. The nicotiana is so wonderful at this time of the evening. Come on, Theo.'

He rose to follow her, grieved that he could not bring her solace, saddened by his own inadequacies. They passed across the flagged floor of the shadowy hall, through the drawing room and out on to the terrace. A cool breeze made Freddy shiver and she tucked her arm inside Theo's, feeling the comforting warmth of his jersey. She could not speak out her love, as Prue had done, but her hold tightened and he returned the pressure, anxious to reassure her, as they walked together in the garden they had shared for nearly forty years.

As they strolled, Theo thought again about Tony. He could see why he would be attractive to women and men alike: good-looking – but not *too* handsome – with an easy camaraderie and chivalrous manners. Men would think of him as a 'good sort' whilst women would find him fun: he would flutter them a little without threatening them. Theo wondered how genuine Tony's affection for Prue was. It would be terribly easy to love Prue – but would that kind of love be enough? Prue needed someone to care deeply for her as John had cared, protectively without stifling her or misunderstanding her ability to love. It was clear to see that Prue was lonely, and that she was going to miss the twins terribly when they went away to their respective boarding schools in the autumn, and it would be difficult to persuade her that it was better to be alone than with the wrong person. During their evening together he had watched them both closely and it was evident that Prue was deeply involved with Tony. He had been sweet with her and, except for the fact that he could not support her, had seemed as responsive and kind as any other man in the same circumstances.

Later, Prue had made Theo promise that he would do his best for them with Freddy and Theo had agreed he would represent the situation fairly. Had he done so? Impossible for him to judge.

'Our coffee will be getting cold,' Freddy reminded him as they turned back towards the house. 'Too many worries, that's the trouble with us. First the children, especially Mole, and now Prue . . .'

'Play for us,' he suggested as they crossed the terrace and re-entered the drawing room. 'It will help to clear your mind and I always feel calmer when I've listened to you playing.'

She went readily to the Bechstein whilst he poured the coffee.

'Any particular request?' she asked as he placed her coffee cup beside her.

'Nothing melancholy, nothing complicated,' he replied as he returned to his chair with his own coffee – and smiled with contented delight as the first notes of Grieg's Holberg Suite filled the quiet drawing room.

Chapter Eight

As the train steamed out of Temple Meads, Prue sat back comfortably in her seat and relaxed for the first time for days. Getting the twins organised for a month's holiday at The Keep was exhausting and Tony had not made things easier. He was not being generous or understanding about Prue's plan to have a week to herself. Clearly he was anxious lest he should lose her – that Prue might decide that she was happier free – and she was rather touched by his lack of confidence. Usually it was she who felt insecure, realising that most men were cautious of taking on a widow with two children. It had never occurred to her for a moment that Tony might be interested in her worldly goods; as far as Prue was concerned these were too few to be impressive. Tony always had lots of good ideas about how he was going to get himself sorted out and had hinted at expectations of his own. It seemed so churlish to keep questioning him when he never asked her to pay for anything and he cared about her so much.

Tony, it seemed, thought that love was more important than wealth and position; that together they would manage. Prue knew that if it hadn't been for the thought of Freddy in the background, she might have already accepted Tony's proposal. She suspected that her anxiety that the twins might not like Tony as a stepfather was merely an excuse for avoiding facing the fact that she was afraid of Freddy. Prue tried to analyse this fear. Freddy had always been perfectly kind to her and very generous. She had provided for them all after Johnny's death, saying that she thought it was important that the twins felt secure and that Prue should not have to leave them so as to earn money. Prue, who had no desire to work, was grateful – but paid the price of being beholden.

To be absolutely fair, Freddy had made the dividends from Johnny's shares payable direct to Prue's bank and she had given the mews house to Prue. Nevertheless, Prue, although she never had to ask Freddy for money, was aware that she was Freddy's pensioner and, from time to time, she felt a sense of frustration. Of course, she could have rejected it all and set out under her own steam – but she knew that she had no skills which might earn enough money to support herself and the twins to the same standard and it seemed unfair to make them suffer. Anyway, life was much more comfortable this way; the twins well educated, the house charming; having to feel grateful to Freddy was a small price to pay for all these benefits.

Fitting Tony into this picture, however, was rather more difficult. It was impossible for Prue to pretend that she was at liberty to move Tony into her home and into her life without consulting Freddy. Theo had confirmed this. His words had remained in Prue's consciousness. '*It isn't the done thing for a healthy*

*young man to live off his wife . . . Freddy has the right
to ask a few questions.'*

Prue thought that Tony had shown up very well
with Theo. He had displayed a serious, thoughtful
side that Prue rarely saw and he had asked intelligent
questions about Theo's war and what it had been like
as a chaplain on one of His Majesty's warships. Theo
had recounted one or two amusing anecdotes, making
light of the hardships, and asked Tony about his own
experiences. Tony had said at once that his own
service had come under the 'Top Secret' stamp but he
had told one or two stories that sounded very authen-
tic despite his discretion. When Theo had asked what
he had been doing since the war, Tony hinted that he
was still employed from time to time in that same
capacity.

Prue had begged Theo not to behave as if he were
her father and Tony a suitor, asking for her hand.
This had made it impossible for Theo to probe more
deeply regarding Tony's income or ability to support
Prue. However, the evening had been a good one and
Tony had come out of it very well. Never had Prue
loved him so much as then, watching him with Theo.
When he and Theo talked about the war there was a
manliness, a hardness which Prue had not noticed
before, a toughness which made her feel weak with
love for him. He was so good-looking, so much at
ease, so charming. Why should he have to be treated
as though he were a young boy seeking favours? Her
resentment on his behalf had made her more generous with her love than ever before and she was
beginning to wonder why on earth she was having this
sabbatical. It was clear that she and Tony loved each

other; it was no one else's affair.

This was certainly Tony's view. The affection she'd shown him after Theo left had been gratifying and encouraging, and he had been surprised when she had insisted that she still wanted a week alone 'to think things through'. At first he had been gently amused and very persuasive. When this had not worked, he had become hurt and rather quiet. Still Prue had remained outwardly unmoved – although inside she'd been churning with guilt and remorse – and he had resorted to accusing her of not loving him, of leading him on. She had been very upset but he had implied that he would only believe in her love for him if they went to bed together. Feeling guilty, afraid of losing him, weak with her own desire and longing for love, she'd given in to him.

Even now, several days later, as she sat in the train, Prue was remembering that afternoon at his flat with a delight which spread glowingly through her whole frame and manifested itself as a smile, lingering almost self-consciously on her lips. Inwardly she sighed. Why on earth *was* she going away? With the twins at The Keep for a month it was an ideal opportunity to be with Tony alone and, even though she must put in a reasonably long appearance with the family, it would be quite easy to pretend that she was spending a fortnight with a girl friend. After all, they had accepted that she was having a week alone at a cottage in Cornwall, lent by a friend. So why had she hung on to her decision in the face of such opposition? Was it the thought of Freddy? Or was it some deep instinct within herself that warned her against this step?

Prue thought: I need time to rest and think and be alone. It's not just Tony. I need a break from everything. It's as simple as that.

Tony, reassured by their lovemaking, had become a little less grumpy but she had been obliged to give him an idea of the location of her friend's cottage and a promise that she would telephone him. With these tokens he had become more content and Prue had been able to give her mind to the children; sorting out shorts and shirts and trying to squash into their cases the various items without which, they insisted, they could not live for four whole weeks. Once on the train, they had bagged the window seats, sitting opposite each other, occasionally kicking each other accidentally-on-purpose, happy to be travelling west. Prue saw them grin at each other and her heart was moved within her by love for them, knowing how she would miss them when they started boarding school in the autumn. Once again fear seized her. Would their happy familiar little circle be changed and spoiled by the inclusion of a fourth person?

Kit leaned across to touch Prue's knee. 'Is it time for our sandwiches yet?' she whispered. She glanced rather shyly at the other passengers, who stared ahead pretending not to hear, whilst Prue looked out at the landscape and tried to get her bearings.

'Taunton's the next station,' Hal told her. He consulted his wristwatch – a Christmas present from Freddy – and made a face. 'It's not quite twelve o'clock. Too early, I suppose.'

'Well . . .' Prue looked at their hopeful faces and relented. They had all been up very early and breakfast seemed a long way past. 'We could have our sandwiches now and keep our apples and the chocolate for a bit later.'

Hal jumped up to reach for the small picnic bag on the rack above his head whilst Prue looked apologetically at her fellow passengers. Travelling with children could be rather trying and she hated to upset people. She sat forward on her seat in an attempt to shield them from any interested looks and they talked quietly together, eating egg sandwiches, planning what they would do when they arrived. She let the twins chatter, wondering what Theo had told Freddy about Tony and whether she would raise the subject . . . Prue passed Hal the flask containing the twins' orangeade and began to fold up the greaseproof paper. At least Theo would be there, waiting for her, supporting her. Theo, surely, would be on her side.

It was very hot. The Keep seemed pinned down in a timeless breathlessness beneath the heat's power; even the birds were silent. Mole had long since abandoned his tricycle in the courtyard and taken refuge in the hall. He liked the hall. Either side of the granite fireplace stood two high-backed sofas, their faded chintz piled with cushions, facing each other across the low, long table. A deep comfortable armchair had been placed at the end of this table, so that these chairs made a little room within the hall. There was a tartan rug on the armchair, for it was often draughty here, and Mole would take the rug and burrow beneath the cushions on the sofa, pulling the rug on top of him, completely hidden.

It was too hot today to hide beneath the rug and Mole climbed on to one of the sofas, rolling himself beneath the cushions. He lay languidly, listening to the silence, breathing in the accumulated scents of old stone, musty fabric, beeswax and dog. It was cooler in the hall and Mole dozed a little. The heat reminded him of Africa and he dreamed that he was back in the low single-storey farmhouse, asleep in the wicker chair whilst the sun streamed through the cracks in the shutters and made patterns on the matting flooring. Dimly he was aware of Fliss's voice somewhere in the back of the house and someone – was it Cookie? – singing to Susanna. '*I had a cat and cat pleased me. I fed my cat by yonder tree. Cat goes fiddle-i-fee.*' He turned his cheek into the cushion, his limbs relaxed, eyelids heavy. Susanna was trying to sing, too. '*Cow goes moo-moo . . .*' She laughed with pleasure at her efforts and Mole smiled in his sleep. He knew that she would never remember the right order for the animals; even Fliss couldn't. Only Jamie ever got it quite right. And Mummy. Mole stirred a little. There was something worrying about Mummy but he couldn't remember exactly what it was. He struggled with a fleeting memory but the heat and sleep held him in their tangled web and his eyelids ceased to flutter and closed heavily again. Other noises impinged upon his consciousness: footsteps; the closing of a door; the sound of a car approaching; voices somewhere above his head. He roused himself a little. Someone was still singing: '*I had a wife and wife pleased me. I fed my wife by yonder tree . . .*' Suddenly Fliss's cry shattered the silence and penetrated Mole's dream. 'They've arrived! They're here!'

He woke, staring about him. He was puzzled by the hall but some great urgency, implicit in Fliss's cry, hurried him off the sofa and across to the door. Dazed and still half asleep he stared out into the courtyard, his thoughts and dreams confused as he watched the car pull up and the door open. He knew that he had been dreaming, worrying about Mummy, Mummy and Jamie, but here they were, home safely after all.

'They're here!' Fliss's voice rang out again and Mole woke right up. He wasn't back in Kenya but here in England, at The Keep with Grandmother, and Jamie and Mummy and Daddy were dead. Yet here was Jamie, getting out of the car, his bright hair shining in the sun, laughing and stretching, staring round him happily. Mole's heart jumped about so violently he had to stop breathing; his throat was dry. It must have been some terrible, awful nightmarish mistake. Jamie was *alive*. He was here, in the court-yard, and Mummy and Daddy must be with him. A woman was climbing out now; he could see the full cotton skirt spilling out of the door, her bare leg extended . . .

Mole gasped, swallowed – and found his voice. 'Mummy!' he screamed. 'Mummy! Jamie!' He ran down the steps and across the grass where the boy and the woman stood as if petrified into stone. 'Jamie!' he screamed and flinging his arms round Hal's waist he turned to look at Prue . . .

He screamed again, this time in confusion and despair, and Fliss was there beside him, her face white, tears pouring down her cheeks. 'I told you, Mole,' she was crying, beseeching, 'I *told* you that Hal and Kit were coming with Aunt Prue. That Fox was fetching them from the station. Ooooh . . .'

She collapsed into tears whilst Mole, shocked, continued to stare disbelievingly at Hal until Prue bent down and took him into her arms and carried him into the house.

Freddy sat on Theo's window seat, hugging her knees. He saw that her face was haggard and he touched her briefly on the shoulder as he passed, going to sit down behind his desk.

'Well, we've certainly had the crisis and it seems that you were right. But can you imagine anything more awful?' she asked at last. There was a long silence.

'But he has regained his voice,' said Theo.

Freddy nodded. 'As you foresaw. The shock freed his voice. Fliss broke down completely. I think that she has just been holding everything inside and this was the last straw. She blamed herself, you see.'

'How could she, poor child? How could any of us know that Mole would think that Hal was Jamie?'

'I should have thought of it,' said Freddy, resting her forehead on her knees. 'I knew how alike they were. After all, their fathers were twins and there has always been a strong resemblance between the two boys. It just never occurred to me.' She raised her head and looked at Theo. 'I shall never forgive myself. Never. Poor, poor Mole.'

'But he is speaking again,' insisted Theo. 'If it achieved that then it was worth it. That and making Fliss grieve. It is dangerous to bury such real sorrow. She will be all the better for allowing it to come out. And Mole, too. He wept with Fliss. Perhaps that was his grief pouring out with hers ... And he is still talking.'

'It was Prue.' Freddy sounded puzzled. 'They absolutely fastened on her. She held them while they wept.'

Theo watched her, wondering if she felt jealous, but she sounded simply surprised.

'Perhaps,' he offered, 'it is because she is . . . motherly. Her children are still young and she is used to sudden storms and disasters. Perhaps she reminded them of Alison.'

Freddy shook her head, baffled. 'Whatever it was, it worked. And it has confirmed my belief that the children need a young person. I am quite certain that I am right about that.'

'I have never disagreed with you,' Theo pointed out. 'It is Ellen you need to convince. Where are the children now?'

'They went with Prue and the twins to unpack. I think you may be right, Theo. It might just have been a blessing in disguise. We shall see how it is at tea. At present I'm leaving them to Prue.'

She swung her feet off the seat and stood up, hesitating, and he smiled at her encouragingly.

'A drink,' he suggested. 'What do you say? I think we both need a restorative after all the drama.'

She looked at him gratefully. 'That's a very good idea,' she said with feeling. 'What have you got?'

He pushed back his chair and went to the wall cupboard. 'Gin,' he offered, peering inside. 'Scotch. Sherry. That's it, I'm afraid.'

'That's more than enough to start with.' Freddy sounded more like herself. 'A Scotch, please. Don't drown it.'

He went into his bathroom to fetch water and

LOOKING FORWARD

Freddy wandered over to the window and looked down into the courtyard. Mole's tricycle stood abandoned at the bottom of the steps and she stared at it, remembering how Peter had ridden round on it, his favourite teddy stuck in the space behind the saddle. Clever, charming Peter; sweet-tempered, affectionate John: her lovely darling boys; running and shouting; playing cricket on the lawn; taking turns on the swing; going off to school; going off to war . . . The tears were streaming down her cheeks and the pain in her heart doubled her up in her agony. She cried out for all those that she had lost, reaching out blindly for them, and Theo came swiftly from behind her and took her in his arms to comfort her.

Chapter Nine

Prue walked in the lane behind the cottage in the hour before supper. She pottered slowly, peering to look at leaves and examine flowers, pausing to listen to the unfamiliar notes of a bird. Even now, a few weeks after that momentous arrival at The Keep with the twins, she felt an amazed elation. After the terrible initial misunderstanding it seemed that nothing she could do was wrong. Mole and Fliss had clung to her, wept with her and had gradually become steady and restored. Only *she* had been able to deal with their grief, sustain their slow recovery, nourish their spirits.

Prue thought: *Not* Freddy. *Not* Ellen or Fox. But *me*.

She gave a tiny skip, enjoying the freedom of slacks and flat shoes, aware of the fresh feel of her bare tanned face and the simplicity of hair tied back casually with a scarf. She felt happy; light and free from anxiety. As the days had passed, so the twins had begun to take some of the responsibility for Mole and Fliss from her. It was clear that Hal was a kind of hero to them. They watched him with awe and fascination, even with a longing; a longing which tore at Prue's heart. She'd explained privately to the still shocked Hal that he reminded them of Jamie, that he must expect a certain measure of their love to be poured out on him. It was only natural to make him a substitute. Hal had knit his brows, feeling a weight that he might not be able to bear, but he had done his best to help his small cousins. They'd responded immediately with a pathetic gratefulness which had touched him and spurred him to greater efforts. Kit had joined in. The scene in the courtyard had horrified and frightened her. To witness such depths of grief had expunged all feelings of jealousy from her heart and she had done everything possible to aid the children's recovery.

Then, when things were on a more even keel, Prue had – quite unwittingly – further consolidated her new popularity at The Keep by casually referring to the sister of a friend of hers, a nanny who was looking for a job. Her charge had started school, her work was over and she had nowhere as yet to go next. Freddy's cry had stopped her short so that she'd lost the thread of her conversation; but Freddy had no longer been interested in Prue's conversation. She'd only been interested in this nanny, this friend of Prue's who needed a job. What was she like? Was she reliable? How old was she? Since Prue had been at school with Caroline's elder sister – it was she who was lending Prue the cottage – she'd been able to answer these questions quite easily. Her stock had risen even higher and, when she'd left for her holiday at the cottage on the borders of Devon and Cornwall, her position within the family was that of a beloved and well-esteemed daughter. Never had she been so popular. No further mention had been made of Tony but she felt certain that no obstacles would now be placed in her way.

Prue took a deep breath of pure pleasure and turned to retrace her steps. The evening was warm and rich with late summer scents. Long fingers of sunlight reached between the trees; deep shadows lay across the dusty lane. The vivid bluish-purple tufted vetch scrambled over the powdery white flowers of the hedge parsley and burned brightly amongst bleached feathery grasses; herb Robert's dark red leaves gleamed in a tangle of nettle and, beneath a dock, a vole crouched. A tiny wren, fossicking in the dry-stone wall, churred indignantly as Prue leaned to pick a spray of pale honeysuckle, alerting a small party of long-tailed tits who flitted over the hedge and away into the woodland beyond.

With the honeysuckle dangling from her fingers, Prue turned into the track which led to the cottage. It was a four-roomed stone and slate dwelling, fairly basic, but comfortable enough and only a short walk from the village. She pushed open the back door and went into the kitchen. Her supper was already prepared; a simple meal of local honey-roast ham with a salad and a brown loaf. The grocer had cherries for sale and Prue had bought some and put them in a blue and white bowl. She took one now, relishing its flavour as she passed through the kitchen into the larder where the food kept cool and sweet. She fetched butter, mixed the salad and put the loaf on its wooden board. There was some good Cheddar cheese and her friend had left several bottles of wine, chilling on the cold slates under the sink in the scullery.

It was a feast, the ham thick and succulent, the

lettuce crisp, the bread soft ... Prue sighed with satisfaction, poured a second glass of cold white wine and bit into another cherry, leaning to touch the honeysuckle as it bloomed in its tiny jar. The click of the door latch made her jump and she was on her feet by the time Tony was inside the door. She gaped at him and he laughed – although there was a tiny edge of anxiety in his laugh. Prue felt a sharp stab of resentment – she had been enjoying her precious moment of peace and isolation – but the wine had relaxed her, dulling her quiet joy to a faint longing for ... for what? She suddenly knew that she had been wanting him, needing Tony to make it all perfect.

'Oh, darling,' she said protestingly. 'What did I say? I might have known I couldn't trust you ...'

'Darling Prue.' He was crushing her against him, determined to stifle any reproaches, however weak, to overbear her uncertainties swiftly by the only means he knew how. He saw the bottle and gave thanks that she was already softened, warming towards him. 'Darling,' he said again. 'You must have known I couldn't bear to be away from you. God, how I've missed you ...'

'Honestly,' but she was laughing, suffering his kisses, accepting them. 'How on earth did you find me?'

He made the usual flattering answers but she was already too needful of him to question the clichés and well-worn phrases. She fed him and they emptied the bottle and opened another – and presently they went together up the narrow stone staircase to the bedroom above.

LOOKING FORWARD

★ ★ ★

Theo took off his spectacles, rubbing the bridge of his nose, letting his book fall shut upon his knee. Freddy, sitting at the Bechstein, had been playing quietly, passing from Rameau to Scarlatti and on to Couperin. Becoming aware of the subtle change in atmosphere she hesitated, played a few more notes, stopped; watching him across the drawing room, gauging his mood, reluctant to disturb his thoughts yet longing to establish a more tangible connection with him. She guessed that he often sat with her out of a sense of . . . duty? Her heart sank a little. Duty was a cold word and perhaps friendship was a gentler, more suitable one. Often, she knew, he longed to be alone, either working or in contemplation, but, this evening, he had sensed her need for companionship and had come to sit with her in the drawing room after dinner. 'Play to me,' he'd said – and she had gone readily to the piano . . .

Rain drummed steadily on the terrace beyond the window and lamps were lit. Pools of light glowed on polished mahogany, reflected off dark wood panelling and gleamed on the brass fender. Long-dead Chadwicks stared down from the walls, watching as Freddy tidied her music with sidelong glances at the motionless Theo. He was staring ahead, his hands linked loosely on his lap, remote from her, unreachable. He had always had the power to withdraw himself mentally, to enter into a world where she could not follow. She respected this need in him, yet the sight of him sitting there, so dear and familiar, made it difficult not to pursue him, to draw him back to her.

'Do you remember when we had the electricity put

in?' She couldn't help herself. 'Poor Ellen. How she hated it.'

'Only at first.' Theo put his book aside, showing a readiness to communicate. 'When she realised that there were no more paraffin lamps to fill and clean she embraced it wholeheartedly.'

'Her conversion was absolute.' Freddy left the piano and came to sit in the corner of one of the sofas, tucking her long legs beneath her, smiling reminiscently. 'It was she who insisted on the Hoover if you remember. Goodness, how hard she must have worked in those early years! Of course, there were girls to help her then . . . How long ago it seems.'

'The two wars have been like watersheds. Afterwards everything changed. Rather like the Industrial Revolution, I suppose. People have new expectations, different approaches.'

'And now all this talk about nuclear power.' She shuddered. 'What is the next generation going into, Theo?'

He knew that she was thinking about Hal and Mole; would they, too, be killed in yet another war? He sought to distract her from these horrors, seizing upon the one subject that he knew would cheer her.

'You never really told me how the children got on with Caroline,' he said deviously. 'I know about your interview with her but nothing else. I liked her very much. What luck that Prue happened to mention her.'

'She was at school with her sister, you see. The children took to her quite quickly. She's such a lively bright girl. Didn't you think so? Just what they need. She dealt so easily with Mole's stammer . . . Do you think that he'll always have that now, Theo?'

Theo shook his head. 'Probably not. Why should he? It's just a result of his experiences. A leftover from his dumbness. I see no reason why it shouldn't go, given time.'

'What a comfort you are.' She smiled at him. 'Of course, it helped that the twins knew her already. Hal's opinion is what matters in the nursery. Caroline was halfway there already.'

'Poor Hal. What a responsibility.'

Her look was anxious. 'Too much for him, you think?'

Theo considered. 'I think that it is fortunate that he doesn't live here,' he said at last. 'He isn't Jamie. He is Hal. None of us must forget that. Especially Hal mustn't. It is so easy – and even tempting – to take roles to ourselves, especially where there is power and adulation.'

'Heavens! Isn't that going rather too far? They are children, after all.'

'My dear Freddy, that is exactly why it is dangerous. If power corrupts the old and experienced, imagine the effect on a young boy.'

'You're frightening me. Surely a little hero worship won't hurt Hal? He's such a sensible boy.'

'You're right, of course.' He nodded, unwilling to alarm her too much. The idea of power terrified Theo; he had seen its insidious effect. 'But it might go to his head if he were around all the time. So the children liked Caroline. And Ellen?'

'Ellen is . . .' Freddy hesitated, attempting to clarify Ellen's position to herself before she described it. 'She is not going to give in too easily but Caroline has won her over. I can tell. It would be a very good idea if we could persuade her to move down into the spare bedroom beside the twins' rooms in the west wing. There's a bathroom right next door. Much more sensible than wearing herself out climbing up and down three flights. Caroline can take charge of the nursery and Ellen can go back to what she was doing before the children arrived. It's more than enough, after all.'

'But will she be happy to relinquish them to Caroline?'

'Oh, I think so. Now that Mole is better and they've all settled down, I think she'll be quite relieved to leave them to Caroline. Susanna is at a very exhausting age. It is simply that Ellen doesn't want to be seen to be capitulating too readily. She has her pride. Thank God Caroline is such a sweetie. She was so tactful, so quick to notice all the little nuances. It is fortunate that she's not *too* pretty.'

'Is it possible for a woman to be too pretty?' wondered Theo.

'The last thing we want is a horde of young men about the place,' said Freddy firmly. 'Caroline doesn't look the type to want to be off dancing or going to the cinema. Her family is army, you know, so she will have learned to be adaptable and she tells me that she loves the country.' Freddy shook her head in amazement at so much luck. 'I simply can't believe our good fortune.'

'And Prue's reward is that there is to be no more fuss about Tony?'

Freddy looked at him sharply and burst out laughing. 'How clever of you. But it wasn't *quite* so deliberate. It is simply impossible, at the moment, to find the will to be cross with her. I don't *want* to be unpleasant, Theo. I want Prue's happiness. From what you said, I think it is unlikely that Tony is going to provide it.'

'I fear you may be right but I also fear that we are going to have to let Prue find it out for herself.'

'All these wretched children.' Freddy uncurled her legs and stretched. 'We are far too old for such fits and starts. I don't want to be responsible for a family that stretches between the age of two and thirty-four.'

'I suppose,' said Theo, after a pause, 'I must be grateful that you don't include me.'

'Oh, I'm used to worrying about you,' said Freddy lightly. 'All those years I spent being desperately social so as to find a nice young woman for you. Julia and I used to plot and plan but it came to nothing. The breath I've wasted trying to persuade you to come back home. Never mind. I shan't despair.'

Theo smiled the slow sweet smile that started in his eyes but barely touched his mouth. 'That's good,' he said. 'I shouldn't like to be despaired about.'

Freddy was silent. Her fingers played over the heavy bun of hair at the nape of her neck and she sat for some moments thus, her head bent. She knew that Theo was about to return to Southsea and she was trying to accept it. The older she became the lonelier she grew. This sounded foolish, given that she was surrounded by people, but she needed someone of her own age, with the same habits of mind and a similar background. It would be so hard to let Theo go without reproaches or pleas, yet she would have been ashamed to show her need. She would manage, as she had managed all these years . . . She raised her head and smiled at him.

Theo, who accurately guessed her thoughts, silently saluted her courage. Instinctively he knew that the time was not yet right for his return; that it would undermine Freddy's strength. She needed to feel that she was in complete control, yet there was something within her which had always yielded to Theo. The relationship worked very well at a distance but he knew that it was too soon to join her at The Keep; that her subconscious desire to submit to him would make her resentful. From the beginning she had been required to be so strong – both mother and father to the twins, owner of The Keep – and those deep feminine instincts and softer ways had been sublimated. Only Theo had ever had the power to shake her confidence, make her question her decisions, rethink her views on important subjects. He had never asked for – and did not desire – this power; he had simply happened to be there; Bertie's younger brother, ready to be his substitute where possible. In those early days he had longed so terribly to be his brother's substitute in every possible way. Instead, she had bullied him and teased him – and relied on him absolutely . . .

He smiled back at her. 'I shall be home for the Birthday,' he said. 'It will be a very exciting one this year. Isn't Mole's birthday at the end of October, as well as yours and the twins'? What a celebration!'

Freddy accepted the comfort he was offering. Two months; she could manage for two months. 'It's so lucky that it falls during half term. The twins look forward to it so much. We shall be a houseful, shan't we? I shall invite Tony along, of course. Well . . .' She glanced at her wristwatch. 'Bedtime? A nightcap, I think. Yes? The usual? No, stay there. I'll see to it.'

He watched her, tall and slim at the drinks table, and felt the long familiar pain.

He thought: I love you, Freddy. I always did, from the first moment. But how could I ever tell you and betray your trust in me? It could never have been the same afterwards. I was only ever Bertie's little brother, although you have come to love me in your way. I can be grateful for that . . .

Freddy thought: What would he think if he knew? If I told him that I fell in love with him from that first moment? That beside him, Bertie could never be anything but second best? How shaming it would be. How unfair on Bertie. And anyway, he was so much younger, or it seemed so then. After a bit I forgot to notice it. Oh hell. Not all that again. It's too late now . . .

She turned with the glasses and passed him his whisky.

'To us!' she said cheerfully – and swallowed back the clear gold liquid.

'Yes,' he said after a moment – and, in the silence that followed, they realised that the rain had stopped and the evening was clear and bright with moonlight.

Book Two
Autumn 1961

———

Chapter Ten

Kit woke early, as she generally did at The Keep, and immediately thought about Graham. The holidays were nearly over and tomorrow she would be going back to Bristol; back to her final year at school and back to Graham. She missed him terribly, terrified that during their separation he might be taking out other girls. He was three years older than she was and much more sophisticated; an art student, twenty years old. She had met him at a student party during the Easter holidays and was completely bowled over by his style. He dressed only in black. This was his trademark: black roll-neck jerseys or shirts with tight black jeans. It accentuated the fairness of his hair and his height and, when she arrived in the small upstairs flat near the university, he was already the centre of a group of girls who giggled and vied for his attention. Kit knew instinctively that this was not the way to get noticed. She had left him alone and talked to another student whom she had met whilst working at the Old Vic during the previous holidays. She had worked at the theatre in King Street for love – running errands, making coffee, sweeping up – and for the sheer delight of being close to the members of the small repertory company and Val May.

She was already in love with Richard Pasco and Michael Jayston, who were amongst the actors working at the theatre for this Shakespeare season, but Graham Fielding, this tall and elegant student, seemed rather more accessible. He was watching her as she discussed the merits of Pasco's Henry Fifth and she tried not to overact as she felt his gaze upon her. He was with a girl, Wendy something, who was clinging to him, tugging at his arm. She had drunk too much and was, for some reason, near to tears.

Kit turned away, feeling sorry for the girl, yet a shade superior. Surely it was clear that such behaviour wouldn't keep a man? She talked to her own friends, collecting her curry and sitting on the floor near them to eat it – and steered well clear of Graham Fielding. Someone mentioned his name, whispering that he was clever and – like Old Man Kangaroo – well and truly run after, and that he was tired of Wendy. Kit ate her curry and drank her wine, pretending only a mild interest. She decided to leave early. The party was breaking up into couples and she didn't want to be the odd one out. Several people had already drunk too much and someone had put a smoochy Peggy Lee LP on the record player.

She hummed the tune as she went to fetch her cloak; a rather stylish garment in gunmetal velvet which fell to her ankles and had a deep hood. Kit loved it, reluctant to leave it on the rather grubby untidy bed amongst the other shabby coats. As she pushed open the bedroom door, she saw that someone was sitting on the bed. It was Wendy. Her face was awash with tears and she looked ill. Graham stood beside her, looking tall and forbidding. Kit could see at once that he was cross. Embarrassed, she smiled faintly and whispered, 'Sorry,' trying not to look at them.

'She's been sick.' Graham spoke as though Wendy was either deaf or insensible. 'Drunk too much, I'm afraid.' He shrugged and looked at Kit with interest.

'Oh dear,' said Kit inadequately. She wanted to make certain that her cloak had not fallen victim to Wendy's excesses but to search for it openly seemed rather heartless. 'Are you OK now?' she asked her, going closer but keeping an eye open. She saw her cloak, lying beneath a tweed jacket and picked it up gratefully, smoothing out the creases. 'Would you like some water?'

Wendy began to cry again, hunched like a child on the side of the bed, and Kit looked at Graham. He smiled at her and her stomach lurched rather peculiarly.

'I'm going to suggest to Liz that she beds down here,' he said confidentially, rather as though he and Kit were confederates and the wretched Wendy a rather tiresome stranger. 'She's been very ill. What do you think?'

'I don't really know,' said Kit helplessly. 'Is she a friend of Liz's?'

Wendy groaned and began to retch and Kit leaped aside as she stood up and groped uncertainly towards the door. She reached the bathroom and began to vomit, still groaning loudly, and Kit frowned involuntarily, though trying to feel sympathetic.

'Come on.' Graham took her arm and led her along the passage. 'Wait for me outside. Shan't be a sec.'

So she had waited beneath the lamppost, heart beating fast, wondering if she was being cheap, until he came running down the steps.

'All dealt with,' he said cheerfully. 'Poor girl. I'll come round in the morning and see that she's OK. Walk you home?'

Kit hesitated. 'There will be a bus along soon,' she said awkwardly, not knowing how to handle this. 'I can catch it outside Maples. It passes the end of my road.'

'Where do you live?' he asked, falling into step beside her.

When she told him he'd smiled down at her. 'Don't you like walking at night? The city is so much nicer in the dark, don't you think? More mysterious and exciting.'

His voice was intimate, slightly teasing, and she felt hopelessly and deliciously out of her depth. She muttered something inaudible and he slipped an arm about her shoulder in an almost brotherly way. Just as Hal might, she told herself, knowing that it was not the least bit like Hal's hugs. He talked easily, guiding their steps, by-passing the bus stop, and it was as if she were mesmerised, already caught in the web of his charm. When he stopped in the shadows between two pools of lamplight she was prepared for his kiss, almost sick with nervousness, yet longing for it. She was well aware of her utter lack of experience but he had plenty enough for both of them and she learned fast. Afterwards, he held her closely and she felt equal measures of bliss and terror. She had managed her first kiss without disgracing herself but she wondered if he'd guessed and was despising her. It seemed not.

'I'm not going to lose sight of you now,' he was murmuring. 'You know that, don't you?'

Kit thought she might faint with the heady surge of joy and power that possessed her. This much-sought-after man was hers . . . but what about Wendy?

'I thought . . . Isn't Wendy . . .?' she muttered, embarrassed but determined to make matters clear.

'It's been over for weeks,' he reassured her. 'Forget her. I'd much rather talk about you.'

That was nearly six months ago. Kit pushed herself up on her pillows and felt the usual mixture of happiness and anxiety. Being in love wasn't as simple as she had imagined. She'd only been prepared to come to The Keep because Graham had taken a holiday job as a waiter at a big hotel in Hampshire. He would be away most of the summer; such a terrible waste when they could have been together. It was so difficult to get away during term-time.

'It'll be great fun,' she'd heard him say to a friend. 'It's right on the beach. And think of all those gorgeous chambermaids.'

She'd laughed with the others, too proud to show her fear, her stomach turning over when she thought of him, loose amongst the girls. He'd written to her regularly, telling her about them in detail, yet always saying that they couldn't hold a candle to her, sending his love in personal messages that reassured her. He'd told her that he missed her and hinted that, on his return they might go further than heavy petting, that if she really loved him she'd show him . . .

She climbed out of bed and wandered over to the window that looked west across the garden. The grass was a silvery grey, drenched with heavy dew, the whole garden painted in soft, pale monochrome. Only the tips of the three tall fir trees at the end of the orchard glowed vividly in this quiet scene, the first rays of the sun touching them with gold. She leaned her forehead against the cool glass, terrified of losing him, terrified of going 'too far'. What if she became pregnant? Graham had laughed away these childish fears. He knew all about it; knew exactly what to do. She had only to trust him.

Kit thought: Trust him or lose him. Oh, what shall I do?

Desperate with love and longing, restless with fear, she pulled on her clothes and went down to walk in the garden.

Perched on the window seat in her small bedroom, high on the nursery floor, Susanna watched her big cousin walking in the early morning dew. The view from this west window would always be connected with her earliest memories of The Keep. The garden lay before her: the sweep of the lawn with the changing symmetry of colour and shape in the border beneath the high wall; the orchard at the end of the lawn with its old, lichen-covered fruit trees, which were smothered with a glorious wash of blossom each spring; the tall banks of rhododendron that hid the kitchen garden away to the right and, beyond the orchard, the three tall fir trees.

For as long as she could remember, the trees had seemed like old friends, guardians that watched over the gardens and The Keep. Although they stood close together she could see their faces quite clearly, their overlapping branches allowing glimpses of the sky which looked like eyes and teeth. The tallest one looked north. His nose and chin jutted strongly and, when the wind blew, he waved his shaggy arms and Susanna could see his sky-white eye glittering fiercely. The second tree stood with his back to the sunset, facing her. He had a wide toothy smile and he seemed to be perpetually chuckling, even as the gales raced over his feathery topknot. The third tree faced south. He had a shy, kindly look about his profile, opening his arms to the birds and squirrels and welcoming the sunshine. She was quite certain that they guarded her window, each facing in a separate direction, waving and bowing to her each morning when she climbed on to the window seat, resting her arms on the sill and staring out across the garden to make certain they were still there.

Now, she was watching Kit. She had felt some change in Kit when she had arrived for the usual few weeks of the summer holiday. There was something different; some abstraction in her voice; a preoccupation in her eyes. When Susanna demanded her attention, wanting her to tell a story about Pudgie and Binker or to teach her to ride Fliss's old bicycle, it was as if Kit must return from some distance, called back to the present by Susanna's insistence. Then she would play as she had always done: wholeheartedly, madly, wonderfully. Susanna adored her.

She kneeled up tall to watch Kit disappearing amongst the trees of the orchard. She would have liked to go downstairs to join her but some instinct warned against it. This same instinct warned her when Mole was having one of his dark moments. She called them that, to herself, because it seemed that some light or brightness disappeared from his face and a darkness overtook him. She became more careful with him, knowing this was not the time to badger him or wheedle him to play or share some toy. She stayed quietly beside him, sensing that he needed her, but going on with her own games, talking to herself. When the darkness drew off, she was ready to carry on wherever they left off quite undemandingly and easily. He was Mole and this was what Mole did; it was how he was.

Kit was different. Hers was a new darkness and Susanna didn't care for it. She didn't understand it and it upset her that Kit might be unhappy, although it wasn't that she *looked* unhappy, exactly . . . Kit had quite disappeared and Susanna suddenly felt bored and restless. She sighed heavily and made a face, seeing how far she could push up her lips to touch her nose; rolling off the window seat and trying to stand on her head. She guessed that it was too early for anyone from the nursery floor to be about, although there was just a chance that Fox and Ellen might be down in the kitchen having a cup of tea. She decided to go and see.

Pulling on her dressing gown – actually an old one that had belonged to Fliss – over her pyjamas, Susanna opened her door carefully, passed Caroline's door on tiptoe and crept down the back stairs to the kitchen. To her delight, Ellen was there, raking out the Aga and making tea.

'And what are you doing out of your bed so early and with no slippers?' she scolded distractedly. 'Get up on the chair, quick. Fox has already taken the dogs out but we'll have a cup of tea together, shall we?'

Susanna opened her mouth to say that she wasn't usually allowed tea – and shut it again. Behind her, the door opened again and Fliss appeared. She was yawning, looking pale and tired in her Jaeger dressing gown, her thick fair hair in a long plait down her back. Ellen clucked disapprovingly.

'Whatever is up with you all?' she asked of no one in particular. 'Fox says that Kit's roaming about in the orchard and now here's you two . . .'

'Hal and Kit go back tomorrow,' said Fliss sadly. 'We want to make the most of their last day.'

Ellen glanced at her sharply. 'Hal won't be up yet,' she said. 'Catch him out of his bed before nine o'clock. Late for breakfast every single day, he's been.'

Fliss and Susanna smiled at each other, feeling all the familiar comfort of the warm kitchen and Ellen grumbling, knowing that Fox was out on the hill with the dogs as usual. The kitchen door opened and Kit came in. Her walk in the garden had refreshed her spirits and renewed her natural optimism. Soon she would be seeing Graham; nothing else really mattered. All would be well as soon as they were back together again. She grinned at her cousins as she pulled out a chair.

'Good morning, darlings,' she said, for all the world as if she were one of the stars at the Old Vic, and with just the right amount of panache. 'And how are we all today?'

Susanna beamed at her. 'I saw you walking in the garden,' she told her.

'Early morning blues,' said Kit briefly, and looked at Fliss, guessing how she would be feeling at the thought of Hal leaving tomorrow. She felt a wave of sympathy and fellowship and kicked her gently under the table. 'You too?' she asked.

Fliss knew that she was blushing but couldn't help herself. 'We shall miss you,' she explained.

'Come and see us,' suggested Kit, suddenly animated by this new idea. 'Come to Bristol for an exeat. We'll have to make sure that the dates work so that we're all out together. Oh, wouldn't it be fun? Hal would love it.'

Generosity made her add this, knowing that it would please Fliss, but her cousin's reaction was lost in Susanna's wail. 'I want to come, too,' she cried. 'Please, Kit. Can I come, too?'

'May I?' said Ellen automatically, stirring porridge. '*May* I come, too?'

'Of course you may, Ellen,' said Kit, grinning mischievously. 'We'd love to have you.'

'And that's quite enough of your sauce, miss,' replied Ellen tartly. 'Take those elbows off the table, please, Susanna. Only the Queen and uncles and aunts are allowed to put their elbows on the table, as you know very well, and if any of you have become uncles or aunts then it's the first I've heard of it. Whatever next, I wonder. Go to Bristol indeed.'

'You make it sound like the North Pole,' said Kit. 'Never mind, Susanna. Let's have a picnic today, shall we? Perhaps we could go to the beach. All in favour raise your right hand. Carried unanimously. Drink up, then, and we'll go and wake Hal and Mole and make an early start.'

'And who's going to be cutting all those sandwiches?' demanded Ellen – but they knew that she approved of the idea.

'I'll help,' Fliss volunteered, looking happy again. 'Susanna can be in charge of rugs and Mole can check the hamper.'

'A good breakfast, first,' said Ellen firmly, as Fox could be heard arriving back, scraping his boots at the door, talking to the dogs. 'Go and deal with your brothers and when we've finished breakfast and cleared away, we'll think about picnics. First things first.'

Several hours later, Hal, with Caroline seated beside him, drove them all out to Bigbury. He was booked to take his driving test shortly after his return to Bristol and he insisted that he needed the practice. Susanna was perched on Caroline's knee, with Mrs Pooter at their feet, and the other three were squashed together in the back with Mugwump, as the puppy, now as big as his mother, had been named. In the boot with the hamper were bathing costumes, towels and rugs, buckets and spades. Hal drove carefully, aware of Caroline's critical eye, and arrived without mishap, parking on the cliff above the bay. The sun was hot but the wind blew strong and cold from the west, whipping white horses across the surface of the sea, and they all stood for a moment, gulping in the fresh, salty air.

The descent to the beach was steep and they went down carefully, clutching their bundles, Mole and Susanna slithering and sliding ahead. The tide was ebbing and they found a sheltered spot behind some rocks which provided a natural pool for paddling, warmed by the sun, big enough and deep enough for Susanna to be able to practise her strokes. Caroline refused to let any of them – not even Hal – swim in the sea, which crashed in huge breakers as it retreated across the yellow, dangerously shelving sand. It was so cold out of the shelter of the rocks that Hal gave in with good grace and devoted himself to teaching Susanna the breaststroke whilst Kit and Fliss took the dogs for a walk along the beach towards Bantham.

Mole was a fairly competent swimmer now, thanks to Caroline, and he splashed along behind Susanna, head up, eyes narrowed with determination. Hal had his hand under Susanna's chin, encouraging her with cries of, 'Well done, Sooz. Nice and even, now. Don't thrash like that. Keep it smooth,' whilst Mole followed in her splashy wake.

Caroline sat in the shelter of the rocks, watching the lesson. Even after four years she still experienced moments of sheer amazed gratitude that she was so utterly accepted as one of the family. She had soon realised that she had neither the beauty nor the easy flirtatious ways that attracted very young men and had gradually learned to be content with the love of small children. She entered wholeheartedly into their lives, sharing their triumphs and disasters, yet seeing them clearly so that her judgement concerning their wellbeing was invariably sound. She had been lucky so far with 'her' children, yet never had she been so happy as she was here in Devon. As she huddled beneath the rock, the wind ruffling her short brown curls, she was sure in the knowledge that she was where she belonged at The Keep and that she was especially important to the three younger Chadwicks. In so far as it was possible she had filled an emptiness in their lives, supplied a sense of continuity. She was a missing link between the generations and she did her best to make up for their terrible loss . . .

She kneeled up quickly as Mole and Susanna came scrambling out, wrapping them in rough warm towels and giving them hot tea to drink from plastic mugs.

'I did s-six s-strokes all on my own, Caroline,' said Susanna, her teeth chattering. 'Did you see me, Fliss? Did you see, Kit?'

'You sound like Roo,' said Kit good-naturedly as she unpacked the hamper. 'Of course we saw you.'

'Jolly good, Sooz,' said Fliss. 'I've peeled your egg. Look. There, with some bread and butter. There's a screw of salt somewhere.'

After the picnic lunch, Caroline organised races using a cricket stump thrust into the sand for a marker. Everyone joined in the three-legged race; Caroline partnering herself with Kit, Fliss with Hal, Mole with Susanna. Hal and Fliss won, Hal almost carrying her along with him, and they all collapsed exhausted on the two rugs, laughing and out of breath and demanding orangeade . . .

'Must we go home?' asked Susanna wistfully, as she sat on a rock some time later, leg held out whilst Caroline wiped the sand from her feet and put on her shoes.

'Your grandmother will want to have you all together for tea today,' Caroline told her. 'Hal and Kit's last day. You wouldn't want to disappoint her, would you?'

'We don't m-mind really,' said Mole, who was cramming damp sandy feet into his sandshoes. 'Do we, Sooz? We'll come again soon.' He shivered inside his navy-blue jersey and jumped about to keep warm, enjoying the gritty feel of his feet inside the canvas.

'Next time we'll ride on the duck over the Burgh Island,' promised Caroline.

This was a great treat. The duck was a specially built vehicle with large wheels and a high platform on which passengers were carried across the causeway linking Burgh Island to the mainland. The children loved to ride on it, especially when the tide was in and the water almost covered the wheels. They cheered loudly and went off to find their belongings, helping Fliss to shake the sand out of the rugs whilst Kit checked the contents of the hamper. They straggled up the slope to the car, reluctant as always to leave, comforting themselves with the thought of tea in the hall with Ellen's home-made scones and jam and clotted cream.

Fliss paused, looking back over the pounding, roaring sea, wishing that the day could last for ever; that the holidays would never end. Sighing, she turned to follow the others up the path, her heart heavy with the knowledge that this precious last day was almost over; already looking forward to the next time they would all be together.

Chapter Eleven

A week or two later, Fox stood on the hill below The Keep, looking intently towards the belt of trees at the foot of the slope. The late September afternoon was mild, the distant hills a misty blue, and the whole countryside was enveloped in a heavy drowsiness. A buzzard hung for a moment, motionless in the clear sky, before climbing upward on a thermal, his shadow moving gently over the land. A cock pheasant croaked and was silent. Suddenly there was an explosion of noise and several figures burst out of the shadow of the trees and came racing up the hill.

The dogs led the way, ears flying, followed by the two children, and Fox laughed aloud in his delight. At this distance, and looking down upon them, Mole and Susanna were difficult to tell apart. Susanna's hair was almost as short as Mole's, and just as dark, and they were dressed identically in shorts and Aertex shirts. Dark-skinned, dark-eyed, strong-limbed, they were the image of their grandfather.

Fox thought: Chadwick's children, that's what they are. True Chadwicks. As for that Mugwump! What a name for a dog. Trust Kit . . .

He remembered that it was then, four years ago

when Kit had named the puppy, that they had all heard Mole laugh aloud for the first time: a rusty kind of noise but oddly infectious.

'M-mugwump?' he'd repeated, unbelieving – and he'd begun to laugh and laugh. Kit had grinned up at him from where she was playing with the puppy on the kitchen floor.

'It's just right for him, isn't it?' she'd demanded. 'Well, *isn't* it?' And Mole had nodded, still laughing, while the others stood about grinning foolishly, too happy to be able to speak. Fliss had had tears in her eyes . . .

Mugwump reached him now, with Mrs Pooter close behind and the children in hot pursuit. Fox bent to fondle his ears.

'Daft bloody dog,' he muttered. 'As for you, you old bitch . . .'

Mrs Pooter pushed past him, indifferent to insult or praise. She was thinking of her dinner, homeward bound, getting a little too old for these excursions. Susanna flung herself upon Fox.

'How fast were we?' she asked breathlessly. 'Quicker than yesterday?'

Fox consulted his watch. 'Four seconds up on your time.' He looked at Mole. 'Did you go right round?'

Mole nodded. 'R-Right round,' he said, 'didn't we, Sooz? We couldn't see you at all.'

'Good lad.' He smiled at Susanna. 'Getting good, you are, maid. Legs aching? Want a piggyback?'

She nodded, her thick fringe flopping, and he crouched so that she could scramble up. He set off along the narrow sheep track, Mugwump ahead, Mole bringing up the rear. Susanna began to sing in a high breathless voice, clinging to Fox's neck with small brown hands.

> 'To market, to market, to buy a fat pig,
> Home again, home again, jiggety-jig;'

Gasping for breath, Mole paused, turning to look back the way they had come. How far down it looked! He could never accustom himself to the way the land seemed to shift and change. From his bedroom in The Keep, the hill opposite looked hardly any height at all. Yet when he was down in the valley it appeared to rise up, tall as a mountain, its smooth green fields so nearly vertical that he wondered how the sheep clung to them. He stared down at the trees, frowning. He hated the moment when he reached the point where he could no longer see The Keep and Fox waiting for him on the hill. It had become a private test; a test which he had not yet passed for, so far, Susanna had always been with him. He knew – and Fox knew – that he could not quite bring himself to go right round the spinney alone. It was not that the path was in any way dangerous; it was simply that some deep-down fear prevented him from being out of sight of everything that represented safety. Supposing that something terrible should be waiting in the shadows of the trees? Death might strike suddenly, unexpectedly, out of a bright summer day. He shuddered, deliberately blocking his mind to the pictures of ambush and blood. This same fear made it necessary that some member of his little family should be around at all times. He was always watching from a window for Freddy to return from shopping in

Totnes, for Fliss to come home from piano lessons. It had been such a relief that they could go to school together, although he had hated being parted from her at the classroom door.

When she was thirteen, two years before, Fliss had gone away to boarding school and Mole had missed her terribly: not only at home but even more at school. A year ago Susanna had been old enough to go with him to the infants school at Dartington and he had known a small glow of confidence at showing her the ropes. Susanna was six now and he, Mole, would be nine at the end of October; old enough to go away to school. There had been talk that this autumn he should start at prep school but it had come to nothing. Perhaps next year . . . Fear clutched at his heart and he began to run, anxious to catch up with Fox and Susanna.

The kitchen was warm and welcoming. Ellen had baked a Victoria sponge, and a pot of her new-made bramble jelly stood promisingly on the table. Mugwump was already lapping deeply at the bowl of cold water in the corner whilst Mrs Pooter had taken up her position by the door, ready to follow Susanna into the hall for tea. As well as being the untidiest eater, she was also given to passing unwanted titbits down to Mrs Pooter's waiting jaws. They worked well as a team, both having a measure of low cunning as well as a strong streak of self-preservation. They understood and respected each other and, consequently, had a very good relationship.

'We did well today,' Fox told Ellen, as he reached for the teapot. 'Up on their time four seconds. How about that?'

She glanced at him, eyebrows raised, but he shook his head at her unspoken question. Both knew that the timing of the run was of secondary importance, a fad that had sprung up after the school's sports day in the summer. Suddenly everything had to be timed – but the run round the spinney had developed into something much more important.

'Four seconds,' Ellen said admiringly. 'Well. Ready for some tea after that, I should think. Into the scullery, both of you, and get those hands washed. Your grandmother will be waiting.'

'He'll do it,' said Fox into the tiny silence left by the children's departure. 'He'll get to it.'

'Course he will,' said Ellen, pouring milk into the two mugs and putting them on the laden tea tray. 'In his own good time. One day he'll surprise us all.'

'He's not ready,' Caroline had said earlier, over a year ago now, staring Freddy firmly in the eye. 'He mustn't go. It wouldn't be right.'

Theo, summoned to attend this important discussion, had felt a sneaking admiration for such straight speaking.

'That's what we have to talk about.' Freddy's tone was faintly repressive. 'That's why Theo is here. We want to talk it over and naturally we need your . . . opinion, Caroline.'

Theo found it hard not to grin. It was impossible to repress Caroline when she felt deeply about some decision regarding the children; not even Freddy was capable of it. She burst out from all angles so that it was rather like trying to hold down a lid on a hot-water geyser.

'Well, there you have it,' said Caroline briskly. 'He's not ready to go away to school this autumn.'

'Thank you, Caroline.' Freddy's look would have quelled a lesser being. 'I think you've made yourself very clear.'

'It might be interesting,' said Theo mildly to Freddy, 'to hear exactly why Caroline should think so.' He smiled at Caroline. 'You do rather make it sound as if there is no room for discussion.'

'I feel very strongly about it.' When Caroline talked, her whole body – hands, shoulders, forehead, even her eyebrows – took part. Her brown curls stood on end and her hazel eyes sparkled. Now, as she looked at Theo, her fists clenched and her face creased up in her desperation to make her point. 'It's not just the stammer – although the other boys would probably tease him unmercifully – he's just not . . . not *strong* enough yet.'

'Strong enough?' repeated Freddy sharply. 'He's perfectly healthy. He runs like the wind and climbs trees like a monkey.'

'I'm not talking about his physical wellbeing,' said Caroline impatiently. 'He's quite fit, I grant you that. I'm talking about his emotional side. He's very insecure. I don't think he's recovered from that terrible thing in Kenya.'

Freddy closed her eyes on a long breath and Caroline looked anxiously at Theo. He nodded, leaning over to touch Freddy's arm.

'We have to face it,' he said. 'He may not be ready yet. Does it matter? Is it so terribly important that he goes away this autumn?'

Freddy sat back in her chair. Something – some

virtue – had gone out from her and she looked tired and old. 'It's hard for a boy to start halfway through prep school,' she said. 'You should know that, Theo. It's more difficult to catch up and to make friends. It's terrible to be on the edge of things and Mole is not naturally gregarious. He would be at a disadvantage. I want the best for him, that's all.'

'He's afraid, you see.' Caroline was quieter now that she seemed to have carried her point. 'He's afraid of losing people. People he loves, that is. He's always terrified in case they don't come back.'

Freddy frowned a little. 'I'd hoped he was nearly over that,' she said. 'I thought there was an improvement.'

Caroline shook her head. 'He's just better at hiding it. As he gets older he learns to put on a show of bravado. It's still there underneath. I think it would kill him to be away from us all.'

It was as if Freddy shrank a little from such extravagance but Caroline nodded vehemently.

'Honestly.' She looked at Theo. 'It sounds silly, I know, but I really mean it. In some way an important bit of him *would* die.'

'We both know what you are trying to say,' said Theo gently. 'You have the most to do with him and I know that you are truly fond of him. I am happy to bow to your judgement.'

Neither of them looked at Freddy, who stirred in her chair. 'Very well,' she said. 'We shall see what happens. Perhaps another year might not be too critical. Let's hope that he becomes more confident. Thank you, Caroline. You've been very . . . helpful.'

Caroline slipped away and Theo reached out again

to touch Freddy's hand. She nodded, accepting his comfort. 'So that's that,' she said. 'Let's go and walk around the garden. I need some fresh air and I want to talk to you about Mole.'

So the idea of small tests had evolved; tiny things in themselves but things which might build Mole's confidence. Freddy would drive into Totnes with him, wondering how she might help him to overcome his fear, trying to think of new ways to strengthen his courage. Sitting at a table in the Quaker House with her cup of coffee, she would 'remember' that she had forgotten to buy the newspaper.

'Now I wonder,' she would say thoughtfully, 'could you possibly manage to save my old legs? What do you think? You know where Cummings is, don't you? Just two shops up?'

Mole would nod, standing beside her, eyes big with anxiety but self-importance inflating his chest. She would pass over the pennies, hating herself, praying that there would be no problems . . . Moments later he would burst back into the café, elated with his success, excited by these triumphs. They would toast his achievement with orangeade or an ice and she would begin to work out the next one. Once she asked him to wait outside Harris's, the ironmonger's shop, standing beside a large heavy parcel while she went to fetch the car. She was delayed and, when the old Morris Oxford finally came chugging up beside him, she was horrified by the white terror on his face and the tense rigidity of his small body.

'I thought you'd g-gone,' he'd said, lips trembling,

and she'd hugged him tightly, cursing herself for cruelty and insensitivity.

Would he ever recover? It was a question they all asked. Fliss seemed to have settled contentedly enough into The Keep. She had passed through her grief and fastened the adoration she had had for Jamie on to Hal; the others had become her family and, though quiet and self-contained, she was happy. Susanna could remember no other world. It had been agreed that she should not know the very tragic details of her parents' and brother's deaths and she was told merely that they had died in a road accident. She accepted it calmly, unable to remember them, and continued to grow, the cheerful child she had always been. Only Mole remained deeply damaged but still the adults of his small world continued to hope that, as he developed, he would heal.

So it was agreed that he should remain at The Keep, going to school with Susanna, growing in confidence. The spinney had become a kind of symbol. One day Mole would run round the spinney alone and on that day they would all know that he had overcome some terror deep within himself; that he was ready to move forward.

Prue woke suddenly, rolled on to her back and yawned. She had been dreaming a confused dream in which she was struggling to get to the school concert. The bus was full and she was obliged to carry Hal's cello; apologising, explaining, weeping with frustration . . . Prue yawned again. How stupid dreams were! It was years since Hal had played the cello. She sat up, feeling with her toes for her slippers, sliding from bed, reaching for her dressing gown. She tied the flimsy garment round her and went into the bathroom.

By the time she finally arrived in the kitchen it was nearly ten o'clock. She was quite alone. Prue stretched luxuriously, revelling in this rare treat. The twins were back at school and Tony was paying one of his regular visits to his brother in the north. Prue had met this brother only once, at the registry office four years before, and could barely remember him.

'We don't really get on,' Tony had said when she'd questioned him afterwards. 'Never have. I feel a kind of responsibility for him, that's all. He's had a rough time. Let's forget him, shall we, darling?'

Yet three or four times a year Tony went to see him and often sent him money. Prue made no fuss, asked no questions. Her own father had been an alcoholic, an actor who seemed perpetually out of work, and her mother had spent her life trying to screen him and protect him. When Prue was twelve they had gone to live with her great-aunt in Edinburgh, a wealthy, kindly old lady who paid for her to go away to school whilst supporting them all, and Prue had been relieved when the war had come and she could finally escape; even more relieved when her father died and she hadn't been required to present him to Johnny – or Freddy. Her mother and aunt had appeared briefly at the wedding and vanished away again and eventually her mother had died of cancer, although the now very elderly great-aunt was still alive. Prue wrote to her regularly, sent photographs of the twins, occasionally visited. She felt guilty that she had minded so little when her parents died. She had tried hard to love them but they had been so self-obsessed and dramatic in the early years; so maudlin and worn down by life as they grew older. Prue had almost envied her sister-in-law, Alison, whose parents had died when she was a child and who was so practical and self-assured. How long ago it seemed that she and Johnny and Alison and Peter had been young together.

Prue made coffee, staring out of the window at the wall of the next-door house. Perhaps marrying Johnny was the only really sensible thing she'd ever done. It had been the most perfect single achievement. It was still amazing to her that handsome, talented, wonderful Johnny Chadwick had chosen her. What glorious fun they'd had and how desperately she'd missed him. Tony had never matched up to him, yet he'd been a good companion despite his moods. With Tony she was never quite certain which way the cat would jump and she was relieved that Kit had wanted to board at Badminton School so that the twins were rarely witness to the rows that occasionally erupted. It also gave Tony and Prue an amount of privacy which had been essential. Tony could be temperamental, easily hurt, sulky, and bed was the best place for solving such problems.

A now familiar anxiety pressed in upon Prue as she perched at the table, staring at the letters she'd picked up on her way through the hall. One bore the familiar crest of the bank and she looked at it nervously. She'd had a communication from them a few months back, pointing out that her account was overdrawn. Prue had been surprised by how much, relieved that her yearly dividend was nearly due and, in the end, had borrowed from Theo. It wasn't the first time in the last four years that she had borrowed from him but she felt guilty about it, always promising to pay him back. Theo had written, enclosing a comfortingly generous cheque and telling her that a large deposit of china clay had been discovered somewhere near Teignmouth, so they weren't quite destitute yet . . .

She picked up the envelope, wondering how on earth she would have survived without Theo. Not just because he baled her out but because he gave the impression that he valued her, cared about her, that she was important to him.

Prue thought: I should have married Theo. Why on earth didn't I?

She laughed a little at the idea as she tore the letter open and pulled out the sheet. She read the words in disbelief, the smile slowly dying from her face, and read them through again. The manager wrote politely but implacably. She was well overdrawn on her account and it had been necessary to return several cheques. She wouldn't be able to use her account until funds were paid in . . . Prue lit a cigarette, her eyes leaping again to the enclosed statement. The shock seemed to galvanise her entire body. Impossible! The entire sum, her *whole* yearly allowance had been drawn out in four large separate payments. Prue shook her head; quite impossible. Some mistake had obviously occurred. She sipped quickly at her coffee, her eye running down the statement, grimacing at those horrid red figures. Presently she put down the cup thoughtfully, checking the items more slowly. There were other amounts, amounts that she couldn't puzzle out. She recognised some: three pounds a week for housekeeping; two pounds ten on a pair of shoes;

one pound nineteen and eleven on a coat for Kit. These she could remember – but what was this one for fifteen pounds? Or this for a hundred and fifty? *A hundred and fifty?* Prue sat quite still. The cheque numbers were listed beside the amount and presently she rummaged in her bag and pulled out her cheque book. She flipped through the stubs, castigating herself for being so casual about filling them in. Only one or two could be checked, yet the cheques had gone; cheques she could not remember writing; cheques she was quite certain she had not written; cheques she *must* have written because they had been torn out to prove it.

Prue smoked thoughtfully. Was it possible that there might be someone somewhere with a duplicate numbered cheque book? Could the bank have made such a mistake? If so, then those cheques, written by someone else, were being drawn on her account. It was the only explanation. If only she were more careful about filling in the counterfoils. She wished that Tony was with her. He always had plausibly comforting explanations for such anxieties; he could make her laugh, cheer her up. True, he could be extravagant, too, but no one could be more generous when he was in funds. She glanced at her watch. He would be back late on Sunday afternoon. No point in worrying, she would talk it through with Tony and telephone the bank on Monday morning. It was clear that some mistake had been made and would have to be sorted out.

Prue stubbed out her cigarette and went upstairs to have a bath.

Chapter Twelve

Chill damp wisps of a sea fog followed Theo up the narrow stairs which led to his rooms. The mist had swirled about the town all day, blowing in from the channel, laying a film of moisture upon everything it touched. Only force of habit had made him take his evening walk, just before the murky light faded altogether, and he was glad to reach the warmth of his flat again and take off his damp ulster. He stood for a moment in the tiny lobby, feeling dispirited. He was missing his book. Finally, after years of work, it had been accepted by a small, reputable if specialist publishing house and, on publication, had received attention from a worthy critic and a leading churchman, both of whom had reviewed it most satisfactorily, the former referring to it as '. . . this most important book . . .' and the latter as '. . . a difficult and controversial subject made fascinating and thought-provoking . . .' Theo had been astonished and delighted; had felt the glow of something achieved. When the small fuss died down he found that he missed his work; it had kept him occupied; given a structure to his day. His periods of spiritual contemplation nourished him but he felt the need of something practical to attempt.

Whilst he was trying to think of some other subject about which he felt he might have something intelligent to say, an old friend asked him to take care of his parish in the Midlands whilst he underwent an operation. Theo gladly obliged but he felt no regrets when his temporary curacy came to an end. He had begun to feel his age. Prolonged immersion in the sea, after the warship on which he was serving was torpedoed, had weakened him and made him subject to bouts of bronchitis. He had never been good at taking care of himself and this indifference was starting to take its toll on his health.

Theo rubbed his hands over his thick damp hair – he had forgotten to put on his hat – and went into the kitchen. He looked with distaste upon his supper – four limp, pallid sausages and a heel of white bread – and felt even more depressed. He felt an insidious longing for one of Ellen's stews with delicious floury dumplings and thick gravy, allowing himself the luxury of imagining her at work in the kitchen at The Keep. His mouth watered as he conjured up the taste of her steak and kidney pie followed, perhaps, by plum tart and clotted cream. He groaned aloud. Why was he starving in a few cold rooms in Southsea when he might be enjoying himself in the comfort and beauty of his home in the West Country? Well, he knew the answer to that. Until he could be certain that he and Freddy could live together, peaceably and with no regrets, he had no right to disturb her hard-won tranquillity.

He was summoning up the energy to get the frying pan out of the cupboard when the telephone rang. It was almost a relief to leave the kitchen in order to answer it, although he was beginning to feel very hungry. He snatched up the only occupant of the fruit bowl as he passed and bit into the withered apple as he picked up the receiver.

'Theo?' Suspicion overlaid some other emotion in the voice at the other end of the line. 'What are you doing?'

Theo swallowed the piece of apple, choked on the tough skin and burst into a coughing fit.

'Sorry,' he gasped. 'Sorry. Something went down the wrong way. Sorry.' He wheezed musically for a moment and recovered himself. 'Terribly sorry. All right now. Is that you, Prue?'

'Yes, it is. Are you OK, Theo? Not having one of your attacks?'

'No, no. Absolutely not. Choked on a piece of apple. How are you, Prue? How nice to hear from you. Are the twins well?'

'Oh, Theo.' Her voice wavered, threatening tears. 'Something rather terrible has happened.'

Theo made sympathetic noises, wondering wildly if his bank account could stand any more of Prue's 'rather terrible' moments. He dug into his flannels pocket for a handkerchief and blew his nose while he listened to her voice telling him that Tony had left her.

'*Left* you?' It was the last thing he had expected to hear. He was well aware that, despite the odd jobs that Tony had found – and lost – during the last four years, Prue had financed the relationship out of her allowance with considerable help from Theo himself. It seemed odd that Tony should abandon such a source of support and easy living. He frowned and marshalled his wits. 'Are you certain, Prue? There's not some mistake here? Why should he leave you?'

'Oh, Theo.' He could hear her trying to control her voice. 'I'm sure he's gone. He went to visit his brother and was supposed to be back last Sunday week. It's Thursday now and I haven't heard a thing. Not a phone call or anything.'

'Is it possible that he's had an accident?' asked Theo anxiously. 'Have you phoned his brother?'

'He's not on the phone. He lives in a very remote spot, way up on the borders. I know he's gone, Theo. He's been . . . Oh God, Theo, he's been forging cheques.'

Theo was silent. With a shock, he realised that his first reaction was not a refusal to accept such a suggestion but to wonder how much damage Tony had done.

'Theo?' She sounded forlorn but there was a kind of weary desperation that made him feel that she had been living with this for a while; that she had not just discovered his deception but had spent some time coming to terms with it. 'Theo, he's drawn out all my money. My allowance had just been paid in and it's all gone. I've been to see the bank manager. The cheques were made out to a woman and she's been cashing them in various parts of the country. He's written other, smaller cheques to pay for things. I haven't got a penny and I'm in the red to the tune of four hundred and twenty-six pounds and a few odd pennies.'

Theo closed his eyes. His hand groped for the chair beside him and he lowered himself on to the seat, breathing deeply.

'My poor girl,' he said at last. 'My poor Prue. This

is terrible. Have you told anyone else?'

'No,' she said quickly. 'No one else. Oh God, Theo. What will Freddy say?'

She sounded so frightened that Theo's heart was touched by compassion.

'Never mind Freddy for the moment,' he said. 'I'll come down, shall I? Shall I come tomorrow so that we can talk things over? I could see the bank manager to put his mind at rest and bale you out for the moment. What do you think?'

She was crying now, sobbing quietly with relief and gratitude. 'Yes, please,' she said at last. 'But I can't bear it, Theo. You've been so wonderful already. How can I borrow any more from you? And how shall I pay it back? Oh, why do I get everything wrong?'

'Hush,' he said gently. 'Hush, child. I feel very honoured that you confide in me. We're friends, Prue, aren't we? Of course we are. This is what friendship is all about. I'll come tomorrow. Usual train. Don't meet me. I'll grab a taxi and be with you by lunchtime. No more tears. Now have a hot bath and a strong drink and try to sleep . . . Yes, yes, I know you do. I love you, too. Until tomorrow, then.'

He replaced the receiver and sat for a moment, trying to grasp and understand all that she had said. At length, with a sigh, he got up and returned to the kitchen. The sausages looked even more limp and pallid, the loaf more stale, and suddenly Theo yearned for a good strong whisky and a juicy steak. He experienced a violent surge of reckless hedonism.

'Damned if I shall eat you,' he muttered, thrusting the sausages back into the meat safe and the crust into the bread bin. 'Damned if I shall.'

He went out into the lobby, seized his coat, remembered his hat and hurried down the stairs and out of the door, heading purposefully for the warmth and companionship of the Keppel's Head.

After church on Sunday morning Mole and Susanna were in their special place in the far corner of the orchard. A small stone building had stood here once and in the crumbling remains, behind a tree, they had made a house. Old crates served as chairs and a table and they came here to play, with food begged from Ellen. Here they could be anyone they chose, depending on which book was the present favourite. Until recently they had been the Children of the New Forest, hunted by the Roundheads, and, before that, Peter Pan and Wendy defying Captain Hook. Sometimes they invented their own games but this morning they were busy cleaning their house with a very old garden broom and a piece of rag. Earlier, Ellen had given them their ration of chocolate, two penny bars of Cadbury's chocolate each, and these, their blue and silver foil removed, lay on the two cracked saucers which served as plates beside a bottle of orange juice ready to be poured into two handleless cups. This was their elevenses. First, however, their housekeeping must be completed.

Spiders ran for cover as Susanna wielded her rag with more energy than success but the earthen floor was brushed fairly clean and the loose covers shaken outside the door. These covers – old, faded curtains – lent a homely touch when spread over the three splintery crates and the little room looked jolly enough. The door – an ancient, rusting piece of corrugated iron – was leaning against the tree so that the light and air could come in; another such piece formed the flat roof, balancing precariously on what remained of the walls.

'For men must toil and women must weep,' said Susanna, quoting Ellen, and flourishing her rag over the old wheelbarrow in which they kept a few treasures – a rusting biscuit tin containing some rather soggy shortbread and some mouldy maps in a wooden box – and heaving a heavy sigh. 'There are spiders galore in all these cracks. Whatever next, I wonder.'

Mole stood his broom beside the open doorway and frowned at the brightness outside. Dust danced in the sunlight and he sneezed suddenly.

'Elevenses,' he announced. 'I'm dry as a chuck.' This was one of Fox's phrases. He sneezed again and sat down on a crate.

'What *is* a chuck?' asked Susanna, joining him with alacrity.

Mole poured the juice with scrupulous fairness and shook his head. 'Some kind of animal?' he hazarded.

'Perhaps it burrows a lot,' suggested Susanna, biting off a piece of chocolate. 'Which is why it gets thirsty. So what's our new game?'

'Supposing . . .' began Mole slowly, 'supposing there was treasure buried in the garden?' Caroline was reading them a carefully abridged version of *Treasure Island*. 'And we had to find it. But another gang was after it, too.'

'What treasure?' asked Susanna excitedly. 'Pieces of eight?'

'If you like,' said Mole. 'We could wrap some

pennies in this chocolate paper, the silver side out, and ask Caroline to hide it for us. We'd need the maps of course. Caroline could make us a map, too. It would be t-top secret and the other gang would be after it.'

He felt a brief thrill of terror at the mere thought of the other gang but Susanna had already jumped up to fetch the box. Mole opened it and took out a map of the moor behind Ashburton which they spread out on the table, carefully holding up their cups of juice. They pored over it together. It already bore several pencil marks but this seemed to add to its authenticity.

'This is the orchard,' said Mole. 'See? And this is the courtyard. X marks the spot. Now then. Where's the pencil . . .?'

A short distance away, beyond the fuchsia hedge, Freddy was working in the herbaceous border that ran the length of the lawn beneath the high stone wall. She was tying back the Michaelmas daisies and the tall Japanese anemones. A south-westerly gale had wreaked havoc in the night, even in this sheltered corner, and she was busy restoring and rescuing. The gale had blown itself out by morning and the air was fresh. Against the deep tender blue of the sky whorls and feathery streaks of high white cirrus appeared to be stationary whilst below them ragged wispy grey clouds drifted quickly, remnants of the storm. A robin sang from the top of the wall and a hardy red admiral spread its wings on the golden fruit of the Japonica.

As Freddy worked, her mind was busy on several

different levels. The children were in her thoughts as usual: Fliss, writing to ask if she might go on a special school trip to Stratford; Susanna, needing a new winter coat; Mole, dithering over an invitation to a party on bonfire night. Then there was Fox, who had been rendered helpless by an agonising attack of sciatica, not to mention Caroline, who had taken his duties upon herself, as well as continuing to deal competently with her own.

Freddy thought: Whatever should we have done without Caroline? What a blessing she has been.

She stepped back on to the lawn, scraping the mud from her thick gardening shoes, and bent to pick up some more twine. Mugwump, who lay at a short distance away gnawing on a dead branch which had been brought down by the gale, wagged his tail a little. He kept an eye on her, lest she might feel the need to remove his branch, but she merely cut another length of twine and moved along the border to tie back the chrysanthemums. Freddy smiled at the sight of him, stretched upon the lawn, remembering a time when she would not have dared to lay anything down within his range for fear it would have been carried off or chewed to pieces. She had spent a great deal of time running after him so as to take back her gloves or a trowel or a bundle of twine. He'd always relished a good tug of war but, in the main, he took the confiscation of his toys in good part. He was less destructive now but she missed his naughtiness.

'We're all getting older,' she told him as she bent to her work again.

Mugwump sensed a touch of sadness in her voice and wondered whether she might enjoy a game. He got up and dragged the branch across the lawn, pushing it towards her and giving an encouraging bark or two. He was pleased to see that she understood him, for she took one end and shook it. At once he seized the other end in his jaws, tugging strongly and growling excitedly. He was disappointed when she let go.

'Take it, you ridiculous animal,' she said, laughing. 'You're too strong for me. I don't want your old stick.'

He shook it again, temptingly, but she had returned to the flowers and he gave up, lying down to resume his gnawing. Freddy's thoughts, meanwhile, had moved on to Theo. She had been tempted to use Fox's disability as blackmail to persuade Theo down to The Keep for a while. The difficulty was that he might take her seriously and feel obliged to take on the physical work which Caroline was managing. Freddy knew that Theo would find it impossible to stand by whilst Caroline chopped wood and hauled coal, mowed the lawns and coped with the vegetable garden. Naturally, she and Ellen were helping Caroline all they could, even Mole and Susanna had been given tasks according to their abilities, but it underlined the problems that were waiting to loom once they all became older and less able. Of course, Theo's extra pair of hands would be very useful, but his bronchitis attacks were becoming rather more frequent of late and Freddy worried about him. She longed for him to come home to The Keep – not least because he would be properly cared for – but she was afraid lest he should overtire himself. Perhaps she should be thinking of employing a younger man on a part-time basis . . . The problem was that she knew how Fox would hate it – or would he? She remembered how antagonistic Ellen had felt about bringing in a nanny when the children had first arrived, yet she and Caroline were now the best of friends.

Freddy finished the tying up and glanced at her watch; nearly time for luncheon and Julia would be arriving at any moment. Mealtimes were another worry. When Peter and John had started their preparatory school she had decided that the time had come for them to eat luncheon with her in the dining room during their holidays; at thirteen they had joined her for dinner. It was years now since she had used the dining room, except for huge family gatherings or for the more formal occasions, but she knew that she should be thinking about it again. When Caroline had arrived at The Keep, Freddy pondered on how and where she should eat. The boys had had a governess for the short years before they went off to school but she had eaten her meals on a tray in her room. Even Freddy realised that those days were past and that Caroline came from quite as good a background as the Chadwicks themselves. Fortunately, Caroline had solved the problem for herself. She had quite easily and naturally stayed in the kitchen with the children, although she occasionally – at Freddy's invitation – joined her in the breakfast room for dinner. Prue and the twins always dined with her now – the twins were, after all, seventeen years old – and Fliss had been gratified, though faintly alarmed, when it was suggested that she should join them during the last holiday. Freddy felt that Fliss had acquitted herself very well, however, obviously enjoying the sensation of being treated as one of the adults.

Soon Mole and Susanna would be old enough to join them and then the dining room would come back into its own. Freddy felt a little daunted by the prospect of the children growing up, leaving school, finding jobs, getting married . . .

She thought: For Heaven's sake! Susanna is only six.

Another fear seized her. Would she still be alive when Susanna was old enough to be looking for a husband? Before she could pursue this alarming idea she heard a voice and saw Caroline coming across the grass towards her.

'There you are!' she cried. 'Gosh! Haven't you got on well! Not too much damage? Good. Mrs Blakiston's just arriving and there's been a telephone call from Theo. He's coming down tomorrow. He'll be in time for tea. Getting in at three forty-five.'

'But why so unexpectedly?' Freddy was dragging off her gloves. 'It's another ten days to the Birthday. Is he quite well?'

'Perfectly fit,' Caroline assured her. 'He said something about a craving for Ellen's stew with dumplings.'

She laughed and Freddy smiled with her, shaking her head at such strange behaviour. Mugwump, pleased to see such jollity, advanced with his branch which he dropped provocatively at Caroline's feet. He could always count on Caroline for a good romp. She grabbed the branch and began to run across the grass, trailing it behind her, encouraging him with shouts. He raced behind her, trying to catch the madly veering branch and failing utterly. Freddy laughed out loud as she watched them. She felt a sense of relief at the news that Theo would soon be with them, deciding to collect him herself and experiencing the usual twinge of annoyance when she remembered that the passenger trains no longer used the branch line to Staverton and that she would have to drive into Totnes. It was an inconvenience they were all getting used to, however, and it would be wonderful to have Theo home. She could share her ideas about a part-time gardener, always assuming that she could afford it . . . Freddy's smile faded a little. The company was supporting so many of them at present, although Peter had been very well insured and Alison had had some money of her own which had gone into a trust for Fliss, Mole and Susanna. Nevertheless it was to be hoped that some of the children would soon be supporting themselves. Hal would shortly be attending his Admiralty Interview Board, although Kit swung about between putative careers, as unsteady as a weathercock, whilst Fliss, as yet, showed no indication towards any particular vocation.

Freddy wasted no time in the garden room as she stowed away her twine and scissors and hurried to change her shoes. Julia was crossing the courtyard as she emerged and they went up the front steps together.

'Summer is over,' Freddy announced. 'It is time to light the hall fire and prepare for the winter.'

'I have a feeling that I should feel depressed by that statement,' Julia suggested as she followed her friend into the drawing room, 'but I find that each season has its advantages.'

'That's because you are fortunate enough to be

independent,' said Freddy, heading for the drinks tray. 'Your social life doesn't stop at the onset of winter. Neither would mine – if I had one. We dash about in our little cars, protected from the weather, not inconvenienced by local transport. I see these young women, freezing at bus stops, weighed down by shopping bags and trying to deal with babies and pushchairs.' She shook her head. 'Bad enough in summer. Intolerable in winter, I should think.'

'Lots of families have their own cars these days,' protested Julia. 'I know that the husbands have the use of them in the week but there is plenty of opportunity to shop together at weekends.'

'Perhaps,' said Freddy. 'Things are easier now than they used to be, I agree, but I feel that you and I were rather ahead of our time, Julia. I wonder whether our friendship would have had the chance to flourish if we had not been able to see each other whenever we felt like it.'

'I'm sure you are right.' Julia took her glass. 'We've been lucky in that respect. We have enjoyed an independence most women do not have. It has been a small recompense for the things that we've lost.'

Before Freddy could answer, Caroline put her head round the door.

'Good morning, Mrs Blakiston,' she said. 'Lunch is ready, Mrs Chadwick.'

Freddy nodded. 'Thank you, Caroline. Tell Ellen that we'll go straight through.'

'Another recompense, I think,' murmured Julia as Caroline disappeared.

'Oh, yes,' agreed Freddy at once. 'A very considerable one. I can't begin to think how we would have managed without Caroline. You'll have to bring your drink with you, Julia. One valuable lesson I *have* learned in life is never to upset the cook. Come along. I want to hear all your news.'

Chapter Thirteen

It was Caroline who lit the fire in the hall; the first of the winter. A mellow Indian summer had made it unnecessary so far but the storm had brought a cool freshness to the air and she decided that a fire would be a real welcome for Theo. There was room for a huge log basket in the deep stone recess which housed the fireplace and, luckily for Caroline, it was full of big dry logs which she laid on the wide hearth which was cleaned out at the end of the season but rarely touched once the fire was lit. Each winter a bed of hot ash would build up gradually as the weeks wore on, and occasionally Fox would remove a few careful shovelfuls of ash lest the bed become too high, but the fire rarely went out. Now, at the beginning of the season, Caroline had to use screws of newspaper and dry twigs to start it but she soon had a good blaze going. Presently she perched on the little stool which was kept in the recess opposite the log basket and where Susanna loved to sit on winter afternoons, the flames glowing rosily on her cheeks. Caroline linked her hands round her knees and stared into the fire, brooding on the past.

In 1939 her mother had been dead for several years

and her father, a serving army officer, had left Caroline in the care of her older sister and their aunt. He had died in North Africa. Caroline had been heartbroken but she was a soldier's daughter and had been taught that this was part of the job. She was a sensible, capable child but she had a longing to be part of a family. As her own had seemed to be gradually disappearing she had decided that she would like to be a nanny, thereby adopting somebody else's.

Now she thought: How lucky I was to come here. Good old Prue. She did me the best turn ever. Hope they don't chuck me out when Susanna grows old enough to go off to school. Wherever would I go? This is home, now. The good thing is, Mrs Chadwick needs me, not just for the children but for all sorts of things. Oh, please God don't let them not want me anymore.

Even though it was four years since she had seen him, thoughts of Jeremy slid into her mind. Jeremy: her last employer, whose children she had cared for, with whom she had fallen deeply in love. His wife had died of some rare disease and Caroline had been convinced that Jeremy would eventually turn to her for more than just the companionship and help which he relied upon so heavily after his wife's death. It had been a humiliating shock when he had returned from a house party announcing that he was in love. He had expected her to rejoice with him, to congratulate him, and she had done her best. Since the youngest child had just started his preparatory school, Caroline took the opportunity to give in her notice; her humiliation was complete when she saw with what alacrity he accepted it. She knew that he would have found it hard to dismiss her after the years of support she had given him. As it was he let her go without a qualm and it was while she had been taking refuge with her sister that Prue had come to stay, to arrange to borrow the cottage. Apart from her sister, only Prue knew the whole story, such that it was. After all, Jeremy had never given her reason to hope that he might love her. Nonetheless, she could not quite forget him . . .

She heard the slamming of the door that led from the back of the hall into the kitchen quarters and jumped up. Ellen appeared with the tea things.

'Everyone will be arriving together,' she said anxiously. 'Mr Theo from the train with Madam, and the children from school. If only we'd thought, they could have picked them up on the way.'

'Never mind, Ellen.' Caroline began to help her unload the tray. 'It'll give Mrs Chadwick time on her own with Mr Theo. I'll walk to meet the bus and hurry them along a bit.'

'That Mole,' said Ellen, counting plates. 'He'll be picking up the conkers from that great tree on the corner. Not that he needs any more. I've got a whole tray of 'em, baking up nice and hard in the bottom oven.'

'He's doing swops with his chums,' Caroline told her. 'He's building up a very good marble collection.'

Ellen put cups into the saucers and added spoons. 'At least he's happy to walk home now without someone meeting him,' she observed. 'Of course, he's got Susanna but it's another little step.'

'It certainly is.' Caroline checked the table and

nodded. 'All present and correct. That cake looks delicious, Ellen. How's Fox doing?'

Ellen clicked her tongue vexatiously. 'Got himself up out of bed, drat the man. He's in the kitchen. District nurse will be in later. She'll deal with him.'

Caroline laughed. 'Poor Fox. He says her hands are made of steel and that he's covered in bruises.'

'She gives him a good pummelling,' admitted Ellen, with a certain satisfaction. 'He'll need hot-water bottles wrapped in flannel afterwards. There now. That looks very good, even if I do say so myself.'

'I hope you've saved some for us,' said Caroline as they went through to the kitchen together. 'I'll have mine with you and Fox today. Anything I can do before I meet the children?'

'You've done more than your fair share, my dear.' Ellen gave Caroline's hand an affectionate pat. 'Go off and meet those children and enjoy the walk. It'll do you good.'

Caroline went, surprised and touched by the gesture; Ellen was not given to showing her emotions. As she passed out through the gates, her spirits rose. Sheep were grazing in the field to the left of the drive and the wind blew strong and clean from the moors. She loved the power of the elements: roaring blusterous winds that bowed mighty trees; towering huge seas that crashed in against the shore; lashing rain that drove into the earth and cleansed it. It pleased her to know that however man might pit his puny efforts in an attempt to harness these great forces, they remained untouched and unconquerable; not cruel but simply indifferent.

She turned her face up to the wind, leaning against

it, feeling its force as it hurried her along the drive. Out in the deep lane the high banks protected her and she ran her fingers through her short curls, feeling invigorated, all humiliating memories blown away. Two small figures appeared round the bend in the lane; Susanna and Mole toiling home from school. Caroline's heart gave a little tuck of love at the sight of them and, raising her hands high above her head to wave, she began to run to meet them.

The study was directly behind the drawing room looking north. Here all the books in the house, apart from the children's books and Freddy's personal reading, were collected on shelves which lined the entire wall space. There was a faintly sombre atmosphere in this quiet room and Freddy had done her best to lighten it with bright rugs and curtains with plenty of rich gold and thick cream colours woven into them. A walnut table was placed between the two windows, with several chairs drawn up to it, and two small sofas, covered in cream brocade and piled with scarlet cushions, faced each other from either side of the fireplace.

Here, Freddy finally ran Theo to earth the morning after his arrival. They had breakfasted together an hour before but various household tasks had claimed Freddy, leaving Theo to his own devices. He had felt too restless to stay in his private quarters, wondering how he could break Prue's news to Freddy, and he'd wandered down to the study hoping to find a book to distract him. He had persuaded Prue that it would be sensible to let him tell Freddy the whole sorry story for, although Prue knew that she was being cowardly, it was clear to see that she was terrified of facing her mother-in-law. Theo decided that it was better for Freddy to think Prue a coward than to risk an absolute rupture between them. Prue was far too shaken, far too nervous, to tell the story clearly and articulately and he knew that Freddy would lose patience long before the half of it had been explained.

Prue gave in readily enough and Theo had set out for the West Country, rehearsing the story in his mind, thinking of ways of presenting Prue in the best possible light. She had surprised him. Despite her terror and shame she had thought of two measures in which she could make reparation and he had known an overwhelming affection for her when she had outlined them to him . . .

The door was pushed open and Freddy put her head into the room.

'I wondered where you'd disappeared to,' she said. 'Looking for something to read or are you fleeing Ellen and the Hoover?'

'I'm waiting to talk to you,' he said seriously, drawing her further in and shutting the door behind her. 'Have you got time to listen?'

'Of course I have.' His tone alerted her and she watched him, chin raised, automatically bracing herself for some kind of blow. 'What is it? Wouldn't we be more comfortable in the drawing room?'

'Possibly.' Theo shrugged. 'And much more likely to be disturbed. Come and sit down.'

She settled herself on one of the sofas but Theo remained standing, hands in his trouser pockets. There was a silence during which Freddy studied him closely. He was wearing an old Aran jersey, which

Ellen had knitted him years before, and his usual grey flannels. His thick hair was rumpled and he looked very casual and attractive and somehow much younger than he had for months. Freddy had the sudden horrid fear that he was going to tell her that he'd met a woman, had fallen in love with her and was going to marry her.

'What is it, Theo?' she asked sharply. 'Stop dithering and get on with it.'

The fear in her voice made him look at her quickly. She stared back at him stonily and he felt a sinking apprehension.

'I've got something to tell you,' he said. 'It's very difficult to know quite where to start.'

She was so certain now that her fear was well-founded that jealousy and anger closed her throat and kept her silent. Afterwards, her relief that this had prevented her from making an ass of herself was so great that she often woke in the night in a cold sweat just thinking about it.

'It's about Prue,' he said – and she thought that she might faint with relief. 'Tony's left her. That is to say, he has been missing from home for a fortnight with no message and Prue has discovered that he has been taking her cheques and forging her signature.'

She could hardly take it in. Her extreme reaction to that first dread had shocked her and she found it difficult to assimilate exactly what it was he was now trying to tell her. She shook her head, as though to clear it, and he went to sit beside her.

'She wanted to tell you herself,' he needed to make this very plain, 'but I insisted that I should be the one to explain it all to you. She's terribly upset.'

'So I imagine.' Her voice was unsteady and she cleared her throat. He put his hand on hers and she turned her own so that she could hold his tightly. How insupportable it would be to lose Theo – and especially to another woman. He was looking at her with a strange expression and she collected her wits and arranged her face into more usual lines. 'Tell me all about it. From the beginning. Sorry. This is rather a shock.'

His look of loving concern almost unnerved her again but it was clear that he suspected nothing and she sent up a quick prayer of thanks. He began to talk, explaining about Tony's trips away, which had now taken on a more sinister light, the many occasions when Prue had found herself overdrawn without understanding how she could have spent so much, and the final deed of drawing out her entire allowance as well as forging other cheques to pay for goods. Freddy listened silently, her own early reaction subsiding as she began to see the magnitude of Tony's deception.

'Oh really, Theo,' she said when he finished. 'I can hardly believe that even Prue can have been so gullible. Or so featherbrained. Does she never keep a check on her accounts? Her whole allowance! Oh, it really is too bad, even for Prue!'

'There are no hard words you could think up that Prue doesn't think she deserves,' said Theo after a moment. 'She is prostrate with humiliation. She has the double humiliation, in fact. First, of being left penniless and second, of being abandoned by her husband for another woman. She has been used and duped very cruelly. Apart from being rather casual about her financial affairs, Prue's only real fault is that she has fallen in love with the wrong person. I suppose we might all be capable of doing that.' Freddy glanced up at him quickly and looked away again. 'Mightn't we?' he asked gently and rather sadly. 'Prue must be condemned for loving someone far too well and too generously.'

Words seethed on Freddy's lips but she swallowed them back furiously. She longed to rail against Prue's weakness of character but Theo had unwittingly spiked all her guns.

'So what is to be done?' she asked at last, somewhat acidly. 'Do you suggest that we let him get away with it? Send him on his way with blessings? I fear my generosity may not be in the same class as Prue's.'

She shut her lips, hating herself, but Theo was smiling at her affectionately. She glared at him.

'We have informed the police,' he told her. 'Naturally he must be apprehended if possible but it is unlikely that we shall see the money again.'

'And how is Prue to live?' demanded Freddy. 'How is the overdraft to be paid back? She is nearly a thousand pounds adrift from what I can make out. It's not just Prue, is it? There are the twins to consider.'

'Prue has thought about it very carefully. She sees that she has cost the estate a great deal of money and she suggests that you sell her house so as to reimburse it.'

Freddy gaped at him. 'Sell her *house*?'

He nodded. 'She told me that, though you had been generous enough to make her a present of it, she has never really felt that it was hers. She thinks it would

173

be best if it were to be sold to raise the money to cover her overdraft.'

Prue's innocent comment came like a blow in the face and Freddy was hurt beyond measure. She could remember how proud she'd been of her generous gesture and how graciously she had dealt with Prue's surprised and stammered gratitude. She writhed inwardly.

'And where would they live?' she asked contemptuously. '*How* are they to live?'

'Prue has found herself a job,' said Theo. His pride in her was so clear that Freddy shrank before it. It was evident that he expected that Freddy should feel as proud of Prue as he did; instead she felt ashamed and small.

'Doing what?' she muttered.

'Starting next week, she'll be working in one of the big department stores in Queen's Road, selling ladies' fashions. She's hoping to find a small flat to rent.'

'And does she really imagine that she can support herself on the wage she will earn as a shop-girl?' Again she hated herself. 'It is ridiculous and quite unnecessary,' she said angrily. 'Does she see me as some kind of wicked stepmother only waiting for the opportunity to throw her out into the snow? As far as I am concerned she is still my daughter-in-law and I shall care for her accordingly. Why should the twins have to live in a poky flat simply because Prue is such a bad judge of character?'

'Not such a bad judge,' Theo pointed out gently. 'She chose John first.'

Freddy's lips shook and she pursed them together fiercely. He should not see how deeply she was hurt, both by Prue's rejection of the gift of the house and by his championship of Prue, which had shown her, Freddy, in such a poor light. Theo only saw that she was upset, imagined that it was the allusion to her beloved John, and put his arms around her.

'Forgive me,' he said.

Freddy took hold of a piece of his jersey, rubbing the stuff between her fingers. 'What shall I do?' she asked.

He was silent for a while, holding her in the circle of his arm, relieved that she had taken it so well.

'I think we should compromise,' he said at last. 'I think Prue should keep the house but I think that it would be good for her to work. It will improve her self-esteem and make her feel that she is doing something useful. She will have to be frugal and sensible and I think that she will make very big efforts to manage. The twins won't suffer, we shall see to that.'

'And the overdraft?' She still held on to his jersey, head bent, her eyes shut.

'Can the estate afford to make it good?'

'I suppose so. But we can't go on looking upon it as a bottomless purse, Theo. There are so many calls upon it at the moment. I want to discuss that with you later.'

'Very well. But I think that if we can afford to clear Prue's debt then we should do so. I have some shares that my aunt left me—'

'No, no,' she said impatiently. 'I'm quite sure that Prue has cost you quite enough already.' She looked up at him shrewdly. 'Hasn't she?'

Her eyes challenged him but he smiled down at her blandly.

'Women are expensive creatures,' he said reflectively. 'I know that much. Don't you want to know what I've brought you for your birthday? And there's Susanna pestering for a new bicycle . . .'

'There's plenty of life in Fliss's old bicycle,' said Freddy shortly. 'As for presents . . .' She hesitated. Theo's presents were rare objects, chosen with love and care. 'So what have you bought me?' she asked carelessly.

He burst out laughing, kissing her briefly and drawing her up from the chair. In fact he'd found a pair of pretty candlesticks in the Bristol blue glass she loved so much. They would look well in her little corner cupboard amongst her treasures.

'Wait and see,' he told her. 'Do something for me. Come and telephone Prue. Be kind to her. She'll be so relieved. Will you do that for me?' He knew that she disliked the telephone, preferring to write letters.

'Oh, very well,' she sighed, a measure of irritation returning, unwilling to part from him, even briefly. 'Then we must talk, Theo. About Fox and . . . oh, all sorts of things.'

'I shall be ready for you,' he said. 'Go and talk to Prue. Tell her you're proud that she's got a job. Bless you, Freddy. I'll be waiting for you in the drawing room.'

Chapter Fourteen

Prue replaced the receiver gently and stood quite still, overcome by shock. The sound of Freddy's voice at the other end of the line had rendered her quite weak with fright – and surprise: she had been expecting a letter – and she had instinctively braced herself. Freddy could be very cool, with a dazzlingly cutting way with words which always reduced Prue to a miserable, inarticulate heap. Ever since she knew that Theo had arrived at The Keep, Prue had been waiting for a communication from her mother-in-law. It was odd how she continued to think of Freddy in that role. Prue wondered what the situation actually was now that she had remarried but it was irrelevant. Freddy would always be her mother-in-law, she was Johnny's mother; the twins' grandmother; provider and supporter . . . Prue went to pour herself a drink. It might be only half-past eleven but she needed something strong.

As she gulped at an aggressive gin and tonic, Prue reflected on the telephone call. True, Freddy's sympathy for her plight had lacked a certain wholeheartedness; her reassurance that Prue need not be anxious regarding the overdraft was the least bit restrained;

her congratulations on Prue's new-found independence contained a faintly acid flavour. It was rather as if Freddy might have been sucking on a lemon throughout the whole conversation . . . Prue giggled suddenly with gratitude and relief – and gin – and flopped down in a chair. It was going to be all right. At this moment, she was so overwhelmed by Freddy's generosity that Tony's defection no longer seemed to matter. The important things were that the bank would be dealt with and that she and the twins would not have to move into some dreary little bedsit. She knew quite well that she could only have afforded the most simple of lodgings and, though she had been prepared to lose the house, she had been unable to shrug off the guilt at having to deprive the twins of their home.

Silently, she raised her glass to Theo. She knew quite well that she owed her survival to him. It was likely that Freddy would have baled her out, if only for the twins' sake, but not with such generosity. It was good of her to let her keep the house. Prue had been expecting that Freddy would say that the whole family must move down to Devon. Theo had warned her to be prepared for this. It was, after all, an obvious solution. The twins were away at school and soon would be leaving home altogether and there was plenty of room for Prue at The Keep. Her heart had plunged with terror at the thought of living permanently under the same roof with Freddy – even if it were a fairly big roof – though she had tried to hide this reaction from Theo. Prue swallowed some more gin and smiled wryly to herself. She guessed that Freddy would feel exactly as she did and, by insisting that Prue should be allowed to keep her little house, was protecting her own position. Whatever the reasons, Prue felt weak with thankfulness. She was more than happy to work in an attempt to redress the balance – that was perfectly fair – but she was deeply relieved that the twins would be spared any suffering as a result of her own stupidities.

The now familiar depression began to creep back. She wondered where Tony was and felt a stab of misery and shame at being duped so thoroughly. It was clear now that, once he'd seen that Prue was not in line for a large inheritance or able to turn any heirlooms into cash, he had begun to lay plans to move on. Looking back, she could see the pattern. She saw how the visits to the north had slowly increased – he had told her his brother was ill – and how he had experimented with forging a cheque here and there. Naturally she had turned to him with her anxieties and he had been quick to explain them away, laughing at her confusion, distracting her with love.

Prue thought: God, what a fool I've been. So easily taken in. I trusted him, made love with him, and he must have been seeing *her* all the time.

She gritted her teeth, hot with shame and anger, but she knew now that, deep down, she did not really love him; that the shame and anger were the products of hurt pride rather than the reaction of true passion. She could remember how she'd loved Johnny. If Johnny had been unfaithful she would have . . . Prue closed her eyes. It would have been the end of her world. Even now, eighteen years on, the thought of Johnny with another woman had the power to inflict real pain. No, she did not really love Tony. It was a pale imitation, brought forth out of loneliness and need, yet the pain caused by his defection and deceit was quite bad enough. If only she had been more cautious . . .

It was over. Prue swallowed the last of her drink and pushed herself up out of the chair. It was finished and done with and she must put it behind her. She had another chance and she intended to take it and show Freddy that she was worth rescuing. Prue went into the kitchen and put the glass on the draining board. She had to buy some new clothes ready for work on Monday; clerical-grey skirt and a white shirt was the uniform required. Thanks to Theo, she had enough cash to be able to kit herself out satisfactorily and she was determined to pay him back out of her first pay-packet. She decided to go out and shop about but first she would write a proper thank-you letter to Freddy. She had been too dazed to thank her properly on the telephone and it was important that Freddy should know how very grateful she was. With a lighter heart than she had known for many months, Prue went into the little sitting room and sat down at her bureau.

'Seems that Tony's left Prue,' said Ellen to Fox as they shared an early morning cup of tea. 'Gone off without a word and took all her money with him.'

Fox stared at her in disbelief and she nodded at him, mouth pursed, chin drawn back, in a 'what did I say?' expression. He gave a long, low whistle.

'Poor Prue,' he said. 'Poor maid. What happens now?'

Ellen shrugged. 'Mr Theo and Madam are sorting

it out,' she told him. 'Prue's got herself a job to help the ship along. Working in a big shop like Spooner's, selling ladies' clothes.'

They looked at one another, silently registering faint disapproval that one of the family should have to resort to such means.

'Another woman is it?' suggested Fox cautiously.

'Trust a man for that,' cried Ellen indignantly. 'Always have to bring women into everything. Why should it be another woman?'

Fox drained his cup and set it back on the draining board. 'Not a question of *bringing* women in,' he said provocatively. 'Get themselves everywhere. You mark my words, there'll be a woman around somewhere, causing trouble.'

Ellen hesitated, torn between the relief of being able to lay the guilt and responsibility at an unknown hussy's feet and admitting that Prue had picked a wrong 'un in Tony. Fox grinned at her dilemma.

'Where be they dogs?' he asked. 'Damned if they haven't gone off without me. See you later, maid.'

'And who said you were fit enough to go walking?' she demanded, distracted by this flagrant disobedience. 'Supposed to be resting, you are.'

'A gentle stroll won't hurt,' he said contemptuously. 'I shall take it slowly. A bit of exercise never hurt nobody . . .'

He disappeared, leaving Ellen fretting.

'Men,' she muttered, banging the porridge saucepan down. '*Men . . .*'

Freddy sat in the pew which had long been designated for the Chadwicks' use and which was directly behind the Rectory pew, and tried to concentrate on the sermon. Despite her long and consistent battle with religion, she always experienced a quiet comfort here, in her familiar corner of the small stone church. The squat grey building with its square Norman tower looked as if it had grown up out of the earth, simple and plain in its quiet graveyard, without ornament or ostentation. It had stood so for nine hundred years and it was reasonable enough to expect a sense of peace in a place where so much worship and prayer had taken place. Freddy told herself that this peace came from having a brief respite from the daily round, from having an enforced rest where nothing was demanded of her but to stand and sit and kneel at the appropriate moments, but the older she grew the more she appreciated the time she spent in this corner.

She glanced along at her family; only five of them this morning. Ellen always attended Evensong so that she could prepare the lunch and occasionally Fox would go with her. At present he was recovering from his attack of sciatica and certainly not mobile enough to attend church. Meanwhile there was Caroline, at the far end of the pew, and Mole and Susanna with Theo between them. Mole sat quiet and still, his eyes fixed on the rector with whom he had struck up an unlikely friendship. The rector collected stamps, a hobby which fascinated Mole, who had inherited the collections belonging to his father and his uncle. Once, when the rector had come to The Keep and had stayed on to tea, he had discussed this hobby with Mole and, a few weeks later, Mole had been invited over to the Rectory to see the rector's interesting collection. Caroline had cycled over with him and stayed to talk to the rector's wife, who was delightfully short and round and made excellent shortbread. It had become a pleasant habit and, on the first Saturday of each month, Mole and Caroline went to tea at the Rectory. On this Sunday morning, Freddy was pleased to see that this closer acquaintance with the rector had apparently given Mole an incentive to listen to the sermon.

Susanna was leaning against Caroline, thumb in her mouth, legs swinging. Freddy frowned a little. She should be encouraged to sit up straight and she was too old to be sucking her thumb. Caroline was wonderful, there was no doubt about that, but she had a tendency to be rather too easy-going with the children . . .

Freddy thought: I'm getting old. It's a sure sign when you start criticising the next generation.

She remembered how she had sat here with the twins and their governess. Miss Smollett would not have allowed either lolling or thumb-sucking – and Peter and John would have been taken out before the sermon, leaving their mother sitting in splendid isolation. Both of them had been married here, wartime marriages with all the necessary stringencies, but Freddy had done the very best she could and she and Ellen between them had put on a splendid show. Hal and Kit had been baptised in this small grey church and so had Fliss and Mole. No wonder she had a fondness for it – nothing to do with faith or God, of course, just a feeling of continuity and family.

Theo glanced sideways at her and she smiled at

him, indicating her amusement at Mole's concentration, thinking of other times during the last eighteen years when her grandchildren had been in this pew with her. When they were small, the twins always behaved much better than she expected – given that Prue rarely took them to church – saying the Lord's Prayer loudly and singing enthusiastically during the hymns. When the three younger ones arrived at The Keep, poor Hal was set up as an example to them all and was obliged to be on his best behaviour whilst Kit read the Psalms during the sermon and helped Mole find his way about the Book of Common Prayer. Freddy remembered Susanna at two, asleep on Caroline's knee, with Mole sitting quietly beside her, whilst Fliss frowned over the prodigal son's brother, feeling that he had been unfairly treated. She took the scriptures very seriously and had been struck by the poor faithful brother's remark: '. . . *yet thou never gavest me a kid, that I might make merry with my friends.*' Her tender heart had been touched, her sense of fair play aggrieved, and, afterwards, she had tackled Freddy. 'But why, Grandmother?' she had asked. 'He'd stayed at home to do all the work and look after the land. Why couldn't he have a party with his friends?' Freddy had smiled with evil cunning upon Theo. 'You must ask your uncle, my darling,' she'd answered with an unbecoming glee. 'He will explain it all to you much better than I could.'

Now, Freddy chuckled silently to herself and she recalled Theo's look. Fliss had become a thorn in his side. Next Sunday it had been the man cured of the palsy. She wanted to know what happened to the roof after it had been broken up to let the man down on his bed to Jesus. What, demanded, Fliss, had the owner of the house said about it? Did he make the man's friends repair it afterwards?

'She has all the instincts of the landowner,' Theo said to Freddy later. 'First the prodigal son wasting his inheritance and now a householder in Palestine who had his roof vandalised two thousand years ago. Just let's hope that 1 Kings 21 isn't coming up as the Old Testament reading before I go back to Southsea.'

Later, Freddy had looked the reference up and saw that it was the story of Naboth's vineyard . . . Dear Theo. She looked at him again; sitting forward, head bent, hands clasped loosely between his knees, he was listening intently. She felt the familiar tug of love and sadness. How hard she had fought over this God business; or was it that? Was she perhaps fighting herself, her love for him, the bitter fate that made her fall in love with a man when she'd just become engaged to his brother. God had made a good scapegoat for her unhappiness; a handy stick with which to beat Theo. It was odd that, loving him as she did, she'd found it necessary to strike at him and wound him, as if she wanted to punish him for being in the wrong place at the wrong time, for not falling in love with her in return, to wring any kind of a reaction from him. It had given her a kind of fierce satisfaction to reject his faith, to mock at him; yet how little satisfaction he'd given her.

'I don't think you care about saving my soul,' she'd said to him once.

'Your soul is God's affair, not mine,' he'd answered. 'It's not a contest, Freddy. You have free will.'

She'd felt snubbed, considering her soul to be something rather special that God was waiting for with baited breath, as an ornament to add to His glory.

'I thought that it was a priest's job to save sinners.' Her tone had been flippant, to hide her feeling of foolishness.

'Perhaps,' he'd said. 'It's not the way I work. I'm not a missionary. God touches people in His own way. When God has touched your heart, there are no more questions.'

She'd felt hurt, rejected. 'But how do you know,' she'd mumbled self-consciously, 'if He . . . touches your heart?'

'You know.' Theo had spoken with finality.

'So if you don't save souls,' she'd asked. 'What *do* you do?'

'I contemplate Him,' Theo had answered. 'I worship Him. And I pray.'

'Prayers aren't answers,' she'd said scornfully. 'I know that.'

'I think you are confusing prayer with the list of demands with which you bombard Him,' he'd suggested. 'People use their religion as a kind of bargaining table. If You do this I'll do that. If You let this happen I'll never do such and such again. That's not prayer.'

'What *is* prayer then?' she'd asked.

'Prayer is waiting in love and longing,' he'd said. 'Waiting in silence upon God. Waiting is all you can do. God will do the rest. It is demanding and wearying and often unrewarding, but occasionally we are taken hold of. It depends on God. It's not a new idea. The psalmist says "*I waited patiently for the Lord; and he . . . heard my cry.*" Isaiah writes: "*They that wait upon the Lord shall renew their strength; they shall mount up with wings as eagles.*" It's all there in the Bible . . .'

Remembering, Freddy was visited by a strange sensation, a kind of inner certainty that her life had been exactly as it should have been, that she had been fighting against something that didn't exist. How unhappy she would have been to betray Bertie with Theo; how dreadful not to have had her twins, Peter and John, Bertie's sons; how glad she had been of Theo's strength and companionship, unmarred by guilt or confused by sex. It had been terrible to lose her husband and her sons, yet she still had these dear children, Peter's children, going on into the future. For one tiny, breathtaking moment Freddy saw quite clearly that death was unimportant; saw a brief vision of a huge infinity with a great Power at its centre and saw how all humanity unconsciously strove towards it, confused and lost in the clamour and fear for survival, yet with a deep-down longing, an unconscious need for a oneness with God, a returning to the Source . . .

The rector was intoning, 'And now to God the Father, God the Son and God the Holy Ghost,' and the congregation was waking up, reaching for hymn books, jingling their collection. Freddy came back to earth with a jolt, her heart beating fast with an exultation which was rapidly fading. Disorientated, she glanced along the pew where Caroline was giving Susanna her threepenny piece and Mole was delving in his shorts pocket for his sixpence, whilst Theo patted absent-mindedly at his pockets, still deep in thought. Freddy found her ten-shilling note and picked up her hymn book as the organist played the opening bars of 'Praise my soul the King of Heaven'. The rector's wife turned to smile at her and Freddy – feeling an unusual sense of warmth, of belonging, even of joy – smiled back at her.

Chapter Fifteen

The following weekend the family collected together at The Keep for the Birthday. It had begun quite simply, as family traditions do. Freddy's birthday fell at the end of October and, when the boys were small, a celebration had been made of it. At teatime they had brought their presents and cards, made under Ellen's watchful eye to begin with and later with Miss Smollet's supervision; presents lovingly wrapped, cards carefully crayoned. Tea was in the hall as usual but it was a special tea with all the delicacies that Freddy and the boys liked best. All through their schooldays, the Birthday had fallen during half term and so, over the years, it had become an institution. When Hal and Kit were born within a day of the date it had given extra cause to celebrate; this happened again when Mole arrived, this time on the day before Freddy's birthday. Now, all four of them celebrated together with one big party, starting at teatime with the giving of presents in the hall and extending into the evening once Hal and Kit were old enough to stay up for dinner. This year Freddy would be sixty-seven, the twins eighteen, Mole nine.

As she prepared for the tea, Fliss knew the exquisite joy of being at home again. How differently she had felt when she'd been going away to school just over a year ago; how great her anxieties. She had been so worried about Mole and Susanna, fearing lest they should not be looked after quite as well without her. They had promised to write to her regularly and she had charged Caroline with endless dos and don'ts on their behalfs. She had missed them terribly, those early weeks of term a misery of loneliness and longing. How she treasured the little presents they had carefully chosen for her, overseen by Freddy: a smart dark blue leather writing case from Mole: a matching address book from Susanna. Simply looking at these precious keepsakes had brought tears into her eyes, making her long for home and her small brother and sister, but gradually she had settled in and made friends.

Now, she stared at herself in the looking-glass on the old washstand, which doubled as dressing table and desk, peering with anxiety at a spot on her chin. She had celebrated her fifteenth birthday in September and Freddy had bought her a pretty sleeveless georgette party frock in sweet-pea tints. The neckline was cut in a modestly rounded curve and the skirt was bell-shaped. To Fliss's eyes it was very grown up, the delicate colours suiting her fairness, the design showing off her slenderness. This evening she would wear it for dinner, longing for Hal to see her in it, to see how mature she looked when she piled up her hair – and now she had this wretched spot. From the shallow drawer Fliss took her powder compact, given to her by Prue for that same birthday, and dabbed some powder on the offending spot. She suspected that Grandmother hadn't quite approved of such a present, thinking her a little young to be wearing make-up, but she had said nothing and Fliss was almost speechless with gratitude to Prue. It was very hard to persuade her family that she was very nearly grown up, although Caroline was usually on her side. The problem here was that Caroline wasn't particularly interested in clothes and make-up and didn't have a clue about the latest colour in lipsticks. Fliss *was* interested, enormously interested, in all these things, and relied on her cousin Kit to help her out. Prue fully expected her daughter to try out lipsticks and experiment with her hair and Kit was very generous in passing on tips, not to mention certain items which had proved to be errors of judgement.

It was Kit who had encouraged Fliss to broach the subject of a brassiere. Stammering almost as badly as Mole, she had found the courage one morning when Ellen and Caroline were stripping the beds.

'Brassiere?' Ellen had sounded almost affronted as she pulled the sheets from Mole's bed. 'And what were you thinking of putting in it?'

Remembering, Fliss blushed almost as much now as she had on that occasion. Caroline had been much more understanding.

'Do the other girls wear brassieres?' she'd asked.

Fliss had nodded, feeling foolish but resentful. Just because she was small didn't mean that she was still a child.

'All the girls in my class wear a bra,' she'd muttered defensively. 'Everyone except me. They tease me about it.'

'Whatever next, I wonder,' Ellen had remarked to no one in particular. 'Brassieres indeed.'

She'd plumped up Mole's pillows with a vigorous and contemptuous hand but Caroline had sent Fliss a tiny wink.

'We'll have a look in Spooner's,' she'd said, 'next time we're in Plymouth. Don't you worry. We'll get something sorted out.'

She had been true to her word and Fliss became the proud owner of two Berlei brassieres; size 32, A cup. Back in her bedroom, she'd tried one on, standing sideways so as to see the tiny mounds. She was certainly no Jayne Mansfield but, as the assistant in the lingerie department had said comfortingly, 'You'll grow, miss. Never fear.' The small cups had soft cotton padding which helped to fill them out and, when Kit saw them, she advised her to stuff them with cotton wool if she wanted extra shape. They'd giggled together and Fliss felt truly grown up; a woman at last, powerful and mysterious. Under her navy-blue jersey, these wonderful new breasts could scarcely be seen but it was a different matter when it came to the thin filmy georgette of her party frock.

Fliss slipped the compact back into the drawer and glanced at her watch. It was nearly teatime. She looked about her room with pleasure, happy to be back at home in it again. Once Mole had recovered from the terrible shock of his parents' and brother's deaths and been able to sleep alone, Fliss had moved into this small room which had, years before, been Miss Smollet's sitting room. Caroline had no need of it, using the room downstairs next to the kitchen which had been turned into a general sitting room for

Ellen and Fox, and so Fliss had taken possession of it. She loved it. The window looked north across the huge sweep of countryside and, though there was not much space and it was a cold room, nevertheless it was hers and here all her treasures were gathered.

The walls were painted white, and opposite the window was the narrow iron-framed bed which she'd used since she'd first arrived at The Keep and shared Mole's bedroom. There were several pretty flower prints on the walls and she'd put one or two of her most precious keepsakes on the painted chest which stood against the wall at the foot of the bed. Here was a flowered china pot in which Alison had kept small pieces of jewellery. Fliss lifted the dainty little lid and looked inside. Her own seed pearl necklace was safe in this pot along with her gold charm bracelet, both of which she would wear this evening. Her father's small alabaster box, which had held his cufflinks, now contained some precious shells, as well as other odds and ends, and her mother's tortoiseshell-backed hair-brushes lay beside a silver-framed studio photograph of the little family.

Fliss stared at it. Peter stood behind Alison, a hand on her shoulder, with Jamie standing proudly beside him. Fliss sat next to her mother, her arm about Mole, who leaned against her knee, whilst baby Susanna lay placidly in Alison's arms.

Fliss thought: How complete we look. How normal and safe and ordinary. Who could have imagined such things would happen to us?

She had learned not to dwell on the tragedy which had shadowed her childhood, to turn her thoughts away from it whenever it threatened to thrust her back into grief, yet she still missed Jamie. Stuck into the mahogany frame around her mirror on the washstand, there was an old curling snapshot of him; hands in pocket, smiling out at her. Fliss bent to look at him, the mere sight of him giving her courage, making her smile back. Below this snapshot was another, of Alison and Peter at the race meeting which was held every Sunday afternoon at Nairobi's Ngong Racecourse. Her father was glancing away from the camera: tall, confident, handsome. Her mother, wearing her old straw hat, looked faintly puzzled, almost censorious, as though she suspected the person behind the camera of inefficiency. Fliss remembered the look. It had kept her up to the mark, on her toes, watchful and prepared. Her mother had expected great things of all of them and there had always been something of a strain in being with her, in living up to those expectations. Her father had been more easy-going with her, swinging her up on to his shoulders when her short legs could no longer keep up with his long strides, reading her bedtime stories whilst she snuggled into the crook of his arm . . .

Fliss turned away and deliberately swung open the door of the hanging cupboard which was built into the thickness of the wall. She took out her lovely frock, touching the soft material, admiring the colours, until the choking sensation passed and she could see her room quite clearly again; the austere whiteness relieved by cheerful notes of colour. There were warm rugs on the dark-stained floor and thick scarlet chenille curtains at the window. This bright glow of colour was repeated in the patchwork quilt which Ellen had sewed through long winter evenings and which Fliss adored. In past years she had made Ellen tell of the pieces over and over again.

'Now this blue velvet was from your grandmother's evening gown,' she'd say, peering closely, her finger smoothing the fabric. 'And this bit of gingham here was from one of Kit's dresses when she was no bigger than Susanna. Now see this cotton square? That was one of Fox's old shirts. My word! Did he make a fuss when he saw I'd torn it up at last. Falling off him it was, bless the man. The flowery squares are your Aunt Prue's summer frock, oh, way back from before the war . . .'

To Fliss the patchwork quilt was a history of her family and, when she lay under it at night, she felt part of them all. She closed the cupboard door and looked at as much of herself as she could see in the mirror, tilting it, bending this way and that. She wore her Black Watch tartan kilt and Shetland jersey, knowing that grandmother would approve, but she was still longing for the moment when she could change into her pretty frock, brush out her thick plait and put up her hair. She paused to look at the other photographs stuck into the frame of the mirror. There was one of Susanna beaming proudly, astride Fliss's old bicycle; one of Mole squinting at the camera with a blurred Fox behind him; one of a kneeling Kit, her arm round Mrs Pooter's neck. Fliss glanced at her watch again; time to go downstairs for tea. Gathering together the presents for her family, she let herself out of her bedroom and went hurrying down to the hall.

While Fliss was pottering in her bedroom, Kit was in one of her most favourite places. Curled up small, she was sharing the huge dog basket with Mrs Pooter. There was something infinitely comforting to Kit to be pressed against warm fur, with the familiar smell of dog in her nostrils, the old prickly blanket under her fingers. From a small child upwards she had always enjoyed curling up with the dogs. Mrs Pooter, who considered Kit's behaviour to be tiresome and unnecessary, grumbled internally for a while before stretching out as much as she could, her head on Kit's thighs. Kit closed her eyes, smelling Mrs Pooter's fur, stroking her ears. Ellen's voice drifted about in the upper reaches of the kitchen, along with the other wonderfully familiar smells of baking: new bread, fresh scones, sponge cake.

'. . . and if your grandmother could see you in the dog basket I can't think what she'd say. You're not a baby now, young lady. Eighteen tomorrow and sitting in a dog basket. Whatever next, I wonder. And I hope you're not thinking of going into tea in those old trousers. Your grandmother likes to see you in skirts, as well you know. Why you should want to dress like a farm hand I simply can't think. Look how nice Fliss looks in her kilt. You just go upstairs and change and remember to wash your hands . . .'

The voice, which somehow had the effect of adding to Kit's feelings of security and contentment, died away as Fox came into the kitchen. He was followed by Mugwump, who came straight across to the basket, sniffing inquisitively, licking Kit's face. She laughed and gave a tiny scream as he attempted to climb in with them. Mrs Pooter protested, a low subterranean rumbling, which made Mugwump draw back a little. Ellen turned her attention to Fox and Kit closed her eyes, thinking her own thoughts. It was the first Birthday weekend that she and Hal had travelled down to Devon without Prue. She was obliged to work all day on Saturdays and, although Freddy had suggested that the Birthday party could be held on Sunday, Prue had declined; it was simply too much to travel down very late on Saturday, only to have to hurry back on Sunday so as to be ready for work on Monday morning. Both women had felt a certain measure of relief at this decision. It was still too soon after the recent trouble for either of them to feel really easy in the other's company but Freddy still felt rather guilty at depriving Prue of the twins' company on their birthday. She had written to her to say so but Prue had telephoned so as to put her mind at rest at once.

'I'm only too pleased that they're coming,' she'd said. 'It's not much fun for them with me working during their birthday and half term. We've decided to have a little party before they come down and another when they come back. Truly. I feel much happier knowing they're down with you all at The Keep. Drink a toast to me, won't you?'

Freddy had assured her that they would but the twins still felt badly about leaving her behind when the time came. They'd hugged her tightly when they'd said goodbye at Temple Meads, had waved madly until the platform was out of sight, and settled down to a rather quiet journey on one of the new diesel trains. Kit was torn by differing emotions. Part of her hated leaving Prue all alone; part of her longed to be at The Keep. She and Hal had been shocked to learn of Tony's defection and dishonesty, but they were not sorry he was gone. Although he had tried to be tactful about leaving them time with Prue, the twins felt that he had broken up their little family group rather than been absorbed into it. He could be moody and sharp-tongued and, although they wanted Prue to be happy, it wasn't too long before it was evident that their marriage was not idyllic. The twins were old enough to realise that this was fairly normal and concentrated on their own lives. Being away at school meant that they hardly ever saw Tony. He'd always tried to arrange for his journeys north to coincide with their holidays, giving them time with their mother alone, so it was not surprising if they didn't miss him.

Kit had been prepared to sympathise with Prue. Her own feelings for Graham gave her a very real idea of how she might be feeling but her mother seemed to be taking it all very calmly. Kit suspected that she was putting on a show for them; nevertheless, what with the new job and sorting out Tony's legacy of problems, Prue was almost too busy to be unhappy.

'It's almost a relief, darling,' she'd admitted to her daughter rather sadly. 'Perhaps I'd been on my own too long to be married again. It was silly of me to think that anyone could measure up to your father.'

Kit had hugged her, made her a cup of tea, tried to be daughterly. She was finding that being grown up was a worrying sort of business, with all sorts of rules to be learned. Though part of her longed to be thirty-six, in a black sheath dress and pearls, in other ways she was glad that she was still at school. It gave her very little free time – she was determined to win a place at university to read English or History – and so Graham's growing demands were held at bay while she tried to sort herself out. She loved him – she was quite certain of it – but terrified of going 'too far'. What worrying words they were. Some of the girls at school laughed at her, insisting that they'd done 'it' and there was nothing to it. She noticed, however, that they were reluctant to discuss 'it' in detail and she suspected that they were as ignorant and frightened as she was herself. She couldn't bring herself to talk to Prue, who was so preoccupied and had so many worries, so she had talked it through with Hal. He confirmed her suspicion that girls who went all the way were looked upon by men as 'easy', to be despised, and she felt even more desperate.

'If he loves you,' Hal had said, rather sternly, 'he should ask you to marry him. Not that you could get married yet, you're too young, but you could get engaged.'

No such proposals, however, had passed Graham's lips and Kit felt even more anxious. He had already hinted that there were plenty of girls – more experienced, more sophisticated – who would be only too ready to be less prudish and Kit was torn between calling his bluff and giving in altogether. Sometimes she desperately wanted to forget all her inhibitions, to relax and enjoy his lovemaking, but fear held her back. She was beginning to see that, though she loved him, she did not altogether like him, and this confused and worried her. At the last party they'd been to together he'd paid a great deal of attention to another girl, trying to make Kit jealous, humiliating her. Remembering the luckless Wendy, Kit had held on to her pride, despite the pain in her heart, and, later, had refused to give up her week at The Keep so as to be with him. She knew that she would be under siege from him and did not trust herself not to give in to him and sleep with him.

It was a relief to be here at The Keep, to be a child again, listening to Ellen's nagging while she curled up in the dog basket. Here there was no tensions, no pressures to be anything but herself . . . She tickled Mugwump's nose with a tiny feather and he sneezed, attracting Ellen's attention.

'Now just you get out of that basket and go upstairs and change,' she said crossly. 'Just look at you! All over hair! Up with you now.'

Fox hauled her out and Kit brushed herself down, grinning at them.

'Keep the old wig on, darling,' she said, giving Ellen a quick kiss. 'I'm on my way.'

She whirled out of the kitchen, humming, and Ellen shook her head, lips pursed, ignoring Fox's smile. 'That girl . . .' she said.

Theo was already waiting in the hall when Freddy came down. He kissed her on both cheeks and, as the children gathered, he handed her a box. It was not wrapped – Theo was clumsy with his hands – and she removed the lid carefully, pushing aside the foaming tissue paper. Inside was a pair of candlesticks in Bristol blue glass; old and delicate and beautiful. She touched them gently, smiling to herself, and glanced across at him. He raised his cup to her – and then the children were exchanging presents, ripping away wrapping paper, exclaiming. Caroline poured the tea, enjoying the hubbub. Unlike Theo, she was clever with her hands and had knitted Aran jerseys for Mole and Hal. Mole's was cream; Hal's was navy blue. They hugged her, holding the jerseys against their chests admiringly, declaring that they were perfect. Kit had already pulled on the knitted beret and matching scarf in bright scarlet wool and was posing dramatically. Caroline grinned back at her, relieved by such wholehearted approval, and hoped that Freddy would like the book she had bought her: a biography of Grieg. Fliss, passing round scones, beamed happily as Freddy draped a feather-light silky shawl about her shoulders and blew her grandmother an appreciative thank-you kiss. Kit was given a garnet and silver necklace which had belonged to Freddy's mother, whilst Hal received a pair of gold cufflinks which had once been Bertie's. Fliss, Mole and Susanna, assisted financially by Freddy, had bought a pretty silver photograph frame for Kit and a set of black onyx studs for Hal.

As the presents and cards mounted on the table and overflowed on to the floor, the party became even more noisy. Mole's pile of toys and books almost filled the armchair and when Ellen appeared, bearing the cake covered in lighted candles, everyone cheered. Fox followed behind her to proffer his congratulations, so that the whole household was gathered as usual to hear Theo's little speech and to join in his good wishes for the coming year. When he'd finished and he smiled round at the assembled company, they knew exactly what he would say and they all chorused it with him.

'God bless us, every one.'

Chapter Sixteen

On the Thursday after the party, a gloriously bright, warm autumn day, a picnic on Dartmoor was mooted. The apple-picking – another great annual event – was over, and Ellen and Caroline had embarked on the making of apple jelly whilst Fox was storing the remainder of the crop, ready for the winter. It was Caroline who suggested that Hal should drive, leaving the adult members of the family at home to get on and, thereby, providing more space in the car. As the children grew bigger it was becoming increasingly difficult to fit them all into the car along with a driver, as well as one or both of the dogs, and Caroline's idea was perfectly reasonable. Freddy, however, was clearly anxious. Hal had passed his test during the summer holiday but he was not an experienced driver. As Caroline pointed out, however, Fox had taken him out often in the old Morris Oxford as a learner and he was very familiar with the lanes and the road to the moors. Freddy knew that Hal was careful – she had allowed him to drive her into Totnes to Heath's Nurseries and had been quite impressed by his expertise – but nevertheless she felt quite faint at the thought of all of her beloved grandchildren being in his care. Everyone gathered in the courtyard to see them off and to assist with the packing of the boot with the hamper and rugs, the rounders bat, tennis balls, Susanna's butterfly net and all the paraphernalia required for an English picnic. Freddy saw to it that the sensible Fliss was sitting in the passenger seat beside Hal, watchful and prepared, alert for any approaching disaster, a second pair of eyes. Mrs Pooter was curled at her feet and Susanna and Mole were squashed in the back with Kit and Mugwump. When all the passengers had been fitted in, Hal prepared to take his place at the wheel.

'Be very careful, my darling,' Freddy admonished him. 'You have a precious cargo.'

He beamed at her cheerfully. 'Fear not, Grandmother,' he said, thrilled to be in charge of the outing and to be entrusted with her car. 'I shall bring them all safely back.'

She was gripped by such a thrill of superstitious terror at his insouciance that she felt an unexpected and atavistic need to propitiate any jealous or capricious gods who might be listening to such boastfulness. Had she been quite mad to think – even for that single visionary second – that death was unimportant? Perhaps she was now to be put to the test. She glanced anxiously at Theo, who was watching her, eyes narrowed with amusement, and she knew that he had guessed accurately at her thoughts. 'Do something,' she said foolishly and, grinning openly now, he extended his arm and solemnly made the sign of the cross over the party. She glared at him and turned to watch the car bump out between the gatehouses, Mole's face peering from the small back window, Susanna's hand fluttering from the side of the car. Fox, Ellen and Caroline disappeared to their various tasks and Freddy and Theo were left alone.

She stood quite still, her arms folded tightly beneath her breast as though she were holding herself together, whilst Theo watched her. Her face was serious, almost grim, and she looked elegant and formidable in her old, smoky-coloured tweeds. He let his love flow silently towards her and presently she turned to look at him.

'I think I know now exactly how Mole feels,' she told him. 'That terrible fear that all those whom you love most might be taken from you at one stroke. It is so easy to think that it is the kind of thing that only happens to other people, isn't it? But it has happened to Mole and he will never be able to feel truly safe ever again.'

'It has happened to you, too,' Theo reminded her. 'Why, suddenly now, do you talk of understanding Mole? You, of all people, must have always known how he feels.'

'Not quite,' said Freddy. 'You see, I was grown up when it happened to me. I was already a wife and soon to be a mother when Bertie was killed. Not a very experienced one, perhaps, but I was an adult. Mole was only four when he lost his mother and father and big brother. Now here, now gone. Four years old, Theo. No wonder he won't run round the spinney alone. He is terrified that when he gets round the other side, we shall all be gone, too.'

'And Fliss?'

Freddy sighed. 'Fliss,' she repeated. 'She was only ten, poor mite, but I think that the growing-up process had already begun for her. Alison would have been a very exacting mother and I think much was expected of Jamie and Fliss. She suffered terribly, of course, but she was immediately required to be in charge and she was given no time to dwell on it. She still misses Jamie and Peter, I know that. Alison probably less so. Fliss is a worrier, as Alison was, but underneath she's very self-contained.'

'And she didn't hear the details,' added Theo. 'Mole had to contend with that, too.'

'They all adore Hal.' Freddy turned towards the house, slipping her arm through Theo's. 'You were worried about that, I remember.'

'I think that Hal feels his responsibility.' Theo's voice was thoughtful. 'But he has great strength. He is very like his father.'

Her fingers dug into his arm. 'Oh, Theo,' her voice was hoarse with emotion, 'when he said that, about coming back safely, he looked so like John, going off to war. I know why I felt so frightened just now. John said almost exactly the same thing. "Don't worry," he said. "I'll come back." But he didn't.'

'We have to let them go. You know that,' said Theo gently. 'If we let them go willingly and trustingly they will always come back to us, unless—'

'Don't say it,' she said fiercely. 'Talk of something else.'

'I must get back to Southsea,' he said, knowing that it would distract her. 'What with Prue and the Birthday I have been away too long.'

'Why?' she demanded. 'What is there to hold you in

Southsea? Why won't you come back where you belong?'

They stood in the shadows of the porch, at the top of the steps, staring at each other.

Freddy thought: Just say 'Yes', Theo. Please come home. If only you were here with me I could bear anything. I need you here to grow old with, to keep my fears at bay, because we are friends.

She stood stiffly, shoulders squared, chin up, and Theo was filled with the long-familiar uncertainties: the fear of committing himself, lest it should be wrong for her; that their joint loves and needs might undermine their individual strengths.

He thought: Is now the time? Is it right, at last, for both of us?

He did the only thing that ever helped him to come to a difficult decision: he emptied his mind and prayed silently for help. It came swiftly. He saw clearly how the time might not only be too early but also – and just as fatally – too late; that in continuing to wait for the right moment, this love they shared might disintegrate, go bad on them, even die. He knew a brief confident certainty but Freddy was already turning away.

'I shall come,' he said – and she turned back to him, radiant with delight and surprise. 'I shall come as soon as I can clear everything up in Southsea.'

'Soon?' she asked quickly. 'It will be soon? You won't change your mind.'

'No,' he said, 'I shan't change my mind. I shall be home by Christmas. You have my word.'

The picnic party arrived safely at Haytor rocks with

only one moment of real anxiety. A car travelling too fast towards them in one of the narrow lanes had caused a frightened Hal to turn the wheel sharply, cursing under his breath.

'*Bloody* fool!' he muttered – and cast a shamefaced glance at Fliss, who was nearly as shocked to hear Hal swearing as she was at the near miss.

She smiled back at him, hiding the shock, not wishing to look prudish. 'He was going much too fast,' she assured him, lest his confidence should be shaken. 'You were jolly quick.'

The three in the back were sorting themselves out, Mugwump pushing his head out at the open window.

'Easy does it,' sang out Kit. 'You had poor old Sooz on the floor.'

Fliss glanced back anxiously but Susanna had already scrambled back on the seat and was asking her usual question. 'Are we nearly there?'

'Very nearly,' said Fliss as they bumped over a cattle grid. 'Not long now. Hold tight.'

Kit gazed out with pleasure across the top of Mole's head, as they reached the open moor at last. The deserted road wound between slopes of bracken-covered moorland which glowed with fiery intensity in the afternoon sun, stretching away to the very feet of the high granite tors. Banks of prickly gorse bushes were bright with enamel-yellow blossoms whose excitingly sweet, nutty scent drifted gently in the warm air. Wind-shaped thorn trees, scarlet with winter berries, offered dappled shade to the grazing ponies, who kicked up their heels and clattered away suddenly as the car approached. A sheep ambled out unexpectedly, crossing the road without a glance, so that Hal had to stand on the brakes and, as the engine slowed and idled, Kit could hear a lark singing somewhere high above them.

'Rabbits!' she whispered in Mugwump's ear – and he strained at the open window, whining faintly.

Hal parked the car near Haytor rocks and they laid out the rugs and the hamper on the springy, sheep-nibbled turf and looked about them, laughing and stretching, finding it a little strange to be all together without one of the older members of the family.

'Tea first?' asked Fliss, who felt that someone should be in charge of the catering department. 'Or climb? Which?'

'Climb,' said Kit at once. 'We shall be too full after tea to want to climb things.'

They stared up at the grey seamed rocks, piled high into strange shapes, reaching stony fists and fingers into the pale blue sky; granite islands in a sea of burning bracken.

'Come on,' shouted Susanna and Mole. 'Come on, you lot.'

They jumped about amongst the bracken, leaping on and off the smaller rocks that lay tumbled about, calling to the dogs questing to and fro, noses to earth, tails wagging.

'Should I stay with the hamper?' suggested Fliss uncertainly, knowing that this was what Caroline did so as to ward off inquisitive ponies. 'What d'you think?'

'No need,' said Hal impatiently. 'It's all quite safe. No ponies about. Roll the rugs up if you're worried. Let's get going.'

'I'll stay,' said Kit suddenly. 'No, really. I want to.

I'm a bit fagged to tell you the truth and poor old Mrs Ooter-Pooter will never make it to the top. She'll stay here with me, won't you, old lady? Good girl, then. Honestly, Fliss. Don't look so worried. I shall stretch out here in the sun. Go on. Bet you can't get to the top in ten minutes. I'll time you.'

They were off at once, the two little ones running ahead, Mugwump at their heels. Kit watched them for a few moments then lay back, the sun warm on her closed eyelids, listening to the skylarks, her fingers playing with Mrs Pooter's ear. She thought about Graham, forgetting to keep an eye on her watch, and presently she dozed.

Hal strode out, filled with a joyful sense of well-being and achievement, breathing in lungfuls of the clear air. It had been quite a near thing, with that ass of a driver pushing them into the hedge, but he'd handled it very well all things considered. He dwelled with private satisfaction on one or two moments of the journey and then glanced down at Fliss, who was almost running to keep up with his long strides. His heart was filled with a new tenderness for her. He had always been fond of his little cousins but Fliss's faithful devotion and admiration had given her a rather special place in his affections. Last Saturday evening, when she'd appeared in the drawing room looking shy but excited in her new dress, he'd felt an almost painful sensation in his heart. She'd looked so sweet, so vulnerable – and so different, with her hair all put somehow on the top of her head, emphasising the slender neck, the swelling of small breasts just evident . . .

He frowned to himself as the climb became

steeper, loose scree slipping beneath his feet. It seemed impossible that little Fliss should be a woman. She was so small and slight, so dear and familiar. Yet, that evening, she had seemed strange to him, alight with some kind of inner mystery known only to herself; a mystery that transformed her. He'd felt oddly shy and rather clumsy, glad that he'd seen Kit change from child to woman and therefore had some sort of experience of this sudden transformation. Kit seemed capable of passing back and forward between the two spheres of childhood and womanhood, so that he often became quite muddled, but the sight of Fliss had made him feel protective – and it had made him feel something else, too. He wasn't sure whether it was wrong to be aroused by the sight of your own cousin and he'd felt guilty – and confused – at this uncontrollable desire because he'd had the strange idea that it was what Fliss wanted him to feel. Yet how could she? She was so young, so innocent – and his cousin.

'Hi!' Mole was shouting from somewhere above him and Hal leaned back, looking up to the rocks where Mole and Susanna danced, waving. Fliss was panting up behind him and he put out his hand so as to haul her up beside him. She was laughing, her face flushed, the shining strands of corn-fair hair blowing loose about her face. She wore an old Aertex shirt that had been Kit's, the faded blue reflecting the colour of her eyes and flattering the warm colour of her skin. Hal felt the strange tightening feeling in the pit of his stomach again as he stared down at her, imagining the breasts which were pressing inside the shirt. He saw her face change, though she still clung to him, and suddenly he wanted to kiss her, knew that she wanted him to kiss her, and he pulled her closer, his heart crashing about, hammering in his ears . . .

Susanna arrived beside them in a shower of scree, skidding down on her bottom, shrieking with joy and impatience.

'Come on. Oh, do come *on*,' she cried. 'Kit's timing us, don't forget. Mole's at the top already.'

They stared at each other for one heart-stopping second longer before following Susanna up the last steep climb to where Mole waited, high in the autumn sunshine.

'Look,' he said. 'You can see for miles and miles. Like when the d-devil tempted Jesus in the desert and offered him the kingdoms of the world if he would only worship him. It must have looked like this, don't you think?'

'Yes,' said Hal, after a moment. 'Just like.'

He seemed to be having difficulty with his breathing, which wasn't surprising after that scramble up, and he didn't look at Fliss, who remained silent.

'Kit's asleep,' said Susanna sadly. 'I've been waving and waving. Now she won't have timed us.'

'Never mind,' consoled Hal. 'We'll do it again soon.'

'After tea?' asked Mole hopefully.

'Perhaps not after tea,' prevaricated Hal. He wished Fliss would say something. She stood tense and still, staring out over the moor towards Teignmouth, across the blue hazy distances, where the silver sea glinted and glittered. 'Although you and Sooz could, if you like, and I'll time you. I can watch you the whole way.'

They cheered loudly and began to jog back down the way they'd come, slipping and sliding and calling to one another. Mugwump shot out of the bracken, where he had been pursuing interesting scents, and raced after them. Hal cleared his throat.

'They've got a mania about being timed for things,' he said awkwardly. 'Everything has to be timed these days, have you noticed? Fox started it with them going round the spinney but now it's getting to be almost anything.'

Fliss nodded, still looking away from him, and he wondered if he'd got all the signals wrong and she was shocked. Perhaps he'd frightened her.

'Fliss,' he said pleadingly. 'Fliss . . .'

She turned to him with a look of such intense love that he was taken aback. So he hadn't got it wrong . . . She did . . . Did what?

'Fliss,' he began again – but she shook her head.

'Come on,' she said – and her voice was light and alive, bubbling like running water. 'Look. Kit's woken up. She's unpacking the hamper. Mole and Susanna are nearly there. Race you back.'

She was gone, crossing the rocks, scrambling down the slope, laughing back at him, her plait falling across her shoulder. He followed her, confused, as though he had somehow lost control of the situation and Fliss had gained it. Something had happened but he was damned if he knew what and he was muddled and faintly irritated. He saw the scene below him: his sister kneeling on the rug, the two smaller children running up, the dogs getting in the way as usual and, as a backdrop, the car. The sight of the car restored his confidence as nothing else could have done, giving him back his sense of superiority and dominance in this family group. He was the eldest, in charge of them all.

He strolled up, hands in pockets, wishing he had a cigarette to add to his show of sophistication, smiling paternally upon them all, avoiding Fliss's eye.

'Tea ready?' he asked. 'So what's it to be afterwards? A game of rounders? Or are you two going to scale Everest again?'

He stretched out on the rug with his hands behind his head, casual and easy, while the girls fussed round, setting out the tea. Susanna fell across his midriff, resting her head on his chest, singing to herself. He tickled her good-naturedly but pushed her off when Kit offered him a sandwich, rolling on to his side, propped on his elbow. Fliss was sitting back on her heels, frowning as she poured tea from the flask, and he suddenly felt that it was good to be young and strong and just setting out. How terrible to be really old, like Freddy and Theo, everything over for them, all passion spent. He'd heard that phrase somewhere and had been struck by the sadness of it. How awful it must be if you could no longer feel passion, not just the sort aroused by pretty girls but passion about driving cars, sailing boats, running, dancing . . .

Fliss was passing him a cup of tea and he grinned at her, winking complicitly, drawing her into a private world of their own. To his delight the colour ran up under her fair skin and she pressed her lips together as though she might laugh with that same ebullient joy that he was feeling.

'So,' he said, confidence absolutely restored, 'rounders afterwards, I think, and then you two can climb the tor again if there's time. Right. So that's that settled. Where are those sandwiches?'

Chapter Seventeen

It had been raining all day. Heavy clouds, the colour of dull pewter, swept in from the west, rolling across the hill and obscuring the countryside in a thick mist. By four o'clock it was dark. Caroline had driven to the end of the lane to meet the children from the school coach and now, tea over, they were ensconced in the kitchen, listening to *Children's Hour*. Freddy had taken herself off to the drawing room, lighting the lamps and putting a match to the fire, which lay ready in the grate. She drew the curtains against the gloom of the November evening and sat down at the piano.

Caroline stood in the hall, listening. She had no knowledge of music but she liked to hear Freddy play. This piece was one of her favourites and, as she listened to it, her heart quickened a little, and she felt somehow both melancholy and exalted. In the silence following, she knocked rapidly and opened the door. Freddy had been sitting quite still. That sonata – Chopin's third in B minor – had particular memories for her. She had played it here, in the drawing room, for Bertie and his brother and Admiral Chadwick on her first evening at The Keep, though not on this piano. The instrument had been an inferior one – none of the Chadwicks played – and she had insisted on bringing her own piano with her when she married. There had been a complete silence when she'd finished playing and, glancing up, she'd seen Theo watching her across the room. In those days the Chadwicks still changed for dinner and she could remember him quite clearly; the dazzling white of his dress shirt against the black of his jacket; his brown eyes fixed on her thoughtfully . . .

'Mrs Chadwick?'

She turned, startled, to see Caroline in the doorway. 'What is it?' Preoccupation sharpened her voice and she made an effort to disguise her emotions.

'I'm so sorry to disturb you.' Caroline came further into the room. 'It's . . . quite important.'

'I'm sure it is.' Freddy swung right round on the stool, smiling at her. 'Don't worry. I'm feeling a little melancholy, that's all. What Kit calls "the blues". It must be the weather. What's the problem? Finding it difficult to settle in again after your holiday?'

'Oh no, not at all.' Caroline shook her head, hesitated – and laughed. 'The truth is that I don't really want to tell you this. It's not in my own interest, you see, but my conscience is nagging me.'

Freddy got up and came towards her. 'Whatever are you talking about, Caroline?' she asked, frowning. 'For heaven's sake, sit down here beside me on the sofa. Now then.'

Caroline sighed. 'I've been away with my sister, as you know,' she said. 'And while I was there a friend of hers came to see her. Actually, she's a friend of mine, too, but she's older, more my sister's age. Well, the long and short of it is that her children are at a school in the New Forest and she was telling us all about it. It's a co-educational school—' she paused – 'that means it takes boys and girls.'

'I know what co-educational means, thank you, Caroline,' said Freddy impatiently. 'Where is this leading us?'

'The interesting thing is that it takes girls from eight to eighteen and boys from eight till fourteen. It's a boarding school and it sounds a first-rate one. Pauline is delighted with it. She has three children there. Two girls and a boy. The boy is about to go away to his public school but the girls are staying on. Well, I immediately thought of Mole and Susanna, you see.'

'In what respect?' asked Freddy, coolly, her protective instinct aroused. She preferred any ideas regarding her grandchildren to be her own.

Caroline, who knew this very well, eyed her cautiously. 'The point is that it sounds such a happy school. There's a lake where the children sail and they do lots of exciting things. Camping in the forest, dancing lessons and theatricals . . .'

'Do they also manage to find time to educate them?' asked Freddy lightly.

Caroline laughed ruefully. 'I'm not doing this very well, am I?' she asked. 'You see it sounded so right for Mole and Susanna. They could go off together when Susanna is eight and Mole is eleven. I asked Pauline and she said that they are quite happy to take boys at that age. The girls give it a different sort of atmosphere and it's more relaxed, if you see what I mean, and they could still be together.' She balled her hands into fists, willing the unresponsive Freddy to understand. 'It sounded a good place for Mole. Somewhere he could go on building his confidence and be watched over to prepare him for big school.'

'I have no thought of sending Susanna to boarding school at eight,' said Freddy flatly.

'I know that,' cried Caroline, frustrated. 'That's what I meant when I said that this is not in my interest. I'd hoped that you'd keep me until Susanna went off to school at thirteen, like Fliss. Don't think *I* want her to go off at eight. It's simply that it's a way of solving Mole's problem and, if you want my opinion, Susanna would absolutely love it. She's a cheerful, easy-going, well-balanced child but I think she'll miss Mole terribly when he goes away and it will be rather dreary for her here with . . .'

'With a lot of old codgers?' finished Freddy when Caroline hesitated.

'Well, frankly yes,' she answered bluntly. 'Or so we must seem to her.' She shrugged. 'I just want what's best for them.'

'Forgive me.' Freddy put her hand over Caroline's clenched ones. 'So do we all. You really think that Susanna would cope?'

'Why not? Look.' Her whole body was tense with the need to communicate her thoughts. 'Don't think I'm prepared to sacrifice Susanna in an attempt to protect Mole. It would be quite wrong. I'm just absolutely certain that when he goes, she'll want to go with him and that she'll be able to manage just as well if not better than he would have done at eight. It's two years away, remember. The thing is that it's such a popular school that you need to get their names down or you won't have a hope of getting them in. After all, you could always change your mind later if it seemed that neither of them was ready.'

'I shall ask the bursar to send a prospectus,' said Freddy. 'What is the school called?'

'Herongate House School. There's a heronry beside the lake.' Caroline looked suddenly tired. 'Well, then . . .'

'It is good of you to put the children's interest before your own,' said Freddy gently, 'and it sounds an excellent idea, but I hope it doesn't necessarily mean that we would lose you.'

Caroline stared at her, surprised. 'But what would I do if the children are gone?' she asked.

'There are the holidays,' Freddy pointed out. 'Half terms, exeats, trunks and tuck-boxes. Getting them to and fro, fitting them out at Daniel Neal's. It's an exhausting business, ask Ellen. No, I don't think we'd want to lose you. Unless, of course, you'd find it hard to spend so much time with just a – how did we put it? – a lot of old codgers?'

'*You* said that.' Caroline tried, unsuccessfully, to hide her happiness. 'You know how much I love it here. You're my family. The Keep is my home. I'd hate to leave it, or any of you.'

Freddy was silent for a moment. 'I thought those kind of qualities had been destroyed by the war,' she said at last. 'Thank you, Caroline. You have become part of my family and I hope we shall never have to part with you.'

Caroline stood up, her eyes wet with tears. 'Thank you, Mrs Chadwick.' It was clear that she was unable to think of anything that might adequately express her feelings. 'I'd better go and help Ellen with the children's supper. Sorry to disturb your playing.'

She slipped out, shutting the door quietly behind her. Freddy sat on, staring into the fire. By what stroke of good fortune had she merited such loyalty? All these years she'd had dear old Ellen and Fox to protect and care for her and now Caroline was carrying on their tradition of service. How lucky, how very lucky she was. Her thoughts became more practical: two years in which to prepare the children for school. Surely, in that time, Mole would have overcome those deep-set fears? He was improving all the time – or was he merely becoming better at hiding it, as Caroline had once suggested?

Freddy thought: Theo is coming home! *He* is the one to help Mole. He will mend him, heal his mind and make him whole and strong.

She felt so happy, so weak with relief, that she continued to sit, simply smiling into the fire until the need to play overwhelmed her and presently she stood up and went back to the piano.

The bus jolted along slowly, its tyres hissing on the wet road, the rain streaming down its darkened, steamed-up windows. The pavements gleamed wetly under the streetlights and people going home from work scurried along, heads bent, hunched against the steady downpour. The passengers on the bus, which was grinding its way through the rush-hour traffic, sat dispiritedly, slouching and swaying in their seats as the bus lurched from stop to stop. No sooner had it pulled away from the kerb, forcing its way into the almost stationary queue of cars, than it was required to take on board another group of soaking passengers. The people standing in the aisle clung to the seat poles as the bus turned into Princess Victoria Street. It shuddered to a halt as the conductor rang the bell and people jostled and pushed to the back, ready to alight.

Prue swung herself off and hurried along the wet pavement, her feet and ankles soaked long before she crossed into Waterloo Street. She let herself in to the hall, switched on the light and dragged off her dripping mackintosh. She hung it on the hall stand, feeling for her comfortable old shoes as she forced the smart drenched ones from her feet. The house was cold and unwelcoming on this dank late November evening and she felt the usual flattening of her spirits as she went into the dining room to pour herself a sherry. She carried her drink into the sitting room, where she switched on the lamps and the electric fire and drew the curtains, before kicking off her shoes and collapsing into an armchair, legs curled beneath her. She rested her head against the back of the chair and closed her eyes. It wasn't that she really minded working, at least not *too* much – the girls were friendly and she loved the clothes – but it would have been heaven to come home to a warm house with supper cooked and a drink waiting. How lucky married men were, who could stroll in at the end of a hard day's work and put their feet up. No food to prepare, no clothes to wash and iron, no chores to do. Although she missed them, she was almost glad that the twins were away at school so that she didn't have to worry about them, too.

She felt ashamed when she thought of some of her colleagues who coped with work, husbands, children, homes, even dogs and cats. Perhaps it was because she'd come to it late – or perhaps it was simply that she was naturally idle. She grimaced to herself and began to relax as she sipped her sherry. It helped that Christmas was approaching. Decorations were being put up in all the departments, and there was an air of festive gaiety, but her heart often felt a little heavy when she wondered whether this was to be her lot for the rest of her life.

At least it had taken her mind off Tony. There was, as yet, no news of him but the hurt was fading, probably because she was generally too tired to feel anything much these days except an intense desire for sleep. She was also longing for her Christmas holiday at The Keep. At one point it seemed that she might not be allowed to take off more than the few days of the bank holiday. In desperation, she went to the personnel manager and explained that she had booked Christmas much earlier in the year – before she had taken this job – and that she and her children simply must have the whole week between Christmas Eve and New Year's Day. He had been very unhappy about it. The January sales had to be organised during those few days, he told her, and it would put a great deal of pressure on her colleagues. Fortunately for Prue, these women had encouraged her to ask for the time off and she was able to press her case. She had promised to do extra Saturdays for them, to make up for it, and offered to stay late during the run-up to Christmas so as to do as much as she could towards the sale. Reluctantly the personnel manager agreed – Prue was a good saleswoman and he didn't want to lose her – but told her that the week would be docked from her fortnight's annual holiday next year. Recklessly, Prue agreed. A bird in the hand was worth two in the bush; summer was a long way off and Christmas only three weeks away. She had hurried back to the department to tell her good news.

Prue was popular and her workmates felt sorry for her, having a husband who had run off, leaving her to cope all on her own. She was natural and open with them and made them laugh and they liked her because she had no 'side', although she was obviously from a completely different background. A great many of the account customers were her friends and she would joke outrageously with them, persuading them to buy things to help her commission, sending them off to other departments for accessories; scarves, handbags, shoes, hats. She enjoyed her work, knowing that it could have been a great deal worse, nevertheless she longed for those happy, easy days before Tony had arrived on the scene. How much she'd taken for granted; how indifferent to other people's pressures and fears.

She had been so lucky to have Freddy to support her and to provide for the children. When she heard about the hardships and problems confronting some of those women at the shop, she felt quite sick with shame at how spoiled she still was. She didn't have the grinding anxiety of finding rent or mortgage, and her children were having excellent educations. It was an eye-opening experience – and she was glad that she'd had it – but oh, how delighted she would be if her old life could somehow be magically restored to her. She was tired and lonely, unused to the exhausting daily discipline. Nobody knew how very much she'd missed the Birthday week, although she realised that it might have been an awkward meeting for her and Freddy. Nevertheless, she was surprised at how she'd longed to go; longed to see them all; Fox and Ellen and the children, dear funny Caroline – and darling old Theo . . .

As she struggled up out of her chair, forcing herself to think about preparing some supper, the telephone rang.

'Theo.' Her voice rose with pleasure. 'I was just thinking about you. How very nice to hear you.'

'How are you, Prue?' he asked. '. . . And the twins? Good. I thought you might not have heard my latest news so I decided to telephone you before anyone else got in first.'

'No, I haven't heard anything.' She stood on one foot, warming the other against the calf of her leg. It was cold and draughty in the hall. 'What's happened?'

'I'm moving down to The Keep,' he told her. 'Permanently, that is. It seems so silly struggling on here alone. What do you think?'

'I think it's wonderful,' she said warmly. 'I know that it's good to be independent but I'm sure it's the right decision. You'll be looked after properly.'

'I simply cannot think why everyone imagines I can't look after myself.' She could hear that he was smiling. 'I've been doing it for fifty-odd years.'

'But Ellen and Caroline will do it better,' she told him, laughing. 'Oh, I'm so pleased. Why on earth try to fend for yourself and go on being on your own, if you don't have to? Although I know you like to be alone, Theo. I know you need it. How will you manage that with all those women around?'

'Your guess is as good as mine. So how are things in Bristol?'

'Cold and miserable,' she answered. 'It's a beastly day and I hate coming home to an empty house. Never mind. Could be worse. So when do you go down to Devon?'

'In a week or two. I shall be there for Christmas. I hope you're going to manage it?'

'I certainly am. For the whole week. Isn't it wonderful? I shall send the twins on ahead because I have to work right up until the night before Christmas Eve. Good thing it's on a Sunday this year or I'd have had to work all day Christmas Eve as well. As it is, some of the staff will be in on that Sunday morning, and I've promised I shall go to give a hand for a few hours, but I'll be down as soon as I can. I shall be there in time for supper with luck.'

'Well done. And things are really all right? Money and so on? You wouldn't lie to me?'

'What would be the point? You'd know at once. I'm fine. Honestly.'

'Take care of yourself, then. God bless. Stay in touch.'

She said goodbye and hung up, feeling strangely weepy. How good and kind he was; a constant point of reference in life's uncharted waters.

She thought: I simply couldn't manage without Theo. Thank goodness he'll be looked after properly. He belongs at The Keep and it means I shall see him more often.

Suddenly Christmas felt like light years away and she wondered how she would live through the days until she, too, could be travelling down to Devon.

Chapter Eighteen

Theo was the first of the family to arrive home for Christmas. He came on a cold frosty day, appearing early in the afternoon. Freddy was waiting for him on the platform at Totnes, hands deep in her jacket pockets, her feet in thick fur-lined boots. They smiled at each other, both afraid of displaying too much emotion, careful to keep the moment under control.

'I hate these beastly new trains,' observed Freddy, embracing him briefly. 'There's no atmosphere with them.'

'And no smuts or smoke either.' He passed one of his bags to her. 'Can you manage that one? It's the lightest. Thanks.'

'Is this the sum total of your worldly goods?' she asked. 'Two suitcases and a bag? Good heavens. Prue brings this much for a weekend.'

He laughed. 'She's so excited about Christmas. The twins are coming down early, I gather.'

Freddy fished in her pocket for the car keys as they passed out through the gate. 'Poor Prue is working early and late so as to earn her holiday and she thinks it will be more fun for Hal and Kit to be with us. She'll have them for a week before they come, even so.

They break up very early these days. I'm sure we never had such long holidays when we were young.'

'But I'm sure our parents *thought* we did,' said Theo drily, putting the cases into the boot. 'It all depends on your viewpoint.'

The Morris chugged over the bridge, heading out towards Dartington and The Keep. Freddy was a good driver, calm and confident, and Theo settled into his seat and looked about at the familiar landmarks with pleasure. It was a sparkling day, with a clear blue sky and bright sunshine which made no impression on the thick frost. Theo found that his apprehension was subsiding. He was coming home at last.

'Why is it that you are such a good driver and I am such a bad one?' he complained. 'I'm sure it ought to be the other way round.'

'Simply because you are a man?' enquired Freddy. 'What nonsense. Different people have different abilities. Nothing to do with male or female. Look at the children.'

'How do you mean?'

'Caroline is right in saying that Susanna could cope with boarding school much earlier than Mole or even Fliss. She's more gregarious, doesn't worry so much, makes friends more easily. She's certainly more capable than Mole was at her age.'

'But is this a fair example? How might they have been without the tragedy in their young lives? There's no question but that it has affected Fliss and Mole, but Jamie was very confident.'

Freddy glanced at him sharply as they approached Shinners Bridge. 'I hope you haven't come home merely to argue with me,' she said.

Theo threw up his hands. 'Perish the thought,' he said. 'You know what a coward I am. So tell me all about this school Caroline has found. It certainly sounds as if it might be the solution.'

'I am beginning to think so,' agreed Freddy as the car hurried through the narrow lanes. 'The prospectus has arrived. I'll show you when we get home.'

Home: the word had a simultaneous effect on both of them. In a silence which was charged with emotion, Freddy put out her hand and touched Theo's, where it rested on his knee. He held it tightly for a moment and let it go.

'Thank you,' he said. 'Thank you for allowing me to feel The Keep is my home. Not many people would be so generous.'

'Don't be a fool,' she said roughly – and he glanced at her quickly. She swallowed and tried to smile. 'Sorry. It's just that it has always been your home as far as I am concerned. I thought you knew that.'

'I think I did,' he said, after a moment. 'Of course I did. Haven't I stayed often enough . . .?'

'No,' she said quickly. 'Never often enough. I can't tell you how delighted everyone is that you are coming home at last . . . And here we are.'

She drove in between the gatehouses and stopped the car. Theo stared at the house: grey, imposing, beautiful, full of memories. She was watching him and he shook his head wordlessly. She nodded, as though agreeing, understanding, and kissed him lightly on the cheek.

'Welcome home, Theo,' she said.

★ ★ ★

The sun was low in the sky when the children came home from school. In the lane the puddles were thick with ice, the muddy cart-tracks frozen into deep, ankle-turning ruts; frost rimed the twigs and stiffened the remaining leaves which clung, brown and fragile, in the hedgerow. Mole paused at the farm gate to stare across the field where the winter stubble was burnished to copper by the last rays of the sun as it sank, flaming, towards the western hills. The trees stood stark and black, their shadows stretching long and thin, locked in frozen stillness. Behind him in the lane, Susanna jumped on the puddles, chanting to herself, trying to break the ice which creaked and splintered beneath her weight but did not give way. He glanced over his shoulder at her and then up at the holly tree beside the gate. Its polished spiky leaves were bright – but not as bright as the berries which glowed redly, brilliant in the last dazzling showers of sunshine.

The image of blood entered his consciousness and was immediately dismissed. He could do that now; deliberately rejecting any image which might resurrect the past. Slowly he had learned that it was the only way to deal with the horror; push it down, seal it off. It worked, freeing him from terror, helping him to maintain control; meanwhile he paid the price in nightmares. He was learning to cope with those, too. He was beginning to be aware of the onset of these dreams, the familiar paralysing sensation of fear which preceded the recognition of the menacing dark figure, although the dreams were not always quite the same. Only the helplessness was always constant; the inability to escape or to be deaf or blind to what might follow. Often he was able to wake himself up, sweating and shaking, before anything happened. Sometimes – but not so often now – he woke shouting or weeping. If he were lucky, nobody heard him. Usually, however, Caroline would come in, ready to comfort, to talk to him, until he could control the shaking. He simply must conquer it before he went away to school. The thought of it happening in a dormitory of other boys was enough to bring on the nightmare itself. Now, it seemed that Caroline had won him a respite; two more years – and Susanna going with him.

He turned again to look at her. Relief washed over his whole body and he let go of the gate as he watched her. Oblivious of anything or anyone she danced in the lane, singing; knees high, arms outstretched, she practised the little dance she had been taught for the end-of-term concert. How he loved her. She was the only member of the family who was untouched by the blood. Everyone else knew, remembered; it was part of their lives. He saw it sometimes looking out of Fliss's eyes and he knew what his grandmother was thinking when she played the piano, her cheeks wet with tears, thinking herself alone. He still had the tendency to hide, to burrow under rugs and cushions, although he was getting rather too big to secrete himself away, and it could be dangerous. You saw and heard things you didn't want to understand . . . Only Susanna was free of that terrible, sickening knowledge; innocent and free, she faced the world. He could never be free of it, Jamie's blood had stained into his very bones, but he could conquer it. He had two years; a lot could happen in two years.

Mole took a deep breath and stepped into the lane. He looked beyond Susanna and his heart almost stopped beating; he felt suffocated by terror. A figure was coming towards them; tall and sinister, with a long black shadow going before him, the man advanced inexorably. This was his dream becoming reality; nowhere to run, nowhere to hide and Death advancing. He knew that when he saw the face it would be smiling with closed lips and wide, blind eyes; grim and triumphant and terrifying. The noise he made in his throat attracted Susanna's attention. She curtsied to her imaginary audience and looked down the lane, following Mole's gaze. Her piercing scream made him quake, closing his eyes for a second, and, in that moment, she was gone; flying along the lane, shouting.

'It's Uncle Theo. He's arrived in time to meet us.' Her voice echoed back to him and he stared unbelievingly as the man opened long arms, picking up the small figure, swinging her round. Heart pumping, almost weeping with relief, he too began to run on trembling legs, reaching Theo as he set Susanna back on her feet so that he could be picked up, gathered to Theo's heart and held closely in his turn; safe.

Fliss had been home for nearly a week when the twins arrived. She saw at once that something had happened to Kit; she was brittle, gay, all her emotions close to the surface. Fliss watched her anxiously before she realised that she, herself, was behaving in rather the same way with Hal. Whenever he was near she found herself adopting that same way of talking and acting; she felt light, breathless, excited. In the general bustle it was barely noticed and, if it were, put down to high spirits and the festive season. Hal noticed but he was being very grown up about it – for the moment.

On the Saturday afternoon, the day before Christmas Eve, when Theo and Hal had taken the children to cut holly, Caroline and Ellen were in Totnes doing last-minute shopping and Freddy was having tea with Julia Blakiston, Fliss came upon Kit in her bedroom, crying as though her heart might break.

'Oh, what is it?' Fliss closed the door behind her but remained rooted to the spot, shocked. In all the last four years she had never seen Kit cry. 'Kit? Are you ill?'

Kit raised her face from the pillow and Fliss saw that, although she was indeed crying, she was in some way jubilant.

'Whatever is it?' she whispered, coming closer. 'Please, Kit. Are you OK?'

Kit reached up and pulled her down beside her on the bed. 'Oh, I can't tell you what a relief it is,' she said. 'I've got the curse. Oh God, I think I shall die with joy.'

Fliss frowned, puzzled, and Kit burst out laughing and hugged her. 'Dear old Flissy,' she said, with a resumption of her stage manner. 'Sharpen your wits. I did it with Graham.'

'Oh,' Fliss drew up her knees and stared at Kit with admiration and alarm.

'And let me tell you, it was nothing to write home about.' She looked more serious. 'Gosh, it hurt. And there were pints of blood. God, it was so embarrassing. But he put this towel on the bed . . .'

'Whose bed?' Fliss found her voice at last.

'His. There was a party and I had a bit too much to drink. Now don't look like that, darling. It happens. Anyway, I went back to his room. He was all prepared . . .' She shivered. 'It made it faintly sordid, somehow, but I was feeling, well, rather happy and . . .' she shrugged, 'it happened. I didn't like it much, although I can see how it might be quite nice if you got used to it.'

'Oh, Kit. Did he ask you to marry him?'

'No, my dear coz, he did not. And I wouldn't anyway. Afterwards I thought that perhaps I didn't like him quite so much and then I began to panic that I might be pregnant.'

'Golly!'

'He wore something,' said Kit evasively. 'And he promised it was OK but I began to worry. You know.'

Fliss nodded. She didn't know but she could guess. 'Imagine telling Grandmother,' she said.

Kit shivered. 'Don't. It's over. Fancy if I'd had to marry him. I've been terrified.'

Fliss stared at her, determined that she would never, ever take such a risk, not even for Hal . . . She began to see how Kit might have felt – but even so . . .

'Oh, thank heavens you're OK, Kit,' she said. 'How awful Christmas would have been. And poor Aunt Prue would have been so worried.'

'I know.' Kit grimaced. 'I vowed that if I could be OK I'd be angelic for as long as I live.' She began to laugh helplessly. 'I've never been to the lavatory so often in my whole life. Every ten minutes, hoping – you know.'

Fliss began to laugh, too. 'You're hopeless,' she said affectionately.

'I know,' said Kit proudly. She got off the bed and stretched, twirling round, still laughing. 'Come on. Fox and Hal have got the tree up in the hall and we're supposed to be finding the decorations ready for tomorrow. Oh, Fliss, I feel so *happy*!'

In the kitchen on Christmas Eve afternoon, Ellen made mince pies and Caroline iced the Christmas cake whilst they listened to the Nine Lessons and Carols from Cambridge on Ellen's wireless.

'Always makes me want to cry,' admitted Ellen, cutting the pastry with an experienced hand.

'Me, too,' said Caroline happily.

There was a short silence.

'Where are those girls?' wondered Ellen. 'Acting strange, they are. Specially that Kit.'

'Just her age, don't you think?' suggested Caroline. 'All those hormones rampaging about. Fliss is getting to be the same.'

'Hormones,' sniffed Ellen contemptuously, dealing deftly with mincemeat. 'Never had hormones when I was a girl. Hormones indeed. Whatever next, I wonder. Here's Fox with the dogs. Get the kettle on, there's a good girl. I'm all over flour.'

Assured by Caroline that Father Christmas would know where to find it, Susanna was hanging one of Ellen's discarded lisle stockings on the hook on the back of the door.

'I haven't got a knob on my bed like you have,' she told Mole, who was watching with interest and faint

237

anxiety. 'Last year we hung it over the chair but this year I want to see it hanging up all full and nobbly when I wake in the morning. Caroline says Father Christmas will know where it will be.'

'I expect he g-gets used to looking about,' said Mole. He shivered. Even the thought of jolly friendly Father Christmas in his room made him feel nervous. Supposing that white beard hid closed, smiling lips? The twinkly eyes might suddenly turn wide and blank and merciless. Last year he had been unable to sleep and had gone in to Caroline until the coast was clear. 'What would we do if we w-woke up and s-saw him, I wonder.'

His tone was studiedly casual but Susanna was alerted, aware of some tension. She frowned – remembering that Mole suffered nightmares – and took the limp stocking off the door.

'I don't like it there after all,' she announced. 'Grandmother said we could hang our stockings by the fireplace in the hall. That's where he'll come down, after all. Shall we do that? Fliss can hang hers there, too. And Caroline. We all will. Then he needn't come upstairs at all.'

'B-but,' protested Mole, striving to be unselfish, 'then you won't see it hanging up when you wake in the m-morning.'

Susanna shrugged, winding the stocking over her arm. 'I don't mind really. I'll wake you up and we'll go down together. It'll be fun to see them all hanging in a row, won't it?'

'I'll get my s-stocking,' Mole said, rosy with relief. 'Let's go down now and see where they can go. Come on, Sooz.' He hesitated, wishing he could repay her, not knowing how. 'I really hope he brings your scooter, Sooz.'

'So do I,' she said cheerfully. 'Come on. Let's go and ask Caroline where we can put them and then it will be time for tea. Mince pies. Yummy.'

By the time Prue arrived later on Christmas Eve everything was ready. When she came into the hall, fetched from the station by Fox, they were all waiting for her. The tree, soaring up to the ceiling, was covered in lit candles, the only light apart from leaping firelight. The tinsel and baubles shone and glittered, and tiny parcels, beautifully wrapped, hung from the stronger boughs. Holly and mistletoe, tied with scarlet ribbon, decorated the hall; mince pies and sherry were waiting on the table before the fire. She stood quite still, just inside the door, and stared in delight while the family smiled at her pleasure.

'It's perfect,' she said at last and – as though she had released them from a spell – they surged forward to greet her, hugging and kissing her, making her welcome.

They gathered about the fire, whilst Susanna and Mole crawled round the tree feeling the presents piled beneath it and Hal, under the cover of conversation, kissed Fliss under the mistletoe. Kit saw them and grinned at Fliss who wondered if anyone had ever died of happiness.

The two girls, with Prue and Caroline, Hal and Theo, went to Midnight Mass. Caroline drove – much to Hal's disgust – but it meant that he could sit in the back with Fliss on his lap, whilst Prue and Kit squashed in beside them. The old grey church was ablaze with candlelight and, when they came out, a cold white moon hung in a starry sky. Their breath smoked in the freezing air and the frost crunched beneath their feet.

As the car pulled into the courtyard, the front door opened and the light from the hall streamed down the steps and across the grass. Freddy stood waiting for them, tall and slim in her high-necked blouse and long velvet skirt, with a shawl about her shoulders.

'The children are in bed at last, stockings hung up,' she said, 'waiting for Father Christmas. Fox has made up the fire and Ellen has just brewed some hot coffee. Come in and get warm. And a very Happy Christmas to us all.'

They stood for a moment, listening to the Christmas bells ringing out across the quiet countryside, smiling at one another, and then they all went inside and closed the door behind them.

Book Three
Winter 1965

———

Book Three

Chapter Nineteen

Theo, oblivious of the wind howling round The Keep, sat at the desk in his study immersed in a yellowing, much-folded document which was nearly ninety years old. He was compiling a history of the Chadwicks. It was Fliss, with her strong sense of family, who had begged him to do it. She pored over old photographs and letters, questioning and examining, demanding explanations, until Theo had given in and agreed to chronicle the family history. He was enjoying it. There was plenty to do at The Keep – more than enough physical labour required of them all to maintain the place – but it was very pleasant to retreat upstairs to his study whenever the opportunity arose to resume work on his project.

He took off his spectacles, rubbing his eyes and stretching back in his chair. Slowly he became aware of the fact that the room was chilly. The short January day was nearly over and the room was in darkness, except for the pool of light shed by the lamp on his desk. Freddy had insisted on the lamp, anxious lest he should strain his eyes as he struggled to interpret faded script or crabbed handwriting. When he had absolutely refused to allow coal to be carried up so that the fire could be lit, she had also supplied him with an electric fire – which he invariably forgot to switch on until he was reminded, as he was now, by the cold clumsiness of his fingers. He stood up stiffly and went to draw the curtains, pausing to glance down into the courtyard where the rain swirled about in the wind, buffering against the windows, battering the climbing shrubs which clung to the high walls. A light gleamed out from Fox's little gatehouse cottage, shining on the wet flagstones, and Theo could see a figure moving around within. Fox was changing out of his damp clothes, no doubt, before coming over for his tea. Theo dragged the curtains together and pushed his cold hands into his cardigan pockets. Even with this warm woollen jacket over his thick jersey he was still cold and he went to switch on the fire, lest Freddy should come to seek him out and be cross at his self-neglect.

To be fair, no one interrupted his work unless he was late for a meal. Freddy had lived alone for far too long, self-sufficient and quite able to deploy her time, to be in constant need of his company. She was tactful and sensible about becoming too demanding and saw to it that he was never disturbed during the regular daily periods – early and late – of contemplative prayer which were such an integral part of his existence. She respected his absolute need to go apart and he suspected that, after so many years alone, she had a similar requirement. Even after three years they were finding the other's daily presence far too precious to abuse it in any way. Both were so afraid of spoiling their contentment that they rather erred on the side of determined self-sufficiency and careful awareness; it was enough for each to know that the other was there.

Theo thought: It was neither too early nor too late for us. By some miracle it has worked.

He had never been so content. There was a special joy in sharing the passing seasons in the company of someone whom you loved, had loved for so many years, and, because he had denied himself so long, this reward was all the sweeter. Theo was still certain that, if he had come back to live at The Keep in the early years, the relationship would have foundered beneath the weight of his own longings and Freddy's pride. He regretted nothing.

Glancing at his watch, he saw that it was teatime; Freddy would already be in the hall. The thought of the blazing log fire and the hot tea drew him out of his study and downstairs. Freddy sat sideways on one of the sofas, head bent as she read the obituary page of *The Times*. She looked up at him sombrely and he guessed that she was reading about Winston Churchill; his research had driven the recent news of the great statesman's death temporarily from his mind but today the newspapers must be full of it. Like Freddy, Theo saw his death as the end of an era and they had reminisced together; remembering the war and how his inspired speech had encouraged those who waited at home and those who were away fighting. It was as if some whole way of life were passing with him; nevertheless he was too old a man for his death to be a shock to the nation.

The tribal, almost sinister reverberations of the Mersey beat seemed to be providing a background for new and frightening discoveries in scientific warfare and in worrying outbreaks of criminal activity and violence: the Great Train Robbery; the Profumo affair; the assassination of John Kennedy; the war in Vietnam. Freddy felt that Churchill's death was symbolic of the loss of some last great bastion of civilised behaviour; the world was heading for disaster. She had said as much to Theo.

'Nonsense,' he'd said at once. 'The last two wars were hardly examples of civilised behaviour. Life has always been violent and crude. History shows a continual cycle. There are peaceful and prosperous interludes between war-torn and violent eras. It's all a matter of luck as to when we are born. If there are grim times ahead it won't be for the first time and we shall come about again. Mankind is surprisingly resilient and resourceful.'

'I can't decide,' she had answered, 'whether I find that comforting or not. I still feel that the storm clouds are gathering.'

'They have gathered before and it has not meant Armageddon, although we sometimes thought it did,' he said. 'The Great War. The Cuban crisis. You and I have lived through two world wars and a depression, Freddy. I expect we shall survive a few clouds.'

'What about the clouds of Hiroshima?' she had reminded him sharply, not wishing to be comforted but wanting him to be as depressed as she was. She felt surprisingly low, old and tired and futile, and his sane realism irked her. 'We wouldn't survive a nuclear war.'

'I don't think we'd want to,' he'd replied lightly, hoping to encourage her back to a more positive viewpoint without appearing to be insensitive. 'You know that Hal says that nuclear power is the ultimate deterrent. Everyone is too afraid of the devastating results to risk confrontation.'

'And what would Hal know?' she'd asked crossly. 'He's barely a sub-lieutenant. Hardly an expert on world safety.'

'True.' Theo began to smile at her determined gloom. Hal – in his last year at the Royal Naval College at Dartmouth – was usually quoted as a leading authority on warfare generally. 'How terrible life is, after all. Shall we tell Ellen to bring us arsenic for two in the study after dinner? Get it over and done with?'

She'd laughed unwillingly but, as usual, he had managed to lift her spirits; had saved her from despair . . .

'Come and get warm,' she said now, casting *The Times* to one side. 'How are you getting on?'

'Not very fast,' he answered. 'At the moment I'm still attempting to sort out some documents and papers regarding a lawsuit in 1850. My grandfather was a very determined and devious man, by all accounts.'

As he sat down close to the fire, stretching his cold hands to the flames whilst Freddy poured his tea, the front door opened and Caroline came in out of the wet, cold darkness. A mackintosh-hat was jammed down over her hair and she was carrying several parcels.

'How cosy you look,' she said, shutting the door and pulling off her hat. 'It's beastly out there.'

'Why don't you put your things in the cloakroom and come and have some tea?' suggested Freddy. 'You look as if you need warming up. And then you can tell us how Fliss is and how you fared in Exeter.'

Theo raised his eyebrows at Freddy as Caroline disappeared through the door at the back of the hall. She frowned slightly and shook her head, indicating that he must wait for Caroline's return. He took his tea, racking his brains in an effort to remember any reference to this trip to Exeter, wondering if it had any great significance. Because of the rain he had been working in his study since breakfast and, as Julia Blakiston had been invited to lunch, he'd had a tray in his room, giving Freddy the opportunity to relish her old friend's company. He was sure that Freddy had said nothing about the trip at breakfast – or maybe his forgetfulness was even worse than he feared. In a few moments Caroline was back, the short curls flattened by her hat, her brown Oxfords very damp, her cheeks glowing.

'So how was Fliss?' Freddy was filling a cup of tea. 'Any luck with the material?'

'We had a really good time in spite of the weather.' Caroline beamed at them. 'Fliss was determined that she should have brocade, you know. She says that it's the "in" thing,' she made a wry face and shrugged her ignorance – 'but when she went to look in Bobby's last week they told her that they didn't keep gold in stock, so she ordered some. You know I haven't got a clue about clothes but I must say it's gorgeous.' She paused. 'I bought a dress for my dinner with Miles.'

'Well.' Freddy exchanged a look with Theo at the mention of a man, as Caroline sipped gratefully at her hot tea. 'So aren't you going to show it to us?'

'Oh.' She was gratified and surprised all at once.

'Well, if you really would like to see it . . .'

'We certainly would,' said Freddy. 'And anything else you've been buying. You seemed to be carrying some interesting-looking parcels. What have you done with them?'

Caroline looked faintly embarrassed. 'I left them in the cloakroom,' she mumbled. 'I didn't think anyone would be interested.'

'Of *course* we're interested,' said Freddy. 'Good heavens! Shopping expeditions are always interesting. Go and get your spoils. Hurry up or your tea will get cold.'

Caroline stood up, hesitating. 'If you're sure . . .'

'I don't think she wants to show us,' said Freddy to Theo – and Caroline grinned and hurried away.

'*Are* we interested?' asked Theo mildly. 'I'm not certain where I stand when it comes to ladies' dresses. Didn't we call them frocks?'

'Don't be tiresome,' said Freddy shortly. 'And for goodness' sake make an effort. She's in love, poor darling. It sticks out a mile. *Do* try to show an interest.'

Theo was still digesting this amazing piece of information when Caroline returned, bearing her parcels.

Freddy pushed aside the tea things so that Caroline could spread the dress on the low table.

'Beautiful.' Freddy ran her fingers over the soft thin grey-green jersey, noting the cross-over bodice and gently flaring skirt. 'Quite charming. Don't you think so, Theo?'

She glared at him warningly whilst Caroline, unconscious of any by-play, gazed upon her new dress.

'The colour is perfect for you,' said Theo unexpectedly. 'It brings out the green in your eyes.'

Both women stared at him, open-mouthed. Caroline recovered first. 'In my *eyes*?' she asked disbelievingly.

'Certainly,' said Theo recklessly. 'I've often noticed it. The true hazel, I think it's called. Very unusual. And beautiful.'

Caroline was quite silenced by such an extravagant and unexpected tribute; Freddy stared at him, her eyes narrowed thoughtfully, lips pursed. He smiled sweetly at her. She inhaled slowly and carefully through her nose, as if suppressing some deep inner conflict, before turning back to Caroline.

'And what's in the other parcel?'

Caroline coloured a little as she carefully folded the dress back into its tissue paper. 'I've been very extravagant,' she said guiltily. 'Although it was in the sale. And Fliss . . .' She paused.

'And Fliss encouraged you,' said Fliss's grandmother. 'I believe you. Go on. Get it out.'

Caroline held up a thick brown winter coat. It was cut full, in a loose swagger, and its collar was actually a long scarf with a black fringe at each end.

'Goodness,' said Freddy at last. 'This, no doubt, is also the "in" thing.'

'Well, it is.' Caroline looked at her anxiously. 'I wondered whether it was a bit *too* fashionable but Fliss was so certain . . .'

'Try it on,' said Theo suddenly. 'Let's see you in it.'

Scarlet with embarrassment, Caroline stood up and pulled on the coat. She stared at them for a moment and then, on impulse, she flung one end of the scarf about her neck and twirled round on her toes.

Flushed and laughing she posed, watching them self-consciously.

'What d'you think?' she asked breathlessly.

They were both smiling. Theo clapped his hands, applauding her, and Freddy nodded.

'Fliss is quite right,' she said. 'You look charming.'

'Honestly?' She looked so relieved that they both laughed at her. 'Gosh, I was worried coming home on the train. I kept peering at it. You know? I'm not used to buying so much all in one go.'

'You've bought very sensibly,' Freddy reassured her. 'It's a good quality coat which will last for years. And as for the dress . . .'

'Well, it's very good of . . . Miles to ask me . . .' Her cheeks were red again as she laid the coat over the arm of the sofa and sat down, picking up her cup. 'It's just dinner with some friends of his, while the others are at the Ladies' Night. Fliss is looking forward to it so much. It should be fun.'

'Ladies' nights are always fun.' Freddy refilled Theo's cup. 'Especially in the Gunroom. Not so stuffy as in the Mess. Well, she'll have to hurry to get the dress made up in time.'

'I know.' Caroline gulped at her tea. 'Saturday week. One of her room-mates is going to help her.'

'So she is well?' Freddy sat back with her own tea. 'Settled in again?'

Theo watched them as they talked, wondering how it was that Freddy, at seventy, should be more elegant and far more beautiful than Caroline at thirty-four. It helped, of course, that she was tall, long-legged and graceful, whereas Caroline was short and stocky and her features unremarkable. Nevertheless, she had youth on her side. He found himself trying to remember who Miles was . . .

'He is Hal's divisional officer,' said Freddy later, when Caroline had gone, clutching her spoils. 'He arrived last term which you would know if you ever listened to anything we said to you. They're driving over to pick up the girls for this Ladies' Night so we'll meet him. Kit is coming down from London. Hal has a fellow officer lined up for her and they are all spending the night at Miles's house in Above Town. He lives out, although he has a cabin in the college, too. He's a widower and a Lieutenant-Commander. Lieutenant-Commander Harrington.' ('Oh, *him*!' exclaimed the enlightened Theo.) 'The girls have been over to parties several times and then there was the Christmas Ball. Poor Caroline is smitten with him . . .' She cast up her eyes in despair. 'I can't believe you haven't noticed. You're hopeless. Hal talks about Miles so often and Caroline goes all starry-eyed.'

'I thought I handled the dress rather well,' said Theo defensively but with a touch of modest pride.

'The true hazel!' Freddy snorted derisively. 'We must hope that Miles is as inventive. By the way, I had a letter from Mole by the afternoon post. Cut yourself a piece of cake while I read it to you . . .'

Kit let herself out of the basement flat of the small terraced house in Scarsdale Villas, ran up the steps and walked briskly along to the Earls Court Road. Her ash-brown hair, fine and feathery, fell below the shoulders of the still much-loved cape, which was now showing signs of wear. The knee-length boots were new however; so new that she kept glancing at them with pleasure as she walked, admiring them as her long legs flashed in and out of the cloak's folds. She'd managed to get a Saturday job in a small gallery in Kensington Church Street and she was enjoying it so much that she was hoping that she might be offered a full-time job when she finished university in the summer. As she turned into Kensington High Street she pulled her cloak more tightly about her. The wind was cold but at least the rain had stopped. Kit hummed under her breath. The basement flat was the best she'd had yet and the other girls – fellow students at King's College – were fun. Of course, she missed those Saturday mornings rummaging about in the Portobello Road for bargains or meeting friends for coffee in the King's Road but the job paid well. Lots of interesting people came to the gallery and she enjoyed meeting the artists. A great variety of work was shown: paintings, pottery, sculpture, photographs. Generally the display was changed each fortnight, which was very exciting. This week it was metal sculptures, strange elongated shapes and designs which fascinated Kit. One in particular, metal loops twisted into the shape of a woman, she would have liked to have bought and taken back to her room in the basement. The price, of course, was exorbitant – yet the things sold. There were two rows of six chairs, placed back to back in the centre of the studio beneath the chandelier, and people came to sit and stare at the paintings or photographs which hung on the plain white walls, or at the pottery or sculpture, which was arranged on plain white boxes.

As she waited to cross into Kensington Church

Street, watching the traffic, she found herself thinking about Devon and The Keep. She'd been down for Christmas but in this last twelve months she'd been back, to Bristol and Devon, less and less. Kit grimaced guiltily and hastened to justify herself. For one thing, a Saturday job made it very difficult to get away for the weekend and, anyway, she had this scene going with one of the two young men who shared a flat upstairs. Jacques Villon – Kit called him Jake the rake – was tall, good-looking and rather fun, and at least twenty-five. He liked classical jazz . . . She suddenly remembered – with a certain amount of embarrassment – the great passion she'd had at the end of her first year. He'd been in his second year at Imperial College and it was all wonderfully romantic. They had declared their mutual undying love and she had taken him home to meet Prue. Paul was twenty, penniless and had only a very hazy idea as to his future. He was an attractive, serious Scot and obviously adored Kit but – to Kit's disappointment – Prue had been very cautious. She made him welcome and was charming to him but, especially when they talked about getting married, there had been awkward silences.

A week later an edict had arrived from The Keep. Whilst the children were supported by the family there would be no engagements or weddings until their educational training – whatever form that might take – was finished. If they wished to proceed without the benefit of financial support or the allowances which would become due on their twenty-first birthdays, then that was entirely up to them. Kit had been shocked by such heartlessness, railing at Prue on the telephone, denouncing the family as cruel and wicked and Prue a traitress. For a week or two she and Paul saw themselves as a latter-day Romeo and Juliet, and she suggested to Paul that they should both go down to The Keep and confront her grandmother. Paul, for some reason, had not been keen on this plan of action and his passion seemed to cool a little. The glamour of being star-crossed lovers inevitably began to fade; their friends grew bored with their declarations; her grandmother dealt kindly but implacably with Kit's impassioned letters; the protagonists were left without an audience. The long vacation started and Paul returned to Scotland. Kit went home to Bristol, to Prue and Hal who, primed by his mother and grandmother, had arranged several jolly outings with some of his brother officers. By the time Kit and Paul were back in London in the autumn it was all over.

Standing on the kerb, huddled in her cloak, Kit marvelled that love could die so utterly. She thought of the entwined walks by the river, the kisses in dark doorways, the hot fumblings in the long grass in the park. She shook her head, feeling worldly and sophisticated. It would never have survived the winter; nowhere to go except the back row of the cinema . . . How long ago it seemed now, how naïve and innocent she'd been to be taken in by such an immature and callow youth, to imagine that she would love him for ever. How wonderful it was to be confident and in charge of your own life, to go to jazz clubs with dark young men who knew just how to flirt and have fun.

She skipped lightly between two tall buses, feeling happy. Next week she would be travelling west, going to Dartmouth for a Ladies' Night with the gang. She wished she'd thought of asking Jake. Hal's brother officers were rather unsophisticated by comparison, although they were more mature than other young men of the same age. Of course, there was Miles Harrington . . . but that was going too far. He must be at least thirty-five. Kit saw the gallery owner approaching from the opposite direction and knew that she was early. This was quite intentional. She must look keen if she wanted to be considered for the job. Kit put Ladies' Nights and dark young men out of her mind and prepared to concentrate on work.

Chapter Twenty

Fliss was travelling home to The Keep early on Friday evening. She had begun the teachers' training course at Rolle College in Exmouth the previous autumn and was settling in very happily. The hall of residence was an old Victorian house only ten minutes' walk from the college and she shared a big downstairs room – no doubt the former dining room or drawing room – with two other girls. So big was this room that each girl was able to have a bed, a desk and a wardrobe. Upstairs, the third-year girls had study-bedrooms and there was a great deal of coming and going and impromptu fun. Despite a new-found independence, however, Fliss's life was still very much centred on The Keep and her family. This evening, as she caught the ferry that crossed the estuary to Starcross, her thoughts were already flying ahead to the weekend. She was barely aware of the low-lying mist which wreathed its milky strands across the dark water, obscuring the hulls of the small boats which lay at anchor. The lights of Exmouth were gradually blotted out behind them as the ferry chugged gently across the wide channel towards the woods and the deer park of the Powderham estate. Neither of these was visible on this early February evening; only a deeper, more solid density of darkness indicated that they were drawing closer to the other shore, until a lightening and diffusion of the fog, growing brighter and finally dwindling into a single point of light, guided them towards the small railway station at Starcross.

As she walked along the ferry pier and on to the station, Fliss thought how wonderful it was to be only half an hour away from home. The train from Exeter was on time and she climbed on and found herself a seat. Since it was too dark to see the sand dunes at Dawlish Warren on the sea, Fliss gave herself up to imaginings and expectations. During Hal's first year at Dartmouth she had still been away at school on the north coast and in his second year, as a midshipman, he had been posted to a cruiser which had sailed for the Far East. Only in the summer holidays had they had the chance to be together and even then she had been too young to be taken really seriously. At last, however, he was back for his final year and she had finished school and was old enough to go to parties and Ladies' Nights.

Fliss gave a huge sigh of delight and longing. How she loved him. There were still those echoes of Jamie about him: the protective caring, often disguised by a friendly impatience; the reliance on her good opinion and support, often disguised by a manly indifference; her feeling of absolute safety when she was with him. She was rendered quite weak with adoration when she saw him in his uniform; tall, blond, confident. Her heart seemed actually to leave her body and speed into his. When they were separated by a crowd, or dancing with other people, his eyes would seek her out and he would give her that tiny complicit wink that was like a hug. She knew that their friends and family regarded them still as almost brother and sister but she had those private magic memories of swift kisses and exciting moments when the electricity was so strongly charged between them that she felt she might die of it.

She stared out into the darkness, wondering how the family would react if they told of their love. Of course there was that old wives' tale about cousins producing batty children, and obviously a lot of in-breeding was dangerous, but there was no such history in the Chadwick family. She and Hal would be the first cousins to marry and it was quite obvious to Fliss that she was much more like her mother than her father; she was small and slight and only the thick blonde hair showed her to be Freddy's granddaughter. Hal, on the other hand, was the image of his own father and very like Freddy. At the thought of her grandmother, Fliss felt a twinge of anxiety. Would she approve? She remembered how swiftly she had dealt with Kit's romance – and now that edict affected Hal and herself. Nevertheless, Grandmother loved them all so much that surely she must want their happiness? It would keep the family even more tightly welded together. She was certain that Kit would be happy for them and Mole and Susanna were still too young to worry about things like in-breeding.

The little frown, which sat so often on her fair feathery brows, deepened. The school in the New Forest had proved to be a brilliant find. Susanna and Mole had settled down very quickly and Mole was as happy there as he could hope to be at any distance from his family. His stammering had become a great deal worse for a while but gradually he had been able to relax within his new surroundings and it had now almost disappeared. The family were delighted by his progress but Fliss still worried about him. Several times during the Christmas holidays she'd heard him shouting at night and once she'd gone out to the bathroom and found him standing, blank-eyed and quite still, in the passage outside his bedroom door. Her heart had almost stopped with fright but she soon saw that he was asleep and she had led him back to bed and sat beside him until he slept naturally, breathing deeply.

Next morning she'd spoken to Caroline about it. The serious expression which appeared on her face had underlined Fliss's fears.

'I think he hides his feelings a lot,' she'd said at last. 'I don't want to worry Mrs Chadwick about it but I keep an eye on him. It's a bit better now that Theo's here. It's good for Mole to have a male member of his family around.'

'But I thought he was so much better,' Fliss had said sadly.

'He is. Honestly,' Caroline hastened to comfort her, not wishing to frighten her. 'But there are bound to be good days and bad days.'

'But *why*?' cried Fliss. 'Of course we shall never forget about . . . about what happened. How could we? But why is it so specially awful for poor Mole? Why does he have to suffer so terribly?'

Caroline had been silent for a moment. Although Fliss knew that Mole had heard the dreadful news in a particularly violent way she still had no idea that he knew the shocking details. She had been told that the car had been ambushed, her parents and Jamie shot, dying instantly. Everyone had waited to see if Mole would speak about what he had heard and, when it seemed that he would keep the terrible details to himself, they had prayed that Fliss and Susanna might never know the real truth. For Fliss, what she had been told was ghastly enough but she still had no real idea of exactly how much Mole *had* suffered.

'It was probably his age,' Caroline had said at last. 'You were just old enough to cope with it, Susanna was too young to know anything. Mole was between the two and he's taken much longer to come to terms with it.'

Fliss thought: I *had* to cope with it. There were no choices. I was the oldest and there was no one to turn to until I arrived at The Keep.

Even now she still felt responsibility for her siblings, which was why being with Hal was such heaven. He was bigger, older, in charge; just as Jamie had been but with all the extra magic. Of course, there was Grandmother, Uncle Theo, Aunt Prue – not to mention Ellen, Fox and Caroline – all of whom took the real weight of the worry from her; nevertheless she felt a special anxiety for Mole and Susanna. The older members of her family seemed changeless – yet she lived with the terror that these beloved people might suddenly die, leaving her alone again. It was odd to her that there was an agelessness about them; they were all exactly as they had been for the last eight years. Caroline was different. She remained unchanged – but in some inexplicable way she, Fliss, appeared to be catching up with her. The gap between them was narrowing and there were occasions – for instance, buying the dress and the winter coat – when their positions were reversed and it was she who seemed the elder. She longed to talk to Caroline about her feelings for Hal but something prevented her.

Fliss moved restlessly in her seat, staring out as the train drew into Newton Abbot. It was as if she were waiting for some sign from Hal himself, something more than the quick, private demonstrations of a love that were more than brotherly or even cousinly; something to show *absolutely* that he was just as serious as she was; some proof . . . She shivered in delicious anticipation of that declaration. Hal would never flout his grandmother's wishes, she felt certain of that, which meant another eighteen months must be got through somehow before she finished at college and Hal had completed his fourth-year courses. It was possible that he felt it would be wrong to commit either of them to anything that could not be openly acknowledged. This, no doubt, was the honourable way, but how she longed for something more definite. She allowed her imagination to wander into the future, inventing an endless variety of scenes in which Hal declared himself at last . . .

It was Caroline who collected Fliss from the station. She did most of the driving now, although Freddy still drove herself into Totnes or over to see Julia at Ashburton. On the platform the girls hugged each other, both equally excited at the thought of the weekend to come, and made their way through the fine misty rain to find the car.

'When does Kit arrive?' asked Fliss, throwing her

bag on the back seat of the Ford Anglia Estate which had recently replaced the old Morris Oxford. 'I can't wait to see her.'

'She'll be rather late,' warned Caroline. 'A tutorial or lecture or something. She says she can't cut it. We'll come in together to fetch her if you like.'

'Oh, yes. She'd love that. What a pity Mole and Susanna haven't got an exeat. It would be such fun for everyone to be home at once.'

'A fortnight adrift, I'm afraid.' Caroline pulled out of the station on to the Dartington road. 'I doubt that Kit will be able to take another Saturday off so soon.'

Fliss made a face. 'What a bore. Still, she seems to really like working in that gallery. So how does the dress look?'

'It's wonderful.' Caroline shook her head, still not quite able to believe the sight of herself in the grey-green dress. 'You were quite right about the colour.'

'I just knew it,' said Fliss contentedly. 'The minute I saw it I knew that it was absolutely right for you. Mine's finished but only just. It's fun that Miles and Hal are coming to fetch us, isn't it?'

'Very nice.' Caroline tried to keep her voice controlled and cool. No one must suspect how she felt. 'I'm glad we don't have to go over in our evening things. Miles says we can change at his house. Much better. They'll be with us in time for tea. I wouldn't have minded driving but it's rather a change to be chauffeured now and again.'

'Poor Caroline.' Fliss peered at her in the gloom. 'You must get fed up with ferrying us all to and fro.'

'Nonsense. I love driving. It's just on special occasions that it's nice not to have to.'

'There's the dear old school,' Fliss said, peering from the window as they passed through Dartington. She laughed. 'It seems so odd that Mole and I used to go there every day. It seems centuries ago.'

'Eight years ago,' said Caroline. 'And you were only there for two years.'

'Age is a funny thing, isn't it?' Fliss was still pursuing her earlier line of thought. 'It seems odd that Mole and Susanna are still children but I'm grown up. And you don't seem to have changed a bit. I feel closer in age to you now than I do to them. It's peculiar.'

'I know what you mean.' Caroline changed gear and swung the car into the narrow lane that led to The Keep. 'People go in fits and starts. Once you reach a certain age you seem to stay that way for years and years and then you do another jump forward.'

'That's it,' said Fliss slowly. 'Grandmother and Uncle Theo haven't changed at all in eight years. They seem to be just the same. And so do you. But Kit and Hal and I . . .'

'You've changed from children to adults. That's a big leap. But there's not much difference from say, thirty to forty-five. Or from sixty to seventy-five. And inside I think we hardly change at all.'

'That must be rather horrid,' said Fliss thoughtfully. 'To feel really young inside and to look all old and wrinkly and grey outside.'

'Horrid,' agreed Caroline. 'But you don't have to worry about that just yet.'

A companionable silence fell between them, each dwelling privately on the delights of the weekend to come, until the car swung in between the gatehouses and came to a halt in front of the garage.

Fliss sighed a deep, happy sigh as she saw the lights shining out across the courtyard. 'Home,' she said. 'Thanks, Caroline.' She reached for her bag and climbed out. 'Come on. I'm dying for a cup of tea and then I want to show you my dress.'

The atmosphere in the car, as it travelled between The Keep and Dartmouth, was so charged with excitement that it was a wonder it didn't explode. Fliss could smell it; the air was full of it. Crushed in the back between Kit and Hal, she felt almost ill with its pressure. Only Kit seemed exempt from its influence – but then Kit had always been able to manufacture her own brand of excitement; she had always had the power to make things happen. Everyone seemed to be talking and laughing at once; everyone except Caroline. Caroline remained silent, speechless with happiness. She had not expected to be handed into the front seat by Hal as though she were the guest of honour. Although the Chadwicks treated her as one of themselves, she was always aware of her position in the household. She was grateful for their generosity and made certain that she did not abuse it. It had never been necessary to remind Caroline of her particular status; she rarely forgot it. To be riding in the front seat beside Lieutenant-Commander Miles Harrington was an honour she had not expected. Her eyes slid sideways, examining him. The two men were dressed in what Hal called 'dog-robbers'; as far as she could see, this meant grey flannel trousers and tweed jackets. Her innate common sense warned her that he was way out of her league – that with his looks and charm he could have any woman he chose – yet the fact that he was unattached raised her hopes a little. She looked at his long-fingered hands as they held the steering-wheel, her glance lingering on his wedding ring . . .

Miles caught the glance and smiled at her, noticing how the flush stained her cheek. He felt tremendously lucky to be included in this family group. His wife had died of leukaemia – a slow, drawn-out dying – and to be plunged back into this young, carefree group was rather like being born again. He'd married young, younger even than Hal was now, in his Mid year. Belinda had been a quiet, gentle girl, who had become a sickly, nervous wife, and he had done his best to care for her and make her happy. Now, nearly five years after her death, he felt as though life were giving him a second chance. He'd liked Hal very much, right from the beginning. Of course, the name Chadwick was a well-known one in the Navy. Hal's father and grandfather had been killed in action and there was a Chadwick hanging amongst the admirals' portraits on the walls of the senior Gunroom. He was glad to be able to put his tall narrow house in Dartmouth at this family's disposal and have a share in their happy-go-lucky fun. Caroline had been persuaded along to one or two parties and it had been Hal's idea that Miles should partner her to the Christmas Ball. It had been such a wonderful evening that Miles had invited them all to his New Year's Eve party.

When he heard that Hal intended to bring Fliss and Kit to the Ladies' Night he gave it careful thought. Here was another chance for a get-together, except that as a staff officer he would not be asked to a

Ladies' Night in the Gunroom. Eventually he saw a
way of arranging it so that he could offer his hospitality; be part of the fun again. He invited them to stay
for the weekend and, as Hal's brother officers were far
too young for Caroline, he decided to invite her to
dinner with some friends in the town whilst the others
were at the Ladies' Night and planned to take the
whole party out to lunch the following day.

Later, when they had changed and he had poured
drinks for them, he stood slightly apart, delighted to
have them all there, fascinated by them. The three
women could hardly be more different. Caroline,
brown-eyed, brown-haired, attractive in her pretty
dress, was very simple and direct. Of course, her age
gave her a confidence not to be expected in the other
two, yet she was in some ways touchingly unsophisticated. She was old-fashioned in the nicest possible
way. Now Kit, on the other hand, was a real dolly-
bird. The long black clinging shift dress had 'London'
stamped all over it and her make-up was subtle but
dramatic; smudgy kohl pencil emphasised her smoky
blue eyes, and her wide lovely mouth was coloured
with pale lipstick. She looked modern, exciting, chal-
lenging, as she listened to her escort, glass in hand,
one narrow black strap slipping from a smooth shoulder. Miles moved a little so as to see Fliss. She was
standing still, hands clasped, watching Hal as he
disputed a point with Kit's partner. Her small face
was intense; pale clear skin, wide grey eyes, pointed
chin. The thick coil of corn-fair hair looked almost
too heavy for her slender neck and there was an
old-world look about her that was charming if vulnerable. Hal turned to speak to her and her face lit up

as she bent towards him . . .

Miles saw that Caroline was watching him and wondered if she'd guessed at his thoughts. He raised his glass to her, laughing almost guiltily, inviting her to laugh with him, and she did so, raising her own glass. They toasted each other, two adults in a party of big children and he glanced back at Kit and Fliss, still wondering whether he'd let his love show, if his expression had been unguarded . . . Hal looked round, drawing him into the conversation, appealing to him for support, and the moment passed.

Hal felt very proud as he ushered his two ladies into the Gunroom with his fellow officers and their guests. The long mahogany table gleamed with glass and silver and the stewards stood smartly to attention, ready to anticipate and serve. Portraits of admirals hung on the walls, gazing down on the handsome young men in their uniforms and the young girls in their pretty dresses. Hal felt that he was carrying on in a great family tradition and he smiled at Fliss, looking forward to dancing with her after dinner. He felt strong and happy, aware of a superabundance of energy and confidence, delighted with his chosen career. Talk ebbed and flowed about him as course followed course and the wine was poured – 'Red or white, ma'am? Red or white, sir?' – by the unobtrusive stewards. The toast was given – 'The Queen, God bless her' – during which, as tradition allowed, the company remained seated and the port had passed.

As they prepared to move into the discotheque next door, Hal smiled down at Fliss.

'Happy?' he asked.

She shook her head, unable to frame a suitably ecstatic reply, and he laughed, delighted with her reaction. Kit, watching them, thought how good they looked together and how unlike their usual workaday selves. Tonight there was a magic about them that lent them a glow so that she barely recognised them. As she followed them out of the Gunroom she saw that they were holding hands.

Chapter Twenty-one

A week later, heavy snow made the lanes impassable and The Keep was temporarily cut off from the outside world. Fox and Caroline, reminding each other of the winter of '63, dug paths to the woodshed and across the courtyard to the gatehouse. They put out crumbs for the robin and hung suet in the rhododendrons for the woodpecker. Mrs Pooter, old and irritable at thirteen, refused to go beyond the yard outside the kitchen but Mugwump was still young enough to need exercise. He and Fox ventured out on to the hillside – against Ellen's express wishes – where the snow had blown into deep drifts, making the countryside unrecognisable; a white and silent world, all familiar landmarks buried or disguised, stretching away to merge with the leaden canopy of cloud in the north. The wind was bitingly cold and no birds or animals were to be seen in this inhospitable landscape. The freezing air rasped in Fox's chest and his eyes watered; if it had not been for Ellen's earlier acid comments about 'no fool like an old fool' he would have turned back at once. Pride carried him on, along the narrow path, until Mugwump leaped recklessly into a deep wall of snow and completely disappeared.

He foundered helplessly, uttering short staccato barks of distress, until Fox managed to take a grip on his collar and pull him out, slipping as he did so and wrenching his ankle. Both soaked to the skin, Fox limping painfully, the two returned sheepishly to the warmth of the kitchen.

'And what did I say?' asked Ellen wrathfully, pushing Fox down into the chair near the Aga and laying hold of his gumboot, whilst Caroline rubbed the lumps of snow and ice from Mugwump's ears with a towel. 'You can always rely on men to make trouble, that's one of life's certainties. There's Mr Theo with one of his coughs and no medicine to be had. Mrs Chadwick worrying about whether those children will be able to get home on exeat next week. Wood to be got in and paths cleared and you have to go out on the hill as if it's midsummer. Whatever next, I wonder. Twisted your ankle, and, I've *no* doubt, started up your sciatica again. Well, you'll get no sympathy from me. Get that kettle on, Caroline. Hot tea's what we need here. As for that dog, dripping everywhere . . .'

Caroline grinned sympathetically at him as she went to push the kettle on to the hotplate and Fox winked nonchalantly, if a little shamefacedly.

'Bitter cold, out there,' he said, making a faint bid for sympathy.

'You don't say so?' enquired Ellen with heavy sarcasm as she put a stool under his foot. 'Would you credit it? And with all that snow and ice about and the wind in the north. What a surprise. And me thinking you'd be bringing back a nice bunch of spring flowers. Put that dog on his bed, Caroline. His mother's got more sense. We must be grateful for that.'

Fox gave an artistic groan, hand to the small of his back and she was round on him in a flash. 'Don't worry,' he said bravely. ''Tis nothing. Just a twinge in the old back.'

Her snort caused several fragile cups on the dresser to vibrate. 'No "just" about it,' she said crossly. 'Well, there's no help for it. I'll have to give you an arnica rub myself. Fat chance of getting the nurse out in this.'

Caroline began to laugh at the expression on Fox's face. 'Tea first,' she suggested diplomatically, 'and a couple of aspirins. I wouldn't be surprised if that does the trick.'

'That's it,' agreed Fox with alacrity. 'Couple o' they tablets and some hot tea. That's the ticket.'

'We'll see,' warned Ellen ominously. 'I shall have my eye on you, my lad. There now. Look at the time. Mrs Chadwick will be wanting her tea . . .'

'You deserve that arnica rub,' said Caroline severely, when Ellen had gone through to the hall with the tray. 'Honestly.'

'I know,' he groaned guiltily. 'It was just her telling me I was too old. Got some pride left, y'know.'

'Feeling better?'

He nodded. 'They tablets work a treat. Thank the Lord we got all the wood in early or I should never hear the last of it. Bless you, maid. You're a good girl.'

Caroline chuckled. 'What a pair you are. Worse than an old married couple.'

'Wouldn't catch me with parson and ring,' said Fox cheerfully. 'Hasn't been born, the woman who could tie me down. Variety's the spice of life, that's what I say . . .'

'And when Valentino's finished giving us the benefit of his experience,' said Ellen, who had come in unobserved, 'perhaps you'd fetch some butter from the fridge, Caroline. *If* you can tear yourself away, that is . . .'

The snow disappeared as quickly as it had come. The wind backed to the west and the rain poured down relentlessly. By the time Mole and Susanna arrived home the wind had strengthened and gales buffeted The Keep, rattling windows, howling at chimneys. In their first year at the school, Caroline or Freddy had driven them to and fro at exeats and half terms, and at the beginning and end of each term. As the time passed, however, Freddy decided that it might be wise to allow them to make one or two trips with Caroline on the train and, when Mole was twelve, they made the journey by themselves.

'It must be the journey home, to begin with,' Freddy had said. 'Too bleak, going back to school by themselves. It will be so good for Mole if it can be achieved without any disasters.'

She and Caroline had pored over the timetables. It seemed impossible to find a train that went between Totnes and Southampton without a change being necessary. Even if they were fetched from Exeter, there was still the change to be made at either Salisbury or Westbury.

'Westbury's a very small station,' Caroline had said thoughtfully. 'And they don't have to come over. Do you think they could cope?'

Freddy had put the suggestion to Mole and Susanna. Mole'd remained silent but Susanna cheered.

'Oh, do let's try,' she'd begged. 'It'll be fun. Lots of other children go on the train on their own and we've done the trip with Caroline.'

Freddy had looked at Mole. He'd smiled but his eyes had been expressionless, oddly blank. 'Why not?' he'd asked with an almost adult lightness. 'We can manage, can't we, Sooz?'

'I should just think we can,' she'd said earnestly. 'Someone will put us on at the other end. It'll be an adventure.'

'We shall meet you at Exeter,' Freddy had said. 'That change is a bit more tricky and it's a long wait. We'll have you home long before the train would.'

She'd looked again at Mole, who had raised his eyebrows and shrugged. 'Well then . . .' he'd said.

Heart in mouth, Freddy had lived through that afternoon in a state of terror. Theo had tried to help her.

'They have promised to ask at Westbury and to double-check before they get on the train to Exeter,' he'd reminded her. 'They are both very sensible.'

Freddy had nodded. She'd felt that if she should open her mouth she might scream; her nerves were rubbed raw with fear. She knew that if something went wrong this afternoon, years of progress with Mole might all go for nothing. His air of control and poise was almost disconcertingly mature, yet she was aware that beneath it he was still insecure. She'd discussed it with Theo.

'We can't have it both ways,' he had said. 'He has to

learn to conquer his fears or to go under. We shan't be here always. If we simply try to protect him indefinitely, then one day he *will* be left alone, with all his terrors a reality.'

'It just doesn't feel right,' Freddy had answered desperately. 'There's a rigidity about him that's almost frightening. I wanted him to be cured of it, Theo, not to have to bury it. Surely that's dangerous?'

'It all depends.' Theo had looked thoughtful. 'He's very young. He's had to work hard to control his fears. Quite often I see him playing and talking quite ordinarily and I hoped that this will become more and more the norm and the controlling part will just be a habit he will require less and less.'

Freddy had been unconvinced. She'd continued to be anxious and, the next time she went to fetch the children, she talked at length to the staff at the school but finally had to be content with their reports that Mole was doing well and had plenty of friends, though no really intimate ones.

On the afternoon of the momentous journey, she had left for Exeter quite an hour before it was necessary. Though Caroline went with her, Freddy insisted on driving. She said she needed something to occupy her mind.

When the children alighted from the train, Mole was white, silent with relief, and Susanna was glowing, voluble with excitement, but, presently, Mole was able to join in as Susanna recounted the whole of their adventure. Caroline encouraged and marvelled whilst Freddy drove silently, quite weak and ill with the tension. A huge tea awaited the heroes and they had to tell the story all over again, first for Theo in the hall and later for Ellen and Fox in the kitchen. It was in danger of becoming an epic – comparable with Hannibal crossing the Alps or the retreat from Moscow – and the children went to bed, exhausted but thrilled by their achievement.

The next morning, before breakfast, Mole had run round the spinney alone.

He stood on the hill, the south-westerly gale roaring above his head, the towering clouds racing before the wind. Shafts of sun, transparent pillars of gold, struck down through the grey masses, briefly illuminating a field of rich red earth or a stand of black bare trees. He braced himself against the strength of the wind, remembering how he had flown his father's kite here with Fox beside him, fearful lest the string should be torn from his hand by the wind's power. He remembered how he had jogged down the narrow sheep tracks on Hal's shoulders; down to the river on quiet summer afternoons, to paddle in the sandy shallows or climb amongst the boulders. Once they had built a dam . . . He thought of early morning walks with the dogs, Mrs Pooter chasing rabbits whilst the sheep scattered before her, and of the races he had run with Susanna, Fox waiting on the hill above with his stopwatch. Finally he looked at the spinney . . .

How clearly he remembered that morning. He had woken with all the thrill of the previous day's success still buoying him up and he had jumped out of bed and dragged on his clothes quickly, lest his nerve should desert him as it had done so many times before. He had gone down to the kitchen where Fox and Ellen were enjoying an early cup of tea.

'I'm g-going round,' he'd said – that was all – and they stared at him.

He'd needed Fox as a witness but he had not waited for him. He had wrenched open the back door and hurried out into the cool morning air, ignoring the dogs in the yard, passing out through the green door on to the hillside. He had run down, jumping and leaping, not daring to look behind him as his plimsolls gripped the dusty tracks, sending up tiny puffs like smoke beneath his feet. Only at the last had he glanced back; at the point where the spinney hid the hillside and the high walls of The Keep, he had thrown one last look upward. Fox had stood there, solid as the house itself, an arm upraised. Heart crashing, throat dry, he had run faster than ever before, his eyes fixed on that further point where he would see all that he loved most once more . . . He'd made it. Weak with effort and relief, gasping for breath, he had begun the ascent. Then Fox was there beside him, grasping him beneath his arms, swinging him into the air, shouting. Only much later had Mole realised that they had both been crying . . .

A voice behind him made him spin round; Fliss was coming down towards him. He smiled, lifting a hand in greeting, but he was watchful, prepared. He knew that she would question him, ask him if he were OK, if he had any problems, if things were going well at school. Her care, which had once been so reassuring, had become something of a pressure. He wondered why it should be so, why Fliss's anxiety was so much more crushing than Susanna's apparent indifference to his handicap. Was it because Fliss *feared* that he might be unable to manage that he felt less *strong* in her presence? Susanna took it for granted that he would behave like other people. Yet she understood him; she knew when he had 'black dog' as he called it to himself, when he needed to be left alone. Perhaps it was simply that Susanna allowed him to be normal, accepting his 'black dog' as normal, too. Other boys had fits of temper, losses of confidence, moments of fear and depression; why should his attacks be any different? Susanna, in her cheerful acceptance, indicated that she thought that they were no different; he was as other boys. Fliss, in her anxious probing, in her carefully worded questions, showed that she did not.

'We wondered where you were,' she said as she came up to him. 'Lunch is nearly ready.'

'I'm starving,' he said as they fell into step together. 'The wind's given me an appetite. Wild, isn't it?'

'It certainly is.' She looked out across the countryside. 'I think it's going to rain. So how are things?'

'Fine. Really good. What about you? Thanks for the letter. The Ladies' Night sounded fun.'

'Oh, it was.'

'And Hal? Is he OK?' He saw the little smile and knew that he was safe for a moment. He had learned quite early to distract people away from himself but, with Fliss, Hal was about the only subject that ever really did this.

'He might be over later,' she said happily. 'He said that Miles might bring him. I'd like you to meet Miles, he's really nice . . .'

Watching her, he felt a sense of ingratitude. He

needed her so much, relied on her so heavily, it was beastly of him to resent her love for him. Anyway, it *wasn't* that he resented it, exactly . . . He smiled at Fliss, noting that he was nearly as tall as she was now, and, with a kind of internal shock, saw that she was just as necessary to him as Susanna was. It was a different relationship, that was all. She was almost as a mother might be, someone to whom he could always turn, on whom he would always be able to rely, who loved him very deeply – but whose caring might well irk from time to time. She was also six years older. He couldn't boss her about and tell her off as he did Susanna . . .

'. . . so we were wondering whether to make a foursome and go over to the Church House for supper. What a pity you're too young to come.'

He pretended a disappointment that he didn't really feel. Now that Fox, Ellen and Caroline had clubbed together to rent a television, holidays at The Keep had gained an extra dimension. The television was in the sitting room that the three of them shared, next to the kitchen, and it was here that Mole and Susanna were to be found most winter evenings when they were at home. The novelty of it hadn't worn off and he was looking forward to an hour of watching before bed. It was probably too much to hope that *Z-Cars* might be on. Sometimes Ellen vetoed it but generally she could be persuaded if he and Susanna pleaded hard enough.

'Never mind,' Fliss was saying. 'You'll soon be old enough to do all sorts of things.'

'It's Hal's Passing Out Parade I'm really looking forward to,' he told her. 'Thank goodness we shall have broken up.'

'Grandmother would have got you special dispensation,' laughed Fliss. 'She's determined that the whole family will be there. It'll be wonderful. And then there's the ball afterwards.'

'Wait till it's my turn.' He spoke bravely, wondering if he'd get through the Admiralty Interview Board. 'Hal should be an admiral by the time I go to Dartmouth.'

'Oh, Mole,' she said, squeezing his arm. 'I'm glad you still want to join the Navy.'

'Course I do,' he said casually, following her through the green door. 'Tradition, isn't it? I *am* a Chadwick, after all.'

After lunch he and Susanna wandered out into the courtyard together. They stood irresolutely, rejecting the idea of a visit to the house in the orchard. The loose covers had been packed away for the winter, their treasures stored in Mole's bedroom, and the little house would be damp and bleak.

'Let's get our bikes,' suggested Susanna. 'We'll cycle up to Dartington and buy some choc. I've got some pocket money left. We'll be the Lone Pine Five when they went off on their bikes in the *Secret of Grey Walls*. You can be David and I'll be Peter. I wish my name was Petronella. Or Georgina. You can't make a boy's name out of Susanna. Shall we?'

'Why not?' He was finding it increasingly difficult to be drawn back into their childhood world of make-believe but he enjoyed himself when he allowed himself to relax and not worry about feeling a bit of a fool. 'We'll take a few supplies in our saddlebags.'

'I'll get one of the maps,' said Susanna gleefully.

'We could come home the other way. It's longer and we don't know it so well. It would be an adventure. You go and ask Ellen for some grog and a few biscuits. Bring any money you've got, too. Hurry. Last one back's a cissy . . .'

Chapter Twenty-two

On Prue's forty-second birthday, Kit cut her lectures and went to Bristol to celebrate it with her.

'Not much to celebrate,' grimaced Prue. 'Oh, darling, I'm getting old.'

'Cheer up, Ma.' Kit leaned against the door jamb, watching her mother sorting through various items of clothing piled on the bed. 'You don't look a day over thirty-five now. I've taken you in hand. Like a drink? There's loads of time. I booked the table for eight thirty.'

'That's a very good idea.' Prue brightened a little. 'I seem to have put on weight. Nothing fits anymore. Not these evening things, anyway.' She glanced at Kit's very brief skirt. 'You should turn some heads, though. The miniskirt hasn't quite caught on yet in provincial old Bristol. It's just above the knee and rising but yours looks like a curtain pelmet.'

Kit grinned. 'Old Hal gets quite stuffy about it,' she agreed. 'His friends like it, though.'

'I'm sure they do.' Prue gave up and sat down on the bed. 'It's no good, darling. You'll have to choose something for me. Suddenly I'm bored with all my evening clothes.'

'I'll get us some drinks,' said Kit, 'and then we'll experiment. Don't move.'

Prue sat still, waiting. She loved it when Kit came home and turned the place upside down with her music and her untidiness. She dragged Prue out to jazz cellars and pubs in King Street or to the Trattoria in Queen's Road, criticised her dreary clothes and took her to Anne Scarlett's at the top of Park Street to have her hair cut.

'Now then, Mark,' she'd say to the handsome young owner of the salon, 'cut out this awful perm and layer it. Soft and feathery. Don't panic, Ma. We know what we're doing . . .' And she'd perch on a chair beside them, long legs swinging, chatting away. Afterwards they'd have coffee in Fortes before they started on serious shopping: shoes, clothes, make-up.

'*Not* those high-heeled things,' Kit would say, when Prue veered towards the stilettos and court shoes. 'Now *these* are really cool . . .' 'These' were flat-heeled slingbacks in soft chestnut-coloured leather. 'Go on. Try them. They look great. Now then . . .'

A French blue linen suit with the skirt hem on the knee – 'I can't,' panicked Prue, 'I'm too old,' – and a short jacket with a narrow belt was the next on Kit's list. 'Looks great,' said Kit, 'specially with the shoes. Short skirts need flat heels or long boots. Now we need something to finish it all off . . .'

The blouse was white cotton with an edging of heavy lace in place of cuffs and collar. 'See how nice that looks under the jacket?' asked Kit. 'Really cool. Now what about a new lipstick? That dark stuff's very ageing . . .'

'You realise,' asked Prue, as they sat with all their

shopping around them, having a restorative cup of tea in the Berkeley, 'that I shall never have the courage to wear it all?'

'Yes you will,' said Kit. 'Come and see me in London to get your courage up. Got to go with the times, Ma.'

To her surprise, she had worn the things – and loved them, revelling in her friends' envious glances. They were too set in their ways to make such changes, nor did their children treat them as Kit treated Prue. The bond of friendship, begun in those earlier lonely days of missing Johnny, had developed into something very precious and she knew that she was lucky. It wasn't quite the same with Hal. Once he'd left school she saw much less of him and he'd been at sea and in the Far East for the best part of the last year. Now that he was back at Dartmouth for the final year – known as the Academic year and concentrating on Mathematics and Languages – he often came home at weekends to Bristol. Unless he was duty officer, or having to take charge of the Junior Division or first-year cadets, he would have weekends to himself. Of course, he looked upon The Keep as his home, too. If he hitched a lift he could be there in half an hour. Prue was not jealous but she *had* resented the hours she'd spent at the shop when they could have been together during the holidays. She adored him; he was so like Johnny that it gave her a shock each time she saw him. Past became present and memories flooded back, bringing a bittersweet pain. Like Kit he was easy and casual with her, which made her feel young again, but there was a more critical side to him which showed in his cautious appraisal of her clothes and hairstyles as orchestrated by Kit. He preferred her to look a little more like a mother than a sister, yet he was very proud of her and clearly pleased when his friends complimented him on having a gorgeous mama. Prue loved it when he filled the house with these young officers and she could cook for them and listen to their endless stories of the injustices of the Naval College . . . 'And he said to me, "Am I hurting you, son?" and I said, "No, chief," and he said, "Well, I ought to be, son. I'm standing on your bloody hair. *Get it cut* . . .' She spoiled them and mothered them and flirted with them, all at once, and missed them terribly when they went and she was alone again.

It had come as a tremendous relief when her allowance had continued to arrive after the débâcle with Tony. He had never been traced and Prue no longer cared. In time a divorce could be obtained on the grounds of desertion and, meanwhile, she decided to resume the name of Chadwick. It seemed right: Johnny's name; her children's name. She felt better immediately. It was more difficult to give up her job. Having made the gesture of independence she found it embarrassing to stop, fearing that it might show that she was only too ready to live off the family again. The job wasn't too bad, she enjoyed the company of the other women, but she tired easily and found standing all day quite exhausting. More importantly, it meant that she hardly saw the twins when they came home for the holidays. In the end she decided on a compromise; she would work two days a week and one Saturday a month.

She'd broached the subject during a visit to The Keep, sounding Theo out first.

'Do you think I ought to continue to work full time even if I don't have to?' she'd asked him anxiously.

Theo had considered the question carefully, wondering what lay behind it. 'Work is an excellent antidote to boredom,' he'd answered at last. 'It can also improve the self-esteem, stretch the mind or keep us fit, depending on the work. But for most people it is simply a means of survival and for a very few it is something they love. Those few are the truly lucky ones. If you are not happy at work, Prue, there is no moral reason why you should continue to do it.'

'I used to get bored sometimes,' she'd said, 'once the children had gone away to school and there was so little to do. Probably that's why I married Tony. I was lonely. I *do* get very tired but the real problem is that I can't spend time with the twins when they're on holiday. I thought I might work part time. Compromise and see how it goes. What do you think?'

'I think it's an excellent plan,' he'd answered warmly. 'Kit and Hal get such long holidays and it's hard that you can't be together. Perhaps it might mean that you could come down to see us more often, too? We don't see nearly enough of you.'

'Darling Theo.' She'd hugged him tightly. 'What do you think Freddy will say?'

'I think she'll be all for it. You don't need her permission, you know. Or mine.'

'I know that.' Prue had frowned. 'The thing is that I'm afraid that if I become dependent on the estate again, Freddy will think I'm skiving.'

'If John were alive he would have his allowance,' Theo had said firmly. 'He'd have supported you and you would have lived comfortably and looked after his children. He wouldn't have wanted you to go out to work unless it was something you wanted to do yourself, I'm certain of that. You've made amends. Now be happy.'

'Bless you,' she'd said rather chokily. 'I'll do that.'

Now, as she sat on the bed waiting for Kit to come back with their drinks, she realised that she'd done exactly that. During the last eighteen months she had been happier than she'd been for years. Her life had a balance to it; some work, some fun – and a measure of peace.

She thought: How lucky I am.

Kit came in carrying two glasses, a parcel clutched precariously under her arm. 'You'd better have it now,' she said, 'though your birthday isn't till tomorrow. You need it tonight. I can see that.' She passed a glass and the parcel to Prue and raised her own glass. 'Happy birthday.'

Setting the glass down on Prue's dressing table, she began to riffle through the clothes, humming to herself.

'Oh, darling . . .' breathed Prue. She held up the silk shawl, heavily fringed and embroidered with flowers the colour of bright jewels: emerald, sapphire, ruby. 'It's absolutely beautiful. Where on earth did you find it? It must have cost a fortune. Oh, Kit . . .'

'No it didn't. Don't panic, Ma. I found it in the Portobello Road on a stall.' Kit pulled out a long crushed-velvet skirt in midnight blue. 'Aha! This is just the thing. Where's that silky top? Now this will be really cool.' She put the two garments together as if Prue were inside and took the shawl from her unwilling hands. 'Now, you throw the shawl round it like *that*. See? You'll look great.'

'Bless you, darling.' Prue stood up and kissed her daughter. 'Thank you for my present and for coming home specially. That's the best present of all.'

'We shall have fun,' promised Kit. 'Now where's your silver necklace . . .?'

Freddy was visiting Julia, who had slipped on some ice during the snowy weather and broken her ankle. Confined, Julia was irritable and restless. She struggled gamely on, swinging between her crutches, refusing to let Freddy help with the lunch until they both relaxed at last with coffee in the drawing room.

'What a stubborn old woman you are,' observed Freddy affectionately. 'Do you never give in? Not even with a broken ankle?'

'I don't hold with giving in,' said Julia grimly. 'It's the first step on the slippery slope to the scrap heap.'

'Surely at our ages—' began Freddy persuasively.

'*Especially* at our ages,' interrupted Julia. 'We must soldier on or the next thing we know we shall be deemed incapable and some bright young thing will be making our decisions for us, telling us what to eat and how much gardening we're allowed to do. No, no. Old age isn't for the faint-hearted, Freddy, we both know that, but I'm damned if I'm going to have a keeper. Mrs Pearse does very well. She keeps an eye on me.'

'Which is just as well under the circumstances.' Freddy laughed a little. 'You're right, of course, but you make me feel ashamed when I think of my army of helpers – Ellen, Fox, Caroline.'

'That's quite different,' argued Julia. 'You had a

family to bring up and a big house to run. Ellen and Fox have been with you for ever. Having someone new at my age would be quite intolerable.'

'Then we must hope that Mrs Pearse can bear up under the strain,' said Freddy lightly. 'She must be getting on a bit herself.'

'We've known each other for forty years,' said Julia with satisfaction. 'She's been coming in three days a week since she was nineteen and just married. We do very well together. She knows my ways.'

'We've both been lucky,' said Freddy reflectively, 'although Ellen and Fox aren't getting any younger. I simply do not know how we would have managed without Caroline.'

'I envy you Caroline,' admitted Julia. 'If I could be sure of finding another Caroline I might change my mind about a companion. Never mind. Pour some more coffee and tell me about Mole and Susanna.'

Caroline put away the last of the plates and hung the teacloth over the Aga's rail. The kitchen was quiet and warm, curtains pulled against the chill February night, the dogs fast asleep on their beds. Ellen, who had been suffering all day with a headache, had been bullied into bed at teatime with a cup of tea and some aspirin, leaving Caroline to cope. She didn't mind. As she wiped down the draining board and the table, she felt an unusual sense of happiness at being alone. She was a person who liked company, people around her, an air of bustle and movement. This was why The Keep was such a perfect place for her: there was always someone to talk to, things happening, people coming and going. The more there was to do, the more she thrived. She was strong and active, hating to sit and do nothing. Even the novelty of watching the television had worn off after a few weeks and she'd soon become restless and bored, entertained only by the gentle bickering between Fox and Ellen as they criticised and commented on the programme in question. Fox was in the little sitting room now, watching the news. She had taken his cup of tea in to him and stayed for a moment while Richard Baker told them about American jets bombing the Vietcong in South Vietnam.

'Here we go again,' Fox had said with gloomy satisfaction but Caroline had come away, not wanting to hear any more, wanting to savour a few moments on her own in the kitchen, to think about Miles. It was significant that ever since she had known him her awareness of the threat of war had increased. All her old fears had returned; the fears attached to loving a military man. She had been ten when the last war had started and quite old enough when it finished to remember the terrors and hardships, old enough to know all about loss.

As she prepared the coffee tray to be carried into the drawing room for Freddy and Theo, her mind was occupied by another problem: if Miles should ask her to marry him, how on earth would they cope at The Keep without her? Part of her felt a kind of shyness at the mere expectation of a proposal; a dread of being conceited, of hoping for too much. He was such an attractive man, popular and in line for promotion, and she had no illusions about her own lack of glamour. Yet another realistic part of her told her that Miles was not a boy; neither was he the sort of man who flirted and enjoyed playing the field. Surely he was too kind, too down-to-earth, to mislead her; but was there any question of misleading? As she waited for the kettle to boil, she mentally thumbed through her small sheaf of special memories. Even she had to admit that it was a rather sparse catalogue. There were no embraces or tender words; these moments were built on other things, often guessed at rather than revealed: an awareness of familiar ideas and hopes; a recognition of shared thoughts and reactions; similar roles. The really special memory was of the evening he had invited her to dinner with his friends whilst the others were at the Ladies' Night. His behaviour had been quite proper, courteous and attentive to her needs, but she felt that it had been an important step. Often it seemed as if she and Miles were set apart from the rest of the group of young people. They were both in positions of responsibility and it was natural that they should draw closer together because of it. Often, as he watched the younger ones enjoying themselves she would see a look of . . . Caroline hesitated here. She could never quite define that look. There was sadness, affection . . . and something else she couldn't quite place. If he saw her observing him he would smile quickly, straightening himself as if he shrugged off something that worried him. The high spirits of his young friends might simply be reminding him of his own youth. Perhaps, and this was more likely, their antics showed him what he had missed. She knew that he had married very young and so tragically. No wonder he sometimes looked sad.

Caroline made the coffee and put the pot on the

tray. Really there was very little on which to base her hope of a proposal. Her experience with Jeremy had taught her that loving someone was not enough; he had to love you back. Yet Miles was so ready to seek her company, to be partnered off with her, to spend time with her. She told herself that marriage was a big commitment and Miles might have grown too used to his freedom to want to take it too readily. He needed time to get used to the idea. Well, there was plenty of time ... but how on earth would they manage without her? How could she bring herself to leave them all?

Balancing the tray carefully, she opened the door which led into the hall – and hesitated. The drawing-room door was slightly open and Freddy was playing the piano. Caroline stood quite still, listening. It was the particular piece of music that she loved, that aroused all kinds of nameless yearnings in her, that made her want to weep. Freddy had told her that it was something by Chopin – but what? She racked her brains for a moment, then shrugged. At least this was something else that she and Miles had in common: a complete ignorance of music. Smiling to herself, she grasped the tray more firmly, crossed the hall and pushed open the drawing-room door with her shoulder.

Theo smiled at her, miming his thanks as she placed the tray on the low table. She set the cups and saucers out quietly, loath to disturb the music, enjoying the peace and warmth of the lovely room and the air of companionship between the two older Chadwicks. She went out, Theo closing the door gently behind her, and she paused again, listening until Freddy finished playing and, after a moment of silence, she heard the murmur of voices and the clink of china.

Caroline thought: How nice if Miles and I could grow old together like that . . .

Chapter Twenty-three

Half term. Once again Mole and Susanna made the journey from the New Forest alone. Mole, his book held up before him, listened to Susanna chattering to a fellow passenger. Travelling with Susanna was an ordeal in itself; she was friendly, open, confiding. Adults responded readily; asking her questions, offering her sweets.

'You mustn't take sweets from strangers,' he admonished her, once the large, chatty old lady had got off the train at Honiton. 'I've told you over and over again.' But she popped the sweet into her mouth anyway. Cheek bulging, she grimaced at him.

'Aagh!' She clutched at her throat. 'I'm just coming to the poisoned bit.' She rolled her eyes, gasping artistically, and he grinned unwillingly, pushing her off as she slumped against him.

'Shut up, you clot. And you know you shouldn't. Caroline told us.'

'I know.' Susanna sat upright. 'But it depends who it is. She was nice.'

Mole sighed. Everyone was nice to Susanna; she seemed to inspire it. Her belief that anyone she met was certain to become a dear old friend was generally justified. He, on the other hand, trusted no one. He was terrified when she went off blithely to the lavatory, fearing that someone might be lying in wait for her, enticing her away with inducements of sweets or toys or a puppy. He'd read about such things in the newspapers, and he'd begged Caroline to forbid Susanna to talk to strangers. Caroline had tried to explain that she did not want to destroy Susanna's faith in people. Of course she must be careful and sensible but no harm could come to her whilst Mole was with her.

'But I'm *not* always with her,' he'd explained. 'I can't watch her all the time . . .'

He'd recognised the compassionate look she'd given him. He was used to it now; knew what they were all thinking.

Mole thought: But I *am* better. I don't think about it nearly as much as I did, but the world is *dangerous* . . .

The thought of anything happening to Susanna made him breathless with terror and he had forced Caroline to promise that Susanna should not be allowed to travel alone once he'd left Herongate House. In the autumn he would start at Blundell's School, where generations of Chadwicks had gone before him, but Susanna would stay on in the New Forest. She showed no signs of anxiety, beyond saying that it wouldn't be the same without him, but he worried about her. In the end he'd gone to Uncle Theo.

'Love is very terrible,' he'd agreed gravely, 'but it is wonderful, too. Even on our pathetic human level it can transform. It can cure and heal but it can also destroy. Do you worry about Susanna for her own sake or for yours?'

'For mine?'

'It's difficult,' Uncle Theo had said thoughtfully. 'Generally it is not clear cut, of course. Love is a muddly old business. Do you worry because Susanna might suffer or because you cannot bear the thought of being without her?

Mole remembered how he'd stood stiff and straight, feeling miserable and confused. 'It's b-both,' he'd said at last. 'I don't want anything to happen to her like in the p-papers. But I . . . *need* her.'

He'd said that, about needing her, angrily, not wanting to admit it. He'd felt ashamed.

'Why not?' Uncle Theo had asked calmly. 'We all' need each other on one level or another. Perfectly reasonable. But you can't put a cage round Susanna and make her a prisoner of your love. It wouldn't be fair to her. She must have her own freedom as you have yours. That's the problem with loving. Instinctively we wish to bind our loved ones to us, for all sorts of reasons, but we must resist it. It is not fair to protect people indefinitely, unless we can guarantee that we shall always be there with them. They must learn to protect themselves. Look upon life as a river. We cannot walk beside it, watching it fearfully, clutching someone's hand. Sooner or later we must get in and learn to swim. Susanna must learn, too, but we shall all be as close as possible whilst she's doing it.'

'But I shan't be with her after next term,' Mole had persisted. 'That's the whole point. Who will be close to her then?'

'In the autumn,' Uncle Theo had said, 'she will

have been away at school for three years. Susanna's been lucky to find her feet with you around. She's made lots of friends who will look out for her. You mustn't worry too much, Mole. It can be terrible to be worried about, you know. Suffocating and enfeebling.'

Although Uncle Theo used funny words, he'd known at once what he meant. It was how *he* felt when Fliss worried about him.

'Can you remember how you felt that first time you travelled alone?' his uncle had asked. 'And how you ran round the spinney the next morning?' Mole had nodded. 'How? How did you feel?'

Mole had hesitated. 'Good,' he'd said at last. 'Sort of . . . strong.'

'Yes.' Uncle Theo had nodded. 'And do you see how one thing led to another? Because you completed the journey alone, it gave you the courage to run round the spinney. Do you see? That's how life teaches us. We go from strength to strength. If we are allowed to. But supposing Grandmother had never allowed you to travel alone because she feared for your safety?'

Mole had stared at him and Uncle Theo had smiled back. 'We were all so worried that day. If anything had happened to you we would never have forgiven ourselves, yet we had to let you do it. To let you grow.'

Mole had been silent, working it out. 'Loving people is terrible,' he'd burst out at last. 'It's . . . t-terrible.'

'Terrible,' his uncle had agreed. 'And wonderful. It is like life. It gives and takes away. It is neither cruel nor unfair but simply the law of nature. There must be laws or the muddle would be indescribable.'

Now, Mole looked out across the estuary. The tide

was ebbing and the small dinghies leaned, showing their keels. Waders ran about in the gleaming mud at the water's edge and a cormorant flew, low and straight, heading out to sea. Out in the deep-water channel boats lay quietly at anchor whilst the seagulls swooped above them, screaming hoarsely. The sun shone from behind rags of cloud, silvering the water. A heron rose with its cranking cry and flapped slowly up the estuary, long legs trailing.

'Look,' Susanna was saying, nose pressed to the window. 'That's where Fliss is at college over there.'

Watching from the train, Mole felt a sense of peace creep round his heart. Here things always stayed the same, quiet and unchanging, away from the busy, dangerous world . . . Susanna was pulling at his arm, showing him the deer under the trees. For a moment their hands touched and held tightly and he felt hot tears at the back of his throat. She always seemed to know . . .

'Well then.' She was back in her seat, feet swinging. 'Not long now. We'll see the sea in a minute. Where's the chocolate?'

Caroline was waiting, waving on the platform as the train drew in. They collected their bags and went to meet her, hugging her, passing out together to find the car. It was Mole's turn to sit in the front, watching for the familiar landmarks as Susanna chattered away in the back: the castle, the Queen's Arms, the water wheel at Shinners Bridge, Dartington School. As the car pulled into the courtyard he felt a sense of relaxation that as yet he had only ever known here at The Keep. Tension and fear dropped away from him and he wondered if there would ever be anywhere else where he might experience this release from pressure. Grandmother was coming down the steps. She moved slowly and he saw, suddenly, that she was old ... Terror gripped, plunging him back into the familiar abyss. For a brief moment of clarity he saw fear for the canker that it is, eating, corroding, destroying, the serpent in the Garden of Eden. Deliberately he fought it down, trampled it underfoot – and climbed out smiling.

'Hello, Grandmother,' he said, stretching up for her kiss. 'Here we are. Safe and sound.'

Three days after the children returned to school, Mrs Pooter died. She did it in her own way, just as she had lived, and with no fuss at all. Although recently she had often opted out of the early walk, on this particular morning she decided to go with Fox and Mugwump. It was a clear bright morning, a forerunner of spring, with swags of cobwebs slung about the gorse bushes and the grass wet with a heavy dew. Catkins hung on the hazel-nut tree and snowdrops blossomed by the wall. Fox walked slowly, keeping at Mrs Pooter's pace, whilst Mugwump ran on ahead, nose to earth. The sky was clear, a tender greenish blue, and the air was soft and mild. Fox breathed deeply and stretched himself, pulling back his shoulders. He looked younger than his seventy-three years. Hard work had kept him lithe and strong, and his skin was weatherbeaten, rough and lined as the bark of an old tree.

He glanced back, checking on Mrs Pooter fossicking slowly in the rear, and stared out again across the hillside where he had walked with her for so many years. The trees of the spinney stood black against the soft green of the hill that rose up behind it and Fox shook his head, whistling a little between his teeth. It was odd that Mole should have run round the spinney again almost as soon as he'd arrived home for half term.

Fox thought: He was testing himself again. No doubt about that. But why *then*? Hardly got in through the door . . .

He shook his head, reaching into his waistcoat pocket for his crumpled packet of cigarettes. The boy was better, no doubt about it, but that sort of thing might come back at any time and then what? This stiff-upper-lip approach was all very well but it could make people hard. He'd seen them in the war; hard on themselves and hard on other people, too. They were bred to lead, to be brave, to take responsibility, and there was no room for softness or weakness. It didn't seem right, somehow, but then how would it be if everyone was soft and weak, wanting to be cosseted and looked after; no one wanting to be responsible for themselves but pushing it on to others? It took all sorts, that was the point.

Fox glanced around again and saw Mrs Pooter standing erect, ears up. A rabbit broke cover and she was after it, just like the old days. He watched, laughing, but she gave up the chase quite soon, coming back panting up the hill, pushing past his caressing hand, just as she had always done, heading for home.

'Old bitch,' he said affectionately and whistled for Mugwump.

When they arrived back in the yard, Mrs Pooter

was drinking deeply from the bowl of cold water but, instead of going into the kitchen as usual, she wandered out into the garden. Fox let her go. He was looking forward to his breakfast and to telling Ellen about the rabbit.

He found her much later, on his way to the greenhouse. She was lying in the orchard under an apple tree, as though she were asleep, and he bent to stroke her before he realised how stiff and still she lay. He crouched then, running his hand over her coat, tears streaming down his face.

'Old bitch,' he muttered, over and over. 'Old bitch . . .'

Caroline found them both as she went on her way to the kitchen garden to sow onions. She stood for a moment, biting her lip, her hand on his shoulder. He looked up at her, swallowing, his face seamed with tears, and presently she helped him up and led him away to the kitchen and to Ellen.

It was Fliss who wrote to Kit. 'It would be terrible for her,' she'd said to Caroline, 'to come home thinking Mrs Pooter was still here and suddenly finding she isn't. Much worse than hearing by letter. I'll tell her about the rabbit and everything. No, we can't telephone. It's stuck out in the hallway and anyone might see her when she cries.'

The letter was put into her pigeonhole in the hall and Kit collected it when she came back late in the afternoon. She was slitting it open when Jake came in behind her. She grinned at him.

'Letter from my little coz,' she said. 'Darling old Flissy. She keeps me up with all the news . . .'

She was pulling the letter out of the envelope as he slipped an arm about her and suggested coffee.

'Mmm,' she murmured absently, her eyes racing over the written lines. 'Why not? *Oh!*'

It was an exclamation of pain and he looked at her sharply. 'What? What's wrong?'

'Mrs Pooter,' whispered Kit. She clenched her fist on the letter, tears slipping down her cheeks. 'Our dog. Oh, I can't bear it. Mrs Pooter's dead and I didn't say goodbye. Oh, no . . .'

She stood like a child in the middle of the hall, weeping silently, the letter clutched in her hand. Students coming in glanced at her curiously and Jake drew her gently with him, towards his flat beside the front door. She went with him unresistingly and he sat her down in an old lumpy armchair while he went to light the gas under the kettle. He came back and kneeled beside her, passing her his handkerchief, holding her hand.

'I've known her for ever, you see,' she burst out. 'Since she was a puppy with huge paws and floppy ears. I named her. She just was . . . you know . . . Mrs Pooter. It's odd that, isn't it? You just know what's right for a puppy . . . The funny thing is that she was an absolute cow really . . .'

Kit put her face down on the arm of the chair and cried in earnest. Presently Jake went out, turned the kettle off, and, coming back, took her into her arms.

It was days before Kit could think about Mrs Pooter without bursting into tears. As she sat at one of the long oak tables in the English library in Gower Street a week or two later, she found Fliss's letter stuffed into her jacket pocket. For a moment she wondered how it had come there – and then remembered how she had read the letter and cried . . . and been comforted. Kit smiled reminiscently. It had been sad and beautiful and very, very comforting. How nice it was when someone took charge of you in that situation, decided what you needed and gave it to you. She reflected on the niceness of dark young men and the various forms of comfort, continuing to smile to herself. Presently she realised that further along the table another young man was sitting watching her, smiling back at her.

Kit stared at him. She did not recognise him, although that was hardly surprising, but he looked rather fun. He had a good strong jaw and his hair was a dark reddish colour. The smile died from Kit's face. His hair was exactly the colour of Mrs Pooter's fur . . . Kit frowned fiercely, shook her head abruptly as tears stung her eyes, and, gathering up her books, she hurried away, leaving the young man staring after her in surprise.

Fliss also wrote to Mole, who broke the news to Susanna. They were both upset, shocked by the knowledge that they would never see Mrs Pooter again.

'I hope they've given her a proper funeral,' said Susanna gloomily as they walked beside the lake together at break time, 'with a cross and things.'

'Fliss says that Fox has put her beside the wall out on the hillside,' Mole consoled her. 'It was where she liked best.' He swallowed, forcing his mind away from death, the heavy earth, corruption. 'Remember how she used to chase the rabbits?'

LOOKING FORWARD

'Perhaps we'll get another dog,' said Susanna hopefully. 'It won't seem right without Mrs Pooter. The
kitchen wouldn't be the same and Kit wouldn't have
anyone to get into the dog basket with.'

'There's Mugwump,' Mole pointed out. 'I expect
he'll use the dog basket now. Mrs Pooter would never
let him before.'

'But we *need* two dogs,' said Susanna. 'We've *always*
had two dogs.'

'I'm sure we'll have another,' said Mole comfortingly. 'Course we will. I wonder what it'll be like?'

'I'd like one that looks like Timmy,' said Susanna at
once. 'Then we could really be the Famous Five.'

'The Famous Two, anyway,' said Mole, relieved to
see her looking happier again. 'There's the bell. Come
on. Don't worry. I bet there will be another dog by the
time we go home again.'

Chapter Twenty-four

After lunch one cold afternoon in March, Freddy sat at the piano in the drawing room. Bright sunshine filled the room but she was grateful for the comfort of the log fire. The delicate scent of some early narcissi drifted on the warm air and sprays of *Garrya elliptica*, with silken tassels of creamy yellow, stood in a jug on a small mahogany table. She had chosen to play Bach's Italian Concerto, which suited her mood perfectly, being both grave and light-hearted, serious yet cheerful. As she played the thick opening chords of the *Allegro* she was contemplating her good fortune and deep contentment whilst, at a different level, she also brooded on the future of her grandchildren. Playing the piano had always helped her to sort out her thoughts and clear her mind. It calmed and soothed her in times of anxiety and stress and cheered her when she was depressed. At this moment she felt none of those emotions. The approach of spring, this well-loved room, the narcissi, all these added to her deep contentment and she sighed with happiness. As for the children, the future looked promising. It seemed unbelievable that Hal had nearly finished at Dartmouth. How quickly those years had passed. His career would continue to follow the familiar pattern; he would complete his fourth-year courses at various naval establishments, before going to sea to get his Bridge Watch-keeping certificate and his Ocean Navigation certificate. He needed these for promotion to the rank of lieutenant. Having achieved them he would, no doubt, be posted to a cruiser or a frigate and go off to sea. He was doing well and she had every confidence that he would follow in the Chadwick tradition of the service but prayed it would be without the tragedy of war.

She smiled a little to herself as she played, thinking of Hal and how like John he was: so tall and fair; purposeful and yet such fun. She was a little surprised that he had not yet brought home a girlfriend, although she was relieved that he was not yet involved with any one girl. She knew that socially he moved in groups of young people and that he would be meeting the sisters of the other young acting sub-lieutenants as well as the girls – usually nurses – who were invited to make up the numbers at naval parties. No doubt he was playing the field and there was always Fliss and Kit to take along if he needed a partner. Soon enough he would arrive with some beautiful and delightful girl: strong and sensible enough to be a supportive service wife; clever and able enough to promote his career; a suitable future chatelaine for The Keep.

Kit, too, would graduate this year and, meanwhile, had a job already. There was talk of her position at the gallery becoming full time after the summer and, although Freddy wished that Kit was nearer home, it was a comfort to know that she would be settled once she had finished her degree course. After that business with the young student in her first year, Freddy had feared that there might be trouble with Kit. She was very like Prue, affectionate, warm-hearted, scatty, but she also had the Chadwick determination and plenty of self-confidence. Kit was Prue's responsibility – as was Hal – but the problem was that Prue might not be capable of exerting the necessary influence when it was required. Of course, she had been very sensible when Kit had wanted to become engaged, telephoning for advice, anxious lest Kit might commit herself unwisely. Freddy had not hesitated. If her grandchildren decided to marry before they qualified then they must do so without her financial support. Kit's letters had been eloquent and touching but Freddy remained unmoved. She had discussed it at length with Theo, who had agreed with her. If Kit's passion was genuine then, no doubt, it would survive two years. As it happened, it had barely lasted through the long vacation.

'The relief!' Prue had said to Freddy on the telephone. 'He was a very dreary boy, you know. Not Kit's type at all, I should have said. Honestly, these children.'

Freddy, remembering Tony, held her peace but she was relieved that the problem was solved whilst at the same time giving the other children a warning shot across the bows. Not that she really had any fears for Fliss. She was so steady and sensible; a quiet dependable child, perfectly happy to be trailed round by Hal as a partner, making up foursomes, fitting in when needed. It was wonderful for her to have this social experience whilst under Hal's protection for, although she was a pretty girl, she was very shy and serious and most unlikely to encourage the young men. No doubt these parties and Ladies' Nights would teach her a few valuable lessons and give her confidence.

As for Mole . . . As Freddy passed on into the quieter mood of the *Andante*, she decided that she felt very confident about Mole. She knew that this feeling might swing back to anxiety at any moment – but today she felt hopeful, happy, positive. Mole was coming to terms with his fears and learning to deal with them. It had been unrealistic to imagine that he would miraculously recover from the tragedy that had shadowed his young life. It had bit too deep and must leave a mark. Nevertheless, he was able to control his terrors and it was to be hoped that, as he grew older, these would fade and dwindle so that he would see them in a more natural perspective. She remembered the day that he had run round the spinney and how he and Fox had come back together, full of themselves. Ellen had brought the news with the early morning tea and for one brief moment their hands had reached out, gripping tightly; no more emotion than that, but it said everything. Mole had been speechless with a sense of achievement, white with excitement. She knew that he wanted to join the Navy but recently he had told her that he wanted to be a submariner.

Theo had laughed at her surprise. He thought it perfectly reasonable that Mole of all people should want to join a branch of the service which was so secretive and subterranean. It was, he reminded her, Mole's nature. On reflection Freddy could see that this was so; still it had come as a bit of a shock. She felt a chill on her skin at the thought of Mole, closed into the sinister black hull, cruising secretly beneath the surface of the sea. However, it was foolish to worry about it so far in advance. It was at least four years before he could sit the AIB and another four – assuming that he passed – before he would take his specialisation. Plenty of time . . .

Freddy played on, thinking of Susanna. Of all her beloved grandchildren this was the one she worried about least. Susanna was such a happy child, cheerful and well balanced, as she had been from those earliest days at The Keep. Mole would miss her when he went to Blundell's in the autumn. She was so wonderfully normal, so refreshingly direct. It was Susanna who had made the observation that set them all thinking one day at lunch, when the whole family had been at The Keep together.

'We shan't know how to be husbands and wives,' she'd said, following a conversation about marriage. 'We haven't got anyone to copy.'

Silence had followed this remark whilst Susanna had ploughed on busily with her steak and kidney pudding, unaware of the reaction. Freddy had looked at Theo, who was frowning at his plate, and then at Prue – who'd said, 'Well, the twins have had me,' rather dubiously, as though she'd expected someone to say that she had not been a very good example.

'But you're not a husband and wife,' Susanna had pointed out. 'You're just a mother.'

'I see what she's getting at,' Kit had agreed. 'There are no actual couples, are there? But does it really matter? Can we be good husbands and wives without an example, Hal? What do you think, Fliss?'

As the melody gently unwound, Freddy remembered that Fliss had gone scarlet. It would have almost been amusing if it hadn't been so distressing. Freddy had thought: she really is too sensitive, poor lamb – and then Ellen had come in to collect the plates and the moment had passed. She'd found herself thinking about it afterwards, however.

'Is she right?' she'd asked Theo when they were alone.

'I've no idea,' he'd answered honestly. 'I do hope not.'

'Trust Susanna,' she'd said, almost crossly – and he'd laughed at her.

'For giving you something else to worry about?' he'd asked. 'John and Peter managed very well without a father as an example. They were good husbands.'

'That's true,' she'd agreed at once, her brow clearing a little. 'At least, Peter was. Poor John hardly lived long enough to find out.'

'He must have been a pretty good husband for Prue to have mourned him for so long,' Theo had said gently.

She'd smiled at him gratefully. 'I think Peter was a good husband *and* father,' she'd said thoughtfully. 'Jamie and Fliss adored him. But I suppose all mothers want to think that their sons and daughters are perfect.'

'Surely even mothers aren't quite so altruistic?' he'd asked provocatively.

She'd scowled at him. 'We *hope* they might be perfect.'

'Clearly a triumph of hope over experience,' he'd murmured.

She laughed aloud, now, as she remembered his remark. How happy she had been since he had returned to The Keep; how lucky they were to be able to live so easily and contentedly together. Now that he was here with her, her need to punish him, to fight against his beliefs, had gradually died away and she wished he had not waited so long before joining her. She regretted all those years when he had stubbornly lived in Southsea when he might have been here. Had there been someone – a woman – who had kept him there? The stab of the old, once-familiar jealousy surprised her. She had thought that this, too, was a thing of the past; it was too humiliating to feel these pangs when you were seventy. She pushed the thought aside by deliberately concentrating on a decision she must make soon: to whom should she leave The Keep? Her instinct was to leave it to Hal. He might reasonably hope to be based at Devonport and his wife would be able to remain at The Keep whilst he was at sea. He would have the means to support the establishment and it would make an excellent back-drop to his career. He was also the eldest grandchild, so like her beloved John, and the most sensible and responsible of them all; but what of the others who lived at The Keep? She must make provision for them, too. It was quite an unlikely scenario but supposing – just supposing – Hal were to marry a wife who refused to give a home to Theo, or to Mole and Susanna whilst they were still growing up; who turned out Ellen and Fox? Supposing she persuaded him to sell it?

It seemed impossible that Hal should marry such a woman; nevertheless Freddy felt a thrill of fear. Fliss and Kit – and, in time, Susanna – would no doubt marry men whose jobs might make it impossible for them to live at The Keep and, if she left it to all five of them, they might fall out over it. There was another solution. It should be left to Theo. Of all of them he had the most right; it had been his home first, before any of them. He would watch over the children and Ellen and Fox. He was, in many ways, the best custodian. For the first time in her life, Freddy wished that Theo was much younger. There was only three years between them, which meant that, in the event of her own death, this problem must immediately be his. Could she be sure he would solve it wisely?

She played on, the Venetian stillness of the *Andante* calming her anxiety. There was a third solution: that The Keep should be left in trust with all sorts of conditions attached and Theo, Hal and Mole could be trustees. It might not seem fair but it was the only possible option. Everybody would be taken care of and each loose end tied up. The Keep was a family home and must remain so; it must continue to be a refuge for any of the children who might need it . . . As the sparkling extrovert notes of the *Presto* filled the drawing room Freddy felt that this was the right decision and her confidence and happiness returned. She would talk it through with Theo and then act upon it.

In the kitchen, the conversation turned upon dogs.

'He misses her,' said Fox, sitting at the table whilst Ellen and Caroline cleared up the lunch things, Ellen washing, Caroline drying and putting away.

'Very likely,' said Ellen, hands plunged in soapsuds. 'So do we all.'

'Pining,' said Fox. 'That's what he be doing. Pining.'

'I expect he'll get used to it,' said Caroline comfortingly, as she stacked clean plates on the table. 'He's bound to find it odd at first.'

'Lost all his spirit,' Fox sighed heavily. ''Tis sad really. He'll be old before his time.'

'As I shall be,' said Ellen sharply, 'if you keep on about it. No more puppies. And there's an end to it.'

Fox gazed mournfully at Mugwump who lay in the dog basket, one eye open, watching. 'He knows we be talking about him.'

'Hardly surprising.' Ellen whisked her cloth vigorously over a saucepan. 'You've done nothing else this last week.'

Caroline looked at Fox sympathetically. He raised his eyebrows; she shook her head. He had asked her to try to soften Ellen's heart in the matter of a puppy but it was clear that Ellen was standing firm.

'We're too old for puppies,' she'd said. 'And *don't* tell me you'll have it down in the gatehouse with you. I've heard it all before.'

'Caroline—' began the persistent Fox.

'Caroline is too busy to be training puppies.' Ellen wouldn't let him finish. 'We've got Mugwump. We don't need any more dogs.'

'It's only being Mrs Pooter's own stock,' he said now for the hundredth time. 'If it were any other puppy, I'd agree with you. But this being her great-granddaughter . . . Funny that her red coat should've thrown up again, isn't it? Looks just like Mrs P. did when I brought her home all those years ago.'

'I had heard talk,' said Ellen ominously, 'of planting early potatoes this afternoon. Or did I hear wrong, I wonder. This weather won't hold for ever.'

With a self-pitying sigh, Fox got to his feet, picked up his cap and went out, Mugwump at his heels. For a moment there was a silence as the two women finished the clearing up.

'*Could* we cope with a puppy?' asked Caroline after a while. 'I'll be responsible for its house-training. He seems to miss her so much. And if this puppy *is* her however many great-granddaughter . . .'

Ellen snorted fiercely. 'Devious, that's what he is. Went back to where he took her pups. Eight years ago that was. He went back just on the off chance. Whatever next, I wonder. Didn't say a word to anyone. Devious, that's what he is.'

'I think it's just that he misses her,' ventured Caroline, who suspected that Ellen wished that she'd thought of it herself. Fox's initiative had annoyed her and she was unwilling to applaud it. 'She was very much his dog, wasn't she?'

'So you said before.'

'I know you looked after her,' said Caroline placatingly. 'I realise how much work a puppy is for you. I'd do as much as I could, of course. It *is* a bit of a miracle, isn't it, that there should be a litter just now?'

'As to miracles,' retorted Ellen, 'I should think that the good Lord has far too much on his plate to be worrying about puppies. As I have.'

'Oh well. You're probably right. Of course, the children would have loved it. Imagine their faces when they arrived home for the Easter holidays and found a puppy waiting for them. I always love that story you tell about Mole's first night here and how Mugwump slept in his bed. I'm sure the dogs have helped him enormously. They're terribly upset about Mrs Pooter, apparently. Fliss wrote to them, of course. It's going to seem so odd to them without her here, isn't it?'

Ellen turned suddenly to face her and Caroline fell silent. 'Very well,' she said weightily. 'Very well, Caroline. You've said your piece and I know when I'm outnumbered. If Madam agrees to another puppy then I shall give in with good grace.'

'Oh, Ellen.' Caroline put her arms round the unyielding form and hugged her. 'Oh, bless you. I'm sure Mrs Chadwick will agree to it and I promise we'll try not to let it bother you.'

'Well then.' Ellen straightened her pinafore. 'You'd better tell him when you go down to the greenhouses. It'll put an end to his pining if nothing else. But you just make certain with Madam, mind. Off you go then. I've got work to do even if no one else round here has.'

Chapter Twenty-five

Miles stood in The Vic deep in thought, the remains of a pint before him on the bar. The end of term was approaching and, with it, the Easter Ball. It was already agreed that he would be included in the party from The Keep and he was considering whether he had the courage to chance his arm and make his intentions a little more open. He had half wondered whether to speak to Hal but had decided that it might be embarrassing for both of them. Another thought was flickering in the back of his mind but, even as he brooded on it, the door opened and a group of young cadets came in. They saw him at once and there was a chorus of 'Good evening, sir,' as they crowded to the bar.

Suspecting that his presence would hamper their flirtation with the pretty barmaid, Miles swallowed down his pint and wandered out into Victoria Road. As he walked home through the quiet streets of Dartmouth, he asked himself if he were mad even to consider marrying again. He was old enough and wise enough to know that he would miss the freedom which he now took for granted; that the effort required to make any relationship really work might

319

be beyond him. He would stay at Dartmouth for little more than eighteen months when, with luck, he would be promoted out of his job as divisional officer and might even be given command of a cruiser. Was it fair to marry a young woman and leave her alone for so long? Belinda had hated it. Miles felt his spirits flattening as he remembered the tears. Of course, neither of them had realised that she was already beginning to suffer from the insidious disease and he had often been impatient with her. He was, after all, a sailor; no good whining if he went to sea. The trouble was that they were in love and, with all the misguided confidence of youth, had imagined that love was enough.

Miles knew now that it wasn't nearly enough; especially in a job where the husband was away so much and the wife carried such a lot of responsibility, whilst at the same time coping with loneliness. The first few years had been happy enough, despite the Navy disapproving of young officers marrying whilst they were still at Dartmouth. Belinda's wealthy father – a widower – had encouraged the match, however, and bought them the little house in Above Town which Belinda loved so much. During their first year together – Miles's third at the college – they had invited his young brother officers to parties and impromptu suppers. They had flirted with Belinda, envied his independent married status and pulled his leg unmercifully on the mornings when he came in looking tired. During fourth-year courses Belinda had followed him around – staying in the most unlikely places and looking after the other young officers' girlfriends – returning to Dartmouth for leave periods and inviting friends to stay. What fun they'd all had together.

It was once the fourth-year courses were over and he'd gone to sea on a frigate that the problems had started. Belinda missed him terribly. With hindsight it was clear that she might have been happier if she'd stayed in Portsmouth, living in a married quarter or a hiring, and getting to know the other young wives. Instead she had insisted on returning to the house in Dartmouth. He could understand that she'd felt safer there, with all her happy memories, but her true happiness was bound up in him and, once he had gone, she'd been left with little purpose. Without the framework of the Navy she'd found it difficult to make friends, and by then she knew no one at the college, although one or two wives of the staff who lived in had made a few attempts to draw her into various activities. She'd been too young to wish to join the clubs and societies to which the matrons of the town belonged and, since she'd had no children, had been excluded from the camaraderie that grows around the school gate.

When he'd returned from sea, Miles had tried to persuade her to move back to Portsmouth so that she might have the support of the other wives but she'd refused. Even now, he could not decide why she had resisted so strongly. She had loved her little house but by then it had become almost a prison. She'd complained of the steepness of the hills when carrying shopping home; the difficulty of crossing the river to catch the train from Kingswear when she'd wanted to visit her family. Her father had offered to buy them a car but – to Miles's chagrin – she'd refused, saying

that she would be too nervous to drive in the narrow
Devon lanes. As the months passed he'd detected a
stubbornness in her character, an intractability, which
had made their lives even more difficult. Gradually it
had become obvious that the slow breaking-down of
the relationship was to be all Miles's fault. His refusal
to give up the sea showed that he loved it more than
he loved her; his impatience with her nervousness
indicated his insensitivity. When her illness was diagnosed there had been a kind of quiet triumph on her
part and he had felt guilty and ashamed. An older
cousin had come to stay with her when he'd gone
back to sea and, when he was lucky enough to be
given a ship refit at Devonport, he'd bought a car
which meant that he could be at home with her most
nights. He had done his best to be caring and loving,
to do everything within his power to make her
happy . . .

As Miles fitted his key into the front door he had
begun to feel a deadening sense of inadequacy. Could
it work for him again? The stubborn refusal to give in,
which was characteristic of him, stiffened his jaw.

He thought: Damned if I won't have a shot at it.

Shutting the door behind him, he lit a cigarette and
sat down by the telephone.

It was Caroline who answered the telephone and
Caroline who let him in the next afternoon after
lunch.

'You're being very mysterious,' she said lightly,
trying to hide her inclination to beam madly at him.
'Mrs Chadwick is in the drawing room.'

He grimaced at her. 'I'm sure you've guessed

exactly what it's all about,' he said. 'I'm being very formal and proper. Wish me luck.'

She showed him into the room and then, collecting Mugwump, took herself off to walk on the hillside in an effort to subdue her excitement. His visit could mean only one thing, yet surely he could have approached her directly without going first to Mrs Chadwick? After all, she, Caroline, was not a child. She shook her head, putting his behaviour down to the fact that he worked within a very formal structure, and looked about her. The weather was still cold and bright and a bitter north-easterly wind raced over the hill. The landscape looked bleached and frozen, any hint of spring caught and petrified in the icy grasp of departing winter. The sky was a clear, pure blue and the sun dazzled in her eyes whilst the wind stung her cheeks. She pushed her hands deep into her jacket pockets and followed Mugwump down the narrow tracks, trying hard not to think about the meeting taking place in the drawing room.

As she watched Mugwump pottering slowly ahead, Caroline wondered how he would greet the puppy, secured by an excited Fox and ready to leave its mother in two weeks' time. Everyone – even Ellen – was looking forward to the puppy's arrival, which would be just in time for the school holidays. Nothing had been said to the children yet, just in case there was some last-minute problem, but she could imagine their surprise and delight. It would help them over their grief at losing Mrs Pooter and give them something else to think about. There would be the usual problem of finding a name and – no doubt – Kit would be called upon to conjure up something different and special.

Near the bottom of the hill she paused to pick a few sprays of catkins from the hazel bushes, wrapping the stems in her handkerchief. A jay, scolding raucously, flew out of the spinney. She turned to watch as, with a flash of blue wing and white rump, it sped round the curve of the hill. As she looked back towards the walls of The Keep she could easily imagine how the small Mole must have felt, terrified of losing sight – even briefly – of all that he loved. Her heart contracted with pain. How could she bear to think of leaving them all? How would they manage without her? Of course, the children didn't need a nanny anymore but she was part of their lives – just as they were part of hers. As for the hard physical work, it shouldn't be too difficult to find part-time help to cope with it; nevertheless . . .

She began the ascent, feeling confused. After all, she loved Miles, wanted to be with him – yet the thought of leaving the Chadwicks was a terrible one. Nearer the top, however, her former excitement began to reassert itself and she found herself hurrying, longing to see him, wondering what he was saying to Mrs Chadwick.

Miles took some time coming to the point and, in the end, Freddy kindly but firmly asked him the reason for his visit. Despite his career in the Navy it was clear that he was in awe of the formidable nature of Freddy's character. She sat across the room, relaxed but upright in her chair, shoulders squared, chin raised, watching him.

'The thing is,' he began awkwardly, all memory of his carefully rehearsed speech deserting him, 'the thing is . . .' He hesitated and gazed at her anxiously, biting his lip. 'Perhaps you've guessed what I'm going to say?' he asked hopefully.

Freddy, privately amused at his sudden and complete lack of poise, smiled sweetly upon him. 'I'm afraid I haven't the least idea,' she told him with no suspicion of regret.

'Damn,' he said, thrusting his hand through his hair. 'Sorry. It's just . . . Oh, *hell*. Sorry. The thing is . . .'

'Do you know, I *think* we got that far before?' she told him. 'Perhaps you'd care for a drink instead of that tea? It must be quite cold by now.'

'No, no,' he said at once, snatching up the bone-thin cup and gulping at the lukewarm tea. 'It's fine. Honestly.'

'Well then.' She nodded encouragingly. 'Where were we?'

He looked at her, discomfited, saw her private smile and began to chuckle. 'I'm making a prize ass of myself,' he said ruefully. 'Right. The thing is, Mrs Chadwick, I've fallen in love with your granddaughter Fliss and I should like to ask for her hand in marriage. I know that she's very young and I haven't spoken to her about this but I promise you that I've never felt like this ever in my life before.'

He stopped. The quality of the silence distracted him from his declaration and he saw that Freddy was staring at him with something like horror. He frowned, puzzled, and she leaned forward in her chair.

'You have fallen in love with Fliss?' she asked sharply. 'With *Fliss*?'

'Why, yes.' He shrugged awkwardly; even he had not expected such a negative reaction. 'I know I'm much older than she is but I hope that need not be a reason to refuse me. I truly love her, Mrs Chadwick. This isn't just an infatuation. At least I'm old enough to know that.' He paused and shook his head with a mixture of despondency and chagrin. 'It's clear that you had no idea.'

'If I thought about it all,' said Freddy carefully, 'I would have supposed that it might be Caroline you had come to love.'

Miles shook his head at once. 'I'm terribly fond of her,' he said, 'but there's never been anything like that between us, she'll tell you that. We're good friends and I'm quite sure that she's guessed how I feel about Fliss. We've been thrown together because of our ages, of course, and I like her enormously, but from the first I've been absolutely in love with Fliss.'

'I see. Does Fliss have any idea of your feelings for her?'

'I should have said that it was impossible *not* to see how I feel,' said Miles frankly. 'I feel like a boy of twenty. It's almost humiliating. But I don't want to frighten her or . . . you know?' He appealed to her understanding of the situation. 'It's rather tricky. I decided that it would be best to approach you first. She's so young and innocent.' He rumpled up his hair again, frowning. 'It seemed rather as though I might be taking advantage, if you see what I mean. I have never been alone with her but I think a more experienced girl might have guessed how I felt.'

Freddy watched him. Despite the shock his announcement had given her, and her growing concern for Caroline, she was impressed with Miles and felt a certain admiration and even affection for him.

'I have to tell you,' she said, 'that I should resist any attempt by you to engage Fliss's feelings before she has finished her training. It is a rule I have found it necessary to apply within the family. She is very young and I don't want her to be distracted and confused whilst she is qualifying. After that, of course . . .'

'But I shall be allowed to see her?' he asked eagerly. 'If I promise not to crowd her? Nothing need change?'

'Nothing need change,' she agreed, smiling at him. 'If you are prepared to wait then who knows what might happen? And now, you know, I think that we should both have a small drink. Whisky?'

'Absolutely,' he said fervently. 'Thank you for listening to me and not throwing me out on my ear.'

'What a strange idea you must have of me,' murmured Freddy as she handed him his glass. 'I appreciate your proper feelings and the spirit in which you have taken my decision. Shall we drink to the future?'

As Caroline came into the hall, Freddy was closing the front door behind her. Caroline frowned, puzzled.

'Has he gone?'

Freddy paused, nodded and came across to her, taking her by the arm.

'Come into the drawing room,' she said. 'I want to talk to you. Come along. That's right. Now sit down here beside me.'

They sat together on the sofa, slightly turned so as to face each other. Caroline felt a tremendous anxiety and she watched Freddy impatiently, waiting for her to speak, placing the catkins on the cushion between them. Freddy, still recovering from her shock, sat silently, trying to bring her ideas into order.

'I simply don't know what to say to you,' she said at last, to Caroline's surprise. 'I think I have guessed how you feel about Miles Harrington, my dear, but I have to tell you that he has been here today to ask how I would react if he were to ask Fliss to marry him.'

Caroline sat quite still. She could not speak; it was as if all her breath had been squeezed out of her body. She shook her head, staring blankly at Freddy, who leaned forward a little and took her hand.

'My dear child,' she said compassionately, 'I had no more idea than you had. I was quite sure that he was interested in you. It seems that he thought you knew how he felt.'

Caroline felt a huge scorching wave of humiliation flood slowly through her whole frame. It was the Jeremy thing all over again. She glared at Mrs Chadwick, daring her to pity her, gathering her pride around her as though it were armour.

She thought: I hate men. I just hate bloody men.

'Naturally I said nothing about my suspicions,' Freddy was saying, 'but I have to ask you, Caroline, whether you think Fliss has any interest in Miles. Forgive me but this has taken me completely by surprise.'

Caroline swallowed and withdrew her hand, crossing her arms beneath her breast. She frowned, as if trying to understand Freddy's words.

'Fliss has no eyes for anyone but Hal,' she said dully, at last. 'She likes Miles but he's so much older . . . He's always very sweet to her and she feels safe with him. No more than that.'

There was a long silence. Caroline was aware of a paralysing lethargy stealing over her, a numbness which made it impossible to stand up, yet she longed to leave the room, to be alone. She struggled feebly against Freddy's love and compassion which was weakening her, making her want to weep, to confide.

'I feel such a fool,' she heard herself say. 'Oh God, what a prize idiot I've been.'

Her voice shook and she put her hands over her eyes. She felt rather than saw Freddy stand up and presently a cold glass was pressed into her hand.

'Drink it,' said the voice above her head. 'You've had a shock. It will do you good.'

She gulped back the whisky, which made her choke, and tears streamed down her cheeks.

'I don't know what to do,' she said miserably. 'I thought he cared about me.'

'I think he *is* fond of you.' Freddy was sitting beside her again. 'It's simply that he has conceived a romantic attachment for Fliss. It seems perfectly genuine but I've told him that there is to be no question of any relationship until she is qualified. She's much too young to know her own mind yet, anyway. He's accepted that.'

'I can't bear it,' said Caroline fiercely – but with trembling lips. 'I simply can't *bear* it if he's going to be coming here and . . . and *adoring* her at a decent

329

distance. I simply can't put up with it. I shall have to leave.'

She winced as Freddy's hand closed over hers, strong and hard, her fingers gripping.

'You can't leave us. We need you.'

Caroline stared at her. 'But what about me?' she cried. 'How do you think *I* feel?'

'I think you feel hurt and probably rather foolish,' said Freddy calmly. 'If it's any comfort, he has no idea how you feel about him. But do you really love him, Caroline? Are you absolutely certain? *Is* it really love – or just an excitement? A kind of glamour that goes with the parties and balls, or a true, enduring passion? Would you really leave us – we who love you and are your family? Would you leave us because of Miles Harrington?'

'That's not fair,' burst out Caroline. 'It's . . . it's blackmail.'

'Oh, my dear girl. I simply don't want you to do anything you might regret. In less than four months Hal will have left Dartmouth and there will be no reason for you to see Miles. If Fliss doesn't encourage him he will soon run out of excuses for coming here. Don't let him frighten you away from where you belong.'

'You say that because you need me,' cried Caroline resentfully. 'What would you do without me?'

'I can't imagine,' said Freddy honestly. 'Of course we need you. I don't deny it. But I think you need us, too. More than you will admit at the moment.'

'I don't want to leave you,' said Caroline at last. 'Why should I? I am so happy here. But I thought . . . I thought he loved me.'

'If that had been the case,' said Freddy gently, 'then we would have all been happy to know that you were going to a home of your own with a man whom you loved. None of us would have expected you to sacrifice yourself for us. But why should you leave us now? Where would you go? If necessary I shall insist that Miles stays away from The Keep. He will see Fliss at social events during the next few months. He need not come here.'

Caroline breathed deeply. She gathered up the catkins and stared at them, remembering how she had felt out on the hill.

'I don't know what I want,' she said sadly. 'Just now, when I thought that I might be going to leave you I felt that I couldn't bear it. But how can I face seeing him again? I can't go to the ball. I simply can't.'

'You don't have to do anything you don't wish to,' Freddy assured her. 'You can simply feel unwell. Any excuse will do. We'll think of something. Just don't make any long-term decisions in a hurry. Promise me you will give yourself time to think and I will promise you that Miles will not be invited here.'

'Very well.'

Caroline stood up, hesitated and, with an awkward clumsy gesture, gave Freddy the catkins. The older woman reached up and, drawing her down a little, kissed her lightly on the cheek.

'Thank you,' she said. 'Thank you, Caroline.'

Caroline went out through the hall and paused outside the kitchen. She could hear Ellen and Fox, their voices rising and falling, a chair scraping back, water running from a tap. She turned away and, with a heavy heart, she began to climb the stairs which led

331

to her room on the nursery floor.

In the sitting room Freddy continued to sit, her eyes fixed unseemingly on the catkins. Several thoughts chased through her mind and one particular sentence, which Caroline had uttered, detached itself from the rest and stood out boldly. One or two things became clearer.

Freddy thought: I've been a fool . . .

She heard the sound of tea arriving in the hall and Theo's voice. Rising quickly she went out to see him, closing the door gently behind her, the catkins still clasped in her hand.

Chapter Twenty-six

Prue sat down at the corner table in the canteen and delved into her handbag for a cigarette. Maureen from Lingerie waved cheerfully at her from another table where she was gossiping with Laura from Millinery. They sat with their heads close together, faces prurient with dangerous knowledge: More and Lore, as they referred to each other, could destroy or build a reputation in minutes. Prue smiled back, half tempted to join them. They could always make her laugh and their gossip kept her abreast of life within the large department store. Although she enjoyed the extra time to herself at home, she looked forward to her two days a week at the shop. Now the girls were moving belongings about, gesturing for her to sit with them, and Prue gave up her idea of reading Freddy's letter and picked up her coffee and her bag.

'Thrills and spills,' said Laura, shifting a little to give Prue more room. 'You'll never guess who June saw in the Llandoger Trow on Saturday night.'

'I don't suppose I shall,' agreed Prue, putting her bag down by her chair. 'Out with it.'

'Only,' began Maureen, huge with the news, '*only*

Jenny from Leather Goods with Richard God-almighty Prior. That's all.' She drew in her chin, lips pursed, eyes round with excitement, and Prue began to laugh.

'I don't believe it,' she said. 'Surely he wouldn't take such a chance?' Richard Prior was the Personnel Manager and a married man. 'What was June doing at the Llandoger Trow anyway?'

'Wedding anniversary,' answered Maureen succinctly. 'A rare old treat. Her old man's usually too mean to give you the droppings from his nose but her kids all got together and booked the table. Must've broke his heart paying the bill. June says she had everything going.'

'And when she looked round, there they were,' chipped in Laura. 'Large as life and twice as natural.'

They looked at Prue, their faces bright with mischief, and she grinned back at them. 'And did Mr Prior and Jenny see her?'

'Trust June for that,' said Laura with immense satisfaction. 'Made sure she went out right past their table. She had to drop her handbag they were that wrapped up in themselves. She says Jenny upset her wine and old Prior went white as death.'

'So I should think,' said Maureen virtuously, 'and him married with kids. It's shocking.'

'Poor old Jenny must be embarrassed,' suggested Prue. 'Has she said anything?'

'June hasn't given her the chance.' Laura bent closer. 'She's over there, watching us now. Bet she knows what we're talking about.'

She stared boldly at the luckless Jenny and Prue knew a moment of deep relief that these women had made a friend of her. Jenny's misfortune was that she regarded herself as a cut above the other shop assistants – and let them see it.

'I told June that she should pop in and ask old Prior for a rise,' Maureen was saying, her eyes snapping with glee. 'What d'you bet she'd get it?'

'We'll get it if we don't get a move on.' Laura was looking at her watch. 'Get the sack, that's what we'll get. Come on, More.'

They gathered up their bags, grumbling as usual about the rules, and hurried away with friendly farewells to Prue and sly glances at the discomfited Jenny. Prue settled down and took out Freddy's letter, avoiding Jenny's half-hopeful smile. She knew that Jenny felt that she should be on her side, that she regarded Prue and herself as two of a kind, but Prue had no intention of becoming involved. She thought Jenny was a snob and a bore and she deliberately immersed herself in the letter so that she need not respond. She was halfway down the first page before she took in exactly what Freddy was telling her. Her attention was now fully occupied and she put out a hand, feeling blindly for the ashtray, her eyes riveted on the sheets of writing paper. She stubbed out her cigarette and turned the page:

. . . I am sure that you will be able to sympathise with how Caroline is feeling and wonder if you agree with me that a complete break might not be a help to her. The Easter holidays will be an especially difficult time and Lt. Cdr. Harrington might very well drop in without warning. Would it be possible for you to invite Caroline to stay for a week or two? I know that I am asking a great deal, dear Prue, at a time when you will be looking forward to seeing Kit and Hal but I should be very grateful if you could help us through this difficult moment.

I am confident that Caroline will recover quite quickly but I hate to think of her suffering any humiliation. Nobody, except me – and now you – knows about her attachment, not even Miles Harrington, and I know that I can trust you to keep a secret. As to his feelings for Fliss, that too remains between him and me and, of course, Caroline. I need to give this some thought but I know I can trust your discretion.

Touching on another matter. I have decided to make Hal my heir (although I am creating a trust which will own The Keep) and I should like to have a talk with him privately quite soon. I also think that it might be time for him to have a car of his own. (I know we agreed that this should wait until we judged him mature enough to be sensible and so I should like to hear your view.) As you know, I have always tried to treat the twins equally and so perhaps you would consult with Kit in the matter of a car. Perhaps she would prefer something else although I know she drives. I think she will understand why I am making Hal my heir. He is, after all, the oldest of my grandchildren. The other children will, nevertheless, be properly provided for and The Keep will remain a refuge for any of the family who needs it. We must talk properly about this, my dear Prue, meanwhile I hope that you will agree to my having a discussion with Hal at the earliest opportunity . . .

Prue scrabbled in her handbag for another cigarette. Never had she received such a letter from Freddy; to be applied to for help; Hal to be heir; cars for Kit and Hal . . . Prue inhaled deeply, staring into space.

She thought: Poor, poor Caroline. And after all that business with Jeremy. Oh God, she'll be feeling desperate. Of course she must come . . .

She could see that it was vital that the invitation appeared to be unforced and she racked her brains to think of some good excuse to invite Caroline so that she would suspect nothing. As for Miles Harrington falling for Fliss . . . Prue smoked thoughtfully. In some ways an older man might be good for Fliss: she was shy and innocent but she was also surprisingly mature. Because she was quiet she tended to be overlooked, standing as she did between the confident liveliness of the twins and the needs of the two younger children; yet there was a steadiness about her, an unchangeability, which made her strong and reliable despite her youth. Kit had said – quite recently – that Fliss was in love with Hal. She'd spoken quite lightly but Prue had been surprised at the depth of her own violent reaction against such a thing. Fliss and Hal were like brother and sister; their fathers had been identical twins and Hal had been the image of Jamie. Fliss might look like Alison but Prue was often aware of a definite Chadwick resemblance – Freddy's lift of the chin, Peter's direct look – and she felt very strongly that any such affection should be squashed.

She'd spoken sharply to Kit, saying that Fliss had always adored Hal, that he had replaced Jamie in her affections and that he was just as a brother to her, to suggest anything else was disgusting. Kit, taken aback by such a forceful reaction, had merely shrugged and let it pass.

Prue drank the last of the nearly cold coffee and replaced the cup in its saucer. It might be interesting to know what Fliss thought of Lieutenant-Commander Harrington, although it would be very painful for Caroline should anything come of it. She found herself wondering why Hal had never brought a girl home to meet her. Up until this point, she had put it down to a combination of Freddy's edict and a young man's tendency to play the field ... Prue frowned. Perhaps it would be a good idea to get away for Easter; to take the twins and Caroline right away. She glanced at her watch and hastily crushed out her cigarette. Folding the sheets of Freddy's letter, she pushed them back into the envelope, tucked it into her bag and made her way out of the canteen and downstairs to the department.

Theo knocked at the door of Freddy's sitting room, waited for her call and entered. Freddy, who was writing letters at her bureau, turned to see him standing there and smiled. Theo recognised the faintly brittle smile that she had been using for the past few days and his serious expression became even more grave.

'Have you a moment?' he asked. 'I should like to talk to you.'

'Yes, of course.'

She gestured to the armchair but remained at her bureau, pen poised. Her head was tilted, her expression alert, almost impatient. He felt that he was being granted an interview and – what was more – granted it unwillingly, but Theo knew how dangerous it was to allow even small misunderstandings to creep into any relationship and he refused to be intimidated. He remained standing and, when he spoke, it was with a directness which her glance did not encourage.

'I have a feeling that there is some kind of conspiracy going on in this house. Am I right, Freddy?'

He saw the familiar tightening of the lips, the upward jerk of the chin, and his heart sank. Until a short while ago he had assumed that this new preoccupation was none of his business and – although he was made anxious by her unusual behaviour – he had been content to allow Freddy to deal with her own problems, whilst remaining ready to offer help if she should require it. Now he watched her, the silence lengthening between them.

'I'm not certain what you mean.'

The cool voice, the faint dismissive shrug, filled him with something like anger. She was lying and he knew it and the look he bent upon her made her bite her lip.

'Yes, you are. Quite certain. Tell me to mind my own business, Freddy, but don't lie to me. I have no wish to interfere but there has been an atmosphere during these last few days which is not a happy one. Can you tell me why that should be?'

'My dear Theo!' Her laugh was forced and unconvincing. 'I know I share most of my troubles with you but there *are* a few things which I prefer to keep to myself.'

'I accept that,' he said at once. 'Nevertheless, this is the first time in all these years we have lived here together – how many are they? Four? Five? – that there has been such an atmosphere. Are you telling me that you are not aware of it?'

She watched him angrily. If she dismissed it as nonsense she knew she would deny and undervalue their friendship; if she admitted to it she would also have to attempt to explain it. His look did not waver and she shrank before it. This was the Theo she understood least, feared most: a Theo who put aside the comforting qualities of his personality and was ready to expose the weaknesses and falsehoods to which people clung. It was the Theo whose good opinion she most valued; the Theo she hated to disappoint. As their wills clashed she felt that they might be standing at a crossroads. Theo knew they were. It was the very situation he had most dreaded; the reason he had stayed away so long. *His* love for her would not allow her to cheat. *Her* pride might never forgive him for it.

She sighed heavily, with an air of exaggerated patience. 'I've been worrying about Hal,' she told him – and he knew instinctively that this was partly true – but her eyes were evasive. 'We've been through this whole thing about him being my heir. I know you favoured putting all the shares into a trust with The Keep and enough to maintain it but you agreed with me in the end that this *was* the right thing to do. However it's not *quite* that simple.' Her tone was aggrieved, even patronising, as if she were explaining something to a particularly stupid child. 'It is still a very big step and there is a great deal to think about.'

There was a subtle accusation here: that he could have no idea of the weight of responsibility she carried. 'I have to think about the other children, to be absolutely certain that everything is dealt with carefully.'

She had turned back to her desk, her shoulders tense, one hand clenched, her jaw rigid. He waited, willing her to speak openly, but there was only silence. He braced himself, emptying his mind briefly, seeking help.

'So,' he said at last, reflectively, 'it has nothing to do with a fear which you and Prue seem to share that Hal and Fliss love each other. A love which, between you both, you are hoping to destroy.'

He saw her swallow and felt a great sense of sadness.

Freddy thought: I *knew* I shouldn't have trusted Prue. Why didn't I think to tell her that Theo didn't know? She would have assumed that I had told him everything. Damn, damn, damn. How he must be despising me now . . .

'Is this the reason for making him your heir, Freddy? For buying him a new car which you were determined you would not do until he'd left Dartmouth? For this sudden decision that Prue and the twins must go away for Easter on holiday?'

'That is because of Caroline.' She was stung at last into defending herself, swinging round to face him. 'Can you imagine how she must be feeling?' She caught herself up. 'I imagine Prue has told you everything?' she asked contemptuously.

Theo sighed. 'She assumed I knew,' he said. 'She imagined that you would have shared it with me. I am sorry that you felt you couldn't.'

Freddy looked away from him. Once she'd heard that simple remark – 'Fliss only has eyes for Hal' – and so many things had slotted into place, she'd suspected that her plans of action would not gain Theo's support. She had no choice – so she'd told herself – but to protect the family.

'I hope you agree,' she said resentfully, 'that it is only fair and kind to get Caroline away. She is hurt and humiliated. As for Hal, he is young. He has his whole career ahead of him. Once he leaves Dartmouth he'll see that it was just a childish infatuation. Not even that.'

'So,' said Theo calmly, 'he is to be given grown-up toys, a house, a car, an inheritance to distract him and to encourage him to look for a suitable wife.' He nodded thoughtfully. 'And what of Fliss?'

'Fliss?' She looked at him, her anger turning to puzzlement. 'Fliss will be here with us.'

'Is Fliss to have nothing to distract her from her pain?'

'Pain? For goodness' sake, Theo, she's a child. She has had this infatuation for Hal since she was a child. She has always worshipped him. And it was you – *you*, Theo – who warned me about it. It was you who said that there was danger in her idolatry. You said that too much power was bad for Hal. But we didn't do anything about it, did we? Now she fancies she is in love with him, her own cousin. More like a brother, in fact. It is our fault as much as hers but it has to be stopped. It is unhealthy.'

'It may be *unwise*,' he corrected her, 'but that doesn't mean that her love should be dismissed so lightly. You and Prue are taking Caroline's love for

Miles Harrington very seriously.'

'Caroline is a woman,' cried Freddy. 'Fliss is a child. She has no idea about love.'

'She is not far off twenty,' he said coldly. 'Your age when you married Bertie and came here. Did *you* have no idea about love?'

She gasped, her hands grasping the arms of her chair, unable to answer him. What could she say? She had misjudged her love for Bertie, yet she had loved Theo – his brother – for fifty years. She had been barely twenty . . . She felt weakness stealing over her. She longed for him to comfort her, to reassure her . . . He was speaking to her but she could barely take in the words.

'You are right to accuse me,' he was saying sadly. 'Only now, with hindsight, we can see that Fliss is far more bound up in Hal than we realised. They are still children to us because we have grown old but we mustn't forget what it felt like to be passionately in love.'

The old jealousy clawed at her heart. 'What do *you* know of love?' she cried furiously, fearfully. 'What do *you* know of its pain?'

He stood quite still, his face expressionless, and she turned away from him, lest he should see her tears. She put her elbows on the desk, her fingers pressed against her mouth, waiting for him to touch her, speak to her – but the only sound was the click of the latch as the door closed quietly behind him.

Chapter Twenty-seven

'A car,' marvelled Kit. 'A car! Can you believe it? I just can't get over it.'

In the cold morning light, the kitchen was definitely a depressing place. A small green transistor, tuned permanently to Radio London, stood on the dusty windowsill alongside a pile of precariously balanced textbooks and a decaying pot plant. The sink and draining board overflowed with the evidence of last night's impromptu party whose remains extended to the table and other flat surfaces. The floor, covered with a faded and cracked linoleum, was just the least bit sticky and someone's dirty washing had been kicked under the chair in the corner. Kit, dressed in jeans and one of Hal's jerseys, leaned against the crowded sink as she read the letter.

'It's all true,' she said. 'Not a dream. Here it is in black and white. My very own car! Think of the things we shall be able to do!'

Across the untidy, Formica-topped kitchen table, her flatmate watched her with a carefully assumed indifference. 'We'll be able to do a ton up the M1,' she suggested idly. 'Or we'll find our buckets and spades and go to the coast on Sundays. Big deal.'

Kit grinned at her, undeceived by this show of sophistication. 'If you like,' she said. 'Why not? The world is our oyster. We can go to Brighton.'

'Gosh,' said the flatmate with studied awe. 'Really? I can't wait. Brighton. Could we survive the excitement? Listen! We could go to Southend and eat jellied eels.'

'You're jealous,' said Kit. 'Make some coffee or something. Don't just sit there.'

'Jealous?' echoed the flatmate. '*Jealous?* Of *course* I'm jealous. Who wouldn't be? I wish I had a grandmother who handed out cars like sweets.'

'It's only because of Hal,' Kit told her. 'She's made him her heir and I think that this is a kind of sop, if you see what I mean? After all, we *are* twins. Why shouldn't I be an heir, too? Split it between us.'

Her flatmate watched her curiously. 'You don't seem too upset about it.'

'I'm not.' Kit shrugged. 'I don't want a big old house down in Devon to worry about. Hal can have the responsibility. I'll have the car.'

'But you love The Keep.'

'And I shall go on loving The Keep. Especially if I don't have to pay its bills. I can still go any time I like. Ma says that's a condition. "The family must be able to continue to use it as a refuge," ' she quoted. 'Those are grandmother's words.'

'Gothic,' yawned her companion. 'Like Jane Austen or something. Listen.' She leaned across the table, pushing back long blonde hair. 'How about me and Hal getting together? He's a real dish. That'd be cool, wouldn't it?'

Kit plugged in the kettle and switched it on. She

looked suddenly serious as she spooned coffee into two cups. 'The thing is,' she said slowly, 'he's had a bit of thing going with my little coz. Nothing heavy. Just a bit of a thing. She's had a crush on him since she was about twelve and he's got used to it. Well, the word's out. It's got to be stopped. To tell you the truth, Ma had a fit. Cousins and all that. You see? So Hal's had a jawing and it's all over.'

'Gothic,' repeated her flatmate, putting her head back on her folded arms, cheek on wrists. 'Medieval.'

'I hadn't really thought about it,' admitted Kit. 'I suppose they might be right. All that about having odd children or something. But I'm worried about my little coz. She's a poppet and she's going to be terribly hurt. I've told Hal that he's got to be really careful with her.'

The flatmate snorted, rolling her eyes. 'Your story has touched my heart,' she drawled, 'and I shall be glad to make a subscription to your worthy cause.'

'Shut up,' said Kit, grinning for a moment – but looking serious again. 'It's real for Fliss.'

The flatmate got up and began to dance slowly, grabbing Kit as she revolved, growling in her ear the words of 'You've Lost that Lovin' Feelin'.'

'Pig,' said Kit. 'Heartless cow. I wouldn't want you for a sister-in-law. We're out of milk. How about dashing round to the vending machine in Earls Court Road?'

'*You* dash.' Her companion sank back on to her chair. 'Don't think I'm going to start sucking up just because you're going to have a car. So what are you going to ask for? An E-Type? Mini-Cooper S?'

'Don't be daft. Grandmother isn't Rockefeller. Hal

thinks he might get a tiny, tiny sports car if he plays it right. I know just what I want. A Morris Minor convertible. They're really groovy. Not overstated or anything. Really cool.'

Her flatmate sighed. 'So much for doing a ton up the M1,' she said, resigned. 'Be lucky if we get as far as Richmond Park. Ah well. Good thing we still kept our jobs, wasn't it?'

'I'm going to get milk,' said Kit. 'You could be getting on with the washing-up. This kitchen is a tip.'

She slammed the door on the shrieks of indignation and ran up the basement steps into the chilly morning air, excited about the car but still thinking about Fliss. Hal had telephoned and talked for hours. As she turned into Earls Court Road, Kit wondered why it was that she sometimes felt centuries older than Hal. It was clear that he took the idea of being Freddy's heir very seriously indeed; she had impressed him with her talk of his being the head of the family when she died and the responsibility that it entailed.

Kit thought: All a bit dated really. Lucky that Hal's in the Navy. He's used to the idea of service and duty and all that.

It was Prue who had really shocked him, however. She was very firm about any future relationship between her son and Fliss.

'To be honest,' Hal had said on the telephone to Kit, 'she took me by surprise. I don't know how she even suspected anything. She feels really strongly about it.'

'And how do *you* feel about it?' she'd asked.

'I don't know,' he'd answered after a pause, 'I'm

terribly fond of Fliss. I like having her around and . . . well . . .'

'And it flatters you,' Kit had assisted, 'to have a pretty girl to show off and to think you're wonderful.'

This time the silence had been longer. 'I suppose so,' he'd said reluctantly. 'But it wasn't intentional, Kit. I didn't mean to hurt or mislead her. It was just . . . fun. A bit . . . naughty. Do you know what I mean? It sounds heartless somehow.'

'I know what you mean,' Kit had said compassionately. 'You sort of both grew into it. It was like a habit. No real harm but something to hide from the grown-ups.'

'That's it.' He'd sounded relieved. 'And it's just been so easy to do things together this last year.'

'I think that Fliss takes it much more seriously than that,' she'd told him. 'You're going to hurt her.'

'Ma says that it would be wrong for me to marry her anyway,' Hal had said. 'To begin with she says that Fliss has had no chance to find anyone else to measure me against and that as she grows up she'll resent the fact that she had no experience. And then there's that thing about first cousins having funny children, especially with our fathers being identical twins. She says that Fliss will certainly want children and if there should be a problem it would break her heart. She says that the best thing for Fliss is for me to break free now. What do you think?'

Kit had suppressed the instinctive observation that their mother was manipulating him into doing what she wanted – and thought carefully. 'Do you love Fliss, Hal?' she'd asked gently.

'Of course I do!' he'd cried. 'She's . . . she's Fliss.

She's so pretty and so sweet and . . . OK, I admit it, it's very nice having a pretty girl thinking you're wonderful, even if she *is* your cousin. But there's a kind of . . . excitement missing. It's fun to kiss her but . . . It's probably because I know her so well but there's none of that real excitement like when I meet other girls. Oh hell, Kit. I feel an absolute bastard.'

There'd been another long silence.

'I think Ma's right,' Kit had said at last. 'It's not fair on either of you. You're both too young to commit yourselves, especially when neither of you has had a chance to look about a bit.'

'I had a few experiences during my Mid year,' Hal had protested, unwilling to be dismissed as a greenhorn. 'But I've been working too hard this year to bother much.'

'And there's always been Fliss to fall back on,' Kit had added. She'd sighed. 'I think Ma's right, Hal, but for God's sake be careful how you put it to Fliss.'

'I suppose,' he'd said carefully, 'I *do* have to tell her.'

'Yes you bloody do! If you think you can just let it dawn on her gradually, forget it. She'd never understand. And don't tell her that it's because Ma has told you to do it. Let her think that you've been thinking things through and that you've decided that it's unfair to ask her to commit herself. Apart from anything else, because of Grandmother's edict Fliss can't get involved with anyone for another two years. You'll be off goodness knows where and it would be unfair to hold her to a promise anyway. But it won't be easy, Hal.'

'You're not kidding,' he'd said grimly. 'Where should I tell her, do you think?'

'Don't ask her out specially,' Kit had said at once. 'She'll think it's something quite different. Wait till you're alone at The Keep and then get out quick afterwards. Don't hang about reminding her. She'll have other people around if she needs them and she'll be where she likes best to be.'

'Oh God.' He'd sounded near to tears. 'Why did I ever start this?'

'You didn't start it,' she'd said sympathetically. 'It started years ago when Jamie died. She latched on to you and it sort of grew out of that. It's not all your fault.'

'Thanks.' He'd spoken awkwardly and she'd felt a great rush of affection for him.

'Would it help if I was there with you?' she'd suggested. 'Not when you tell her, of course, but afterwards?'

'Could you be there for Fliss?' he'd asked – and the tears had pricked behind her eyes.

'Yes,' she'd said. 'I'll be there for Fliss. Just let me know when.'

'Soon. I want to get it over with but I want to try and keep our friendship going if I can. I want to make sure she enjoys the Easter Ball and goes on looking forward to the Passing Out Parade and things. I've got to do it so that she stops thinking there's something secret between us but at the same time we stay close. I'm going to make sure that we're a big party for the ball. You're coming down for it?'

'Try to keep me away,' she'd said. 'And then we'll be going off to join Ma and Caroline right afterwards.'

'It'll have to be next weekend then. Oh God, Kit . . .'

'*Courage, mon brave.*' She'd attempted lightness. 'Look upon it as good practice for being head of the family one of these days. And, Hal, I think it *is* the right thing to do.'

'Thanks,' he'd said. 'Thanks, Kit. Next weekend, then. I'll be waiting for you. Let me know what time you'll be getting in.'

'I'll do that.'

She'd hesitated, hating to say goodbye to him, but he'd hung up quickly.

Now, as she rummaged in the pockets of her jeans for a coin to put into the vending machine, she thought about Fliss: her love of both The Keep and the family; her loyalty and stability; her sweetness and her level-headedness. Was she not, in many ways, the perfect wife for Hal? Kit headed for home, clutching her carton of milk, wondering if they just might all be making a terrible mistake.

Theo stared into his suitcase as it lay half packed upon his bed, his hands full of shirts. There seemed something so wrong about leaving; it was as if he were running away. Yet he could think of no way out of the impasse he and Freddy had reached. Since their confrontation, a few days previously, they had been careful to keep their feelings hidden from Ellen and Fox. Caroline was too bound up in her own misery to notice too much but he wondered how long it would be before someone became aware of the change. It was not unusual for Theo to have lunch in his rooms while he worked, and Freddy had managed to get herself invited over to Julia for one whole day, but it was impossible to continue under this strain, especially with the children due to arrive home from school.

He left his packing and wandered across to the window of his sparsely furnished bedroom. The wintry landscape rolled away in muted tones: earthy browns, chalky blues, silvery greens. The sky was white, brooding quietly over the still and waiting land, and so great was the silence that the sound of running water could just be heard as the river raced noisily over the rocks and boulders in its narrow bed far below. Theo stuck his hands in his pockets, head bowed. For the hundredth time he analysed the situation, trying to decide exactly on his position. It was not that he objected to Hal being made Freddy's heir. He and she had discussed it endlessly – she had even mooted that he, Theo, should inherit, which he had refused – and he had agreed that it was the most sensible way of disposing of the estate. Freddy wanted Hal to be the head of the family, confident that she could trust him to look after his cousins once she and Theo were gone. He agreed with her; Hal was very like his father and his uncle. He would take his responsibilities seriously and he already had a sense of kindly caring for his sister and his cousins.

Theo sighed heavily. That was where the trouble had started, of course. Hal had been positively encouraged to look after his little cousins; especially Fliss. He remembered how he had been fleetingly aware of the danger all those years ago but, somehow, he had ceased to notice Fliss's growing infatuation. Perhaps it was because he had ceased to have the observant eye of the outsider; he had moved in, become one of the family, and his awareness had become blunted. It was only as Prue had talked to him on the telephone, pouring it all out, that things became suddenly clear.

He had been almost angry with her implied conspiracy; that he must approve what she and Freddy were planning to do. He realised now that he had been unfair in imputing Freddy's decision regarding the inheritance to mere bribery. Nevertheless, her silence on the subject – prior to Prue's conversation – lent a suspicious aspect to this convenient decision. He knew that she'd feared he would disapprove of their joint methods of disentangling Hal and had hoped to carry the whole thing off without arousing his attention.

The foolish thing was that the only part which had really upset him was their cavalier treatment of Fliss. Caroline must be protected, Hal must be distracted – and Fliss must just get on with it. In attempting to protect her it was unfortunate that he had ventured into the unknown territory of love. Freddy could not know how he had loved her through all these years, or the pain of his unrequited passion. How could she? But to challenge her love for Bertie, whom she had loved so much, had been unforgivable. She had been right to ask him those questions – but how could he possibly have answered her? It was for these reasons that for years he had feared to return to The Keep, lest their friendship should founder on hidden, secret rocks. Yet how could he abandon Fliss? It was right that she should be considered and dealt with carefully. This is what made his decision about leaving such a difficult one. It was clear that Freddy must wish him gone, would understand now why he had hesitated to return in the first place, but might Fliss need him? As always, he dithered over this question, never sure whether he was an asset or a liability.

A knock at the door distracted him and he called, 'Come in,' expecting Ellen to summon him to lunch – or was it teatime?

It was Freddy. She stood just inside the door, chin up, but her swift glance passed over the case and she took a short, quick breath.

'My dear Freddy,' he said, hoping that she would not use that brittle smile upon him, 'do come in. As you see, I'm packing. I wondered if you might prefer to be alone for a few days.'

'Why?' she asked sharply. 'Why should I? To whom are you going?'

It was such an odd question that he looked at her in surprise. She was watching him with an expression he couldn't quite place and he smiled, hoping to engender some of the old warmth, some friendliness between them. The most painful aspect of the whole situation had been the cessation of that familiar love, as though a current had been abruptly switched off.

'I thought to visit my old friends in Southsea,' he said. 'I . . . I want to say how sorry I am that I said certain things to you. Unforgivable things. But I have had no opportunity. I was concerned for Fliss. I still am—'

'You were quite right,' she interrupted him, 'to remind us of Fliss's . . . feelings. I promise you that I have not spoken to Hal about this. Prue has suggested to him that they are both too young to make any commitment, especially as he will be going away soon. That is all we have done.'

He watched her with distress, knowing that she was seeking his approval. He felt confused. 'You are the children's grandmother and guardian—' he began.

'No, no,' she cried. 'You can't have it both ways. You reserve the right to criticise and then deny any responsibility when I act upon it.'

'Freddy,' he was holding her hands tightly, 'please let us understand each other. I was – *am* concerned for Fliss, that her feelings should not be dismissed lightly because she is young. I feared that you might be bribing Hal. I might have been wrong about that. However, I said other things for which I have wanted to apologise but you have avoided me.'

'You were only partly wrong.' She stared at him proudly – but clung on to his hands. 'I *was* preparing to bribe him. But not with the car. The car is merely to give him independence from Miles. It isn't fair on either Fliss or Caroline to have Miles bringing Hal to and fro. I think Miles is a very determined man, as well as being a very likeable one, and I have no intention of encouraging him at the moment. I would have given Hal the car at the end of the summer term anyway. You must believe that this was the reason I changed my mind about the car.'

'I do believe it,' he said at once.

'But I *did* intend to bribe him through his sense of honour. Through his obligation to prove himself in his career and because it would have been unfair to extract some sort of commitment from Fliss which could not be fulfilled for two years. I intended to use my power as far as I could to detach him from Fliss. I admit it. I did not do it, however. We only talked about his inheritance and his duties as far as they relate to it. I promise you I made no attempt to influence him—'

'Please.' He managed to interrupt her at last. 'I accept that you are telling me the truth and I am delighted that you resisted the temptation to use your power. Please believe that.'

'Then why are you leaving?'

He released her hands and turned away from her. 'Because I thought you wished me gone. The strain has been truly awful. We can't go on living in this way, Freddy. So . . .' He gestured, both hands upraised, and suddenly smiled at her, feeling the current miraculously flowing once more between them.

She smiled back at him, sighing with relief. 'But now we've talked it over, can't we be friends again? Please, Theo. I hate this.'

'My dear Freddy, I should be only too happy to unpack these things, if you are quite certain . . .?'

'Of course I'm certain,' she said crossly. 'Don't be a fool, Theo. I've done the best I can to put things right, although,' she glanced slyly at his back as he turned to bend over the case, 'I cannot be answerable for Prue.'

He was bundling things away, putting the case on top of the wardrobe.

'For Prue?'

'She feels strongly about cousins marrying. And Fliss and Hal's fathers *were* identical twins. I don't know what *she* might say to him.'

She stared at him almost defiantly and he raised his eyebrows, guessing at the speciousness of this remark.

'Theo,' she said quickly. 'I need you. We will watch over Fliss together. Please don't leave us.'

'I shall stay,' he said – and his eyes narrowed into a smile as he stretched out his arms to her. 'I shall stay with you at The Keep and we shall watch over all our children together.'

Chapter Twenty-eight

Mole stood on the shores of the lake watching the heron. A sudden gust of wind ruffled the smooth grey water, chopping its cold light into a million refracted shards and sending tiny wavelets into the dry bleached reeds that rustled uneasily beside the path. He shivered, pushing his hands into the pockets of his brown cord windcheater, trying to shelter beneath the tall banks of rhododendron whose leaves clattered restlessly. His fingers closed on Fliss's letter, making him think again about the new puppy. Fliss and Grandmother were the letter writers of the family. Occasionally, on important examination days, for instance, Kit – prompted by Fliss – might send a card, and Caroline scribbled off a line from time to time, but never had he received anything but birthday and Christmas cards from Hal or Theo. Fliss's letters were his favourite. Grandmother's were encouraging, supportive, sustaining, but Fliss's were full of news, descriptions of events, even jokes – usually told to her by Hal and Kit. As he read them he could hear her voice, picture her gestures as she described things, and he would experience a warm sensation, as though he could feel her arm about his shoulders.

The heron was pacing slowly along the shoreline, each leg slowly lifted clear of the water, narrow head drooped reflectively. The older children rowed about on this lake in warmer weather and the new smaller pupils sailed toy boats and paddled. Mole knew that he would miss Herongate. The old Georgian house set in its parkland had an odd feel of The Keep. He couldn't really decide why. Architecturally it was quite different and the grounds were sweepingly open; the whole place was far more gracious and imposing than his home in Devon. Yet there was a feeling of peace and continuity here, a sense of timelessness which reminded him of The Keep.

He brought out his letter, smoothing the envelope, drawing out the sheets. He wished that *he* was able to catch a train and be home in half an hour, as Fliss could. She had already seen the puppy and had described it for him . . .

She's absolutely sweet. Huge paws and long floppy ears, just like Mugwump was when he was small. You remember, Mole? Only she's smaller, being a bitch, but exactly the same colour. Fox says she's the image of Mrs Pooter when she was a puppy. Isn't it lovely to think that this is her granddaughter? I hope we can go on for ever with Mrs Pooter's descendants. Kit's home this weekend so I expect she'll come up with a name for her. Hal's home, too. Just for Saturday . . .

Mole folded the letter thoughtfully. It was unlike Fliss to remind him of any occasion which might be painful for him and he wondered whether she was beginning to acknowledge his strength or if she'd simply been too excited to remember ... In his mind's eye he saw Ellen coming into the bedroom, pausing to look down at Fliss, turning to see him wide awake, watching her. He remembered how she had sat quietly on his narrow little bed, absently smoothing back the hair from his forehead, while she thought about things. He had gone with her, though longing for Fliss to wake, into the room which was now Caroline's – and there were the dogs. He could still feel the warmth of the puppy, cuddled against him once they were in bed again, and the relaxation that had come stealing, soothing his mind, sending him to sleep. How terrible that time had been; his throat locked against the blood; his head seething with dark and terrible images. How far he had come ... Even the spinney was beginning to lose its terror.

There were shouts and laughter in the bushes behind him, the sound of pounding feet, and he pushed the letter into his pocket and turned back towards the school. He must find Susanna and tell her about the puppy; Fliss would be relying on him to do that. She never sent the same news to both, knowing that they would exchange information, but regularly wrote to each of them in turn. Susanna would be delighted to hear about the puppy. He looked for her amongst the milling throng in the large concrete area, called 'the playground' because of the swings and climbing frame, searching for her dark head, his heart beating a little faster with excitement. In two weeks they would be home for Easter.

★ ★ ★

As Hal drove from Dartmouth to The Keep, in the second-hand frog-eye Sprite, his heart was not nearly so light. His pride in this new red car was dimmed by the prospect before him. In the last two weeks he had rehearsed all the things which he might say to Fliss. None of them seemed appropriate. The thought of hurting her filled him with horror: she was so dear to him. Even now he was incapable of sorting out his true feelings for her. He was so confused and unhappy that even the ownership of a wonderful new car was bringing him much less joy than he had expected. He knew that until the interview was over, he would be able to take no pleasure in anything. With the optimism of youth he hoped that, once the difficulties were explained, he and Fliss could continue in their friendship and he was absolutely determined that the Easter Ball should be a happy evening for her.

Even now, he couldn't quite decide when the excitingly flirtatious side of the relationship had crept into their almost sibling friendship. He could remember confusing occasions – when Fliss had seemed to encourage him to look upon her in a different light – but he knew that he should never have gone along with it. He was older than she was, responsible for her, and he was ashamed that he had ever done anything which had given rise to the sort of emotions which had so disgusted his mother. As the car passed through Harbertonford, heading towards Totnes, he felt hot with embarrassment as he remembered her disgust. She was generally so easy-going that her reaction had had a powerful effect on him, although he had attempted to defend himself and Fliss. After all, nothing had happened except for a few kisses. He had said as much, hinting at his affection for Fliss, thinking at first that she was accusing him of behaving callously and requiring proof of his affection. He'd soon learned differently. Never had he seen his mother so distressed nor heard her so eloquent. By the time she had finished he'd felt like some depraved libertine and, although he had protested that cousins *did* marry, that it wasn't *so* shocking, she had pointed out that their fathers were identical twins and that, in their case, it was practically incest.

The word had shocked him. It felt all wrong to be having such a conversation with his mother, close though they were, and he had promised to talk to Fliss if only to be freed from the embarrassment, hoping to shut her up. She had talked on, however, showing him how unfair it was to lead Fliss into believing that they might have any kind of future together as man and wife. Even if they had been in a position to marry, she'd said, it would be madness to tie themselves down so young. His career was just beginning; the world was his oyster, and so on. She'd reminded him that he would be going away to sea whilst Fliss had only just begun her teachers' training course and that the best thing he could do for her was to explain that she must be free to experiment, to give herself the opportunity to grow. He was relieved that nobody was really blaming Fliss. It was understood that their mutual affection had got a little out of hand but now must be ruthlessly controlled . . .

As the car fled down the hill into Totnes and turned off on to the back road to Dartington, he rehearsed those words about experimenting and growing for the fiftieth time, hoping that Fliss would accept and understand that he was thinking about her welfare. He passed The Cott Inn, resisting the temptation to stop off for a pint, and drove through the village. As he turned into the network of lanes which led to The Keep, he was so nervous that his hands trembled on the wheel. He knew that Kit would already be there. She had been able to get away early and Caroline had fetched her from the train as usual. Hal briefly wondered how they would all manage at The Keep without Caroline. She certainly deserved a holiday although he was surprised that she was taking it just now, with the Easter holidays at hand. His mother was borrowing a friend's London flat for a few weeks and had persuaded Caroline to join her. She wanted to go to the theatre – she had a passion for musicals – and do some shopping but felt that it wouldn't be much fun alone. When he pointed out that Kit would be at hand, she'd said that his sister was working hard for her approaching Finals and had her job at the gallery. Anyway, she'd said firmly, it would be fun to have another woman to chat and shop with and the change would do Caroline good, too. Caroline, it seemed, had readily agreed.

Hal knew that his own invitation to London was disguising his mother's desire to have him clear of The Keep during the holidays and he was quite ready to go along with it. He knew that it was sensible to keep away from Fliss for a few weeks and he was relieved to have this excuse . . . He cursed himself, feeling cowardly and weak, but not knowing what else to do. Thank goodness Kit would be at hand to comfort Fliss.

Hal thought: I *do* love her, that's the trouble. In a

funny kind of way I feel we belong together. Why should it be wrong? Oh hell . . .

He turned in through the gatehouse, hoping, even in his misery, that someone might be at hand to witness his arrival. The top was down despite the cold weather, and his ears were freezing, but nothing except drenching rain would have made him put up the hood. He climbed out, stomach churning, and glanced across the courtyard. The front door opened and Kit came out on to the steps. She raised her hand to him and, with a sinking heart, he crossed the grass towards her.

The house was very quiet. Since Freddy was lunching with Julia, Theo had remained in his room, working. The two girls had eaten in the kitchen with the others and, when someone had telephoned for Kit, Fliss had wandered into the drawing room and seated herself at the piano. She liked to play, although she was nowhere near Freddy's class, and she selected a Beethoven sonata from Freddy's music. It was here that Hal found her.

She swung round to greet him, her eyes alight with pleasure at the sight of him. He looked cold and almost stern as he stood beside her, rubbing his hands to warm them. As usual she found it difficult to speak when they were quite alone and so she simply sat smiling at him, waiting for him to say something. When he did begin to talk to her she was unable to take it in. She frowned, watching him, feeling suddenly frightened. His words sounded stilted, as if he had been practising them, and he continued to look aloof. At one point she put out her hand to him, hoping to stop him, to make him look at her properly. He held her hand tightly but dropped it almost immediately.

'It's you I'm thinking of, Fliss,' he was saying. 'You're very young and then there's all your training to get through . . .'

He sounded quite desperate – and very unhappy. She shook her head, puzzled, wanting to comfort him. Surely he must know that she'd wait for ever for him? Now he was talking about being cousins, the problems, children . . .

'We couldn't take the chance, you see. Think how you love children. Supposing you . . . we were to have a child that wasn't normal. It would break your heart. We mustn't take the risk. It's bad enough for ordinary cousins but our fathers were identical twins. It was silly of us to get carried away but we'll go on being close, won't we?'

There was silence. His voice had stopped and she could hear the grandfather clock ticking weightily, the wood sighing into ashes in the grate. He stood quite still beside her and she noticed that he was wearing his old blue Shetland jersey which was very slightly too small for him. Presently she looked up at him. His face was pinched with anxiety, clenched with misery.

'But I love you.' She said the words quite simply, as if they would cure everything.

She watched him close his eyes and pass his hands over his face, saw his breast lift with a deep sigh. He laid the back of his hand to her cheek, touched her thick bright hair.

'It's no good, Fliss,' he said gently and very sadly, looking at her properly at last. 'We have to accept that it wouldn't work. Everything's against us. I love you, too. But it's got to be a different kind of love from now on.'

'But how? How are we just to stop?' she asked dully. His misery was passing into her, filling her up so that she could barely breathe.

'We just must.' He was crouching beside her, watching her anxiously. 'Don't look like that, Fliss. Please don't. I can't stand it. Look. You've never had a boyfriend. You simply don't know what you want yet. *Please*, Fliss.'

His last plea pulled her together as nothing else could. She saw that he was suffering, too, and instinctively wished to protect him from it, realising that she must be the strong one now. She swallowed, nodding, accepting. He gripped her shoulder, relieved, grateful.

'Try,' he pleaded. 'Try not to let it change us, Fliss. We can still be close. Don't let this spoil everything.'

She shook her head, agreeing, her smile woefully awry. 'No . . . No, I won't.' Tears blinded her and she turned away. 'Go on, Hal. Just leave me. I'll be OK. Only please go away now.'

He stood up awkwardly, remembering Kit's advice, pausing only to kiss her neat fair head before plunging out of the room . . . She had no idea how long it was before Kit came in. She felt her cousin's arm about her shoulders, drawing her from the piano stool, over to the fire, where a cup of hot tea stood on the fender.

'Come on, little coz,' Kit was saying. 'Drink this. God, isn't life hell? Go on, have a good cry . . .'

Later, she let herself out through the green gate and on to the hill. She felt calmer now. Kit had talked to her, explaining it all over again, making terrible sense of Hal's words. She knew that he was attempting to protect her, to do what seemed right for her, but she only knew that she loved him, would always love him. The weather was warmer and she stood beneath the high wall, staring out at the familiar scene, hardly seeing it yet gaining comfort from it. In this moment it seemed that she had reached some important part of her life: her childhood had abruptly come to a close and the rest of her life stretched before her, apparently arid and empty. She shivered, crossing her arms across her breast, her eyes hot and heavy with weeping.

Fliss thought: I thought it was the end when Mummy and Daddy and Jamie died but it wasn't. I came through that. I must get through this too.

She became slowly aware of an unnatural silence on the hill and she suddenly saw that the world was being blotted out by a storm of snow which came sweeping in from the north, covering the trees and fields and filling the air. It fell upon her, where she sheltered beneath the wall, waiting breathlessly. Time seemed to be suspended in this quiet landscape, held between this last, late blast of winter and the sure and certain promise of the warm, gentle spring; and she was held with it; waiting for a sign; something that offered some kind of promise to which she might cling.

She stared upwards, the snow falling gently on her face, and, in the midst of the whirling white flakes somewhere high above her, she heard a skylark singing.

Book Four
Spring 1970

Chapter Twenty-nine

The garden was full of birdsong; the clear warm air ringing with its clamour. Freddy pottered happily, enjoying the comfort of the sun on her back as she pruned the fuchsia hedge which divided the orchard from the lawn. As she cut back the new wood she paused from time to time to gaze with delight upon the scene in the orchard. Soft floods of purple and gold and blue spread beneath the branches of the old trees: a tender tide of crocus and squills washing over the brilliant green of the grass, lapping against the rough, grainy trunks, spilling across to the high, restraining walls. Beside her in the trug lay twigs of forsythia alongside sprays of yellow *Ribes odoratum* whose fragrance she inhaled luxuriously from time to time, sighing with pleasure. As she worked, to the accompaniment of a friendly and vociferous robin perched amongst the scarlet flowers of the japonica, she put the pruned wood straight into the wheel-barrow placed beside the hedge by Caroline. This last winter had been a testing one for the older members of the family. Freddy had been subjected to giddy spells and faintness – 'Nothing but old age,' she'd said impatiently. 'Don't fuss' – and Theo had suffered more than usual from his attacks of bronchitis. In February an influenza bug had swept through The Keep, affecting them each in turn and leaving Theo and Fox weakened and tired. This was only to be expected in Theo's case but Fox's inability to recover fully had frightened them all – especially Ellen.

'We have to remember,' Freddy told her gently, 'that he's not far off eighty. He's so active that we don't think of his age.'

'Nothing makes you older quicker than thinking about your age,' Ellen had responded tartly – but Freddy had seen the tears in her eyes and laid a hand on Ellen's shoulders, bowed beneath the flowered overall. They had stood quietly thus for a moment, each acknowledging the other's strength, sharing affection and respect . . .

Freddy dropped the secateurs into the trug and straightened up. Fox was pulling round now, helped by these warmer days, but it was necessary to have a boy to help out with the heavy work. She laughed to herself as she put the trug into the wheelbarrow and pushed the whole lot down past the rhododendrons to the bonfire. The 'boy' was probably twenty-six, the same age as the twins, but he seemed a mere child to Freddy. He cycled over from Dartington to chop and saw and carry wood and to dig and turn the heavy earth. Fox watched impotently, humiliated by his incapacity, forbidden by Ellen to attempt to assist.

'Should be turned out to grass,' he'd mutter, stumping back to the warmth of the kitchen. 'Fit for nothing. That's me now.'

Joshua, the boy, though polite, wasted few words. He lived with his widowed mother in Staverton and had been brought up to respect his elders. Freddy guessed that he was smart enough to see that there was a long-term job for him here at The Keep if he were patient. He was treading warily, deferential to Fox but certainly not a novice. He and Caroline had a good working relationship and she spoke with enthusiasm of his strength and willingness, though not in front of Fox.

Taking her trug from the wheelbarrow, Freddy turned back to the house. Caroline would scold her for pushing the barrow round to the bonfire but Freddy liked to hold on to her independence and Caroline had more than enough on her hands. What a great day it had been for the family when Caroline had arrived amongst them; what a tower of strength she had become; how closely Freddy had watched over her after that terrible misunderstanding with Miles Harrington five years before. She frowned as she bent to pick some daffodils from the bank beneath the rhododendrons. How quickly those five years had passed; how much had been achieved. Caroline and Fliss had both slowly recovered from their unhappiness . . . At least, Caroline had recovered. Freddy suspected that Caroline's heart had never been fully engaged, that it had been a romantic interlude from which she had emerged unscathed. As for Fliss . . .

Freddy placed the daffodils gently in the trug. She feared that Fliss might still be clinging to her love for Hal. No other young man had emerged to take his place although Miles Harrington had remained faithful. He had made no attempt to crowd her but, once he had been promoted out of Dartmouth after only a year, he had started to write to her regularly. She had accepted his invitations willingly enough, often accompanying him to balls and parties, but it was clear that she considered him simply as a friend, although a very dear one. Try as she might – and Freddy knew that she'd tried very hard indeed – it was almost impossible for Fliss to be indifferent to Hal whilst he was still a regular visitor to The Keep and it had almost been a relief when he'd sailed for Singapore after his fourth-year courses. The subsequent two years had given him and Fliss time to come to terms with their feelings. Freddy felt fairly confident that Hal had put his youthful romantic love behind him but she suspected that Fliss had not made a full recovery. Perhaps she never would. Her love for Hal was bound up in the tragedy of her parents and her brother Jamie, and it might be too complicated ever to disentangle it from the cousinly affection that she also felt for him.

As she crossed the lawn Freddy brooded on how the tragedy had affected them all. Sudden violent death must always leave its mark on those who are left but would it have been easier to come to terms with the deaths of Bertie and John if they had died of illness or simply – in Bertie's case – old age? In times of war there was the faint comfort that you were not suffering alone; that thousands of others were undergoing the same experience. War – senseless though it might be – forged a common bond, a sense of unity and commitment. Losing John had been terrible enough but Peter's death had left the deeper wound. Was it because he had been murdered with his wife and son whilst going peacefully about his business?

No doubt the Kikuyu tribesmen – or the secret political society called Mau Mau – who were trying to drive European settlers from their land, would have considered themselves legitimately at war. When, wondered Freddy, does a terrorist become a freedom fighter? Why is a British spy a hero whilst a German or a Russian spy is looked upon as an evil monster?

Freddy thought: Killing is killing. So why is it that the twins have not been so affected by John's death as Fliss and Mole have been by Peter's?

She reached the garden room and put the trug down on the table. There were many differences, of course. Fliss and Mole had also lost their mother and big brother, and the manner of the telling had been shocking. They were old enough to know what was happening, whilst the twins had been babies when John had died at sea. This must be a relevant point. Susanna had grown up barely affected by the loss of half her family. She couldn't remember them, any more than the twins could remember their father. This must be the key of it. Perhaps pain and suffering only became real and intolerable when you knew and loved those who suffered? Freddy sat down in the wicker chair to pull off her overshoes, still brooding over something Julia had said very recently. 'If you seriously contemplated world suffering you'd go mad with the agony of it. You have to be in the saint class to be able to deal with it . . .' She felt faintly depressed, the joy of the morning fading.

I'm getting old, that's the trouble, she thought. It's been such a difficult winter. Shall we all survive another one . . .?

The scent of the *Ribes odoratum* drifted gently,

filling the garden room, whilst the birdsong poured in through the open door. These manifestations of spring slowly penetrated Freddy's consciousness. She looked at the massed yellow flowers of the forsythia, at the golden trumpets of the daffodils, her depression receding a little. Almost imperceptibly her shoulders straightened and she took a deep breath. Before she could rise to her feet, Theo appeared in the doorway.

'I have been sent to bully you,' he said smilingly. 'Caroline has decided that you have done more than enough for one morning. It's nearly lunchtime. Come and have a drink.'

'Now that is an invitation I shall not refuse,' said Freddy, allowing herself to be drawn up from the chair. 'Oh, Theo, I was having a fit of the glooms here, all on my own.'

'Never be miserable alone,' he advised her, picking up the trug. 'It's even worse than drinking alone. Are these coming in?'

'Later,' she said. 'Put their feet in water, would you, please? There's a bowl in the sink. Thank you, Theo. I'll arrange them after lunch.'

'So,' he said, opening the door and ushering her through into the drawing room. 'What glooms were these on such a wonderful morning?'

'Oh, you know. Worries. Missing the children now they've all gone back to school. Black dog, Mole calls it, doesn't he? General gloom and doom.' She shrugged. 'We're all getting old, Theo.'

'It is certainly impossible to debate that point,' he agreed cheerfully, pouring her a generous quantity of gin with a restrained amount of tonic. 'But at least we're all doing it together.'

'That's part of my terror,' she said, taking her glass. 'That one of us might stop.'

'It's inevitable,' he said gently. 'We all know that. But don't let the knowledge of it spoil what we have.'

She nodded reluctantly, feeling oddly tearful, needing his comfort.

'I'm a daft old woman,' she said.

'Another impossible point to debate,' he observed, sipping thoughtfully.

She glared at him and he beamed back, raising his glass to her, but, before she could retaliate, Caroline arrived to tell them that lunch was ready and they all went in together.

Prue, who had not long since celebrated her forty-seventh birthday, was also feeling low in spirits. There was an aching beauty about the spring that caught at her heart and made her melancholy. The longer, lighter evenings filled her with restlessness and loneliness and, unable to remain in the house on this Friday evening, she went to walk above the Avon Gorge where she could look down on the river and the great cradle of the suspension bridge. The tide was high, covering the mudbanks, sweeping in between the wooded banks of Clifton and Leigh and she remembered how she and the twins had gone picnicking in Nightingale Valley. How long ago it seemed and how she longed for those days when Hal and Kit were children and she was never lonely.

Prue thought: But I've always been lonely for Johnny. I've never got over him. Probably because we didn't have time to tire of one another. It was still new and exciting.

As she stood beside the Observatory tower watching a small coaster chugging up on the tide, she wondered why it was that neither Hal nor Kit ever really fell in love: had neither of them inherited that deeply romantic streak which she and Johnny had shared? Hal, she suspected, had been more in love with Fliss than she or any of the family had guessed. He had taken the whole business very hard and she grieved for him – but she couldn't regret her decision. It would have been quite wrong for Hal and Fliss to marry, she still held firm to that, but she could sympathise with both of them. At least Hal was enjoying himself, no question about that, but one never quite knew with Fliss. She was so quiet and self-contained that it was impossible to judge how she felt. According to Kit, Fliss had no idea that the other members of the family had been involved. This meant that she could continue to be perfectly at ease with them although she had all the pain of thinking that it was Hal himself who had dealt the blow. Prue knew that Hal resented being pushed into the role of executioner, although he accepted that it was the only way to make a clean break. She had convinced him that marriage with Fliss would be absolutely wrong – therefore it was essential that, once the blow was dealt, Fliss had the family to whom she could turn without resentment or humiliation. Kit was the exception – but Kit and Fliss were so close that this did not matter. Kit could sympathise, side with Fliss, share in her unhappiness. Prue knew – to her own shame – that it would be so much easier for them all if only Fliss would find herself a serious boyfriend, someone of her own to love . . .

Kit, on the other hand, had a whole raft of boyfriends, all of whom she brought to Bristol in turn, all of whom she seemed to love equally. When Prue asked – as she did at regular intervals – when she was going to settle down and get married, Kit would open her eyes in horror at her.

'But how could I possibly choose just one?' she'd ask dramatically. 'What a terrible decision to make. Don't you just love men, Ma?'

A young couple passed her, entwined together, making for the bushes, and Prue smiled to herself. How wonderful to be young and passionately in love. Even now, thirty years on, she could remember how Johnny had made her feel; warm and weak with longing, yet strong and young and confident. No one had ever matched up to him, though she had tried to find his successor. She had been deceived by her own need, endowing other men with Johnny's special qualities, but it had never worked. She thought of Tony, remembering how desperate she had been to find something of Johnny in him, and shook her head. What a fool she'd been. Tony was nothing like Johnny.

Turning for home, she thought of him as he was when she'd first met him at a party during the war: tall, fair-haired, vivid . . . Prue caught her breath. He was walking towards her over the short turf, the long, loping stride and the carriage of his head unmistakable, his fingers loosely clasping the hand of a young girl. He raised his free hand to her, laughing, calling to her . . .

'Hal,' she whispered in a dry throat. 'Oh, Hal. What a shock you gave me.'

'Hi, Ma.' He was hugging her. 'What's up? You look like you've seen a ghost. I knew you'd be here. I said to Maria, didn't I, darling? "She'll be looking at the river." So we came on up . . .'

Darling? Prue swallowed, nodding, smiling at Maria. She could have been especially invented for the modern age: long, dark shining hair swinging on her shoulders, a neat, perfect little face, big brown eyes outlined like a panda's. Her woollen shift dress barely covered her bottom and her long lovely legs were encased in knee-length boots. Hal was making introductions and Maria was shaking Prue's hand: charmingly parrying Hal's extravagant remarks, laughing helplessly, shrugging hopelessly.

'He's impossible,' she said to Prue. 'Honestly . . .'

'I made her come,' Hal was saying proudly. 'We only met last week, Ma, but it was love at first sight. Can you blame me? Brace yourself, Ma. We're going to get married. No good fighting it.'

'I'm so sorry, Mrs Chadwick.' Maria was biting her pretty lips, pretending anxiety, unable to keep from smiling. 'You mustn't be cross with us. We simply can't help ourselves.'

'My dear child, I'm delighted.'

Prue thought: This is what I've been waiting for, longing for. Just like me and Johnny all over again.

Remembering how coolly Freddy had looked at her nearly thirty years before, Prue leaned forward and kissed Maria on the cheek. 'I'm delighted,' she repeated warmly.

'Oh.' The girl gave a great sigh of relief. 'I can't tell you how terrified I've been all the way from Portsmouth. Only Hal *would* come . . .'

'You should have telephoned,' said Prue to her triumphant son. 'I've got nothing to give you.'

'We're all going out to dinner,' he said. 'Celebration. I wanted it to be a surprise, Ma.'

'It's certainly that,' she said as they began to walk home, one each side of her. '*Well*. I shall want to know everything.' She began to laugh. 'Oh, Hal. How dare you spring this on me without warning! The house is in a mess – and so am I . . .'

'You look lovely.' Maria squeezed her arm. 'Just like Hal described. Bless you for not throwing a fit. Only I *do* love him.'

'Oh, my dear.' Prue was utterly disarmed. 'So do I.'

They laughed together whilst Hal smiled tolerantly. This was just as it should be, exactly as he'd imagined it. It was wonderful to feel like this when he'd suspected it to be impossible, that his love for Fliss might destroy any other chance of happiness. Then he had seen Maria . . . he had felt tremendous relief and a desire to grasp at this new happiness with both hands, possessed by an odd terror that there was not a minute to lose, that to wait would be disastrous.

Prue, glancing up at him, was struck by his expression. Anxiety seized her and she took his arm. He looked down at her quickly and her hold tightened.

'It's the real thing,' he said, almost as if he were seeking her reassurance, needing to convince himself.

'I can see that,' she said happily, wanting him to see she approved and relieved to see his smile return. Maria was leaning forward to look at him and he winked at her. Prue, holding an arm of each, drew them closer to her. 'I've got a rather nice claret tucked away so at least I can toast you,' she said, 'even if it isn't quite the same as champagne. And then we'll book a table somewhere really special. Can you stay the whole weekend? Till Sunday morning? Oh, what fun. Here we are. Now then, where's my key . . .?'

Chapter Thirty

'So it's happened at last.' Kit returned from her telephone call, looking both elated and anxious. 'Hal's got himself engaged. Mother is euphoric.'

'Fab,' said her flatmate morosely, washing up with bored deliberation. 'Great. Let joy be unconfined.'

Kit seized the teacloth and began to dry up. She had risen in the world – quite literally – in the last year. The promotion at the gallery, combined with a tiny allowance from Freddy, had enabled her to move to a roomy second-floor flat in a Victorian terraced house in Pembridge Square. She was within walking distance of Whiteleys and Queens Ice Rink, and had a key to the delightful little garden in the centre of the square. Her former flatmate, who now worked at the British Museum, had moved with her. To begin with, this silent, cautious girl had remained nameless and anonymous amongst her fellow students. When pressed she reluctantly admitted that she had been baptised Cynthia Janice – 'Oh dear!' Kit had declared. 'Nothing to be done with that, I'm afraid' – but, once she'd been invited to make a fourth at the basement flat in Scarsdale Villas, a change began to occur. As she shed her sensible middle-class upbringing, emerging from a stiflingly hidebound chrysalis into a butterfly child of her time, it became evident that there was only one possible name for her. Kit, as usual, had been the one to see it and, as she had named various puppies with such success, so she had renamed Cynthia Janice by simply but devastatingly shortening the first of her Christian names.

'This is Sin,' Kit would announce casually – and men of all ages would take one look at the sombre eyes and blonde mane, the boyish figure and endless legs, and pray devoutly that she spoke the truth. At The Keep, Sin had a mixed reception. Kit had driven her down in the Morris convertible – called Eppyjay because of its number plate: EPJ 43 – and had watched the effect on her family with interest. Theo had been in the courtyard when the car pulled in and he had come across the grass to meet them. It was the first time that Kit had ever looked upon Theo as a man and not just a component part of her family. The girls climbed out and Kit had said nonchalantly, 'This is Sin, Uncle Theo,' and, after a long moment, Theo had said thoughtfully, 'Yes, I can well imagine that it might be.' Sin had taken his hand, shaking back her mane, staring up at him, and Kit had suddenly seen how attractive Theo was: tall and spare, thick greying hair and the smile that creased up his eyes but barely touched his mouth.

'Wow!' Sin had muttered as she and Kit unpacked the car boot together. 'Double wow! Why didn't you tell me about him?'

'I've only just noticed,' Kit had said, honestly. 'For God's sake watch out for Grandmother, though.'

Freddy, however, had accepted Sin quite naturally and with faint amusement, treating her as she treated her grandchildren. It was Fox and Ellen who'd resisted Sin, unable to come to terms with such flagrant sexiness. Mole adored her, Susanna was indifferent, Fliss treated her calmly as Kit's friend. Hal was terrified of her.

'Funny, isn't it?' Sin had said, on the way back to London. 'Older men are just terrific. It's because they *know*. And you know they know. That's what's so sexy about them.'

'But not about all of them,' Kit had pointed out.

'No,' Sin had replied thoughtfully. 'Not all of them. Isn't it odd? Oh, Kit. I've fallen in love with Theo.'

'Well you can't.' Kit had been torn between pride that she had an attractive uncle and shock that he should be looked upon in such a light. 'He's a priest.'

Sin had stared out at Cullompton, drowsing in the afternoon sun, as Eppyjay sped down the A38. 'We were made for each other,' she'd said dreamily.

Even now, several years on, Sin insisted that she loved only Theo and that all her other conquests were as nothing beside her passion for him. This evening, however, Kit was not thinking about Theo.

'I wonder how Fliss will take it,' she said anxiously. 'I've been dreading this. I think she's still in love with Hal.'

'Just like me and Theo,' said Sin, sighing. 'Made for each other yet kept apart by cruel circumstances—'

'Shut up,' said Kit. 'I'm serious. Poor old Fliss. And I bet I shall have to be the one to tell her. Ma said not to mention it to anyone just yet but I bet Hal will lose his nerve and ask me to.'

'Look,' said Sin, drying her hands on the roller towel behind the kitchen door. 'This is probably the best thing that could happen for Fliss.'

Kit stared at her. 'How come?'

'Look,' said Sin again. 'It's been agreed that Hal and Fliss are never going to get it together. Right? Well, until Hal is put right out of her reach poor old Flissy is going to keep hoping. There will be just that tiny, tiny glimmer that one day a miracle is going to happen and he'll suddenly be hers. Enough to prevent her from ever committing herself to anyone else. See?'

'I hadn't thought of it like that,' said Kit slowly.

'Well, think of it now,' advised Sin. 'Cruel to be kind and all that jazz. She'll probably shack up with that Miles. Lucky old her. Do you remember when she stayed here for that party and he came to collect her?' Sin made appreciative noises. 'Really cool. Can't think why she wants a callow youth like Hal when she's got Miles just waiting to carry her off.'

'Miles *is* rather dishy,' agreed Kit thoughtfully, 'and you can see he adores Fliss. Do you really think she might . . . you know?'

'Why not?' shrugged Sin. 'It's a bit like being blinded, isn't it? She meets your big brother when she's in a terrible state and just grows up loving him. Can't see anyone but him. Remove him from her line of sight and she might be able to see someone else for a change. Old Miles is obviously smitten. I changed into my Biba special, ready for when he brought her home, and he didn't even look at me. Well, not more than twice, anyway.'

'You're unspeakable.' Kit began to laugh. 'No man is safe from you. Thank God I've never been seriously in love. When that day comes I shall move. I shan't let you near him.'

'You're no fun anymore,' yawned Sin. 'So then, let's hear all about brother Hal and don't miss anything out. New readers start here . . .'

Kit was wrong, however. It *was* Hal who told Fliss. He telephoned her on the following Friday evening at the little flat she used at the private school in Gloucestershire, where she had found her first job after qualifying. Although she had enjoyed her three years at college, she knew that part of the attraction had been its proximity to The Keep and, after nearly ten years away from home, it would have been so easy to settle down with her family; the temptation to live at home was enormous. It was pride that had made her accept the job in Gloucestershire. She had been almost glad that there were no vacancies at any of the local primary schools and, although Freddy would have been quite happy for her to wait until a post fell empty at one of these schools, something drove her to make a complete break.

Everyone accepted it calmly enough. After all, there were the long school holidays when she could come home to be with them all, as well as half terms. Only Kit guessed how lonely she was, how much she missed them all, but Fliss resisted any attempt to move back. She needed to show herself that she could manage alone whilst she got over her love for Hal. It was so much easier when she wasn't seeing him or listening to the others talking about him. Things had been a little better when he was out in the Far East but now that he was back and based in Portsmouth all the old feelings had come rushing back.

Fliss wondered whatever she would have done without the steady undemanding affection which Miles Harrington had shown her. She was no good at meeting people, no good at flirting with men as Kit did, or at chatting them up. She was too shy and, even if she became seriously interested in a man, Hal's image would interpose itself, making the whole exercise pointless. This was where Miles was so wonderful. He was almost part of the family, part of her life when she and Hal had spent such happy times together. She felt safe with him as she had only ever felt with her father or Jamie – and, of course, Hal himself . . .

When she heard his voice at the other end of the line she experienced all the old sensations. Her heart hammered so hard that she became breathless and she sank down in the chair beside the telephone. He sounded strained and distracted and when he finally plunged into the reason for telephoning she closed her eyes, sick with disappointment.

'I wanted to be the one to tell you,' he said. 'I . . . I don't know what else to say, Fliss.'

Pride drove out her weakness, her longing to weep and plead with him, the jealousy which pierced her heart and made her stomach churn. Pride stiffened her spine and helped to control her voice.

'I'm really pleased for you,' she lied bravely. 'Honestly.'

'Oh, Fliss. You know that you're still very special to me, though. No one can ever take your place. I've told Maria all about you. She can't wait to meet you.'

She gritted her teeth, hating him.

'Me too,' she said lightly. 'Let me know when you both next go down to The Keep. When . . . When are you planning the big day?'

'Soon,' he answered. She could hear the relief in his voice. Had he expected her to scream or cry? 'No point in delaying. Maria's always wanted a June wedding. Her parents are very happy about it. Susanna is to be one of the bridesmaids. I suppose . . .?' He hesitated.

'No,' she said quickly. 'Thanks but no thanks. Susanna will be delighted.'

'I thought you wouldn't want to. Kit says the same but Maria said I should ask.'

'Do thank her,' said Fliss. She shut her eyes again in disbelief. Were they really saying these things to each other? 'Tell her I can't wait to meet her. Look, I'm just on my way out. Got a date. We'll talk again soon.'

'Oh. Right.' He sounded surprised, almost put out. 'Is he nice?'

She clenched her fist and studied it for a brief moment. 'Very. 'Bye then.' She replaced the receiver and sat staring at the wall.

Fliss thought: I am angry. I hate him . . . But what else could he do? Did I really think that he would change his mind one day?

Misery and desolation swept over her. How could she bear to meet this Maria, this girl with whom he had fallen in love? She wondered whether she should speak to Kit but felt incapable of communicating with any of the family. Yet how could she bear to sit alone knowing that her last faint hope was dashed and her life finished? She sat silently, fighting to control her unhappiness, refusing to give in to it. The weekend stretched miserably and emptily ahead. Presently she picked up the receiver and dialled Miles's house in Dartmouth.

For months afterwards Miles would break out in a cold sweat when he remembered how easily he might have missed her telephone call. He actually had his hand on the latch of the front door, on his way out to The Vic for a pint, hoping for a quiet weekend at the little house in Above Town after a busy week at his desk in Whitehall.

'Fliss?' He could barely believe his ears. 'How are you? *Where* are you?'

Her voice sounded off: light and breathless. He frowned, plucking at the telephone cord, trying to read the message behind the words she was saying. She'd felt suddenly lonely, dreading the weekend, wanted someone to talk to . . . Excitement began to build in his chest, an elation caused by the knowledge that, for the first time, she had turned to him, chosen him.

'Wait a minute,' he said. 'I'm on my own this weekend, too. Why don't I come up and see you tomorrow? Even better. Why don't I bring you back here for the weekend? It's such glorious weather. We could go for a walk at Blackpool Sands and I'll buy you dinner at The Cherub. Can't say fairer than that, can I?'

He was laughing, preparing to be rebuffed, praying that she'd accept. She was saying something about a netball match on Saturday afternoon and having to supervise the players' tea, perhaps she could get someone to switch with her . . .

'Please,' he begged. 'Please try, Fliss. It would be such fun and I'd love to see you. I could be there in two hours and the spare bed's made up ready.'

He thought he'd better put that in just in case she thought he was trying it on – but she was already laughing at his eagerness, her voice a little shaky, as though she were moved by his undisguised longing.

Miles thought: For goodness' sake, she must know how I feel about her by now.

Some instinct told him to make a real push, that this was his moment.

'I simply shan't take no for an answer,' he told her firmly. 'Get yourself sorted out. I'll be there at—' he did a quick mental calculation – 'ten o'clock, give or take. We'll be back here in time for lunch.'

He put down the receiver on her confused thanks, feeling puzzled. Why suddenly now, after nearly five years, had his luck turned? Miles shook his head, glancing round anxiously to check that the house was in good order – a local woman came in once a week to clean – wondering if he'd have time in the morning to do some shopping on the way, mentally checking on the contents of the fridge . . . Jubilation washed over him.

Miles thought: She telephoned *me*, not her family. Oh God, please don't let me die before I can get to her.

She was waiting for him at the end of the drive, clutching an overnight bag, her face strained until she saw his car pull up and prepare to turn in the wide gateway. He jumped out, opening the door for her, taking her bag, settling her comfortably. Fliss felt an odd sense of inevitability. In a brief moment of insight she knew that in surrendering at last to Miles's strength she was, in some part, relinquishing and denying her own. She looked at him, confused and indecisive, as he climbed into the driving seat and turned to smile at her, raising his eyebrows, inviting some response. His familiarity, the proximity of his broad-shouldered physical power, his innate air of command, all these aspects of him disarmed her. It was so tempting to give in and to rest upon him.

'Thanks for coming,' she said – and he leaned across and kissed her swiftly on the mouth.

It was a deliberate statement, quite different from earlier gestures of affection, and she seemed to accept this, watching him gravely. For a long moment they stared at each other, as if some message were being exchanged, before he started the engine and headed back towards Devon. She sat in silence, closing her mind to her unhappiness and confusion, allowing him to amuse her and care for her. There was no hitch in any of his plans and, afterwards, he marvelled that the two days should have been so perfect. Fliss responded readily to his suggestions, fell in with all his plans, and was deeply grateful. His adoration was balm to her hurt, his kindness almost an aphrodisiac. She desperately needed the love that comes from someone outside the family, who loves because they choose to do so, not because of blood or duty. His faithfulness – especially from such an experienced and mature man – was a tremendous compliment and she felt it as she had never done before.

Looking back, Miles realised that he had been

inspired in his decisions; even the weather conspired with him. After lunch at the Royal Castle he drove out to Blackpool sands where they wandered on the beach in the warm April sunshine, watching the sea creaming in over the sand, listening to the seagulls screaming as they swooped and dived above the cliffs. Later, they had a cream tea at The Sea Breezes at Torcross before driving slowly through the deep, narrow lanes, out to Start Point. Miles could feel the tension slipping from her as they strolled down to the lighthouse, the waves crashing against the rocks below them, the tremendous arc of sky above them a deep and tender blue. The sheer immensity of the sea, stretched like taut blue silk as far as the eye could see had the power to reduce all anxieties, put problems into perspective.

After baths and a change of clothes, they strolled along the Embankment, watching the boats. The river blazed and shimmered, liquid fire in the reflected light of a flaming sunset, and they paused to marvel at it before turning back into the town for dinner at The Cherub. Fliss ate very little. She seemed to be trying to come to some sort of decision – and Miles knew exactly what it was. He watched her as she grew quieter and more thoughtful, noticing that an electric shyness seemed to be settling between them. His own determination grew, preparing to crush the last remnants of her indecisiveness. He refilled her wine glass – and she drank obediently, almost absently – and presently, when he'd settled the bill, he drew her to her feet and took her back to his little house, his arm about her, pressing her close to his side.

When they got inside, he removed her coat, kissed her and took her upstairs. There was no question of the spare room. She went with him into his bedroom and he made love to her and held her in his arms until the morning.

Chapter Thirty-one

It was Freddy who broke the news to Caroline. Fliss's letter had not taken her altogether by surprise; once she'd heard the news of Hal's engagement, she had been waiting for some reaction from Fliss. She read the letter at breakfast and silently passed it to Theo. He frowned over it, stirring his coffee round and round until Freddy was ready to scream at him.

'Well?' she asked impatiently when she could bear it no longer. 'I see that she has forbidden Miles to ask for her hand formally. Old-fashioned, she calls it. Of course, she doesn't know that he's already done it.'

Theo looked at her, still frowning. 'Done it?' he repeated sharply.

'He telephoned,' said Freddy reluctantly. Theo's reaction was unnerving. 'He thought it was proper. She's very young and we have to remember that she doesn't know that he had already asked for it five years ago. He told me that, with my permission, he was going to ask her to marry him and had every hope of success. Fliss's letter confirms that he was right.'

Her anxiety receded a little as she remembered the conversation. Miles had been almost incoherent with joy that Fliss had finally turned to him, accepted his love at last.

'Fliss thinks it's old-fashioned to ask permission,' he'd said, 'but I shall feel easier in my mind to have your approval, Mrs Chadwick. You know how much I love her, even more than I did five years ago, and it's going to get stronger and stronger . . .' He'd laughed helplessly. 'You'll have to forgive me for behaving like a lunatic but how *do* you behave when your dreams finally come true? I don't mean to be presumptuous or jump the gun but I just *know* that she's going to say "Yes" and I feel exactly like a five-year-old on Christmas morning.'

Freddy had laughed with him, liking him enormously, promising to keep the telephone call a secret from Fliss . . .

Now, made uneasy by Theo's silence, she buttered a slice of toast, dropped it back uneaten on to the plate and pushed her breakfast aside. 'Whatever is it, Theo? *Don't* you approve?'

'I wish that it had not happened at this time,' he answered. 'I would prefer to think that it is not a direct reaction to Hal's engagement.'

'Obviously,' she said irritably – this was her own worry. 'Of course we all would. Nevertheless, it has happened. What can we do? We can hardly ask her to examine her motives for suddenly seeing Miles in a new and attractive light.'

He smiled a little at her acerbity, recognising her anxiety beneath it, but his serious look returned. 'Can't we?' he asked.

She stared at him. 'Are you *quite* mad?' she asked. 'Do you seriously suggest that we open all those wounds again? Ask Fliss whether she's marrying Miles because Hal is now absolutely lost to her? Or whether it's a defiant gesture? How do you think she would feel?'

'I'd rather she was unhappy for a while than committed to a man she doesn't truly love,' he answered calmly.

'Very likely,' said Freddy sharply. 'But then we don't know that she doesn't love him, do we? She's seen a great deal of him in the last few years. There are other kinds of enduring love than that which is described as "love at first sight". He is in love with her and he can look after her. Fliss will be happier with an older man.'

'Will she?'

Freddy closed her eyes and breathed in deeply through her nose, expressing a silent desire for patience. 'Have you any reason to believe she won't be?'

'I think,' he said slowly, 'I think that a myth has grown up around Fliss because of the way Peter and Jamie died. She missed the influence of the father and older brother, the comfort of having someone older and stronger to rely on, and so she turned to Hal. It was natural enough but it was out of proportion because of the tragedy she suffered. She never grew up and out of it as she would have done if Peter and Jamie had lived. Now she has turned to Miles. She is using his strength to help her over this painful time and is committing herself in so doing. I think that she has enough strength of her own to deal with it, if she is given the space to develop it. I like Miles very much but I suspect that he has seen his advantage and is, quite naturally, seizing it.'

Freddy was watching him curiously. 'You think she would be happier alone?'

He was silent for a moment. 'Women have been trained to think that men are stronger and wiser, to allow them to decide and act for them,' he said at last. 'It is not necessarily true. Men may be physically stronger and they are used to being in the workplace and making important decisions and taking responsibility. Those women who are capable and have great emotional strength may well come to resent men who do not allow them to exercise their potential abilities. They might be temporarily seduced by the power men wield, some instinct may urge them to submit, but ultimately there will be some point of conflict which will be dangerous.'

There was another silence.

'That is why you stayed away so long,' she said quietly. 'You stayed away lest you should influence me.'

Theo hesitated. It was not all of the truth but he could not admit the rest of it; that while they were still young, his love might have been too great to hide.

'It sounds presumptuous,' he admitted. 'But yes, I feared it might be so.'

'Why did you come when you did? Did you imagine that your power was diminished?'

'Say, rather,' he answered quickly, 'that your own strength was too well developed for me to fear influencing it.'

'Yet you did,' she told him. 'Over the Hal business. When I planned to bribe him. You were angry then.'

'I was jealous for your own integrity,' he said. 'It— You are very dear to me. It was important that it should not be corrupted— For heaven's sake,' he interrupted himself, 'what a self-opinionated prig I am. Shall we return to the subject of Fliss?'

'I don't quite know what to say,' she said. She was deeply moved, understanding many things, feeling humbled yet exalted. 'Are you saying that Fliss must cope alone?'

'Not at all,' he said strongly. 'If I knew that Fliss loved Miles, deeply and absolutely, then I would be delighted that she had found someone with whom to share all her troubles – and all her joys. My fear is that she thinks she needs his strength and she is giving up herself in return for it. Later she might well resent it and they will both suffer. I don't blame Miles. He loves her, no question about that, and sees that she needs him. It is natural that he should take the advantage offered to him. I am frightened for them both.'

'So what are we to do?'

'What do you suggest?'

She smiled, noticing that he made no attempt to accept the power she offered him. 'It's not fair,' she remarked, 'to point out all the disadvantages and then retire gracefully.'

'You did not seem to care for my idea,' he corrected her, 'of suggesting to Fliss that she should wait.'

Freddy frowned. 'How *can* I?' she asked. 'How can I possibly question her motives?'

Theo shrugged – but remained silent. Freddy glared at him as she pushed back her chair, throwing down her linen napkin upon the table.

'I must speak to Caroline,' she said. 'At least I can prepare her for the news.'

She went out – but Theo remained at the table, sitting quietly in thought, absently stirring his long-cold coffee.

Caroline was mowing the grass in the courtyard, putting the cuttings into the wheelbarrow. Freddy sniffed appreciatively as she approached.

'The smell of new-cut grass,' she said. 'So evocative of summer.'

'Bit early yet,' replied the prosaic Caroline. 'Only April. Warm as June today though. Fox says we shall pay for it later.'

'Which is a very good argument for living in the present,' said Freddy. 'I've just had a letter from Fliss.'

'Oh yes?' Caroline leaned on the handles of the Qualcast, watching her. News from any member of the family was generally shared but she detected something odd in Freddy's manner. 'How is she?'

'She is about to become engaged to Miles Harrington,' said Freddy gently. 'I'm sorry, Caroline. There really is no other way to tell you.'

Caroline drew a very deep breath. 'I see,' she said.

Freddy studied her anxiously. 'I had hoped that it might not matter too much,' she said tentatively.

'It doesn't,' Caroline assured her. 'Just a twinge, you know. A kind of residual tug at the heartstrings. I was very fond of him but I wonder if I am the marrying kind. I like to be amongst a group of people where there's a certain amount of coming and going. And I like to be in charge. I realise that now. I would have been very good whilst Miles was at sea but I'd have resented it when he came home and wanted to take over things.'

Remembering the conversation which she had just had with Theo, Freddy found herself acknowledging Caroline as one of those independent women of whom he had spoken. Was Fliss such another?

'Do you think Fliss will be happy with him?' she asked impulsively.

Caroline frowned a little, pushing back her hair. With a shock, Freddy saw that there was grey amongst the brown. She looked upon Caroline as one of the children and it was impossible to think of her as a middle-aged woman, yet she must be over forty.

'Don't look so worried,' Caroline was saying, mis-understanding her change of expression. 'She'll be as happy with Miles as with anyone. Why not? He's kind and he loves her. Just because she didn't fall in love with him at once doesn't mean anything. She's had time to appreciate him, I expect, and now that Hal's getting married it's probably given her a jolt.'

Freddy looked at her sharply. 'A jolt?'

Caroline shrugged. 'She was always a little in love with him, wasn't she? A childish infatuation she never quite grew out of. Fliss isn't like Kit. She's not the "love them and leave them" sort. I'm sure she'll be happy with Miles. She'll have lots of babies and bring them all here whilst Miles is at sea. Are you ready for the next generation, Mrs Chadwick?'

'I wasn't ready for this one.' Freddy began to laugh. 'You can't imagine how my heart sank when I saw those three children standing on the platform at Staverton. I thought that I was too old to cope with them and I felt ill with terror.'

'Well, you've got me now,' said Caroline sturdily. 'Don't worry about Miles. It's all over, truly. I'm just so glad he never knew. At least my pride is intact.'

'My dear girl,' said Freddy warmly, 'I'm just so selfishly glad it worked out as it did.'

Caroline watched her walking away, still tall and elegant at seventy-five years old, and sighed. So Fliss was to be married to Miles. As she bent again to her mowing, Caroline tested herself, thinking of Miles, remembering how she had felt about him. Only the merest flicker remained; a slight warmth about the heart; a faint weak echo of desire. She paused to stare up at The Keep; at its imposing stone face with its castellated outline; the two wings slightly set back; the steps leading up to the porch and into the hall. She thought of the family who came and went within its strong safe walls and the continuity which stretched back into the past and was now being carried forward into the future.

She thought: I belong here, too. It has become my place, my home. I regret nothing.

In the kitchen after lunch, Ellen made pastry whilst Fox put a new washer on the tap. There was still plenty for him to do, despite the fact that Josh had taken over the heavy work in the garden. Mugwump, grey of muzzle and portly at the waist, lay stretched before the Aga. In her great-grandmother's basket, Polly Perkins – 'Oh, *pretty* Polly Perkins,' Kit had cried on seeing her for the first time – generally called Perks, was curled into a red-brown ball.

'So,' said Ellen, rolling out the floury dough. '*So*. Two weddings. And all in a matter of months. Whatever next, I wonder. Two weddings. How is it to be done, I ask myself. Madam says that Fliss wants a quiet do. Commander Harrington being a widower and so on. But Hal will want a proper affair. Big naval wedding and the full works, no doubt.'

'Bride's family will see to all that,' said Fox, busy with his wrench. 'No call to be worrying, maid. Won't be here, will it?'

Ellen's face fell a little but she had no intention of giving Fox the satisfaction of knowing that he had thought of it first.

'There will be plenty to do,' she said. 'Mark my words. I think we should've met her. Engaged and Madam hasn't seen her yet.'

'Prue's the boy's mother,' pointed out Fox, although secretly he agreed with Ellen. Freddy was head of the family and should be consulted on all matters. 'If Prue's satisfied, no doubt we shall all like her.'

Ellen sniffed eloquently, indicating her opinion of Prue's ability to judge. 'Hope she's not like that Sin,' she said gloomily. 'Sin, indeed. These girls. I wish Fliss was marrying someone nearer her own age. Seems a shame somehow, marrying a widower nearly forty. She's such a pretty girl. Would have been a beautiful bride with all the trimmings.'

'All done.' Fox turned away from the sink, gathering up his tools. 'Funny how she's never shown much interest in the boys. Not like Kit. Always talking about this one or that one. In love twice a week.'

'That Kit,' said Ellen. 'Get herself into trouble one of the these days. Fliss is more steady. More serious.'

She cut the pastry with a practised hand and laid the floury circlet on the dish which held the very last of the Bramleys from the orchard, stored over winter.

'Bit too serious perhaps?' It was a suggestion not an

403

accusation. 'Boys like a bit of fun, don't they? Bit of a joke and a laugh.'

'Fliss likes a bit of fun.' It was a protest – but he could see that she was thinking about it. 'She's the worrying type. Like a mother to those two young ones still.' As she dusted the pastry with caster sugar another thought struck her. 'I wonder how Mole will take it. Miss her, he will. Used to having her about during the holidays.'

She put the apple pie into the oven and pushed the kettle on to the hotplate. Fox, seeing an unscheduled cup of tea on the way, sat down at the table.

'He'll miss her,' he said thoughtfully. 'Course he will. But it won't be long before he's off himself. Maybe they'll finish up in the same base together. He'll be at Dartmouth in the autumn. No time for missing people, then.'

'If,' Ellen reminded him, '*if* he passed the Board.'

'Course he'll pass,' said Fox contemptuously. 'He's a Chadwick through and through. Course he'll pass.'

'She'll have to give up the teaching, I suppose,' mused Ellen, bringing cups and saucers from the dresser and producing a large square biscuit tin depicting scenes of the coronation of the young Queen Elizabeth. 'Stands to reason. She can't be stuck in a school somewhere with Commander Harrington off all over the place. Waste of all that training. Still, it might come in later.'

'She'll be wanting children,' said Fox, accepting a piece of shortbread, understanding that this was by way of being a private celebration between the two of them. 'Wait till she starts coming home with babies.'

Ellen brightened a little. 'Be a houseful, then,' she commented.

'Hal's too,' said Fox, munching appreciatively. 'Hope we're up to it.'

Ellen sat down, the teapot beside her. 'Won't see so much of *his* children,' she said. 'Girls go home to their own mothers with their babies. Doubt they'll be down here often.'

Fox frowned as he spooned sugar into his tea. 'But Hal's the heir,' he said. 'One day The Keep will be his. His children will need to know it and feel at home here.'

Ellen looked at him. 'Have you ever thought,' she asked casually, 'what might happen to us if Madam . . . died?'

'Happen?'

'Mmm.' She nodded, pursing her lips. 'What would happen if Hal moves in and this new wife of his doesn't take to us?'

Fox stared at her, his shortbread forgotten. 'How do you mean?'

'What I say,' she said impatiently. 'If Madam's gone and Hal's wife thinks we're all a bit too old to be coping with babies and the garden and such, what happens then?'

'Nobody can turn us out,' said Fox slowly. 'Madam told us that, remember? Anyway, Hal wouldn't think of such a thing.'

'*Hal* wouldn't,' agreed Ellen meaningfully. 'But things could be made difficult for us, if you see what I mean. Depends on what sort of girl she is. There're Mole and Susanna to think of, too.'

'I can't see Hal going against his grandmother's

wishes.' Fox shook his head. 'Nor I don't see him marrying that kind of girl. You've been watching too much television, maid.'

'Perhaps I have.' Ellen saw that he was genuinely upset and felt remorseful. 'It's the shock's unsettled me, I expect. Two weddings at once. Not a one for change, me.'

'There won't be hardly any change,' he comforted her. 'Hal's never here these days, except for flying visits, and Fliss is only home for holidays. She'll come home often, you mark my words. When the Commander goes back to sea, she'll be here more than she ever is now. Babies and all. As for Madam dying, all I can say is I never saw anyone look as well as she does. Could take her for sixty, easy. If anyone's going to be dropping down, 'tis more likely to be me. Me or Mr Theo . . .'

'And that's quite enough of that talk.' Fear flickered behind her anger and her hand shook a little as she refilled his cup. 'Fine ones we are. Talking about dying when we're s'posed to be celebrating weddings.'

'Well then. Here's to Hal and Fliss.' He raised his cup, smiling at her. 'Don't start crossing bridges, maid. Time enough for that.'

She touched his cup gently with hers, feeling comforted. He was right – but she would feel happier once she'd met this Maria and sized her up for herself. She suddenly wished that she could stop the march of time; turn back the clock twenty years, when they'd all been younger and stronger and the children safe around them. He was watching her compassionately and she jerked her chin, deriding her own foolishness, mocking her fears.

'Hal and Fliss,' she repeated after him. 'Pity they couldn't marry each other. That would have been just right for everyone, that would. Pass that tin over, *if* there's anything left in it . . .'

Chapter Thirty-two

Mole closed his bedroom door behind him and stood quite still. The moonlight cast dark bars across the carpet, filling the room with an unearthly light. He remained for a moment, watching the pattern, listening to the cry of the owl, before crossing over to the window and kneeling on the window seat. Outside, pure white brilliance poured down on the silent countryside, robbing it of any depth of colour. Trees and hedges were etched black against the ghostly grey of grass and the moon itself was cold and white, reducing the stars to mere pinpricks of light. The small pale patchwork fields stretched away to the black horizon but, below in the valley, the mist was rising. It curled up, wispy and ethereal, wreathing round the dark boles of trees, floating above hedges, drifting against the hillside.

The upper half of the sash window was pushed right down and Mole rested his folded arms on the wooden ledge, breathing in the chill air. He heard the scream of an unwary rabbit as the owl swooped above it, talons outstretched, and a faint shudder passed over him. Sudden death, striking out of the darkness – or out of a bright sunny day; it was the stuff of which his private nightmares were made. A dog barked and fell silent. The creak of the turning door handle turned him to ice: frozen, immovable, helpless. He would not look round. In his mind's eye he could see the face of his assassin; smiling with closed lips, eyes wide and blind in the moonlight. He *must* turn: he must confront his terror . . .

Susanna's whisper rendered him weak with relief – and shame.

'I heard you go to the lavatory,' she was saying. 'I can't sleep. Couldn't you sleep either?'

He swallowed. 'Something woke me,' he muttered. 'Probably the moonlight. Why can't you sleep?'

'Too excited.' She clambered up beside him. 'I can't wait to meet Maria tomorrow, can you? She wants me to be chief bridesmaid.'

She had told him a dozen times already. He studied her profile as she gazed out, awestruck by the scene beyond the window. She was not beautiful as Fliss was; fair and delicate and ethereal. Susanna's was an earthy beauty, made up of colour and strong lines. Her heavy hair was longer these days, held back with clips, so that he could see the dark thick brows slanting towards her temples, the curve of glowing cheek, the firm round chin. Her nose was short, almost blunt, her lips full, made for laughter. He knew that they were alike, but he could see no resemblance to his own features in this lively face. Yet other people remarked on it.

Susanna shivered and he reached behind him to the chair where his dressing gown lay.

'Here.' He draped it round her. 'You'll catch a chill. It's cold tonight.'

'But so beautiful . . . Are you OK?'

'Why shouldn't I be?' He leaned beside her, staring out.

'Just . . . you were a bit quiet earlier.' She waited; calm, understanding, her warm arm pressed against his own.

'It'll be odd. Fliss being married.' He brought out the words with difficulty, attempting an air of casualness.

'Mmm.' She shifted beside him. 'Nice though, in a way.'

'In what way?'

'Well, it's another person, isn't it?'

'What is?'

'Miles is. When people get married they bring more people into a family, don't they? Husbands and wives, like Miles and Maria. Then babies. So it goes on growing. I like it. I shall have lots of babies. You'll be an uncle.'

Mole thought of Susanna having babies; the risk involved. Babies. More people to love – to lose.

'You . . . wouldn't be afraid?' he asked at last.

'Oh no.' Her devastating indifference to her own safety was breathtaking.

'I would be,' he said honestly. 'I'm a coward.'

'No you're not,' she answered comfortably. 'It's just that you're a man. Men do other frightening things. I'd be scared to death to go under the water in a submarine. I'd rather have a dozen babies.'

He felt soothed by this but the other thing was still weighing on his mind.

'Babies are a responsibility though, aren't they? They're so . . . helpless. You get to love them and then they m-might . . . Anything might happen.'

His heart surged with terror at the thought of the loss. He longed to beg her not to have babies, not to marry, but she was already offering her own particular brand of common sense.

'Everything's dangerous though, isn't it? Going in cars and aeroplanes, catching things from other people. Even cooking can be dangerous. You wouldn't do anything in the end. Might as well be dead. Think how dangerous it might be in a submarine.'

'That's different.'

'Why?' she asked, interested.

He couldn't explain the absolute necessity to prove himself, to do what his father had done before him, what Hal was doing now. Joining the Navy showed that he was a perfectly ordinary Chadwick; upholding tradition and, in doing so, keeping fear at bay.

'It just is,' he mumbled. 'Anyway, Hal says that if there's a nuclear war, a submarine is the safest place to be.' He closed his mind to the horror of a nuclear holocaust; his family spread about, being unable to get to them, to save them. 'But there won't be one. Nobody would be crazy enough to start it.'

'Are you worried about the AIB?' she asked.

'Course I am,' he answered irritably. 'It's all very well for Hal to say it's a walkover. I'm not Hal.'

She reached out from under the dressing gown and squeezed his arm. 'Shall I come to Gosport with you? I could wait for you and we could go up to London afterwards. Go and see Kit and Sin. They could book some tickets for the theatre or something. Wouldn't it be fun?'

Already she was turning it from a day of terror into

a jolly, the AIB something casual to be dealt with before turning to the really important things, yet he knew that she was well aware of how vital it was to him.

'You'll be at school,' he said – but she knew that he had understood and accepted her love. His voice was relaxed again, the tension gone from him.

'I'd better go back to bed,' she said, scrambling down. 'Big day tomorrow. What luck we've got an exeat. Even Fliss is coming home.' She paused, just inside the door. 'Will you sleep now?'

'Sure. Go on. Go and get in before Caroline wakes up. You need your beauty sleep if you're going to be a bridesmaid. *Chief* bridesmaid.'

She made a face at him and vanished silently. He bent to pick up his dressing gown, took one last look at the night and climbed into bed, but sleep eluded him and the moon was sinking away to the west before he finally fell into a deep, dreamless slumber.

Fliss, travelling home by train, was more nervous than she could ever remember. The thought of seeing Hal and meeting Maria was almost overwhelming. How would he behave to her? Had he told Maria? She burned with humiliation at the thought, turning her hand so that she could see Miles's ring, taking comfort from the pretty sapphire and diamond twist. He had chosen it himself, bringing it from London and giving it to her after a little dinner *à deux*, putting it on her finger in the time-honoured way . . .

The thought of Miles warmed her heart and gave her courage. She half wished that he would be at The Keep for the weekend but some instinct had told her that it would be better if it were just the family – not that Maria was part of the family yet. The wedding was planned for June. Fliss felt a deep sense of relief that Maria's family were undertaking the whole business of the wedding. How bitter a pill it would have been to see The Keep *en fête* for Maria. Fliss felt ashamed but defiant. Maria had Hal – had him with all the approval and blessing of the family – but at least her wedding would not overshadow Fliss's quieter ceremony.

For a brief moment, Fliss allowed herself to imagine her wedding day had her mother and father and Jamie still been alive. She closed her eyes, the better to see it all: clouds of white tulle, crates of champagne, flowers, laughter, panics, excitement: her father, tall and handsome at the church door, offering his arm to her, his eyes full of love and pride; her mother, emotional but steady, the event orchestrated to the very last detail so as to be perfect for her pretty, beloved daughter; Jamie, surrounded by his friends, teasing but protective . . . She swallowed away the tears, staring fixedly out of the window lest the other passengers should see, thinking determinedly of Miles, of her family at The Keep, already planning her special day, determined that it should be just as she wanted it.

Fliss thought: But how *do* I want it? What am I doing? Oh God, please let me be doing the right thing. I love Miles. I do. He's so kind and loving. I can make him happy . . .

She stared at her ring, remembering the night at the house at Dartmouth. His absolute authority had been exactly what she required. Had he hesitated, questioned her, waited for some sign, it would have been fatal. His confidence and experience had overwhelmed her and she had rested on his strength and given herself up to him. It had been such an immense relief, a laying down of a heavy burden . . . Why, then, this faint feeling of regret, of loss? She shook her head impatiently. People had cold feet just before they committed themselves to marriage, everyone knew that. Miles was probably terrified. The thought made her smile a little. He was so happy, so extravagant, unable to contain his joy that she was his at last.

Five years; he had loved her for five years. Yet she had hardly noticed him at first. He was just there, part of the group, Hal's divisional officer.

Fliss thought: It is true that love is blind. Not only to the loved one's faults and failings but to everything else that is happening around them. All I could see was Hal. He was sharp and clear and everything else was slightly fuzzy. I never noticed that Miles was in love with me. If anything I should have said that Miles liked Caroline best. She certainly liked *him* . . .

The thought made her blink. Caroline and Miles. Had Caroline cared for Miles? Fliss racked her memory for any signs that might indicate a real affection on Caroline's part. She remembered how much Caroline had enjoyed those parties and balls; the outings to the pub; the trip to Exeter to buy the grey dress . . . The grey dress had been for a dinner party with Miles; Caroline had been so excited about it. Fliss sat quite still, her brain doubling to and fro, desperate to remember. How terrible if Caroline loved Miles; how must she be feeling now?

Deliberately she calmed herself, reminding herself that all this had happened five years before and, during those years, Caroline and Miles had hardly seen each other and certainly not in the last two years. She realised that, because of her unchanging feelings for Hal, she might well become oversensitive regarding other people's pain and loyalty. Miles had never mentioned Caroline and she was not the type of woman to languish after a man who showed no interest in her.

The train was pulling out of Exeter and Fliss watched for the familiar and well-loved landmarks that showed that she was coming home. For ten years she had travelled this line – as a schoolgirl, as a student, as an adult – coming home again. As she looked across the smooth waters of the estuary to Exmouth, she remembered how she had caught the ferry to Starcross on Friday evenings, anticipating magic weekends . . . Fliss turned quickly away, looking for the deer in Powderham park, watching for the sea, her heart beating faster as the train drew nearer home; Dawlish; Teignmouth; Newton Abbot. It was slowing down, pulling in at Totnes . . .

Heart hammering, Fliss reached for her bag and made her way along the swaying carriage. As she stepped out on to the platform she saw Caroline. She stood as she always stood, feet sturdily apart, curls on end, staring at the train, watching the doors. So she had stood to welcome her home at exeats, at half terms, for holidays; Caroline, who had packed tuckboxes, bought Fliss's first bra, sewed on nametapes; been there when she couldn't sleep, soothed her through illness, watched over Mole and Susanna in her absence. How inconceivable to imagine life without Caroline; how unbearable to hurt her in any way at all. No one, not even Miles, was worth such a betrayal.

Fliss stumbled into her arms and was held tightly, blinded by tears. It seemed as if they would never stop hugging and Fliss suddenly realised that she was praying silently, pleading that Caroline was not hurt. When she finally looked at her she saw that Caroline's eyes were clear, unshadowed, happy. Tenderly she touched away the tears on Fliss's cheeks, smoothing away the tendrils of hair, as though she were still a child.

'Welcome home,' she said – just as she had always said. 'And every happiness, Flissy dear. We're all thrilled to bits. Does Miles know just how lucky he is?'

Fliss's fear vanished away as mist before the sunshine but she held on to Caroline's arm as they went to find the car.

'I feel such a fool,' she admitted. 'I came over all peculiar, seeing you there as usual just like you've always been. You won't ever leave us, will you, Caroline?'

Caroline smiled at her across the top of the car. She looked strong and confident and Fliss felt a tweak of envy for such independence.

'I need you all, too, you know,' Caroline was saying. 'It works both ways. Where would I be without you? You're my family now.'

Fliss climbed into the car feeling happier, able to face the weekend to come.

'So,' she said, as they drove out, craning as usual

for the glimpse of the castle, 'have Hal and Maria arrived yet?'

How easily she spoke their names. She marvelled at her insouciance, her confidence increasing.

'Not yet,' said Caroline. 'They should be here for tea. Kit hopes to be in time for lunch. She had to work late yesterday so as to have the morning off.'

'The whole family except Aunt Prue home together. Quite an occasion.'

'Well.' Caroline began to laugh. 'It's not often we get two engagements in as many weeks. It's infectious. Kit will be next.'

Fliss laughed too. 'That'll be the day. She and Sin are a pair. They egg each other on with the men in their lives. I bet Susanna's thrilled about being a bridesmaid. I've had a letter at least twenty pages long.'

'She is quite beside herself. Not just about being a bridesmaid. She's equally thrilled about being your flower girl as well.'

'I am right, aren't I, Caroline?' asked Fliss, after a moment. 'A big white wedding would be wrong with Miles as a widower, wouldn't it? It's just . . .' she shrugged, 'well, wrong.'

'I know what you mean,' agreed Caroline. 'I think you're perfectly right to have a quiet wedding. It's still a church ceremony, after all, and all your friends will come back to The Keep for the reception. It will be a lovely day, you'll see. Exactly right for you and Miles. We all think so.'

Fliss relaxed gratefully, watching for The Queen's Arms, the water wheel, the school . . . 'Is Mole OK?' she asked presently.

'Mole's fine,' Caroline said reassuringly. 'He's taking a while to adjust to all the excitement, you know Mole, but he's beginning to see that there won't be too much change. He won't be losing you altogether.'

'Miles and Hal might be based at Devonport,' said Fliss lightly, 'and then we'll be home all the time. You'll all be sick to death of us, Mole included.'

'I think he's brooding a bit about the AIB,' said Caroline. 'It's only natural. It'll be a relief to get that over.'

'It must be a terrible strain to be following in your family's footsteps,' said Fliss thoughtfully. 'Having to measure up to them. Poor Mole. I'm sure he'll make it. What do you think?'

'I'm fairly confident,' said Caroline. 'No reason why he shouldn't pass. He's fit. Quiet as ever but stronger in himself, I think. He'll be delighted to see you. He and Susanna wanted to come to meet you but Ellen was insistent that they finished their chores. There's rather a lot to do with everyone coming home at once.'

'Good old Ellen,' grinned Fliss. 'Not even two weddings would make her change her routine.'

'I thought it was a bit hard on them,' admitted Caroline, 'but I would never dare to interfere once Ellen has spoken.'

They were both laughing as the car drew into the courtyard and Freddy, who had been waiting anxiously for them, drew a deep breath of relief. One awkward corner had been successfully negotiated – now for the rest of the day . . .

'My darling,' she said, stretching out her hands to Fliss, 'welcome home. Many, many blessings and

every happiness. My dear child, we are all so happy
for you.'

Fliss stared up at her grandmother, surprised to see
tears in her eyes, that her lips were trembling, so much
at odds with the erect carriage, the lift of the chin.
Swiftly, instinctively, she took her into her arms,
reaching up to press her smooth young cheek against
her grandmother's soft wrinkled skin. She held her
tightly but, before she could speak, Mole and
Susanna came running down the steps with Theo
behind them. For a moment Freddy held her close,
then, with one last long look between them, Fliss
turned to greet the rest of her family.

Chapter Thirty-three

Hal's arrival at The Keep was faintly reminiscent of a young prince entering into his kingdom. The red sports car swung in between the gatehouses, its hood down to reveal Maria, wearing sunglasses, her hair protected by a headscarf whose ends crossed under her chin and knotted at the back. As Hal switched off the engine and leaped out she sat gazing at The Keep, pulling off her scarf and shaking her hair loose, pushing her sunglasses up so that they rested on the top of her head. She was wearing Hal's blazer over a white shirt, tucked into tight denim jeans, and, as she swung her long legs out and stood gracefully beside him, she looked elegantly casual, gorgeously under-stated, subtly sexy. The too-large blazer gave her a slightly vulnerable, little-girl look and, as Freddy appeared on the steps, she went to meet her, pushing up the sleeves almost nervously, smiling with charm-ing shyness.

'Pretty good act, isn't it?' murmured Kit in Fliss's ear. 'It was exactly the same when I met her in London. Sin said that you feel she's got a producer just round the corner setting the scene.'

Fliss, staring down into the courtyard from Kit's

bedroom window, remained silent, watching the foreshortened figures being introduced, gesturing, embracing. Their voices rose quite clearly to the open window.

'How are you, Grandmother? . . . Yes, a very good trip. This is Maria.'

'I'm so pleased to meet you at last, Mrs Chadwick. What a perfectly wonderful house.'

'How do you do, my dear? Well, we're naturally very fond of it.'

'Hal's told me so much about it.'

'Has he made you travel all the way from Portsmouth with that wretched hood down? Really, Hal . . .'

'Now you mustn't be cross with him. I love the fresh air. Truly, I'm not a bit cold.'

'It's warm as summer, Grandmother. She's tougher than she looks, aren't you, darling? This is my Uncle Theo . . .'

'How do you do, Maria? May I offer my best wishes on your engagement? Congratulations, Hal.'

'Oh, how kind. I've heard so much about you I feel I know you all already.'

'. . . And my cousins. This is Mole . . . yes, a family nickname, he's Sam, really.'

'May I call you Mole? I know I'm not *quite* one of the family yet . . .'

'And this monster is Susanna.'

'Aha, my chief bridesmaid. How pretty you are. Now I can see with your wonderful dark colouring you'll simply have to wear pink. Not a sickly pale colour but a very deep rose . . . Don't you think so, Mrs Chadwick?'

'I'm sure that would be very charming . . .'

'Never mind all that, darling. It's tea we need, not bridesmaids' dresses. You must come and meet Ellen and Fox. I'm simply dying of thirst . . . Are Fliss and Kit here? Maria's met Kit already but I want her to meet Fliss . . .'

'I'm sure you're ready for some tea, Maria. Perhaps you'd like to wash your hands . . .?'

'Thank you, Mrs Chadwick. I'd love some tea. Perhaps Susanna would show me where the cloak-room is . . .?'

They disappeared into the porch and there was silence.

'I can't do it,' said Fliss desperately. 'I simply can't go through with it.'

'You have to,' said Kit flatly. 'Two minutes and it will be over. You'll never have to do it again.'

'Why didn't you tell me how beautiful she is?'

Kit made a rude face. 'She's OK, I suppose.'

'*OK?*' Fliss turned to look at her. 'Are you blind or something?'

'Oh, she's pretty enough,' said Kit impatiently. 'But there's something contrived about her. If you're not a bloke or very young like Susanna, you're just not taken in. That's all.'

'Obviously Hal has been,' said Fliss bleakly.

'Look, honey,' said Kit urgently, 'pull yourself together. Don't give her the satisfaction of feeling that she's some little princess come to queen it over us. Right? *You're* the little princess here. The Keep is *your* home. You're our Flissy, little coz. OK, so she's done the Lucy Clayton Charm Course. So what? She's pretty and glamorous and she knows how to get out

423

of low-slung cars elegantly and how to drink tea without leaving lipstick on the cup but it all goes just as deep as the make-up. I'm sure she's sweet and blah, blah, blah. She'll probably make Hal a terrific wife. So great. But you're heaps more beautiful. Real deep-down, bone-deep beautiful. Inside and outside. OK? Look. Hal couldn't marry you. He *couldn't*. You know the reasons. So. You've got Miles. A real sexy man who could take his pick. Even Sin goes weak at the knees when she sees him. And he's chosen *you*. Don't chuck it all away for some romantic dream about Hal. He's going to be here in a minute and if you let him see that Maria's beaten you, I'll *kill* you. OK?'

The sharp rap at the door made them both jump. They stared at each other, Kit's grip on Fliss's arm tightening so that she bit her lip to prevent herself from protesting.

'Kit?' It was Hal. 'Are you in there? May I come in?'

Kit gave Fliss a sharp, grim nod, gave her arm a last shake – and released her. 'Sure,' she called easily, strolling over to sit on the window seat. 'Come on in.'

As the door opened Fliss straightened her shoulders and raised her chin. Watching her, Kit had the uncanny feeling that she was looking at a very young Freddy but there was no time to ponder on it. Hal was coming in, his hands held out to Fliss, barely acknowledging his sister. He took her head in his hands, looked at her for one long moment and kissed her full on the lips.

'That's the last time, Fliss,' he said quietly, as though there were just the two of them. 'It has to be, doesn't it? You have Miles and I have Maria. I've told her that you're the most special person in my life and the most beautiful girl I know. She's terribly jealous and terrified of meeting you. Will you come down with me now and be nice to her?'

'Well, you've told her nothing but the truth,' drawled Kit into the deep silence that followed this. 'You should have warned her about those jeans, little brother. They must have killed Grandmother. Wait till Ellen and Fox see her.'

Hal did not glance at her but held out a hand to Fliss. 'Please? Maria's not nearly as confident as she looks. Underneath she's rather unsure of herself. She's been almost ill with worry about meeting the family today although she won't let it show. I hope you'll be friends. I know it's a lot to ask . . .'

'Of course I'll come,' said Fliss calmly. 'We were chatting, I'm afraid. We should have been there to meet you and Maria.'

She spoke the name without hesitation, her voice composed and friendly, but she prayed that he would not notice that her hand was icy cold and trembling. As they went out together, she glanced back at Kit. Her cousin raised her hand, the finger and thumb making a circle, and winked at her approvingly.

'Well done, little coz,' she murmured. 'Well done indeed' – and prepared to follow them down to the hall for tea.

Freddy thought: She's behaving beautifully. I am very proud of her.

She glanced at Caroline, who smiled back, guessing at her thoughts, understanding and agreeing. Fliss, looking cool and composed, had come into the hall with Hal, greeted Maria with warmth and poise and sat down beside her. It was Maria who fiddled with her teaspoon and dropped a scone, whose voice was a shade too high and whose laugh was too sharp. Freddy and Caroline, anxious for Fliss, were not aware of the undercurrents but Kit, strolling in behind her brother, observed everything with interest. She saw that Maria's eyes – alert and nervous behind the quick, charming smile – slid continually to Hal's face. Hal, however, seemed to have eyes only for Fliss. He watched her with a kind of tenderness which Maria obviously misunderstood. Often she called his attention back to herself. '. . . Didn't you, Hal?' '. . . wasn't it, Hal?' '. . . do you remember, Hal?' – but having answered her, his attention returned to Fliss as she helped Caroline provide the family with tea.

Theo and Mole were having a long conversation about being at sea at night and Susanna was bombarding Maria with questions about her bridesmaid's dress – which Maria answered distractedly – whilst Freddy beamed proudly upon Fliss. When she saw Ellen's perfect sponge being crumbled between Maria's fretful fingers, heard Maria's laugh become more shrill, even Kit took pity on her. She decided to take a hand.

'So,' she said, into a lull in the conversation, 'tell us about the wedding, Maria. What fun it's going to be. Will there be room for all of us?'

'Yes, of course.' Maria looked surprised. 'We shall certainly want all of you there with us, won't we, Hal?'

She looked at him, delighted to have his full attention at last, smiling intimately at him, determined that they should all see his adoration for her. He smiled back.

'Of course we shall. Your mother has kindly invited all of us, even Ellen and Fox.' ('But of *course* they must come, too,' declared Maria prettily.) 'And Miles as well, naturally.' He was looking at Fliss again. 'Good old Miles. He wrote to me, you know. He's like a cat that got the cream. So he should be. Lucky blighter . . .'

'And may I bring a friend, too?' asked Kit demurely, seeing Maria's face, hoping to deflect Hal.

'Friend?' It worked far better than she'd hoped. Hal laughed derisively. 'Don't tell me you've got a serious boyfriend at last?'

Kit arched her brows at him. '*All* my boyfriends are serious,' she said reprovingly. '*I'm* the one who isn't. But I can't invite them all, honey. We'd need Westminster Abbey to fit them all in. No, I'm talking about Sin, of course. She simply adores weddings. Cries all the way through, every time.'

She saw Hal glance quickly at Maria, saw the flash of anger on her face. So Maria hadn't liked Sin. Kit chuckled internally, watching Hal's dilemma.

'I don't see why not, do you, darling?' he asked, leaning across the low table towards her. 'Other people's weddings are the only sort that poor old Sin is ever likely to attend.'

Although Kit knew why he'd said it and sympathised with his situation, nevertheless she felt a flash of anger of Sin's behalf.

'Quite right,' she said lazily. 'Not that she doesn't get a proposal a week on average but it's simply that she's madly in love with Uncle Theo. He has ruined her life.'

Maria stared from Kit to Theo in surprise; Freddy

shook her head, amused at Kit's naughtiness; Hal and Fliss laughed.

Theo smiled his peculiarly sweet smile. 'I've been resisting sin all my life,' he said. 'I'm afraid I'm too old to change my ways now.'

He looked at Freddy, who smiled back at him. It was a private exchange of a deep affection that comes only with years of sharing and Kit, who witnessed it, felt a pricking of tears behind her eyes and a lump in her throat. Suddenly she felt rather cheap and she stood up abruptly.

'I'm going to see the dogs,' she said. 'See you later.'

'And I must phone Miles.' Fliss prepared to follow her. 'I promised I'd phone at five. He panics if I'm not on time. Do excuse me.'

Stepping past legs and over feet, she disappeared through the door at the back of the hall. There was a moment of silence.

'More tea, Maria?' asked Caroline.

'Yes,' said Maria with relief. Suddenly the hall felt less threatening. 'Yes, please.'

She looked at Hal with a kind of pleading intensity and he stood up and went to sit beside her. 'Me too, please, Caroline,' he said, 'if there is enough. So, Mole. AIB getting closer? How are you feeling about it?'

The talk passed gently into calmer waters. Presently Freddy and Theo went off together; Mole and Susanna decided to find Fliss and have a good chat about her wedding; Caroline piled up the tea things and tactfully left Hal and Maria alone together.

'You see,' he said leaning back contentedly. 'It wasn't so bad, was it?'

'Oh, Hal.' She snuggled under his arm, delighted to be alone with him, needing reassurance. 'Do you think they liked me?'

'Don't talk daft, woman,' he said. 'They loved you. Who wouldn't? I know I do.'

His hold tightened and he bent his head to hers. Caroline, returning for the last plates and the teapot, withdrew quietly. When she went into the kitchen Fox and Ellen were sitting at the table having their own tea and Kit was curled up in the dog basket with Perks.

'Looks like the cake went down well,' commented Ellen, eyeing the empty plate with a certain satisfaction.

'It was delicious,' said Caroline. 'A lovely tea, Ellen. And what did you think of Maria?'

'Very nice manners,' said Ellen, whilst Fox nodded approvingly. 'Very prettily behaved. A proper lady. Not like some people I could mention who like to lie about in dog baskets, all over hairs.'

'But did you like her jeans?' questioned Kit idly, tickling Mugwump with the end of Perks's tail, knowing that Fox and Ellen had been thrilled by their personal invitations to the wedding made charmingly – if briefly – by Maria before tea. 'You were very rude about poor old Sin when she came down here in her Levi's. What's so different about Maria?'

'It's not so much what you wear,' began Ellen, 'as how you behave while you're wearing it.'

'You mean that Sin is much more sexy,' said Kit. 'Well, I agree with you. You've either got it or you haven't. Doesn't matter what you wear or how much make-up you plaster on . . .'

'Maria certainly didn't have make-up on,' said

Ellen, rising indignantly to the bait. 'Lovely skin she's got. I thought she looked every inch a lady.'

Kit snorted. 'Just because she was wearing her pearls . . .'

''Tis a pretty name,' observed Fox suddenly. 'Maria. Reminds me of something . . .'

'*West Side Story*,' said Kit promptly. ' "Ma-ri-a!" ' she yodelled theatrically, rolling her eyes and clutching the startled but passive Perks to her bosom. ' "Ma-ri-a!" '

'That girl,' said Ellen to no one in particular whilst Caroline began to laugh. 'Never mind lying there singing. Just you get up and give a hand with the washing-up. If you've got nothing better to do than lie about in dog baskets . . .'

'Methinks I've heard all this before,' said Kit, hauling herself out and brushing down her skirt. 'Come on, Caroline. You wash, I'll dry.'

'Maria's gone up for a bath,' said Hal, appearing suddenly with the remains of the tea things. 'Anything I can do?'

'Yes,' said Kit at once. 'You can help Caroline to wash up whilst you tell them all about your lovely Maria. They're dying to know all about the wedding. She's made a terrific hit, you know.'

She thrust the teacloth into his hand and whirled off out of the kitchen and down the passage, her voice floating back to them. ' "Ma-ri-a!" '

'You're happy then?' Mole was asking Fliss, whilst Susanna peered into the looking-glass, a dark pink scarf held up near her face. 'Really happy?'

'Really happy,' she told him, sitting beside him on

the narrow bed. 'You like Miles, don't you, Mole?'

He nodded. 'He's very sound, old Miles,' he said, copying Hal in his new deep voice. 'I like him a lot. He's not . . . a bit old?'

'Not for me,' said Fliss quickly. 'I like older men. You . . . you can depend on them, if you see what I mean.'

Mole nodded; he could understand that. 'I just want you to be happy,' he said awkwardly.

Fliss swallowed, grateful for Susanna, who swung round to ask, 'Does pink *really* suit me?' before turning back to the glass.

'Of course it does,' Fliss told her. 'Maria's quite right. We must discuss your dress for my wedding, too. We'll look at some pictures, shall we?'

Susanna beamed upon her. 'Shall I get Ellen's pattern book?' she asked. 'There might be something in there. Shall I?'

She dashed off and Fliss looked at Mole, sitting quietly beside her.

'I want to ask you a favour,' she said. 'Something special. I didn't want to write it to you like I did to Susanna about being my flower girl. This is a bit more important.' He was watching her now and she frowned a little. 'It's just that when a girl gets married her father gives her away. Do you know what I mean? It's as if he stops being responsible for her and passes her into her husband's keeping.' She paused. Mole nodded. He'd seen it in films on the television. 'Well,' said Fliss, 'we haven't got a father to do it for me, so I'd like *you* to do it for me, Mole. Will you? Will you give me away at my wedding?'

He stared at her, amazed. 'Me? N-Not Uncle Theo?'

'No,' she said firmly. 'He would, of course, but I want *you*, Mole. You're my brother, my closest relative. This is the biggest day of my life probably. I want you beside me. Oh, Mole, please say you will.'

'Of course I will,' he said. 'Of course. I shall be very proud. I don't want to give you to anybody but I expect old Miles is OK.' He was holding her tightly now, whilst she wept against his shoulder, weeping for Peter and Alison; for Jamie and for Hal. He valiantly swallowed his own tears, desperately seeking for something which might comfort her. 'We'll have to share you. You must be with us here when old Miles is at sea. Who knows, we might all finish up together somewhere . . .'

'Yes,' she sobbed, sitting up and scrubbing at her face with her sleeve. 'Yes, we might. Sorry, Mole. It's just . . . you know, all a bit much. Sorry.'

'Nothing to be sorry about,' he said nonchalantly. 'Emotional things, weddings. Do you . . .? Would you like a drink? I expect that's what Kit would say, don't you? You need a drink.'

'She's probably right.' Fliss was smiling now, much to his relief. 'Good idea. We'll all have one. Let's find Susanna and Kit and we'll have a little celebratory drink. Thanks, Mole. And bless you for being . . . Mole.'

'No problem,' he said with studied carefulness as he followed her out of the bedroom. 'Nothing to it. You can always rely on me, you know.'

Chapter Thirty-four

Theo opened his eyes, the sense of joy fading a little as the sounds of an early morning in late spring were borne in upon his consciousness. He felt the usual pang of desolation as the peace of his contemplative silence gave way before the awareness of the world but he was strengthened and nourished by the spiritual encounter, comforted by the knowledge that he could return. '. . . *They that wait upon the Lord shall renew their strength; they shall mount up with wings as eagles; they shall run, and not be weary; and they shall walk, and not faint.*' How much these words had come to mean to him. He climbed to his feet and went to the open window. During his periods of silence the sun had risen and the countryside was washed with a clear brilliant light. Down in the spinney tender new leaves of fresh green were opening, forming a high lacy canopy that rustled in the gentle breeze; below this flimsy roof, the dim interior would soon be brightened by a vivid drift of bluebells. Across the valley the lush emerald fields were studded with pale and gold primroses whilst, in the hedgerows, blackthorn blossom sheltered the young fledgelings in their nests.

Of all the seasons this was Theo's favourite: this period of renewal, beginning with the miracle of the resurrection, was one of continuing delight. He loved the delicate yellows and deep blues of the spring flowers, the cool blue of rain-washed skies, the bright misting green of growing crops planted in rich red soil. The longer days, the strengthening of the sun's power, the return of the swallows: the fulfilment of all these promises filled his heart with grateful joy.

On the north side of The Keep the walls were covered with ivy and in its dense foliage, amongst the thick branches, there were dozens of nests. Theo leaned from the window to watch the sparrows, busy and noisy in the ivy below him. A blackbird, poised for flight, saw him and flew away with its stuttering warning call whilst its mate remained crouching on her eggs, watchful, hidden in the glossy density. Two brimstone butterflies executed a dazzling dance, shimmering in the sunshine, and in the woods across the valley a yaffingale was laughing. This spring morning the whole of nature was obsessed with new life.

Theo realised that he was thinking about Fliss. Was he right in assuming that Hal's sudden passion for Maria had pushed Fliss into her engagement to Miles? Why, having known him for so many years, should she choose this very moment to decide that she loved him? He had hoped that Freddy might find some opportunity to talk to her but there was a determination about Fliss which made it difficult to approach her. Theo recognised the brittleness, the gaiety, the barriers which might be invisible but which were proof against confidential conversation. He had attempted it himself but with little effect.

'Are you certain that this is what you want?' he'd asked during a rare moment alone with her.

They were together in the courtyard, looking at the fat buds and springing leaves on the climbing shrubs, marvelling at the wonders of nature. He saw a faint stiffening as she prepared to answer him and his heart sank.

'By "this" do you mean getting married?' she'd asked politely – and he guessed that had he been a contemporary she would have given him short shrift.

'Will you forgive me if I say that we are sometimes influenced by others,' he'd said gently. 'Getting married is a heady business, rather like going to the sales. You buy things you don't want and certainly don't need, lest someone else might beat you to it.'

She'd smiled at him then, a warm genuine smile, and he'd felt a humble gratitude and relief at her generosity.

'Whatever do *you* know about going to the sales, Uncle Theo?' she'd asked. 'I'm sure you've never done anything so rash.'

'I bought an umbrella in a sale once,' he'd said reflectively, surprising her. 'It was green, you know, and I was in two minds about it until the man standing beside me reached out for it. Suddenly I saw it in all its glorious desirability and I seized it. I still remember my sense of triumph as I bore it out victoriously into Oxford Street.'

She'd been laughing at him and he'd joined in with her. 'Are you likening Miles to an umbrella?' she'd asked, amused. 'And who else wants him? *He's* not in a sale, you know.'

'It was a poor allegory,' he'd admitted. 'Forgive me.

We put a quite unreasonable burden on you with our love. We wish to be assured of your happiness, which is quite nonsensical. Even if we knew how to define happiness, there is no reason why you should be one of the fortunate few who attain it.'

She had been taken aback by his realism. 'I – I hope I shall be happy,' she'd protested.

'There are other things which are more important,' he'd said gravely. 'Do you know that the Yurok Indians have only one law? It's a simple one.' He'd paused for a moment, as if attempting to recall the words accurately. '*Being true to yourself means giving your best to help a person in need,*' he'd quoted.

'And you think I am not being true to myself?' The lift of the chin was Freddy's legacy but the anxious little frown was Alison's. 'Why should I not be?'

Theo had shaken his head. 'Only you can truly answer that,' he'd told her.

She'd looked away from him, her cheek stained pink. 'I love Miles,' she'd said stonily.

'That's excellent then,' Theo had returned calmly. 'That is all that matters. We know that *he* loves *you.*'

'I know what everyone is thinking,' Fliss had said mutinously. 'They're thinking it's because of Hal. Everyone is wondering why I should decide to marry Miles now, when I've known him so long. That's what you meant, wasn't it? That all this business about Hal's wedding has gone to my head and I don't want to be left out?'

'Something like that,' Theo had admitted, giving thanks that Fliss had no idea that the family knew how she really felt about Hal.

He'd thought: Does she think we are blind or

simply stupid? Yet we only see it so clearly now because we *know*. Because of that chance comment of Caroline's to Freddy. Even Caroline hadn't guessed the real truth.

'Well, it isn't,' Fliss had said almost crossly. 'I *do* love Miles but it has taken all this time for me to realise it. You can get used to people, can't you? You take them for granted and then, one day, you suddenly realise how terrible it would be if you lost them. That's how I feel about Miles.'

Theo knew that he should have persevered, asked what it was that had shown Miles in this new light; he knew that he should have encouraged her to examine her feelings honestly, lest she make a terrible mistake, but Caroline and Susanna had appeared and the moment had passed.

Now, as he stood at the window, Theo wondered whether he had been right in letting it pass so easily, neglectful in not seeking another opportunity. Yet was Fliss strong enough, mature enough, to examine her own character ruthlessly and deal with the findings? Harm might result and, anyway, who was he to assume that he could demand it? Theo experienced the corroding, deadening confusion that had pursued him all his life and he shook his head, exasperated with his own weaknesses, defeated by his sense of failure. As he brooded, the sounds of the spring morning pressed in on him again; piercing the fog of his preoccupation; lifting his spirits. The thin, high, plaintive cry of newborn lambs echoed up to his window whilst across the valley – most evocative of all the springtime sounds – the cuckoo called: once, twice, thrice . . . Theo took a deep breath, feeling his strength flowing back; the glorious promise of the resurrection reasserting itself, giving him new hope.

Below him, on the hill, Fox heard the cuckoo and turned to watch its flight. Like Theo, the spring was a special time for him, although Fox loved all the seasons. Lately, however, the advent of autumn and winter – especially the winter's cold, wet days which exacerbated the stiffness of his joints – were no longer so welcome a part of the natural changing scene. Now he preferred the warmer, kinder weather that the longer days brought with them. Fox had been woken by the cacophony of birdsong, the friendly chatter of the house martins beneath the eaves of his little cottage. He was delighted to see them clinging to the wall, inspecting their old quarters, making preparations for the new season. He slept less well as he grew older and he was always glad to see the dawn, to hear the beginning of the chorus which swelled gradually as the sun rose up in the east and touched the world with its warmth. This morning, very early, after a long, disturbed and tiring night, he had fallen into a heavy sleep and woken later than usual. Only the thought of Ellen preparing breakfast in the warm kitchen had made him drag himself out of his bed. He'd felt slow, his mind drugged, his body aching, but now, out here on the hillside with the dogs, his old resilience was flowing back. He stretched in the sunshine and was pierced with sudden joy at the sound of the cuckoo's call across the valley.

He looked about him for the dogs. Mugwump was pottering a little way ahead. At thirteen he was still quite lively, if a little stiff and rather too fat, and he enjoyed his forays out on the hill. Fox remembered the puppy that had been there to welcome the children when they arrived from Kenya – and he thought of Mrs Pooter.

'Old bitch,' he muttered, swallowing hard. 'Old bitch, she was.'

Her great-granddaughter, who had been detained by an interesting scent, came wagging up, pushing against his leg, pausing to have her ears pulled. She had a much nicer temperament than her ancestor and, though in a different way, Fox loved her just as much. Dogs were like most people, he had concluded: none alike, each with some redeeming trait. Perks, distracted by the sight of Mugwump sniffing at some new smell, hurried off to inspect it and Fox wandered slowly after them.

The Keep was quiet now after the busy weekend – only the usual inhabitants going about their business – but there was plenty to talk about and exciting plans to make. Two weddings coming one after the other were bound to disrupt the routines and patterns of daily life. Fox and Ellen were in absolute accord. They approved of both Maria and Miles, agreeing that Hal and Fliss had done very well. Ellen was still a little distressed by the age gap between Miles and Fliss but Caroline had persuaded her that Miles would be a devoted, caring husband as well as being successful in his career. He had just been appointed as Staff Operations Officer to the Admiral in Devonport, which meant that he and Fliss would start their marriage with a shore job very close to home. They could live in Dartmouth at the house in Above Town and Fliss would be able to come visiting at The Keep very regularly. Everyone – especially Miles – was delighted.

As for Maria . . . Fox began to whistle appreciatively through his teeth. Hal had found himself a real prize; even Ellen was completely bowled over. By the time the weekend had ended she'd won all their hearts. She was so pretty and friendly and so obviously longing for their approval.

Fox thought: No need to worry that she'd ever throw us out. Hal's done himself proud. Wouldn't hurt a fly, that little maid wouldn't.

She'd invited them so charmingly to the wedding in Wiltshire. Her parents were offering to accommodate all Hal's family at a local hotel and there was no question but that Ellen and Fox were part of Hal's family. There had been nothing patronising about her invitation, nothing which Ellen could possibly see as an injury to her pride or to which either of them could take any offence. Now the talk was nothing but plans: how they should travel; what they should wear; what present they should choose. Caroline was organising it all in conjunction with Freddy; nevertheless it was great fun going over the details, anticipating it all . . .

Before the great day at the end of June, however, Fliss's wedding would take place at The Keep. It had been decided that it would be right and proper for Miles to take up his new post as a married man and so this wedding would precede the other by two weeks. Although it was to be a quiet affair there was still much to be arranged. The whole family was determined that Fliss's day should be the most wonderful The Keep could produce and nothing should be allowed to spoil it for even a second.

Despite the warmth and beauty of the morning, Fox felt a longing for the kitchen; for hot tea and porridge and the company of Ellen and Caroline. Occasionally he allowed himself the terror of imagining himself alone, without family or real friends, trying to cope, struggling to survive. Only yesterday he had spoken to Freddy about his feelings of inadequacy, trying to express his gratitude at being her pensioner now that he could add very little to her wellbeing. She had listened to him thoughtfully, frowning a little.

'It must be hard for you,' she'd said at last, when he'd stumbled to a halt, 'but, you see, you are part of my family. You must be gracious now and accept our care for you in the future as we have accepted your protection and service in the past. It is no more than you deserve and, anyway, we still need you. You have been with me from the beginning, Fox, and we shall see things out together, you and I.'

She had touched his shoulder and left him, walking away, tall and straight in her old tweeds, chin high, shoulders squared. Fox had suddenly seen the young Freddy striding away from him, the corn-gold hair piled on her small head, hands thrust into her jacket pockets; one of a string of the cairns she'd loved gambolling round her feet; her two small boys, Peter and John, running ahead. His eyes had filled with tears as he saw how the long years had passed in a flash of precious time, spent, now, and nearly over. He had felt deep pride and overwhelming love – and an invaluable sense of belonging . . .

Now, as he turned back, calling to the dogs, he wondered how it would be when the first one of them

441

died. How would he manage without Freddy; without Ellen . . .?

'What's the matter with you?' asked Ellen sharply as he came into the kitchen. 'Lost a shilling and found sixpence by the look on your face.'

To her surprise he put an arm about her shoulder and kissed her wrinkled cheek.

'Don't leave me, Ellen,' he said – and went to the Aga for the teapot.

Silenced by such an unexpected display, moved by his gesture, Ellen was for once at a loss and it was left to Caroline, coming in behind them, to release the tension.

'What a morning!' she exclaimed. 'What a perfect day. Now this is just what we need for Fliss's wedding. The garden will be looking at its best. I don't see why we shouldn't make a good sowing of runner beans outside today. What do you think, Fox? Josh is coming up later. Anything you want him to do?'

He knew that she deferred to him so that his pride should not be wounded, so that he still felt needed, and he smiled at her gratefully.

''Tis between you and him, maid,' he said without rancour. Freddy had taken away the sting that threatened to poison his contentment and he could be at peace and take an honourable ease. ''Tisn't fair to a young man to be waiting on an old one. He be a good lad. Nothing you can't cope with between the two of you.'

A glance flashed between the two women as Fox turned back to replace the teapot on the Aga. Caroline raised her brows; Ellen shrugged.

'Well then,' said Caroline, after a moment. 'Well . . .'

'Breakfast,' said Ellen, regaining her composure. 'Breakfast first. We'll worry about the garden later.'

'Mole must be getting nervous,' said Caroline, assisting her to change the subject. 'He's off down to Gosport on Thursday. I'm bringing him home on Wednesday for the night. Early start the next morning.'

'Hal's primed him,' said Fox confidently, sitting down to his porridge with relish. 'Told him what to watch out for. All the little tricks they play. He'll do, Mole will.'

'Course he will,' said Ellen, relieved to see Fox more like his usual self. 'Goodness, when you think of that little mite, unable to speak.' She shook her head. 'Well, we've all made a good job of him, even if I say it myself.'

'Quite right,' said Caroline, seeing that the party was in the mood for a little self-congratulation. 'Do you remember when he ran round the spinney, Fox? What a great day that was. You were the one waiting for him. He was clinging to you when you came back, I remember. Mole was crying with joy.'

'So was I,' admitted Fox. 'Remember, Ellen?'

'Course I remember,' she said gruffly. 'He appeared down here one morning, just about this time and he said, "I'm going round," and he was gone. Fox didn't even finish his tea. He was out there after him.'

'He trusted you,' said Caroline thoughtfully. 'He just knew you'd be waiting when he got round the other side, that you'd never let him down. He needed that.'

There was a silence. Fox blew his nose noisily. 'He's had that from each and every one of us,' he said.

'We've always been here. Seeing it through together. That's what families be about.' He looked at them, smiling. 'So then. I've got a terrible hunger after all that fresh air. Any chance of a piece of toast?'

Chapter Thirty-five

The warm weather took an abrupt turn back to winter and cold rain swept in from the west. Prue, hurrying indoors out of the wet, shivered as she took off her mackintosh and went into the sitting room to turn on the electric fire. The sudden change in temperature, however, could not dampen her spirits. She felt as though life had suddenly revved up again after years of simply ticking over, of idling along and going nowhere. She laughed to herself. That was a habit of Johnny's; thinking of life in terms of engines. How proud he would have been of Hal, how delighted with Maria. Prue sighed with deep satisfaction and went to pour herself a drink. Hal had driven her to Wiltshire to meet Maria's parents at their surprisingly modern and quite excitingly unusual house near Salisbury. Her father was an architect and had branches of his practice in Salisbury and Winchester; her mother worked part time in an antiquarian bookshop. They had made Prue welcome, fussing over her and cosseting her, making it quite clear that they were very ready to accept Hal as their son-in-law. Maria was their only child and it was evident that nothing was too good for her. Hal, it seemed, had passed the test with flying colours.

Watching him, Prue had been reminded vividly of Johnny; his easy charm and good manners combined with a sense of humour and boundless enthusiasm must always win him friends. There was a genuineness, an openness, that appealed to all ages and Maria's parents were frankly delighted to give their daughter into the care of a popular and successful young naval officer. In her own home, Maria was more confident than she had been in Bristol. Now that they were officially engaged she behaved in a delightfully proprietorial way towards Hal which made Prue feel quite choky. She hoped that these two would have the long and happy life which she and Johnny had been denied, and she was already making plans for her grandchildren.

'We want to get straight on and have children, Ma,' Hal had told her as they'd driven back to Bristol. 'I can afford it and we want to have them while we're both young enough to really enjoy them. I shall be twenty-seven this autumn. Can you believe it?'

Prue had been silent. It seemed quite impossible that Johnny had been dead for so long. Hal had glanced sideways at her and covered her hand briefly with his own. She'd smiled quickly at him.

'Oh, darling, you can't have them quick enough as far as I'm concerned. I adore babies, you know that. What fun it will be.'

'She's a great girl, isn't she?' he'd asked. 'She was really shy down at The Keep, you know. I wish you'd come. She seems so much at ease with you.'

'It was probably wrong of me,' Prue had admitted,

'but I wanted your grandmother to have you both to herself. That sounds silly since the place was full of people, but you know what I mean. She's been so good to you that I wanted to stay out of the picture and let her feel it was her show.'

'Well, poor old Maria was a bit overwhelmed. Fliss was sweet to her, though.'

There had been a certain defiance about this statement but she had calmly and readily acknowledged Fliss's generosity and gone on to talk of Kit; if only she, too, could find someone and settle down. Prue was secretly horrified that Kit was nearly twenty-seven and still showed no signs of becoming attached. It wasn't that there was a lack of boyfriends, quite the contrary, simply an inability on Kit's part to be content with just one of them. As the little car sped on towards Bristol Prue had confided her fears to Hal. She was afraid that Kit might miss the boat.

'If she's not careful,' she'd told him, 'she'll find that she's left with widowers and divorcees. She's brought home some lovely young men. Oh, Hal, *why* can't she fall in love, like you and Maria?'

Looking at him, his fair hair blown about by the wind – he had persuaded her to travel with the hood down – his hands lightly but confidently grasping the wheel, she had detected a faint air of smugness; a complacency which made it difficult for him to concentrate on other, less fortunate, people's problems whilst he was obsessed by his own happiness. She'd waited for him to dismiss her anxiety lightly, with platitudes: 'Oh, she'll find someone one day,' or 'You worry too much, Ma. Plenty of time . . .' Instead he had given it serious thought.

'The thing is,' he'd said at last, 'what you have to take on board is that Kit is really happy. She absolutely loves life. If she were a bachelor you wouldn't bother, would you? But because she's a woman you think she ought to be settling down with a husband and babies.'

'But don't you think so too?' she'd asked curiously. Hal was so conventional in his views on the woman's role that she'd been taken aback. Didn't these views extend to his sister?

Now, as Prue sat in front of her little fire, she remembered his answer with the same sense of surprise – even shock – that she had experienced at the time.

'Kit isn't like most other women,' he'd said slowly, as though he were dragging up his thoughts out of some deep subconscious. 'She never has been. She's a strange mix. She loves men, quite at ease with them, no droning on about their weaknesses and failings like some women, but she's very independent, too. She enjoys her job, her freedom. It's the way men have always been, Ma, but it's not so common in women. The times they are a-changing and all that. I think Kit is able to be herself without being odd. Twenty years ago she'd have been labelled an eccentric, these days she's just doing her own thing. It's allowed now. Sin's rather like her. That's why they get on so well. No demands, no fusses.'

There had been a little silence.

'It's odd though,' Prue had ventured at last. 'Don't you think so? I'm very conventional . . .'

'Are you?' he'd asked quickly. 'Are you sure? You didn't marry again, did you? Oh, I know there was

Tony but he was a kind of mistake, wasn't he? And we were thirteen years old by then. You didn't exactly hurry to tie yourself up to another man, to . . . well, become dependent again, did you?'

'I wanted to,' Prue had confessed. 'I missed Johnny so much—'

'Hang on,' he'd intervened. 'You tried to replace our father, at least you wanted to, but when you saw that you couldn't, you stopped trying. With the truly conventional woman I think almost any man is better than no man at all.'

'Perhaps,' Prue had said honestly, 'it might have been different if I hadn't had Freddy behind me. Financially I was always secure.'

'But you got out there and worked when you had to, didn't you?' he'd insisted. 'You didn't sit about weeping or looking for someone else to take the weight.'

Sitting by her little fire, sipping her sherry, Prue felt a tremendous glow as she remembered those words. It was as if he had given her a brief glimpse at her life as seen from a different angle; as if she hadn't been quite so foolish as she thought.

'I wanted to make amends for being so stupid as to be taken in by Tony,' she'd admitted to Hal. 'I was a fool . . . I was lonely . . .'

'That's what I mean,' he'd said eagerly. 'You could have had a husband any time you chose. I remember there were always men hanging around you. When we went off to school it must have been awful for you and it was then that you got married. And let's face it, Tony was great fun.' He'd shrugged. 'So it was a mistake but you never made another one, did you?

Even though you were still lonely and your job wasn't exactly a piece of cake. What I'm saying is that perhaps we're not all as conventional as we think we are. Our father doesn't sound particularly conventional. And look at Uncle Peter, swanning off to Africa because he found life boring in peacetime. And what about Grandmother? Living down at The Keep bringing up her boys alone, tough as old boots.'

'And you?' she'd ventured. 'How do you see yourself?'

'I am probably the most conventional of us all,' he'd said slowly. 'I want a wife who will always be there, who will put me and the children first. But I want her to be independent, too. I don't want a wife who's going to start whinging when things get tough. I need a wife who will be able to cope with separations and problems. It's not easy, being a naval wife.'

'And you think Maria will be able to manage?' Prue had asked. 'She's very young.'

'I think she will as long as she's got the usual safety net. You know what I mean? Other wives, the naval support scene, knowing she's not alone. I shall make sure she's well in with the other wives.'

'And there's the family,' Prue had said. 'We shall all be there if need be.'

'Yes,' Hal'd replied. 'There's the family . . .'

Even now, a week later, Prue recalled the odd note in his voice and the courage she had needed to broach the important question. She had known that it must be asked and the shadows finally driven away.

'Is . . . everything well between you and Fliss?' She'd kept her voice light. 'You loved each other, didn't you? I'm so sorry, Hal.'

She'd seen his face harden a little, the chin lift defensively. 'Yes, we did. Fliss was all those things I've talked about, you see. I came first with Fliss but she's strong, too. People don't always notice that. There's a tendency to say, "Oh, poor Fliss," because she had a rough deal and she's quiet and the little ones tend to get all the attention and Kit gets all the laughs. But Fliss is strong. She's like Grandmother. I still love her, if that's what you're asking. I always shall – but there's not that excitement that there is with Maria. There was to begin with, when we were all growing up, but that was just puberty or something. Young boys are easily aroused, aren't they? Later it was as though I knew her *too* well . . .'

Prue sighed as she finished her drink, feeling guilty that she had made him define his feelings but sure that it was best out in the open, lest damaging mysteries grew up about Hal and Fliss and they continued to see themselves as a pair of star-crossed lovers. Maria's love of fun, her prettiness, her adoration, all these would drive out any lingering regret, and when the babies started coming . . . She gave another sigh, this time of pure happiness at the thought of Hal's children, and went to pour herself another drink.

'Are you sure,' Miles was asking Fliss at almost the same moment, 'are you sure you'll be happy here? We could sell it, you know. Buy something else. It doesn't have to be Dartmouth.'

'Honestly.' She was laughing at him, putting her arms round him. 'Stop fussing. I love this house. I'm not bothered because you chose it with Belinda or because you lived here with her. Why should I be?'

He held her tightly, wanting everything to be perfect, knowing it couldn't be. 'I love you,' he mumbled against her hair.

'Then make me some tea,' she said lightly. 'I'm gasping. All this way I've come and you don't even offer me some tea.'

He kissed her, said, 'Don't be too long then,' and disappeared downstairs. Fliss dropped her jacket on the bed and wandered over to the window. She stood staring out over the huddled rooftops across the river to Kingswear, wondering why she didn't mind that Miles had lived here with another woman.

Fliss thought: Perhaps it's because the dead have always been so much part of my life. We shouldn't deny them their part in our present. We pack them away so quickly.

She had noticed – and felt sad – that the photographs of Belinda had disappeared. There had been two here in the bedroom on the chest of drawers; a studio portrait and a smaller photograph of Miles and Belinda together on a beach, laughing at the camera. Fliss thought of the photographs, back at The Keep, that were part of her life, part of her history. Did it make so much difference that Belinda had been Miles's wife? Should she be jealous? Staring out into the cold, wet evening, Fliss examined her thoughts. It seemed impossible to be jealous about something that had happened so long ago, about a woman she'd never met. Clearly there were different kinds of love. Her love for Miles was deep and strong but did not admit to wild passion or moods of jealousy and despair. Fleetingly she thought about Hal and Maria, comparing her love. The stab of pain was swift but she stifled it, denying it, her face grim as she stared out. There must be no weakness. If she and Hal had been allowed to show their love openly it might all have fizzled out in a matter of months; its very secrecy had added to its charm. They would never quite know – but they were no longer children and the game was over.

Fliss knew that she was at a crossroads. She could go forward with Miles, allowing no thought for what might have been, or she could continue to wallow in self-pity and romantic dreaming. She straightened her shoulders, raising her chin. There was no contest. Miles had so much to offer: she had so much to give. Why waste precious life in repining?

'Tea's up.' He was back, watching her from the doorway, aware of her mood.

She turned to smile at him, loving his care for her, his anxiety that all should be as she would wish.

'I love this view,' she said at random. 'But what have you done with the photographs?'

He coloured so deeply that she wondered if it might have been best to let it pass.

'I . . . I wasn't quite sure,' he said awkwardly. 'It seemed wrong somehow . . .'

'For me or for you?' she asked.

'Oh hell, I don't know.' He rumpled up his thick dark hair and shrugged. 'It doesn't matter to me. That sounds wrong, too, doesn't it? As if I don't care.'

'Miles.' She went to him, taking his hands. 'You mustn't worry so much. I love you. It's going to be all right. Belinda was part of your life. She helped to make you what you are. Don't cut her out as if she had no share. It's . . . it's cruel, somehow.'

'I didn't want you to imagine that . . .' He bit his lip and began again. 'This is *your* home now. I just don't want you to feel . . . anything,' he finished lamely.

She started to laugh, holding his hands tighter. 'Well, if you don't want me to feel *anything*,' she said, 'we'd better go downstairs quickly and have that tea. Mind you, I shan't promise not to feel *anything*, even if we're only drinking tea.'

'Wretched woman,' he said, kissing her, 'you know exactly what I mean.'

'Tea.' She slipped out of his arms and went down the steep, narrow stairs and into the big room which was both kitchen and dining room. 'I must have my tea. Oh, it's such a dear little house, Miles. I'm going to love it here when you're at sea. I shall feel so safe here.'

He opened his mouth to explain that Belinda had felt quite differently – and shut it again. Apart from anything else, it sounded so disloyal. She was watching him, holding her cup, leaning against the stainless-steel sink, eyebrows raised.

'Look,' he said urgently. 'I know what you're thinking. You're thinking that I'm trying to hide things or that I'm afraid Belinda might come between us. But it isn't like that. If I start whinging on that we weren't terribly happy and that she hated it when I went to sea it sounds as if I'm looking for sympathy. But to be honest, once Dartmouth and fourth-year courses were over, Belinda *wasn't* happy. She didn't want a husband who was away at sea and I wasn't very sensitive about it. It struck me as unfair to marry a sailor and then complain when he had to do his job. I always felt so guilty, if you see what I mean, and then when they diagnosed her illness it was almost as if she was *pleased* about it. Oh, I know, I know,' he raised his hands defensively at the expression on her face, 'but it was *like* that. As if she was saying, "There now, see what you've done with your selfishness." I know it sounds crazy but it was almost as if she *liked* having something really tangible that she could legitimately complain about. So there you are.'

He turned away from her, staring down the narrow strip of garden with its high walls, his lips compressed. There was a long silence followed by the click of Fliss's cup being put back into its saucer. He felt her behind him, her arms about him, her cheek against his back, resting on the rough wool of his jersey.

'I'm sorry, Miles.' He could barely hear her. 'Sorry for both of you. It must have been very difficult. It's just that I don't want anything between us, you see. Say what you like about Belinda, good things and bad things, memories, whatever. Just don't feel you can't, that's all, and don't feel I shall be judging one way or the other. Why should I? Belinda is gone. I am here with you now. I love you.'

He turned quickly, dragging her into his arms, hugging her until she could barely breathe. 'Oh, Fliss,' he mumbled, 'oh, Fliss.'

'Well, all I can say,' she muttered in his ear, 'is, if you don't want me to feel *anything* you're going a very funny way about it and now that I've had my tea . . .'

'God, I do love you, Fliss,' he said. 'I really, really do.'

'Well, stop talking about it then,' she said, 'and start showing me.'

Chapter Thirty-six

Kit put an LP of the soundtrack from *The Graduate* on to the record player and stretched out full length on the sofa. During the last good spell of weather, she'd become used to wandering over to Hyde Park after her day at the gallery. She'd go in through the Marlborough Gate and stroll along beside the Serpentine, enjoying the fresh air, revelling in the unmistakable signs of approaching summer. During the last few days, however, the weather had been chilly and damp and she was obliged to forgo her walk and come straight home. It was good to live close to the park, to have the little garden belonging to the square to sit in on sunny Sunday afternoons, and she was looking forward to the long summer evenings.

This particular wet and gloomy evening – as she lay comatose, her eyes closed, listening to Simon and Garfunkel singing the melancholy 'Scarborough Fair' – she thought about her forthcoming holiday at The Keep and helping with the preparations for Fliss's wedding. Contented though she was with her life in London, it was always good to go back to The Keep. There, she could cast off her grown-up skin and be a child again. She wondered what it must be like when there was no one left who could remember you as a child; no one to whom you could say, 'Do you remember . . .?' She knew that she was lucky to have two places – in Bristol and in Devon – to which she could return; lucky to have so many varied relationships. Ma, for instance, was almost like a chum, but, though her mother fussed over her when she went home, Kit felt a kind of responsibility for her. She worried about her, bullied her and laughed with her.

It was different at The Keep. Though Fliss was just like a sister, Mole and Susanna seemed to belong to a different generation – more like a niece and a nephew perhaps . . . Kit pondered on this. There was quite an age gap here. Mole was ten years her junior, Susanna even younger. At the moment this was a gap which made itself felt. No doubt when she, Kit, was fifty and Mole was forty there would seem to be hardly any difference between them. She tried to imagine Mole at forty – herself at fifty.

Kit thought: That's older than Ma. How weird to think of myself as older than Ma . . .

As for Grandmother and Uncle Theo, they had hardly changed at all throughout her whole life. It had been impossible to keep Grandmother's age a secret because of the Birthday party. At various times through the years, one or other of the children had innocently demanded her age – when she was cutting the cake or opening her presents – and she had told them quite readily, although it had meant very little to them. She would be seventy-six in the autumn. Kit brooded over it. This meant that Grandmother was already nearly fifty when Kit and Hal were born, yet for twenty-seven years she had seemed exactly the same. Seventy-six . . . With a sudden clutch of fear Kit tried to imagine The Keep without her grandmother, without Uncle Theo, or Ellen and Fox and Caroline. She snatched up a small cushion and held it to her chest, eyes tightly shut, imagining the horror of it. What would happen to them all without that framework of love and support? Who would replace them?

Kit thought: We take so much for granted.

She comforted herself with the thought that it was unlikely that both her elderly relatives and Ellen and Fox would all die at once – and Caroline would still be there for ages yet – but, even so, she felt a strange sense of insecurity. Hal and Maria living at The Keep wouldn't be the same thing at all. How, for instance, would she be able to lie happy and relaxed in the dog basket with Maria working in Ellen's kitchen, cooking on Ellen's Aga? Despite herself, Kit began to laugh. It was such a ludicrous picture. Maria wouldn't understand at all. She'd be disapproving: not as Ellen was disapproving but unsympathetic, disgusted even. Fliss would understand, of course, but that was because she had known Kit for ever; Fliss would always be there to say, 'Do you remember . . .?'

Kit thought: I wish Grandmother had left The Keep to Fliss. She's the one who should be there. She *belongs* there. We all need her, Mole and Sooz and Hal and me.

Kit suddenly knew that she couldn't bear the thought of anything happening to Fliss. She lay quite still, staring at the ceiling, her heart hammering. Fliss was the linchpin of their generation: stable, caring, safe. None of them could manage without

Fliss somewhere in the background . . . She jumped violently as the door shut sharply behind her. Sin wandered in and stood staring down at her.

'Do I gather from your relaxed attitude,' she asked, 'that my supper is prepared? The duck à l'orange timed for eight o'clock? The Bollinger chilling in the fridge?'

'No, it bloody isn't,' snapped Kit. 'Anyway, it's your week for cooking.'

Sin sat down in an armchair and studied her narrowly. She sighed deeply, rolling her eyes, mimicking despair. 'Life isn't what it was before the war,' she observed wearily. 'Standards have dropped. You simply can't get the staff, you know.'

Kit grinned unwillingly. 'I'm feeling miserable,' she informed Sin. 'I was thinking about people dying.'

Sin pursed her lips and nodded. 'And why not? Whatever turns you on,' she said, shrugging. 'Can anyone play? I mean, just how big is the canvas here? Can it be any old people? People we know? People we hate? I'd like to start with all the people on the tube this evening. Match that if you can. Highest number wins. Loser cooks the supper.'

'There *isn't* any supper,' said Kit crossly. 'You were going to do some shopping. Remember?'

'Did I say that?' mused Sin. 'Are you sure? Didn't we agree that we were on a diet?'

'No we didn't,' said Kit firmly. 'And I'm starving.'

'It'll have to be the Roma,' said Sin. 'It's too late for shopping. Everything's shut. We'll go round to the Roma and I'll treat you to a porterhouse steak. Can't say fairer than that, can I? Take it or leave it.'

'I shall take it,' said Kit, sitting up and casting

aside her cushion. 'Why is the thought of food so comforting?'

'*Has* anyone died?' asked Sin cautiously. 'Or was it some kind of weird mental exercise? I simply ask because I want to know.'

'I was thinking about the family,' said Kit, frowning, unwilling to have her feelings mocked. 'And I suddenly realised how awful it would be if anything happened to Fliss.'

She glowered at Sin, lest she should be tempted to make fun of her, but Sin was watching her thoughtfully.

'I can see that,' she said. 'She's the next generation's mother figure, isn't she? If you come from a big family there's always someone holding the reins, being there for everyone else. It gets passed on. You've been really lucky with all those old darlings down in Devon. Spoiled, you are.'

'I know,' said Kit guiltily. Sin and her parents were always at loggerheads and she rarely saw them. 'I know I am.'

'It's not your fault,' said Sin magnanimously. 'You couldn't help it. At least you're prepared to share them round. Anyway, I thought you were thinking about weddings these days, not funerals.'

'I'm being silly,' admitted Kit, 'but I'm OK now. And I'm ready for my steak. Come on. Let's go and eat.'

During the two days of Mole's AIB, The Keep was wrapped in a fog of nervous tension. The whole family knew exactly what was in store for him; all of them had been through it before; first with Peter and

461

John and then with Hal. They were able, as it were, to live through the days with him: 'Now he's arrived; now he'll be doing the practical tests . . .' and so on. On the morning of the second day they stopped telling each other that everything would be all right, that he was prepared and capable, and each of them began to relapse into silence. Fox appeared in the kitchen at regular intervals, hovering anxiously about, until Ellen dropped a plate and snapped at him in frustration, her nerves stretched to breaking point. After a lunch eaten in a strained atmosphere, Caroline disappeared to the greenhouse and Fox took the dogs out on the hill whilst Ellen, at her own request, washed up in sole – and peaceful – possession of the kitchen.

Freddy and Theo fared a little better, not least because Theo emanated a kind of calm confidence which Freddy found, on the whole, infinitely soothing, although she would not admit as much to him. He refused to be panicked or irritated by her occasional fits and starts of alarm and anxiety but remained steady, quietly assured of Mole's success.

'But *why*?' she demanded at one point, when he refused to be drawn into a discussion on how they would cope with Mole if he failed. '*Why* are you so sure?'

Theo reflected on the certainty of his mental and spiritual state. 'I just feel it,' he said at last – and began to laugh at the expression of frustration on her face. 'My poor Freddy,' he chuckled. 'I know that you would prefer signs and portents. A burning bush, perhaps? What about that potentilla that's not doing so well? Or some assurance written in tablets of stone? The big slab at the bottom of the steps would suit nicely. It's no good, you know. I can't help you, I'm afraid. It is one of those moments when we have to listen to St Paul. "*For we walk by faith, not sight.*" The old boy had the habit of hitting the nail right on the head.'

'There are times, Theo,' she said, biting off her words with careful emphasis, 'when I find you extraordinarily tiresome,' and she went away to the drawing room to play the piano. Theo remained by the fire, certain now that he had been right to keep his love for Freddy a secret, private thing. The very act of denial had strengthened and nourished their relationship, lifting it on to a higher level. At peace with himself, he relaxed and reached for the newspaper.

So it was while Theo was in the hall, waiting for tea and reading an article in *The Times* regarding the cancellation of the South African cricket tour, that the telephone rang. It was Mole. The Board was over but he had stayed behind to telephone to The Keep, wanting them to know how he had done. Theo listened, moved and delighted, as Mole's voice – confident and excited – reassured him that all was well. He recounted a few amusing incidents, whilst Theo roared with laughter, and then asked to speak to his grandmother. Theo passed him over to Caroline, who had materialised at his shoulder and was watching and listening with hopeful anguish, and hurried through the hall to the drawing room.

Freddy was playing the third and most melancholy of Grieg's lyric pieces and brooding on her life and her love for Theo. How glad she was now that she had never told her love; how much more satisfying to enjoy the happiness and dignity of their deep, abiding friendship. How much might have been sacrificed for a brief, self-indulgent moment of passion? She allowed herself to become absorbed by the music but she turned at once, her fingers stilled, as Theo came in.

'It's Mole,' he said, smiling at her. 'He wants to talk to you. Everything's fine. He's in high spirits.'

He was left talking to thin air; Freddy had fled away to the telephone, taking the receiver from Caroline, who beamed upon her, signalling joy, before hurrying off to relay the news to Ellen and Fox . . .

Theo was waiting for Freddy in the hall. She came in to him, obviously in the grip of some great emotion, and they stood silently for a few moments, looking at each other, unable to think of any words that might fit the occasion.

'I've never heard Mole sound like that before,' she said at last, feeling her way along the back of the sofa as if she were lame or blind. 'He was so excited. So certain. Oh, Theo . . .'

'I know,' he said quickly, going to her and taking her hands. 'I know we shan't hear for another week but I am sure he has passed. So is he. From what he was telling me he has done all the right things. I'm sure he's made it, Freddy.'

She looked up at him, her eyes full of tears. 'I feel it now, too,' she told him. 'How strange. It was in his voice. Oh, Theo. We have *come through*. Whilst I was listening to him, all I could see was a picture of the three of them, Mole and Fliss and Susanna, waiting for me on the platform at Staverton all those years ago. I was so afraid that I might fail them.'

'And now Fliss is to be married and Mole has made it through the AIB,' he was holding her hands tightly, 'and Susanna is a happy, healthy child. Yes. They have all come through.'

'And not just the children,' she said gently, 'but you and I, Theo. We, too, have come through. But now what?'

'Now we go on,' he told her, 'because there is really no beginning or end. No starts and finishes. There are only small plateaux where we may stop for a moment to enjoy the view so as to refresh ourselves for the next struggle.'

'Thank God,' she said gratefully, 'that we are all doing it together.'

He bent to kiss her and she held him close for a brief moment until Caroline and Ellen could be heard emerging from the kitchen with the tea tray.

Mole came out through HMS *Sultan*'s main gate and stood for a moment in Military Road, gripping his overnight case. It was rather too early for his train but there was one thing he wanted to do and now he would have plenty of time for it. He turned towards the Cocked Hat roundabout – named after the pub which stood beside it – wondering whether to catch a bus to the ferry slip. Suddenly he felt exhausted. The Interview Board had been much better than he had expected but he felt strangely flat and disorientated after his exultant telephone call to the family. Caroline had offered to drive him to Gosport and stay overnight, so as to bring him home afterwards, but he'd refused. He knew it would look more adult to arrive on the train, unaccompanied. Now he almost wished that he'd accepted her offer; almost but not quite. Everything had gone so splendidly. He was lucky that he'd had Hal to prepare him for the ordeal which started when he'd caught the ferry from Portsmouth Harbour. He and the others who had travelled down on the train with him had been picked up on the Gosport side of the river and, from that moment, things had proceeded exactly as Hal had foretold. They'd been driven to *Sultan*, shown their dormitories and told to change into their gym kit ready for the practical tests.

'Keep your eyes open,' his cousin had said, 'and don't be first in. See how the others tackle things, especially in the practical tests.'

These had been difficult; getting your team across a chasm – the area of floor between two rows of chairs – without touching the floor and with the sole aid of several lengths of rope suspended high above from the ceiling, and some long pieces of wood, none of which was quite long enough. However, Hal's advice had paid off surprisingly quickly. Mole had looked round, weighing things up, and there in the corner stood a very useful boat hook. He was the only candidate to be successful in getting his team across and he began to realise how useful his years in the CCF at Blundell's had been, giving him confidence in leadership and quick thinking.

He'd been warned that the session with the psychologist might be unnerving – that he would attempt to undermine Mole's confidence, to make him angry – but even his callous references to Mole's family and the tragedy in Kenya had not succeeded in catching him off guard. After all, he had had years of practice

at hiding his feelings, controlling his emotions . . .
The words and numbers tests had followed and, next
day, the group discussion and the interview with the
Board. Now he had to wait for a week until the result
arrived. If he had been successful he would be asked
to attend a medical at the Empress State Building at
Earls Court.

Mole shifted his case into the other hand and set
off down the Military Road. It was going to be a long
journey back to The Keep and now that the ordeal
was over he longed to share it with someone – going
back over it, perhaps even bragging a bit – yet he had
been quite happy to see the other candidates hurrying
away and had made no attempt to detain them. He
had wanted to speak to Uncle Theo and Grandmother, revelling in their pride, and he felt oddly cut
off once the telephone receiver had been replaced and
the miles between him and The Keep rolled back
between them.

Mole thought: What you need after something like
this is someone you know really well. Someone to
relax with . . .

His heart bumped as a shadow detached itself from
the high wall and moved into his path; it was a girl
dressed in a miniskirt, her hair swinging in a shining
bob, big eyes, good legs. He stared in amazement,
suspecting his own eyes of playing tricks . . . It was
Susanna.

'Whatever are you doing here?' he gasped. He took
in the briefness of the miniskirt, the exuberant make-
up, and glanced around, drawing her aside with him.
'How on earth did you get here?'

She was grinning at him. 'I've got the afternoon

off,' she told him. 'I begged and begged and they said I could. It was only tennis, after all. But I've got to be back by six o'clock. Oh, Mole. How did it go?'

He continued to stare at her. 'I simply don't believe this,' he said – and suddenly he began to laugh. 'Honestly, Sooz. Wherever did you get the gear? And that make-up?'

'Borrowed it.' She twirled round. 'What d'you think? I told one of the sixth-formers and she took pity on me. Good job she's like Twiggy. I've had to do the skirt up with a pin as it is.'

'Don't tell me you just strolled out like that.' His spirits were rising, excitement was flooding over him. She was laughing with him.

'Changed in the ladies' loo at Southampton station,' she told him. 'I thought you might have your chums with you and I didn't want to show you up in my blazer and a straw boater, did I? I thought you were never coming. I saw several boys come along that looked as if they'd been doing the Board, too, and they looked at me rather oddly. Have I overdone the make-up bit?'

He studied her pink cheeks, the eyes made huge with pencil liner, the glossy lips.

'You look terrific actually,' he said seriously – and she beamed at him, lips compressed with pleasure, overcome with a sudden shyness.

'So tell me all about it,' she muttered as they walked along Privett Road. 'Let's go and have some tea somewhere. There must be a café although I didn't notice when I came from the train. I was terrified I was going to be late and miss you.'

'We'll catch the ferry and go to The Black Cat in

Portsmouth High Street,' he told her. 'But there's something I want to show you first.'

'What is it?' she asked, impressed by the solemnity of his tone.

'You'll see,' he said. 'Look. There's a bus coming. Quick. It'll save a long walk down to the ferry.'

They climbed aboard and sat down halfway along the bus. Susanna looked at him eagerly.

'So how do you think you've done?' she asked. 'Was it really difficult? What were the other boys like?'

'It was fine,' he told her. 'I just know it's OK. I did really well. They were pleased with me, I could tell. Thank God old Hal briefed me first. Some bits were tricky though.'

He began to describe things, exaggerating, making her gasp, making her laugh. He felt wonderful. His exhaustion had vanished and he felt strong and happy; confident that he had passed, delighted to be sharing it with her. There was something so right about having her here with him, even in those ridiculous clothes and the make-up. She looked about eighteen . . . Suddenly his heart contracted with the old fear; that something might happen to her.

'You'll change before you travel back, won't you?' he asked her urgently – and she looked at him in surprise.

'Course I will,' she said casually. 'Catch me strolling back into school like this.'

'Where will you change?' he asked. 'You could change at Portsmouth.'

'Can't,' she said nonchalantly. 'Left my uniform in a locker at Southampton. I couldn't bring it with me, could I?'

'Well, watch out on the way back. You could get picked up looking like that.'

'Could I?' Her eyes sparkled as she looked at him. 'Do you think so? Really? How old do I look?'

'You look like a kid dressed up,' he said, exasperated by her obvious delight at the possibility of being mistaken for an adult. 'Just watch it, that's all. There are some funny people about.'

'I'll be careful.' She grinned at him and he grinned back, unable to help himself.

'How will you get that make-up off?' he asked curiously.

'Soap and water,' she said. 'And loo paper. Here's the ferry. We'll have to get off. Come on.'

They climbed off by the ferry slip and looked about them. There was a ferry waiting but Mole shook his head.

'Wait a bit,' he said. 'I want to show you something. There's plenty of time. We can see them from here.'

He led her along by the water, away from the ferry, inland a little, and then stopped and pointed across the water.

'Look,' he said quietly. 'See them? Hal showed me when I came down to see him once. Look, Sooz. It's HMS *Dolphin*, the submarine school, and those are the submarines. That's the future of the modern Navy and that's where I'm going to be, Sooz.'

She stared across the water, impressed by the seriousness of his voice, aware that this was a momentous occasion. The long black boats rocked gently at their trots, two or three abreast, the trot-sentries on watch. Despite the afternoon sunshine there was something sinister in the curved hulls, something menacing and powerful, secretive and dangerous . . . Mole realised that he was holding his breath. He looked down at Susanna and saw the awe in her face. She took his arm, holding it tightly so as to show her confidence in him; her belief in his dreams and her pride to be sharing them with him.

'I just know you're going to make it,' she said, smiling up at him with tears in her eyes. 'It's terrific.' She shook her head, trying to take it all in, as they stood there, side by side, close together, looking at the future. 'Oh, Mole.' Her voice was so quiet that he had to bend close to hear her. 'It's such a very long way from the spinney.'

Second Time Around

To Sue

Chapter One

Market day. The town was busy although there were far fewer visitors about now that the school holidays were over and September was more than halfway through. Tourists jostled to examine the contents of the stalls set up on the quay whilst others made for the café with its tables placed beneath bright umbrellas. It was quite warm enough to sit outside and enjoy a cup of coffee in the sunshine.

Isobel Stangate shifted her weight from one foot to the other and held her collecting tin a little higher. She had positioned herself outside Boots the chemist in a cunning attempt to intercept shoppers as they crossed the road from the car park opposite – and she had not been unsuccessful. She glanced at her watch and fixed her eye meaningly upon a young man who stood on the pavement, waiting to cross. He looked quickly away from her purposeful gaze and, in an attempt to avoid her altogether, sheered off hastily across the road, nearly falling beneath the wheels of a passing car. The driver shouted imprecations and Isobel grinned maliciously as the young man fled, his ears burning with embarrassment.

Years of being dragooned into helping on flag days had given Isobel a cynical outlook. She knew that ladies of a certain age who dressed in navy blue would always put something into the tin. They had stood too often themselves, smiling hopefully and shaking collecting boxes encouragingly, to ignore a fellow sufferer. Young mothers generally allowed their offspring to put a few pennies into the slot and smiled tolerantly as the sticker was placed somewhere upon the child's person. Expensively dressed visitors stared at her brazenly, either passing by without a qualm – or an offering – or pausing to tell her that they wished someone would start up a charity on *their* behalf. The locals would sigh and say, 'What is it *this* time?' as they felt in a pocket or scrabbled for a purse, whilst the lonely ones seized the opportunity for a chat. There were those who would ostentatiously peer at the charity's name on the box and then shake their heads, frowning a little, as if to say, 'Oh, no. I couldn't contribute to *that*.'

Isobel, who was a soft touch and could be relied upon to respond to a cry for help from a busy organiser or committee member, knew them all. She smiled down at a tiny elderly lady, wrinkled and wizened as a nut, who had stopped at her elbow and was peering at the tin whilst struggling to extricate her purse.

'Always someone 'ere,' she said complainingly. 'Ev'ry week. Must think us old age pensioners be made o' money. 'Tis us what should 'ave a collection.'

'Couldn't agree with you more,' agreed Isobel cheerfully. 'You get it organised and I'll come and hold a tin.'

The old woman put ten pence into the box whilst Isobel stuck the paper disc to her ancient jacket.

'Don't forget to take it off when you wash your cardigan,' she said, 'otherwise the glue will make it go all gungy.'

' "Devon against Drugs".' The old woman snorted, squinting down at her newly adorned chest. "Ow do they afford 'em in the first place? That's what I want to know! I can't 'ardly afford a packet o' tea. 'Ow come these kids can afford drugs?'

'By banging you on the head and stealing your pension,' said Isobel promptly. She smiled at the woman who unexpectedly grinned back at her.

'If you're still 'ere when I come back I'll bring you out a cuppa,' she said.

Isobel laughed. 'I'll hold you to that,' she promised. She watched her pass through the swing door into the chemist and suddenly felt depressed. The poor old thing probably couldn't afford that ten pence. She held the heavy tin invitingly towards a smartly dressed couple who, having parked their brand-new BMW in the car park, had been having coffee at the café on the quay. The woman pretended not to see but her companion smiled patronisingly.

'There's too much giving done in this country,' he told Isobel. 'Make people stand on their own two feet, that's what I say. Charity begins at home.'

His wife pulled at his arm, muttering through thin blood-red lips, whilst Isobel suppressed a desire to swing the collecting tin at his smug head. Her depression increased and she looked again at her watch; her two hours were nearly up. She'd promised to stand in for someone at the last moment, agreeing to take the nine-to-eleven stint, and then had woken late and only just made it into

Kingsbridge in time to fetch her tin and sheaf of stickers. Having missed breakfast she longed for a cup of coffee and had every intention of stopping off at the Harbour Bookshop when her stint was over. She knew that Pat Abrehart would probably have the kettle boiling. Pat had offered her a part-time job at the bookshop when Isobel's lover had left her and her husband had refused to take her back.

Isobel knew how lucky she was to have even a part-time job in these difficult times and looked forward to her two days each week at the bookshop.

She bent down to allow a small boy to put some pennies into her tin, smiled at his mother and decided that she'd had enough. She folded up the remaining sheets of stickers, tucked the collecting tin under her arm and headed for Mill Street.

Later, feeling refreshed after some coffee and a chat with Pat, she drove out of Kingsbridge and away towards the coast. When Mike had left her, quite callously and suddenly after nearly a year, it had not been the shock that her friends imagined. For several months Isobel had known that she'd made a terrible mistake in leaving Simon; but how to admit it? Everyone – her daughter, her parents, most of her friends – had condemned her for leaving the gentle, loving, caring Simon for the irresponsible rogue that Mike so obviously was. Even now, knowing her mistake, living continually with the results of that mistake, she did not ask herself *why* she had been such a fool. She knew exactly why. After twenty years in a relationship of the utmost security she had been overwhelmed by utter madness. She

4

was bored with kindness, consideration and safety – and the glitter in Mike's eyes and his reckless pursuit had swept away her habitual feelings of loyalty and love.

As she turned on to the lane that led out to Start Point she remembered those exciting days. She had become a stranger, not only to her family and friends, but to herself; a different woman whose only desire was for fun and laughter. The sensible Isobel who organised dinner parties and drove Helen to dancing classes vanished as though she had never been. The passion she felt for Mike reduced the love she had for Simon to a pale cold emotion and she was dazzled by the power of her feelings. The world about her and everything in it seemed larger, brighter, louder, happier; to resist was quite impossible.

Isobel, driving now between tall hedges of dusty fading foliage, sighed for the fool she had been. She had thrown away love, respect, contentment, security; she had mistaken the shadow for the substance and now must live with the consequences. Helen, just sixteen, had been mortified by her mother's behaviour.

'How can you?' she'd cried, resisting Isobel's attempt to draw her close to her, deaf to her explanations. 'Don't touch me! It's disgusting. A woman of your age! How can you do this to Daddy?' She'd refused to see Isobel, despite even Simon's attempts to reason with her.

At what point, wondered Isobel, had she realised that, all through those heady days, Simon's love for her had been like a safety net swinging beneath her as she cavorted on the high wire? Impossible to say. The fever had passed and she had woken one morning thinking of Simon, missing him, wanting him. The game was over but her pride made her hold out a little longer. She went to meet Simon, as she had at intervals, to talk about Helen who still steadfastly refused to see her. Her secret knowledge made the meeting somehow exciting. His continuing love flattered her and she flirted with him just a little, knowing that soon – very soon now – she would make it all up to him. He had watched her, smiling a little, his affection for her still apparent in his eyes. She'd hugged him when they parted and felt his unguarded response with a kind of triumph. Soon, very soon now . . .

When Mike left it had been almost a relief and she prepared for her return with all the confidence of the Prodigal Son but with none of his humility. Simon had been gentle but adamant. Yes, he loved her; yes, he missed her but he would never be able to trust her again. He was not prepared to risk himself. He listened to her explanations and her pleas but refused to be moved. Knowing that stubbornness was one of his less attractive traits, Isobel withdrew and went to see her mother with whom Helen was spending a few days of half term. Her mother received the news of her proposed return coolly. Her sympathy had been completely with Simon, whom she loved, and her adored granddaughter. Presently Isobel found herself alone with Helen.

'What did you expect?' asked her daughter. 'Did you expect him to fall on his knees and kiss your feet?'

'No,' said Isobel wearily – but she knew that she had expected just that. 'Please, Helen, try to understand. I made a terrible mistake. Can't you forgive me?'

'No,' said Helen baldly. 'I just feel shame for you. Poor Daddy . . .'

'Look!' cried Isobel. 'Look! I fell in love with Mike. It was like a kind of madness. An illness. You're seventeen, Helen. Haven't you felt like that about a boy? Mad about him one day, gone right off him the next . . . ?'

She stopped and shook her head hopelessly. Helen was regarding her with scorn.

'Surely at your age you know the difference between real love and infatuation, don't you?' she asked contemptuously.

'Obviously not.' Isobel tried to smile. She knew how badly she had hurt her daughter and that Helen's cruelty was the measure of that hurt. 'I know now that it was Daddy I loved all along.'

'That's your problem,' said Helen.

Now, two years on, nothing had altered. Isobel changed down into second gear and swung into the track that twisted off from the road and bumped its way down towards the sea. She negotiated the sharp bend to the right, worrying as usual about the car's suspension, remembering her first visit to this remote, hidden-away cove. She'd seen the advertisement in the *Western Morning News* when she was wondering where she should go and what she should do. The offer of a small cottage and use of a car in return for cleaning and shopping was too good to refuse and Isobel accepted the conditions and

settled in with relief. Simon, it seemed, was prepared to support her but Isobel's pride rebelled
against it. She needed to be independent of him but
wanted to stay near Plymouth in case Simon underwent a change of heart. Perhaps his pride needed
time to recover. When Helen went off to university
Simon sold the Plymouth town house and moved to
Modbury. Now he was barely twenty minutes away
from Isobel.

The beach opened out fanwise before her. Here
the track divided. The left-hand fork ended in an
open area behind an old stone house. She drove the
Morris Traveller into a dilapidated building built
into the rock behind this odd-looking house, which
was constructed on three levels and faced out to sea,
and, having collected her shopping from the back
seat, she followed the track along the back of the
beach. Across the small cove from the stone house a
tiny cottage perched above a boathouse, backed into
the cliff on its small plateau of rock. This had been
her home for nearly two years; her wage from her
job at the bookshop plus a minute income from the
legacy her father had left her just enabled her to
survive.

Isobel climbed the rocky steps to her door and
went inside. This door, set in the side of the cottage,
opened into a small lobby. Opposite the front door
was the door into the kitchen, behind which was
the bathroom and lavatory. A second door led from
the kitchen into the sitting room. The cottage was
both cramped and damp but the view from all four
windows was more than enough to compensate for
these inconveniences. She recalled how she had run

up the stairs which rose from the sitting room to the two bedrooms above and how she had gone from room to room, gazing out on to the sea and the cliffs, her worries forgotten, her heartache soothed. She refused to be alarmed by the spectres of damp and cold, of sea mists and gales. This was where she wanted to be. The owner smiled sceptically at Isobel's delighted ravings and suggested a three-month trial.

As she packed away her shopping Isobel chuckled to herself as she remembered Mathilda Rainbird's expression. It was, she'd pointed out in her precise old voice, an exceptionally mild and sunny November day. Perhaps Isobel should restrain her excitement until she'd experienced a few weeks of wet weather? Isobel had insisted that she loved the rain. Mathilda inclined her head politely and suggested that Isobel should look over the house which it would be her duty to clean. It was one of the strangest houses she'd ever seen. Each seaward-facing room on all three floors had its own balcony and the views were just as spectacular as those from the cottage. The kitchen-living room and the dining room – now relegated to a storeroom – took up most of the ground floor along with a walk-in larder, a scullery and a lavatory. A solid-fuel Rayburn which, thought Isobel with dismay, must have been with Mrs Noah in the ark, kept this floor warm and dry and helped to heat Mathilda's bedroom which was directly above it. There was a second big bedroom on the first floor and a bathroom. Above again were the drawing room and a study.

As they toiled from floor to floor, Mathilda gave

Isobel a brief history of the place. Her father had bought the three buildings at the end of the nineteenth century. At that time they had belonged to an estate which was being broken up; the cottage had been derelict and the boathouse unused. Her father was an Oxford professor, a botanist who studied the plant communities indigenous to the sea-cliffs of the South-West, and he bought the house for a retreat to be used during the long vacation and as a base from which to pursue his studies. He and Mathilda's mother had come to love the place and, after Mathilda was born in 1910, the three of them spent as many weeks together as could be spared each year in happy isolation.

Her mother had died of Spanish influenza in the year following the Great War. As soon as she was old enough Mathilda was sent away to school but, each holiday, she and her father returned to the house in the cove. At the end of the Second World War her father suffered a stroke. Mathilda who had worked with him, collating his notes, writing them up and cataloguing his collections, continued to do so and after his death, and with his College's permission, went on with the great mass of work left to her. Often she undertook similar work for his colleagues and newer research students of the college and so the years passed, calmly and uneventfully.

Now, at eighty-four, she spent a good deal of time reading but, when the weather allowed, she still took out the launch which was kept in the boathouse. Isobel had been alarmed to see her setting off alone for a day's fishing but she grew accustomed to the sight and to hearing the boat puttering out on those clear moonlit nights when Mathilda was unable to sleep. She was undemanding, self-sufficient and undoubtedly odd but Isobel had grown tremendously fond of her. She seemed indifferent to comfort and, should the fire burn low or go out whilst she was immersed in her book, she would merely wrap herself in the old blanket which was thrown across her chair and go on reading.

Isobel cleaned the house, did the washing and the shopping and kept the Rayburn alight. The coke occupied a shed beside the back door and each morning and evening, whatever the weather, Isobel was to be seen lugging in the scuttle and carrying out the ashes. She could understand that gas or oil might be impracticable, so far as they were from other habitations, but she did tentatively mention that an electric stove might be more convenient.

Mathilda raised her eyebrows and Isobel could almost see the words, 'For whom?' forming themselves upon her lips; she began to laugh.

'Apart from which,' pointed out Mathilda, exactly as if the exchange had taken place aloud, 'what should we do when we have a power cut? We have a great many in the winter, you know.'

This was true. When the great south-westerly gales brought the seas thundering into the cove – almost to their very doors – and the ground seemed to shake beneath her feet Isobel was glad to huddle in the big kitchen beside the Rayburn, whilst Mathilda continued to read by the light of one of the many oil lamps which were placed in handy positions around the house. Sometimes, on these occasions, Mathilda would suggest that Isobel stay the night and, tucked up in the second bedroom clutching a hot-water bottle, Isobel would wonder at life's vagaries that through one foolish action, one terrible mistake, she should be in this undreamed of situation; cut off from her husband and child, with only an old woman for company, listening to the noise of the gale battering against her window.

Chapter Two

The cove lay at the edge of a rocky combe which ran inland between the cliffs and opened out into a wide valley, rich in pasture and deep woods. A small brook had cut a bed through the combe, running down beside the track and issuing forth on to the beach. In high summer it was little more than a damp patch that barely wet Isobel's shoes as she passed across the sand between house and cottage: but in the winter it gushed out from between the rocks and dug such a deep channel across the beach that a granite slab had been placed so as to make a bridge where it issued forth from the combe.

Overnight the weather had changed from summer to autumn. Late in the afternoon clouds massed in the west and, as the sky darkened, so the sea turned a dull lightless grey. During the evening the wind increased in strength and the waves rode in, high and white-flecked, to crash against the rocks. Towards dawn rain fell in torrents, drumming on the roof, filling the rutted holes along the track and flattening the sea. With the first light the storm passed away to the east but the wind was still high and the water poured down from the moors in a thousand streams and issues.

Mathilda Rainbird paused to watch the brook bubbling over the beach, stepped across the slab and continued her early morning walk. As usual she carried an old plastic bag over her arm and, as she strolled, she kept an eye open for driftwood. It was neither parsimony nor poverty which prompted Mathilda; merely that she liked to watch the blue and orange flames that flickered over the bleached and salty wood. It was a habit formed in childhood. She bent to pick up a piece which was whiter and smoother than her own old fingers and put it into the bag which already had a very satisfactory bulge. The fruits of the storm; that was what her father had called their gleanings. Sometimes the previous eighty years merged together for Mathilda and she was both child and middle-aged woman at one and the same time. She remembered running along the beach, shouting for the sheer pleasure of the feel of gritty sand beneath her bare feet and the wind tugging at her hair; and, too, she was the older woman who had walked more sedately beside her father's research assistant and protégé, discussing his work as they watched the fishing boats heading out to sea.

She missed Nigel. She had loved him, not with passion but as she might have loved a brother. Their minds chimed together; their habits were similar; each was completely at ease in the other's company. He was in love with a married woman and was content to admire and languish from afar and, after Mathilda's father died, he had continued to spend all his vacations with her at the house in the cove. She had known the fulfilment of hard work and the contentment of a quiet mind. Inexperienced as she was, she knew that no man could ever replace Nigel.

14

She had not the temperament for passion or jealous scenes nor was she disturbed by sexual urges. She enjoyed the companionship of a man who thought as she did but she neither desired him physically nor did she have any tendencies to mother him. She more often than not left him to fend for himself; debating and discussing with him as they prepared their separate meals in the big warm kitchen; reading aloud to him to underline some point as he washed his clothes at the deep ironstone sink. When he died of a brain tumour she felt truly alone for the first time in her life.

It was he who had suggested that the cottage should be renovated so that she could offer accommodation to someone in return for some care and attention. He had worried about her as she grew older; concerned that she seemed unaware of damp or cold and was liable to forget to eat. Often she had nothing in the larder even if she had remembered. She had shrugged at the suggestion, prevaricating about cost. Knowing that Professor Rainbird had left her with sufficient income to put the house in order, and seeing this as the only method of protecting her, he bullied her until the job was done and a woman installed. To his relief the system worked. The young woman, a widow, was hardworking and grateful for a roof for herself and her small child. She and Mathilda rubbed along well enough although in almost all respects each might have belonged to a different planet. Then the young widow met a man and was lured away.

By now, Nigel was gravely ill. Mathilda left the cove for the first time for twenty years to travel to

Oxford. She was with him at his end and, at the wishes of Nigel and his sister, brought his ashes back with her. On the first clear night following her return she took the boat out of the boathouse, chugged quietly into deep waters, switched off the engine and cast what remained of Nigel upon the smooth silky bosom of the sea. For some while she sat quite still, the boat drifting on the gentle swell, and made her final farewell to her oldest, dearest friend. He had been the last link with her past and now there was no one with whom she could share the mild jokes that had grown up over the years; no one who had known her parents or remembered her as a girl. For the first time Mathilda felt truly old.

When the young woman went away with her lover, Mathilda advertised again. She accepted, now, that it was sensible to have another human being close at hand. To begin with she was unlucky. The first tenant had three noisy children and an estranged husband who would appear from time to time, the worse for drink, and create scenes on the beach or in the cottage – if he could gain access. One day an inspector from the social services arrived in the cove to make certain enquiries; there was a matter of payments for five children and a claim for rent allowance on the cottage. A puzzled Mathilda explained that there were only three children, not five, and that the woman worked in lieu of rent. She pointed out, however, that the three children *seemed* like five. The inspector, who lacked a sense of humour, made notes and went away. A week later, mother and children had disappeared and the cove was restored to its erstwhile serenity.

The next occupant was a pale, thin, earnest woman in her thirties who had a passion for practising the Alexander Technique stark naked on the beach each morning. This predilection came as rather a shock for Mathilda, taking her first early morning walk after her new tenant's arrival, but she decided that a polite 'Good morning' was all that was required and passed on her way merely hoping that the woman might not take a chill.

She took more than a chill. It seemed that she had eschewed what she referred to as 'death-dealing' foods – with which, she claimed, the supermarket shelves were packed – and had taken to feeding on the fruits of the hedgerows and the beach. Mathilda found her collapsed on the kitchen floor, vomiting, and silently blessed Nigel, who had insisted that a telephone should be installed. The ambulance carried the woman away and she, too, was seen no more.

Cautiously Mathilda advertised yet again. When Isobel arrived, Mathilda was relieved to note that she looked reassuringly normal and appeared to have no dependants or strange habits; no children to be drowned if not watched; no husband waving cans of beer and bellowing drunkenly; no tendencies to dance unclothed upon the sand. It was apparent from the shopping which she brought home in the elderly Morris that she believed in good old-fashioned death-dealing food and what was more – and this was a tremendous bonus – she could hold an intelligent conversation and play a mean game of Scrabble. Mathilda relaxed and began to enjoy life once more. During the ensuing months life in

17

the cove settled down and the two women became easy in their companionship.

During the winter evenings a closer relationship developed. This was because Isobel was lonely and had a need to talk to someone rather than because Mathilda was a natural confidante. The fact that she had been so much alone meant that she had lived through few of the experiences which Isobel described and she listened with surprise as Isobel explained how she had felt and the recent dramas she had undergone. Mathilda, who was used to a more cerebral approach to life, began to be interested in these emotional outpourings. It was impossible for her to enter into Isobel's feelings but she listened to her intelligently and reserved her conclusions until Isobel demanded them.

This was a whole new procedure for Isobel. Her friends were only too ready to join in, cite their own similar cases, offer advice. Her mother argued, but not necessarily constructively, and Simon gently but firmly stonewalled any discussion which became too personal. Mathilda took these outpourings on to a completely different level which forced Isobel to think more carefully than usual.

'Surely you can see,' Isobel would cry, banging pans about upon the Rayburn – she had taken to cooking for Mathilda, fearful that she would fade away entirely if left to fend for herself – 'surely *anyone* can see why I left Simon! Isn't it natural to seize happiness when it's offered?'

At this point her mother would have talked about duties and responsibilities and her divorced friends would have muttered sympathetically. Mathilda, huddled in the Windsor chair beside the Rayburn with the inevitable book upon her lap, would remain silent until Isobel looked at her.

'Honestly, Mathilda,' she would say pleadingly, 'don't you think that happiness is the only thing that matters in the end?'

Confronted, Mathilda would raise her still beautiful slate-blue eyes from the pages of her book.

'It all depends on what you mean –' Mathilda was a disciple of Professor Joad – 'it really all depends on what you mean by "happiness".'

'Oh, for heaven's sake!' Isobel would groan, bashing about with a spoon in the soup. 'Not that "it all depends what you mean" stuff, Mathilda.'

'But how do you define happiness? Do you mean joy? Or do you mean contentment? If you mean some kind of ephemeral excitement bound up with physical gratification, then I must reject your values. It certainly is not all that matters in the end.'

Sighing deeply and rolling her eyes in frustration, Isobel would ladle the soup into bowls.

'How would you know?' she'd grumble. 'Stuck down here for most of your life.'

'Why ask me then?' asked Mathilda serenely, standing up and moving to the table.

Seated opposite – it had been agreed that, since Isobel had taken over the cooking, she should feed with Mathilda and at her expense – Isobel wondered why. She recognised that there was something tough in Mathilda, some unchanging point of reference, against which she could measure her own ideals. It was rather odd, and she would never admit it, but she felt as if she were growing; developing in some vital manner. She'd grinned at the old woman across the table – a misused and mistreated mahogany Georgian breakfast table on a carved pedestal leg – and sighed with a curious contentment.

'I don't know why,' she'd answered.

Remembering this conversation on the quiet grey morning after the storm, Mathilda glanced up at the windows of the small cottage perched on its rocky plateau. The curtains were still tightly drawn. Isobel was not an early riser and it was a while yet until she needed to be off to the bookshop. Mathilda reached the furthest point of the cove and stood for a moment staring out to sea, thinking about Nigel. She was beginning to realise how lucky she'd been to have shared such a satisfying relationship with him; lucky that he'd been content to adore his beloved from afar. To one of Mathilda's temperament, Isobel's life sounded too fraught to contemplate.

She turned back across the firm wet gleaming sand at the water's edge, her bag bumping gently against her leg. It had been in her mind to suggest that Isobel should move into the house for the winter but something prevented her; some inner conviction that it was wise to preserve that small measure of independence and privacy that existed between them. Privacy had always been a necessary part of Mathilda's existence and she was never lonely. It was fortunate that the cove could only be reached by the track from the landward side and although boats occasionally anchored off the beach during the summer and people swam from them and picnicked, few ever ventured ashore.

She entered the house by the side door and, dropping the bag of firewood at the bottom of the stairs, went on into the kitchen to prepare some breakfast. This was the one meal of the day which the two women rarely shared, both agreeing that early morning was a time for silence. Even when Isobel stopped overnight with Mathilda they still breakfasted separately simply because Mathilda rose so much earlier. Now she took some bread from the crock and, dusting off the green mould which adhered to its crust, she placed it on the bread board and proceeded to hack two uneven slices from the parent loaf. She was too indifferent to food to make any effort to make a meal attractive or appetising. Pushing the slices with difficulty into the toaster she rooted around for the butter and found a plate and a knife. She shoved aside the usual muddle of letters and papers and books, which lived permanently on the once beautiful table, assembled her breakfast and sat herself down.

However hard she tried, Isobel was quite incapable of keeping Mathilda's living areas tidy but at least everything was clean. The old cream-coloured Rayburn had cost her some despairing moments but the kitchen looked welcoming, even if it was not the modern idea of a work station. She had realised that Mathilda liked to live in the kitchen as well as to cook and eat in it and that the shelves of books, the aged sofa by the French windows which led on to the balcony and the ability to use the table as a desk were far more important to Mathilda than dishwashers, microwaves and high-speed mixers.

Mathilda finished her breakfast, put the plate and knife in the deep old sink and, collecting her bag of wood, began the climb upstairs to the study. Here she was working on an idea which had occurred to her very recently and she went at once to the large kneehole desk, with its scratched green leather inlay, which resided opposite the fireplace. She stood for a while, looking at papers, studying her notes, frowning a little. It was a large room with glass-fronted bookcases in each of the alcoves on either side of the fireplace whilst the remaining areas of faded wallpaper were almost hidden by the paintings which covered the walls; some originals, some prints. Above the fireplace hung a tapestry which Mathilda's mother had worked nearly eighty years before. The floor was carpeted by a thick Turkey rug whilst several sagging but still comfortable armchairs were placed strategically about the room. Here Mathilda was happiest.

Presently she crossed to the French windows and, pushing them open, went out on to the balcony. There was a brightness now to the morning and she saw that Isobel's curtains had been drawn back. Even as she watched, Isobel came hurrying out, almost running, the long skirt flapping round her bare ankles, a silk scarf floating at her throat. Mathilda watched her leap across the brook and disappear behind the house. She heard the sound of the Morris's engine start up and gradually fade as it bumped its way up the track. As it did so, Mathilda remembered the rest of the conversation she'd been thinking of earlier.

'And did you find happiness?' she'd asked Isobel

at length. There had been a long silence.

'No,' said Isobel at last. 'But it was worth trying for, surely?'

'That rather depends,' replied Mathilda, 'on what you lost in the attempt.'

There had been a longer, deeper silence and finally Isobel had risen to fetch the cheese and had begun to talk about something entirely different.

Mathilda stood for some time on the balcony, lost in thought. The golden glow behind the cloud brightened and the sun's warmth began to shred the mist, drawing it up, dissolving it. The small wavelets broke decorously against the sand and the brook gurgled cheerfully in the combe behind the house. Mathilda went back into the study and settled herself at the desk.

Chapter Three

A week later the autumn made its presence known with a more determined ferocity. The equinoctial gales roared in from the west bringing heavy rain. The trees bowed beneath their passing and the last plums and apples were shaken from the boughs. Sailors hurried to secure their boats or take them off the rivers and estuaries for the winter and the locals put away their espadrilles and placed gumboots in readiness by back doors. The swallows had left for the south and only the martins were still to be seen, swooping and diving for insects, their second brood still in the nest.

The pub car park was nearly empty. Isobel halted the Morris beside Simon's hatchback and switched off the engine. She felt the usual uprush of excitement at the thought of seeing him and she altered the angle of the driving mirror so as to peer at herself in the gloomy light of early evening. She'd dragged her dark hair back, securing it with a clip at the nape of her neck, and she still could not decide whether this made her look sophisticated and distinguished or merely older and rather severe. Perhaps her face was too thin, too bony to take such a style? She grimaced at her reflection to give herself courage, collected her bag and slid out of the car with her coat round her shoulders to protect

25

her from the rain. As she locked the door she bent to peer through Simon's window. His car was both clean and tidy, inside and out, and she sighed as she remembered how she'd teased him about his habit of cleaning it every weekend.

He was sitting in a corner, well away from the bar, but got to his feet the moment he saw her. She experienced the familiar shock of seeing as a stranger he who had been her lover, husband, father of her child. This knowledge lent an underlying excitement to all her dealings with him and sometimes she felt almost breathless with longing for him. He bent his head to receive her kiss and she was seized with a desire to hold him and shout at him. 'Let's stop all this politeness and pretence!' she wanted to cry. 'It was a silly mistake. It's all over and I'll never do anything like it again. It's cost too much! Please let's go back to how we were.' Instead she sat down and smiled at him.

'Spritzer, please. Everything OK?'

'Everything's fine.'

He turned away to the bar and she watched him order the drinks. He looked easy and relaxed in his jeans and sweatshirt, his greying hair a little longer than when they had been together. He was head of the English department at one of Plymouth's comprehensive schools and he was both popular and effective. Isobel mentally prepared the questions she would ask about Helen – the supposed reason for this meeting – and wondered why he had never invited her to his new home at Modbury. It had been a tremendous shock when he'd told her that he wanted to sell the house in Plymouth. Still in thrall to Mike she'd made no protest and had signed the forms obligingly but it had come as an unwelcome surprise to see Simon make such a decision without her advice. That was when she'd realised that, although she was happy with Mike, she was still counting on Simon being there.

I wanted to have my cake and eat it, she thought, watching Simon pocketing his change and picking up the two glasses.

It had hurt when he had chosen the house in Modbury without consulting her, although he had asked her which pieces of furniture or ornaments she would like to take. She knew then that she'd wanted her erstwhile home to stay exactly as it was and, after some reflection, she'd taken only one or two small special things of her own and suggested that he kept the rest himself. Since the Modbury house was smaller than the town house certain items were now superfluous and, having decided between them what was no longer required, it was agreed that these things should be sold or taken to the dump. Later, Isobel decided that she was glad that Simon had made the move. It might be easier to start again in a new place . . . except that there was no suggestion that a new start was desirable to him.

Isobel took her glass and sipped at her spritzer. Simon sat opposite, took a pull at his beer and raised his eyebrows.

'So . . .' He let it hang in the air; not quite a question.

'I just wanted to ask about Helen,' Isobel said quickly. 'How the holidays went, whether there's

27

any sign of relenting. That sort of thing. Has she gone back to Durham?'

'Yes, I drove her up at the weekend.' Simon moved a little in his chair, rather as if he found the subject an awkward one. 'Term doesn't start for a week or two but she's moving out of hall and going into a house with a group of friends. Very nice it is too. A little Victorian crescent near the cathedral.'

Isobel was silent. The pain made it impossible for her to speak. That she was not allowed to take part in her daughter's life was unbearable and she quite suddenly remembered Mathilda's words. '*That rather depends on what you lost in the attempt . . .*' Oh, far too much, she cried silently.

'She's fine,' said Simon gently. 'Honestly. She's got some really nice friends and she's doing well.'

Isobel nodded, swallowing hard and trying to smile. 'I'm so pleased,' she said. 'I just wish that I could see her. You know . . .'

'I know,' he agreed. 'I'm really sorry, love. But now that she's over eighteen it's up to her. I do my best to make her see it all rationally.'

'I know you do.' She smiled more easily; the endearment had been absurdly comforting. 'I know. It's just the years are going by.' She looked at him. 'And how are you?'

'Oh.' He seemed taken aback by the direct question. 'Oh, OK. Much the same.' He looked away from her intense stare, made uncomfortable by it.

'Oh, Simon,' she sighed. 'It all seems so silly. Such a waste.'

'Yes. Well . . .' He hesitated, unwilling to point out that it was her doing.

'I know,' she said quickly. 'It's my fault. Do you think I don't tell myself that?'

'Please, Isobel.' He looked extremely distressed. 'Please don't go on. I'm sure that Helen will come round. She's growing up. You must be patient.'

'It's not just Helen,' she said – and stopped.

'I know it isn't,' Simon said, so bleakly that she looked at him quickly, hopefully. 'Oh, Izzy...'

There was something almost despairing in his tone and, at the sound of the nickname he had used so often in the past, she found the courage to reach out and touch his hand.

'Honestly, Simon,' she said, 'I never really loved Mike. I know that now. It was like I was ill or something. Mad. You know? Couldn't we...?'

'Look.' He took her hand and held it tightly, biting his lip, searching for words. 'The thing is...' He sighed and released her. 'It's no good,' he said flatly. 'There's someone else, Isobel. Sorry, but it's best to say it straight out.'

She sat back quickly, clasping her hands together. 'I... see.'

'I should have said something before,' he continued wretchedly. 'I knew how your mind was working but I couldn't bring myself to hurt you.'

'That's generous of you, in the circumstances,' she said. She picked up her glass and took a long swallow. Simon stared at the table. 'Do... do I know her?'

He hesitated so long that she knew that she must and her shocked mind ranged briefly over their friends.

'It's Sally Curtis,' he said at last.

29

Sally Curtis. Sally of the long brown hair and green eyes who taught History; Sally who had lost husband and child in a car crash and had bravely started a new life; Sally whom she had invited to a barbecue at the town house and with whom she had sympathised; Sally who had encouraged Helen with her history; Sally . . . He was watching her compassionately.

'She's been a good friend,' he said.

'Yes,' said Isobel. 'I'm sure she has. And Helen adores her.'

'That is a bonus,' he agreed. 'I'm sorry, Isobel—'

'No, no,' she interrupted him quickly, 'I should have guessed there was someone. After all, why shouldn't you and . . . and Sally . . .'

'Shall I get you another drink?' he asked anxiously.

'No,' she said abruptly. 'No. Just go, would you, Simon? Sorry. It's just . . . Please go.'

He finished his beer and stood up, his eyes genuinely worried. 'Will you be OK?'

'Of course I will. I just want to sit quiet.' Go, she begged silently. Just go before I burst into tears or do something bloody humiliating. For God's sake *go*!

'I'll be in touch.' She felt his hand briefly on her shoulder. 'Take care.'

She didn't look up until she heard the door close behind him. She stared straight ahead, seeing nothing. So that was that. What a fool she'd been! Humiliation swept over her, staining her cheeks. Simon and Sally Curtis . . . Sally who was only thirty-something; Sally whom Helen adored and now Simon adored also. The pain was so acute that she could barely breathe and she sat for some moments making an attempt to calm herself. The young barman – probably a student – came to collect Simon's empty glass. He glanced at her curiously and Isobel attempted to smile at him. It was a failure. Her lips shook and she picked up her bag and went out into the windy car park. A gust of wind drove the rain horizontally and she held her coat over her head as she hurried to the car. Once inside she fumbled with her keys and realised that her hands were trembling. Suddenly she wanted to be back at the cove, tucked away inside her little cottage or – better still – with Mathilda in her tall grey house. Just being with Mathilda would calm and strengthen her.

Isobel started the engine and switched on the windscreen wipers. They wiped away the rain but not her tears and she dragged her hand angrily across her eyes before she pulled out on to the road and headed for the cove.

The kitchen was empty. Out of habit Isobel went round tidying up, locking the French windows and drawing the curtains before going upstairs. Having reached the landing she paused to listen at Mathilda's bedroom door before climbing on again, up to the top floor. The study was empty so she opened the drawing room door and looked inside. Mathilda sat reading beside a fire which had burned down to little more than ashes, undisturbed by the rain which streamed down the darkened window panes or the wind which rattled at the catches.

'Honestly, Mathilda.' Isobel shut the door behind her and crossed the room to the French windows.

'You could at least keep the fire going. Aren't you cold?'

Mathilda raised her eyes from her book and watched Isobel drag the curtains together. Even she detected a brittle note in the younger woman's voice.

'I didn't notice,' she said. 'Is it dark already?'

Isobel sighed and began to rake the ashes together, putting on small pieces of wood until the fire blazed up. 'You're hopeless,' she said.

'So you keep telling me,' said Mathilda without rancour.

Isobel laughed. 'Hopeless and impossible. Have you had any supper?'

Mathilda's brow wrinkled thoughtfully. 'Soup?' she suggested cautiously.

'That was lunch,' sighed Isobel. 'I left you a casserole in the bottom oven. I *did* tell you.'

'Well, now we can share it.' Mathilda put a marker between the pages of her book and prepared to rise. 'Are you hungry?'

No, thought Isobel. It would choke me to swallow even a spoonful. She remembered that she had planned that she and Simon would be eating together this evening, so sure had she been that he was weakening.

'I've had some supper,' she said aloud. 'But I'll come and watch you eat yours.'

'Good idea. And then we'll have a game of Scrabble.'

Isobel piled some more logs on the fire and put the discarded book on the table beside Mathilda's chair. She was not surprised to see that it was Alain-Fournier's *Le Grand Meaulnes* in the French. It might easily have been *The Hunting of the Snark*. Months ago she'd asked Mathilda how she was able to read Lewis Carroll one day and Descartes the next. Mathilda pondered. 'They were both mathematicians, you know,' she'd said at last.

Later they sat together, a low table drawn up between them before the fire. After the crowded, active atmosphere of the study the drawing room was almost stark in its austerity; one or two large paintings on the otherwise empty walls; a long sofa against the wall opposite the fireplace; two armchairs pulled up to the fire; a bureau in an alcove. There were the usual bookshelves in the second alcove but it seemed to Isobel that all of Mathilda's taste and personality had been crammed into the study.

Isobel rearranged the Scrabble tiles on her rack and wrenched her mind away from Simon and Sally. Instead she thought of an article she'd read only that morning.

'Do you believe in euthanasia?' she asked abruptly.

Mathilda began to place her tiles on the board. 'Of course I do,' she said.

Isobel stared at her, surprised at such a swift and unqualified reply. Mathilda met her gaze and raised her eyebrows.

'I must believe in it,' she said reasonably. 'After all, it exists. It happens. How could I not believe in it?'

'Oh, honestly!' said Isobel impatiently. 'You're so pedantic, Mathilda. You know what I mean.'

'If you are asking if I *approve* of it then you

should say so,' replied the old woman. 'If I am pedantic, you are sloppy. You were a teacher. You should know better.'

'I taught very young children,' said Isobel, as though that excused it.

'All the more reason for accuracy,' observed Mathilda.

'But do you?' persisted Isobel. 'Do you approve?'

'It all depends,' began Mathilda – and smiled at Isobel's groan. 'It depends on the state of the person at the time. If he is terminally ill and in his right mind I think that he should have as much right to choose the manner of his death just as he has chosen the manner in which he has lived.'

'I notice you say "he"?'

'A manner of speech,' murmured Mathilda, who had been thinking about Nigel.

She had visited him in hospital after his chemo-therapy treatment. Even now the remembrance had the power to shock her. 'That's right, love. Come to see your dad?' the man in the next bed had asked. Mathilda, who was several years older than Nigel, had looked down on the yellow, bald, mummified head, too horrified to explain that they were not related. Nigel had been unable to communicate and she had sat clutching the claw that had been his hand, staring into the open lashless eyes, her heart pierced with pain.

'But is it right for someone to kill another person? Even if it is a mercy killing?'

I would have killed Nigel, thought Mathilda. I would have released him from the terrible indignity of those final weeks.

'And don't say "it all depends",' warned Isobel.

'But it does, you see. It depends whether the killer is able to bear the responsibility. Whether the sufferer actually desires release or whether the killer merely thinks he – or she – does . . . It is all extremely complicated.'

'People cling to life,' mused Isobel. 'They say, "Oh, knock me on the head if I get like that," but when the time comes they decide they've changed their minds.'

'This life is all we know,' said Mathilda putting her last tile in place. 'It is the human condition to cling to what we know.'

'Even if it's pretty awful. Mathilda! You can't have that! *Pribble*? I've never heard of it.'

'Look it up.' Mathilda pushed the dictionary towards her. 'It's a perfectly good word meaning "pointless chattering". Go on. Look it up.'

'If you will use a pre-war dictionary,' grumbled Isobel. 'Pre-Boer War . . .'

'Are you going to stay the night?' asked Mathilda, taking more tiles from the bag.

'I think I will,' said Isobel, listening to the sea pounding against the rocks, the windows rattling beneath the assault of the wind. 'If that's OK?'

'Of course.' Mathilda felt relieved, although she was not quite certain why. It would never have occurred to her to question Isobel but she was aware of a tension in the younger woman.

'Thanks.' Suddenly Isobel dreaded the moment when she would be alone in bed, unable then to postpone any longer the pictures of Simon and Sally together. She gave thanks that, because she slept so badly, Mathilda generally went to bed late. 'I'll make us a hot drink when we've finished this game,' she promised. 'OK. My turn. Wait till you see this one!'

Mathilda jotted down her score carefully. Her thoughts of Nigel had disturbed her and she was in some measure glad of Isobel's company. The fire burned cheerfully, the casserole had been delicious, and she was grateful for the younger woman's care which went far beyond her duties. She wished that she could help Isobel but did not know how. At least they could bear each other company through this wild night and maybe in the morning the storm would have passed.

Chapter Four

It was a few days after her meeting with Simon before Isobel took in the whole meaning of what he had told her. Just as she had – albeit subconsciously – used the knowledge of his love as a safety net during her affair with Mike, so had she regarded their eventually coming back together as a certainty. Simon had loved her so much, with such care and consideration and loyalty, that she could not seriously contemplate his love ever dying. She had even rather enjoyed their meetings, seeing them almost as a prelude to a new, more exciting relationship. Although she had been taken aback when he did not immediately 'kiss her feet', as Helen had put it, deep down she had been sure that she would win him back.

The shock of realising that there had been someone else numbed her and occupied her every waking thought. She recalled each single meeting and conversation she had ever had with Sally, even morbidly wondering if Simon had been attracted to her before Mike had appeared on the scene. She pictured them together and made herself miserable by contemplating Sally's happy, easy relationship with Helen. It was at this point that Isobel began to think about her own future. With Sally around it seemed unlikely that Helen would ever need her own mother again.

Isobel knew now how much she had counted on resuming her marriage with Simon as a route back to her daughter. When she and Simon were living together once more Helen would be confronted with the necessity of seeing and communicating with her. It would be unavoidable, unless Helen gave up coming home altogether. Isobel had been confident that this would be the last hurdle. Now she saw her hopes and plans crumbling to nothing. She was the outsider with no rights to either Simon or Helen. She tried to deal with this as she went about her work, looking after Mathilda, shopping, cleaning and working at the bookshop.

She was grateful for those two days a week in Mill Street. She and Pat often laughed – sometimes rather bitterly – when customers or friends observed what fun it must be to work in a bookshop. They seemed to imagine that the days passed in a leisurely manner, poring over this book or that and drinking coffee. These people had no notion of the business of unpacking boxes of books, ordering new ones, talking to suppliers, tracking down books for customers who had very few details apart from the titles, answering the telephone, wrestling with the computer; nor how much one's feet ached at the end of the day. Most lunchtimes Isobel sat out in the back office with a sandwich but generally the telephone would ring or a customer would appear and her sandwich would have to be abandoned, bites snatched at odd moments during the afternoon. Occasionally she would escape next door to The Hermitage and in the warmer months would sit out in the garden with her drink, gratefully breathing in the fresh air.

It was Pat who made her think about her future. When Isobel told her what had happened, Pat's concern was for how Isobel would survive. She pointed out that she could offer her no more than her two days at the bookshop; perhaps she should think of going back to teaching? Isobel, who had not yet considered this aspect of her troubles, had remarked that she had Mathilda.

'But for how long?' asked Pat.

During the next few days Isobel brooded on this. Until Simon had shattered her hopes she had seen the future somewhat hazily. She could manage on what she was earning but she had never looked upon her work, either at the bookshop or with Mathilda, as a long-term arrangement. At some point she and Simon would be back together in the house at Modbury and all would be well. She had applied for teaching posts, which were very few and far between, but the competition was fierce and she had not been lucky. Then her job with Pat had turned up, along with Mathilda's advertisement, and she had put the idea of teaching on the back burner, so to speak. Now Pat's question haunted her. Mathilda was old and frail. What would happen if she should die? Isobel began to scour the papers in the hope of seeing teaching posts advertised and wondered who would inherit the house in the cove.

This question was answered almost immediately. The storms subsided and gentler, warmer weather set in. Isobel wandered on the cliffs above the beach but even the breathtaking beauty of the scene failed to raise her spirits. The sea appeared to be resting peacefully against the land, a world away from the recent storms. Beneath the cliffs the water was a pure translucent turquoise fading away, as far as the eye could see, to a softer blue which reflected the cloudless sky until both sea and sky seemed to merge into infinity. Isobel followed the tracks through heather and gorse, which had flowered together in a blaze of colour, and turned inland across the stunted grass towards the fields. A chiffchaff sung his two notes from a hazel bush and the hedges were full of blackberries. She untied the cotton scarf she wore at her throat and began to pick the berries. Mathilda might enjoy a blackberry and apple pie.

Her heart was heavy, however, and even this task seemed pointless and exhausting. Everything tired her and her natural vitality and enthusiasm had deserted her. She sat down upon a boulder, turning her face to the sun, her fingers picking idly at the crumbly dry lichen on the rough pitted stone. At the sudden beating of wings and the raucous cry of a gull she opened her eyes and stared out across to Start Point; at the jagged bony spine of the cliff as it descended towards the sea and at the white column of the lighthouse. The tranquillity of the scene, the sheer timelessness of sea and rock, soothed her and presently she picked up her handkerchief and its contents, strolled back across the cliff and descended the steps which led down to the back of her cottage. Soon the cove would be in shadow and she shivered a little as she thought of the winter drawing on. She knew that she simply must not allow despair to swamp her nor self-pity deaden her will to survive. She let herself into the kitchen which was still warm from a day of sunshine and put the blackberries on the table, determined to make a pie for supper.

Her kitchen was hardly less basic than Mathilda's but at least she had a microwave and an electric mixer. The room was filled with the light from the sea; a white shaking light which continually formed, dissolved and re-formed into watery patterns on the whitewashed walls. On certain days Isobel felt that she was living underwater. She loved it and she loved the sound of the sea shushing across the sand; hissing and sucking at the land as if it were loath to leave it behind as it retreated; whispering secretly across it as it returned.

At first she had been fascinated by the changing scene; the colour of the water as it reflected a cloudy sky; the dark outline of the Mew stone; the tall day beacon above Kingswear shining white in the evening sunshine. She had sat late at her bedroom window watching the moon rise clear from a skein of cloud and ride high above the black silk of the sea, its silver path running almost to her very door; and had woken early to see the sun rolling up out of the cliffs to the east to set the water blazing with orange and gold. After a while she had learned to close her curtains against these temptations lest she be too tired to work; but she never grew indifferent to her surroundings. Even now she was aware of the glory all about her and, even if it did not set her spirits leaping with joy, it brought a measure of comfort to her unhappy heart.

Isobel took off her jacket and concentrated on the pie. Now that she did so much cooking for Mathilda she was always finding that certain items were no longer to hand. This afternoon it was her pie dish which was missing; no doubt languishing in Mathilda's kitchen where it had been washed up after they had eaten their last pie together. Isobel debated with herself. Should she run over to fetch the dish or take the ingredients and make the pie in Mathilda's kitchen? She knew that the pie would taste better if cooked in the Rayburn – apart from which she needed company. Gathering up the things she required, she piled them into a basket and went out across the cove. The shadow of the cliff stretched nearly to the water's edge and she was glad to reach the warmth of Mathilda's kitchen. She set the basket on the table, checked the Rayburn and glanced at her watch. Whilst the Rayburn pulled up a little to the necessary temperature she would make Mathilda a cup of tea.

Mathilda was in the study, working at the big desk. Isobel set the tray on the fender and paused to throw a log on the fire.

'Tea,' she announced. 'I'm making a blackberry and apple pie for supper but the blackberries taste a bit funny. Sort of mushy. I hope it'll be OK. Isn't the Devil supposed to spit on them at Michaelmas or something?'

'I think,' said Mathilda, without turning round, 'that the blame should be laid at the door of the flesh fly. He dribbles saliva on them so as to be able to suck up the juice.'

'Eeuch!' Isobel made a face. 'Honestly, Mathilda,

I wish you hadn't told me. That's disgusting, isn't it?'

'That depends on whether you are a flesh fly,' replied Mathilda. 'Thank you. I should like some tea. I'm trying to work out my family tree.'

'Heavens!' Isobel kneeled down by the fender and began to pour the tea, attempting meanwhile to expel the taste of flesh fly saliva from her mouth. She scraped at her tongue with her teeth, quite certain now that it was coated with it. 'Whyever?'

'I'm looking for a beneficiary,' replied the old woman. 'I've decided to change my will.'

Isobel's hands were arrested in the act of adding milk; the flesh fly was utterly expunged from her mind – and mouth. 'Your will?'

'Mmm.' Mathilda swivelled round in her chair to look at her. 'I had decided to endow a studentship at my father's old college but I disapprove of their new policy of giving the highest proportion of places to foreign students who can afford to pay huge fees. And now I hear that they are intending to discontinue his field of study in favour of the peat bog. Apparently, with all this fuss about preserving peat it is hoped that it will attract more funding.'

'I see,' said Isobel. She carried the cup across and placed it on the desk. 'So how far have you got?' Her heart was hurrying a little as she tried to frame the words as carelessly as possible. 'I hope you're not planning to pop off just yet, Mathilda?'

'Not just yet,' said Mathilda comfortably, 'but I do want to get this sorted out.'

Isobel stared down at the papers upon which Mathilda's neat writing was quite clear. Names stared up at her. 'Who are Maria and Albert Holmes?' she asked.

'Maria was my father's sister.' Mathilda sipped her tea. 'She married Albert Holmes and had three children. Ruth died young and Peter and John were both killed in the Great War but John had already married a woman called Ada and had a son by her.'

'It's fascinating.' Isobel peered at the names and the dates. 'What about your mother's family?'

Mathilda shook her head. 'I never knew my mother's family. I can very vaguely remember an old woman who might have been my grandmother but I think she must have died whilst I was still very young. My mother died when I was ten and my father was not good at keeping in touch with relatives. Even with his own family.'

'I can believe that,' murmured Isobel, who guessed that Mathilda was much like her father. 'And who are William and Edith Rainbird?'

'William was my second cousin and died at Dunkirk.' Mathilda frowned. 'It's all rather complicated.'

'And how have you tracked down these people?'

'Some of it was in the family bible and I found a few notes amongst my father's papers but a friend of mine in London is putting in the real work,' admitted Mathilda. She replaced her cup in its saucer and looked at Isobel. She noticed that she was looking thinner, sharper around the nose and cheekbones, and the old woman studied her for a moment. 'Perhaps you should have a holiday?' she suggested.

Isobel, surprised both at the sudden change of

subject and that Mathilda should make such a personal remark, looked at her quickly. 'Do I look as if I need one?'

'You do rather,' said Mathilda bluntly. 'Are you losing weight?'

'I'm worried in case you're thinking of turning me out,' replied Isobel lightly. 'In favour of all these relations.'

'Oh, I shan't do that.' Mathilda shook her head. 'You will have all the rights of a sitting tenant. No one shall turn you out.'

'That's a comfort.' Isobel tried to maintain her lightness of tone, wondering whether the beneficiary would require a housekeeper and, if not, how she, Isobel, would afford the rent of her little cottage. 'So which one have you decided on?'

'There appear to be three possible contenders,' said Mathilda. 'Edward Holmes married the year after I was born so, though it's unlikely he's still alive, he might have offspring. Then William married in 1914. He was the one who died at Dunkirk. Apparently he had a son but we have been unable to find him as yet. We *have* traced the third possibility down to the last decade at which point the entire family appear to have vanished without trace.'

'But what will you do if you find them all?' Isobel's question had a certain self-interest behind it. 'How would you decide? Would you interview them?'

Mathilda finished her tea and passed the cup to Isobel. 'Yes, please. I should like another if there's any in the pot. It's a rather difficult decision. There might be an obvious candidate, you see. On the other hand I might decide to leave it to several of my father's descendants.'

'That sounds fraught with difficulties,' said Isobel, pouring the tea and feeling more nervous by the minute. 'They could hardly be expected to live here all together. Surely they'd simply sell it all up and divide the spoils?'

'You may well be right.' Mathilda looked at her papers thoughtfully. 'We are not a particularly *fruitful* family,' she observed. 'Perhaps there will be no one left to inherit after all.'

Isobel carried the tray down the two flights of stairs and set it on the wooden draining board. She felt frightened and lonely; what would happen to her with Mathilda gone? She stared at the blackberries and suddenly remembered the flesh fly. With an exclamation of disgust she heaved the whole lot into the pedal bin and, sitting down at the table, put her head in her hands. She tried to imagine Mathilda's descendants arriving at the cove; going all over the house with an eye to its value, laughing at its old-fashioned kitchen and deciding to turn the house and cottage – not to mention the boathouse – into a kind of holiday park. In her mind's eye she could see it; the house split up into letting units; the cottage frizzed and powdered into the kind of twee 'fisherman's cott' one saw in the glossy brochures. The boathouse with its huge attic room where Professor Rainbird had once worked would be ideal for keeping sailing dinghies and sailboards, as well as a launch – but not Mathilda's old boat – for trips along the coast. She could imagine children on the small stone pier and the cove resounding to their shouts. Even the long winding drive would no doubt be laid down to tarmac and proper garages built into the cliffs behind the house where the Morris now lived in solitary splendour.

Isobel wiped away a tear or two and sighed. Whatever happened would have to be faced. Perhaps she could raise the money to buy the cottage ... Perhaps Mathilda might be right when she said that, after all, there might be no one left to inherit.

Chapter Five

Tessa Rainbird sat at the small table in the little back bedroom of a house in Shepherd's Bush. This had been her home almost ever since her parents and small brother had been gassed to death when a volcano erupted in the Cameroons where her father was working as a petrochemical consultant. At the time Tessa had been at her school in England but even now, eleven years on, she suffered nightmares in which she was desperately trying to save her adored baby brother. Sometimes the nightmare took the form of wreckage, amongst which she crawled whilst explosions and screams reverberated about her. At other times the nightmare had that well-known quality of helplessness: her legs refused to run, her voice died in her throat, and she was unable to warn her brother or her parents or rescue them from their terrible fate.

Her mother's second cousin had stepped into the breach when Tessa's paternal grandmother died two years after the accident. Tessa's father was an only child but her mother, whose parents were dead, had a sister in New Zealand who had offered to care for Tessa. Tessa could barely remember her aunt and dreaded leaving England and the friends she had made at school who had been so kind to her during these years. At last it was decided that she should

stay on at her boarding school and go to Cousin
Pauline in the holidays. She was already elderly; a
quiet, gentle woman who watched a great deal of
television and was no companion for a thirteen-year-
old. Gradually Tessa began to accept more of the
invitations to stay for the holidays which issued
from her friends, and spent very little time at the
terraced house in Cobbold Road. She knew that
Cousin Pauline had taken her out of duty rather
than love and, though she was grateful, Tessa knew
that her presence was not an advantage except as a
pair of young legs and hands to help with the
household tasks.

When Rachel Anderson arrived at the school on
the south coast the two girls took to each other at
once. Rachel, a warm-hearted, eager girl, was
horrified at Tessa's tragic history whilst Tessa was
immediately drawn to the family to whom Rachel
belonged. Her father was a naval officer, her mother
a natural homemaker – wherever she was posted
with her husband – and the small twins were the
same age that Tessa's brother, Timmy, would have
been had he lived. As for Sebastian . . . At seventeen
he was the most handsome young man she had ever
seen. Tall, fair-haired, hazel-eyed, he treated her
just as he did his younger siblings; he teased them,
hugged them and for the most part ignored them.
Tessa, who had so desperately missed family life,
was enchanted by the Andersons and never refused
an invitation to stay.

By the time she was seventeen she was wondering what she should do with her life. She could see
that a university degree was not the passport to a

career that it had once been and she knew that she was not brilliant enough to be one of the lucky few who, in these difficult times, found jobs easily. Once again it was through the Andersons, who gave her help and encouragement, that she discovered, quite out of the blue, what it was she really wanted to do. At the end of the spring term Rachel received a letter from home.

'Doom and gloom,' she announced to Tessa, with whom she shared a study. 'The dog lady can't come, apparently. She's broken her ankle and Granny's down with flu. Looks like our holiday's up the spout.'

'Dog lady?' Tessa knew that the Andersons were going skiing as soon as school broke up for Easter.

'You know,' said Rachel. 'The woman who dog-sits when we go away. Mummie's quite desperate. It's the first leave that Daddy's had for ages that fits in with school holidays.'

There was a silence whilst Rachel read her letter and Tessa was visited by an exciting answer to the Andersons' problem. She thought it through carefully.

'I've had a thought,' she said at last. 'Is there any reason why I couldn't do it? After all, Baggins and I are old friends. I'd be quite happy to look after him.'

Rachel had stared at her for a few moments, letting the idea sink in. 'Brilliant!' she'd said. 'Fantastic! Are you sure? It's a great idea. I'll phone Mummie.'

That was how it had started. During those quiet weeks in the Andersons' house Tessa began to see how she could earn her living. She adored dogs, preferred the country to the town and never minded her own company. She still missed her parents and her brother quite dreadfully but she had already learned that it is better to be alone than to be with the wrong people.

Sebastian and Rachel approached the suggestion of her new career with their usual enthusiasm. Sebastian immediately drew up a list of naval families who might require her services and Mrs Anderson recommended Tessa to these friends and wrote a glowing reference. In the following year – her last at school – she had four jobs during the holidays and a growing clientele.

Now, at twenty-two, she worked almost two-thirds of the year. Between jobs she came back to London but she longed for a little place of her own. Her work took her all over the south and west so it was difficult to decide where she might base herself and whatever she chose to rent would be empty for the greater part of each year. The money from her father's estate would come to her when she was twenty-five but it was by no means a large sum. It had paid for her education – which included driving lessons – and her trustees had advanced enough for her to buy an estate car so that the dogs could be taken for walks or to the vet in an emergency – owners did not always leave transport available – but meanwhile she lived on the interest which was paid quarterly. It amounted in all to approximately two thousand pounds a year, which came in very useful.

Tessa bent thoughtfully over her diary. The weeks were filling up very satisfactorily and tomorrow she was off to Devon; a week on Dartmoor. She sighed with pleasure. Kate and David Porteous were probably her favourite clients. David was an artist – an RA – who often went to London whilst Kate tried to juggle their lives between their town house and the country. Kate, who once had been married to a naval officer, knew the Andersons very well and had been quite willing to give Tessa a try. It had been one of Tessa's earliest jobs and she was desperate to do well. She took at once to Kate's large golden retriever, Felix, fell in love with the moor, and now Kate was a regular client.

Tessa shut her diary, picked up her bag and ran downstairs. She had promised to go to the Spar shop in the Uxbridge Road and it was very nearly lunchtime. She put her head into the sitting room, where Cousin Pauline was watching *Neighbours*, told her where she was going and went out into Cobbold Road. As she hurried along, crossing by the library and turning right by the Askew Arms, she was barely aware of her surroundings. Only one thought sustained her; tomorrow she would be in Devon.

As she drove out through Ashburton and headed for the moor, Tessa was thinking of Sebastian. This was not unusual; Tessa spent most of her time thinking or dreaming about Sebastian. From those earliest days she had been in love with him and she had plenty of hours in which to weave fantasies about him. Yet it was fairly clear that, fond of her though he was, Tessa was little more to him than Rachel's friend. At one time, when he was at university, Tessa believed that their friendship had blossomed into love. He had invited her to a party

53

in London and they had both drunk too much. She had told her love and he had very kindly and considerately relieved her of her virginity. Afterwards she wished that she could remember more about it but the act alone convinced her that he must love her, too.

This sadly had not proved to be the case. He was still as affectionate as he had always been but nothing, it seemed, had changed. Tessa had been shocked and then desperate. Had she thrown herself at him? Had he been just using her? She could hardly ask Rachel, frightened that she might confront Sebastian, and there was no one else in whom she could really confide. Sebastian put things right himself.

'Are you OK, kiddo?' he'd asked, next time they'd met. 'I hope you're not angry with me. It just seemed the natural thing to do at the time. The first time is rather important for a girl, isn't it? And I wouldn't like you to be hurt or anything like that by some insensitive lout.'

She'd swallowed and nodded; her experience did not allow for this kind of conversation.

'Well then.' He bent and kissed her lightly and instinctively her arms went out to hold him. 'That's all right. But don't drink too much at parties.'

So that was that; but Tessa had not stopped loving him. One day, she was quite convinced of it, he would suddenly realise that he'd loved her all along. Meanwhile she dreamed about him.

She passed Ausewell Cross and a few minutes later was pulling in at the Roundhouse at Buckland-in-the-Moor. She always got up on to the moor as quickly as she could and the Roundhouse was always her first stop. She climbed out of the car and stretched, sniffing at the wind that blew across the hills. The Roundhouse, with its little shop and gallery of artists' studios, was attached to the farm and three generations of Perrymans – if you included young Colin who helped out in emergencies – ran it all. She wondered if Mrs Perryman would be around or whether one of her twin daughters – or perhaps both – would be working today. She looked forward to seeing their friendly smiles and hearing their soft Devon voices just as much as she longed for the delicious coffee. Tessa smiled to herself with anticipation; she felt exactly as though she were coming home.

'The usual dramas!' announced Kate when Tessa had settled into the big Victorian house on the edge of Whitchurch Down. 'Felix has cut his pad and David has left half his belongings behind. Oh, and I think I've found you a new customer.'

'Oh great!' Tessa sat at the kitchen table stroking Felix, who had come to lean against her. 'Who is it?'

'Hang on, I've written it down somewhere.' Kate leafed distractedly through the muddle on the table. 'They're over towards Ivybridge way. Two labradors. Here we are. Carrington. She's a widow, rather elderly, who likes to visit her daughter in the Midlands. Dear old thing she is and the dogs are very well trained and far too fat and idle to do anything antisocial like running away. I'm sure you'll get on very well.'

'Thanks, Kate.' Tessa inspected the piece of paper

which Kate pushed across to her. 'I need all the help I can get.'

Kate looked down at the feathery blonde hair cut short and the neat little face with the wonderfully expressive golden eyes; lion's eyes. She admired Tessa who was making such an effort to create a decent career for herself, despite a lack of family to support and encourage her. Sue Anderson had told Kate all about Tessa's past.

'She's an absolute sweetie,' Sue had said. 'We all love her. She longs for a family. It's quite heart-rending, really. Nothing but some old aunt who watches the box all day long. We met her at the school once. Poor Tessa.'

'I've heard that you're doing splendidly,' Kate said now, giving Tessa's shoulder a little squeeze. 'Give Mrs Carrington a buzz while you're here and then go over and see her. You'll love Romulus and Remus.'

Tessa burst out laughing. 'Really?' she asked. 'Romulus and Remus? Good grief!'

'The breeder was having a Roman period, apparently,' said Kate. 'At least Mrs Carrington didn't choose Ptolemy or Nero. One must be grateful for small mercies.'

Tessa grinned up at her. 'It's nice to be back,' she said.

Later, after she'd driven Kate into Plymouth to catch the train, Tessa took the limping Felix for a little stroll. The late October sunshine was warm on her shoulders and she restrained an urge to run and shout. These huge spaces filled her with a sense of freedom and she took great lungfuls of air, still hardly able to believe her good fortune. She might have been stuck in an office somewhere – or in a shop. What luck to have fallen into this job and to have such good friends to help her! Tessa paused to pat Felix, who hobbled beside her, and then turned to the car: she mustn't let him overdo it.

Back at the house, she unpacked and began to settle herself in properly. She always had the little spare room which she had almost come to look upon as her own and, having put her things away, she made her usual tour of the house. Everything was in order and with a sigh of contentment she went into the kitchen and pushed the kettle on to the Rayburn. Felix, stretched on his rug in the corner, watched her, his tail beating a tattoo on the floor. She went to him, crouching beside him and stroking him.

'She'll be back soon,' Tessa told him. 'Don't worry.'

He stretched himself out contentedly and she got up and wandered round the kitchen, peering into the fridge, checking the larder – Kate was always very generous – and pausing before her favourite painting; a moorland scene done by David himself. It was of a bridge over the River Dart and a part of the bank with a group of foxgloves glowing against the sun-warmed stone. The light danced on the water and, in the corner of the picture some words were scrawled, partly obscured by the mounting: 'Bless you for everything. It's been perfect.' The rest of the writing was too hidden to read. The painting never ceased to hold her attention and engage her emotions. Presently a new frame on the dresser caught her eye and she picked it up curiously. It was a photograph of two young men. Tessa had often seen photographs of Kate's twins from her first marriage. They were dotted about the house; in Kate's bedroom on her chest of drawers; in a montage of family photographs in a frame in the downstairs loo; in the bedroom – which was obviously kept ready for them – standing on the bedside table. There were the twins as babies at either end of a huge pram; the twins as toddlers, each clasping the other's hand on a beach; the twins as small boys in uniform, going off to school. This, however, was a very recent one. Tessa stared at it. They were very alike – both tall and dark – but one looked more serious, almost forbidding, frowning a little; the other smiled, his eyes crinkled against the sun, his hands dug deep in his pockets.

Tessa replaced the photograph and sighed a little. Families: everyone seemed to belong to someone.

'Everyone except me,' she said aloud sadly, and Felix opened an eye and sat up.

She smiled ruefully at her self-pity and pulled herself together.

'You wait,' she said to him. 'One day I'm going to have lots of children and at least two dogs. And I shall live here on the moor. You wait and see!'

Felix sighed deeply and lay down again, putting his head on his paws and watching Tessa whilst she moved to and fro making herself some tea. The kitchen was warm and presently he dozed. Tessa sat on at the table, drinking her tea, listening to the slow ticking of the clock, staring across at David's painting on the opposite wall. It comforted her to be in such surroundings; in a family home with an old dog lying asleep in the corner. For this moment in time it was her home, her dog, her kitchen. She sighed, looked again at the piece of paper lying on the table and, slipping quietly from her chair, went to telephone Mrs Carrington.

Chapter Six

In the end the Christmas holiday turned out to be very different from all that Isobel had imagined. Out of the unhappiness that had dogged her through the autumn a desperate hope had been born. She became convinced that when Helen came home for Christmas she would have relented a little, become mature enough at least to be prepared to communicate with her mother. The few telephone conversations Isobel had with Simon confirmed that Helen was growing up and Isobel allowed herself to believe that the season of goodwill might extend its promise of happiness to her. Simon agreed to have a serious talk with Helen and, when they had discussed the best approach and Isobel had made her points – as much for Simon's ears as Helen's – as to her regrets and guilt, she suggested tentatively that he might meet her for a Christmas drink for old times' sake.

He hesitated so long that her pride almost made her say, 'Forget it! Don't bother! Another time, perhaps?' but her need kept her silent and he reluctantly agreed. As she went about her work she buoyed herself up with the knowledge that, as yet, Sally had not moved in with Simon. Their relationship might still come to nothing. As she shopped and cooked and spent her two days a week at the bookshop she allowed herself little fantasies in which Simon realised that he still loved her and that Sally had merely been a kind of sop to his injured pride; a consolation. She imagined Helen coming home at the end of a busy, happy term with a sense of fulfilment and contentment which might blossom into a generosity towards her mother. All these things were possible and Isobel clung to them.

The blow fell two weeks before Christmas when Isobel and Simon met for their drink. She was at the Crabshell before him and her heart described its usual upward leap as she saw him come in. She stood up and waved to him across the crowd and he smiled in recognition and grimaced comically at the noise and the quantity of people crammed into the bar. Her spirits soared; it was going to be all right, she just knew it. He pushed his way to her table and gave her the usual kiss on the cheek. His face was cold against hers and he wore a thick jersey over his jeans.

'What a row!' he said. 'Is the whole of Kingsbridge here?'

'I think so.' She felt so happy she could only smile and smile at him. She was still clutching his arm and he made no move to shake her off.

'You were very lucky to get a table,' he told her.

'Aren't I clever?' She grinned at him and his expression softened as he looked down at her. There was that strange feeling of familiarity accompanied by the knowledge that they were, somehow, strangers which excited Isobel and made her heart bump.

'Very clever,' he acknowledged. He moved a little

away from her and she was obliged to release him. 'Are we eating?'

'I thought so.' Isobel sat down again, glowing with this new happiness. 'I've just come from the shop. It's been hell today. Everyone ordering books. We're really busy.'

'Well, that's good, surely?' Simon sat down and picked up the menu. 'It would be worrying if you weren't busy two weeks before Christmas. What are you eating?'

Isobel shrugged. The food was of secondary importance. 'I think I'll have some pasta. The seafood tagliatelle is good. What about you?'

'Steak and kidney pie.' Simon shut the menu and looked towards the bar. 'I'd better order if we want it this side of Christmas.' He glanced at her glass. 'More wine?'

Isobel shook her head. 'Not just yet.'

She watched him as he fought his way to the bar and then stretched herself with a kind of nervous excitement. She'd been into Rainbow and treated herself to a new outfit she couldn't afford: a long skirt in soft lambswool and angora with a matching wrapover cardigan which belted tightly round her narrow waist and was worn over a cotton polo-neck jersey in the same earthy shade. The tweedy terracotta colours lent a glow to her paleness and she had been so delighted with the result that she had bought a pair of dark brown leather ankle boots to finish off the ensemble. Her dark hair was loose, held in place with a twisted silk scarf and she felt a delicious sense of luxury and confidence. She sipped her spritzer and saw that her hand trembled a little.

When Simon returned he was carrying a glass of wine as well as his pint. 'I decided I would,' he said, putting it beside her. 'I'm not sure I can face that again in a hurry.'

'Very sensible,' she agreed. 'So how are you? How's the play coming on?'

Simon always produced the sixth-form play at the end of the Christmas term and he was perfectly happy to discuss it at length. They were still talking about it when the food came. Simon unwrapped his knife and fork from their paper napkin and said, '*Bon appetit*' and Isobel raised her glass to him and finished her spritzer, revelling in their new-found intimacy. She realised that she had missed lunch and that she was very hungry, and she forked up her pasta with relish. Simon asked after Mathilda and she made light, as she always did, of the strange relationship she had with the old woman in her isolated cove. She told him about Mathilda's plans to divide her property between her unknown relations and Simon frowned a little.

'But where would that leave you?' he asked her. 'After all, she's getting on a bit, isn't she?'

Isobel felt her nervousness returning. She put down her fork and swallowed back some wine. 'She says I'll have the right to stay put,' she said, trying to sound unconcerned, 'but it was a bit of a shock. I've got to think about it, of course. Have you . . . ? What are your plans? Any news? When's Helen home?'

Simon finished his pie and pushed his plate aside. 'That's one of the things I wanted to talk about,' he said.

He looked so serious that Isobel took another gulp at her wine and picked up her fork again. 'I'm longing to see her,' she said, spearing a shrimp. 'Have you mentioned anything to her yet? About ... you know. Me longing to see her.'

'The thing is,' he said slowly, 'the thing is – she isn't coming home.'

'Isn't ...? But why not?' Isobel felt a jolt of disappointment but, underneath the disappointment, a tiny hope flared up that she and Simon would spend Christmas together.

'A girl she shares with has parents who have a house in Italy,' he was explaining, 'and she's invited a group of them to go home with her. There's skiing, apparently and goodness knows what and naturally Helen can't resist.'

'Well, I can't say that I blame her.' Isobel's hope was expanding. 'I can send her present to Durham. With luck she'll get it before she goes.'

'I'm sure she will.' He smiled at her, relieved by her philosophical reaction. 'Anyway, she'll be back after the New Year. She's coming home then for a week or two.'

'Well then,' Isobel grinned at him, warmed by his smile, confident that all was going to be well. 'That just leaves you and me.'

His face was suddenly suffused with colour. He looked so distressed that Isobel put down her fork, a sudden anxiety seizing her.

'I shan't be here either,' he said abruptly. 'Sally and I are going to the Lakes. When I heard that Helen wasn't coming down we decided to have a little holiday. Her parents live near Kendal.'

They stared at each other. Her disappointment was so great that Isobel was silenced. She had been so sure . . . This is the second time, she told herself. The second time I've made a fool of myself in a pub. Pride made her pull herself together and she nodded, trying to smile.

'I'm really sorry about Helen,' he told her. 'Maybe when she comes down later on . . .'

She knew that he was offering her a way out; that she could pretend that it was only Helen she cared about.

'It would be wonderful,' she said quickly. 'It means so much to me, as you know.'

'Of course.'

She couldn't bear the pity in his eyes. 'Well, I'll send her present on, then.' She racked her brain for something to say and smiled at him quickly. 'Look, I really ought to be getting back. I must make supper for Mathilda and . . .'

She was on her feet gathering her belongings together and he stood up awkwardly, unable to help her. Politely, like strangers, they wished each other 'Happy Christmas', uttered meaningless inanities, kissed briefly and then Isobel found herself on the quay, the cold frosty air cooling her hot cheeks. She hitched the long strap of her bag over her shoulder and stared down into the inky water which reflected the fairy lights strung along the embankment. The pub door swung open and a gust of noise and laughter spilled out, light shafting across the quay towards her. Hastily, lest Simon should come out and see her with the tears wet on her cheeks, she turned aside and hurried away to the car.

* * *

Mathilda was sitting at the kitchen table, eating rice pudding directly from the dish, a book propped against the sugar bowl. She glanced up as Isobel came in, brows raised questioningly.

'I thought you were dining out,' she said. 'Oh dear. Have I got it wrong? I'm afraid I've nearly finished this delicious pudding.'

Desperate though Isobel was she gave a short laugh at the sight of Mathilda's comically rueful expression. 'You might have put it on to a plate,' she said, 'but at least you remembered to eat it. It's too much to hope that you had some macaroni cheese first?'

'Much too much,' agreed Mathilda cheerfully. "Was there some? Never mind. This is extremely filling.'

Isobel shook her head at her and sat down at the table. She knew quite well that everything was now finished between herself and Simon and the overwhelming misery that had engulfed her when he had first told her about Sally was flooding back. She had been a fool to allow herself to hope; to persuade herself that the affair with Sally was a passing one . . .

'Is something wrong?'

Mathilda's voice broke in upon her thoughts and Isobel pressed her lips firmly together lest she should burst into tears. She shook her head, trying to smile, and Mathilda stood up and went across to the Rayburn.

'Tea, I think,' she said reflectively.

She pottered to and fro, giving Isobel time to

regain her control, and presently the younger woman laughed. It was a rather desperate sound, which almost immediately turned into a sigh, but Mathilda turned to look at her enquiringly.

'I was just thinking,' said Isobel. 'The song is quite wrong. All that business about love being lovelier the second time around. Remember it? Something about it being much more comfortable with both feet on the ground? Quite the reverse, in my case.'

Mathilda was silent. 'I don't think I know it,' she said at last.

This time Isobel's laugh held a note of genuine amusement. 'No, you wouldn't,' she said. 'Now if it had been by Hugo Wolf or Benjamin Britten . . .'

'Possibly,' agreed Mathilda, placing a mug of tea at Isobel's elbow. 'I suspect, however, that each composer tends to write about his own experience. Love is a subject which is far too general to pin down to one person's view of it. It's as foolish as saying that the Italians are wonderful lovers or that the French are marvellous cooks. It is hardly realistic to generalise about the entire population of any country. I imagine that it is the same with love. We each have a different experience.'

Isobel sipped her tea gratefully and wondered what Mathilda's experience had been. Was it some betrayal that had led to her solitary existence in the cove? She knew she could not ask.

'At least you didn't say, "It all depends what you mean by love",' she said rather bitterly.

Mathilda chuckled a little. 'I didn't feel that you were quite in the mood,' she admitted as she sat down again at the table.

'I'm not,' said Isobel miserably. 'Mathilda, what shall we do for Christmas?'

Hearing the desperation behind the question, Mathilda brought her mind to bear on it. She guessed that it was very important that Isobel should be distracted from whatever was making her so unhappy and given some sort of work or responsibility. She needed, thought Mathilda, to be made use of, to be kept busy. With a tiny inward sigh she prepared to make her own sacrifice.

'If you are going to be free,' she said, 'I should like to ask a favour of you. It would be foolish, at my age, to think that I shall live for much longer,' she held up a thin hand at Isobel's protest, 'and I should very much like to see an old friend before I die. Delia is really too elderly to travel to Devon and if you would be prepared to take on the responsibility – and if you think the car can cope – I should very much like to go to Oxford to see her.'

'Really?' Isobel was staring at her in amazement. 'You mean you'd leave the cove? Good heavens, Mathilda, I never thought to hear such a thing!'

'Oh, I've been known to go visiting occasionally.' Mathilda watched Isobel thoughtfully, noticing the new interest in her eyes and the colour returning to the pale cheeks. 'So. Could you manage it, d'you think? It will take some organisation. I'm afraid that my friend is just as hopeless as I am so there will be the travelling to arrange and itineraries and so on. She asks me every year but I have never had the courage to go alone.'

'We'll go together,' announced Isobel, 'that is ... will she mind ... ?' Her thoughts ranged anxiously over the cost of hotel rooms. 'It's just that . . .'

'You will be her guest,' said Mathilda firmly. 'She has always suggested that I bring a companion. You will incur no costs and seats for the Christmas Eve service at the chapel in St John's are part of the inducement.'

'It sounds like heaven,' said Isobel. 'But aren't we a bit late? It's only two weeks to go . . .'

'Shall we go upstairs and make some telephone calls?' suggested Mathilda. 'It's certainly not too late, but now that we are agreed on it perhaps we should start the ball rolling?'

Isobel followed Mathilda up the stairs, her heart full of gratitude. It would be such a relief to have something to plan, something to take her mind off her unhappiness and the thought of the empty frightening future. She was suddenly filled with determination that Mathilda should thoroughly enjoy her Christmas and, as she made up the fire in the study whilst Mathilda searched for her address book, she was already considering which route they should take and what presents should be bought. If this friend were anything like Mathilda it might be wise to do a big bake before they set out. She'd need to know all about her before she made any final decisions, of course . . .

She piled more logs on to the flames, preparing for a busy evening, her mind turned resolutely away from pictures of Simon and Sally enjoying themselves in the northern hills. Love *isn't* lovelier the second time around, she told herself fiercely, though it might be for Sally and Simon . . .

'I've got a strange tone.' Mathilda's voice interrupted her thoughts. 'I must have misdialled. Could you . . . ?'

Isobel jumped to her feet and hurried across to the desk. 'Shall I dial for you?'

Mathilda passed the receiver over meekly. She could read Delia's number perfectly clearly but her ploy had proved a useful distraction. She had not cared to see such an expression of despair on Isobel's face. Mathilda looked about her study sadly. She would hate to leave it but some instinct warned her that the sacrifice was a necessary one – and it would be good to see Nigel's sister again . . .

'I've got Delia Burrows on the line.' Isobel's hand was over the mouthpiece, her eyebrows raised hopefully. 'Is she . . . ?'

Mathilda nodded and took the receiver; the die was cast.

Chapter Seven

Tessa spent Christmas in a rather ugly little bungalow on the edge of Dartmoor. Her client, Freddie Spenlow, had been introduced to her through Kate. He, too, liked to spend regular periods with a friend in London and was deeply relieved when Kate assured him that his large Newfoundland, Charlie Custard, would be quite safe with Tessa. Kate had warned Tessa, however, that she might find Freddie's place rather basic.

'I've been over and sorted him out,' she told Tessa on the telephone a few weeks before she left London for Devon. 'If you have a problem we're only fifteen minutes away. Give me a buzz when you've settled in.'

Tessa approached the bungalow with a certain amount of trepidation. She parked the car in the track, noticing that the small garden had a gate leading into an adjoining paddock. At least there should be no problem in exercising this great dog. Kate's description had prepared her for something between a bear and an elephant and her heart beat a little faster as she rang the doorbell. There was no answering bark but presently the door was opened by a broadly built man in his middle thirties whose smile was so eager and welcoming that Tessa's nervousness began to fade.

'Hello,' she said. 'Mr Spenlow? I'm Tessa Rainbird.'

'Hello. Come in. This is wonderful.' He was attempting to shake hands, lead her in and shut the door all at once and she laughed as they stood together in the narrow hallway. He laughed, too, rumpling his thick brown hair and grimacing at himself. 'It's just such a relief,' he said, taking her coat. 'I wasn't planning to go away and then something blew up and poor old Custard ... Well, he doesn't really care for the bright lights and he's not an easy dog to farm out. I can't tell you how pleased I am to see you.'

Tessa followed him into the kitchen. It had nothing of the charm of Kate's kitchen or the cosiness of the Andersons', nor did it have the streamlined efficiency she had become used to in the homes of some of her richer clients. It was a simple ordinary room but any detail, for the moment, escaped her. Her whole attention was taken by a huge black dog who was sitting sideways on a shabby old sofa under the window. He leaned heavily against the back of the seat, his back legs stretched forward to their full length, his head resting wearily on a grubby cushion. His eye rolled towards Tessa but he made no move.

'Is that Charlie Custard?' she asked. She realised that she had lowered her voice, as though she might be in the presence of some great personage. 'Is he OK?'

'He's exhausted,' said Freddie, bustling to fill the kettle. 'Aren't you, Custard old chap? He's been to two Christmas parties and he's absolutely worn out.'

The dog sighed heavily and shut his eyes. Tessa watched, spellbound.

'*Two* parties?' she asked, rather awed by Charlie Custard's social commitments. 'Gosh!'

'You know the Lampeters?' asked Freddie. 'Well, their Jessie is one of my dogs. Did Kate tell you I bred them? Not any more but there are still a few of mine about. The Barrett-Thompsons? Yes? Know them? Well, Ozzy is Jessie's litter brother. Custard is their father. We have a get-together every now and again.'

Tessa advanced cautiously upon the sofa. 'Hello,' she said, stroking the big black head. 'Who's a beautiful boy?'

Charlie Custard was unmoved by this show of adulation. He sighed again but opened an eye to look at her. Tessa laughed. 'You're an old fraud,' she said. 'Worn out, indeed. I suspect you've been coming the heavy parent with your offspring.'

Custard's tail moved languidly once or twice and Freddie chuckled. 'You're right,' he said. 'Don't be alarmed at his size. He's very obedient.'

'I do hope so,' murmured Tessa, gazing at the dog's huge bulk and hoping that a clash of wills would not occur.

'You'll be fine,' declared Freddie confidently. 'And you don't need to take him beyond the paddock if you're not happy about it.'

It had needed only a day or two with Charlie Custard to give her confidence, however. She was used to the Lampeters' Jessie – although she saw now that Jessie was quite a small bitch compared with this male of the species – but Custard was a gentleman and, more importantly, a very lazy gentleman. He strolled peaceably at her side and even should a sheep break cover at his very paws or a rabbit hop into his path, he would merely prick up his ears and stare in amazement at such effrontery. In the evening, as she sat before the wood fire in the ugly tiled fireplace in Freddie's little sitting room, Charlie Custard would come to lean against her legs and the chair would slowly but steadily run backwards under his weight until it came to rest against the wall or some other obstruction.

She had been deeply touched to find a tiny Christmas tree standing on a table beside the fireplace. It was a small plastic thing, with fairy lights attached to its tinselly branches, and beside it were several gaily wrapped parcels – two for Tessa and two for Custard. The labels bore Freddie's good wishes and Tessa stared at them, a lump rising in her throat. She had been surprised to find that she was always much in demand over Christmas and the New Year. The elderly went away to visit their families and many couples went skiing. She was relieved not to be spending a quiet Christmas with Cousin Pauline, who spent the festive season watching the James Bond reruns on television and eating chocolates, but it was nevertheless a very lonely time for Tessa.

However hard she tried she could not help but remember those wonderful holidays with her own parents and her brother and, as she sat alone in some stranger's house, she would feel all the force of her loneliness. It was while she was fingering the presents beside the little tree and swallowing back her tears that the telephone rang.

'Everything OK?' asked Kate. 'Custard behaving himself? Good. So what time shall we expect you on Christmas morning?'

Tessa was quite silent. 'Christmas morning?' she asked at last.

'Of course.' Kate sounded surprised. 'I hope you weren't thinking of leaving David and me in solitary splendour. Guy got himself married last week and he and Gemma are off on honeymoon to some romantic place abroad and Giles is on a photographic job in America and won't be home till the New Year, so we're counting on you.'

'Oh, Kate.' Tessa bit her lip and blinked away her tears. 'I should love to come. If you're sure?'

'Don't be a twit,' said Kate.

Mathilda was glad to be back in the cove; glad, too, that she'd made the effort to see Delia. She knew that they would never meet again, in this life, and it had been a comfort to take such a gentle satisfying farewell of Nigel's sister, who was her oldest friend. After Christmas Isobel had driven them both to visit a mutual friend, now in a nursing home. This was a mistake. The old lady was beyond recognising them or holding any kind of conversation. She sat smiling vacantly, slipping in and out of sleep, waking to make disconnected remarks. Her hair was greyish-white and tufty, like sheep's wool caught on barbed wire, and there were gravy stains on her cardigan. A television, large as a young film screen, blared in the corner, and relatives and friends sat with desperate smiles attempting to communicate with their unheeding loved ones.

Mathilda and Delia were silent during the journey home whilst Isobel railed against the system and deplored the loss of the extended family.

'Poor old thing,' she said indignantly. 'It's so undignified. What a way to finish, amongst strangers. Hasn't she any children who could look after her?'

'I've always thought that it must be so humiliating to be "looked after" by one's children,' mused Delia. 'One comes full circle. As if one's life and achievements have gone for nothing. Perhaps it is better to disintegrate in the privacy of a nursing home without inconveniencing one's family. At least there would be no guilt.'

'Why should there be guilt?' demanded Isobel, changing gear noisily – the Morris did not take kindly to dramatics – and pulling in outside Delia's house. 'The elderly should be treated with love and dignity by their families.'

'Invariably?' asked Mathilda. 'As a right? Even if they have been cruel or tyrannical or selfish to their children?'

'Yes,' said Isobel. 'Well . . . How d'you mean?'

'I was merely testing your theory.' Mathilda prepared to alight. 'If you believe that old age confers such rights automatically then at least your own mother need have no fear for her future.'

Isobel climbed out thoughtfully, trying to imagine her mother aged and infirm, toothless and incontinent. She saw herself dealing with criticism and chilly silent disapproval, not as she did now with argument and defensive rudeness, but with unstinting, generous, unquestioning love. Mathilda was smiling sweetly at her. Isobel glared back and slammed the car door with more force than was usual – or necessary.

'I am very lucky,' said Mathilda to Delia as they went up the path together. 'I have my independence but I also have care and protection. I don't quite know how I'd manage without Isobel.'

'You are very lucky indeed,' agreed Delia, fumbling for her key. 'Long may it last. Just in time for tea, I think. Come along in out of the cold . . .'

Isobel locked the car broodingly. Mathilda had taught her that arguing from the particular to the general was fraught with danger; that an argument was worthless if it could not be taken to a logical conclusion. Sometimes Isobel wondered whether, before Mathilda, she'd ever *really* thought at all. She realised that she found it easier to be with Mathilda than with her own mother; that in some ways she was fonder of her, too. Confused and feeling guilty and rather cross, she followed them into the house.

It was early spring before Tessa went back to Devon. This time it was to look after Romulus and Remus whilst Mrs Carrington went to see her family in the Midlands. She was a kindly gentle woman whose thoughts centred on her daughter and her new grandchild. Whilst she showed Tessa round the cottage and gave her lists and instructions Mrs Carrington talked about her only child with tremendous pride. Tessa listened eagerly and looked

79

at photographs of the young family with genuine interest. Family life never ceased to fascinate her. It was clear that Mrs Carrington was making sacrifices to help them as much as she could and this included the sale of a delightful little bureau.

'The young man is coming to collect it in a day or two,' she told Tessa. 'Here is his card and his leaflet. Please let him do what is necessary but please remain with him at all times. You simply can't tell . . .' She looked at Tessa anxiously. 'Perhaps I should wait until I'm back. It's just that the money would be so useful and these people take so long . . .'

'Don't worry a bit,' said Tessa reassuringly. 'Have you telephoned this number? You know, just to check it out?'

'Oh yes.' Mrs Carrington nodded. 'I did it as soon as he'd left. It's all quite above board. Such a nice girl answered and suggested I visited the office if I felt the least bit anxious. Quite out of the question, since it's in London but I was reassured by her attitude.'

'That's OK then. Don't worry, I shan't leave him alone with all your lovely things. If there's any trouble I'll set the boys on him.'

Mrs Carrington looked at the two dogs wheezing asthmatically on their beds and laughed. It was a rather sad laugh. 'They're getting old, poor darlings,' she said. 'And they miss my husband. We all do.'

'I'm so sorry.' Tessa cast around for a happier topic. 'I see you've been knitting for the baby.'

The older woman's face cleared and she picked up the soft mass of apricot-coloured wool from the table. 'Isn't it pretty?' she asked. 'I was so glad that

Julie had a little girl. I'm used to girls and you can make them such lovely things. I'm keeping it out so that I can get some done on the train.'

'And if the young man comes to take the desk away shall I telephone you?' asked Tessa.

Mrs Carrington's cheeks flushed and she looked embarrassed. 'Perhaps not . . .' She hesitated. 'Oh dear. It's just I don't want Julie knowing . . . You see, I haven't told her that I'm not *quite* so well off as she thinks I am. The thing is that the young man tells me he can squeeze as much as three hundred pounds for the bureau and I don't want to give him time to change his mind. He says there are one or two around at the moment so I can't afford to dilly-dally. But he must leave cash and some sort of documentation. No cheques, mind!'

She looked very severe and rather anxious all at once and Tessa longed to hug her.

'Not a penny less than three hundred pounds! And a receipt for the bureau,' she said. 'Don't worry. I shall deal with it.'

It was not the antiques dealer who arrived on the doorstep the following morning, however. It was Sebastian. He hugged her, dealt graciously with her cries of delight and followed her into the cottage.

'You're doing very well, I hear,' he said, pausing to pat Romulus – or Remus – who had waddled over to greet him. 'Loadsa clients. Loadsa money.'

Tessa laughed, digging her hands into her jeans pocket lest she should go on hugging and hugging him. 'Not quite. But it's building up. Did Rachel tell you I was here?'

'No. I telephoned Ma to say that the ship is in

Devonport for a few days. Engine problems. She told
me that you were down here, too, and I thought you
might like to come out for a drink. I couldn't get a
reply when I phoned so I drove over.'

From the beginning, Tessa had left her current
telephone number and address with Mrs Anderson
in case of emergencies but this was the first time
that Sebastian had ever taken advantage of it. Tessa
felt quite weak with excitement and love but she
attempted to keep her voice under control.

'Sounds great,' she said. 'So have you hired a car
or what?'

'I thought I might as well get about while we're
here.' Sebastian, a lieutenant on a naval destroyer,
was based in Portsmouth. 'I've got to be back on
board at six. Can you leave the dogs?'

'Oh yes. They've had a long walk up to Wrangaton
Beacon.' Tessa was wishing that she wasn't in her
old jeans and faded sweatshirt. 'I'll just go and
change, shall I?'

He glanced indifferently at her clothes. 'You
look fine to me. Tell you what, we'll drive over to
Dartmouth and look up one or two of the old haunts.
Have some lunch. How about that?'

'Terrific,' she said fervently. She didn't care what
they did as long as she could be near him. 'I'll bed
Romulus and Remus down in the kitchen . . .'

'Romulus and Remus?' He burst out laughing. 'No
kidding? Rommy and Remy.'

'I know. But they're dear old things. You mustn't
laugh at them. It's not their fault, is it, boys? Come
on. On your beds and you shall have a biscuit.'

He watched her as she stroked their golden heads

and gave them each a biscuit. 'Be nice to her,' his
mother had said, when she'd given him the address.
'She gets very lonely, you know. And she's so fond of
you.'

He'd puzzled a little over those words as he drove
out from Plymouth and now, as Tessa rose to her
feet and beamed rather shyly at him, he wondered
if his mother might be warning him. He remembered how he'd made love to Tessa and suddenly
felt ashamed of himself. He'd drunk too much and
taken advantage of her affection for him and she'd
accepted his explanation – which had been partly
true – and made no demands on him. He took in
her slender figure and mop of bright hair, the small
face and golden eyes, and smiled at her.

'OK, kiddo?' he asked gently – as he'd been asking
for the last eight years – and she grinned at him,
unable to hide her excitement.

'OK,' she said.

'Let's go, then,' he said – and Tessa grabbed her
bag and followed him out, locking the door behind
her.

Chapter Eight

Mathilda finished the letter to her lawyer and leaned back in her chair. The day was mild for early April and sunshine streamed in through the window, which was open on to the balcony. Without moving she knew the exact state of the tide. It was on the turn, the heavy swell crashing against the wall of sand where it shelved sharply and dangerously, far out at the edge of the cove. Presently, the waves would flatten, rolling above the shelf, surging over the rocks, to run in across the beach, creaming up to the high-water mark. It was the time of the full moon and the springs were at their highest, leaving a line of seaweed and other gleanings way up on the sand.

Mathilda pushed back her chair and wandered out on to the balcony. Behind the house, high on the cliffs, seagulls screamed as they swooped above the nesting colonies and the scent of flowering gorse was sharp on the salty breeze. Beyond the mouth of the bay a fishing boat had hove to, and two men were busy hauling up the lobster pots, bracing themselves against the heavy seas. Mathilda watched them, leaning her elbows on the railings, shivering a little despite the warmth of the sun. The doctor's diagnosis was always with her now; the knowledge at the back of her mind whilst she read or walked, or played Scrabble with Isobel. The lump in her breast had become too big to ignore and she had no intention of allowing matters to be taken out of her own hands.

She had summoned her GP whilst Isobel was at the bookshop and he had examined her in silence and then told her what she'd guessed already. They both realised that it was too late to hope that there was time to save her but, nevertheless, he wanted her to have an operation, treatment . . .

'What is the point?' she'd asked him. 'If my life cannot be saved, what is the point of such a waste of resources on an old woman? What you have described would cost thousands of pounds. Why? So that I can die in six months' time instead of three? Less.'

He was silent, staring out of the window across to Start Point lighthouse gleaming white in the sunshine that shone out between scudding thunder clouds. Stabs of light pierced the dark green seas which pounded on to the beach and the wind howled and shuddered against the old house.

'Why did you wait so long?' he'd asked. 'We could have done something if you'd come to me earlier.'

She'd shrugged. 'I didn't notice it until recently,' she told him honestly, 'and when I did I suspected that it would have spread. Secondaries, d'you call them?'

'It's worth having a try,' he'd said – but she detected a lack of conviction in his voice and shook her head.

'Surely,' he'd said gently, 'you don't want to just give up. Look at this place. Your view! Isn't it

86

worth fighting for? Life is very precious . . .'

'Ah, no,' she contradicted him. 'Not at any price. It's the quality of life that is important. I've had eighty-four years. It's enough.'

He'd shrugged then, his expression changing, frowning a little. 'There may be no choice, you know. I can't give you a shot in the arm to put you out of your misery.'

She'd smiled at him. 'I realise that. I need time to think.'

He'd looked at her, taking in her frailty, the yellowish tinge to her skin, the strained lines on her face.

'The pain won't get any better,' he said brutally, hoping to shock her into compliance. 'Please be sensible. Let me help you. You have no family?'

Common sense warned her not to arouse his suspicions. 'No,' she admitted. 'You're right, of course. I can't just ignore it. Please allow me some time to adjust . . .'

He'd nodded, taking advantage of her more rational approach. 'Of course. But not *too* long. I'll give you a prescription but I want to see you soon.'

'I quite understand,' she said quickly. 'Of course. Just a few days to come to terms with it.'

After he'd gone the storm had broken; hail clattered on the roof whilst out at sea the lightning sizzled and the thunder rolled round the bay and resounded back from the cliffs. Presently Mathilda had turned away and sat down by the fire, huddling into her rug, remembering Nigel . . .

The fishermen had emptied the pots and the boat was heading back towards Dartmouth, seagulls wheeling in its wake. Mathilda was visited by a moment of utter loss and despair. She knew now why people cling to life; its joys and simple pleasures and all the dear familiar things. How difficult to relinquish them of one's own free will; how much easier to allow oneself to be deprived of them. There would be, she knew, a sense of relief in giving in, in letting some other person take control of her life, of being officially terminally ill.

The sound of the Morris bumping down the track had the effect of stiffening her spine. Her hands clenched for a moment on the balustrade and then she turned back into the room, slipping her letter into the drawer to be put in the post box by the back door later on. She heard the kitchen door bang and went out on to the landing.

'Hi. Mathilda?' Isobel's voice echoed up the stairwell.

'Coming,' she called back, and began to descend the stairs.

'It's cold out there.' Isobel was unpacking bags, putting the shopping away. 'Don't be deceived by the sun.'

Mathilda smiled at her, her heart warmed by affection. 'I shan't be. But I'm thinking of going out fishing tonight. Don't be surprised if you hear the boat.'

'Fishing?' Isobel paused in her labours to stare at her almost indignantly. 'Well, of course you're quite mad. Fishing! Honestly, Mathilda . . .'

'You know I'm more than capable,' said Mathilda calmly. 'You've seen me going out often enough to know that now.'

'You're not getting any younger,' grumbled Isobel. 'Supposing you couldn't get the engine started or something? Sitting there in the freezing cold . . .'

'It will be a beautifully clear night,' Mathilda told her peaceably as she sat down beside the Rayburn. 'Full moon and a gentle swell. The forecast's good. Please don't fuss.'

'Wouldn't make any difference if I did!' Isobel pushed the pan of soup on to the hotplate and put some rolls in the oven. 'Go and drown yourself and see if I care!'

'Of course I know that you're longing to meet these relations of mine.' Mathilda watched her as she laid the table for lunch.

'Well, I must say that I think you're mean not to invite them down so that we can give them the once-over,' said Isobel, stirring furiously as she brought up this old grievance. 'I almost feel as if I know them. I've got a picture in my mind.'

'We don't know yet that they are alive,' Mathilda pointed out.

'Don't be a spoilsport.' Isobel filled two bowls. 'Come and have some soup. And for heaven's sake wrap up tonight and don't forget to take a flask . . .'

The boat rocked gently alongside the small stone quay. Mathilda stood at her window, watching it. She wondered if she had the courage to do what was needed and whether it would work. Even if it did not, she reasoned to herself, she would be no worse off. She was aware of the house all around her, silent, washed in moonlight; her refuge for so many years. She allowed the happy memories to filter in to her mind, dwelling on each and then letting it go. Finally she thought of her father after his stroke and Nigel in the hospital in Oxford . . .

Abruptly she turned from the window and went downstairs. On the table stood the flask which Isobel, fearing that Mathilda might not bother, had filled for her earlier. She picked it up and put it in the duffel bag that stood by the door and, with one last look round, went out into the dark. She crossed the beach as quietly as she could, her plimsolls scrunching on the sand, and, with a glance at Isobel's curtained window, dropped the bag into the boat and untied the painter.

Mathilda had neglected to take the launch round to Salcombe for its winter overhaul and the engine started reluctantly at the second try. She pushed the gear lever forward and headed out to sea. As she had forecast the moon was full and the water fractured into a thousand splinters of silver as a capricious breeze shivered across its surface. The beam from the lighthouse which swept the sky was pale and insignificant beside the brilliant glory of the night.

Mathilda set course for Start Point but her chin was on her shoulder and she stared back at the cove until the cliffs hid it from her view. She was conscious of the engine puttering gently, the only sound except for the restless sea, and she huddled herself more deeply into her jacket as the boat moved out of the shelter of the land. When she was some way out, over the place where she had flung Nigel's ashes on to the surface of the deep waters, she switched off the engine. She sat for some while watching the moonlight and listening to the slap of the waves against the hull; thinking about her life, trying to decide about her future.

Her intention – to slip over the side and let the sea take her – needed more courage than she had imagined. Here, in the cold empty indifferent spaces, her resolve wavered; her desire to cling to warm, vital life strengthened. Sunk in her thoughts she had not realised that the tide had turned and that the wind was rising. The water was choppy now, and broke unevenly in little wavelets, rocking the boat. The breeze was cold. Mathilda, disturbed from her reverie, glanced around her and saw that she was being carried further round the Point. Suddenly she was frightened. She saw the rocks beneath the cliffs and, getting to her feet, reached to start the engine. There was no response. Terror in her heart, her hand shaking, she turned the key again. The engine puttered into life only to die again almost immediately. The tide was running strongly now but the wind was backing round behind it, driving the little boat closer and closer to the shore.

Mathilda struggled for'ard to find the starting handle. The boat lurched and she stumbled, bruising her shoulder on the thwart before she regained her balance. Trembling, she managed to fit the handle into its bed and, summoning all her energy, she swung it. The engine's flicker of life was extinguished almost immediately and, with a super-human strength, Mathilda swung the handle again; nothing. Dropping it she crawled into the well beside the engine. The boat was now in shallower waters and the waves broke over the gunwales,

soaking her with their spray. She opened the duffel
bag with shaking fingers and pulled out her heavy
waterproof. Her only hope was that the boat might
lodge itself between the rocks where she could wait
until help arrived. She dared not look. The thundering of the sea against land warned her that she was
close under the cliffs and she lay down, wrapping
herself in the coat, wedging herself firmly between
the engine housing and the thwart.

A wave lifted the boat and flung it amongst the
rocks, jarring Mathilda where she lay. The boat
twisted and caught between two boulders as the tide
continued to recede. Shivering, Mathilda raised
herself a little; the boat rocked ominously. The
moonlight showed her that she was held fast under
the cliffs and would soon be left high and dry by the
falling tide. Cautiously she stretched her hand
towards the bag and felt for the flask. The movement caused the boat to settle itself lower on to the
rocks and Mathilda lay motionless, hand still
outstretched. Presently she caught the bag in her
fingers and dragged it slowly closer. The smooth
rounded body of the flask evaded her cold, damp
grip but she found the handle of its plastic cup and
drew it carefully out of the bag. Barely moving she
unscrewed the cup and then the top of the flask,
blessing Isobel's thoughtfulness. The smell of hot
coffee brought tears to her eyes and she began to
cry weakly as she dribbled the liquid into the cup.

The pain, which was always with her now,
threatened to overwhelm her and she felt inside her
jersey for the little bag of painkillers which she had
put on a leather thong around her neck. She

managed to insinuate three tablets into her mouth and washed them down with a gulp. A last wave surged up against the rocks, jolting the boat and spilling the coffee, and Mathilda grasped at the flask, feeling for the lid. She gulped back another mouthful but resisted the urge to finish it, knowing that she would need some later. Weakness engulfed her as she pushed the flask into the bag and tried to make herself comfortable. The boat seemed to be firmly held and she prayed that an early fisherman out of Salcombe would spot her; or perhaps the incoming tide would lift the boat free. She burrowed into the waterproof, pulling it across her face and felt the nagging pain begin to recede. Consciously willing her muscles to relax she felt exhaustion overtake her. She seemed to be sinking into a cold dampness which received her kindly, numbing her gently into insensibility . . .

The moon sank into the west and the chill light of dawn showed bright fingers of light along the horizon. The sun rose. A fishing boat motored out of Salcombe harbour and headed for the fishing grounds. Others followed but no one noticed the small boat half hidden amongst the rocks. A walker, taking her early morning constitutional on the cliffs above, was the first to spot it. She shouted down to the bundle curled on the bottom boards and, receiving no reply, began to run as fast as she could back to Hope Cove.

'I told her,' wept Isobel. 'I told her that she shouldn't go. That she was too old.' She stretched her arms across the kitchen table to the young coastguard who watched her sympathetically. 'I said – I actually said – "Go and drown yourself and see if I care!"' Isobel put her head in her hands and cried in earnest.

'We got the boat off,' he told her. 'The engine wasn't working. Our guess is that she was carried round the Point by the tide and swept into the rocks.'

He pushed the mug of tea closer to her elbow. He was a local boy and he'd recognised Mathilda's boat at once. As soon as he was able, he'd driven down to the cove and found Isobel frantically telephoning the coastguard. He told her that Mathilda had died of hypothermia and exhaustion and that the doctor had also noticed advanced stages of cancer. Shocked and silent, Isobel had sat staring at nothing while he made tea and attempted to comfort her. All at once she had begun to cry, the tears spurting from between her fingers, and he'd wondered if he should call her doctor or take her to the surgery.

'She did it on purpose.' Isobel sounded a little calmer, although sobs burst from her uncontrollably. 'She wouldn't have wanted operations and things. If only I'd known. Oh God . . .'

'You can't know that,' he said uncomfortably. 'She was always going out on her own, wasn't she? My dad said she'd done it all her life. No reason why she shouldn't go last night. Lovely clear night, it was.'

Isobel looked at him. 'Yes,' she said dully. 'Yes, I'm sure you're right. Sorry.'

'Nothing to be sorry about. Look, I've got to go. I'm a bit late for work. Only I don't like to leave you. Is there somebody you could phone up? I could give you a lift.'

'No.' Isobel shook her head and attempted to control her trembling lips. 'I'm OK. You've been great. Honestly, I'll be all right.'

'Well, if you're sure . . .'

He tucked his chair under the table and she followed him out on to the beach, raising a hand to him as he climbed into his car and disappeared up the track. Keeping her eyes resolutely away from the empty house, Isobel wandered down to the sea. The sun shone in her eyes and a gull cried mournfully as it drifted above her, white wings outstretched. She thought of Mathilda, of the fear that she must have known during the long cold night, and the tears streamed unchecked down her face. She tried to imagine her own life without Mathilda; without her dry humour or her companionship; without the refuge she had given her against the storms. Now she had no one. Isobel sat down on a rock and, bending her head towards her knees, gave herself up to grief.

Chapter Nine

Sunday morning. The June sunshine slanted through the arched windows of the chapel, touching the heads of the smaller boys in the front rows and lingering on the bowl of yellow roses placed at the altar. The drowsy peace was briefly disturbed by the frantic fluttering of a butterfly as it beat its tortoiseshell wings against the glass. Abruptly it abandoned its struggle for freedom, dropping down to rest on the stone sill. The scent of the roses drifted faintly on the warm air and the headmaster's scholarly voice was soothing – almost soporific – as he read the gentle words of St John . . .

'Behold what manner of love the Father hath bestowed upon us, that we should be called the sons of God . . . Little children let no man deceive you . . . He that committeth sin is of the devil . . . For this is the message that ye heard from the beginning, that we should love one another . . .'

Matron, ever vigilant from her vantage point in the choir, watched the small boy opposite. His face was dreamy and peaceful as he unobtrusively slid his fingers under the thigh of his even smaller neighbour and pinched the bare flesh. The cry of anguish was frozen on his victim's lips as she leaned forward to look sternly at both of them. They stared back at her with innocent guileless expressions – but she saw the sharp jab of an elbow in retaliation and smiled to herself.

' . . . My little children, let us not love in word, neither in tongue; but in deed and truth . . .'

Matron sighed deeply; thirty-five years in the company of boys between the ages of eight to thirteen had given her a rather cynical outlook. The first twenty years of her career had been at a boys' preparatory school in Dorset. When the headmaster retired she decided that she, too, should make a change and she had come here to this small school on the edge of the New Forest. It was the right decision and she had been very happy. A succession of little boys had passed through her capable, caring hands and, after they left, she continued to learn of their achievements through the pages of the school magazine and their occasional visits. How she would miss them! She looked down into the body of the chapel and wondered how she would cope with retirement. Her glance picked out the familiar head of the History master. She knew without looking how he would be sitting; hands in his pockets, legs crossed at the ankles and thrust out into the aisle, chin on chest. He was unconventional, sometimes outrageous, an inspired teacher – and the boys adored him. She had regulated her love for Tony Priest so that only she knew of it. It was so humiliating to have such feelings when one was over fifty;

especially if the object of one's desire was a married man. Yet the thought of leaving him, the school, the boys, was a terrible one. Her closest friend, a widow, assumed that they would enter into old age together at her little house in Winchester; or there was the option of buying a small flat, here in the town, not far from the school. She pursed her lips thoughtfully as she mentally reviewed its advantages. The most prominent of these was its cheapness but also important was the comfort in the knowledge that she would be able to keep in touch with the school; to see Tony Priest from time to time. She thought of the letter she had received yesterday from a lawyer in Plymouth; some distant relative had left her a share in a house. She had never heard of this distant cousin and was surprised that she should have been mentioned in her will. It had been suggested that she travel to Devon to see the house but really there was no point. On the other hand the money would be very useful indeed . . .

The rustle of hymn books brought her to her feet with the other members of the choir and she felt for the reading spectacles that swung from a chain around her neck. The small boy sitting directly in front of her sniffed juicily and wiped his nose with the back of his hand. Matron poked him sharply in the back and he turned to stare up at her, aggrieved. 'Handkerchief!' she hissed and he fumbled obediently in the pocket of the grey shorts of his Sunday suit.

Tomorrow, she thought, as he blew with exaggerated ardour into the grubby square of linen, tomorrow I shall write and see what it's all about . . .

* * *

Isobel dragged the sheet from her bed and the cover from the quilt and bundled them into a pile on the floor. She carried the quilt to the window so as to hang it out in the warm sunshine and stood transfixed, one hand outstretched to open the window wider. Below her, on the beach, was a girl. She was standing quite still, with her back to the sea, staring up at the house. The sun glinted on the short blonde hair and her whole attitude was one of tense expectation. Suddenly she swung round and extended her arms, fists clenched in a gesture of triumph, head flung back, eyes tight shut.

Isobel realised that she was still clutching the quilt to her breast; her hand gripping the window latch. She had the strangest feeling that she was spying but, before she could turn away, she saw a man emerge from the house and stroll down the beach. The girl had heard his approach and stood easily now, her hands thrust into the back pockets of her jeans. Nevertheless, Isobel was aware of a kind of joy emanating from the slight figure. Her own heart beat quickly as their voices mingled with the shushing of the tide upon the sand and she saw the man – whom she now recognised – gesture towards her own cottage.

Isobel dropped the quilt and went downstairs and out into the sunshine. James Barrington – Mathilda's lawyer – raised a hand to her and she was aware of the girl looking at her keenly as she went to meet them.

'Good morning, Isobel.' James smiled and held out his hand. 'How are things with you?'

'I'm fine.'

Isobel liked James. He had recently moved back to the West Country from Oxford and had inherited Mathilda from a retiring partner of the Plymouth law firm where, as a law student nearly fifteen years before, James had worked during his holiday placements. He lived somewhere near Dartmouth and had been very willing to come out to the cove and talk to Mathilda about her quest for her unknown relatives. She had been very taken with him and the three of them had spent several immensely enjoyable evenings together. On one occasion, at Mathilda's request, he had brought his wife, Daisy, and their small boy for Sunday tea.

'This is Tessa Rainbird,' he was saying. 'She is Miss Rainbird's cousin, several times removed. This is Isobel Stangate.'

The two women looked at each other.

'So he found you,' said Isobel lightly. 'Hello.'

Tessa's hand was warm in hers and the golden eyes looked anxious.

'I never knew her,' she said. 'Isn't it terrible? I didn't know about her, you see. And I've been down in Devon so much in the last couple of years. Oh, it's such a waste!'

'Never mind.' Isobel was taken aback at her intensity. 'She didn't know about you, either.'

'But she was *family*,' said Tessa sadly. 'I wish I'd known her. And now it's too late.'

'Yes.' Isobel winced at the stab of pain which reminded her of her own loss. 'I'm afraid it is.'

'Mrs Stangate will be able to tell you all about

her.' James's voice was comforting. 'She looked after her, you know.'

'Well, up to a point.' Isobel looked at Tessa and felt curious. 'Do you like the house?'

'I love it,' said Tessa simply. 'All of it. The house and the cove. It's . . . Well, it's magic, isn't it?'

'It's rather special,' agreed Isobel. She was feeling confused. She had been prepared to dislike on sight these relatives who were to supplant Mathilda and turn the cove into a kind of holiday camp – but this girl wasn't quite what she had envisaged.

'I want to live here,' Tessa was telling her, 'but I have to wait to see what the other beneficiaries want to do.'

Isobel looked at James who shrugged. 'Perfectly true, I'm afraid. If they want to sell it'll be two against one.'

'I can't bear it.' Tessa screwed up her eyes as though she might burst into tears but laughed instead. 'Silly, isn't it?'

'Love at first sight,' said James sympathetically. 'Often painful. Want another look round before we go?'

'Yes, please,' said Tessa at once. She hesitated but James knew what was in her mind.

'I'll leave you to go round alone,' he said. 'I'll have a chat with Mrs Stangate, if she can spare the time.'

Tessa's face lit up. 'Great!' she said. 'Shan't be long.'

'Take as long as you like,' said Isobel, who had every intention of pumping James for information. 'Come in for some coffee when you've finished.'

* * *

Tessa went slowly from room to room, touching the furniture and ornaments with gentle fingers and reading the titles of the books in the bookcases. Her plan to buy a cottage and live on the moor had been abandoned instantly as soon as she had entered the house. The rooms were full of trembling pearly light and the sound of the sea was like distant music. All was just as Mathilda had left it. Isobel had tidied the rooms and went in daily to dust and air the house but there was an atmosphere of friendly welcome, as though the owner had just popped out and would be returning at any moment. Tessa opened the windows in the study and went out on to the balcony. It had shocked her to learn that she had had a relative of whom she knew nothing; a woman with the same name as her own, with whom she shared a common ancestor, someone of her own flesh and blood who had lived in this magic place.

She leaned on the balustrade and watched the great white sails of a yacht filling with the gentle breeze that ruffled the turquoise sea. On the horizon a tanker appeared to be stationary, painted against the shimmering sky, its great length rendered toy size by distance. The tide washed gently in, hardly seeming to encroach upon the shore, and the sun shone on the stone of the old house and warmed Tessa where she stood in desperate longing.

I want it! she told herself silently. I want it.

She remembered James explaining the terms of the will. There were two other relatives involved so that even if they loved the place as much as she did there must inevitably be certain complications.

'It might be difficult,' James had said thoughtfully,

103

'all mucking in together, if you see what I mean.'

'Maybe,' she said hopefully, 'maybe they'll just want to come for holidays or weekends or something.'

James was silent. Tracking Tessa down had not been easy and her reaction – in light of her own losses – was not particularly surprising. He forbore to point out that almost invariably his instructions in these cases were to get the property sold as quickly as possible and split up the proceeds. After all, there was no question of Tessa buying out her fellow legatees. Despite the fairly primitive conditions in the house, its position alone ensured a high asking price. Properties of this nature were rare and it would be snapped up quickly. He realised that she was watching him, willing him to agree.

'We must wait and see,' he'd told her gently.

Tessa thought about Isobel. She had the right to stay on in the cottage as a sitting tenant. James had explained that sitting tenants sometimes made a place difficult to sell . . . A cormorant skimmed the water, flying south with steady wingbeats. The tanker had disappeared below the horizon and the yacht had sailed round the headland towards Salcombe. Tessa went downstairs, locked the door carefully behind her and crossed the beach to the cottage.

'I always thought it was a crazy idea,' Isobel was saying. 'Leaving it to three people. I mean, why not just one? It's bound to cause trouble.'

She thrust the sugar bowl at him, glaring at James as he maintained a judicious silence. His brief description of Tessa's background had filled her with a maternal concern and she felt cross that the two other as yet unknown relatives would destroy the girl's prospects before she could enter into them.

'Honestly!' she exclaimed. 'It's cruel, isn't it? To see this place and fall in love with it and then be unable to hang on to it! Poor Tessa. I really feel for her.'

James sipped his coffee. He was aware that it must be just as hard for Isobel to have lost her own security and, more importantly, her friend. He suspected that Isobel's anger at Mathilda's will was indirectly aimed at Mathilda. She couldn't forgive Mathilda for dying, for leaving her. James knew how close the two women had become and how important it was for Isobel to have someone to look after, to love, to worry about. It seemed that she was about to transfer her allegiance to Tessa.

'Don't sit there looking so smug!' cried Isobel. 'Sorry.' She caught herself up and sat down at the table. 'I have this terror, you know, of these relations turning the cove into a kind of up-market Butlins.' She folded her arms on the table and shook her head. 'I miss her so much,' she admitted.

Her mouth turned down at the corners and James thought briefly of his own small son when he was hurt or frightened. Just so did he look – although a comparison between a two-year-old boy and a forty-something woman was faintly ridiculous.

'Mathilda had some strange ideas,' he said evasively. 'I don't know quite what was in her mind but she seemed very set on having her way.'

Isobel snorted. 'Nothing surprising about that,' she said tartly. 'But I still don't see . . .'

105

There was a knock on the door and Tessa put her head in. 'Hi,' she said rather shyly. 'Am I interrupting anything, Mrs Stangate?'

'Of course not.' Isobel jumped up and fetched another mug. 'And call me Isobel. We were just discussing these tiresome relatives of yours.'

James looked at her warningly but she made a face at him. Tessa laughed a little.

'I've longed for a family ever since . . . well, since I've been on my own. But I must admit that I could do without these two.'

'Of course you could.' Isobel put the mug beside Tessa's elbow and pushed the milk and sugar towards her. 'So come on, James. Tell us all about them. Don't put on your lawyer's face. We shall know sooner or later.'

James remembered that Mathilda had taken Isobel into her confidence over her will, how she had always been quite frank before her at their meetings, and gave in. He explained that Beatrice Holmes worked in a boys' school in Hampshire and that Clarence Rainbird had recently retired from his administrative post with the United Nations and had been widowed three years previously. He lived in Geneva. Both had been informed of their inheritance but, as yet, he had received no acknowledgement from either of them.

'Geneva,' said Isobel thoughtfully. 'Listen. Perhaps he'll let Tessa rent his bit of the house from him and he can use it for holidays. How about that?'

James sighed. 'It's no use speculating. We must wait. No good getting hopes up only to be dashed.'

Isobel looked at him. 'Do you ever have the urge

to be wildly indiscreet?' she asked. 'To make uncon-sidered remarks? Commit yourself irrevocably?'

'Not to two women at once,' answered James, shocked. 'Although I have been known to have a haircut on the spur of the moment, without taking advice or making an appointment.'

Tessa laughed. 'It's up to you, Isobel,' she said. 'When they turn up I rely on you to persuade them. Convince them that it would be criminal to sell. I simply can't bear the thought of losing it now I've seen it.'

Chapter Ten

Will Rainbird – he had adopted his second name, preferring it to Clarence, on his first day at school – parked his hired car at the top of the track, tucking it well in beside the hedge, and climbed out. He stood for a moment, looking about him, aware of the drone of bees in the honeysuckle that grew in the hedge beside him, smiling with pleasure at the trailing tangle of fragile dog roses. He sniffed, luxuriating in the salty scented air and patted his pockets absently as he craned about for signs of habitation. The jolly lady at the little bakery in the village up on the main road had been very helpful in describing his route to the cove. He had made no secret of who he was, although he had not yet advised the lawyers that he was in the country, and there had been a mild if discreet sensation when he had told the bakery people his name.

Well, here was a track, precisely where the lady had said there would be a track, but there was no sign board to indicate that it led to the cove. Will located his pipe and his matches and strolled slowly down the dusty path. Cow parsley leaned out at him, its creamy crumbly flowers brushing his arms. Red valerian and sulphurous yellow stonecrop clung in the crevices of the stone wall which bordered a field of grazing sheep. The afternoon was hot and still, with a hint of thunder in the air, and the great spaces of sky, now a purplish bruised blue, hinted at the proximity of the sea. Will packed tobacco into his pipe, his eyes fixed on the blue horizon, and listened to the sea birds screaming on the cliffs.

The track dropped downwards and, as he came round the sharp right-hand bend, Will caught his breath at the view of the sea which appeared briefly before him. He found that he was hurrying, his feet slipping on the small stones, and as he came out on to the small fan-shaped beach he gave an inarticulate cry of delight. He stared up at the house, swung round to look about the cove and smothered another exclamation as he saw the figure stretched out on the beach. She lay on her face, head on arms, and he studied the long tanned slender limbs and the dark shining hair that fell across her wrists.

Will stood still. He guessed that this was the tenant of the cottage and he glanced quickly at it perched on its rocky plateau before taking a cautious step forward, clearing his throat noisily. Isobel raised her head, rolled over and sat up swiftly. He took another step towards her, his hands raised in a kind of supplication.

'I'm sorry,' he said, 'so sorry to disturb you.'

He saw that she was older than he had first imagined but he found her tremendously attractive and smiled apologetically as she pulled a T-shirt over her head and fastened a long cotton skirt around her waist. Her brown eyes were angry but there was a touching vulnerability about her mouth.

'I'm so sorry—' he began again – but she interrupted him.

'This is a private beach,' she said as she slid her feet into espadrilles. 'You're trespassing.'

'You've been crying,' he said distressfully, seeing the marks on her cheeks and swollen eyelids, and coloured as he saw her look of outrage. 'Forgive me. It's just . . .' He shrugged at his tactless ineptitude. 'I'm Will Rainbird,' he said simply.

Isobel came closer. It was true that she had been crying. Earlier that morning, on an impulse, she had rung the cottage in Modbury and had been both terrified and delighted when Helen answered. She had countered Isobel's eager questions with monosyllabic replies, refused her invitation to lunch and blocked further conversation by saying that she must go but she would fetch her father to the telephone. Simon had been kind but firm in his refusals to meet 'just to talk things over' and had hung up at the earliest opportunity. Isobel wandered out on to the beach, hurt and unhappy, and had lain down hoping that the heat of the sun would relax her so that she might sleep. Instead, she had wept bitterly then drifted into a brief uneasy doze – and now here was this stranger walking across the beach, catching her at a disadvantage, acting as if he owned the place . . . as indeed he did.

Will held out his hand and, as she took it, Isobel found herself looking into Mathilda's eyes. The shock was so great that she clutched convulsively at his hand. The slate-blue eyes smiled at her as though they quite understood but she pulled herself together and hastily withdrew her hand.

'I do apologise,' she said rapidly. 'I didn't realise

who you were. Just for a moment . . . I was asleep, you see.'

'I shouldn't have come unannounced,' said Will, trying hard not to stare at her. 'To tell the truth I wanted to have a look around on my own, d'you see? Just to get the feel of things without lawyers breathing down my neck.'

'I quite understand.' Isobel, too, was trying not to stare. He could have been Mathilda's much younger brother, so strong was the likeness, and, after her initial irritation, she felt strongly drawn to him. 'I'm Isobel Stangate. I live in the cottage.'

'Thought as much,' said Will, though whether his obvious pleasure was the satisfaction of his successful methods of deduction or from knowing that she was his tenant she could not quite decide. 'Not too much to hope then that you've got a key to the house?'

Isobel began to laugh. 'I certainly have,' she agreed. 'Though whether James would approve of what you have in mind I can't imagine.'

'James?'

'James Barrington. Mathilda's lawyer. Never mind. What the eye doesn't see . . . and all that.'

'My view exactly,' he beamed at her. 'You looked after my cousin, I understand.'

As they walked across the beach together, Isobel explained her role. Suddenly she thought of Tessa. 'I'm hoping that you'll all agree to keep the house,' she told him. 'Then I can stay here and look after you. Rent-free, of course. That was the arrangement with Mathilda. I've met your cousin Tessa. She's all for it.'

She gave him a quick guided tour of the house and then left him to it, hurrying back across the beach and feeling strangely excited and apprehensive.

Will, standing at Mathilda's bedroom window, watched her go. Presently he turned his gaze seawards.

He saw the clouds massing on the horizon and looked westward at the spiny huddle of rock on which the lighthouse stood. He felt a strange sense of belonging; a crazy desire to accept this unexpected inheritance and start a whole new life. After all, what was there to keep him in Switzerland now that Bierta was dead and he had retired? His life had been a quiet one, his administrative work unexciting – rather like his marriage. His Swiss wife had been older than he but he had been attracted by her calm blonde beauty, her smiling good-natured charm. Later – too late – he had discovered that her calm good nature masked an unthinking indifference to life but Will was a loyal man and no one, least of all Bierta, guessed at his disappointment. Their only child was stillborn and with it his last hopes of real happiness died but Will was by nature a positive man and had learned to look for those small precious moments of joy which are vouchsafed at unexpected moments.

Now, it seemed, life might take an exciting turn. His trip to England had been quite impulsive. He had been visited with a desire to have a little holiday; to take a look at this house in its cove, although he had fully expected that, having instructed the lawyers to sell it, he would return to

Switzerland leaving the whole business in their hands. His gaze wandered back to the cottage. What if he should decide to keep the house? Of course there were the wishes of the other beneficiaries to be considered but if he sold the flat in Geneva he could probably buy them out. He remembered that Isobel had mentioned his cousin, Tessa Rainbird. Tessa, she had said, wanted to keep the house. Will's hands went automatically to his pockets, feeling for his pipe as he made another tour of the house. There was no reason why it should not be divided into two flats. It would need a bit of thinking out, of course . . .

As Will left the house fat warm drops of rain were beginning to fall, splashing on the rocks and pocking the gleaming surface of the water. Far out at sea a fork of lightning stabbed across the darkening sky and thunder growled in the distance. Without warning the rain fell in vertical shining rods and Will raced across the sand to the cottage where Isobel waited with the door held wide.

Tessa sat in her favourite corner of the Roundhouse, pouring a second cup of coffee from the pot which Marie, one of the Perryman twins, had brought twenty minutes earlier. For once she was not thinking of Sebastian – from whom she had not heard since that sudden appearance more than three months before – but was brooding on Mathilda and her house in the cove. She felt that she might die of frustration if her other relatives did not soon appear and make their decisions known to her. For the thousandth time she racked her brains for a solution should they both wish to sell. The small trust set aside for her would hardly be enough for a deposit and, even if it were, how on earth would she manage a mortgage? She had been shocked when James had mentioned the sum the house and cottage might reasonably be expected to fetch and now she knew the desperation of helplessness; the frustration of being powerless.

She glanced up as the door opened and her face lost its anxious look. Kate, accompanied by a tall young man, came in, glanced around and waved as she saw Tessa in her corner.

'What are you doing here?' Kate smiled down at her. 'I didn't know you were around. This is Tessa, Giles. My life-saver. Have you met Giles?'

Tessa recognised him at once. It was the young man she'd seen smiling out of the photograph of the twins, on Kate's dresser. She shook hands with him and he slid on to the bench opposite whilst Kate wandered away to order some coffee.

'I feel I know you,' Tessa told Giles mischievously. 'All those photographs.'

'Oh God!' Giles grimaced. 'That's an unfair advantage.'

'But they're very good photographs.' She grinned at him. 'Especially the one of you on the beach.'

He laughed. 'No point in trying to make an impression if you've seen that one.'

Kate appeared beside them. 'What's the joke?' she asked. 'How are you, Tessa? Are you on your way back home or have you just arrived?'

'I'm on my way to Honiton.' Tessa moved along so that Kate could sit beside her. 'A new client. I said

I'd be there about teatime so I could have time to settle in properly. They're off tomorrow morning. I've been at the Lampeters' all week.'

'Ah,' said Kate thoughtfully, studying Giles's face as he watched Tessa. He looked as though he'd just discovered something rather special. She decided that a certain amount of encouragement was in order. 'In that case why don't you join us for lunch? We're going to the Church House at Rattery. It's not far off the A38. On your way, more or less.'

Giles glanced at his mother quickly, eyebrows raised. Kate smiled blandly back at him and he gave a little shrug. This by-play was not lost on Tessa.

'Well . . .' She hesitated, longing to accept but wondering what that glance had meant.

'Take no notice of Giles,' said Kate, knowing that Tess had intercepted their little signal. 'We're meeting my other son and his wife. Gemma will love to meet you.'

'Which implies,' said Giles, making room as Marie arrived with their coffee, 'that Guy won't. It's only fair to warn you that Guy takes a little time to relax with people he doesn't know.'

Tessa remembered the uncompromising stare of Giles's twin as they stood together in the photograph.

'Perhaps he won't like me butting in,' she began, understanding the exchange between Kate and Giles. 'I don't want to be—'

'Rubbish,' interrupted Kate roundly. 'It's my party. Anyway Guy is old enough now to cope with strangers. Gemma has helped no end with that side of his character. She's such an outgoing girl. Thanks, Marie. How's the family?'

While Kate and Marie talked, Tessa was suddenly seized with a fit of shyness. She stared at Giles's hands as he poured coffee and found herself absolutely tongue-tied. At the same time she felt an odd sense of familiarity; as though she had known him for ever.

'It must be great fun working with dogs,' he was saying. 'Mum says that you've been to Freddie's. How's Charlie Custard? I remember . . .'

He talked easily and amusingly and presently she found herself recounting stories of her own whilst Kate sat by, smiling to herself. Presently she glanced at her watch.

'Mr Perryman's made some new bowls,' she told them. Mr Perryman, as well as being a farmer and carver-in-chief on Sundays at the Roundhouse, produced beautifully crafted wood-turned work. 'Marie says he's around somewhere so I'm going to have a word with him. Back in a minute.'

She disappeared through the door that led to the artists' studios and there was another silence.

'So you live in London,' mused Giles. 'I've got a studio flat in Chelsea. It's tiny but rather nice. Where do you live?'

'Shepherd's Bush,' said Tessa so glumly that he burst out laughing.

'Come on,' he said. 'It's not that bad.'

Tessa wrinkled her nose, shrugged and then quite suddenly found herself telling him about Mathilda's legacy, Cousin Pauline and the tragic loss of her parents and her brother. She told him about her nightmares, how she'd started dog-sitting and how she thought she might die if she couldn't live in the house in the cove. Giles listened in silence, his eyes on her face. Kate had already told him something about her and he felt an old-fashioned urge to be allowed to look after her; to protect her. Whilst she talked he restrained these out-of-date feelings and poured himself more coffee.

'So you see,' said Tessa, sighing heavily, 'I just can't see how it can possibly work. I telephoned James Barrington – he's the lawyer – yesterday, and he says that he's had a letter from one of the others instructing him to sell. She doesn't even want to see the house. I begged him to ask her at least to look at it and he's agreed to give it a try.'

'It's a bit odd, isn't it?' he asked. 'Leaving it to three people. I agree with you. How *could* it possibly work, apart from selling it?'

'I wish I could buy them out,' said Tessa wistfully, 'but it seems to be worth rather a lot. I'm hoping that the other two might like to use it for holidays and I could live there between jobs.'

'Could it be divided into three?' asked Giles. 'And what about this cottage?'

Kate, looking through the glass panel in the door, saw the two heads close together and gave a sigh of satisfaction. She decided that she might have a browse in the little shop; perhaps buy a card or two or some mugs. No need to disturb them yet; there was at least another ten minutes before they had to leave.

Chapter Eleven

Beatrice Holmes – who had ceased to be Matron for two whole months – sat listening to the rain drumming on the conservatory roof whilst Norah's voice drummed just as relentlessly in her ears.

'. . . and so I told him that I thought it was quite disgraceful. A whole three pence overnight! Of course, he cheeked me. "Everything goes up," he said. "I have to cover my costs." Well, you can imagine. "Cover your costs!" I said . . .'

Bea fiddled restlessly with the letter in her lap and wondered at what point Norah had become so penny-pinching. She had arrived to teach English at the preparatory school in Dorset when Bea had been Matron for five years or so. In the heavily male-dominated society they had automatically drawn together and, when Norah married and moved into Hampshire, they had remained good friends. Each summer Bea had spent some part of the holidays with her and Bernard, and they had always joked about how they would be tiresome old ladies together. She had sympathised with Norah's irritations at Bernard's feckless ways; his extravagance, his generosity to the undeserving, his tendency to pop round to the pub. He had always effaced himself, leaving the two of them to their own devices, but in the last two months Bea had begun

to realise that it must have been no self-sacrifice on
Bernard's part.

'. . . of course, the man's a saint but how on earth
he puts up with it I can't imagine. She never leaves
him alone for a minute and when I found her there
fiddling with the flowers although she knows *quite*
well it's *my* week . . .'

Norah had passed along from the supermarket
to the church with its long-suffering vicar and her
archenemy, Miss Knowles. Bea thought regretfully
of the little flat near the school. It had been snapped
up two days before she – rendered brave by the
thought of her inheritance – put in her own offer.
There was nothing else that appealed to her that
she could afford and she had given in to Norah's
pleas for company. Bea had insisted on a trial run.
Now, she gave thanks that she'd had the foresight.

'. . . The standard's dropped quite shockingly. "Tea
bags," I said. "I never thought to see that here." Oh,
they trotted out the usual excuses . . .'

Norah had come to rest in the tearoom and Bea
decided that she should stay there for the present.
She smoothed out the letter and got to her feet.

'Where are you off to?' Norah eyed the letter.
'Something wrong?'

'No, no,' answered Bea soothingly. 'It's the
lawyers again. Asking me to go to see them. They're
suggesting that I might like to look at the house.'

'But you've told them to get on and sell it,'
protested Norah. 'Surely they don't expect you to go
all the way to the West Country to look at a house
that's going to be sold?'

Bea racked her brain for inspiration. 'The thing

is,' she said mendaciously, 'that there might be one or two of my cousin's things that I should like to have as keepsakes. He's suggesting that I have a look before the sale.'

'But you didn't know her,' objected Norah. 'How can you have a keepsake of someone you don't know?'

Bea was visited by an urge to see how Norah would look wearing a potful of geraniums but resisted this unworthy impulse and smiled instead.

'Well, you know what I mean. There might be one or two valuable things that I should like . . .'

'I should have thought the money would be more useful. I've been thinking. Supposing we build a small extension on at the side beyond the kitchen? You know you were saying that we should have a sitting room each . . .'

'Let's wait and see what happens,' said Bea quickly. 'That's why I thought I'd go down and see the place. It's really not that far and it will give us a better idea of what I can afford.'

'I suppose so,' said Norah grudgingly. 'Look.' She brightened a little. 'Why don't I come with you? Make a holiday of it. I haven't been to Devon for years. Bernard always liked decent weather and it does rain so down there. Why not, Bea? You can go any time, can't you? Let's go together.'

'It sounds a wonderful idea . . . but it has to be next week,' lied Bea with an ease born of desperation. 'This whoever-he-is,' she waved the letter, 'is going on holiday.' Lie followed lie. 'Next week's a busy one for you, isn't it? You've got Townswomen's Guild and meals-on-wheels. And haven't you invited

Andrew Owen to lunch after decorating the church
for Harvest Festival?' Andrew was the vicar and
Norah was silent. Bea, scenting victory, shrugged a
little. 'Of course, Miss Knowles could take your turn
at the WVS and I'm sure she'll be more than happy
to feed Andrew. Still . . .'

Norah bridled a little in her chair. 'Do you have
to see this particular chap?' she asked peevishly.
'Surely there are other members of the firm who
can take you round the house?'

Bea breathed heavily through her nose and
resorted to further untruths. 'It seems my two
cousins will be there, too,' she said, wondering if it
was thirty-odd years in the close proximity to little
boys which enabled the lies to roll so convincingly
from her lips. 'He's suggested that it's sensible for
us to be there together so as to ensure fair play.'

'Oh well.' Norah looked annoyed. 'Then I suppose
there's nothing to be done. I can't leave poor Andrew
to Miss Knowles's tender mercies . . .'

Bea made her escape, feeling as though she had
been let off detention.

'Oh, Bernard,' she muttered into the ether as she
went to her room to find her writing pad, 'I'm sorry
I said those things about you.'

As she sat in the train travelling west, Bea thought
about Tony Priest and wondered how soon she might
find another suitable flat in the town near the
school. She knew now that she could not possibly
consider spending the rest of her life with Norah.
She began to think that she had never really known
her at all. In those early days they'd been on several

holidays together as well as seeing each other daily at school but Bea wondered if the friendship would have survived if it had been formed in any other environment. It was only to be expected that, over the years, they should have grown apart and to imagine they could live together had probably been madness. A few weeks together each year was one thing; the rest of their lives together was quite another.

Bea gazed out over the Exe estuary. The September day was misty and the silvery sea, creeping in over the mud flats, merged with the soft grey sky. She leaned forward to watch a group of dunlin running before the tide; to smile at the sight of a heron hunched in solitary contemplation. A sense of peace stole into her soul and she settled back contentedly, deciding to enjoy her little holiday. The lawyer had written to her offering to meet her at the station in Plymouth but she had refused, saying that she would take a taxi to his office. There was no earthly reason why she should go to see the house but there might very well be a few items of furniture that would be useful if she were going to be setting up in her own flat. Her thoughts drifted back to Tony Priest but she forgot him when the train pulled in at Dawlish and she saw seagulls perched on the breakwaters and the sea breaking against the great sandstone rocks. It was years since she had made this journey and she gave herself up to the pleasure of recognising certain landmarks.

As the train approached Plymouth, Bea put on the jacket of her grey flannel suit, checked the contents of her handbag for the lawyer's letter and lifted her small case from the rack. She was one of the first off the train and the first into a taxi. The offices of Murchison, Marriott were situated in one of the city's Georgian crescents and Bea looked at the tall house approvingly as she paid the driver. Inside, at the reception desk, a young woman telephoned the news of her arrival and led her upstairs. She opened the door and smilingly bade Bea enter.

'Good afternoon,' James leaped up to greet her and then paused as Bea turned from thanking the receptionist and fixed him with a piercing, assessing stare. The years swung back and he found that he was hastily smoothing down his hair and sur-reptitiously wiping the toes of his shoes down the backs of his trouser legs. 'Good grief,' said James involuntarily. 'It's Matron!'

Isobel bumped down the track towards the cove feeling tired and irritable. The day at the bookshop had started badly when she found the brewer's lorry parked outside The Hermitage, blocking Mill Street whilst the driver sat enjoying a cup of coffee in the bar. This amiable young man nodded cheerfully at her and said that he would call her when he had finished unloading. Cursing, Isobel left the Morris – Mathilda's bequest to her – parked behind the lorry and hastened into the shop. The day had gone from bad to worse. She had been driven to curtness by a customer who wanted a book on gardening without knowing its title, the author, or its publisher but was convinced that Isobel *must* know which book it was because it had been so well reviewed. At lunchtime she lost her purse – although it was found and dropped into the shop just before closing time – and later in the afternoon she was ticked off by a mother for reproving her child who was pulling books off the shelves and dropping them on the floor. The door banged behind mother and child and, with a speaking glance at Pat and Laura, one of the two regular assistants, Isobel went through to the back of the shop to make coffee. The return of her purse cheered her a little but she was glad to get out into the fresh air of the early autumn evening.

She knew that it was tension that was making her so crotchety. Will, who was staying at the Royal Castle in Dartmouth, had made it clear that he was unwilling to sell the house and James had written to Tessa to tell her so. Unfortunately, having no other point of contact, he wrote to the house in Cobbold Road where the letter sat with her other post until she should return. Meanwhile Tessa was in Wales, dog-sitting two Weimaraners, longing to telephone James but afraid of being a nuisance or of hearing unpalatable news. Isobel also knew that, as a result of Tessa's pleadings, James had agreed to write to Beatrice Holmes again with the suggestion that she might like to choose some keepsake from amongst Mathilda's belongings, and in the hope that she might fall in love with the house whilst she was so engaged.

As she turned the Morris into its usual parking place she saw that James's car was already parked at the bottom of the track. She climbed out and stood undecidedly near the door into the kitchen remembering how she would once have gone in, shouting cheerfully to Mathilda, drawing curtains, checking that Mathilda had eaten her lunch. Swallowing hard she stared out to sea, watching the breakers crash against the shelf of sand and thinking of past evenings by the study fire playing Scrabble. The sound of a car's engine made itself heard above the sound of the surf and she turned to see Will's hired car pulling in beside James's Peugeot.

Her heart lifted at the sight of his cheerful countenance and raised hand, and she went to meet him, her loneliness abating a little.

'Have you met her?' he called with a conspiratorial glance towards the house. 'What's she like?'

'Met who?' Isobel began to feel excited. 'Is she here? The schoolteacher?'

'James phoned to say she arrived yesterday,' he told her. 'She's come down to see if there's anything she wants. Clever ruse, that.'

'But even if she likes the place,' argued Isobel, 'what then? Could you all squash in together?'

'Well, I can't afford to buy her out,' said Will gloomily. 'I had no idea it would be so valuable. It's fifty years behind the times inside.'

'It's the position,' said Isobel, equally gloomily. 'If you sell it the developers will move in. Oh, I can't bear it!'

Will smiled at her encouragingly. The whole affair had made him feel years younger. He had spent the last two weeks exploring the area and he was becoming more and more attached to the beautiful South Hams. One day he and Isobel had taken a picnic up on to Dartmoor. She had navigated, showing him the thickly wooded river valleys and the high bleak uplands with their outcrops of granite. There were still a great many holiday-makers about and, unable to find a quiet place to park, they had abandoned the idea of the picnic and Isobel had directed him to the small grey moorland town of Chagford where they had lunched in the Ring O' Bells, looking out over the market square. Afterwards they drove down to Fernworthy Reservoir, a tiny shining lake hidden amongst tall encircling pines, and had walked at the edge of the water and watched the mallard paddling idly in the reeds. Later, Will fetched the hamper and they drank their coffee at one of the picnic tables, nibbling the buns that Isobel had made. The sun was hot, dazzling from the surface of the reservoir where a rowing boat rocked quietly as its occupant bent over his rod.

Isobel talked non-stop about Mathilda until Will gradually built up a shadowy picture of his cousin and had become even more determined to hold on to her house in the cove. They discussed ways and means of dividing the house so that he and Tessa could share it and had almost discounted the third beneficiary until they learned the value of the house and cottage.

Now, as they stood together on the beach, Isobel smiled back at him. His silvery grey hair, like Mathilda's, was always ruffled and slightly untidy and he had an eager look which gave her confidence and hope. The door opened and James appeared followed by a tall well-built woman in a grey suit. Her glance at them was keen and Will instinctively dropped his arm lightly round Isobel's shoulders as they moved forward to meet her. James was looking surprisingly cheerful and Isobel's spirits rose as she shook the woman's hand.

'Isn't it amazing?' James was saying. 'This is Matron. From my prep school. I simply couldn't believe it. She hasn't changed a bit.'

'Which only goes to show,' said Bea, shaking Will's hand, 'what an awful old bat I must have been in my forties.'

'To an eight-year-old anyone over twenty is decrepit,' said Will consolingly. 'I'm your cousin, Will Rainbird. But I can't call you Matron . . .'

'Sorry,' said James hastily. 'This is Miss Holmes.'

'Bea,' she told Isobel, smiling at her. 'How d'you do?'

'I never thought of it being you,' said James. 'I didn't recognise the name. We always called you . . . Matron.'

She smiled at his hesitation. 'Or Busy Bea?' she suggested. 'And other less complimentary things with an emphasis on the B?'

Isobel burst out laughing at James's discomfited expression. 'I'll leave you to discuss in peace,' she said. 'You know where I am if anyone wants anything. Come in for a cup of tea if you feel like it.'

Bea, puzzled, watched her walk away and turned to James. 'Is she not my other cousin?'

'Sorry.' James looked even more confused. 'I should have introduced you properly. That's Isobel Stangate. She rents the cottage. I haven't been able to contact Tessa yet.'

'I see.' Bea looked thoughtful.

'So,' said Will, more heartily than he had intended. 'So what's your verdict?'

She raised her eyebrows. 'Verdict?'

'Now that you've seen the place,' he said, 'what d'you think of it?'

'The position is excellent,' she said slowly, 'if you like deserted coves. I'm sure it will fetch a good price.'

He stared at her in disappointment. 'You still want to sell then?'

She looked at him in surprise. 'What else do you suggest we do with it?'

'I hoped we might keep it,' he said slowly.

'*Keep* it?' She looked at him as though he were mad. 'For what purpose?'

'To live in,' mumbled Will, embarrassed by her penetrating stare. 'I'd like to hang on to it. So would Tessa. We hoped you might feel the same.'

Bea looked at James as though waiting for him to enlighten her. 'They both love the house, you see,' he explained rapidly, rather feeling that he was excusing a particularly muddy rugby shirt or a lost sock. 'They were wondering if the place couldn't be kept and used by the three of you.'

Bea frowned a little, as though she were doing a particularly difficult mental calculation. 'You seriously imagine that the three of us could live here together?' she asked. 'But why? There's nothing here.'

She glanced around her. The tide was swirling in across the sand, bursting in white foam against the rocks, filling the pools; above the cliffs away to the east a new moon hung, just visible in the deepening blue of the night sky.

'I suppose,' said Will slowly, 'it all depends on what you mean by nothing.'

Bea looked sharply at him but James intervened. 'Shall we take advantage of Isobel's offer of a cup of tea?' he asked diplomatically. 'And then I'll drive you back to Plymouth.'

Bea hesitated and then nodded. Will stood for a moment, watching the sky change colour as the darkness gathered and the stars appeared, and then followed them across the beach to the cottage.

Chapter Twelve

The farm gate stood open. Tessa applied the brakes and the two dogs in the back of the car were caught off balance, claws scrabbling. She reversed back along the lane and sat for a moment looking in at the close-cropped turf. She had found that farmers rarely objected to people walking their dogs in fields where there were neither crops nor stock but she always felt safer where the gates were open and the grass very short. She had once been surprised by a flock of sheep being driven into an empty field whilst she and her somewhat excitable charge were at the furthest corner from the gate. It had been an interesting moment.

Here, however, it seemed that the field had been well and truly cropped and Tessa reversed back to a wider part of the lane where she could park safely. She had also learned never to block gateways with the car. The farmer might arrive on a tractor at any moment to feed the field with some kind of fertiliser and be justly annoyed at being denied entry. The clumber spaniel – who bore the unlikely name of Sidney – looked anxiously from the rear window. He hated travelling backwards; it gave him a feeling of insecurity to see objects hastening towards him. He moaned briefly.

'Shut up, Sid!' muttered Tessa, as she negotiated

the verge and the thorn hedge. 'Don't be such a baby. Harry doesn't make a fuss.'

Hearing his name, the Jack Russell who had been standing on his hind legs – forepaws on the wheel arch as he peered eagerly from the side window – let forth a series of staccato barks. Tessa, clad in jeans, gumboots and a warm padded jacket, climbed out and released them and then stood for a moment to breathe in the sharp early morning air. Sidney, happy to be free of the confined space, padded to and fro along the verge, sniffing amongst the brambles and the faded willowherb. Harry, scenting rabbit, vanished into the field, his excited barks echoing in the quiet spaces of the Wiltshire uplands.

'Come on, Sid.' Tessa slung their leads round her neck, pushed her hands into her pockets and followed Harry into the field.

Sidney, his noble mien managing to convey a wounded expression at being called Sid, lifted his leg against a large dock and ambled slowly in her wake. Inside the field Tessa felt a familiar sensation as she gazed across a rolling expanse of chalky fields and gentle dun-coloured slopes. Small cottages, slate grey, nestled in the folds of the hills and mist clung in the valleys. A charm of goldfinches, feeding on thistle seed, swirled up into the cool air and a robin in the branches of an alder sang a stave or two before dipping over the hedge and out of sight. The welling up of joy in Tessa's heart reached the point where she knew it must be expressed in some action lest she burst with gratitude at the beauty spread out before her.

She began to run down the field, calling to the

dogs, arms outstretched. Harry joined in, skittering round her feet, barking madly whilst Sidney watched from his refuge under the hedge, pained at such unrestrained and plebeian behaviour. The field descended to a small stream, trickling between nut and alder trees, and Harry paused to drink copiously, stumpy tail wagging furiously, short legs planted foursquare. Sidney approached cautiously and Tessa bent to stroke his silky white coat and large domed head.

'It's not right, is it, old boy?' she murmured. 'Leaving you with a ratbag like Harry. Poor old chap.'

Sensing sympathy and a proper awareness of his dignity, Sidney sighed deeply. He consented to drink a little, one drooping eye on his regenerate companion. Tessa watched, smiling to herself. The decision that Harry's owner, a newly divorced woman with two small children, should join Sidney's mistress – also divorced with two children – on a holiday in France had been made at the last moment. It seemed that the two women could share the driving and the expense of the villa which could accommodate them all at a pinch; but what about Harry? Rather reluctantly, Tessa agreed that she would look after both dogs and hoped that Harry would be able to adapt to his new surroundings. Fortunately there was an outhouse where he could sleep, so leaving Sidney in possession of the kitchen and his rather smart beanbag. Harry, unused to such niceties, sniffed about and settled down happily on his torn old blanket to the marrow bone with which Tessa had the foresight to supply him.

Sidney had observed these proceedings somewhat dolefully from the safety of the kitchen door but Tessa had been firm with him.

'It's no good, Sid,' she said, shutting the outhouse door firmly and going with Sidney into the kitchen. 'Your missus said, "no bones." That's what comes of being so aristocratic, see? Your digestion's too delicate. Can't have you throwing up on this nice carpet.'

Sidney watched anxiously from his beanbag, fearful that this strange young woman who addressed him so disrespectfully might also forget his night-time Bonio. Tessa pottered, unaware of the distress in Sidney's breast, but talking to him all the time. Finally, however, she opened the cupboard and took out the familiar box. Sidney heaved a relieved sigh as Tessa placed the biscuit beside him, tugged his long ears gently and wished him good night.

Now, as they climbed the grassy slopes to the gate, Tessa was feeling more confident that she could cope with them both and her thoughts slid back inevitably to the house in the cove. She had not been able to meet Beatrice Holmes but Tessa knew now that Bea had no desire to keep the house although James had asked her to think about it, which she had agreed to do but with no real hope of changing her mind. Meanwhile, Will and James were trying to think of some way of buying her out. Between jobs, Tessa had fled down to Devon to meet them. The meeting was held at James's office.

'I know you wanted to meet at the cove,' he told Tessa when she and Will had been introduced. 'But

I felt it best that Isobel should be left out of this discussion.'

The two Rainbirds looked at him and he felt an almost hostile reaction. Part of him was pleased that Isobel had made such a favourable impression on them but it did not give him confidence in what he was about to suggest.

'I like Isobel,' Tessa said. 'She's like one of the family, isn't she? She's told me so many things about Mathilda I feel I knew her, too.'

'Exactly!' Will beamed at her, liking this girl who seemed barely more than a child but who had carved her niche with such determination and courage. 'Must have been quite a girl, Mathilda!'

'Yes.' James leaned his elbows on his desk. 'Yes, she was. And Isobel is a very nice woman but we have to consider this from all angles. The point I wish to make is this. If we could sell the cottage it would probably raise a significant sum towards buying Matron out. Sorry.' He shut his eyes and shook his head. 'She'll always be Matron to me.'

Tessa, who had heard the story from Isobel, grinned but almost immediately looked serious. 'But Isobel has the right to stay on in the cottage,' she pointed out. 'And even if she hadn't, where would she go?'

James stared at his desk top, hating himself. 'I think that if she knew that the sale of the cottage would make it possible for you to hang on to the house then she would look elsewhere for accommodation. There are other houses for rent, you know.'

'We *couldn't* ask her to go,' cried Tessa – to Will's

relief. 'How could we? She cared for Mathilda and she loved her, too. She misses her dreadfully. She loves the cove as much as we do. It's her home.'

Will watched her gratefully, glad that it had not been left to him to defend Isobel's position. 'There's another point, too,' he said. 'Would we want strangers living in the cove? In such close proximity the whole atmosphere of the place could be ruined.'

Tessa was staring at him in horror, remembering Isobel's story of Mathilda's tenant with the drunken husband. James raised his hands and shoulders in a helpless gesture.

'I agree it's a risk. But it *is* a way of keeping the house.'

'And where would Isobel go?' asked Tessa somewhat belligerently.

'Well, you might offer her accommodation in the house,' suggested James, 'although I think it's unlikely that she'd accept. No doubt she'd find another cottage. I take your point about undesirable neighbours at very close quarters but every avenue has to be explored.'

'I've had another idea,' said Tessa. 'It just occurred to me that if Mr . . . if Will –' she spoke his name rather shyly and he nodded at her encouragingly – 'is prepared to sell his property in Switzerland and we put the proceeds together with my trust we might just raise the money for Matron. We'd probably have to take out a small mortgage but I don't mind paying that if I can.'

The men looked at her in surprise. 'I thought your trust didn't materialise for several years,' said James.

'Two years,' said Tessa. 'But do you think Matron might be prepared to wait if we asked her? She could use the house, of course, and perhaps we could pay her interest or something.' She shook her head. 'I don't know the details but perhaps we might persuade her just to hang on. What d'you think?'

'It's not a bad idea,' said Will slowly. 'Of course, she wants to buy her own place, doesn't she? She might not want to wait.'

'I'll talk to her,' said James. 'It might work. Certainly worth a try. But first I need all the details about this trust, Tessa.'

Will sat back in his chair whilst the other two talked, watching Tessa. It was interesting that neither he nor she had questioned for a single moment their compatibility to share the house. It would be fun, he thought, to have such a bright, cheerful girl around and he could look after the house during her absences; make sure that it was a warm welcoming place to which she could come home. Home; that was the word, thought Will. Perhaps that was the link between them. They had both instinctively looked upon the cove as home; something neither of them had truly experienced. We must make it work, he thought. He was not yet prepared to admit to himself how important Isobel was to his plans but he was glad that Tessa had reacted as she had. Isobel belonged to the cove, too. She was part of the family . . .

Tessa had been unaware of Will's thoughts; she only knew that they were of the same mind and had been pleased to think that this man was her cousin, if a rather distant one. Now, as she lifted the tailgate so that Sidney and Harry could jump in, she thought about Will. She could see no reason why they shouldn't share the house. After all, it was a very big place for one girl who spent most of the time in other people's houses. To Tessa's young eyes Will, the wrong side of sixty, was much too old to be considering any romantic entanglements and she could imagine them settling down well together. He would have Isobel for company when she, Tessa, was dog-sitting and he had already professed himself willing to undertake much of the work which was needed to restore the house and bring it up to date.

The whole thing turned on Matron. Tessa, with boarding school not far behind her, had adopted James's name for Bea with no difficulty at all. Tessa imagined a severe, starched, difficult individual who would have no compunction in overturning her hopes and dreams. She drove the car into the ramshackle wooden garage which clung to the side of the small cottage, released the dogs and went inside to make herself some breakfast. Sidney followed her, collapsing on to his beanbag as though he had walked miles. He watched, nose on paws, as she fetched muesli and toasted bread and, unable to resist the hope in his eyes, she gave him another Bonio which he crunched with great gusto.

She heard the soft plop of letters on the mat and went out to fetch the post. Harry was barking at the postman and she opened the door to reprimand him, smiling an apology as she hauled Harry inside and slammed the door. Harry trotted into the kitchen and went at once to Sidney's beanbag to investigate the crumbs. Because of his soft mouth,

Sidney was a messy eater and Harry obligingly cleaned up after him, even licking round Sidney's jaws, much to the clumber's indignation. He looked to Tessa for support but she was opening an envelope. She had asked Cousin Pauline to forward her letters and, amongst them, was a postcard of Edinburgh Castle. She turned it over, puzzled. 'Stuck up here in the frozen north,' ran Sebastian's scrawl. 'How are things? Thanks for last time. See you soon.'

Tessa waited for the surge of excitement with which she had greeted Sebastian's missives over the years but it was not forthcoming. She felt a small glow of pleasure but it was oddly muted and she read the card again so as to work herself up to it. It was no use. Frowning, she looked through the rest of her post which consisted mainly of circulars, apart from a request from Mrs Carrington for a booking for Christmas and the New Year, and a letter from James. This was mainly to confirm all that she told him at their meeting in Plymouth, nevertheless she noted that her heart bumped much faster as she opened this envelope than it had when she'd read Sebastian's card.

As she sat down to her breakfast she castigated herself for putting the anxiety about the house above her love for Sebastian. Mentally she re-designed the house so that it could contain a married couple as well as Will. With Sebastian at sea and herself away so much, she was sure that it could be achieved without too much difficulty ... Pushing her plates aside she folded her arms on the table and shook her head sadly. Marriage with

Sebastian was as distant a dream as it had been when she was fourteen. Their day out together had been lovely but she was aware that, to him, she was still just a little sister. There was none of the excitement that should be there – well, certainly not on his part. It seemed that he needed to be partly drunk to feel that sort of thing.

She found herself thinking about Giles and how differently he had treated her. The expression in his eyes had been flattering and oddly disturbing, giving her flutters in her abdomen. The lunch at the Church House Inn at Rattery had been great fun. True, Guy had been rather distant to begin with but, after a pint or two, he had soon thawed and Gemma was so friendly and funny. Giles had made sure that Tessa was never left out and for those few hours she had felt part of a family group.

Family; she had an obsession about it. Despairingly Tessa began to clear away her breakfast things. She knew that it was this sense of family and deep affection that she saw and loved at the Roundhouse at Buckland-in-the-Moor where the Perrymans worked so happily together; the cheerful banter of the twins, Clare and Marie; the warm motherliness of Mrs Perryman; Sunday lunchtimes when Mr Perryman came in to chat to his regulars; young Colin old enough now to wait at table . . . these were the things that drew her back and gave her a feeling of safety.

Tessa pulled herself together, propped Sebastian's card on the windowsill and began to do the washing-up.

Chapter Thirteen

It was at James's suggestion – and with the permission of the other beneficiaries – that Will moved into the house in the cove. Will gratefully accepted the offer. He had enjoyed staying at the Royal Castle and exploring the busy town of Dartmouth but, as the autumn drew on, he found himself more at one with the countryside than with the urban scene. He drove home on a windy cold afternoon, through the coastal villages of Stoke Fleming and Strete, his eyes drawn again and again to the great sweep of coastline which embraced Blackpool Sands and Torcross beach and stretched away to Start Point, misty and ethereal in the autumn sunshine. He swung left, down the hill and on to Torcross Line where the sea crashed in against the long stretch of shingle to his left and the chilly breeze ruffled the calm waters of Slapton Ley on his right.

He slowed to watch a flock of starlings sweep low over the Ley where two swans sailed, calm and indifferent to these noisy visitors, and ducks swam amongst the reedy edges and huddled together on the tiny beach. The flock of starlings, like a ragged cloud overhead, broke and re-formed and swept away inland. Will sighed with deep pleasure and drove on. The low sun sent long sharp shadows across fields whose red soil glowed richly in its rays, touching the dying bracken in the hedgerows with its fiery glance so that the whole countryside was bathed in brilliant colour.

The entrance to the track was familiar to him but he remembered when he had first seen it in the hot August afternoon. There was no honeysuckle now; the red and gold berries of the black bryony trailed across bare branches which shivered and creaked in the cold rush of the wind and bramble leaves burned darkly in the ditch. Will drove gently down the track wishing that some conclusion could be reached. He had a very adequate pension – and some savings tucked away – but living in a hotel and using a hired car was expensive. Of course, if the house were to be sold then he need not worry about money ever again but if he and Tessa were able to keep it they would need every penny.

As he negotiated the sharp bend to the right and saw that first tantalising glimpse of the sea his heart knocked fast in his breast. He parked the car beside the Morris and climbed out, hearing the boom of the surf as it thudded against the sand shelf out at the mouth of the cove. The beach was deep in shadow but the sea reflected back the blue of the overarching sky above it and, as he walked out on to the beach and looked up at the house, he saw that lights were shining out from the kitchen and the study.

Isobel; at the thought of her his heart became even more unruly and he pushed open the kitchen door eagerly. The room was empty but the smell of casserole assailed his nostrils and he saw an apple pie placed in the middle of the Georgian table. He looked about him; at the scratched but polished table, at the delicate china newly dusted on the dresser shelves, at the battered Rayburn and the beautiful glass bowl of the old paraffin lamp which stood on an oak trolley. On the lower shelf of the trolley was a pile of books. Curiously, Will bent to read the titles. He took the top book out in disbelief.

'*The Hunting of the Snark*,' he murmured with amusement and sank into Mathilda's chair beside the Rayburn . . .

Isobel found him some moments later. The shock of seeing him there, looking so like Mathilda as he gazed up at her with a book in his hand, rendered her momentarily inarticulate. She wavered between delight, at seeing him here where she felt he belonged and at the easing of her own loneliness, and rage at giving her a fright and making her think – for one brief wonderful moment – that Mathilda had returned to her. Delight won.

'Oh, Will,' she said, stretching out her hands to him. 'Welcome home.'

Bea swept the iron rhythmically to and fro across the board, carefully but insistently pressing out the creases of her best white shirt. Norah sat behind her at the kitchen table, her voice pressing just as insistently at Bea's mind, forcing itself into the corners of her thoughts, exactly as the iron pushed relentlessly into the stiff cotton of Bea's shirt.

'Never go back, Bea. It's always disastrous. These old sayings may be clichés but there's a lot of truth in them. I was saying as much to Andrew. He feels that you'll be making a mistake . . .'

Bea clenched her teeth on a spasm of irritation as she thought about Norah discussing her private affairs with Andrew Owen, priest or not.

'... and we agreed that this is exactly the trouble with Miss Knowles. Because she lived here as a girl she feels she has the absolute right to come back, now that she's retired, and behave as though she's been here all her life. She has a most unpleasant air of complacency ...'

Bea peeled her shirt from the ironing board and hung it on a coat hanger. She selected a nightgown from the pile of laundry on the table beside her and stretched it out across the ironing board.

'... of course, the man's a saint. He'd never noticed that smug look on her face but I was able to point out that I've come up against a *very* stubborn streak in her character. Absolutely *determined* to read one of the lessons at the carol service. I know that one member of the congregation is always asked but I flatter myself that I have a better reading voice than most ...'

Once again, Bea found herself thinking about Bernard; understanding those smiling silences, the disappearances to the pub. Why had she allowed herself to be drawn in to this trap? When she told Norah how much she was missing her friends at school and in the nearby town she had brought a deluge round her ears. This was their third conversation on this subject and Bea, though exhausted and sorry for Norah, was standing firm.

'... simply because her father was curate forty years ago she feels that the church is her property. Unless I'm mistaken it will lead to a great deal of heartache. She should have remained where she was, among her own friends. She simply doesn't belong here any more. And that's what *you'll* find, Bea. You simply don't belong there any more.'

'If that's true,' said Bea, speaking for the first time, 'then at least I shall have discovered it for myself. I did tell you at the beginning that we must have a trial run. I'm very fond of you, my dear, but I had no idea how much I would miss the school . . . and the town. You must let me make this experiment.'

Norah exhaled noisily. Without looking round, Bea envisaged her face; chin drawn in, mouth turned down, a self-pitying expression in her eyes.

'Well, if you insist.' She emitted a short mirthless laugh. 'I don't have much choice, do I?'

'Try to understand,' said Bea gently. 'Retirement has come as a bit of a shock. I need time to adjust. The lease on this little flat I've found is for six months. By then I should know one way or the other.'

Norah shrugged – but her reply was lost in the ringing of the telephone. Bea sighed as she folded the nightgown. She had acquiesced to James's request that Will should reside in the house whilst he waited for the outcome to this new suggestion. Bea selected a Viyella skirt from the pile and turned the iron's dial to a lower heat. It was true that she was not desperate for the money from the sale of the house and cottage; nevertheless two years was rather a long time to wait. Thoughtfully Bea smoothed the soft folds. One thing was certain: that she could not live with Norah. It was odd, almost prescient, that Mathilda had left her house to the three of her relatives who had no homes. Of course, that was not strictly true, Will had his flat in Geneva and Tessa had her base in London. As for herself . . . Bea shook out the skirt and slipped it on to its hanger, remembering that James had told her that they were the only three surviving relatives; all three single or alone. For a moment she pictured the cove and heard Will's voice saying, 'It all depends on what you mean by nothing.'

Surely it would be quite impossible for them all to live there together? Perhaps if the cottage were to be vacated . . . She recalled Isobel's anxious face and Will's eager one and laughed aloud as she thought of James's cry of, 'Good grief! It's Matron!' He had been an earnest and very endearing little boy and it was plain that he was just as keen as these others that their hare-brained scheme should come to fruition. James, in his letter, had suggested that she might like to use the house for weekends and holidays during those two years and, meanwhile, Will and Tessa had felt that she should be recompensed for being deprived of her share whilst they waited for Tessa's trust to mature.

Norah was back, clucking with a kind of delighted impatience over some poor soul's inadequacy concerning the preparations for the Townswomen's Guild's Remembrance Sunday's buffet lunch. Bea hardened her heart, grateful that she'd had the sense to leave the bulk of her belongings in the headmaster's attic. She could probably slip away under cover of the new burdens which Norah, with so much joy, was preparing to shoulder. She would write to James, agreeing to his proposal, and settle into the little flat near the school. Bea took her pyjama jacket from the pile. She smiled at Norah, her thoughts elsewhere. Soon she would see Tony Priest and all her boys . . .

Isobel lay in bed staring at the ceiling. Her pleasure at Will's arrival in the cove had been overshadowed by a letter from Simon asking for a divorce. He and Sally wanted to get married, he wrote, and he felt this would be no difficulty now that he and Isobel had been living apart for nearly four years. Isobel had sat for some time, staring at the letter where it lay on the table: nearly four years. She tried to remember that year with Mike – to recapture the madness, the excitement, the fun – but it eluded her, remaining just beyond her mental grasp. Was it really she, Isobel, who had danced and laughed and made love with the energy of a twenty-year-old? She shook her head. The affair seemed to belong to some other person's remote and distant past but the reality was that, because of it, she had lost Simon – and Helen.

Now, the next morning, she rolled over in bed, huddling into the quilt, thinking of her daughter who was a stranger to her and of her husband who now belonged with Sally. Isobel lay quite still, her eyes shut. Mathilda's death and the arrival of her descendants in the cove had enabled Isobel to keep her own heartache and loneliness in abeyance. It closed in again as soon as she was alone but, though she tried to talk herself out of it, she knew beyond doubt that it was Simon whom she still loved, and the idea of him married to Sally was a dreadful one. Just as she had relied on his unchanging love all through her affair with Mike, so she had hoped that one day he would come back to her. Despite her head's certainty that he was irrevocably lost to her, her heart insisted that he still loved her.

The letter had come as a blow to her hopes. Isobel wrapped her arms about herself, squeezing her eyes closed against the morning light. She knew, with heart and head alike, that once he married Sally he was lost to her for ever. And what of Helen? Why should Helen ever bother with her again? Simon had not succeeded in changing his daughter's mind, although she had received a prim little birthday card with her daughter's signature scrawled across the bottom; no message of love, no best wishes, but Isobel had seen the card as a breakthrough and had carried it with her for weeks and, even now, used it as a bookmark. She had comforted herself with the thought that perhaps Sally wasn't quite so wonderful as everyone thought she was. Perhaps Simon was tiring of her and Helen was realising that she was not a substitute for her own mother . . .

Now, Isobel wondered if it had been Sally who had persuaded Helen to send the card. The humiliating thought made her clench her fists and bury her face in the quilt. She would rather not see Helen at all than to know that it was at Sally's prompting. Such knowledge filled her with shame and tears forced themselves out of her eyes. After all, it was she who had wrecked her marriage; she who had abandoned her husband and child in a wild grab at happiness. What right had she to dictate terms now? In her head she heard Mathilda's voice: '*And did you find happiness?*' How many people, wondered Isobel drearily, refused to recognise the happiness at their own doorsteps and spent their lives searching for some mythical bluebird?

Mathilda had injected a kind of strength into her, making it possible to both face the knowledge and bear the result of her mistake. Without her, Isobel felt as though she were drifting off course. She was not yet aware that she was beginning to look towards Will, as she had looked to Mathilda, for courage; but his coming had given her renewed hope which the letter had destroyed. She lay, listening to the continual music of the sea, watching the changing, trembling shift of light on the walls and ceiling, unable to summon the will or energy to get up. The sound of the telephone bell impinged upon her misery and, at length, she swung her legs over the side of the bed and went downstairs.

'Yes?' she said curtly into the receiver. 'Who is it?'

'Hello, Isobel.' It was Tessa. 'Did I get you up? I'm awfully sorry.'

'It's OK,' said Isobel, peering at her watch and seeing that it was twenty past eleven. 'I wasn't asleep. What's the problem?'

'No problem really. I just wondered if Will had moved in.' She sounded hopeful and excited, and Isobel felt her own troubles receding a little. 'I had an idea, you see.'

'Will's in,' said Isobel as cheerfully as she could. 'He's enjoying himself no end. What's the idea?'

'Well, I'm leaving here tomorrow morning and I've got a week's gap. I was just wondering if I could come down to the cove instead of going back to London. What d'you think?'

'Of course you can come,' said Isobel warmly, as though she were the owner of the cove. 'Why not? You have just as much right as Will, and I know he'd be delighted to see you. So would I. When will you be arriving . . . ?'

Isobel replaced the receiver feeling perceptibly happier. She must air sheets, make up a bed and prepare a special supper. It was important that Tessa should feel at home in the house in the cove – and, anyway, it was good to have someone to plan for and to look after. She belted her dressing gown more tightly round her waist and went into the kitchen. Through the window she could see Will walking on the beach, and she paused in her act of filling the kettle to watch him. He pottered, as Mathilda used to; picking up shells or stones so as to examine them; collecting driftwood; stopping to watch the waves. He made no attempt to disturb her privacy or encroach upon her time, always waiting for her to approach him. Her heart warmed towards him and it was with a lighter spirit that, having switched on the kettle, she went running upstairs to dress. She must tell Will of Tessa's imminent arrival and maybe they would go into Kingsbridge together to buy in some supplies, stopping off at Frogmore Bakery to buy some bread from Mary . . .

Isobel pulled on leggings and a warm jersey, thrust her feet into thick socks and hurried back downstairs. The day that had stretched so emptily before her was filled with new purpose.

Chapter Fourteen

Tessa's week with Will at the cove was an un-qualified success. At first he had been anxious lest there might be some awkwardness about sharing the bathroom or appearing unexpectedly in his dressing gown but these fears were swiftly dispelled by Tessa's own attitude. She had spent most of her life either at school or in other people's homes and she was perfectly natural with him. This allowed him, in turn, to be easy and relaxed and soon it was as though they had known each other for years. They prowled about the house together, exploring, investigating, poking into cupboards and generally making themselves at home.

Tactfully, Isobel left them alone as much as possible and it was Will who showed Tessa the countryside, took her in to introduce her to Mary who made such delicious bread at Frogmore Bakery and drove her to Kingsbridge to shop. She exclaimed with pleasure as they passed over Bowcombe Bridge, where the river ran out from between its thickly wooded banks into the wider shining waters of the estuary. The small grey town which clung to the side of the hill, with its slate-hung houses and old cottages and the estuary at its feet, made her think of other small Devonshire towns. She was aware of a sense of timelessness – despite the bustle and the traffic – and a sense of belonging. The weather was cold and bright, with frosty mornings and starlit nights, and Tessa was happier than she had been for many years.

As the week passed an idea was maturing at the back of Will's mind. He was reminded of it by something Tessa was telling him as they sat by the sitting room fire one early evening, making toast. She had told him many stories of her dog-sitting adventures and described her employers and their houses so graphically that he began to feel that he knew them almost as well as she did. At the moment she was embarked upon a description of Mrs Carrington and her daughter in the Midlands. When she reached the part about the sale of the bureau, Will let out an exclamation. Tessa paused and looked at him enquiringly.

'Sorry. Didn't mean to interrupt. Just reminded me of something. Carry on. So did the young man come and fetch it?'

Whilst she buttered toast Tessa finished her story and, putting the plate in the grate to keep warm, she began to pour the tea. 'Poor old thing,' she said. 'It's really a squeeze to make ends meet and that daughter of hers knows she's a soft touch. You can tell.'

Will shook his head sympathetically but his mind was already busy with his new idea. 'It made me think of something,' he told her, pushing the logs back together so that they could begin to burn again. 'You know, there are an awful lot of valuable pieces in this house.'

'Pieces?' Tessa looked puzzled.

'Furniture.' Will accepted his cup. 'Some of it's terrifically old. Now, it occurred to me that if we sold some of it and split the money three ways you and I could put ours towards buying Matron out.'

'But they're Mathilda's things,' said Tessa slowly. 'Family things.'

Will smiled a little. He wondered if it had ever occurred to Tessa just how well off she'd be if they were to sell up. 'I appreciate that,' he said gently. 'But they're our things now, too, d'you see? If it were a choice between selling some of the furniture or selling the house . . . ?'

He let the remark hang in the air whilst he ate his toast, watching her. She sat staring into the fire, deep in thought: presently she looked about the room.

'It wouldn't be the same without her things,' she observed wistfully.

He bit back his impatience, realising that it was the sense of continuity that was important to her. He had seen her, touching the furniture, picking up ornaments, taking down a book, and had known that she was identifying with Mathilda and feeling part of the pattern. Here Mathilda had stood to watch the sea; here she had sat to write and work; here she had slept. Some of the furniture must have belonged to Mathilda's parents, possibly even to her grandparents. There had been Rainbirds here for more than ninety years . . .

'We might only need to sell two or three pieces,' he said. 'Don't think I want to but I'd rather lose a few pieces of furniture than the house.'

'Two or three pieces?' She shook her head. 'Mrs

155

Carrington only got three hundred pounds for her bureau.'

'Perhaps Mrs Carrington's bureau wasn't very valuable,' suggested Will, who was interested in antiques and had a very good idea of just how valuable some of Mathilda's things were. 'It's only a thought. To keep as an emergency. James is hoping that Matron will be prepared to wait.'

Tessa drank her tea. 'Perhaps as an emergency,' she agreed at last.

Will heaved a sigh of relief. 'It will all have to be valued. Perhaps James has had it done already. I'll talk to him. Let's hope it won't be necessary.'

'I hope not but it would be silly to lose the house if we had the means to save it. Oh, I can't tell you what it means to know that I've got this to come back to.' She took a deep breath and nodded. 'We simply must hold on.'

'I'll have a word with James.' He cast about for something to distract her and his eye fell on Mathilda's Scrabble board. 'Ever played Scrabble?'

She began to laugh. 'Not for years and years. I used to play with Rachel and Sebastian. He always won but we said he cheated.'

'Let's have a game.' Will was clearing away the tea things. 'Look, here are the score cards.' Together they studied Mathilda's small precise writing; the two columns of figures headed M and I. 'She must have been quite a player,' he said, chuckling. 'Beat old Isobel nearly every time by the look of it.'

'There are more in the box.' Tessa picked them up. 'These columns are headed M and N. I wonder who N was?'

'Sounds like the old Catechism,' said Will cheerfully, setting out the board and the racks on the low table. ' "What is your name? N or M?" '

Tessa fingered the yellowing paper thoughtfully. Will glanced up at her, surprised at her silence, and felt a sudden surge of affection for the small figure with the serious down-slanted face and its aureole of bright hair. Sensing the slight change of atmosphere, she looked at him and they smiled at each other with deep satisfaction and contentment.

'It'll be all right,' he told her confidently. 'Come on. You can draw first.'

Sunday morning. The chapel was full but the faint warmth from the heaters had not yet dispelled the chill of the frosty December morning. The boys' breath appeared in smoky puffs and they rubbed their hands together and blew out their cheeks, exaggerating the cold. Bea sat at the back of the chapel, trying not to feel superfluous. Her arrival back in the environs of the school had received a mixed response. At first her old friends had greeted her welcomingly and with affection but, when they realised that she was not just on a visit but had rented a flat in the town, their reactions altered. There was a certain raising of eyebrows which indicated surprise and, in some cases, faint disapproval. Bea hid her disappointment and anxiety and tried to make herself feel at home. The shopkeepers knew her and were friendly enough but, now that she was no longer officially attached to the school, there was a very real sense of exclusion.

As she tried to make her new flat comfortable

she told herself that she was being oversensitive. After all, she'd lived close to the town for fifteen years and had as much right to retire here as anyone else. She looked critically at the indifferent furniture with which the flat was furnished and tried not to feel lonely. She had not been ready to deal with the impression that, to her ex-colleagues, she was already an outsider. On the odd occasions when she'd popped into the school for a chat there had been an undercurrent of suspicion; a 'What's *she* doing here?' atmosphere which had made her feel uncomfortable. The new matron, fresh from a school in the north, was openly hostile and even the headmaster, when he saw her chatting to the boys as they came off the playing fields, seemed reserved. Although he offered her tea he looked relieved when she refused, and hurried the boys away to the changing rooms.

Bea spent hours wandering round her three rooms, fiddling with the small personal possessions which gave the flat a less bleak look, and trying to decide how she could overcome this hurtful sense of hostility. The boys had been pleased to see her, waving when they saw her coming down the drive from the school so that she'd strolled over to watch the game. She'd stood with them on the sidelines whilst they cheered their team on and they'd talked easily and naturally with her, as though she were still part of their lives.

No one could have guessed what courage it took for her to make this appearance at the Sunday morning service. She sat just inside the door, dressed in her grey flannel suit and navy felt hat, and stared at the back of Tony Priest's head. She had seen him briefly and only at a distance. He had noticed her as she passed out through the hall from the secretary's office – mercifully June was just as friendly as she'd ever been – and he had raised a long arm in greeting before turning back to the small boy who stared earnestly up at him. She'd paused, pretending to study some photographs pinned to the notice board, but pride had made it impossible to hover there indefinitely.

This morning his wife sat beside him, thin and elegant in soft lambswool, her fine fair hair cut in a short bob. Bea clasped her hands on her grey flannel lap and stared down at her ample, cotton-covered bosom. She had surprised a disapproving stare from Marian, the headmaster's wife, and a glare from the new matron and she felt as miserable and alone as any new boy. She knew now that Norah had been right but she simply could not go back to Winchester. She would rather stay here and risk the snubs . . .

The headmaster's voice, reading the lesson for the first Sunday in Advent, caught her attention. '". . . *it is high time to awake out of sleep . . . The night is far spent, the day is at hand: let us therefore cast off the works of darkness, and put on the armour of light . . ."* '

Bea, moved as always by the Epistle for Advent, thought that this was probably the most exciting time of the whole school year. Christmas loomed ahead with the promise of the carol service and the Christmas party; the decoration of the tree that stood in the hall and the rehearsals for the nativity play which took place in the chapel. The Advent hymns had always thrilled her with a sense of anticipation and there was an ongoing atmosphere of happy expectation. Surely they would not exclude her from all that lay ahead? There must be some part she could play; some area in which she could make herself useful?

As the organ played the opening bars of 'Lo he comes with clouds descending', Bea rose to her feet determined to make a very great effort to be integrated back into her old familiar world. She had yet to collect her few odds and ends from the headmaster's attic and, whilst doing it, she would talk to Marian and let them see that she was no threat. On reflection, she realised that she should have thought of this before. Perhaps the new matron felt that she might be undermined by Bea's presence; perhaps it had been a little thoughtless to turn up unannounced . . . Encouraged, Bea held her hymn book higher and, with her eyes on Tony Priest's broad shoulders, sang the well-known words with new-found confidence.

Giles stretched out his hand to the telephone, dithered and, folding his arms across his chest, tucked both fists into his armpits. His stepfather, seated at the kitchen table, maintained a tactful silence but Kate drew in her breath and closed her eyes in frustration.

'Giles,' she said in a low dangerous voice, 'will you please pick up that telephone and talk to Tessa?'

Giles looked at her. 'The trouble is . . .' he began but stopped as Kate slapped both hands flat on the table and gave a cry of anguish. David courteously but silently drew back his newspaper and Kate glared at him briefly before returning her attention to Giles.

'And *don't* tell me what the trouble is,' she said warningly. 'You've already told me what the trouble is. Once on the phone from London. Again on your arrival yesterday lunchtime and all over again last night after supper. We know how you feel about it. We know that your photographic business might not be able to support a wife; we know you feel that you're not in a position to enter into an ongoing relationship; we know that Tessa has a crush on Sebastian Anderson. We decided, on the telephone and again when you arrived yesterday, and for the third time last evening – or rather at two o'clock this morning – that none of these things matter since you are merely going to invite her out to lunch.'

The word 'lunch' came out on a rather high note and Kate paused and cleared her throat. Giles and David watched her anxiously.

'The thing is, old chap,' said David after a moment of pregnant silence, 'that the girl probably won't give a hang about your job or your bank balance. You're not proposing marriage. Just lunch.'

'I don't believe this.' Kate sat down at the table and ran both hands through her hair. 'No wonder you're thirty years old and not married, Giles. Do you ever manage to ask any girl to go anywhere? I thought that young girls were free and independent and self-sufficient. Why the third degree?'

'Tessa's special,' said Giles simply.

Kate stared at him, her irritation evaporating. 'Oh, darling,' she said. 'I know. At least, I think you could say we suspected. Oh hell! Can't you see that's why we want you to phone her?'

Suppressing a desire to howl with frustration she fetched a bottle of wine and the corkscrew and put them down on the table in front of David.

'Sorry,' said Giles miserably. 'Only it means a lot and I'm afraid of cocking it up. I know she's very independent and all those things and I seem to be a bit old-fashioned where women are concerned and they don't care for it much . . . And then there's Sebastian.'

David and Kate exchanged a glance and David pushed a glass of wine across the table towards Giles where he stood, leaning against the dresser, hands now thrust deep in his trouser pockets.

'Giles,' said Kate carefully, 'please try to be sensible about this. It's one thing being honourable and another being stupid.' David winced and looked quickly at Giles, who was staring into his wine glass. 'Tessa has had a schoolgirl crush on Sebastian for years and, because she rarely gets the opportunity to meet any other young men, she hasn't grown out of it. From what I've read between the lines he treats her like a little sister and has never given her a serious thought. If you're going to let that stand in your way then you're a twit. For heaven's sake, give her the chance to choose for herself.'

Giles stood his glass on the table and looked at the telephone.

'Got an idea.' David smiled at him. 'Why not use the extension in my study? More private.'

'I'll do that.' Giles picked up the address book, nodded at them and disappeared into the hall.

'And now I shan't hear what he says,' groaned Kate. 'I shan't be able to spur him on if he needs it. He looked just like he used to when I left him at school. It's ridiculous.'

David reached a hand across the table to her. 'As you said, my darling, he's thirty years old. Got to let go sometime.'

'I've been letting Giles go since he was eight and he went off to prep school,' said Kate wretchedly. 'I've hardly seen him for the last twenty-two years. Where did I go wrong? Perhaps I wasn't motherly enough.'

'I notice he still telephones when he's got a problem,' said David. 'I think he looks upon you more as a friend than a mother. Nothing wrong with that. Stop fretting. This is the first time I've seen Giles like this in the four years that I've known him. It's love, that's what it is, poor chap.'

'He's been in love before.' Kate swallowed some wine. 'It was a girl he was at university with. Went on for years. Giles is very faithful and loyal and had great difficulty when he knew that it was over for him but that she was still keen. It was hell! For all of us!'

David began to laugh. 'Then why are you so hellbent in putting us all through it again?'

'Shh!' said Kate. 'He's coming . . .'

Giles came in, looking self-conscious. He paused, grinning at their expectant faces and then punched the air with both fists.

'No problem,' he said. 'Sounded very pleased.

She's bringing Charlie Custard and we'll take him for a walk afterwards.'

Kate let out a gasp of relief. 'Thank God for that! Let joy be unconfined. Stop hogging the bottle, David. I need another drink!'

Chapter Fifteen

Tessa replaced the telephone receiver and stroked Charlie Custard as he leaned heavily against her leg.

'That's nice, isn't it, Custard?' she said. 'We've got a lunch date for tomorrow at the Elephant's Nest. Giles is coming here first. We'll have to go in my car so that you can come too.'

She glanced at her watch and saw that it was nearly lunchtime. As she opened a tin of soup she thought about Giles, remembering how easy he had been to talk to, and how he'd made her feel rather special. If it hadn't been for Sebastian ... Tessa switched on the heat under the saucepan and put two slices of bread in the toaster. Charlie Custard watched hopefully but Tessa was deep in thought, remembering her visit to the Andersons a few weekends before. It was Commander and Mrs Anderson's thirtieth wedding anniversary and Tessa had been invited to the party. It was lovely to see the twins and Rachel, who was now a hard-working lawyer in the City, and even more wonderful to see Sebastian, who was on leave from his ship. When she saw him in the flesh she wondered how on earth she had been so indifferent to his postcard. Not exactly indifferent, she told herself as he hugged her, but simply preoccupied with the house. He was delighted to see her, ready to listen to her news about the cove, and – when he'd had a few drinks – more than ready to kiss her while they were supposed to be looking for extra glasses in the kitchen.

By the time the weekend was drawing to its close, she was convinced that this was the turning point she'd been hoping for; the moment when he saw her as a woman. Even Rachel noticed a difference in his attitude and teased them about it, embarrassing Tessa who feared it might frighten Sebastian away. He, however, merely laughed and took Tessa out for a walk and then into the pub, where they sat in a corner and he said the things to her that she'd always longed to hear. They arrived back in time for supper and there was no more opportunity then to be alone. Tessa was sharing a bedroom with Rachel, just like the old days, and they talked until the early hours and parted the next morning promising that they wouldn't let it be so long before they met again. Sebastian slept late and Tessa was obliged to leave for Wales before he appeared.

As Tessa poured the soup into a bowl and put the toast on a plate she relived the disappointment she'd felt when he telephoned later in the week to tell her that he wouldn't be driving to Wales to see her after all. His father needed the car, he'd said, and the train journey was too complicated, but when he was next on leave they must spend some time together ... They'd talked for a while and Tessa had managed to joke and laugh with him and not let him guess how hurt she was. A naval wife needed to be strong and independent and he must see that she would be able to cope with separations. Since then there had been no word but the weekend remained like a warm glow in her heart.

Now she had lunch with Giles to look forward to as well as her very first Christmas at the cove. It was Isobel who had suggested that she should come across from Mrs Carrington's for Christmas Day. It was barely half an hour's drive and she could bring Romulus and Remus with her. Isobel and Will had tried to persuade her to come on Christmas Eve and stay over for Boxing Day but Tessa was firm. Part of her duties was to look after the house as well as the dogs and she felt that it would be wrong to leave it empty at night. They made no attempt to dissuade her from what she rightly saw as her responsibility but promised that the three of them should have the best Christmas Day ever.

Tessa broke a few crusts into her soup bowl and put it down for Charlie Custard to lick, remembering how he and she had spent last Christmas together. She thought of the presents Freddie had left under the little tree and how Kate had invited her to lunch. This year she would be spending most of Christmas Day in her own home. She repeated those last three magic words aloud to herself, hardly daring to believe them, and, unable to contain herself, wrapped her arms round the dog's great neck and gave him a hug of pure joy. She wondered what she'd do without all these long-suffering dogs to talk to and cuddle when she felt happy or miserable, and it struck her that she led a very strange life. Even when she went back to London, Cousin Pauline very rarely talked to her; she was much more interested in the latest television soap. She had shown a faint animation when Tessa told her about the cove but it had quickly faded. Refusing to allow a tinge of self-pity to depress her, Tessa pulled on her coat and, taking the rope halter which served as his lead, she and Charlie Custard went out into the raw winter afternoon.

Isobel, too, was thinking about last Christmas. She remembered the humiliating scene with Simon and how he'd told her that he and Sally were going to the Lakes together. She had come rushing back to Mathilda and they had planned their trip to Oxford together. Isobel shook her head and swallowed hard. Only a year ago . . . and now Mathilda was dead; even then she must have been dying. The bitter thing – the thing she could not come to terms with – was that Mathilda had not confided in her. Isobel had believed that they were friends and yet Mathilda had kept her illness a secret and had gone to her death as she had lived – alone. No matter what other people might say or think Isobel was convinced that Mathilda had taken the boat out that night intending to take her own life. She remembered quite clearly their conversation on euthanasia and Mathilda's words: *'If he is terminally ill and in his right mind I think that he should have as much right to choose the manner of his death just as he has chosen the manner in which he has lived.'*

She knew now that Mathilda had consulted her doctor and a few nights later had taken the boat out. How had she seen her end? Had she switched off the engine and let the boat be washed on to the rocks? If so, how would she have known that she would die? Isobel suspected that Mathilda had set out intending to slip over the side when she was too far out to be able to swim back. She guessed, too, that Mathilda had been unable to carry out the plan when the time came. *'This life is all we know,'* she had said. *'It is the human condition to cling to what we know.'* It was Isobel's private nightmare that, when Mathilda's courage had failed, the engine had failed with it and she had been swept helplessly to her death. Over and over she imagined her terror and her loneliness and blamed herself that Mathilda had been unable to confide in her. Worse, she blamed herself because she had not noticed that Mathilda was ill; that she had never suspected that she was dying. She had been too absorbed in her own problems and she writhed when she remembered her words to Mathilda; 'Go and drown yourself and see if I care!'

James was quite right in suspecting that Isobel couldn't forgive Mathilda for leaving her but she couldn't forgive herself either for what she saw as her own failure. Because of her selfishness Mathilda had been denied the solace of unburdening herself or sharing her fear. If she had been able to talk to Isobel openly and frankly she might not have felt desperate enough to contemplate suicide.

On her worst days, Isobel saw herself as a complete failure; she had failed in her marriage to Simon, she had failed her daughter and, finally, she had failed Mathilda. Guilt lived and flourished in her like a malignant disease and, when it became too painful to bear, she let herself out of the cottage and went to find Will . . .

This morning he was clearing out the room across the passage from the kitchen; the room which had once been the dining room. She leaned in the doorway watching him and feeling comforted merely by the sight of him in his baggy cords and his shapeless old Guernsey.

'So what's all this in aid of?'

Will beamed at her, grey hair on end, flushed with exertion. He pulled a pile of boxes nearer to the door and sat down on the edge of a half-full tea-chest, wiping his brow with a large red handkerchief. Already he loved her so much that he could sense her deep unhappiness but he did not know yet how he could help her.

'It occurred to me that we would need an extra bedroom,' he told her. 'It could just be that the three of us might be here together, d'you see? It would be best if the two girls had the bedrooms. This will do very nicely for me if I can get the rubbish out and give it a lick of paint.'

'You're certain then that you'll be able to stay here?'

'Oh, I think so. Bea has agreed to give us time to raise the money and my flat is up for sale. I've got a buyer.' Will had returned to Geneva for a few days to sort out his affairs and was going back again after the New Year to tie up loose ends. 'Can't give up now.'

'I was thinking.' Isobel wrapped her arms around her body; it was chilly in this unused room. 'If I were to vacate the cottage you could sell it. That would give you what you need, wouldn't it?'

'Absolute nonsense.' Will stood up and began to root in the box. 'You belong here as much as we do. More. You knew Mathilda. You're our link with her. Wouldn't want strangers in the cottage.'

Isobel blinked back her tears and tried to smile, accepting his gesture of friendship. 'Looks like you've got your work cut out. Want some help?'

'Now you're talking.' Will hid his relief – he dreaded the idea of Isobel leaving the cove – and straightened up again. 'I thought that I could pack all this away somewhere. In the garage, perhaps. There's acres of papers and notebooks and all sorts of odds and ends. If we could store it away for the time being, we could have a chance to look at it later when the others are here and I could get on with decorating this room.'

'Won't you mind being down here?' Isobel glanced round the room. 'It looks damp to me.'

'I shall rather like it. Get some heating into it and regular airing and it'll be fine. And I shall have my freedom, d'you see? I'm a bit of a nocturnal animal and when young Tessa is here I'm afraid that I shall disturb her if I go wandering about in the middle of the night. It'll be handy being just across from the kitchen.'

Isobel remembered how she and Mathilda had stayed up late on stormy nights and how comforting it had been to tuck up with a hot-water bottle, knowing that Mathilda was pottering about or in the next bedroom. She wondered if Tessa felt the same about Will.

'You're very like Mathilda,' she said. 'It'll be nice

171

for Tessa to have company. She must get so lonely, all on her own in strange people's houses with only dogs for company.' She watched him for a moment and then shook herself mentally. 'Look, I'll find the key and get the boathouse opened up. It would be better than the garage. It's got a huge loft room. We can pile all this stuff in and you can start painting.'

After her second trip across to the boathouse she went into the kitchen to push the kettle on to the hotplate. Presently Will came to join her. He had just finished washing his hands when the telephone rang. He dried his hands quickly and picked up the receiver. 'Rainbird.' Isobel sipped her coffee, her eyes on his face but mentally reviewing how much more was to be done in preparation for Christmas, now less than two weeks away. 'Of course. Of course you must come,' he said. 'We shall be delighted to see you.' Isobel came out of her reverie and looked at him with renewed interest. He grimaced at her. 'Come to Totnes,' he said, 'not Plymouth. That's right. Let us know and we'll be able to fetch you. No trouble at all. The more the merrier. Yes, we'll all be here. Look forward to hearing from you.'

'Who was that?' asked Isobel curiously as he replaced the receiver.

'It was Bea.' Will looked thoughtful. 'It seems that she'd like to spend Christmas in the cove.' He smiled at Isobel's amazed expression. 'Looks like it's going to be a real family Christmas.' He gulped at his coffee. 'I'd better get on. We're going to need that extra room sooner than we thought.'

'She could come over with me,' offered Isobel. 'I've got a spare room.'

Will stood, brooding. 'No.' He shook his head. 'I think the three of us must make shift together. Don't want anyone to think they don't belong in the house, d'you see? If Tessa or Bea suggest it that's different but to begin with we must share equally.'

'Well, it's there if anyone wants it.' Isobel hesitated. 'Will, I'm still not happy about living rent-free.'

'Look,' Will began to pat his pockets for his pipe, 'we talked that over with James. It was how it was arranged with Mathilda and until the estate is finally sorted out that's how it stays.'

'But I looked after Mathilda,' cried Isobel. 'Well.' Her face changed. 'I tried to.'

Will saw the bitter twist to her mouth but he held his tongue. Now was not the time to find out what was eating away at Isobel's peace of mind.

'And you're looking after us,' he said. 'You clean the house up after me and cook delicious meals. And you've worked like a slave getting things ready for Christmas. No more arguments. Please.'

'OK.' Isobel gave in gratefully. 'Let's make a start on your bedroom. You must be psychic, that's all I can say.'

'It has been said of me,' said Will modestly, hoping to make her smile, 'that I can see further through a brick wall than most.'

He was rewarded by her grin and later, when they set off happily together to buy paint and brushes, Isobel realised that her depression had dissipated and she could look forward more cheerfully and with a lighter heart.

Chapter Sixteen

Once again, Bea was travelling west. She was grateful that she had managed to find a vacant seat next to the window; at least she wouldn't be obliged to make friendly noises at other travellers. The young man in the seat beside her sat with his eyes shut, plugged into his Walkman, oblivious to the noise around him. The train was full of people going home for Christmas and Bea tried to persuade herself that she was doing the same. Slowly and painfully during these past weeks the unpleasant fact had been borne in upon her consciousness; she had no home and no roots.

Her tired eyes looked out unseeingly on the muted colours of the winter countryside. The frosty grass was washed pale gold by a thin faint sunlight and the trees looked like iron against the lemon sky. The bright berries of a holly bush were a shock of colour in the quiet landscape. Bea was seeing none of the beauty that streamed by silently beyond the window. Superimposed over the shadowy reflection of her own face was that of Marian Goodbody – the headmaster's wife.

' . . . so Angus felt that it was only right that we should mention it. You know how fond of you we all are but we have to look to the future. Try to put yourself in Matron's place. She feels that you are undermining her position. The boys know you so well and she feels that it makes it much more difficult to relate to them whilst you are around . . .'

Bea sat on the stiff cretonne-covered chair in Marian's drawing room and watched Marian's mouth moving in her large pale face. Bea's belongings, fetched down from the attic, stood beside her on the carpet whilst Marian continued to render Bea's past valueless and her future bleak.

' . . . and I do feel that it is never wise to try to turn the clock back. It would be so difficult to live on the edge of a community, not quite part of it. Of course, we shall always be glad to see you. Good Heavens! You've been part of our lives for so long . . .'

How triumphant Norah would be, thought Bea observing the squareness of Marian's teeth, to know that she was right. How humiliating to have to tell her.

' . . . but I'm sure that you can sympathise with Matron's feelings. Put yourself in her shoes. Children are so fickle, aren't they? So ready to play one adult off against another. She's going to find your act *quite* difficult enough to follow as it is . . .'

Bea stared at Marian's mouth stretched wide, now, in an encouraging smile whilst her head nodded archly as she tossed Bea this sop to her pride.

' . . . so difficult for the staff. It's a question of loyalty, isn't it? Of course, we all miss you but life goes on and we have to look forward not back . . .'

Bea stood abruptly. Marian stopped mid-speech, head flung back as she stared up at her.

'If you've finished, Marian. I'll be getting on.

Thank you for your little talk. Very interesting. Have you ever thought of taking up counselling professionally?'

The headmaster's wife flushed a dull and unbecoming red. 'I'm sorry that you should take it like this, Bea.' Her mouth no longer smiled. 'I've tried to be tactful . . .'

'Have you?' Bea smiled a little. 'Well, no doubt it's difficult to tell someone that they're superfluous to requirements. Have you any objections to my remaining in the town or will that upset Matron's delicate sensibilities too? Perhaps we should ask *her* where I should be allowed to live? Perhaps it should be brought up at the next staff meeting?'

'That's a very insulting thing to say.' Marian got to her feet. She looked upset and Bea felt a twinge of remorse. 'I am merely doing what is best for everyone . . .'

'I think it is quite breath-taking that you should imagine you know what is best for everyone. Shall we take the rest as read?' They stared angrily at each other. 'I think that Pete is waiting to help me with my belongings. Shall we call him? Thank you for storing them for me.'

In silence Bea waited whilst Marian went to find the groundsman; in silence they carried the things out to his pick-up truck. When they were safely stowed, Bea turned to Marian and held out her hand.

'I shall be away for Christmas,' she told her. 'Thank you for everything.'

Marian took the proffered hand and held it briefly, her lips compressed, and turned back into the house without a word.

'What's eating her?' asked Pete curiously, as Bea climbed in beside him.

Bea felt guilty; they should not have allowed their feelings to show before the staff. A tiny voice reminded her that Marian had never been popular and a sense of wicked rebellion filled her. Why should she worry about Pete guessing that a row had been going on in the headmaster's drawing room? Such things – as had just been firmly pointed out – were no longer her problem. Momentarily, loyalty deserted her.

'She's been giving me the sack,' she said.

He gaped at her as they moved off down the drive. 'Sack? Thought you'd gone already.'

'So I have.' Bea pulled herself together and reassembled her ideas of duty and responsibility. 'Just a joke. Keep your eyes on the road.'

Bea shifted in her seat as the train drew in at Newton Abbot. She watched a young woman struggling along the platform. A baby lay against her chest in a sling, a toddler clung to one of her hands whilst, in the other, she carried a suitcase. A man and a woman broke free from a crowd of people and went to greet her. As Bea watched, the man swung the toddler into his arms and gave him a hearty kiss, the woman touched the baby's cheek, embraced her daughter and relieved her of the case. Moving as one unit, chattering all together, they moved towards the exit.

Bea found herself remembering Will's voice when she had telephoned to tell him at what time she would be arriving at Totnes. He had made her feel that nothing could have given him – or Tessa and

Isobel – more pleasure than to know that she would be joining them for Christmas. Her sore heart had been warmed by his friendliness and she had spent the remaining days choosing presents for them in the town. She had warded off curious looks and questions, glad that she had somewhere to which she could escape. The thought of spending Christmas alone in her flat was a chilling one and there had been very few offers of hospitality.

During those lonely days after Marian's 'talk' she realised how important her job had been. It had given her status, a title and a position within the community. Now she was no one; Matron no longer, nobody's mother or wife or child or aunt, just Bea. As she had stood, staring out of the flat window at the shops opposite, a thought had slipped into her mind. She had cousins, now; cousins who wanted her to make a home with them and to share their inheritance and their lives. Bea stared thoughtfully out into the gathering darkness. Once Tony Priest had issued from the bookshop across the road and raised his hand. For one golden moment she thought that he was summoning her. Almost she hurried down to meet him but, hesitating, she saw his wife emerge from somewhere below the window and cross the road to him. He made some laughing remark and she gave him a friendly push. Slipping an arm about her shoulders they vanished into the evening. After a moment or two, Bea turned back into the shadows of the darkening room and sat down. The next day she had telephoned to the house in the cove . . . and now here she was, collecting her belongings, stepping over the legs of the recumbent young man and

179

going to meet Isobel and Will at Totnes station.

'I wonder why she's coming,' mused Isobel for the fiftieth time as she and Will drove through Harbertonford.

For the present, they were sharing the Morris. Will had managed to sell his own car whilst he was in Switzerland and was now looking around for something to replace it. Isobel had suggested that, instead of spending money on a hired car, he should use the Morris until he found what he wanted. Will readily agreed. For one thing it meant that he and Isobel did so much more together. It was sensible to make joint journeys to go shopping or to the library and, on the days when Isobel was at the bookshop, Will was more than content to potter in the cove. Slowly he was pulling the house together, unobtrusively giving it a face lift, and, as he worked quietly and happily, he thought about Isobel. He was surprised at how strong his feelings were for her. He remembered that it had taken him quite a while to approach Bierta; not because of shyness but because he was cautious.

Will had inherited the Rainbird qualities of self-sufficiency and the ability to live alone, as well as a low physical drive. He, like Mathilda, was not cut out for passion or dramatic scenes; jealous rages and extravagant reconciliations were unknown to him. Bierta had charmed him but the qualities which he attributed to her had been, very largely, in his own imagination. Isobel was so different in almost every way to Bierta and he had loved her as soon as he had seen her on the beach. 'No fool like an old fool,' he told himself. This was very different from his love for Bierta and he had no intention of declaring it. For one thing he must be at least twenty years older than Isobel and for another he knew that she was unhappy. Quite soon she had begun to tell him about her marriage and how she had left Simon and had an affair. Gradually she told him how it had come to nothing but that it had destroyed her marriage. Her husband had found another woman and was now seeking a divorce.

'I still love him, you see,' Isobel had said, staring away from him, looking out over the sea. 'That's the whole bloody irony of it. I threw it all away.'

Will had remained silent. Everything he thought of to say sounded trite or inadequate. Presently she had looked at him and shrugged.

'Do you think happiness is important?' she'd asked him.

There had been an earnestness in her voice and she had watched him eagerly while he thought about it. He felt ill-equipped to answer such a question and that odd tenseness about her made him nervous.

'I suppose it all depends on what you mean by happiness?' he'd said slowly at last and she'd given a great cry, covering her face with her hands. 'What is it?' he'd asked. 'What's the matter?' He felt almost angry with her, as though she was making him play a game without telling him the rules.

'Nothing,' she'd said, shaking her head, but she'd looked distressed. 'It's just that you're *so* like Mathilda. You even speak like she did. She always used to say that. "It all depends on what you mean . . ." That's how she always answered.'

'I'm sorry,' Will said helplessly. 'I don't think I'm being much use.'

'Yes, you are.' She'd jumped up and gone to the window. 'It's a lovely afternoon. Come on. I'll show you Bolberry Down. It'll be glorious up there. We'll watch the sunset.'

Her words struck a chord in Will's memory. He'd taken Bierta to watch the sunset on the lake once, early on in their relationship. Afterwards she'd been cool and evasive and years later he'd heard her say rather bitterly to a friend, 'Will's the kind of man who takes you to see the sunset and then actually expects you to sit and watch it!'

He'd realised that she'd thought his invitation was an excuse to get her alone in a romantic setting and he'd wondered how often he had failed her in that area of their lives together. Luckily, Isobel had expected him to watch the sunset and afterwards they stopped for a drink at the Cricket at Beesands and had come home to one of her delicious casseroles. She treated him with the ease and affection of a long-standing friend and he was grateful. He had no intention of rocking the boat with presumptuous declarations but he wished that Isobel had been his first love rather than his second.

When Bea telephoned, Will had sensed that all was not well with her and he hoped that she was not coming to tell them that she'd changed her mind and wanted to sell the house after all. If that were the case then he and Tessa would have to fall back on his plan to sell some of the furniture. James had confirmed his suspicions that some of it was very valuable and had agreed that, if Bea changed her mind, then it would be wise to sell some of the pieces and buy her out.

Now, as they drove through Harbertonford, Will shook his head at Isobel's question. He had not voiced his fears, no point in panicking unnecessarily. Anyway, Bea hardly needed to come for Christmas to tell them that she wasn't prepared to wait after all.

'I thought she was sharing a house with a friend,' he said. 'Perhaps they've fallen out.'

'Fatal, I should have thought.' Isobel pulled her scarf higher round her neck. The Morris's heater was extremely inefficient. 'Fraught with difficulties.'

'Don't say that.' Will glanced at his watch. 'Plenty of time. Like some coffee?'

'Oh, yes please. But why do you say "Don't say that," in that tone of foreboding?'

'Because,' he said, turning into Cistern Street and heading for the car park, 'it is what we are all attempting to do. Well, me and Tessa and probably Bea as well, by the sounds of it.'

'Well, it *will* be fraught with difficulties,' said Isobel frankly. 'No good pretending. Bound to be. You'll manage.'

He pulled into the Heath Nursery car park, smiling at the confidence in her voice. 'You'll have to be referee,' he told her. 'Got any change for the meter? Just time for a quick cup of something hot in Rumours if we get a move on.'

They were waiting for her on the platform, taking her case, walking on each side of her, hurrying her

183

out to the car. Isobel insisted that Bea sat in front and leaned over her shoulder so as to point out the old castle ruin as the Morris chugged up the hill on the Kingsbridge road.

Bea settled back in the seat and began to relax a little. Her fears that they might have been dreading her arrival, that she would be in the way, began to fade a little. Isobel explained that Tessa was coming for Christmas Day.

'It's such a pity she can't come for longer,' she said, 'but we must make the most of it. She's bringing Romulus and Remus.'

Bea turned to look into the face so close to her own. 'She's bringing *who*?'

They laughed at the expression on her face and explained as the Morris turned off into the five-mile lane and wound its way down to the coast. The short winter day was drawing in and the sea looked like grey slate as they parked behind the house and drew her inside. They took her up to the sitting room where a Christmas tree sparkled in the alcove with a pile of presents waiting temptingly beneath its boughs. Will made up the fire and Isobel drew the curtains and went to make tea. Bea sat looking at the tree with its tiny wooden carved figures, and at the shimmering glass balls and the tinsel, and then she looked about the room, cosy and welcoming in the firelight.

So it was that Bea came home to the cove.

Chapter Seventeen

The young man who had bought Mrs Carrington's bureau sat in his car, parked unobtrusively in the quiet road, and watched Tessa pull in at the gate and stop her car in the drive. She climbed out, shut the gates and released the two labradors from the back. They flopped out heavily and went to drink at a large bowl by the back door. Tessa let herself in and the dogs lay down, panting stertorously, on the concrete apron in front of the garage. The young man had his eyes on his watch. Two minutes passed, three, four ... He imagined her kicking off her boots, hanging up her coat, going into the kitchen and filling the kettle ... He switched on the engine and drove along to the gate.

Romulus and Remus heaved themselves up and, with a bark or two as a token of their vigilance, came wagging to greet him. He touched their heads perfunctorily, his glance alert; no one seemed aware of his arrival. He went to the front door and rang the bell. After a moment Tessa opened the door. She was still wearing her woollen hat and on her feet were thick socks.

'Sorry.' He managed to appear both slightly surprised and apologetic. 'I was hoping to have a word with Mrs Carrington. Is she about?'

'I'm afraid she's away. Back tomorrow.'

He bit his lip, frowning. 'Oh, that's a pity. I was hoping . . . Never mind. You look as if you were on your way out. I don't want to keep you.'

'On my way out? Oh . . .' Tessa swept off her hat and shook her head. 'I've just come in actually.' She hesitated, studying him. 'Don't I know you?'

'Amazing!' He laughed in his relief. 'You've made my day. I remember you, of course. Who wouldn't?' He made a gallant little bow. 'I came to collect Mrs Carrington's bureau last Easter.'

'Yes.' She grimaced ruefully at her forgetfulness. 'Sorry. I remember you now. Is there anything I can do?'

'Well . . .' He looked thoughtful, rubbing his chin as he stared past her into the hallway. 'Since I'm in the area . . . She suggested that I might come back and have a look at one or two things . . . Oh dear. Am I being indiscreet?'

'Of course not.' Tessa stepped back and opened the door wider. 'I'm sure she won't mind if you have a look. Although I'd better stay with you, if you don't mind.' She shifted uncomfortably. 'You know how it is?'

He smiled at her as he preceded her into the hall. 'Don't give it a thought. I understand perfectly. You are responsible in her absence.'

'That's fine, then.' Tessa relaxed. 'Come on through. Where do you want to start?'

The young man looked about him. 'There were one or two things in here and a chest of drawers in her bedroom.' He sighed and shook his head. 'I have the horrid feeling that Mrs Carrington would really rather not part with her treasures.

Sometimes my job is not a nice one.'

Tessa looked at him sympathetically, liking him for his compassion. She thought of all Mathilda's things, glad now that the fear of selling them had receded for the time being.

'Have you one of your leaflets?' she asked him. 'Or a card?' If an emergency cropped up and they were obliged to sell any of Mathilda's pieces, this young man would at least be sensitive about it.

He was digging in his pocket, staring at a small inlaid table which stood under the window. 'I hope *you* haven't got to part with some family heirloom.'

'Not yet.' She took his card and studied it. 'Are you Adrian Pearson?'

'I am.' He made her another little bow. 'And you . . . ?'

'I'm Tessa Rainbird.' They shook hands a little awkwardly. 'I look after people's dogs and houses.'

'Quite a responsibility. Especially in these lawless times.'

'I must admit that there are one or two places where I feel rather nervous.' Tessa perched on the arm of a chair and watched him examine the little table. 'Just a couple of the houses are fairly remote. I have to rely on the dogs to protect the stuff. And me.'

He laughed with her, dropping down to balance on his heels whilst he examined the table underneath. 'I think I'd better give you some of my leaflets to take round with you.'

'Well, I could I suppose.' Tessa sounded a little reluctant. She shrugged. 'Why not?'

He looked at her quickly as he straightened up.

'Well, I was joking actually but I suppose it's not a bad idea. You never know when people might need some ready cash. You'd get a commission, of course.'

She frowned and he saw that he might have looked too eager. 'Don't be offended. It would be only fair, if you think about it. You have access to places I could never hope to find. I wouldn't be happy if you weren't rewarded for your trouble.'

'Well, it's hardly a trouble to leave a few leaflets about but it's nice of you to offer.' She slipped off the chair. 'Finished?'

'I think so.' He was making notes in a little book. 'If I could just have another look at that chest?'

'Of course.' She led the way to the bedroom and stood at the door watching. 'It's pretty, isn't it?'

'Very.' He ran his hands gently over the polished rosewood of the little bow-fronted chest.

'We've got one like that.' She spoke without thinking. 'Well, it looks like that. I don't know anything about antiques.'

'That's at your home, is it?' He spoke absently, running the drawers in and out, examining them closely.

'Yes.' Tessa smiled to herself. 'It's at my home.'

Isobel and Will had given her Mathilda's bedroom and the little chest stood against the wall bearing a tiny bookcase of strange old books, so small that she could hardly read the writing. It was wonderful to go into that room and shut the door and feel that she belonged there . . . Adrian was watching her curiously and she smiled quickly, defensively.

'Sorry. Just daydreaming. All done?'

'All done,' he agreed. He glanced at his watch. 'If

you're quite serious about those leaflets . . . ?'

'Absolutely,' she assured him. 'It's no problem.'

'If you're certain.' He looked concerned. 'I feel that I offended you over that commission business. I was clumsy . . .'

'No, honestly.' It was her turn to look distressed. 'Don't give it a thought.'

'If you say so.' He smiled at her. 'Look, I've had an idea. It's nearly lunchtime. Perhaps I could take you out and buy you a drink and you could give me a contact number and I'll give you the leaflets. Please,' he said pleadingly as she hesitated. 'Then I know you've really forgiven me.'

'Honestly . . . OK.' She gave in. 'But I mustn't be too long. We could go to the Pack Horse in South Brent and have a sandwich.'

'Wonderful.' He looked so pleased that she felt flattered. 'I'll wait in the car while you lock up.'

Tessa called the dogs inside and, dragging off her thick socks, slid her feet into her trainers. As she laced them up she found that she was thinking about Giles and their lunch together at the Elephant's Nest. He was so nice . . . She grimaced a little at the word. He had made her laugh about his job as a photographer and had listened in turn – and with a concentration she was unused to – as she recounted some of the more amusing moments of her work. She remembered how he'd listened to her at the Roundhouse and how, hardly knowing him, she'd talked to him so openly. She wondered if it might be because he was so much older, or because she felt she already knew him through Kate. She had arranged see him again when she was next in London . . . Tessa dragged her thoughts away from Giles, locked the back door and hurried out to where Adrian waited patiently for her in his car.

'The thing is . . .' said Giles. He paused and Kate braced herself, knowing that these words generally prefaced a confidence. 'The thing is – I didn't want to rush it.'

Kate and David studiously avoided meeting each other's eye. They had been having supper at the London house when Giles had arrived. He had sat with them, drinking wine while they ate and now, with supper cleared away, the moment for which Kate and David had been waiting had arrived. Even as a child it had taken Giles some time to come to the point. 'But he's more open than Guy,' Kate had once told David. 'Guy never tells me anything at all.' Giles thought things through carefully and rarely did anything on the spur of the moment. He was not over-confident but he was kind and sensitive to the needs of others.

'Well.' David cleared his throat as the silence lengthened interminably. 'I wouldn't say that two meetings in three months is absolutely rushing it, old boy. No need to fear that.'

Kate who, in her anxiety had drunk too much wine, knew an urge to giggle hysterically. She made a strange noise – a cross between a groan and a scream – and David glanced quellingly at her.

'That's true.' Giles swirled his glass of whisky thoughtfully. 'I was just wondering whether . . . I can't decide . . . If she's down there with Felix . . .'

'Giles!' said Kate sharply. 'Come to the point!'

'Sorry.' He looked guiltily at her. 'I was wondering if I might just pop down to see her. You know. Just for the day or something.'

'Wonderful idea,' said David easily. 'Poor girl must get terribly lonely with only old Felix to keep her company. I should go . . . if I were you.'

'Would you?' Giles looked at him eagerly. 'You don't think she'll wonder if I'm . . . well, pushing it a bit?'

Kate clutched her glass tightly and closed her eyes for a moment. She took several deep breaths lest she should scream with frustration. David smiled quickly at Giles.

'Shouldn't think so for a moment.' He pursed his lips and shook his head as though giving the matter serious thought. 'After all, it's your home, isn't it? No reason why you shouldn't be there.'

'It might be embarrassing for her. That's what I was wondering. There on her own. As if I'm hoping that . . .' He took a quick gulp at his whisky. 'Well, you know what I mean.'

'Perhaps she might like it,' said Kate. Both men stared at her. She stared back at them. 'Don't look at me as if I'm some kind of pervert,' she said crossly. 'Do you know what I think, Giles? I think you should go down to Devon and tell Tessa exactly how you feel. Just do it! Stop pussyfooting about! Stop trying to find the answers before she's even thought of the questions. Stop wondering if she might be offended or shocked. Just go down and . . . and *do* it!'

Giles looked at her with an expression of such hope and excitement that Kate felt a great surge of love for him – followed by a pang of guilt. Was it because of her unhappy marriage and subsequent divorce that her sons were both so chary of relationships with women? They seemed so afraid of committing themselves – but could she blame them? They'd witnessed at first-hand a disintegrating and unhappy situation; was it so surprising that they were unwilling to take the risk? She knew that it was the girl who had taken the initiative in Giles's first relationship and she had seen how he had been prepared to be miserable rather than break it up. She guessed that if he finally committed himself to Tessa, he would remain loyal whatever happened. No wonder that he wanted to be certain that it was absolutely right. He was unable to enjoy casual sex. In a rare moment of confidence he had once told her that for him sex, without love, was no good. She respected him for it and was relieved, too, in these dangerous days but she wished that he could find love and be loved in return. He had a good many friends of both sexes but she suspected that he was often lonely. Had her own mistakes put happiness out of court for him?

She smiled at him, wondering if it were possible to pass through life without feeling continually guilty. It corroded and destroyed and prevented her from seeing clearly; she overreacted in an attempt to compensate. She knew that her guilt would encourage her to sympathise with Giles; it made her afraid to be tough with him lest she spurred him on to actions which he would regret or which would hurt him – leaving her with more guilt. Deliberately she hardened her heart, remembering her instinctive reaction to the sight of Giles and Tessa together at the Roundhouse. She must not allow him to dither.

'Honestly, Giles,' she said quietly, 'I really think you should go. I think that you know in your own heart how you feel about her. Tessa may be young but she's grown up in a hard school. There's nothing precious or silly about her. She'll be honest with you, either way. You've got nothing to lose and everything to gain.'

He stared at her, impressed by her serious tone, feeling his fears sliding away. He knew that he tried to cross too many bridges, to make certain that no one would be hurt, to legislate for every eventuality. Usually his relationships sank beneath all these anxieties before they ever got launched and usually it really didn't matter too much. He had been surprised – and rather frightened – at just how much Tessa mattered.

'You're right,' he said, with so much conviction that David looked at him in surprise and Kate felt her heart lift. 'Absolutely right. I'll go down first thing in the morning. Should I telephone first? Warn her?'

'No,' said Kate instinctively. 'Take her by surprise. Pretend you forgot we weren't there or something. Don't look so shocked! I know you hate telling even the whitest of lies but trust me. Honestly, I just know that this is right.'

'And the frightening thing is,' she said to David when Giles had gone and they were washing up together, 'that he believes me. Like when I told him that he would love school or that he could get to university if he tried. The responsibility is frightening.'

'The trouble with bringing up children,' said David, who had a daughter of his own, 'is that by the time you know you got it wrong it's too late to do anything about it.'

Kate dried plates silently, fighting fear and guilt. Why had she been so confident? Supposing she was wrong and Giles was right to proceed cautiously? Why did she feel that she always knew best when she'd managed to make such mistakes in her own life?

'Oh, David,' she said miserably. 'Why did I open my big mouth?'

'Because he needed you to.' David dried his hands and took her into his arms. 'Don't fight it, my darling. It's impossible to get it right. Sins of omission or commission, we err either way. Just accept it.'

'But it's his life,' she cried against his chest. 'Oh, why do I always interfere?'

'He'll be fine. He's simply got to have a shot at it. Look how happy Guy is. If he can make it then so can Giles. Surely you've no regrets about Guy?'

'Oh no, of course not! But he and Gemma have known each other since they were babies and she's so good for him. Yes, Guy is happy. Perhaps you're right . . .'

'Of course I am,' said David comfortably, returning to his washing-up.

Kate went back into the sitting room and stood staring into the fire. She had felt so certain earlier but now she was eaten up with doubt. David had put his finger on the problem of parenthood; you saw the results of your mistakes when it was too late to rectify them and the anxieties continued long after the children were grown up. She knew that she would be feeling just as worried if she had urged Giles to go cautiously. Kate sighed, put the guard round the fire and went upstairs to have her bath.

Chapter Eighteen

After the New Year a mild spell set in; there were violets growing in the lane and hazel catkins trembling in the hedge. Bea, stooping to look at an early primrose, was possessed of a desire to start afresh. The soft air, which presaged spring and new life, touched her cheeks and filled her with hope. She straightened up and, breathing deeply and eagerly, walked on between the banks that sheltered the lane. The centuries had eroded this track long before it became a metalled lane; ground to dust each summer, scoured by winter rain, so the track had sunk until now, beneath the dry-stone walls, the very rock could be seen. Beech mast, acorn and seeds had rooted in the earth that covered the stones so that the hedges that flourished along the top of the walls grew high above the sunken lane. Their roots had pushed down through the soil, displacing stones, gaining a foothold. These thick gnarled roots were covered with lichen and moss and ferns, supporting small ecological worlds, sheltered from the west winds which roared above their heads.

Bea watched a company of long-tailed tits swinging in the bare branches of an oak tree above her head. They flitted busily, darting from branch to branch, until the whole party took wing and swooped away. She saw a tiny wren, fossicking amongst the drifts of beech leaves in the ditch, and felt a sense of satisfaction and gratitude. The holiday had been a great success. She had been both surprised at the warmth with which Tessa had greeted her and aware of the efforts Will had made to ensure that all three of them felt at home. He insisted that he was very happy in his room downstairs with its proximity to the kitchen. This morning Bea had woken, unusually early, to the smell of frying bacon and had thought herself, for one brief moment, back at school. She lay for a while, thinking; if she were to settle here in the cove then the pattern of life must be set from the beginning. It seemed that Tessa would rarely be with them for any length of time so it was important that she and Will should work out a plan for living compatibly. She hoped that, having spent most of her life living in an institution, she had a head start. Will had been married, so he was used to having females – or at least one female – about the place. It was clear that he and Tessa had very quickly established an easy relationship and Bea knew that it was up to her to maintain the family atmosphere.

Rising from her bed, she had pulled on her thick plaid dressing gown, pushed her feet into sheepskin slippers and descended to the kitchen. Over the Christmas holiday she had breakfasted late, fully dressed, having given Will plenty of time to have his own breakfast and finish his chores. Up until now she hadn't wanted to be in his way but this morning she had felt differently. If Will had been surprised to see her he gave no sign of it. There was a large pot of tea on the table and he took a cup and saucer from the dresser and put them beside her.

'I always like to stoke up for the day,' he'd told her. 'If you have a good breakfast then it doesn't matter too much what happens after that. Care to join me?'

'Who can resist the smell of frying bacon?' asked Bea, pouring herself a cup of tea. 'I certainly can't!'

'My wife could.' As Will dropped a few more rashers into the frying pan he looked uncomfortable; as though he felt that he had been disloyal. 'Had a delicate stomach, d'you see?' he said. 'Had to be careful what she ate.'

'How very tiresome,' said Bea bluntly. 'For her,' she added politely – but she had seen the small grin with which Will had accepted her gesture of under-standing. 'Living with small boys tends to destroy one's sensibilities. I doubt I ever had any in the first place.'

Whilst they ate they had exchanged family back-grounds, trying to trace their ancestry back to Mathilda. Bea discovered that Will was two years the elder and that his father had been killed during the evacuation of Dunkirk; they had both lost their mothers fairly recently.

'I suppose,' said Bea, chasing a mushroom round her plate, 'that I always imagined that I'd look after my mother in her old age. I spent most of the school holidays with her. We were very poor. My father was not particularly strong. He was on convoy duty during the war and was torpedoed twice and I don't think that he ever fully recovered from it. I re-member him as a quiet nervous man. He taught History but he was only fifty-two when he died. My mother was eighty. I was fully expecting to look after her for a few more years yet.'

'It must be difficult,' said Will thoughtfully, 'to retire from your kind of job. Must feel at a bit of a loose end, I should think. It's a way of life, isn't it? Not just a job.'

'Yes,' said Bea, after a minute or two. 'That describes it rather well. I stayed for a while with an old friend. She's newly widowed and rather lonely. We hoped that it might solve both our problems.'

Will remembered his conversation with Isobel in the car. 'Sounds fraught with difficulty,' he suggested.

'Why?' asked Bea sharply. 'Why should it be any more difficult than what we are contemplating here?'

'Because it's *her* home,' answered Will promptly, although he sounded much more confident than he felt. 'She would have to be a very generous sort of woman for you to be able to feel that you had as much right in it as she did. This is your home as much as mine. Quite different I would have thought.'

Bea was silent, mollified by his reply, rather surprised by her flash of aggression. It was evident that she was still feeling rather sensitive when it came to the question of belonging.

'It is different,' she admitted, watching him spread marmalade on his toast with a generous hand. 'But it's rather difficult to feel at home in a house you never saw before in your life.'

'And with two people you never saw before in your life?' He was smiling at her. 'Are we crazy to try it? Is that what you're thinking?'

'No.' She shook her head. 'It's just that I'm not particularly looking forward to telling Norah that I've finally made up my mind. She'll think I'm quite mad. And I have to go back to pick up my belongings from the flat. I hope the landlord can find someone to take it over.'

'Like me to come along?' Will made the suggestion lightly but his heart beat anxiously. He had no wish to patronise her.

'Come with me?'

'I wondered how much stuff you've got? Could you manage it on the train? We could drive up and pack it in the back of the Morris. It's amazing how much she'll take if you drop the back seat.'

It occurred to Bea that it would be a great deal easier to cut the ties to her old life with Will's comforting presence in the background but she was not used to people sharing her burdens or shouldering her problems. It sounded rather tempting . . . Her independent spirit struggled against such weakness. She sat with her eyes on her empty plate, attempting to justify an acceptance of his offer. Will watched her.

'Difficult trying to struggle with it all on the train,' he pondered, hoping to ease her into seeing it as a sensible proposition whilst maintaining her pride. 'Of course you could hire a van but it seems a bit daft with the old Morris out there. Or maybe I'll get on with getting us a car. We'll need one, won't we? Or would you prefer that we had one each? I can understand that. Perhaps we could try sharing one for a start.' He beamed at her. 'It's going to be great fun. Don't you think? Lots to look forward to.

Look, I'd be very glad to come with you. I'd like to see the school and where you worked for so long. Fills in the blank bits, d'you see? And it would be a bit of a jolly.'

She looked at him and discovered that she could accept his friendliness. 'Thank you, Will,' she'd said. 'That would be very kind.'

Now, as she walked in the lane she wondered what Norah would think of him . . .

'. . . and I think it's just too bad of you,' hissed Norah, when Will had excused himself and disappeared to have a pipe in the garden, 'to bring this cousin – or whatever he is – along with you. I'd have preferred to talk with you alone.'

'He is my cousin,' said Bea calmly. 'No whatever-he-is about it.'

'And furthermore,' continued Norah, discounting this observation, 'I have to say that I think it's quite mad. Going back to your old friends at school was foolish enough . . .' She looked at Bea sharply. 'Well, it was, wasn't it? I was right, wasn't I?'

'Yes, Norah,' sighed Bea. 'You were right.'

Norah nodded, smug self-satisfaction writ large upon her face. 'Of course I was. You can't go back. I warn you, it never works.'

'But I'm not going back,' said Bea. 'I'm going forward.'

Norah stared at her with a rather unpleasant look on her face; it had an avid, unhealthy kind of eagerness mingled with a measure of contempt.

'So you're going to live with this . . . cousin?'

'With Will. Yes.' Bea looked back at her and felt a

sense of revulsion. 'For goodness' sake, Norah. Don't look so . . . so *prurient*. There's nothing like that about it at all. We are sharing the house, the three of us. We have a young cousin called Tessa. I told you all about it in the letter. Please try to accept it. I hope you might come and visit me there. It will be lovely in the summer.'

Before Norah could reply, there was a light knock on the door and Will appeared. He smiled at them both.

'Sorry to break up the party but we ought to be getting on . . .'

'Of course.' Bea was on her feet, trying to hide her relief. 'Forgive me, Norah. I'll be in touch. Don't forget that invitation. Give my regards to Andrew.'

They kissed goodbye, though Norah's face was stony and she barely acknowledged Will's farewell . . .

'What invitation?' asked Will suspiciously after they had been driving for some miles in silence. Bea snorted and then she began to chuckle.

'I've invited her to stay,' she admitted, and burst out laughing at Will's horrified expression. 'Don't worry. She won't come.'

'I hope you're right,' said Will fervently. 'Please forgive me if this is tactless but how on earth did you imagine you could live with her?'

Bea felt a twinge of guilt mixed with relief. Norah was an old friend and it was disloyal to laugh about her. At the same time she was glad that Will saw the difficulties involved in living with her; it made her feel less guilty. She told him so. He shook his head.

'It wouldn't have worked,' he said. 'Best to find out early before damage is done.'

Bea stared out through the windscreen and prepared herself for the meeting with Marian Goodbody, the headmaster's wife. She had decided not to collect her belongings and sneak away like a thief in the night. Instead she had telephoned Marian and arranged to have tea with her. After their last meeting Marian had been cool but Bea said that she had some news to tell her and Marian's curiosity had got the better of her pride, especially when Bea asked if she might bring a friend.

'A friend . . . ?' Marian had hesitated and Bea had grinned to herself. 'Why, yes, I suppose so . . .'

'His name's Will Rainbird,' she had told her. 'See you at three o'clock then.'

As they drove into the quadrangle and parked outside the headmaster's house, Bea was overcome by a fit of nerves.

'I have the feeling that I am about to behave very badly,' she told Will. 'Marian and I have never hit it off.'

Will looked alert – Bea had reluctantly told him something of her last interview with the headmaster's wife – rather like someone preparing for a scrap.

'Nothing to lose,' he told her. 'Aha! Is this She Who Must Be Obeyed?'

Bea saw that Marian had appeared at the front door and nudged him in the ribs. 'Yes,' she said. 'For heaven's sake, you're supposed to be helping, not encouraging me.'

From that moment, or so Will told Isobel

afterwards, the meeting went downhill.

'How nice to see you, Bea,' Marian stood at the top of the steps, looking graciously aloof. 'And this is . . . your friend.' She took in his cavalry twills and tweed coat – Bea had bullied him into dressing for the occasion – and extended her hand. 'How nice . . .'

'Will Rainbird,' said Bea nonchalantly. 'This is Marian Goodbody, Will. She is the headmaster's wife.'

At this point Will seemed to lose his nerve. He took Marian's outstretched hand and kissed it. Marian coloured a little, smiled upon him, obviously affected by this courtly and unexpected gesture and led them inside. Behind her back Bea stared at Will outraged by this overfriendly, if not downright sycophantic, behaviour and Will gazed back help-lessly; shoulders, hands, even eyebrows, raised, in abject apology.

'Sorry,' he whispered, 'Got carried away . . .'

Bea pushed him irritably ahead of her into the drawing room where tea was laid and Marian waited, her eyes on Will.

'Do sit down,' she said. 'This is very nice. I admit that I can't wait to hear your news, Bea.' She looked girlishly excited. 'Now you mustn't think I'm being inquisitive, Mr . . . er Rainbird . . . what a delight-fully unusual name, isn't it? But Bea and I are old friends, aren't we, Bea, dear?'

'Certainly old, anyway,' snapped Bea rudely – and tried desperately to control her uprush of anger. 'We've known each other for many years.'

With a look of patient resignation, Marian turned to the tea-tray. Her glance at Will said that, whatever kind of friend he was, he had her sympathy. Will tried to look non-committal. She began to deal with the tea.

'The thing is,' said Bea, sitting upright on the cretonne, 'I've really come to say goodbye.'

She paused whilst Marian continued to pour, head politely inclined, waiting for Bea to continue. Bea glanced at Will who sent her a tiny wink. Encouraged, she cast around for inspiration.

'I'm so glad,' said Marian fatally, 'that you saw the wisdom about not remaining in the town.' She smiled at Will. 'Don't you agree, Mr er, Rainbird, that it is better to make a clean cut when certain parts of our lives come to an end? I'm sure you see the wisdom in Bea making a new life for herself. You can imagine how hard it would be for her to be on the edge of a community that she has served so faithfully.'

'Don't talk about me as if I'm deaf, Marian,' said Bea, irritation returning. 'Don't do that "Does she take sugar?" stuff.'

Marian passed her a cup, her lips tightening. Will absently patted his pocket for his pipe but, remembering where he was, took a cup of tea instead. She looked at him meaningly but he was afraid to smile back lest Bea should see and misinterpret his smile. He busied himself with the sugar bowl.

'I had no intention of upsetting you, Bea,' said Marian, maintaining her saintly air of tolerance. 'I have been very worried for you. Though you mayn't believe it, I have your welfare very much at heart.' She looked at Will. 'It will probably come as no surprise to you, Mr er Rainbird,' ('Oh, for goodness' sake call him Will,' said Bea, 'and have done!') 'that Bea has been a somewhat unconventional, if extremely popular, matron. If I may venture such a remark without being taken to task again.' She shot an unfriendly glance at Bea and smiled again upon Will. 'Naturally we are all concerned for her future.'

'I'm very gratified to hear it,' said Bea acidly, 'though I'm sure you'll understand when I say that it comes as a bit of a surprise. Anyway, there's no need to concern yourselves further. I'm delighted to tell you that I've inherited a considerable estate in Devon and I'm moving down there. In fact I have already moved. I'm sure, given your anxiety for my welfare, that you noticed that I wasn't about over Christmas or the New Year.'

Marian, who had come to attention at the words 'considerable estate' ignored the jibe. She goggled at her. 'An estate? But who . . . I didn't realise that you had . . .' She stopped.

Bea grinned evilly. 'You didn't know that I had respectable relations? Landed gentry, even? No, neither did I. I am as surprised as you are, dear Marian. However, it solves the question of my future. I must be in Devon to oversee it.'

'I see.' Marian looked dumbstruck. 'And er, Will. Are you . . . ?'

'Oh, I come with it, d'you see?' said Will easily, avoiding Bea's anxious eye. 'A kind of factor or land agent. She has to put up with me, too, I'm afraid.'

'I think she's extraordinarily fortunate to have you,' she answered crisply. 'So tell me.' She settled more cosily into her chair, trying to hide her envy, 'where exactly is this estate? How large is it?' She laughed a little, making big eyes at Will. 'We shall expect an invitation, you know. What fun! I don't know Devon too well.'

Will inhaled heavily through his nose and sent up a prayer of thanksgiving. 'It's on the south coast,' he said casually. 'Tucked right away by the sea. Difficult to find.'

'This is so exciting. A considerable estate, you said. Is the big house in good order? How much land . . . ?'

'It's in very good order,' said Bea recklessly. 'Much too big for me, really. Will has a little cottage in the grounds. And there's a dower house in the private cove with a cottage for staff and a boathouse . . .' She gulped at her tea.

'Well!' Marian closed her mouth which had been hanging open during these revelations. 'Well, I must say. We shall look forward to visiting you. Now where . . . ?'

Will shot his cuff and looked at his watch. 'Sorry, Bea. We really ought to be on our way.'

Bea jumped to her feet. 'Absolutely. Look, we'll pop in later, Marian. We've got to collect my bits from the flat . . .'

'Sorry,' she mumbled later to Will as they drove back to Devon. They had left a message for Marian saying that they'd had to rush away, lest she should demand an address or a telephone number. 'I warned you that I might behave badly.'

'I think you were splendid,' said Will. He pulled hastily into the inside lane as a Mercedes snarled past, its driver gesticulating rudely. 'Perfectly ghastly woman.'

'I don't know why you had to go kissing her hand,' grumbled Bea, staring out at Somerset.

'Neither do I,' admitted Will guiltily. 'It just came over me. She unnerved me, standing up there on the steps . . .'

Bea glanced sideways at him, his hair rumpled, his slate-blue eyes fixed anxiously on the road, and was filled with remorse. 'You were terrific,' she said. 'I behaved shockingly. She always brings out the worst in me.'

' "Considerable estate",' quoted Will, beginning to grin. ' "Dower house in the cove", "cottage for the staff".'

'Don't!' said Bea guiltily – and burst into hearty laughter. 'Her face,' she moaned. 'Her face when I was telling her!'

'And what's all this about being unconventional?' he asked, settling down to a steady fifty, which was all the Morris was capable of doing comfortably. 'We have an hour or so before us. New readers start here . . .'

Chapter Nineteen

Isobel watched the growing friendship between Bea and Will with interest. Occasionally Bea was seized with fits of independence and would fret at Will's refusal to be hurried or bullied. Will allowed these moments to wash over him and would carry on with the job in hand whilst Bea betook herself to the cliffs or the lane to walk off her irritation. The domestic decisions were generally taken, however, with very little difficulty or friction.

Having settled the sleeping quarters to everyone's satisfaction the next question was one of a shower room for Will. It was Tessa who insisted that it was unfair that he should have to wait his turn for the women to use the bathroom and that it would be fairer all round if a shower unit could be put in beside the lavatory behind the kitchen. This was undeniably true and so it was costed out and the three of them voted that it should be done as soon as possible. Another problem was how the bills should be divided. It was obviously unfair that Tessa should pay as much as the other two but she wanted to pay her share on the upkeep of the house and on its improvements.

Isobel could understand that; it made Tessa feel that the house was truly hers and that she had a say in it. She came back to the cove between jobs as often as she could and fitted in as easily as if she had never been away. Isobel wondered if the reason why it all worked so well was because the three of them made no emotional demands on each other. It was like being aboard a small ship; each assigned his various tasks for the wellbeing of their small community but with no messy, emotional muddles.

'It's not the same as being married,' she told Will, as they walked on the beach one wild March evening. 'You can argue and discuss and do your own thing and no one gets uptight. Not in the same way that husbands and wives do, or lovers. You know what I mean?'

'I think that's true,' he agreed. 'The problem within an emotional relationship is that both parties need to feel that they are put first. You get the "what about me?" syndrome.'

'That's so true,' sighed Isobel. 'But what's the answer?'

'The answer must be that each trusts the other to put him – or her – first.'

Isobel paused for a moment to watch the waves thundering in across the sand. They were both shouting to make themselves heard above the boom of the surf. Will thrust his hands deep into his pockets and looked far out where the white horses hid the horizon. A gust of wind buffeted them and they braced themselves against its force.

'It's all a question of trust,' said Will, as they turned towards the house. 'You need to feel safe. To be able to say, "I don't have to worry about myself because my partner is doing that for me. This leaves me free to look after her – or him," d'you see?'

'You must have had a pretty good marriage,' said Isobel, as they reached the warmth and silence of the kitchen. Bea and Will had invited her to supper and inviting smells issued from the aged Rayburn. She put her hands to her ears which still seemed to be ringing with the sound of the wind and the sea. 'That's a very idealistic approach to a relationship.'

'I didn't say that I had achieved it,' he said cautiously as he followed her upstairs. 'I was answering your question about the "what about me?" syndrome. You don't have to worry about "me" if someone else is doing it for you.'

'Most marriages are the reverse.' Isobel, entering the sitting room, had to resist the urge to draw the curtains or put a log on the fire. So little had changed that she still half expected to see Mathilda sitting in her chair, reading. 'More like open warfare.'

'I think that married people do often regard their partner as an enemy. Someone to be outwitted. There is a kind of triumph if one wins a skirmish or dupes the other. A desire to win points or to use emotional blackmail. It seems to be a series of battles rather than a love affair.' He watched her thoughtfully, wondering if this was a moment for a confidence. It was at such times that he learned about her life. 'Was your marriage like that? A series of battles?'

'Oh no.' She came to sit on the low stool beside the fire, staring into the flames. 'We rarely quarrelled. Simon is very sweet-tempered and certainly put me first. The trouble was that I am a restless kind of person. I took him for granted.' She pulled up her knees and wrapped her arms around them. 'I'm the kind of person that likes to stir things up. If the water gets too peaceful I heave in a bloody great rock just to see what will happen.'

She glanced around and sighed with satisfaction. It was good to be here. The Scrabble board was in evidence on the small fireside table and, in the corner of the sitting room, a jigsaw puzzle was spread out on the gate-leg table. It was Bea who did the jigsaw puzzle. 'Bringing order out of chaos,' as James described it on his last visit to the cove. 'Just like being Matron. She needs something to organise.'

It was evident that she was delighted to see him; that his reference to her as 'Matron' brought back happy memories. They talked about the boys and recalled amusing incidents.

'Of course,' Bea had said thoughtfully, 'I should have guessed that James was destined to be a lawyer. From a small boy he liked things to be explained very clearly to him and he always abided by the letter of the law. The rule stated that on Sunday mornings each boy must put a clean handkerchief in his suit pocket. Towards the end of term I noticed that James seemed to have lost most of his handkerchiefs. As I watched him in chapel one morning I saw that he was getting quite portly. He looked like a baby Michelin man. Afterwards I examined his suit. He had ten handkerchiefs crammed about his person, all quite clean and unused. He had obeyed the rule exactly.'

James had laughed with the rest and Isobel smiled as she remembered the story. She wondered where Bea was; probably in the study. It was she who had suggested that the study should be a 'quiet room'. It was impossible for each of them to have a private sitting room and, whilst they could go to their bedrooms if they wished to be private, it was agreed that the study should be a place where letters could be written or peace and quiet could be found. A notice bearing the words 'In Use' was made ready to be hung on the door handle at the appropriate times.

'We must hope,' Will had said to Isobel, 'that we don't all want to be quiet at once.'

Isobel listened to the wind howling round the house. No longer did she tuck up in the spare room with a hot-water bottle on these wild nights. She felt quite certain that no one would have minded if she used Tessa's room but she would never have asked. In many ways she felt that she no longer belonged as she had when Mathilda was alive. After Bea's arrival she had continued to do a certain amount of work about the house but Bea was not happy at watching Isobel work whilst she looked on; nor did she need Isobel to shop for her. Isobel began to feel nervous that she would soon be redundant. She did not know that Will had intervened on her behalf. He had explained to Bea on what terms Isobel had the cottage; Bea looked thoughtful, frowning a little.

'I think that Mathilda would have wanted us to honour her agreement,' he added, looking unhappily at Bea's stern face. 'I don't think she can afford the rent, d'you see?'

'I understand that,' said Bea, 'but it goes against the grain to be idle while someone works round me. I'm not that old yet.'

'I know that,' said Will pacifically. 'But we have to think about Isobel's pride.'

'Do we?' asked Bea sharply. 'I don't quite see that Isobel's pride is my problem.'

Will felt the tiny frisson of anxiety that he always experienced when Bea's antagonism surfaced; there had been several moments when he had felt the need to tread warily.

'I think it might become our problem if she were to leave,' he said, 'and we had some stranger living in the cottage.'

'So what do you suggest?' Bea's voice was cool.

'I don't know.' He shook his head. 'She knows that she's not earning her keep, so to speak. She suggested leaving when we first arrived but I really do feel that in such a small community our neighbour is terribly important to us. And she was very good to Mathilda. We mustn't overlook that. I should hate to appear ungrateful.'

'I can't quite see why *you* need be grateful,' said Bea, shrugging a little. 'I think we should keep things in proportion. Isobel did a job for which she was paid, in kind. Mathilda left her the Morris as a sign of gratitude. If Mathilda had wished her to live rent-free in the cottage no doubt she would have left her that, too.'

'That's true.' Will tried to keep calm. He knew that his personal feelings for Isobel coloured the situation but he also knew that championing of her cause would only antagonise Bea further. 'Would you prefer to let the cottage to someone else who could afford to pay rent?'

'I agree with you that it is better to have someone

we know and like at the cottage,' said Bea at last. 'What I can't understand is why Isobel should not try to find some other employment and so be able to pay her rent. It is clear that her arrangement with Mathilda no longer works with us. I see no reason why she should not work on the days when she is not at the bookshop. Even if she paid a nominal rent it would be better for her self-respect and better for us, too. Our pensions are not so enormous as to allow us to be foolishly philanthropic.'

'I think that's perfectly fair,' said Will after a moment's silence. 'In Isobel's defence I would merely say that I think she has been waiting to see how things worked out with us. If we don't require her help then I shall put it to her that she tries to find some other employment and that she pays a nominal rent until she can afford the full amount. I think she will do her best to do that. She doesn't want to be a parasite.'

'I have never thought that she did.' Bea coloured a little, feeling that he was accusing her of being hard-hearted. 'But I really think that it would be the best solution. There must be something she can do. She's a bright intelligent woman.'

'I'll talk to her,' said Will. He had done so at the first opportunity.

Now, watching him as he filled his pipe, Isobel felt her heart warm towards him. How kind and tactful he had been to her on that occasion! She remembered how frightened she had felt. Here was change indeed. The house in the cove was no longer her second home; to wander about in, cook in, draw the curtains and make up the fire. With Bea's arrival there had been a subtle change. Although Will made it clear that Isobel's friendship was important, and he included her as much as he could, she missed those early days when it had been just her and Will in the cove. It had almost been like having Mathilda back. She liked Bea, however, and when Will told her how unkind Marian Goodbody had been Isobel, who knew how it felt to be rejected, had secretly sympathised with Bea's resentment and loneliness.

She could see, however, that things must change and she was grateful that they did not wish her to leave and were prepared to be very generous about the rent. She started once again to apply for the very few teaching posts that were advertised but, although she was once short-listed, she was never offered a post. Eventually she managed to find a job working the lunchtime shift in one of the local pubs at the weekends and two days a week, and thus was able to squeeze a small amount of rent out of her earnings. Now, when she came to the house, she came as a guest and was careful not to wander in unannounced. She had invited Bea to the cottage for lunch and had found her an amusing, if forthright, companion and Isobel was determined not to rock any boats.

As she stared into the flames she wondered if, once she heard that Simon and Sally were married, she would feel some kind of change in her own life. It was as if she were afraid to leave the cove and the safety it represented – or was it because she still hoped that Simon might yet change his mind and that he and Helen would be restored to her . . . ?

'Penny?' Will was watching her.

She smiled and shook her head. 'Not worth that much, I'm afraid.'

She wondered why she never found his questions intrusive; perhaps it was because she felt that he really cared about her. When Will listened she felt that he really *heard* what she was saying. He thought about it and genuinely entered into her fears and ideas. So many friends listened with half an ear, her problems merely striking a chord in their own breasts so that, when she'd finished, their response was invariably, 'Oh, I know *exactly* what you mean. When I was . . .' and she knew that they weren't really interested in helping her but had been waiting for the opportunity to tell their own story. Or, 'I know *just* how you feel.' Whilst she was grateful at this attempt to sympathise she had an urge to scream, 'No you *don't*! How I feel is unique to me. Please respect it. Try to understand me.' Even worse was the flat, 'Tell me about it,' which Isobel always saw as a put down; as a 'I've been through all that and far worse than you could be suffering it. You can't tell me anything about pain . . . or loss . . . or loneliness . . . or being broke . . .' or whatever it was that she had been about to communicate. 'Tell me about it' always shut her up at once. She had a fear that her own problems had been brought about by her own selfishness and that she really had no right to sympathy. To have Will to talk to was a tremendous luxury.

The door opened and Bea put her head round. 'There you are,' she said cheerfully. 'I'm just going down to check on the supper. Drinks time, Will?'

As Will went with alacrity to fulfil his job as barman, Isobel felt a lifting of the heart. She was lucky to be here; to be just across the cove. She pushed away all thought of Sally and Simon and of Helen's continued coolness. With her usual optimism she told herself that, even yet, things might work out and, when Will brought a glass of wine across to her, she raised it to him with a smile.

Chapter Twenty

Indigo clouds towered above the high tors and rolled eastwards, swallowing the tender blue sky and spilling heavy drops of rain on the wide spaces of the moor. The crabbed and twisted thorn trees, their branches flushed soft green with new young leaves, bent lower beneath the wind's cold breath as it fled across the bleached rustling grass. The river, stained brown with peat and white-flecked, raced beneath the old stone bridge and the flooded boglands reflected back a brief bright glint of sunshine.

As Tessa turned right at Moorshop and plunged into the lanes behind Mary Tavy the rain descended suddenly, drumming on the car's roof and streaming down the windscreen. Even with the wipers at their speediest she could barely see out. She pulled into Freddie's drive and sat for some moments, waiting for the storm to abate. When it showed no sign of stopping she took her coat and, with it held over her head, made a dash for the back door. Freddie opened it as she reached it and she followed him in, shaking her jacket and pushing back her hair.

'What weather! So how are you?' He herded her before him into the kitchen where Charlie Custard was lounging gracefully in his favourite position on the old sofa. 'Look who's here, Custard.'

The dog waved a languid tail and then heaved

himself off the sofa and came to greet her.

'Good grief!' said Tessa. 'I feel very honoured. You didn't have to get up for me, Custard.'

'We're feeling very proud,' said Freddie, unable to hide his delight. 'Custard has passed his PAT test. He's got his badge to prove it.'

'Oh well done!' Tessa patted Custard's broad head. 'So how does it feel to be a fully paid-up Pet as Therapy? All those people patting you and telling you how wonderful you are.'

'He did very well when he went for his test,' said Freddie. 'A friendly gentle temperament is the great thing but they have to be immune to sudden noises. He didn't flinch when they dropped a tin tray behind him. It was as if he'd been doing it for years. Of course I've been training him intensively. He was brilliant, weren't you, old chap?'

Charlie Custard yawned deprecatingly and looked suitably modest. Having allowed Tessa to demonstrate her admiration and affection he returned to his position on the sofa and slumped down, exhausted by such an effort.

'Congratulations, Freddie.' Tessa beamed at him. 'So now you and Custard'll be round at the nursing home every minute, bringing down the blood pressure like mad.'

'We shall spread ourselves about,' said Freddie grandly. 'Custard's going to be a great hit and if anyone wants to stroke or cuddle me as well, I shall make myself available. Now then. I think everything's ready for you. I'm catching the three o'clock train so we've got plenty of time. Have you eaten?'

Tessa nodded. 'Stopped off at the Roundhouse,'

she said. 'We'll take Custard with us and I'll give him a walk on the way back from the station. If it isn't raining . . .'

As she drove home from Plymouth she felt the usual happiness at being back on the moor. The cove must be her first love, now, but the moor ran a very close second. The storm had passed. Huge gold and white clouds sailed majestically in the rain-rinsed sky and the full moon hung, serene and pale, in the east. The wind had dropped but the breeze was chill and Tessa huddled into her jacket as she and Custard walked on Gibbet Hill. She was glad that the nights were drawing out. The long winter evenings were nearly past and her job always seemed less lonely in the summer. Her brief returns to the cove had begun to show her how much she was missing in companionship. It had been such fun to draw the curtains against the dark and sit beside the fire playing Scrabble with Will whilst Bea pored over her jigsaw and chuckled at Will's expostulations at Tessa's spelling. It was only after she had left and was back at work that it occurred to her that there had been no television at the house in the cove. Usually she would have been barely able to exist without the company of the television to while away the endless hours. It must be bliss, thought Tessa, to have company instead of being alone all the time. She thought of Giles. He had turned up quite unexpectedly in the middle of the morning at Whitchurch and her first exclamation had been one of distress.

'Kate isn't here,' she'd said, disappointed for him.

'Oh, what a shame. She's up in London.'

He had looked taken aback and she had hastened
to make him as welcome as she could before she
remembered that it was his own home and was
promptly overcome by embarrassment. They had
stood for a moment in silence, neither of them quite
knowing what to say next, and then Giles had
laughed.

'This is silly, isn't it? Sorry to take you by surprise. It's great to see you. How's life in the cove?
Come and tell me all your news.'

They had sat in the kitchen together, talking and
talking . . . or rather she had talked and Giles had
listened. Later they had driven over to the Royal
Oak at Meavy and had a drink and some lunch
and then taken Felix for a walk above Burrator
Reservoir. As they looked down on the lake, set in
the hills beneath Sheepstor and surrounded by
woodland, Giles began to tell her of his childhood.
He recounted amusing tales of naval quarters but
explained that they had lived mainly here on the
moor. He showed her Dousland, below them in the
trees, where Kate had rented a bungalow, and
pointed out the roof of Meavy school which he and
Guy had attended until they went to Mount House
at eight years old. He told her about the break-up of
his parents' marriage and how he had feared the
later visits to his father. Tessa listened in silence,
aware that this was no light thing for Giles. She
guessed that he was not given to unburdening
himself. She remembered how she had talked to him
at the Roundhouse and suddenly felt very close to
him.

They drove over the moor whilst he showed her his past; where he and Guy had played and picnicked and where they had walked Felix's forerunners, Megs and Honey. They looked across the playing fields to Mount House school and stopped to have a stroll at Bellever Bridge where the twins had paddled in other earlier summers. When they got back to Whitchurch he had lit the fire whilst Tessa made the supper and the evening had stretched ahead, relaxed and comfortable, until bedtime.

As Tessa called to Charlie Custard and strolled back to the car, she remembered how she had felt at that point. It seemed almost wrong to separate and go to bed in different rooms. It would have been nice, she thought, to have continued in that feeling of closeness, to have wandered in and out of bathroom and bedroom, talking with that same sense of familiarity and easiness; to have shared the warmth and comfort of their bodies. She suspected that Giles felt the same but would have never mentioned it, feeling that he was pressing home an unfair advantage. Afterwards she wished that she'd had the courage to suggest it – and then felt rather ashamed.

'It would have looked so pushy,' she told herself as she opened the tailgate so that Charlie Custard could jump into the back of the car. 'And what about Sebastian?'

She felt the usual sinking of the heart when she thought about Sebastian. She had received another card from him and a telephone call. There was definite progress but not enough to satisfy Tessa.

Being a part-owner in the cove had given her a measure of confidence and she was beginning to find it difficult to be grateful for Sebastian's crumbs of affection; only beginning though. She had been in love with him for so long that he was a habit that she could not quite break – nor did she want to; he was still special.

The telephone was ringing as she opened the kitchen door and, leaving Charlie Custard to follow her in, she hastened to answer it.

'Hi!' said Sebastian. 'So how's my favourite girl?'

Tessa sank down on a kitchen chair and began to laugh. 'You must be psychic,' she told him. 'I was just thinking about you.'

'So I should hope.' He didn't sound surprised. 'Want to guess where I am?'

'Are you in Plymouth?' Her heart began to beat faster. 'Is the ship in?'

'It is indeed. I phoned up your people and got your number. Clever, aren't I?'

Tessa glowed at the casual phrase 'your people'. 'Was it Bea or Will?' she asked eagerly.

'It was a chap,' answered Sebastian. 'Gave me the third degree before he'd part up with the number, I can tell you.'

'Dear Will.' She smiled at Will's protectiveness. 'He's allowed to give it to one or two special people.'

'I see. And who else is special?' His bantering tone suggested that he was not overly anxious.

She decided to tease him a little. 'Oh, one or two girlfriends and Giles, of course . . .'

'Giles?' He sounded just the tiniest bit put out. 'Who's Giles?'

'A boyfriend,' she said lightly. 'Anyway. Are you in for long?'

'For a few days.' He still sounded faintly aggrieved. 'I was wondering if you might like to come down and meet me? That is if your social diary isn't overloaded.'

'Down where?' she asked. 'To the dockyard?'

'That's right. I shall need the registration number to get you through the gate. Are you on your own?'

For a moment she was puzzled by the question. 'Well, there's Charlie Custard,' she said.

'Charlie *who*?' His amazement made her laugh. 'Who *are* all these chaps?'

'He's a dog,' she told him. She glanced at Custard who was reclining indolently on his sofa. 'You wait till you see him?'

'So I can stay?'

'Stay?' She swallowed. 'You mean . . . ?'

'I mean "stay". As in "the night".' His voice, emphasising the words, was suddenly intimate and she remembered the things he had said in the pub when they'd last met and how he had kissed her. 'I've been really looking forward to seeing you again.'

Confused, she stared unseeingly at Freddie's curtains. Part of her was angry that he imagined that he could telephone out of the blue and expect her to sleep with him; part felt as though she were dissolving with the old treacherous longing.

'I don't know,' she said weakly. 'This isn't my place. It's a bit . . . a bit . . .'

'Nonsense,' he cut in robustly. 'These people can't expect you to live like a nun just because you're

227

looking after their dogs. Look, give me the registration number of your car. It's a Peugeot, isn't it? I'll give you directions to the Camel's Head Gate and they'll tell you what jetty we're on. I'll be looking out for you . . .'

Tessa replaced the receiver and stood for a moment, lost in thought. Charlie Custard watched from the sofa, hoping that she was thinking about his dinner. She shook her head, folded her arms across her chest, changed her mind and stuck her hands in her pockets. There was an air of anxiety and uncertainty about her whole demeanour and Charlie Custard began to feel uneasy. He had had a demanding and exhausting week. He had been patted and stroked and talked to by a number of strangers whilst other inconsiderate people dropped things and made sudden noises behind his back. He stretched out his back legs and rested his head against the top of the sofa, an ear cocked for the familiar words: 'What about dinner, then?'

'Come on then, old chap,' said Tessa. 'We're going out. Come on.'

Custard stared at her in disbelief. *Going out?* He'd only just come in after a tiring trip in the car and a quite unnecessary walk. Going out? Surely she meant 'What about dinner?'

'Get a move on.' She was collecting car keys and picking up the coat she'd dropped on a chair as she'd hurried into the house. 'Come *on*, Custard!'

There was a fraught note in her voice which he distrusted. Sighing heavily, he climbed down off the sofa and, with a meaning look at the cupboard which contained his dinner, he followed her out to the car.

As the engine burst into life the telephone started ringing.

Will hung up with a sigh. He brooded for a moment and then decided that it wasn't important. As he peeled some potatoes for supper he ran through the conversation again. It was obvious that the young man – what was he called? – knew Tessa fairly well and there could surely be no harm in his coming over. On second thoughts, however, it seemed that he didn't know her *that* well.

'Is that Mr Rainbird?' the voice had asked. 'You don't know me. I'm a friend of your daughter, Tessa. Is she about?'

'I'm afraid not.' Will did not correct his mistake. 'She's away for a few weeks. Who is this?'

'My name's Adrian Pearson. Away is she? Mmm . . . I'm sorry to miss her . . .'

Whilst the young man hesitated, Will had time to unhook the sheet containing a list of names which hung by the telephone. He peered at it; Adrian Pearson was not one of those to whom he was allowed to give Tessa's working telephone number.

'It's just that the last time I saw Tessa – we were having lunch together actually – she mentioned that you have some pieces of furniture that you might want to sell. I'm an antique dealer. I should have mentioned that earlier. Sorry if I'm speaking out of turn. It's just that I'm in the area for a few days . . .'

There was another pause. Will thought quickly. Obviously Tessa had seen this young chap at the time when they were debating how they might raise some money to buy Bea out. He and Tessa had talked about the possibility of selling some of Mathilda's pieces and perhaps she had seen this Adrian fellow and mentioned it to him. It was a coincidence that Bea had raised this subject only that morning at breakfast. What with the few items of furniture which she had inherited from her mother and Will's personal bits and pieces, the house was rather overcrowded. They had talked about installing a modern stove and perhaps putting in some central heating and had wondered whether the sale of an item or two might not be a good idea. They both knew that Tessa felt strongly about Mathilda's things, nevertheless there were certain repairs to be done and they needed to keep warm . . .

All these thoughts ran through Will's mind whilst Adrian made tentative noises on the other end of the line. Will made a decision. There would be no harm in this young man coming to look at, and perhaps value, a few things. Obviously Tessa thought that he could be trusted.

'If you would like to check with the office,' Adrian was saying, 'I can give you the number. Or you could speak to Mrs Carrington at Ivybridge.'

'That's all right,' said Will, who remembered Tessa talking about Mrs Carrington and her bureau. 'Since you're in the area why not come and see us? Tomorrow morning? About eleven? Excellent. Now you'll need some directions . . .'

Will dropped the last potato into the saucepan. After all, no decisions need be taken at once and it would be interesting to see how accurate the young man would be in his valuations. Will tried to remember what had happened to the inventory which James had given to him; in Mathilda's bureau, perhaps? He decided that after supper he would hunt it out.

Chapter Twenty-one

Tessa lay watching the moonlight streaming through the window. Sebastian, curled beside her in the narrow bed, was heavily asleep. She wished that she, too, could fall into such deep oblivion. She was wide awake and as confused as she had been when Sebastian had telephoned the previous evening. On the journey into the dockyard – aware of Charlie Custard's reproachfulness emanating from the back of the car – she had tried to analyse her feelings. She knew that she must not let Sebastian take her over; that she must resist his attempts to override her own wishes.

'But what do I want?' she asked herself as she drove into Plymouth. She still had not answered this question when she reached the Camel's Head Gate. Sebastian had been waiting for her at the end of the jetty. He flung his grip on to the back seat, said, 'Good God! Did you know you had a bear in your car?' and guided her out of Devonport en route to the nearest off-licence. It was impossible to remain uninfected by his high spirits and witty remarks and, by the time they were back in Mary Tavy, she had relaxed and was enjoying his company.

He was unimpressed by Freddie's bungalow – and her plans for supper – and took her out instead to the Elephant's Nest, leaving Charlie Custard to enjoy his long-awaited dinner. It was strange to be sitting at the same table where she and Giles had had lunch together and she felt an odd qualm which disappeared when Sebastian took her hand and told her how he had missed her. As usual his physical presence undermined her doubts: he was Sebastian. So she laughed at his jokes – and wondered what would happen when they got back to Freddie's. Since she was driving she drank only one glass of wine but, once they were at home again, Sebastian opened the carrier bag from the off-licence and produced a bottle of Chardonnay and some cans of beer.

They sat together in front of the fire, Charlie Custard snoring heavily on the hearth rug, and Tessa was soon aware that willpower was ebbing away and when he kissed her she responded readily.

Now, as she watched the shadows on the wall, she felt confused. There was something missing, she told herself, but what? Her inexperience was unable to supply the answer. She loved him and, even though she had remained uneasy about having him here for the night, she had enjoyed his lovemaking. Gently she eased her body away from his inert form and slid from the bed. She stood still, waiting, but Sebastian did not stir. Taking her dressing gown from the chair and picking up her slippers, she went quietly out and down the passage to the kitchen.

Charlie Custard, stretched on his sofa, opened an eye and felt a twinge of misgiving. He hoped that more patting and stroking would not be necessary. He decided that he was not cut out for social work after all and, groaning gently, he settled himself more comfortably. Tessa – clad now in dressing gown and slippers – stood staring out of the window whilst she waited for the kettle to boil. Moonlight stippled the grass with silver and the shadows lay long and black across the meadow. The lean form of a fox prowled in the shelter of the hedge, disturbing the small roosting birds in the bare branches above him. On an impulse Tessa opened the back door and wandered out, hunching her shoulders against the cool breeze. Charlie Custard raised his head to watch her. Now what? Curiosity hauled him from sleep and he padded out after her, sniffing at the air and following her down to the meadow. The fox slipped silently away and somewhere to the east a cock crowed.

In Tessa's bed Sebastian stirred and came suddenly awake. He lay quite still, reviewing the events of the past night and wondering where Tessa had gone. Needing a cigarette, he slid out of bed and went to feel in his trouser pocket. As he picked his trousers up from the chair his attention was caught by a movement outside and he paused, staring out of the window. Across the pale-washed grass of the meadow Tessa walked, slim and straight in her long dressing gown, the great dog at her heels. There was something almost medieval in the scene and Sebastian was moved beyond his usual desires and sensations. For the first time he saw Tessa as other men might see her; not as the adoring girl who could be picked up and put down as his whim took him – but as an intelligent, successful and desirable young woman. She had enterprise, property and a great deal of generous charm. As he stood watching her, he remembered the name she had mentioned earlier: Giles. She had spoken of him again in the pub. 'Giles brought me here,' she'd said.

Sebastian took his cigarettes and lighter from his pocket. He lit up thoughtfully, staring out at Tessa as she stopped, looking at something beyond his vision, her hand on the dog's head. His heart moved in his breast as he imagined a future with Tessa in the background; waiting for him when he came home from sea, gracing ladies' nights and parties, pouring out her love upon him. Turning abruptly away, he dragged on his shirt and trousers, crammed his bare feet uncomfortably into his shoes and went out through the kitchen and into the meadow.

She turned as he came through the gate, standing still, her hand still resting on the dog's head. She looked remote and unapproachable in the ghostly light and he knew a moment of fear. He came up to her, taking her by the elbows and staring down into her face.

'I love you,' he said. 'I've just realised it. Will you marry me?'

She stared at him in amazement, wondering if it might be some kind of joke. 'Marry you?'

'Yes.' He shook her slightly, frightened still further by her remoteness. Surely she loved him? 'I thought you loved me.'

'Yes,' she said slowly. 'Yes I do. But—'

'No.' He crushed her against him. 'No buts. It's right. I just know it. It is, isn't it?'

'Yes,' she said – but a kind of terror possessed her. Was it right? He began to kiss her and the terror ebbed and relief took its place. Of course it was right. This was what she had longed for; waited for all these years. 'Yes,' she repeated and began to tremble.

'Come back inside.' He was dragging her with him. 'You're shivering. Come in and we'll have some hot coffee. Oh, Tessa. I do love you.'

They went inside, forgetting Charlie Custard who wandered around for a while before pushing the back door open and padding into the kitchen. There was no sign of them but Tessa's dressing gown lay in a pile on the floor. He sniffed at it, climbed on to the sofa and settled himself to sleep.

Adrian Pearson sat for some moments in his car at the head of the track. He was taking a tremendous chance. Supposing that Tessa's father had telephoned her to ask about this young antique dealer? She would say, no doubt, that she had never said that her family wished to sell any of their belongings. He knew he could bluff it; say that he'd muddled her with someone else or completely misunderstood something she'd said. He'd carry it off and, after all, the old bloke had asked him to come. Tessa had let out a few things over the sandwich in the Pack Horse; not much, but enough to get him started. She'd talked of the old house in the cove somewhere near Kingsbridge and he'd looked up the name of Rainbird in the telephone directory. There were very few of them . . .

It was always worth a chance. He'd discovered that. In these hard times, there was a good chance that someone – generally an old person, living alone – was in need of ready cash. It was easy to disarm them with his sympathetic approach and public school voice; and he never rushed or harassed them. He made it clear that there were other pieces around and that they should give it serious thought. The touch about phoning the office was a good one, especially as the 'office' – a small back room where his girlfriend manned the phone – was in London. Many people had telephoned it but, since his targets were always in the West Country, no one as yet had turned up on the doorstep.

'If anyone wants to come, make sure they make an appointment,' he'd told her. 'You can be well away. Otherwise keep the door locked. Don't worry. No one will bother.'

His cards and leaflets were very professional; his own local contact number was his mobile telephone. He had had one or two frights but he was making a very nice profit, selling the pieces on to a friend in Essex who fed them at discreet intervals to a London showroom. It was worth taking a few chances. A hunch had led him to the cove. He had a sixth sense which was invaluable to him. He spent a great deal of time getting to know each small area that he targeted. He would sit in cafés, watching lonely old women who talked to the waitress about how hard the times were and how they longed to see their grandchildren; he sat in pubs and listened to lonely old men who missed their wives and were struggling to manage on their pensions. He generally avoided the younger women, who might need cash for their student children, but were fairly well clued up on the value of old furniture. He did very well out of the old and vulnerable. Adrian glanced at his watch, started up the engine and swung the car into the track.

Will was filling the coal hod at the bunker by the back door. He straightened up and watched Adrian park, wishing that he could have had a word with Tessa. He had telephoned earlier but there was no reply.

'I hope she's all right,' he had said worriedly to Bea.

'Probably walking the dog,' she'd answered. 'Stop fussing.'

Will dusted his hands on his old cords and went to meet the smart young man who was climbing out of the car. They shook hands and exchanged banalities. Will led him inside, introduced him to Bea in the kitchen and took him upstairs to the drawing room. Adrian's eyes were making a quick inventory although his remarks were studiedly casual.

'What a place you've got here, sir!' He strolled to the window trying not to show his excitement at the sight of the bureau in the alcove. Putting his hands in his pockets he stared out over the sea, wondering if they knew that they were using a valuable Georgian table in their kitchen or that the chest on the landing was probably Jacobean. 'Fantastic!'

'Pretty good, isn't it?' agreed Will genially. 'My cousin is making us some coffee. Sit down, won't you?'

Bea arrived, somewhat out of breath, with the tray. 'Never mind central heating,' she muttered to Will. 'What we need is a dumb waiter.'

He laughed and gave her a tiny private wink. 'Good for the waistline,' he said. 'I hope we haven't got you here on false pretences, Mr Pearson. I'm not certain what Tessa said . . .'

'Don't worry about that, sir—' Bea, pouring coffee, raised her eyebrows at the 'sir' – 'I was hoping to see Tessa, actually. That's the real reason I telephoned. The other was of secondary importance but if there's anything I can do while I'm here . . .'

'Why not?' Will shrugged. 'It's always nice to know if one owns anything worth having. We've inherited a lot of this stuff. Haven't got a clue, have we?'

He smiled ruefully at Bea who shrugged non-committally and retired with her coffee to a distant chair.

'Some of it looks like jumble sale to me,' she said. 'That old table in the kitchen . . .' She shook her head and sipped at her coffee.

Adrian felt his excitement rising. 'It's often a disappointment to people,' he said, 'when I make them an offer for their treasures.'

'I believe you,' said Will. 'Never mind. Luckily we're not desperate yet, are we, Bea?'

'Aren't we?' she answered grimly. She snorted. 'If you say so.'

Will looked terribly embarrassed. He laughed a little, smoothed his hand over his hair and coughed awkwardly. 'I expect you're kept pretty busy, Mr Pearson . . . ?'

'Please call me Adrian, sir.' His voice was earnest and kind. 'Try to see me as Tessa's friend who happens to have some knowledge of antiques.' He glanced at Bea. 'She's a delightful girl, if I may say so.'

'You may say what you please, young man,' said Bea. 'I am not responsible for her genetic brew nor did I bring her up.'

'Please, Bea,' murmured Will. He shot a distracted look at Adrian who gulped back his coffee and rose to his feet. 'Shall we . . . ?'

'Where would you like me to begin, sir?'

'Let's start in the study,' suggested Will. 'Through here.'

Bea sat perfectly still in her chair, listening to their voices. Presently they reappeared. Adrian was making notes in a small book; Will was jotting figures on a piece of paper. He glanced at Bea, who swallowed the last of her coffee and stood up.

Will smiled at her. 'If you'll excuse us for a moment, my dear?'

She stared at him for a moment then collected the cups and the tray and went out. Will shrugged and blew out his lips a little. Adrian smiled sympathetically, his eyes on the bureau.

'I've noticed,' he said tentatively, 'that the women seem more ready to part with their treasures than the men . . .'

'Well, there you have it,' said Will with a measure of relief. 'I'm reluctant to part with things, d'you see? Pure sentiment, according to my cousin, but there it is. And she's right. We need a new stove and central heating . . .' He sighed heavily. 'Never mind. You don't want to hear my problems. Let's get finished. By the way, not a word to her for the moment, if you don't mind.'

'I quite understand, sir,' said Adrian. 'And if you need to contact our office, just to put your mind at rest . . .'

'No need for that, my boy,' said Will. 'Now what about this bureau . . . ?'

A piece of cake, thought Adrian as he drove away. The old biddy's got her claws into him, all right. He'll be back. No wonder he didn't want her to see my quotes. He's probably going to snaffle a bit on the way through. Good luck to him.

He turned on to the main road and began to make some very satisfying mental calculations.

'The man's a crook,' said Will softly, his eyes gleaming. 'I laid all the traps and he walked right in to them. You were splendid, Bea.'

Bea looked modest. 'Good thing we'd decided on a code. What made you suspect?'

Will shook his head. 'Some gut feeling. On the phone first, just a twinge, and then when I saw him. I don't know what it was . . . but I was right.'

'So what shall we do?'

'I'll phone the London office for a start. No.' He looked thoughtful. 'I'll try and get hold of Tessa first. See what she really said to him and how he got on to us. I'm sure she didn't give him our address.'

'But he had our number,' Bea pointed out.

'Could have got it from the book. He certainly knew her name and there aren't that many Rainbirds about. Hang on. Let me try Tessa again.'

Bea watched whilst he dialled and stood waiting. 'Hello. Tessa? Oh good. I was trying to get you

242

earlier but there was no reply . . . Gone to what . . . ? But who . . . ? Well, of course I am. It's just rather sudden . . . Yes. Yes, I see. Well, it's wonderful . . . For tea? Why not . . . ? Yes, and Charlie Custard, too . . . See you then. 'Bye, my dear.'

'Will,' said Bea, infuriated, 'whatever are you talking about? Who is Charlie Custard and why didn't you ask her about Adrian Pearson?'

Will sat down suddenly at the kitchen table. 'I didn't feel I could,' he said. 'She's just got herself engaged to be married and she's bringing him over to tea.'

'She's got herself engaged to someone called *Charlie Custard*?' Bea shook him by the shoulder. 'Pull yourself together, Will. What's going on?'

Will sighed; he looked anxious. 'Some childhood sweetheart called Sebastian has turned up out of the blue and they've got engaged. They've been to Plymouth to buy the ring and she wants to bring him over to meet us. What could I say? It was hardly the time for talking about crooked antique dealers. The child is over the moon. She was hardly coherent.'

'So I gather,' said Bea grimly. 'And who is this Charlie Custard?'

'He's the dog,' said Will wearily. 'He's coming, too.'

'All I can say,' said Bea going to the larder, 'is that dogs these days have very silly names. What with Romulus and Remus . . . However. What are we going to do about Adrian Pearson?'

'I shall talk to James.' Will looked happier as this thought presented itself. 'See if he's got any advice.'

'Good idea.' Bea brought out the scales. 'I shall

make a cake for tea and then I'll see if Isobel's around. If Tessa is going to get herself engaged I'm sure that Isobel will like to have a look at him, too.'

Will, finding James's office number, decided that he would never understand women. The relationship between Isobel and Bea was too complex for him. Bea was insistent that Isobel should pay her rent, yet was anxious that she should meet Tessa's young man. As for Tessa getting engaged . . . He put the problems of his womenfolk out of his head and dialled the offices of Murchison, Marriott.

Chapter Twenty-two

Two days after the announcement of Tessa's engagement, Isobel received a letter from Simon. She picked it up from the hall floor and turned it over in her hands, examining the handwriting and the postmark. At last it had come. Isobel had no real doubt that the letter contained the news of his marriage to Sally and, with its arrival, came the realisation that she had no desire to read the words that would destroy her last hope. She put the letter in her shirt pocket and wandered into her living room. The cottage had been furnished with saleroom pieces but Isobel had contrived to give it a character of its own and this was a cheerful room. The shabby armchair and the sofa were made bright with huge heavy cotton throws in old gold and bright scarlet. A cream Indian cotton bedspread covered the scratched table which stood under the window, and pine-framed reproduction posters hung on the cream-washed walls. Rag rugs hid the worst spots of the threadbare carpet and the kitchen chairs at the table had been rubbed down to their original pine and given padded cushions of scarlet. The patterned curtains in thick chenille seemed to embrace all these colours in a rich warm glow.

A second-hand wood-burning stove had been fitted in the wide stone fireplace, and Isobel kneeled

on the hearth rug and opened the glass doors. The
weather was still cold and she was keeping the fire
in overnight so that there was a centre of warmth
in the house. She put some wood into the stove and
let it blaze up. Presently she took out the letter and
tore open the envelope almost indifferently. She
scanned the words quickly, then read them properly.
Simon had been as tactful as was possible in the
circumstances; the wedding had been a very quiet
one at Sally's home in the Lake District and they
were spending the Easter holidays there in a holiday
cottage. Helen would be staying with friends. He
sent Isobel their best wishes and hoped she was
well . . . She screwed up the paper and flung it into
the flames. So that was finally it; no more pretending that he might come back to her. It was over.
She had told herself this several times in the past
but soon hope had come creeping back. For some
reason Isobel found herself remembering Tessa's
face when she had introduced Sebastian to them.
She had looked happy but there had been something
else as well; a kind of hopeful anxiousness . . . ?

Isobel shook her head. She couldn't really pin
down Tessa's expression but she had found herself
praying that Tessa would be happy. Certainly
Sebastian was a nice enough young man. His
manners were excellent and he was extraordinarily
good-looking. He had been charming to Bea, deferential to Will, sweet to Tessa . . .

'I know now that I'm really old,' Will had said
afterwards. 'I've never been "sirred" so much in one
day in my life. First Adrian Pearson and then
Sebastian . . . Ah well.'

At the thought of Will a faint ray of comfort found its way to Isobel's unhappy heart. It became even more important now that she should be able to remain in the cove. She must redouble her efforts to get a worthwhile job and so be able to pay the proper rent. She knew that Will would not care about it but Bea was a different proposition and she realised that it was important to show that she was really trying to pull her weight.

Isobel drew up her knees and rested her forehead on them. She was well aware of Will's affection for her and for a brief moment she knew a temptation to trade on it; to rest against him and let him take the weight. What a relief it would be to pass all her problems over to Will. She knew that it would be easy to make him really love her and she wondered if she could love him enough to repay him for all that he would give her . . .

Suddenly, in one swift movement, she got to her feet – as though physically rejecting such ideas – and passed into the kitchen. It was shameful to think of Will in such cold-blooded terms she told herself as she began to wash up the breakfast things, along with last night's supper plates. She caught herself thinking of Tessa again. How would Sebastian fit into the cove? Would Tessa give up her job and move around with him, living in married quarters? Even if she did they would want to come home to the cove for leaves and weekends. What then? Would Sebastian share Tessa's room, next door to Bea; and what about when the babies came along?

Isobel stood staring out across the sea, her hands

still in the soapy water. The obvious thing would be for Tessa and Sebastian to have the cottage – but where would she go then? She couldn't imagine herself sharing the house with Bea and Will. She thought of Helen and wondered how she liked sharing a house with Sally and Simon. The thought of Helen made her feel even more desperate as the knowledge of her loneliness and failure seized her and filled her with pain. As she emptied the bowl and dried her hands she saw Bea walking on the beach. She carried a bag into which she put her 'gleanings'. The sight made Isobel remember Mathilda and her loneliness became an intolerable weight. She simply could not bear to be on her own today.

She came out of her door and raised a hand to Bea. 'How are you?' she called in a remarkably steady voice. 'Have you recovered from your shock?'

She went to meet her and they strolled forward together, the early April sunshine pleasantly warm on their faces.

'Will has been talking to James,' Bea told her. 'It seems we can do nothing about this wretched young man.' For one mad moment Isobel thought she was talking about Sebastian. 'You see he is too clever to state his opinion of the worth of the items he purchases. He merely tells you what he is prepared to offer. According to James that is no crime. He doesn't force you to sell, you see. Will said he was very cunning in what he said. He didn't actually admit to anything although he unerringly picked the most valuable pieces.'

'How frustrating,' said Isobel. 'Surely there must be something we can do?'

248

'We're thinking about it. Will would like to set a trap for him and expose him but it's rather complicated. As James says, no one is obliged to take his money.'

'Did you tell Tessa about it?'

Bea shook her head. 'We didn't feel that it was quite the right moment.'

'And what did you think of Sebastian?' asked Isobel, after a moment.

'He seemed a nice enough young man,' said Bea cautiously.

Isobel sighed. 'I hope she'll be happy.'

Bea looked at her sharply. 'You don't sound too sanguine.'

Isobel laughed. 'Don't take any notice of me,' she said lightly. 'I had a letter this morning from my ex-husband to say that he has just remarried. Not a day for too much optimism, I'm afraid.'

They stood at the edge of the cove, looking out over the calm sea in silence.

'I understand that there is a very good market in Totnes on Friday mornings,' said Bea at last. 'I do enjoy a market. Will's tied up this morning. No chance, I suppose, of us going together? I'm sure I could find my way alone but it would be very pleasant to have your company if you can spare the time.'

'I should love to,' cried Isobel. 'It's a wonderful idea. It's my day off and I must say it's not a good day to have too much time to think.'

'Perhaps you wouldn't mind driving the Morris?' suggested Bea, who felt that, in her present state, it would be better if Isobel were to be kept occupied.

She had been looking forward to exploring Totnes alone; preferring to take her own time rather than be worried lest the person with her was bored or waiting at some pre-arranged spot, an eye on the time. On her own she could truly relax, although she enjoyed her jaunts with Will who was an unexacting companion. She suspected that Isobel would rush her from place to place, chattering and requiring regular stops for coffee. Nevertheless, it was clear that Isobel needed company and some task which would take her mind off her troubles. Bea had not been deceived by the brightness of Isobel's voice. 'We could go in the other car,' she said, 'and you could navigate but since you know these lanes so well I should prefer it if you would take charge.'

'No problem,' agreed Isobel promptly. 'We'll take the Morris. I shall really enjoy showing you round. It'll be fun. Market day is really busy.'

'In that case,' said Bea, 'perhaps we should make a start?'

Isobel looked at her gratefully, rather surprised by this gesture. Apart from the fortnightly stock-up at the supermarket and the visits to the library which she did with Will, Bea usually went off alone to do her private shopping. For some reason Isobel was reminded of Mathilda and their trip to Oxford. She did not wait to analyse these feelings but she felt a rush of affection for the older woman and, agreeing to meet her by the car in five minutes, went hurrying back to the cottage.

Will waved them off and returned to scraping down the woodwork of the downstairs windows. There was much to be done but he was enjoying even the most laborious of tasks. As he scraped away the peeling paint, he thought about Mathilda. What inner resources she must have had to live in near isolation yet remain the person Isobel had described to him. Will had remarked that, under such circumstances, most people went a bit potty.

'Mathilda wasn't potty,' Isobel had said indignantly. 'She might forget to eat or not notice the fire going out but she was so clear-sighted. It was Mathilda who made me really think about things. There was something . . . something . . . Oh, how can I put it? She was always the same, never deviating from her real self. There was an absolute serenity deep down inside her. Oh, I can't explain it.'

'You were very fond of her.' It was a statement.

'Yes.' Isobel, who had been talking eagerly, looked suddenly bleak. 'I loved her. We were friends but I let her down at the end.'

'How d'you mean?'

Isobel was silent for a long moment. 'I never knew she was ill,' she said at last. 'I was too busy with my own troubles to notice and she obviously didn't trust me enough to confide in me.'

Will felt a pang of anxiety. This was something which had gone very deep and was corroding Isobel's peace and despoiling her memories of Mathilda. 'I think you may have that round the wrong way,' he said gently.

She'd looked at him quickly. 'How d'you mean?'

'Put yourself in her place. Here is a woman who has lived alone, by choice no doubt, but nevertheless alone. She is someone who prefers her own company to that of the wrong people. You come along and she finds that with you she can talk and joke and play Scrabble. What a joy you must have been to her! What a bonus! You give her plenty of freedom and space but you care for her, keep her warm and well fed and allow her to live happily and do exactly as she pleases. One day she suspects that she's ill.' Will looked directly at Isobel. 'If she had confided in you can you imagine how your relationship would have changed? Gone would have been that ease and fun that you had together. You would have been watching her, worrying, waiting. She would have felt the weight of your anxiety, reminded constantly of her illness, unable to forget it for a moment. I think that Mathilda chose to preserve the quality of her life right up to the end and that your ignorance of the truth enabled her to do it. She would have been relieved that she could hide her knowledge from you and I am quite certain that she never meant to hurt you by her silence nor imagined that you'd feel guilty in any way. From what I know of her and the relationship you shared, I suspect that she assumed that you'd understand.'

The silence seemed endless. Will thought that he'd never made such a long speech and he prayed that it was the right answer. Something told him that it was how Mathilda had felt. He slid a sideways look at Isobel.

'She talked about the quality of life,' she said slowly, 'but surely, if you love someone, you notice if they're not well?'

'Not if they're deliberately hiding it from you,' he answered promptly. 'I think Mathilda did that. She sounds like a woman with very great strength and courage. You are wronging her in dwelling on what you see as your shortcomings. You should be remembering what you had together and being happy and grateful for it. You are debasing the great friendship you shared.'

He heard her swallow at the harsh words and longed to throw his arms around her. Instead, he began to pat about his pockets for his pipe.

'She killed herself,' said Isobel in a small voice. So far she had kept this dreadful thing from Mathilda's relatives. They had been told that Mathilda died by accident, rendered helpless by the weakness caused by her illness and by the onset of hypothermia. 'I know she did. We talked once of euthanasia and she said that she would rather die than face the indignity of suffering. She felt very strongly about it. When she knew she had cancer I think she decided to take her own way out.'

'How wonderful then,' said Will calmly, 'that she had the courage of her convictions. Most of us talk but few of us act.'

'I don't think she did.' Isobel's eyes were dark with horror as she looked at him. 'I think she went out that night intending to drown herself.' She swallowed again, always remembering those fatal words of hers, and her lips trembled. 'I think she *did* lose courage. I think that she changed her mind but the engine wouldn't start. She hadn't bothered to get the boat overhauled. I think that when the storm got up it swept the boat into the rocks and she died of exhaustion and hypothermia. She took a flask with her but that's because I bullied her. I joked and said,' her voice trembled and Will braced himself, 'I said, "Go and drown yourself and see if I care!" But I went over later and made a flask of coffee for her and put it on the kitchen table beside her duffel bag. I knew she wouldn't bother or she'd forget to do it. The flask was half empty when they brought it back. I think she lost her nerve when the time came and then she couldn't get back.' Isobel began to weep. 'I can't help thinking how frightened she must have been. Oh God. I did love her and if only I'd realised I might have saved her.'

'Saved her from what?' Will gave up and put his arm about her shaking shoulders, holding her close. 'Saved her from painful treatment and being a vegetable and dying a humiliatingly undignified death? Would you honestly have brought her back to that, given that you loved her? Can't you see what a blessing it was that fate took things out of her own hands? In the end she died peacefully and painlessly and at that moment of fear she had the warmth and comfort of the flask you made her. In those last moments you gave her what she needed; what you'd been giving her for the last years of her life: The tangible comfort of your love and caring for her.'

Isobel put her head in her hands and gave herself up to violent weeping but, when the storm had passed away, her guilt had been washed away with it. She looked at Will with swollen but clear eyes, the dark grief gone.

'I did love her,' she said shakily. 'She was . . . Mathilda.'

He smiled at her. 'Then give thanks for her and

for your opportunity to love her,' he said. 'It is a great privilege to be able to love someone whole-heartedly. Don't throw it away or debase it in grief and guilt and self-indulgent remorse.'

Now, as he felt the sun warm on his back, Will straightened up and watched a cloud of gulls screaming above a fishing boat as it plied its way towards Dartmouth. He remembered his own sense of guilt after he had talked so confidently to Isobel but the change in her convinced him that it had been the right thing to do. Thanking God that he had been given the means to help her, Will stretched and bent again to his scraping.

Chapter Twenty-three

The woods were full of birdsong. Tessa, hands in pockets, strolled slowly with Sidney pottering in the rear. A shower of upflung leaves and earth showed that Harry was far ahead, scratching busily at a hole deep in the roots of a tree, and quite unconscious of the squirrel who watched him slyly from a branch high above his head. A jay flashed between the trunks of two great oaks, disturbing a wood pigeon who rose with a clapper of wings and, with its odd curving flight, dipped into the meadow where lambs played at the edge of the wood. The pale gold of primroses gleamed from amongst beech mast and dead leaves, wood anemones glowed ghostly in the shadows beyond the path and the constant chuckle of water hinted at the presence of an unseen stream.

Tessa, who had hoped to spend Easter at the cove, was back in Wiltshire. The two families had once again united for a repeat trip to France and Tessa had been unable to refuse their pleas for help. She was not yet in such a position to be able to turn down work and she knew that these two women, struggling to make ends meet, had made great sacrifices to be able to take the children away on holiday for the week.

'It's rather a lot of driving,' Sidney's owner had

admitted, 'but it's a wonderful break and the kids love it. Having you here is a great luxury but I couldn't put Sidney in kennels. He's much too neurotic. He was my husband's dog, you see, and when he went off it broke Sidney's heart, and his new woman wouldn't have him near her. He might slobber on the chair covers. Cow! So he stays with me. Poor old Sidney. He hasn't really got over it.'

It occurred to Tessa that he hadn't got over Harry, either. Despite a second week together, there was still a certain amount of tension on Sidney's part although his gentlemanly instincts obliged him to endure in silence. Harry, with all the insufferable confidence of the street urchin, never even noticed.

Tessa stood still and whistled. There was a scurrying as Harry appeared from nowhere and barged past them – he always had to be ahead – and, with Sidney fairly close to heel, she turned back towards the road where the car was parked. She yawned, feeling terribly tired, and realised that she had felt this weariness for some while. It was odd that, having achieved her heart's desire, she should feel such lethargy now that the first excitement was over. Her limbs were heavy and her brain was dull; unable to be stimulated to happiness, even by the thought of Sebastian or the sight of her engagement ring. As she walked she stretched out her hand so as to stare at the pretty hoop of sapphires, remembering how they had rushed in to Plymouth to choose it and then gone on to the cove so that Sebastian could meet Bea and Will.

Tessa had been swept along on a rising tide of excitement and happiness. Sebastian, having had his eyes opened at last, had behaved perfectly. For the few days that she was at Freddie's it was almost as if they were a couple in a film or an advertisement; he bought flowers and champagne, raced across beaches with her, sang as they drove along in the car, took her out to dinner. It had, she thought now, a sense of unreality about it: tremendous fun but quite unrelated to anything that had happened before or since. It was as if they were both playing parts in a brief moment of romance that had nothing to do with real life.

Tessa yawned again and felt irritable. Why couldn't she be satisfied? For nearly ten years she had yearned after Sebastian and, now that she had him, all she felt was a dull exhaustion. Perhaps it was bound to be like this, she told herself as she let the dogs into the car. There was bound to be some sort of anticlimax after ten years of longing and hoping and waiting. She climbed in, switched on the engine and began to turn the car. Sidney whined miserably as she backed towards the hedge and she felt another surge of irritation.

'Shut up, Sid,' she said crossly. 'For goodness' sake! Nobody's hurting you!' She caught sight of his big domed head and sad eyes in the driving mirror and remembered what his owner had told her. 'Sorry,' she said, filled with compunction. 'Sorry, Sid. I'm being a cow!'

She drove along the lane, a now-familiar sense of confusion making her even more depressed. Deliberately she thought about Sebastian and how happy the Andersons had been when she and Sebastian had telephoned the news of their engagement. She thought of how sweet he had been to her and how he had made love to her – and her heart remained obstinately heavy.

'I'm tired,' she told herself. 'I need a holiday. A real one. Not just bits and pieces here and there. It's been a pretty exhausting year one way and another.'

Comforting herself with this reason for her contrariness, she drove back to the cottage. To-morrow she would leave Wiltshire. She had a few days to herself before her next job and she had planned to spend them at the cove; not as long as she would like but better than nothing. As she opened the door she could hear the telephone ringing and ran to answer it. It was a few moments before she realised who was at the other end.

'I've been ringing and ringing,' said Harry's owner, sounding near to tears. 'It's terrible. Poor Caroline's been taken really ill. We think it might be some seafood she had. She's in hospital. There's no way we can get back tomorrow. Can you hang on for a few days?'

Tessa shut her eyes for a moment, seeing her precious holiday disappearing. She tried to summon some sympathy for Caroline. 'I'm sorry,' she said. 'How awful for her. For all of you. I can stay three more days. I've got to be somewhere else after that.'

'She's really poorly.' The voice was trembling. 'The doctor says she might not recover. She's vomiting all the time. I don't know what to do . . .'

Tessa was shaken out of her lethargy and disappointment. 'How awful for you! Poor Caroline. Are the children all right?'

'We're all fine. Only she would have the mussels.' She began to cry. 'It's food-poisoning, you see. Her mum's coming over.'

'I'm so sorry.' Tessa felt inadequate. 'Look, don't worry about the dogs. I can cope here until Tuesday. Stay in touch though, will you? I'm just . . . Well, I don't know what to say.'

'No. I know. I can hardly believe it myself. And I don't know what to say to the kids. I'll be glad when her mum arrives.'

'Of course you will. Try not to get too upset.'

'No. I'll phone again tomorrow, then. 'Bye.'

Tessa replaced the receiver. She felt frustrated and guilty for being more concerned about not being able to go to the cove than she was about the poor, sick Caroline.

'Shit!' she muttered. 'Damn! Blast!' She kicked off her boots whilst Sidney watched her anxiously. 'Sorry,' she said, automatically, seeing his distress. 'Sorry, Sid.' She stroked his silky head. 'How about a biscuit?'

As the day progressed, her frustration and depression settled back into a mild lethargy. Longing for some communication with the outside world she wrote a letter to Sebastian who was back in Portsmouth – a specially loving letter so as to assuage her guilt – and decided to ring Will and Bea to explain that she might be delayed. There was no reply and she spent some time trying to remember Isobel's surname and cursing herself for not having had the foresight to ask for her telephone number.

After lunch, worn out with so many negative

emotions and the tiring boredom of having nothing to do, she fell asleep on the sofa in front of the television with Sidney stretched out on the floor beside her. Harry was patrolling the garden, a sharp eye out for the neighbour's cat with whom he had an ongoing sparring match. The telephone bell jerked Tessa out of a deep slumber and she hauled herself upright and stumbled out into the kitchen.

'Oh God!' said the voice of Harry's owner. 'It's awful. Caroline's dead. She's dead. Just like that. Isn't it terrible? I can't believe it.' She began to sob.

Tessa stood holding the receiver, trying to comprehend the horror of it. 'I'm so sorry,' she repeated meaninglessly. 'So sorry.'

'Thank God her mum arrived in time. It's awful here. Look, I'm coming back tomorrow morning. It's not fair on my kids to keep them here now. They're in a terrible state. Caroline's mum is coping with her two. They'll be staying here for a bit to arrange for . . . things.' She began to cry again.

'I simply don't know what to say,' said Tessa honestly. 'It's the most awful shock.'

'I know. It doesn't seem possible, does it? Alive one minute – and the next . . . nothing. I can't bear it.' She gave a kind of retching gasp. 'Look, I must go. The kids are waiting. See you tomorrow about three o'clock.'

Tessa filled the kettle and switched it on. The shocking news had penetrated the dullness of her spirits and she was filled with horror. The woman's words repeated themselves in her head. 'Alive one minute – and the next . . . nothing.' So it had been with her parents and her brother. Her old companions of loneliness and isolation weighed upon her so terribly that she became desperate to speak to someone. The need to dispel the terrifying awareness of the transitory nature of man's existence was acute. She simply must smash through her fear and communicate with some warm, living, understanding human being. She found her address book and went back to the telephone. To whom should she speak? She found herself thinking of Giles but gave herself a mental shake. She could hardly phone him up out of the blue and weep down the telephone at him, especially now that she was engaged. Instead, she picked up the receiver and dialled the house in the cove . . .

Only much later did she remember that it had never occurred to her to try to contact Sebastian.

Giles lay on the sofa-bed in his small studio, listening to some jazz and thinking about Tessa. He knew that his mother would have been disappointed at his lack of initiative but he was pleased with the way things were going. He and Tessa had spent two magic days together and, though nothing concrete had been said and he hadn't so much as kissed her, he was certain that progress had been made. On his return to London he had been obliged to leave almost immediately for Ireland, to take photographs for a series of articles on Celtic Britain. Afterwards he had travelled on to Scotland and so he had been away for several weeks. He wished that it was not quite so difficult to contact Tessa. Because she was never in the same place for very long she had given him a contact number and, having arrived back and gathered up his confidence, he had dialled it. There was no reply. Later he had tried again . . . and again – but the number had been engaged for hours.

Giles settled himself more comfortably and closed his eyes. It was true that his upbringing had given him a wariness about entering into relationships, which reinforced his genetic inheritance. Until Tessa, he had never felt strongly enough to make the effort required to sustain such a relationship but, now that he felt as he did about her, he was determined that nothing should go wrong. He was frightened of hurrying her but afraid of losing her. He knew how she felt about Sebastian Anderson which, to begin with, had made it impossible to approach her. Now, he was more of his mother's persuasion; all was fair in love and war. The two days he had spent with her had convinced him that this, at last, was the real thing; now he was ready to fight for her.

He propped himself up a little and pressed the redial button on the telephone. Will answered the telephone so quickly that he took Giles by surprise.

'Hello,' he said. 'Mr Rainbird? My name's Giles Webster. Tessa gave me the number. I'd like to get in touch with her.'

'Ah, yes.' Will appeared to be dithering. Giles did not know that he was checking his list. 'Yes, of course. Giles Webster. The thing is, Giles, she's had a bit of a shock. I've just been speaking to her, as a matter of fact. The woman she's dog-sitting for died abroad yesterday and Tessa's just had to deal with the woman's friend and children collecting the other dog.'

'Died?'

'Shocking, isn't it? Food-poisoning apparently. Poor Tessa's a bit overwhelmed. She was supposed to be coming home today but she's stuck with the dead woman's dog, d'you see?'

'How terrible. Poor Tessa. And poor woman, whoever she was. I'm sorry.'

'Quite. Well, I'll give you her number but I warn you, she's a bit low.'

'I should think so. Thanks for the warning. Don't worry, I'll be as tactful as I can. Yes. I've got a pencil . . . Thanks.'

He dialled the number and waited. Tessa, when she answered, sounded tired and unhappy and Giles was filled with a new, strange tenderness.

'Tessa,' he said, 'it's Giles. I just phoned the number you gave me and Mr Rainbird told me the sad news. I'm terribly sorry. What a shock for everyone. Are you OK?'

'Oh, Giles.' The caring note in his voice warmed her. 'Oh, isn't it awful? I've been talking to Will. I couldn't bear to be on my own, if you see what I mean. The terrible suddenness of it brought everything back.'

'Poor Tessa. Look.' He decided to take a chance. 'I'm just back from Scotland and Ireland before that. I've got a few days off. Would you like me to come and see you? Where are you?'

'I'm in Wiltshire. Oh, it would be lovely. I must admit I'm feeling silly and feeble. I shall probably cry all over you.'

'That's OK.' Giles felt full of protective love. 'Is there a pub I could put up in somewhere at hand?'

'Yes. I suppose ... It's a bit tricky...' She sounded confused. 'Giles, I ought to tell you ... It's embarrassing because it sounds as if ... Oh shit! ...'

'What's the matter?' asked Giles, puzzled by the change in her voice. 'What have you been doing?'

Tessa gave a deep sigh. 'I hope this won't make you change your mind but I feel it's only right to tell you. Sebastian and I are engaged ...'

'I see. I hope you don't expect me to congratulate you.' He tried to keep his voice light.

'Oh, Giles.' She was trying to laugh. 'I can't tell you how much I'd like to see you.'

'Then I'll be there,' he said calmly. 'But if the pub's shut you may have to find me a bed.'

'Come straight here,' she said recklessly. 'Please, Giles. There're plenty of beds and I'm sure it won't be a problem. If you really want to come ...'

'I'll be with you in a couple of hours,' he said. 'Give me the address and the telephone number ...'

When she'd rung off he sat staring at the telephone. To his surprise the news of her engagement had served to stiffen his resolve. He had been able to hide his anger and disappointment – he had no intention of antagonising her – but now his fists clenched involuntarily as he thought of Tessa and Sebastian together. 'Shit,' he muttered through clenched teeth. 'Shit, shit, shit!' As he packed a few things his mind was busy. It came as a revelation to him that he was not prepared to let her go. Usually he would have backed down at once, never dreaming of trying to come between an engaged couple, but not now. He knew that he was prepared to make a fight for Tessa but he would need to be careful. As he drove west, Giles laid his plans.

Chapter Twenty-four

Bea strolled on the cliffs above the cove, her eyes fixed on the hazy horizon. It was a cold damp afternoon and the watery sun had disappeared behind a thin veil of cloud but she was unaware of any physical discomfort. Her brisk walk had warmed her and she was deep in thought. It seemed strange that she had settled so quickly here in this remote cove, far away from her friends and all that had been familiar. A few nights before, as she and Will played Scrabble before the fire, she had mentioned it to him. This, in itself, was surprising. She had come to the cove almost resentfully, simply because she did not know what else to do. To admit that it was working was tantamount to saying that there had been nothing in her previous life that was worth retaining. Normally she would not have allowed anyone to suspect such a thing but somehow Will was different. She could trust him to understand; she could expose weaknesses, put weapons into his hands, knowing that he would never use them against her.

'I feel the same,' he'd said at once. 'Odd, isn't it? All those years in Geneva and now it's as if they never happened. Not true, of course. We carry our experience and memories with us. We're lucky, you and I, Bea. We had no ties to keep us from starting a whole new life.'

Bea fiddled with her tiles, thinking of Norah and of Tony. She knew that these friendships had been part of her school life and that it had been unrealistic to think that they would survive beyond it.

'It's sad though,' she'd said, thinking particularly of Norah. 'Rather selfish to pass people over when they no longer fit in to your life.'

'It all depends on what you mean by "passing people over",' remarked Will. 'If you're thinking of Norah then I think you'll find that she's just as happy, if not happier, without you. It wouldn't have worked, you know, and then you'd have fallen out. As it is, you're keeping in touch with her. She'll probably come down to see you in the summer and the friendship remains ready to be called upon in an emergency.'

Bea sighed and began to arrange tiles upon the board. 'You're probably right,' she said. 'Why does one feel guilty when the right thing just happens to be the thing that one wants? I can't help feeling selfish in knowing that what is right for Norah is exactly what I want.'

Will smiled. 'Poor Bea,' he said. 'What an uncomfortable companion a conscience is. Cheer up. When she comes down for a week you'll soon see it in perspective.'

'You're a cynic,' Bea had said – but she was laughing. She knew that he was right. A day or two of Norah's self-righteous whining would bring all her own intolerance to the surface. 'But you've got a point. We're better apart.'

Will jotted down her score whilst Bea delved for

some more tiles. 'Anyone else you're regretting?' he'd asked casually.

The silence had been a long one. 'Not really,' Bea had said at last. 'Just . . . just someone I rather cared for. Married, of course. Nothing to it except my own foolish imagination.'

'Very painful, that sort of attachment,' said Will thoughtfully. 'Best to get free of it, perhaps?'

He'd left the question hanging in the air and Bea had remained silent.

Now, as she walked on the cliff she thought about Tony Priest. She conjured up his image but, for some reason, it no longer had the power to disturb her. He seemed remote, unreal, and she wondered that she had ever allowed herself to become so romantically attached to him.

'Like a schoolgirl,' she muttered, 'with a crush on a film star.'

She took a deep breath, as though she would dispel all such negative and humiliating thoughts, and looked about her. So immersed in thought had she been that she had not noticed that the mist was rolling in from the sea. The sun had completely disappeared and the soft grey clouds were now pouring across the cliffs, shrouding tree and rock and obliterating the familiar landmarks. Bea knew a moment of real anxiety. Trying to be calm, she stood quite still and listened. If she could hear the sea then at least she could keep well away from the edge of the cliff. She could work her way back to the field and make her way along the hedge.

She strained her ears but was unable to hear any noise. The mist, clothing her now in moisture, had

271

the effect of deadening all sound. Bea pushed down
a tendency to panic. She had been walking back to
the path that led down to the beach, therefore the
sea was on her left; but which was her left? She had
stopped to look about her and now she couldn't
decide which way she had been facing. Bea felt
utterly disorientated; afraid to go either forward or
back. Tentatively she took a few steps in what she
hoped was the right direction. She stepped into a
hole, stumbled, and fell to her knees amongst some
gorse, crying out with pain as her hands plunged
down amongst the spines and prickles. Kneeling
there she gave a dry little sob, raising her head and
straining to hear some sound that might guide her
forward. Silence. The mist flowed over and around
her, thick and wet, chilling her. She cried out, her
voice thin and insubstantial. Scrambling to her feet
she shouted again but the clouds seemed to bear
her voice downwards, drowning and muffling it. As
she stood helplessly, near to tears, she heard a noise.
Straining every muscle and nerve, she peered about
her. 'Help!' she screamed again. 'Help! Please!'
Something appeared suddenly out of the mist beside
her and she stifled a scream. The collie from the
neighbouring farm, gave a brief wag of the tail and
hurried on. He had been rabbiting on the cliff but
he knew it was time to start for home.

'Wait!' cried Bea. 'Stay! Sit! Come back. Please.'

The dog paused, looking back enquiringly and
already barely visible as the mist washed over him,
and Bea ran to him and grasped his collar. Holding
on to it tightly she stroked his head with her
free hand, feeling a measure of comfort at the

feel of his warm hairy body against her leg.

'Good boy,' she said. 'Now then, go slowly. Good boy, then.'

The dog was puzzled but his tail wagged once or twice as he watched her with bright intelligent eyes.

'Come on then,' she encouraged him. 'Good boy. Come on.'

He set off again, Bea almost running at his side, but he did not keep to the short turf or the well-worn path. He was heading for the farm and he took her across country; her feet stumbling into shallow holes, her ankles scratched by gorse and heather. By now the mist was all-enveloping and she could see nothing. The dog, however, trotted confidently forward and she clutched at his collar, grateful for his presence. Suddenly he paused and braced himself. Bea, grasping even more tightly at his collar, sensed that he was about to jump.

'Wait!' she cried. 'Wait a minute.'

She thrust her hand forward and cracked her knuckles on the wooden bar of a farm gate. Pulling him with her she felt for the bolt, praying that it wasn't lashed up with binder twine as was so often the case. Her fingers encountered the smooth clammy iron of a thick hook and she lifted it up and pushed the gate open, shutting it carefully after they had passed through. On they went, across the cropped grass of a field laid down to permanent pasture. The going was easier now but Bea was panting as she hurried along with him. The next gate stood open and Bea found herself splashing through mud and water where the cattle had poached the path into the farmyard.

She caught back a cry of alarm as a tractor loomed from the mist beside her and she shook her head at her fear. She saw the shapes of the farm-buildings and knew that she was safely at the farm in the lane. The track down to the cove was a few hundred yards away. The dog had stopped politely, clearly anxious to find warmth and food. Bea patted him as she released him, flexing her stiff fingers.

'Thanks,' she said. 'Good boy.'

He disappeared towards the outbuildings and Bea picked her way carefully out into the lane, watching for the entrance to the track. She turned into it, her heart beating fast with relief, her feet slithering on the loose stones. She realised that she was trembling, and tried to pull herself together. Near the bottom of the path she heard voices calling to her. She recognised Will's deeper voice chiming with Isobel's anxious one and, with an answering cry, she went to meet them.

Will and Isobel had been in the kitchen when the mist rolled in. Tessa had just telephoned and Will was discussing this call with Isobel.

'I'm a bit confused,' he admitted. 'Apparently Giles is staying with her. Do you know this Giles?'

Isobel, perched on a kitchen chair, feet on the rung, shook her head. 'Sure it's not Sebastian?'

'Quite sure.' Will sat in Mathilda's chair by the Rayburn, frowning. 'He phoned us for her number, d'you see? This Giles. He's on the list she gave me so I could give it to him. It seems he went straight down to her when he heard the terrible news.'

'It's awful.' Isobel shivered. 'Poor Tessa.'

'Quite. So this Giles goes haring down. Nice chap, by the sound of it.' He glanced at Isobel. 'What did you think of Sebastian?'

She pursed her lips and wrinkled her nose. 'OK,' she said. 'He's nice. Good-looking. It's just . . . I felt he wasn't quite right for her. And she was . . . nervous. Or something.' She shook her head. 'I don't know. What did you think?'

'It's difficult,' said Will. 'I'm not sure I can judge. I'm so fond of her that I'm afraid I might feel that no one was quite good enough for her. Anyway, they're coming home together. With Sidney.'

'Sidney? Who's Sidney?'

Will sighed. 'He's the dog. The other woman turned up to collect her dog, d'you see, and she told Tessa that it will be some time before anyone will be thinking about what to do with Sidney. The mother lives in a flat in London and the children will be going to their father.'

'Can't he have the dog?' asked Isobel, faintly confused. 'What's the problem? Surely Sidney would be a comfort if they've just lost their mother?'

'Tessa explained it to me,' said Will, 'but it was all the least bit confusing. The father has re-married and his new wife won't have Sidney in the house. I told Tessa to bring him here for the time being.'

Their eyes met; Will's guilty, Isobel's alarmed.

'What will Bea say?' asked Isobel. 'She's not too keen on dogs, is she? Oh hell!'

'I know,' said Will miserably. 'But what could I do? Poor Tessa is in a frightful state.'

'Perhaps it'll be OK. I could have him in the

cottage. Where *is* Bea? Is she still out? There's a mist rolling in.'

They both glanced involuntarily at the window. 'Heavens!' said Will. 'It's come down a bit, hasn't it?' He stood up and went to the back door.

'Is she up on the cliff?' Isobel followed him. 'God! It's really thick! She'll be frightened. Oh, Will! I hope she's OK. Let's go and meet her.'

She was pulling on her coat, awful visions of Bea alone on the cliff, and worse. Will was already out of the door, much the same thoughts in his head.

'She might have gone up the track,' he said. 'She often walks in the lane.'

'Shall we separate?' asked Isobel anxiously. 'I'll go up the cliff path. You go up the track.'

'Certainly not,' said Will sharply. 'Then I'd have both of you lost up there.'

'Oh, Will.' Isobel sounded frightened. 'People fall off the cliff sometimes and the coastguard gets called out. Well, it's usually dogs, actually, or people cut off by the tide. Should we telephone the coastguard?'

'Wait,' said Will. 'Just wait a minute before we get panicky. We'll go a little way up the track and, if there's no sign of her, we'll try the cliffs.'

'But if she's on the track she'll be OK,' argued Isobel. 'It's the cliffs I'm worried about.'

'I see that,' said Will, more calmly than he felt, 'but if she's on her way home it's pointless for us to go crashing about on the cliffs. Let's just check.'

Isobel took his arm, thinking about Mathilda and imagining Bea stuck on a ledge – or . . .

Will squeezed her arm beneath his own. 'Let's shout,' he suggested. 'Ready?'

Their voices sounded reedy and Isobel shivered. 'Bea!' she shouted again, with more energy, and Will joined in with her. They stopped abruptly, each clutching the other, as an answering hail came from the mist ahead.

'Oh, Will!' cried Isobel, nearly weeping in her relief. 'It's her. She's on the track. Oh, thank God!'

When they drew the shivering Bea into the warmth of the kitchen, they both exclaimed at the state of her hands and feet.

'What's happened to you, Bea?' asked Isobel. 'All those cuts on your hands – and it looks as if you've been paddling in mud. Your trousers are soaked.'

'It's nothing serious,' said Bea, kicking off her shoes, and finding that she was still trembling uncontrollably. 'Honestly. Please don't fuss.'

'Tea,' said Will, getting busy, 'and then a hot bath and clean warm clothes. You'll soon be right.'

'Were you worrying?' asked Bea, with an attempt at lightness.

'We were when we saw that the mist had come down,' said Isobel. 'Before that we were engrossed in Tessa's problems.'

'What's happened now?' Bea was glad to have the attention taken away from her own plight. She was not quite ready yet to admit to her fear or that she hadn't been keeping an eye on the weather.

'Well,' began Isobel – and paused as Will shot her a warning glance. 'Well, someone called Giles telephoned for her number and when he heard about this terrible tragedy he went rushing down from London to see her.'

277

Bea frowned a little. 'Giles?' she repeated. 'I thought his name was Sebastian?'

'Another chap,' said Will succinctly. 'Old friend. Nice chap. Tessa's on her way home and he's coming with her. They're driving in tandem. Tessa's a bit overwrought so he's coming along to keep an eye, as it were.'

Bea raised her eyebrows as she accepted a large mug of hot tea. 'Thank you, Will. It sounds a very philanthropic gesture to me. Old friend or not.'

'That's what we thought,' said Isobel eagerly. 'Why isn't Sebastian there?'

'Be fair,' said Will. 'Can't just jump ship like that. The Navy has responsibilities. There would be chaos if every sailor thought he could dash off each time some drama occurred on the home front.'

Isobel looked sceptical; Bea sipped her tea thoughtfully. Will passed a mug of tea to Isobel, wondering how to approach the next part of the story.

'She's got a bit of a problem,' he began carefully. 'Woman dead, two children to worry about, not to mention the dog. Woman's mother still out in France. Terrible thing! Tessa's bringing Sidney with her, just until things are sorted out, d'you see?'

'Sidney?' Bea looked at him enquiringly. 'Sidney? Is he one of the children? How are we going to cope with a child here?'

Will sighed. He had a sense of *déjà vu*. 'Sidney's the dog,' he explained. 'He's a clumber spaniel. Tessa can't just leave him alone in the house until they all come back from France. I said she could bring him but I know that I should have checked with you first. Trouble was, it was all a bit sudden, d'you see? You weren't here and Tessa was naturally very upset . . .'

He stopped, aware that he was gabbling. He and Isobel watched her anxiously, waiting for her usual criticism on the unsuitability of names given to the modern dog. Bea sat quietly sipping her tea, remembering the collie's patient intelligence and bright eye; the feel of his soft hair under her hand; the comfort of his warm body against her cold legs; the way he had unerringly led her to safety. She smiled a little, catching the worried glance that slipped between the two of them.

'I'm sure that we can manage,' she said serenely. 'He'll find it strange in a new place. I hope Tessa's remembered to bring his bed.' She finished her tea and stood up, a little shakily. 'I'll go and have that bath,' she said, 'and then we must think about what to give Tessa and Giles for supper.'

Chapter Twenty-five

Giles drove carefully along the A303, his eyes on
the tailgate of Tessa's car. From the back window
Sidney watched him mournfully, cocking his head
occasionally when Tessa spoke to him but turning
back again to watch Giles in the car behind. He had
made a great hit with Sidney. Giles felt a tiny surge
of triumph and elation as he remembered Tessa's
greeting. She had been waiting for him, the front
door open the moment he pulled in outside the gate,
hurrying down the path with Sidney at her heels.
She had hesitated momentarily and then flung
herself into his arms.

'Oh, Giles, I can't tell you how good it is to see
you.'

He had held her without fuss, taking no advantage
of this warm greeting, merely comforting her.

'It's a beastly thing to have happened,' he said.
Still holding her in one arm, he bent to pat Sidney
who was sniffing cautiously at his jeans.

'That's Sidney.' Tessa released herself, ashamed
of her outburst. 'He's feeling it a bit. He's one of
these dogs who can't cope with a bad atmosphere.
The other family came and took Harry and there
was a bit of drama, obviously. The poor woman is
completely gob-smacked by it all.'

By this time they were inside the cottage. Tessa

took him into the kitchen and began to heat some soup, already prepared and waiting in a saucepan on the electric cooker. Giles looked about him and sat down by the table. Immediately Sidney came to sit beside him, head on Giles's knee.

'He slobbers a lot,' warned Tessa.

She sounded more cheerful now and Giles looked at her, taking in her leggings and big sweatshirt and rumpled hair. She'd smiled at him and his heart had crashed about in his breast making him feel breathless. He bent down to stroke Sidney's head, hiding his expression. He was determined to abide by his plan.

'I don't mind a bit of slobber, do I, old chap?' he'd asked. 'Used to that with Felix, aren't I?'

'He's even worse,' said Tessa, taking relief in light chatter. 'His mouth is so loose and soft. But he's a sweetie, if somewhat neurotic.'

'So tell me all about it.' Giles rested an elbow on the table, his feelings for her under control. 'Mr Rainbird told me a bit but I'm not exactly sure what's happened.'

Whilst she explained, serving up the soup and taking hot rolls out of the oven, he watched her intently and presently they sat down together to eat their supper.

Now, as he drove behind her, he marvelled at the strangeness of his feelings. All his life he had been diffident, cautious of change, wary of any alteration to the status quo. He knew that it was a fault in him, to be so unwilling to commit himself, and it worried him as much as it worried his mother. He knew that Kate suffered on his behalf; encouraging and pushing him, yet fearful lest she should be misjudging him. He also knew that she blamed herself for the problems that he had inherited from her unhappy marriage.

He had told her that, from his point of view, the divorce was far from being responsible for his dilatory and unconfident character; on the contrary, he had been relieved when his parents had parted and especially when his father, Mark Webster, had emigrated to Canada when he had not gained his promotion in the Navy. From his earliest days his father's inconsistent approach – now indifferent, now stern and bitingly sarcastic – had unsettled Giles and he was always much happier when Mark returned to sea. Guy, his twin, had been able to cope better and had tried to protect Giles from tongue-lashings and other subtle psychological forms of cruelty when they had visited their father after the divorce. Guy had been more successful in his dealings with Mark and had done his best to stand between his father and his twin.

Giles wondered how he would have coped without the steady kindness of his uncle Chris, his mother's brother, and, later, David Porteous. Seeing David with Kate had restored some of Giles's confidence in the married state but the thought of committing himself to a long-term relationship still filled him with anxiety. He had seen, both with his parents and with his friends, how extraordinarily fragile these structures were. He thought of the responsibility involved and felt a faintness of heart. This, he told himself, was nothing to do with his dilatoriness. It was simply a fear that he would be unable to sustain what was required when the time came.

He was old enough to realise that, once you became a husband or a father, expectations followed close behind. Your wife and children made demands, had requirements, and how were you suddenly to know the right answers? Being a husband or a father did not automatically invest you with knowledge, patience, understanding. Supposing you were unable to supply these quite reasonable demands? If you could not, then you let down your wife and children – and what then?

When his father was Giles's present age, he and Guy had been seven years old. Giles shuddered at the thought. Would he be able to deal with a seven-year-old son? He wondered whether his father's behaviour had been a mask for his own in-adequacies; his weakness and fear had taken the form of verbal bullying and psychological arm-twisting. Might not he – his father's son and the recipient of his genes – react in the same way with his own children? He had read that abused children often became abusers and he felt horrified at the idea of being cruel in his turn to a vulnerable child.

He had been amazed when Guy – more like Mark and less social than Giles – had married Gemma Wivenhoe. That Guy, who found most women a bore, should marry the light-hearted Gemma – who was, moreover, nearly nine years younger – had come as a shock.

'What happened?' he'd asked his twin bluntly. 'Gemma's a sweet kid but you've known her all your life. Why suddenly?'

'Probably because I've known her all my life,' replied Guy honestly. 'I feel safe with her. We know each other. Or, more to the point, she knows me. She knows how to deal with me.'

It was typical that he hadn't mentioned the word 'love'. Giles could see, however, that Gemma adored his brother.

'How does she do it?' he'd asked Kate later. 'She teases him and makes fun of him and simply won't let him bark and bite. What's even more amazing, I don't think he wants to!'

Kate had laughed, shaking her head. 'She's just like her mum,' she'd answered. 'Cass is so good-natured that it's almost impossible to be grumpy when you're with her. You forgive her anything. Gemma's just the same. Guy is very lucky but, thank God, he knows it and he's working at it, too. He'll need to. He's very like Mark. So like him that sometimes I feel ill with terror. I couldn't bear it if he were to hurt Gemma.'

It was then that Giles had told her how he felt about himself and marriage; that his indecisiveness was something apart from a natural fear of committing himself to another human being. She had remained silent for some time.

'I think it *is* part of the same thing,' she'd said at last. 'Sorry, Giles, but you can't separate them. They're part of the same instinctive anxiety. Your natural urge to dither merely underlines your fear of letting people down. I understand and I sympathise but you must try to overcome it. Your reluctance to commit yourself is a really negative trait. You'll miss out on so much. OK, so you'll get things wrong. So do we all. You will hurt and be hurt. It's life. It can be painful but it's better than never living at all.'

'But you say *you* feel guilty because you got it wrong,' he'd argued. 'It's you who say that your mistakes have affected our lives, too. Supposing I turn out like Dad and repeat the pattern all over again?'

'Oh, Giles, I know.' She had looked at him with compassion and remorse. 'It's just that you're not much like Mark and, more importantly, you're aware of your weaknesses and attempt to overcome them. I just hope that when the moment comes it'll sweep you along and you'll forget all these misgivings.'

Giles put a Gerry Mulligan cassette in the car tape deck and listened to the mellow notes of the saxophone. Kate had been right. When Tessa had told him of her engagement to Sebastian all his doubt and caution had been swept away. He knew quite surely that he loved her and that he was going to make a fight for her. He knew, too, that this must be a calm, quiet, determined fight – but he had a strange conviction that he was going to win it.

Tessa, peering in her mirror, checked to see that Giles was still behind her. His quiet strength had been exactly what she needed and she felt grateful.

'I'll drive behind you,' he'd said firmly, 'then you can set the pace and stop when you want to have a cup of coffee or if you feel tired. Don't worry. You won't lose me.'

Nor had she. Every time she overtook a vehicle

or a car pulled out directly behind her, she would glance anxiously in the mirror until she saw Giles's little hatchback closing up behind her. Sidney watched, too. He had been drawn to Giles's calm approach, a pleasant change after the tension of the previous few days, and he wanted to keep him in sight.

'He's nice, isn't he, Sid?' said Tessa. Sidney's ears cocked at the sound of her voice but he continued to stare out of the back window. 'I really like him,' said Tessa thoughtfully. 'I feel like I've known him for ever but there's something about him . . .'

Her voice tailed away. She was remembering with faint embarrassment how she had rushed into his arms. He had taken it all very naturally – and she had been able to regain her composure quite quickly – but she was surprised at the strange conflict of emotion which she had felt in that moment when he had held her closely. The old confusion was back. Why had she not thought of telephoning Sebastian? Because, said an inner voice, he wouldn't have really wanted to be bothered with it all. Tessa felt the need to come to Sebastian's defence. He had been brought up in a service family and was used to seeing his mother cope with all kinds of disasters. The Navy couldn't let its men go on leave each time there was some small domestic crisis or there would be no fighting force left. She knew that she must learn to manage alone and that it was not Sebastian's fault that he could not be on hand every time she felt emotional.

She brooded on this, her respect for naval wives increasing. What a lonely life it must be. Suddenly she remembered something Kate had said to her when she was talking about her divorce from Mark Webster.

'The Navy taught me to live without my husband,' she'd said, 'and then I found I could. It's like giving something up for Lent and then discovering that you don't need it any more.'

Tessa could understand that and, after all, it was no lonelier a life than the one she was leading. She felt an affinity with Mathilda who had lived so contentedly by herself in the cove. No doubt she had known loneliness but she had learned at some point that it was better to be alone than to live with the wrong person. Tessa felt a deep satisfaction at the knowledge that Mathilda, Will, Bea and she, Tessa, shared the same great-great-grandfather. No doubt they also shared similar character traits. Bea had managed quite happily, unmarried, and Will seemed quite ready to move to the relative isolation of the cove. All three of them recognised something familiar in the others; they were family.

Tessa slowed a little to allow Giles to catch up. She tried to see Sebastian fitting in at the cove once they were married and frowned. He had been very polite to Will and Bea but there had been something missing.

'Nice old things,' he'd said, as they drove away up the track with Will waving goodbye on the beach. 'And Isobel's OK. Let's hope she moves on soon and then we can have the cottage when I'm on leave. Can't imagine us bouncing about in bed with that old biddy in the next room. You can tell she was a matron. She's got all the hallmarks. I'd probably be impotent at the mere thought!'

Tessa had tried to laugh with him but she'd felt hurt and upset. Bea and Will were her people and she hated it when he laughed at them. On the other hand, it was exactly as he talked about his own parents. Perhaps, because it was so long since she'd had a family of her own, she was being oversensitive. Tessa felt the now-familiar confusion. She knew that he was right and that it would be quite impossible to make love with Bea in the next room; but she had never contemplated such a thing taking place until they were marrried, any more than she would have considered sharing Sebastian's bedroom at the Andersons'. She tried to be reasonable but simply remained confused. This was what she had longed for and dreamed about for so many years but there was something not quite right somewhere.

She glanced at her mirror. Giles was driving easily, arms relaxed, head on one side. He looked as though he might be listening to music. She knew instinctively that he would not mock Will or Bea, nor suggest that he and she make love in the house in the cove. She felt quite hot at the thought of making love with Giles and experienced a sudden sinking sensation in the pit of her stomach. At that moment she feared that she had got things terribly muddled.

'Surely,' she said aloud – and Sidney turned to look at her – 'surely I'm just being silly and over-emotional? Oh God! Don't let me have got it wrong.'

She bit her lip, driving a little slower now as she tried to sort things out. Could her childhood passion for Sebastian have blinded her? Had she been so infatuated with him that she had never bothered to consider whether they were truly suited? She realised that she was slowing right down and looked quickly in her mirror. Giles flashed his headlights at her and gave her a little wave. She waved back, knowing a desire to burst into tears. His friendly caring gesture confirmed her terrors. She had got herself engaged to the wrong man. She remembered how delighted Mrs Anderson had been, how she'd hugged Tessa and said how thrilled she was to have her as a proper daughter at last. She thought of how Rachel, her oldest friend, had shrieked her joy down the telephone. She recalled the kindnesses of all the Andersons over the last ten years when she had been so lonely and unhappy. Tessa stared miserably at the road before her. She had become engaged to the wrong man and there was absolutely nothing she could do about it. She could never hurt the Andersons after all that they had done for her; without them she would not even have her job.

She was aware that Giles was flashing his head-lights at her and pointing ahead where the bright and cheerful sign of a Happy Eater café glowed. Tessa understood what he was trying to tell her and pressed her indicator. She guessed that he had read her slowing down as a sign of weariness and was suggesting that it was time for a break. Grate-fully she pulled into the car park and began to reverse into a space by some grass. Sidney whined anxiously.

'Shut up, Sid,' she said automatically. 'Don't fuss. I'm just about to give you a run.'

Somehow the familiar action of opening the

tailgate and freeing Sidney had the effect of calming her and she was able to greet Giles with a smile.

'Good idea,' she said. 'I was getting a bit tired.'

'I thought you might be,' he said as they strolled behind Sidney. 'You must be exhausted after all the traumas. Shall I go and order some coffee?'

'I suppose . . .' she began reluctantly, not wanting him to go, willing him to remain with her. 'If you . . . Yes, why not?'

'It'll save a bit of time,' he said, pretending not to notice her hesitation. 'Don't want to hurry Sidney. See you in a moment.'

He disappeared through the swing door and Tessa felt a moment of despair. She longed for him to put his arms round her, kiss her, tell her he loved her. Instead he was behaving as though he were a very nice elder brother.

'What else can he do?' she asked herself drearily. 'Oh shit, hell, damn.'

Giles watched her from the window, longing to rush out and seize her but knowing that he must hold back: his moment had not yet come. He pulled the cups closer and began to pour coffee for them both.

Chapter Twenty-six

Adrian Pearson, his car parked in a lay-by in a quiet lane, was making calculations on a small pad. He raised his head, his brain busy, and stared unseeingly at a cow in a neighbouring field. He was doing very well indeed. Mentally he reviewed his list of victims and wondered which of them he should next approach. Mrs Carrington had nothing else of value but there were one or two others in this area . . . Adrian tapped his pen thoughtfully against his teeth. The Rainbirds had not yet contacted him. He frowned, turning the pages in the pad until he came to the inventory he'd made at the house in the cove. As he read it through, excitement began to mount; he couldn't possibly let this one pass. He remembered the desperation which the old buffer had not quite been able to hide and wondered if he were still trying to overcome his scruples or his sentimentality for the pieces. The old bat had been ready to sell, he'd swear to it.

Adrian gave a sigh of pure irritation and snapped his notebook shut. Maybe the time had come for a tiny nudge, a gentle reminder . . . He wondered what the old couple had said to Tessa – and did it matter? After all, they clearly needed to raise money and selling some family heirlooms was the obvious way to do it. He shrugged, flicked the book open again and picked up his mobile telephone. The woman answered almost immediately.

'Ah.' Adrian was caught slightly off balance. For some reason he had expected Mr Rainbird. 'Hello. Miss Rainbird? It's Adrian Pearson here.'

'She's not here,' said the woman. 'Who did you say it was?'

Adrian was puzzled. 'It's Adrian Pearson. The antique dealer. I think we met when I came down to the cove.'

'Ah, yes,' said the woman. 'Of course. Well, Tessa's not here. Shall I take a message?'

'Oh, I see.' He laughed in a conciliatory way. 'I do apologise. I thought that you were Miss Rainbird too, you see.'

'My name is Beatrice Holmes,' she said flatly.

'Yes,' he said awkwardly into the silence and cursing her lack of friendliness. 'Well, I seem doomed to miss Tessa, don't I? Uh . . . any other thoughts about the conversation we had? Any movement there? I'm in the area again for a day or two. I'd be very happy to pop over.'

'I'm sure you know my feeling in the matter, Mr . . . er. My cousin, however, is full of the finer feelings and is having difficulty in bringing himself to the point. It's only a matter of time.'

'I see.' Adrian's spirits began to rise again. She might be an old cow but she was much easier to deal with than these dithering old idiots who wanted to hang on to their relics. He chuckled, trying to introduce a more friendly note into the proceedings. 'Is he there? Would you like me to have a little chat with him? You know? Encourage him a bit?'

The conspiratorial note seemed to soften her a little. 'We-ell, it's not a bad notion, I suppose. He has to be pushed into every decision he takes. Quite exhausting! I'm afraid he isn't here at the moment. Perhaps you could try again later. Have we your telephone number?'

'It's on the card,' said Adrian quickly. 'The London office and my mobile. There's no point in giving you any other number. I move around such a lot. Have you still got my card?'

There was a pause whilst paper was shuffled about at the other end of the line. Presently her voice read out the number of his mobile telephone.

'That's it!' he said cheerfully. 'Excellent. Well, I'll give you a bell later this afternoon, shall I? Meanwhile you can get hold of me on that number unless I'm with a client.'

He switched off and stared out through the windscreen. It looked as if all would be well. 'It's only a matter of time,' she'd said – and there had been no mention of Tessa. Adrian took a deep breath and beat the steering wheel lightly with a triumphant fist. He glanced at his watch. He had one other call to make and then he would be free. The old chap might be back by then and he could give him a nice gentle going-over; a hint that he might not be able to place the pieces if he didn't have them soon; an indication that he might have to drop his offer because of other pieces he'd seen of greater value . . .

Adrian put his notes into his briefcase, shifted in his seat and fastened his seat belt. With luck he might have the whole thing sewn up by this time tomorrow.

* * *

'I gather that it was my name that you were taking in vain?' asked Will, placidly turning the page of the *Kingsbridge Gazette* at the kitchen table. 'Was it our nice friendly crook?'

'It was.' Bea sat down opposite. 'What are we going to do about him?'

Will crossed his arms and brought his mind to bear on Adrian Pearson. 'According to James, there's nothing we *can* do,' he said regretfully.

'Nothing legal, perhaps,' said Bea. 'I know we can't get him locked up but perhaps we could give him a good fright.'

Will looked interested. 'Got any ideas?'

'Not yet,' she admitted. 'All this business with Tessa has put him out of my mind but surely if he knew that we know he's a crook . . . ?'

Will ran his hand through his hair and gazed into the middle-distance; Bea watched him with well-concealed affection. She tried to analyse these new sensations and decided that they were summed up in the word 'contentment'. Her life with Will was without passion but it was deeply satisfying. He was companionable, but left her room to breathe, and his cheerful kindness made him an ideal person with whom to share her home and her life. It was hardly odd that she was barely able to contemplate a different existence.

Bea looked about her. The French windows stood open to the balcony and the room was filled with bright trembling light. Sidney lay stretched out in the May sunshine and she realised that his presence was fast becoming as familiar as the gentle, persistent whisper of the sea. The cries of the gulls could be heard above the sound of the Morris jolting down the track. Isobel was home.

Will, too, had heard the engine and straightened a little in his chair. He could not prevent the upward leaping of his heart at the thought of seeing her; dark, tall, eager. He hated to think of her being unhappy; longed to shoulder her burdens and surround her with his love. Sometimes he imagined her accepting that love, marrying him; would he ever have the courage to ask her? Sometimes, when her loneliness brought her across to the house to sit and talk or play Scrabble, he thought that he might. He knew that he had helped her with her grief and guilt about Mathilda but he was sure that she still loved Simon and that his marriage had hurt her deeply. So, too, had the continuing indifference of her daughter. Like Mathilda before him, Will knew that Isobel was happiest when she was needed.

Sidney raised his head. He, too, had heard Isobel's approach and his tail began to thump. He was happier than he had ever been, since his master's defection, here in the cove and he padded in through the French windows so that when Isobel opened the kitchen door they were all waiting for her.

Her hair was constrained by a twisted silk scarf and she wore a cherry-coloured T-shirt tucked into a long swirling skirt of navy and red, her waist clasped by a wide leather belt. She was carrying a bunch of narcissi in one hand and a bottle of claret in the other and she looked radiant. Will clamped himself to his chair with both hands, lest he should leap up and embrace her, and it was left to Bea to say: 'How summery you look. Goodness! Are they for me?' as Isobel deposited the flowers beside her and held out the wine to Will.

He freed his hands and took it, smiling at her. Something wonderful had happened to her, he could see that at once, and he wondered what could possibly make her look like a young girl in love. He was filled with a horrid foreboding. Perhaps Simon had come to his senses at last and wanted her back. Will stood up quickly so that she should not see the anxiety he was, for the moment, unable to hide and he was grateful for Bea's calm voice asking Isobel what good fortune had blessed her.

'Oh, it's the most fantastic, unbelievable thing,' she was crying as she sank down at the table and hugged Sidney. 'You'll never believe it. *I* can't. I've waited so long.'

Will kept his back to the table, pretending to fiddle at the draining board so that they should not see the sudden tremor of his hands.

'Don't keep us in suspense,' Bea was saying. 'We don't know whether to offer you coffee or champagne. Not that we've got any. So what is this fantastic and unbelievable thing?'

'I've been into Kingsbridge,' she said, trying in vain to control the joy in her voice, 'and I popped into the shop, just to give a message to Pat, and she had a letter for me. Oh, it's just so amazing! I didn't recognise the writing to begin with – well, it's been so long – and I thought it might be a customer. Just occasionally they write to thank you for getting a book or something, so I just shoved it in my bag and went over to Somerfields. And when I'd done my shopping I was just sitting in the car getting my keys out and I saw the letter and opened it.' She took a great breath, half laughing, half sobbing. 'Oh, you'll never guess. It's from Helen. She couldn't remember my address, you see, so she sent it to the shop. She's written from Durham and she's asked if we could meet. Oh, can you believe it? I feel that I might just burst into tears,' said Isobel – and did so.

She stretched her arms out on the table, buried her face in them and wept. Sidney watched her anxiously and moved closer to Will who, weak with relief, turned round at last to look at her. Bea grimaced comically at him and patted Isobel on the shoulder.

'It is certainly wonderful news, my dear. Definitely bottle-worthy. How about that wine you've got there, Will?'

'Absolutely.' Will pulled himself together. 'Or perhaps something a little lighter. I've got a rather pleasant Chardonnay, haven't I, Sidney old chap . . . ?' He talked to himself and Sidney, attempting to reassure Sidney and bring himself under control. For one terrible moment it had seemed that he might be going to lose Isobel. 'Glasses,' he murmured. 'Corkscrew . . .' He touched Isobel briefly on passing and she gripped his hand, still sobbing. He held on tightly, swallowing a little, and smiled at Bea, who watched tolerantly. She had no idea of Will's real feelings for Isobel but saw that he was moved by her happiness.

'I thought I'd never see her again, you see,' explained Isobel, mopping her cheeks. 'Sorry. I'm just completely over the top.'

'And why not?' asked Will. 'I am so happy for you. Does she suggest a time for this meeting?'

'Well, she's just about to do her finals.' Isobel fished the letter out of her bag. 'And it seems that she's been offered a research job at Bristol University.' She glanced down the page. 'She's coming down at the end of June and has asked if we could meet then. She doesn't say much else.'

'It must have been a rather difficult letter to write,' remarked Bea thoughtfully. 'After all this time.'

'It is a bit tentative,' agreed Isobel, 'but it's a start. I shall write back at once. No reproaches or recriminations. I shall say that I can't wait to see her.'

Will smiled at this eager generosity. 'Good for you,' he said. 'Where will it take place?'

'Here,' said Isobel at last. 'At the cottage. I know it's on my ground but she has no place down here and I can hardly go to Modbury. I don't want to meet in a pub or some public place.'

'Well, here's to a new beginning.' Will distributed glasses. 'May the meeting be crowned with success . . .'

It was after lunch, when Isobel had disappeared to the cottage to write her letter to Helen, that the subject of Adrian Pearson resurfaced. Will dialled the London number and spoke to a young woman who confirmed that Adrian Pearson was one of their agents. She told him that the items purchased were distributed to various showrooms throughout the country. The agents were given a list of pieces that were required so that they were usually placed very quickly, often to a waiting customer, which was why the agents were able to pay cash at once.

'No joy there,' reported Will to Bea, 'although I should like to have a look at that office. Pity London is so far away. They count on that, I expect.'

Bea stared at him. 'Giles!' she said, as one inspired. 'Giles could go and check it out.'

'Brilliant!' said Will softly. 'So he could. That would be a start.'

'Once we know what's going on that end,' said Bea, 'we might have some idea as to how to lay a trap for him. Meanwhile, perhaps we should let him visit us again. Just to keep him on the hook.'

'I'll phone Tessa for Giles's number and then I'll phone Mr Pearson,' said Will. 'I must say I rather liked that boy.'

'Giles?' Bea began to stack the washing-up on the wooden draining board. 'Mmm. I think he's in love with her.'

'It sounds silly,' said Will, picking up the tea cloth and standing by, 'but I felt that he was more right with her than Sebastian, if you know what I mean.'

'Well, he's older, of course, less bumptious,' Bea plunged her hands into the soapy water.

'I hope she's not making a mistake,' said Will worriedly.

'What an old mother hen you are,' said Bea affectionately. 'First Isobel. Now Tessa. Perhaps it's as well that you had no children to worry about.'

Will began to put away the plates, glad that Bea

assumed that his feelings for Isobel were purely paternal. There was no need yet to rock the boat. He knew that Bea would not like the idea of him and Isobel getting together, although they need not be far away; he could move over to the cottage, leaving the house for Bea. And Tessa and Sebastian? Of course, the boathouse could be converted . . .

'Come on.' Bea was hustling him. 'Make that phone call. I feel just in the right mood for a bit of a run-in with our Mr Pearson.'

Will abandoned his musings with relief. It was rather complicated working out the logistics of fitting everyone into the cove but he had no doubt that, given time, it could be done. Drying his hands he went to find Adrian's card.

Adrian switched off his mobile with relief. It was so much more satisfactory to have the clients ring rather than having to chase them up. Looking too keen was a very bad mistake. The old chap had invited him to tea. Adrian grinned to himself; very couth. Mr Rainbird had been trying not to sound too anxious but that might simply be because the old bat was breathing down his neck.

He laughed a little, the usual exhilaration sending the adrenalin flowing through his veins. How he enjoyed the chase and the kill! He turned off the A38 and headed towards Kingsbridge, planning his campaign. He'd start by being less confident, this time; notice a few flaws he'd ignored on that first visit; show a little anxiety as to where he might place the stuff. He'd get them on the run all right and tie the whole thing up. He thrust his foot down on the accelerator and overtook a tractor dangerously and at speed. Those lovely pieces were as good as his.

Chapter Twenty-seven

Isobel lay on her face on the beach, the sun hot on her back. Will and Bea had taken a picnic up on to the moor and she had the cove to herself. The heat seemed to press upon her, relaxing her but sapping her energy. The excitement of the last few weeks had exhausted her. She had written a long letter to Helen and then lived in terror lest she had overdone it. She worried as to whether she had been too eager, too gushing, and feared this might frighten Helen away. She was like her father, calm and quiet, and, on reflection, a gentle approach would have been more sensible. Her relief, when another letter arrived from Helen a week later, was overwhelming. The content of this letter had been more relaxed and Helen wrote that she was revising like mad and feeling very nervous about her exams. She agreed to come to the cove, when she arrived back from university, with the proviso that there should be no one else present but she and Isobel.

Isobel guessed that this was because she had written enthusiastically about Bea and Will – not to mention Sidney – and Helen feared that a reception committee might be waiting for her. There was no danger of that. Isobel wanted her daughter absolutely to herself. There was so much catching up to do; nearly five years of lost time. As she thought about this, Isobel became increasingly nervous. It would be like meeting a stranger. When she left Simon, Helen had been a child still; now she was an adult. Isobel stretched her arms out and dug her fingers into the sand at the edge of the rug. How, she asked herself for the thousandth time, could she have abandoned her husband and daughter for a man like Mike? How could she have flung away all that she had for a moment of madness? She wondered how many other women, on the brink of middle age, lost all that was precious and dear to them, all that they'd worked for and achieved, because of a brief descent into boredom and restlessness. Her misfortune had been to have a Mike ready to distract and charm her; to alleviate that boredom and soothe the restlessness with placebos that brought only temporary relief. She had seen her life with Simon as dreary and uneventful; a domestic desert, especially now that Helen was growing up. Mike had offered excitement and fun which she had believed to be happiness.

'But how do you define happiness?' she heard Mathilda asking. *'Do you mean joy? Or do you mean contentment? If you mean some kind of ephemeral excitement bound up with physical gratification, then I must reject your values.'*

How well she summed it up, thought Isobel, rolling over and crossing her arms across her eyes. Ephemeral excitement bound up with physical gratification expressed it very neatly but it certainly did not add up to happiness.

'I was mad,' she said aloud. 'Quite mad. And I've paid for it.'

Now, however, the dark clouds had drawn back a little and the sunshine was breaking through. Helen was coming to see her. The familiar mixture of joy and terror gripped Isobel's stomach. It simply had to work between them; there must be no more misunderstandings. Again she wondered what had made Helen write the letter. Why this change of heart? Was it simply that she was growing up at last and could approach the whole subject with more tolerance? Perhaps she herself had experienced an unhappy love affair? Perhaps it was simply that she missed Isobel? She was, after all, her mother and, however wonderful Sally might be, there was no blood tie. It might be that Simon was more pre-occupied with Sally now that they were married and had less time for his daughter. Was that why Helen had not asked him for her address but had sent the letter to the bookshop?

Isobel stretched lazily. Speculation was useless. It might be any number of things but, in the end, it really didn't matter. Helen was coming to see her. She started up violently as Sidney thrust his cold nose into her neck. It was rather hot for him in the car and, since the moor offered very little shade, it had been decided that Sidney should remain at home. Isobel had agreed to look after him and he had been left in the kitchen until the car had disappeared up the track, lest he tried to follow them. He preferred to have Will within sight or sound but Isobel made a fairly satisfactory sub-stitute. As soon as the car was gone, Isobel let Sidney out so that he could stretch full length on the slate path in the shade behind the house.

Now he was in need of company and Isobel sat up and slipped an arm around his neck. He licked her nose briefly and sat staring out to sea, his silky white coat glistening in the sun.

'How about a little walk?' she whispered into his long ear, which twitched slightly as she blew on it. 'It'll be a bit cooler up on the cliff and you might see a rabbit.'

Sidney's tail moved slightly at the word. Since he'd come to live at the cove he knew all about rabbits. Not that he'd ever caught one but he lived in hope. Isobel stood up and wrapped a cotton skirt about her waist, thinking about Sidney's family; the poor dead mother and the two children. Tessa had told her the story and Isobel wondered how much the children missed Sidney; how they were coping with a new stepmother who hated dogs and who had refused to have Sidney in the house. Isobel wondered, too, how this dog-hater had taken to the two children and why the father had left them and their mother in the first place. Perhaps the man, like herself, had been seeking after the elusive bluebird of happiness. As she strolled towards the cliff path, Sidney trotting expectantly before her, Isobel remembered Mathilda's question and her own answer.

'*And did you find happiness?*'

'*No. But it was worth trying for, surely?*'

Isobel looked out over the dazzling brilliance of the sea, hearing Mathilda's voice in reply.

'*That rather depends on what you lost in the attempt.*'

Until now the answer to that had been, simply,

'everything'. Now it was different. Helen was coming to see her.

Giles emerged from his dark room and went into his tiny galley kitchen to make himself some supper. His work derived mainly from catalogue and fashion photography but he was being used now by the tourists boards and glossy magazines which dealt with country pursuits. His reputation was at last beginning to build and he was able to convince himself that he could make a fairly good living from his work. As to whether or not it was good enough to support a wife, he could not yet be certain. As he stir-fried his vegetables he thought of Tessa. He had enjoyed his trip to the cove and had taken immediately to Will and Bea. He fully understood how Tessa felt about this new family of hers and was moved by their evident affection for her. To be sure, Bea's keen glance had given him cause to wonder if he needed a haircut and made him wish that he'd cleaned his shoes but the feeling soon passed. Will had been interested in his work and he'd been surprised at how readily he'd opened up to him, telling him of the pitfalls and the disappointments of his career.

It was rare for the reticent Giles to be so forthcoming but Will was easy to talk to and genuinely interested. In the end they had persuaded him to stay the night. The woman from the cottage, Isobel Stangate, had offered her spare room and Giles had readily accepted. It had given him an opportunity to spend more time with Tessa and to become more familiar with the place she now knew as home. He had fallen in love with the cove and the cliffs above it and had taken some photographs – Giles never travelled without his photographic equipment – which he was hoping to use in conjunction with the South Hams Tourist Board.

Giles tipped the food on to a plate and took it into his living room. It was a studio flat and this room doubled as his bedroom, the sofa opening out into a bed. It was the darkroom that had persuaded him to look at a flat in such an expensive area; that and the fact that his mother had inherited some property and money from a friend who had died in rather tragic circumstances. Kate, at a loss as to what to do with such unexpected wealth, had insisted that Giles accepted some help from her. Guy had recently made the trip to Canada to see his father, and had returned with enough money to set up his chandlery business in Dartmouth, but Giles could not bring himself to visit the man who had caused his mother and himself such unhappiness. Naturally, therefore, no money was forthcoming from his father for Giles's career and, in the end, he had accepted his mother's assistance with gratitude.

He wondered now, as he ate his supper, whether it was the manifestation of their father's unsociable genes which had pushed him and Guy into careers which relied on no one but themselves to operate. Obviously both of them relied on clients but these remained on the periphery of their lives. Giles felt his old anxiety returning and quickly fixed his mind on Tessa. He must not weaken. Each time he saw Tessa he was confirmed in his certainty that he could be a marriageable viability. Although the least conceited of men, he felt sure that she loved him. There was a rightness that gave him confidence. He was well aware of her difficulty and this was the thing that exercised his mind a great deal. He knew how much she owed the Andersons and how much it would upset her to break the engagement. Her loyalty would be called into question and the friendship threatened.

As he sat with his long legs stretched out in front of him, his dark head bent over his plate, Giles racked his brains for some painless way of extracting Tessa from the engagement. He wondered if Sebastian truly loved her or whether it had been some momentary madness. After all, it had taken him long enough to get round to it. Giles forked up the last mouthful and set the plate on the cushion beside him. On his return to London, he had telephoned Kate and told her the whole story. She had listened in silence until he had announced his decision to fight for Tessa.

'Great,' she'd said briefly. 'Go for it.'

He'd laughed – and then hesitated; a shadow of his former fear looming. 'You don't think . . . ?'

'No,' said Kate. 'I don't. I know Sebastian and I'm quite certain he isn't right for Tessa. And her infatuation for him is just part of all that tragedy of losing her family. It's her need to love and be loved. It just happened that he was there at the vital moment. Don't dither! Go for it.'

'I just don't know how she'd cope with breaking the engagement. She owes the Andersons so much.'

'That's true,' said Kate thoughtfully, 'but there's

no need to immolate herself as a sacrifice on the altar of friendship. No good to anyone. But I take your point. And then again she must feel an awful twit, poor girl.'

'Why?' asked Giles, indignant at even the least slight on Tessa.

'Come on,' said Kate scornfully. 'Think about it. She's been mad about him for years and suddenly he asks her to marry him just when she falls in love with someone else. Poor old Tessa! She must be kicking herself.'

'Of course we don't know that she's . . . you know . . . fallen in love with me.' He felt rather embarrassed at saying the words but at the same time, filled with exultation.

'Yes we do,' said Kate. He could hear the smile in her voice. '*You* do.'

'How d'you mean?'

'Why do you think you're suddenly behaving like Attila the Hun and his boys?' she teased. 'Ah, 'tis love, 'tis love . . .'

'Shut up!' he'd said – but he was laughing too. 'OK. But keep your fingers crossed.'

'And everything else,' she promised. 'David and I will try to think of some way of getting her out of this mess.'

'Are you going to tell him?' he'd asked, rather disconcerted, his usual reticence up in arms.

'Only David,' she'd said wheedlingly. 'No one else, I promise. But I must share it with him. He won't say a word, honestly.'

Giles stood up and took his plate into the kitchen and rooted in the freezer compartment of the fridge for some ice cream. It would be hard to share one's thoughts and fears with another person; to allow them in to all those secret places of the mind and heart. He took his pudding back to the sofa and had just taken an icy mouthful when the telephone rang. It was Will. Giles hastily swallowed and felt the coldness run down inside his chest.

'How are you?' he asked. 'Are you all well? Thanks again for a wonderful time the other week. I really love your cove.'

As Will's voice quacked busily, Giles sat listening, his ice cream melting in the dish.

'OK,' he said at last when Will had related the whole Adrian Pearson saga. 'Let me get a pencil and I'll telephone them and ask where they are. No, I take your point. I won't let them know I'm in London but I shall need the address, shan't I? No, I'll try not to frighten them off. Hang on.'

When Will had finally hung up, Giles looked with distaste at his plate and, taking it into the kitchen, dumped it in the sink and ran water on it. As he stood watching the ice cream disappear the telephone rang again. This time it was Tessa.

'Has Will phoned?' she asked. 'Did he tell you about this awful man who's going round robbing people?'

'He did.' His heart was pounding and he could hardly keep from smiling as she talked indignantly into his ear. 'I'm going to check out the office.'

'Bea's trying to think of a way of giving him a fright, since he can't be stopped legally. Isn't it infuriating? Oh, when I think of poor Mrs Carrington . . .'

'How are you?' he asked at last when she'd talked herself breathless.

'OK.' Suddenly she sounded shy. 'It was fun, wasn't it? Our trip to the cove with Sidney. He's settled in wonderfully which is just as well since they won't have him back. Apparently he's very happy in the cove.'

'I'm not surprised,' said Giles lightly. 'I could be very happy in the cove myself.'

'Yes,' she said – and there was a long silence.

'Tessa,' said Giles gently, when the silence had really said it all, 'this may not be fair or gentlemanly or whatever – but I have to say it. I love you.'

'I think I guessed,' she said faintly. 'Oh, Giles . . .'

'Don't worry about it,' he told her. 'Just think about it sometimes.'

'I think about it all the time,' she said almost inaudibly, 'but there's nothing I can do about it. I *can't* let the Andersons down.'

'I understand how you feel,' he said calmly. 'Try not to worry. I just want to be sure you know. It's important, although I don't want to make things difficult.'

'Of course it makes things difficult,' she cried almost angrily. 'But I don't want you to stop,' she added, suddenly forlorn.

'I shan't stop,' he assured her.

She hung up abruptly and he sat for some time, staring at nothing. He knew that, whilst her engagement stood, Tessa would find it impossible to tell him that she loved him but Giles was in no doubt of it; he felt moved and elated by the exchange. Presently he stopped thinking about

314

Tessa and concentrated on Adrian Pearson. Slowly but gradually an idea began to take form.

Chapter Twenty-eight

Tessa drove slowly up the lane and parked the car on the wide grassy space at the top. Here she could look up at the high hills of the moor to the west and away across the misty valleys to the thin line of sparkling sea to the south. Already it was hot although it was barely half-past seven. Tessa released Romulus and Remus and wandered down the lane towards the field where the grass had recently been cut for silage. It was good to get the two old dogs out on to cool grass before the sun's heat became unbearable. She sniffed, luxuriating in the warm-scented summer smells, and smiled to see the two labradors going down the field at a gallop in pursuit of a rabbit. She pulled on her old denim sunhat and followed them slowly.

In the stillness of the morning a lark rose up somewhere close at hand, the cadence of his song falling back to earth in clear flutelike notes. Small brown moths fluttered lightly in the tall feathery grasses below the hedge; above them a bee, droning heavily, lumbered amongst the delicate flowers of the convolvulus. A rabbit raced across the grass, white scut bobbing, and vanished into a hole almost hidden in the twisted roots of a great beech tree. Strolling down the field, Tessa wondered why her problems seemed so much easier to handle when she was out in the open air. Here it became possible to confront Sebastian and tell him that she had made a terrible mistake; simple to explain the situation to Mrs Anderson and Rachel. In these sunny spaces, with the green springing turf beneath her feet and the blue sky arching into eternity, everything was possible . . . Everything was possible until she saw Sebastian in the flesh or heard Mrs Anderson's voice on the telephone asking if they had made any plans for the date of the wedding.

Fortunately Sebastian had refused to be pinned down to this. There was talk of a staff job in Washington which he was keen to pursue though not, it seemed, as a married man. He had been rather cagey about it when he telephoned Tessa, reluctant to tell her too much, anxious to indicate that it would be difficult to arrange the wedding before he took up the post. Mrs Anderson had been plainly embarrassed by his reluctance and was quick to talk about career structures and dedication to the service, lest Tessa should be hurt. There had been some kind of personality clash, apparently, and Sebastian was in the right place at the right time to be hurried out as a replacement.

For the first time for several weeks Tessa saw a ray of hope. She told Mrs Anderson that she quite understood the position and, gathering all her courage together, suggested that perhaps she and Sebastian should rethink the whole thing; perhaps they'd rushed into it . . . ? Before she could finish Sue Anderson was protesting strongly: . . . never heard so much rubbish in her life . . . break Sebastian's heart . . . simply a question of patience ... Tessa must go out to Washington to stay ... such fun ... By the end of the conversation Tessa had felt convinced that she would never have the courage to tell the Andersons the truth.

Later, Sebastian had rung again. He was charming and persuasive and Tessa guessed that his mother had been talking to him. She suspected that Sebastian knew that Washington would be more fun if he were single and his mother had taken him to task over it. Tessa decided to test him a little and, heart in mouth, had asked if it wouldn't be possible to have a simple ceremony before he flew out or perhaps on his first leave? Instantly he became defensive and even a little sulky; he didn't want any hole-and-corner business, he said, and his mother and Rachel would be so disappointed if they were denied all the panoply of a proper wedding. Moreover, it was absolutely essential that he gave all his time and energy to this important job which would almost certainly lead to promotion if he played his cards right.

Now, as she watched Romulus and Remus panting towards her, Tessa wished that she'd had the courage to be honest with him. Then had been the moment in which she could have pointed out that she wasn't prepared to wait two years for him. Perhaps she had hesitated because Sue Anderson's voice was still too clear in her ears. She suspected that, should she really make a stand, the Andersons would bring pressure to bear on Sebastian and she would find herself married to him after all and flying out to Washington with him.

She bent to stroke the two golden heads and

turned back to the gate. As one dog they panted their way to the corner where, for most of the year, there was a standing puddle. The hot spell, however, had dried it to a hard mud bed at which they sniffed, puzzled. Tessa lifted the tailgate and produced a big plastic bowl and a container. She stood the bowl on the grass and filled it with water for them and they stood side by side, lapping gratefully. As she waited for them to drink their fill she thought about Mrs Carrington and how difficult it had been to see her again knowing, as she now did, about Adrian Pearson. Anger rose within her. It was one thing unwittingly to find a bargain or make a reasonable profit but to set out deliberately to cheat the weak and vulnerable made her speechless with fury. She decided to say nothing to Mrs Carrington; better that she remained in ignorance than to know that she had been duped.

'In you get, boys,' she said. Already the brief courage she had experienced in the field was deserting her. How could she reject Sebastian without hurting his family or losing their love and respect? Guilt settled back like a cloud, obscuring the bright morning. Reversing the car, she headed off back down the lane.

Far out at the edge of the cove, Will swam in the cold sparkling water. Despite it being past midsummer and hot into the bargain, the water of this coast remained breathtakingly icy. Nevertheless, Will swam as often as the weather allowed. As he pushed through the gentle swell he finally made up his mind. As soon as Isobel had seen Helen and sorted things out with her daughter, he intended to ask her to marry him. Just as he had wondered if he should exploit Isobel's loneliness by offering her love and support, so now was he tempted to take advantage of her happiness. She was so warm, so affectionate; a hundred times he had been on the brink of proposing marriage to her but always, at the last moment, he had held back. He knew in his heart that it was unfair to her; that he should wait until she had come to terms with what might lie ahead before she should be asked to take such a decision.

Will rolled over on to his back and floated, allowing the tide to take him. Part of him still recoiled at offering himself to her. He was so much older; his muscles flabby, his hair thinning. She seemed unaware of these things. They swam together, lay in the sun and talked, walked on the cliffs. She had never by glance or word showed that she found him repulsive. A summer in the cove had made him hardy. He had trimmed off any surplus weight and was deeply tanned and looked better than he had for years. As her affection and friendliness grew, so did his confidence. The one thing that remained a real problem was the effect of this – should Isobel accept him – on Bea. He could not decide how much she relied on him. He spent even more time with Bea than he did with Isobel and they had developed a relaxed easy companionship which was important to both of them. If he moved across the cove, how would Bea fare alone? Of course she would hardly be alone with he and Isobel so close at hand but he had the intelligence to realise

that three single people do not add up to the same
sum as two married people and one single person.
He wondered if she would be as contented as
Mathilda had been; after all, Tessa would be coming
home often. Of course, once Tessa was married it
might become a little more complicated . . .

He pulled up his knees sharply, disappeared
briefly beneath the surface and then began to swim
back strongly to the shore. Sidney, watching anxiously from the beach, wagged his tail with relief as
Will waded out, wiping the wetness from his eyes,
water streaming on to the hot sand. He picked up
his towel and gave Sidney a pat. Bea had gone into
Kingsbridge early to the library and Isobel was at
the bookshop. He was at liberty to spend the
morning how he chose. Before he could decide
exactly how he should employ his time, he heard a
car's engine in the track. Tying his towel around
his waist he waited to see who his visitor might be.

He smiled to see Tessa's old Peugeot bump into
sight and park behind the house. He and Sidney
went to greet her.

'No dogs?' He bent to peer in at the back.

'Too hot,' she said, hugging him. 'I've left them in
a nice cool kitchen. Anyway, it's not fair to Sid. This
is his territory now. How are things, Sid? You're
looking good.'

'Which is more than can be said for you,' said
Will bluntly. 'You've lost weight.'

'You sound like Bea.' Tessa laughed a little but
she was grateful that he cared enough to notice. 'I
couldn't resist hopping over to see you all. How are
things?'

'Not bad at all. Look, let me get dressed and then we'll have a nice cold drink and exchange all the gossip. Yes?'

'Sounds wonderful. I'll stay out here if that's OK.' She looked about her, breathing deeply and visibly relaxing. 'It's lovely to be back.'

'Shan't be a moment.'

He hurried indoors, leaving her in possession of the beach, but reappeared in record time, a rug over his arm and carrying a tray.

'Been talking to Giles,' he told her, placing the tray with its burden of two glasses and a jug of fresh lemonade in the shade beside a rock. He spread the rug on the sand. 'Bright lad, that. We've thought up a pretty good plan for Mr Adrian Pearson.'

Tessa, whose heart had bumped erratically at the mention of Giles's name, sank down on the rug. 'Tell me,' she said. 'I'd do anything to frighten the wits out of that little toad.'

'I'm glad to hear you say that,' said Will, filling her glass and passing Sidney a Bonio. 'You may have to. I have to say that Giles and I are counting on you.'

He grinned at her surprise and, whilst she sat in the shade of the cliff and sipped her cold lemonade, he explained the scheme that he and Giles had planned so carefully together.

Sue Anderson cursed as the telephone rang for the fourth time in ten minutes, dumped the laundry basket on the step and hurried back into the house.

'Yes?' she cried impatiently. 'Oh, sorry, darling. It's been one of those mornings. How are you? Still in the dockyard?'

'Yes. Still here. Sorry to spring this on you, Mother, but I've got to talk to you.'

'Talk to me about what?' Sue's heart sank at his serious tone. 'What's the problem? Not *another* enormous mess bill? Oh, Sebastian, you promised me you'd make an effort—'

'It's nothing to do with my mess bill,' he interrupted impatiently. 'It's just that I've been thinking about this posting to Washington and, honestly, Mother, I think it's wrong to ask Tessa to wait until I come back before we get married.'

'Well,' Sue perched on the chair beside the telephone and pushed the hair off her face, thinking furiously. 'It would be the most awful rush but we could probably get something sorted out before you go. After all, Tessa's got hardly any family to worry about so that side would be quite simple. We've agreed that she's got nobody to arrange a wedding for her. She feels that it would be a bit much for her elderly cousin. Do you want me to start organising?'

'I think so. What I feel is, that if we don't do it now then it will never happen. I've got the most terrible attack of cold feet. I know it's unforgivable but I think that I got carried away and now I'm scared to death I've got it wrong.'

'Oh, darling.' Sue clutched the receiver. 'Oh hell. Look, most people get terrified at some point or other, you know. It's a big step but you know Tessa so well and she absolutely adores you.'

'I know that.' He sounded irritable and her heart sank even lower. 'You and Rachel have been telling me that for the last five years. So now we're engaged. If you don't mind the rush then we'll soon be married. Everyone will be happy.'

'Are you saying that you don't love her?' asked Sue sharply, frightened by the heavily sarcastic tone of his voice.

'I tell you I don't know *what* I feel any more,' he cried. 'She's a sweet kid. I'm very fond of her but I don't know about love. What does it mean? All I'm saying is that if we don't get married before I go then it won't happen at all. I know that much.'

'Oh, Sebastian. I . . . I don't know what to say. If you don't love her then you shouldn't marry her.'

'I don't know whether I love her or not.' There was a long pause and when he spoke again the aggression had vanished from his voice. 'How do you think she'll react if I back out?'

'I don't know,' said Sue slowly, remembering her conversation with Tessa and how she'd suggested that she and Sebastian should rethink the situation. Sue had put it down to hurt pride because Sebastian was unwilling to set a date for the wedding but there might just be the faint chance that Tessa herself was having second thoughts. 'Damn!' she said, recalling her own remarks about how such a thing would break Sebastian's heart. 'What a muddle.'

'Can I assume from this that you would not be suicidal if we were to call it off?' he asked her. 'I don't understand women. You and Rachel were so excited.'

'My dear boy,' it was Sue's turn to sound exasperated, 'I love you and Tessa far too much to want either of you to be unhappy. I certainly don't want you to marry Tessa because she's been like one of the family. On the other hand . . .'

'Quite,' said Sebastian, correctly interpreting the pause, 'if she does want the wedding to go ahead we've got problems. I don't want to hurt her.'

'You'll hurt her more in the long run,' said Sue, 'if you don't love her.'

'I've told you,' he said wearily, 'I simply don't know.'

'Have you . . . you know . . . slept with her?'

'Of course I have, Mother,' he said crossly. 'For heaven's sake! She enjoyed it as much as I did. And yes, I took precautions. It was good but then it's been good with other girls.'

'Oh, Sebastian,' she said. 'I'm sorry. I know it's not my business. I was just thinking that if you hadn't . . . with Tessa, then it might be quite sensible. Probably get your feelings sorted out more clearly. But since you have . . .'

'Then it's not going to help us either way,' he finished.

'You know the old test?' she said at last. ' "Do you want to touch her; do you want to see her; do you want to hear her"? I might have that the wrong way round but you get the sense of it. Do you?'

'Not often,' he said frankly. 'Sometimes. Honestly, Mother, I can't answer the only necessary question. So what do I do?'

'You must go and see her,' said Sue at last. 'Go and talk to her and tell her what you feel.'

'Shit!' he muttered. 'What if she . . . Oh Christ!'

'I know. But you've got to,' she said. 'It's the only way. I can't help you except that we'll try to back you up without abandoning Tessa.'

'Thanks.' He gave a short laugh. 'Sorry about all this.'

'Don't give it a thought. I just want you both to be happy. When can you see her?'

'We're going down to Devonport next week for sea trials. She's in Devon, too. I'll see her then. No chance before. She's up in Wales somewhere. If we do decide to go ahead would you be able to cope?'

'Of course I could. Don't worry about that but . . . Oh, Sebastian, I don't know what to say. Stay in touch.'

'I will. Thanks. 'Bye.'

The line went dead and with a heavy heart Sue went to hang the washing out in the hot sunshine.

Chapter Twenty-nine

On an overcast morning in July, Helen arrived at the cove. Since first light Isobel had been wandering about her cottage; tidying, smoothing, puffing up cushions, rearranging the roses in the living room, straightening pictures. Her fingers shook a little and she drank numerous cups of coffee and wished that she'd never given up smoking. Just before ten o'clock she saw Will and Bea emerge. She had taken Bea aside some days before and asked if it would be possible to have the cove to herself just for that particular morning.

'I know it's pushy,' she said, 'but I'm afraid that Will might be over-anxious. Helen's such a strange girl and I'm terrified of anything going wrong. I know it sounds melodramatic . . .'

'I quite understand,' Bea had said. 'You'll be able to relax better. Don't worry. I want to have another look at Tavistock. Pray for a cool day so that we can take Sidney.'

'I can cope with Sidney if necessary,' Isobel said, relieved that Bea wasn't offended. 'It's just that I'm so uptight about this. Bless you for understanding, Bea.'

Now she watched Bea encourage Sidney into the back of the hatchback whilst Will stowed the hamper on the back seat. Presently the sound of the engine died away and there was silence.

Except, thought Isobel, as she drifted back into the living room and stood staring aimlessly out of the open window, that it's never silent when you live this close to the sea.

The tide was running out, the wet sand gleaming under the grey sky. The dark, opaque surface of the sea was splashed with pools of dazzling silver which showered down through breaks in the thick blanket of cloud. A seagull balanced on a newly exposed rock, one yellow leg drawn up as he watched the waters receding. The soothing, rhythmical shushing of waves calmed Isobel and she turned back into the room, feeling relaxed and able now to prepare herself for the coming meeting.

It was just after eleven when she saw the car – Simon's car – emerge from the track and hesitate. Controlling an impulse to run out, Isobel waited. She saw the car pull in beside the Morris and presently Helen climbed out and stood looking about her.

She looks like I did at her age, thought Isobel, watching from the kitchen window. She took note of the dark hair cut in a short shining bob, the slim square shoulders beneath the baggy cotton shirt, the long legs in faded denim. She recognised the quick nervous gesture as Helen pushed back her hair and came on long, easy strides towards the cottage. With a deep breath Isobel went to meet her.

'Hi.' She stood looking down at her daughter who had paused at the bottom of the steps. 'This is . . . wonderful. Come on in.'

With the same anxious gesture, Helen ran her

hand through her hair and climbed the steps.

'What a terrific place.' Nervousness sent her voice up the scale a little. 'That's some view.'

'Pretty good, isn't it?' Isobel was determined that no hysteria should creep in. 'It's the light that gets me. Like living at the bottom of the sea. Although it's a bit dull today... Coffee?'

'Thanks. Got any decaff?'

'I have.' Isobel gave silent thanks for her foresight. 'Milk? Sugar?'

'No thanks. Just black.' Helen looked around the kitchen. 'Oh, you've still got the picture of Soot.'

'Of course.' Helen had drawn the sketch of the family cat when she was just fifteen but it was a very accurate and charming portrayal and Isobel had had it framed. It hung on the wall beside the dresser. Isobel made coffee, sensing that Helen was examining the photographs on the shelves beside the plates; photographs of Helen as a little girl, posed alone and with Simon. The silence lengthened but Isobel refused to blunder in with foolish observations. 'Here.' She passed Helen her mug. 'Let's go into the living room.'

She led the way, sitting down at the table under the window and gesturing to Helen to sit opposite. She slid on to the chair, staring about the room, taking it all in. It gave Isobel the opportunity to study her more closely; to see the drawn look and the tiny frown between the dark level brows. Helen's gaze came round to meet her own and they looked at each other for a long moment.

'So,' said Isobel lightly. 'Where shall we start?'

She had resolved that there should be no more

apologies and explanations; that Helen must try to accept what had happened and be prepared to move forward. It was a pointless exercise to dig up the old bones of their relationship and chew on past grievances and recriminations. Nevertheless, she was not nearly so calm as she appeared and she sipped quickly at her coffee.

'It's difficult.' Helen glanced away, out of the window. 'I'm not sure I know where to start.'

'That makes two of us.' Relieved that the old antagonism was absent, Isobel relaxed a little. 'You've changed so much. Grown up.' She laughed a little. 'Stupid thing to say. Of course you have.' She became serious. 'It really is very good to see you, Helen. Thank you for coming.'

'I wanted to.' She continued to stare out of the window. 'I know that I behaved like a prig. I wanted to say sorry. I understand better now.'

Isobel swallowed, crushing down a longing to explain all over again; justify her feelings, explain her actions. 'I'm . . . glad,' she said. 'At least . . . I'm glad if it means we can be friends. Not so glad if you understand as a result of some problem of your own.'

Helen looked at her, studying Isobel's face, the frown more in evidence as she concentrated. Isobel met the scrutiny steadily, wondering if Helen would be candid with her. Suddenly the meeting had moved on to a much deeper plane and Isobel felt the stirrings of panic. Helen pushed her hair behind her ears and picked up her mug in both hands.

'I couldn't understand, you see,' she said – and took a tiny sip of the black liquid. 'It was terrible to have to believe that you loved that man more than you loved me. That you could leave me for him.'

Isobel's heart sank. So the bones were to be disinterred yet again; she prepared herself for battle. 'I tried to explain—' she began – but Helen shook her head.

'I know you did. But it wasn't that simple. Not then. I think it was something I had to experience for myself. I understand now what you meant when you said it was like an illness. It sort of possesses you and when it goes you can't think what came over you.'

'Yes,' said Isobel sadly. 'That's about it. And then it was too late. For me, that is. Not, I hope, for you.'

'I'm sorry,' said Helen again. 'Really sorry. About Dad and . . . Sally.'

'Yes.' Isobel bit her lip. 'It was a shock. Are they . . . happy?'

Helen nodded, watching her, and Isobel nodded back and tried to smile.

'Do you still love him?' she asked compassionately.

'Oh, yes.' Isobel tried to sound matter-of-fact. 'I always did. The other was just a kind of madness. A very cruel and expensive madness. So. How about you? It's all over now, is it? Was he at university?'

Helen nodded, staring at the Indian cloth. In the silence Isobel wondered how far she should go. She dreaded to pry or open old wounds but how could she help if she did not know the facts? Helen had said that it was finished; that she did not know what had come over her. If she no longer loved whoever-he-was then it shouldn't be painful, unless . . .

'Is he married?'

Another nod; the frown deepened.

'Well,' said Isobel comfortingly, 'being married never made anyone immune. Does his wife know?'

A shake of the head; the lips were pressed tightly together. Isobel was puzzled. So what could be the problem? She guessed the answer at exactly the moment that Helen told her.

'I'm pregnant,' she said – and began to weep.

Instinctively Isobel pressed her hand to her lips; the next moment she was kneeling beside Helen, her arm around her. 'I'm sorry, so sorry.' She murmured the words over and over whilst Helen wept, her head buried in her arms. When she straightened up, Isobel hesitated for a moment and then went back to her chair. She felt she must leave Helen her space and her dignity.

'I want to keep the baby,' said Helen rapidly. 'I can't bear the thought of an abortion or adoption.'

'No,' said Isobel. 'No . . . I see. Does he . . . the father know?'

'No,' she answered fiercely. 'I don't want him to know. It's *my* baby. He has children. I don't want to get rid of it.'

She stared desperately at Isobel whose brain, behind her deceptively calm expression, was desperately seeking some kind of solution.

'But your job?' she said. 'Your job in Bristol? How will you manage? Oh, if only I could help you.'

'Oh, Mum.' The old familiar word slipped out and Isobel's heart lurched with tenderness. 'Would you help?'

'But of course I will,' said Isobel. 'It's just I don't see quite how. I have to work myself, you know. I could try to help out with the baby.' She frowned, wondering how this could be achieved. 'Does Daddy know?' she asked suddenly.

'No.' Helen looked defiant. 'I don't want them to know yet. I can only handle telling you at the moment.'

Isobel experienced another stab of tenderness but it was mixed with a less generous emotion. She felt a triumphant sense of pride that Helen had turned to her rather than to Simon and Sally. Helen was watching her anxiously and she smiled at her.

'Let's not panic,' she said. 'When is the baby due?'

'December. At Christmas. I've been thinking about it,' said Helen, 'and I've thought of a way through. It's an awful lot to ask, especially after . . . after what's happened. I feel very badly but I don't know what else to do. I don't expect you to agree to it.'

'Tell me,' suggested Isobel, wondering if she was going to ask if she and the baby could come to the cove. How would they manage? She felt anxious and even frightened. 'Tell me what your plan is?'

Helen began to speak very quickly, her fingers pleating and repleating the cloth, her eyes on the sea. 'When I knew for certain, I panicked a bit but after a while I began to think it all through. I spoke to the research department at Bristol University and they agreed to give me time off to have the baby, providing that I go back afterwards full time with no problems. There are all sorts of crèches and baby-minding agencies so I told them that I'd got it all fixed. There were a couple of small flats that go with some of the university posts so I've taken one. It's quite nice and it's cheap . . .'

'So what's the problem?' asked Isobel gently, when Helen fell silent. 'It sounds as if you've got it all sewn up. Do you want to come here to have the baby?'

'No. No, I don't want to stay round here with all my friends nudging each other and Dad and Sally fussing.' Helen looked at her mother. 'I'm moving in to the flat next month and I want you to be with me when I have the baby and to look after him when I start work. I don't want to shove him into a crèche or with some baby-minder. How can I bear to leave my brand-new baby with strangers?' Her eyes filled with tears. 'I wouldn't mind if you were with him.'

'But . . . but how could I?' Isobel sounded dazed. 'I'd have to give up my job and . . .' she looked around her as if seeing it for the first time, 'and my home.'

'I know.' Helen wiped her tears on the back of her hand. 'That's why it's such a lot to ask. It's just that I'm not sure that I can cope with it all. A baby and a new job. I know that it's all my fault and I have no right to ask anyone for help but I feel so terribly alone.'

'Oh, darling.' Isobel stretched her hand across the table and Helen took it and gripped it tightly. 'Of course I'll help. I'll do everything I can. It's just . . . It's just such a shock.'

'I know,' said Helen miserably. 'It's been awful, trying to concentrate on exams with all this hanging over me. But it was my fault, you see. I pestered him and wouldn't let him alone. I was sure I could make him happy. I had all these silly fantasies. And then one night we were both at a party. He was on

his own. We drank a bit and then we . . . You know.'
She frowned, smoothing out the cloth. 'I can't
explain but after that I felt differently. It was all
gone. All the excitement and the feverishness.
I didn't even like him much. And then when I
realised . . .' She shook her head and lifted her hands
in despair.

'I'm sorry,' said Isobel inadequately. 'I understand
as far as anyone can understand another person's
predicament.'

'I knew you would.' Helen pushed the cold coffee
aside with a sigh. 'And I know how selfish I'm being.
I'm asking you to give everything up for my
stupidity. Other people manage alone in these
situations, why shouldn't I?'

'I don't want you to manage alone,' Isobel told
her, but her heart was heavy. 'We must think it
through carefully. Don't worry. You won't be alone.
I'm going to make us some more coffee.'

Leaving Helen sitting slumped at the table, she
went into the kitchen and rinsed the mugs. As the
kettle boiled, she stood staring out at the familiar
and much-loved view. Her heart ached for her
daughter but a small corner of her mind was
rebelling. How could she bear to uproot herself from
the cove and go to Bristol to live in a small flat with
Helen and a baby and how would they survive
financially? Would she ever be free again to take up
the threads of her old life; would they still be there,
waiting for her? Isobel felt a sickening panic as she
stood, gripping the edge of the sink, her eyes on the
water. She could not bear to leave Will and Bea; to
give up her job in the bookshop; part with her

cottage. Why should she? Helen had refused to see her for five years. She had ignored her and hurt her and now expected her mother to sacrifice herself for her own mistakes. Her resentment faded and guilt seized Isobel's heart. If she had not abandoned Helen when she met Mike it was possible that none of this might have happened. Was it the shock of seeing her father absorbed with Sally that had turned Helen's love towards an older man? It was impossible to know the truth but Isobel had a cold feeling that it was time to try to make amends for her own selfish actions.

As she turned away from the window, Isobel heard a muffled sound. She paused, her hand on the kettle's handle. It was the despairing sound of Helen weeping. Isobel took a deep breath, imagining her daughter's unhappiness and her loneliness. What a terrible way to start her young life! Bleakly Isobel recognised the fact that there were no choices here; she could not abandon Helen a second time. If she wished to rebuild the love and friendship between them then, somehow, they must manage this together. Isobel made the coffee and, summoning every ounce of courage and optimism, she picked up the mugs and went back to her daughter.

Chapter Thirty

Sebastian stood at the bar of the Skylark at Clearbrook buying drinks. He'd managed to wangle a few hours' leave from the ship but his time was limited and he'd hardly been five minutes at Kate's house at Whitchurch before he'd suggested that he and Tessa should go out for a drink. Sebastian hunched his shoulders and jingled the coins in his pockets as he watched the beer frothing up the glass. Tessa had not realised that this invitation was because, at the sight of her standing at the door, he had completely lost his nerve. As he'd driven out towards Tavistock he had made up his mind to be absolutely honest with her but, when he saw her small figure waiting for him, his courage had deserted him. How could he let her down? He remembered the tragic events which surrounded her younger life and the brave way that she had taken opportunities and carved out a life for herself. He also remembered her unwavering devotion to him and the occasions when he had taken advantage of it.

She'd smiled as he climbed out of the car and approached her but there was an odd expression in her eyes, almost as if she had guessed his cowardly intentions. Desperately he tried to resurrect the feelings he'd had when he'd seen her wandering ethereally in Freddie's meadow but all he could see was the old, familiar Tessa in jeans and sweatshirt, a younger sister of whom he was very fond. He knew from past experience that, when he'd had a beer or two, a certain amount of the magic would return, after all she was a very attractive girl, but being permanently inebriated was not quite how he wished to spend his married life.

Well, it was rather too late to think of that now. The damage was done. Sebastian took a pull at his beer as he waited for his change. He knew now that he was not capable of dealing the blow that would break the engagement. He comforted himself with the knowledge that it could be a great deal worse; she was pretty and very sweet and she loved him. It would simply have to be enough.

From her table in the corner Tessa watched him with a sense of despair. Each time she saw him she was reminded of the past; of all those weekends and holidays when the Andersons had taken pity on her and welcomed her into their home. She remembered how she had first seen him and fallen in love with him and, from that moment, had idealised him. She knew now that the real Sebastian was far removed from those fantasies but how could she possibly explain that to him? His voice on the telephone had been almost curt and, for one glorious moment, she had hoped that he might be coming to tell her that he'd changed his mind. When he arrived, however, he had hugged her in the old friendly way and since then had been chatting perfectly normally. Certainly the new passion he had shown on that night at Freddie's was not apparent, he was much more like his old self, but this was a flying visit and he was probably preoccupied with the ship and her coming sea trials.

Whilst she'd waited for him to drive out from Plymouth she had steeled herself to tell him the truth. She rehearsed what she would say to him, how she would explain her feelings, but, the moment she saw his tall figure, she was swept back into the past with all its memories and obligations and she knew that she would never be able to hurt him or his family. She told herself that he would be away a great deal and that he was kind and good-looking but, when she thought about Giles, she felt as though her heart were being squeezed to death. Her only hope was that, whilst Sebastian was in America, he might meet someone else or change his mind.

She smiled as he set the drinks down and tried to think of something to say. 'Thanks. Well, this is a nice surprise. Here's to the trials.'

'I'll drink to that.' He drank deeply. 'I've got something to suggest, actually. It's a bit sudden but I'm sure you'll understand.'

She looked at him quickly and once again he saw that odd look in her eyes. Could she possibly have guessed at his real feelings? If she had, then at least what he had to say would put her mind at rest.

'I've been thinking.' He put down his glass and reached for her hand. 'You know I think I was wrong to say that we should wait to get married until after Washington.' She stiffened a little and he held her hand more tightly, knowing that she had been hurt at his refusal to go along with her idea of a quiet ceremony before he took up his post. 'I've changed

341

my mind. What about fixing the wedding as soon as possible. Mother's perfectly happy to organise it. What d'you say?'

'Have you spoken to your mother about it?' She was staring at their joined hands; at the winking of the stones in her engagement ring.

He thought quickly. 'Well, I have. Don't be cross with me. I had to clear it with her. To make sure she could cope before I asked you. It'll be a bit of a rush and you did say that you felt your cousin couldn't be expected to deal with it.'

'I know I did. Don't worry. I wasn't accusing you of anything. What did your mother say?'

'She said that it could be done. It would be a bit hectic but that she's perfectly happy to take it on.'

'I see.' So that was that. Her escape route was closed.

'You don't look too certain about it?'

He was watching her with a strange expression in his eyes and she was distressed lest he should be hurt by her lack of enthusiasm.

'Sorry.' She made a tremendous effort and smiled at him as brightly as she could. 'It's come as a bit of a shock. I'd . . . well, I'd resigned myself to waiting. In fact,' she made one last try, 'I had a tiny suspicion that you might be changing your mind.'

She was staring at him so desperately that he felt a stab of guilt followed by a rush of tenderness for her. 'What rubbish!' he said and leaned over to kiss her. 'Just too much on my mind, that's all. So what about it?'

'Wonderful.' She raised her glass. 'Here's to us.'

For a moment he thought that she had tears in

her eyes and he sighed inwardly. How could he possibly have imagined that he could hurt her?

'Here's to us,' he said.

Bea ordered coffee and went back to the table in the corner where Sidney, waiting obediently by her chair, wagged his tail and lay down with a sigh. Bea sighed too as she looked about her and settled herself more comfortably in her chair. Isobel had brought her to the Bedford Hotel, several months before, and she had been struck by the quiet comfortable bar where locals and residents alike sat talking over pots of tea or coffee or reading the newspapers. Well-behaved dogs were welcomed and Bea felt content to sit here in this peaceful atmosphere and wait for Will. She glanced down at Sidney who was attracting attention from a couple at a neighbouring table. Clumber spaniels were by no means a common sight and his square sturdy body and big domed head drew much praise. Strangers approached crying, 'Oh, isn't he beautiful. But what is he?' and Sidney stood patiently as they stroked his silky coat and gently pulled his long ears.

Bea stretched out a foot and patted him with her toe, smiling at the couple. She was secretly enjoying the vicarious admiration which he attracted and was becoming resigned to white hair on the carpet and slobber marks on her skirt. This surprised her but she knew that there was always a price to pay if life was to be lived fully; the mess a cat or dog made; the ash and dust from a wood fire; the clearing up after the preparation of a delicious meal. It was tempting – and Bea knew that living alone she might easily have been so tempted – to simplify life, to pare it to the bone, cutting out anything that made unnecessary work. The trouble was that this nihilistic attitude could lead to boredom and emptiness. Bea was grateful that Will saved her from this temptation. Will lived with great enthusiasm and Bea was very happy to be taken along with him.

The coffee arrived and Bea shuffled forward on her seat so as to pour herself a cupful. She was reaching for the sugar when the sound of her name, uttered with great surprise, arrested her action. Hand outstretched she stared up at Tony Priest.

'It *is* you,' he said with the lazy smile that had caused her such flutterings in the past. 'Well, well.' His eyes took in the casual shirt and sailcloth skirt, her tanned skin and well-cut cropped hair. 'I must say you're looking extraordinarily fit. Being a landowner obviously suits you.'

Bea swallowed and dropped a lump of brown sugar into her coffee. 'It . . . has its moments,' she said, wondering whether Will was likely to arrive and unwittingly show her up. She remembered her mother saying, 'Oh, what a tangled web we weave, when first we practise to deceive,' and took a deep breath. 'How are you, Tony? How's everyone?'

'Fine.' He glanced down at the slumbering Sidney and, to Bea's dismay, sank into the chair opposite. 'Missing you, of course.'

He smiled at her again and she remembered how he had enjoyed making her a little confused, delighting in her silent admiration. Bea looked away from him – outraged that she had ever been fool enough to have given him such satisfaction – and saw Will come in and look about him. The expression on her face caused Tony to glance round, giving Bea just long enough to make a warning face at Will. He came across, smiling at Bea and noticing the wariness with which she greeted him.

'This is Tony Priest,' she said. 'The History master at my old school. This is Will Rainbird,' she told Tony. 'My land agent. He met Marian when we came to collect my things.'

'So I heard.' Tony had risen and was shaking Will's hand, looking at him appraisingly. 'She was very impressed . . . with the whole thing, of course.' His implication that Marian had been taken with Will was left hanging in the air and there was a moment of awkwardness. Bea remembered how he had loved to create these little frissons, often very amusing ones, and how he liked to stand back and watch the effect. Generally – and flatteringly – he had invited Bea to be a fellow spectator. This time she refused to play his game.

'Oh, Marian was all over him like a rash,' she said dismissively. 'Poor Will. Very embarrassing wasn't it, darling?'

Tony's eyes opened wide and he looked sharply at Will, who was patting himself all over, his face expressionless.

'Dreadful woman,' he said, producing his pipe. 'Terribly obvious. What an afternoon! Now then, my darling, are you ready or do you want more coffee?' He took her hand and held it for a second and then turned back to Tony, who watched this by-play with amazement on his face. 'Sorry. Am I butting in? Are you staying in the hotel?'

'We are.' Tony took a grip on himself. 'Nicola will be along in a moment. Why don't you stay to see her?'

Bea, who was dithering between fleeing whilst there was time and a desire to brazen it out, looked at Will. It was clear that, having given her the opportunity to escape, he was leaving the next move to her. She remembered that he'd had no coffee and that Sidney would probably not be welcome in any of the other cafés. Moreover, she had not yet drunk her own coffee.

'Good idea,' she said easily. 'You need some coffee, Will, after the drive over. Why not order some. Tony?'

'No, none for me,' he said quickly. 'I had plenty at breakfast. So, Bea.' He sat down, looking at her intently as Will went to the bar, the old teasing smile willing her to share her secrets. 'What a dark horse you are.'

She refused to be drawn or flattered. 'Oh, not particularly,' she said, meeting his eye provocatively. 'I just take advantage of what life sends. Don't we all?'

'We do indeed. Ah!' He got to his feet. 'Nicola. Over here. Look who's here?'

Bea looked at the slim, smart, pretty woman and realised that she no longer felt inadequate, nor clumsy and plain. She smiled, raising her eyebrows at Nicola's surprise.

'What fun,' she said calmly. 'How are you, Nicola?'

'I'm well thanks, Bea. And you, I hear, have become a wealthy landowner.'

Her sharp eyes examined Bea coldly: Bea laughed.

'Old Marian does like to be first with the news,

doesn't she?' she asked admiringly. 'I expect the whole school knows. Probably the town, as well. Did she tell you about Will, too?'

'Will?' Nicola looked faintly discomfited. 'Well, I'm not absolutely certain . . .' She looked at Tony, who was obviously enjoying the encounter enormously.

'No need to be prissy, Nicola,' said Bea impatiently. 'I'm sure she did. And here he is. Will, darling, this is Nicola, Tony's wife. This is Will Rainbird, my land agent.'

'How d'you do?' Will shook her hand warmly. 'Perhaps I should have ordered more coffee.' He sat down beside Bea, leaving the other two standing, and stroked Sidney who groaned and rolled over on to his side.

'Did he come with the estate, too?' asked Tony, still looking amused.

'He comes from a broken home,' said Will blandly. 'He's learning to trust again. We're a very happy little community, aren't we, my darling?'

He beamed at Bea, who smiled at him with genuine affection. 'We certainly are,' she agreed. She looked up at Tony and Nicola. 'Do sit down,' she said, a testy note creeping into her voice. 'Are you sure you won't have some coffee?'

'Perfectly sure.' Nicola stared disbelievingly as Bea laid her hand upon Will's and their fingers intertwined. 'We must go. So nice to see you, Bea. Come on, Tony. We shall be late.'

Tony looked down at Bea with a little smile as Nicola turned away. 'I have a feeling,' he said softly, 'that I underestimated you. What a pity.'

Bea raised her cup to him. 'Good luck,' she said.

'Don't forget to give our love to Marian. Off you go. Nicola's waiting.'

When they'd gone she sat back in her seat with a gasp of relief. Presently she began to laugh. Will's coffee arrived and he began to pour, smiling at Bea's reaction.

'We shall have to be careful,' he said. 'Who knows who else may pop out of the woodwork?'

'She'll go rushing back to Marian with the news,' said Bea with enormous satisfaction. 'Her eyes were like organ stops. Talk about Lady Chatterley!'

They laughed immoderately and drank their coffee companionably, temporarily forgetting about Isobel and her meeting with Helen at the cove. It was pleasant to be at leisure together and presently they fastened Sidney's lead to his collar and wandered out into the town. The weather was brighter and they pottered slowly. Since Isobel had asked them to give her plenty of time with Helen they had the whole day before them. Bea, delighted with her routing of Nicola, took Will's arm.

'Just in case,' she told him demurely, 'they're still about.'

'Quite right,' he said, giving it a squeeze. 'And if I see them approaching we'll go into a clinch and pray that Sidney can cope with a sudden display of unbridled passion.'

'I wish I'd thought of that,' said Bea wistfully. 'That would have really given them something to think about.'

'There's still time,' said Will cheerfully. 'They're staying at the hotel. We'll go back for lunch and give 'em a treat.'

Chuckling together, arms linked, they strolled across the road and disappeared into the market.

Chapter Thirty-one

Sebastian put down the telephone receiver, glanced at his watch and shrugged at his oppo, Rob Walters.

'She's not there,' he said. 'I've left a message on the ansaphone.'

'So you'll come anyway?'

Sebastian nodded. 'Why not? She's probably only walking the dog. It's a pity to waste time and if you really don't mind me coming on with you if she's not there . . . ?'

'Not a bit. Barbara will be pleased to see you again. She was rather miffed that as soon as we bought a house down here I got posted to Pompey. She's settling in but she'll be pleased to see a friendly face. She's thrilled that we've got more problems and the ship'll be stuck alongside for a day or two. Let's get going then.'

'You can spare a minute to see Tessa, I hope,' said Sebastian, as they went down the gangplank together. 'Seeing that you're going to be best man.'

'Can't wait to meet her again,' said Rob, feeling for the car keys. 'We must all get together while the ship's in.'

'Good idea,' said Sebastian – but he sighed as he waited for Rob to unlock the door. He was determined to be positive but it was not quite as easy as he'd hoped.

* * *

Adrian Pearson drove slowly past the church looking for the house which Tessa had described to him.
He had been wary when he'd first heard her voice
on his mobile. How was she going to react to his
visits to the cove? His second visit had been un-
productive. The old boy had checked the figures over
again and indicated the one or two pieces he might
be prepared to sell. One of these was an elegant, if
simple, Regency writing table and, although the
sabre legs had been repaired with brackets and the
leather top was scored and marked, it would easily
bring five and a half thousand pounds. The old
buffer had been delighted at an offer of four hundred
pounds for 'that old table', as the old aunt or
whatever-she-was had called it, and had promised
a final decision soon.

Adrian, peering through the windscreen, had
been quickly reassured by Tessa's call. She had been
friendly, apologised for not getting in touch before
and explained that she had some rather interesting
pieces to show him. He felt the familiar excitement
begin to build. Should he, he'd asked, give the owner
a bell? Tessa answered that the owner was away
but that she, Tessa, had permission to show him a
few pieces with a view to selling. Could he come
over to Tavistock? she'd asked. He could.

So here he was, turning in through the gate of a
Victorian house set well back from the road, and
there was Tessa opening the front door. She led him
straight through to the kitchen and invited him to
sit down while she made coffee. He glanced about
him; nothing particularly exciting here but that was

often the way. It was surprising how many people had just one or two really valuable things, inherited over the years and regarded with the contempt that familiarity brings. These were the kind of customers he wanted; not those whose homes were stuffed with goodies and who knew their value down to the tiniest silver thimble. He looked at Tessa and smiled to himself. Perhaps he hadn't misjudged her after all. She could lead him to all sorts of treasures but he must make certain that she was on his side.

'How are things?' he asked, bringing his charm to bear on her. She was not really his type – but business is business. 'I tracked you down to the cove, you know, but you weren't there. I've been hoping that I would see you again.'

She smiled at him and he realised that there was none of that early caution he remembered. She leaned against the sink and looked at him appraisingly.

'I've been thinking about you, too,' she said.

Her smile was a peculiarly intimate one and he raised his eyebrows, smiling a little in return. He was surprised – and a faint excitement stirred which had nothing to do with profit-making.

'I'm flattered,' he said lightly. 'You shouldn't be so elusive. Those relations of yours are very efficient guard dogs.'

She laughed and shook her head. 'What a pair of old dinosaurs they are. I inherited the property with them, you know, so we all have to rub along together.'

He grimaced sympathetically. 'Not too easy, I should think. The old . . . um, Mr Rainbird seems a nice enough chap but your aunt is a bit fearsome, isn't she?'

'She's my cousin.' Tessa turned away to make the coffee. 'She's been a matron in a boys' school all her life.'

'I should have guessed.'

He studied her, wondering how far this might lead. She was wearing a denim mini-skirt and a T-shirt and, as he watched her moving about, the excitement increased.

'So.' She turned round so suddenly that she caught his eyes on her legs and once again she smiled that intimate knowing smile. 'Making a valuation?' she asked provocatively.

He burst out laughing, throwing his hands up to signify that she'd scored a hit. 'I admit it. Should I apologise?'

She shrugged, pushing his coffee towards him. 'That depends on the valuation.'

'Out of my league.' He pretended despondency. 'I've known it all along really.' He sighed. 'But you can't blame me for trying.'

'Oh, I don't.' She leaned her elbows on the table, mug in her hands and stared at him. 'I'm wondering how truthful I can be with you.'

He pulled down the corners of his mouth. 'That sounds very serious. Totally, I hope.' He conjured up the sympathetic interest he reserved for the Mrs Carringtons. 'Got a problem?'

'Uh-huh.' She nodded. 'Between you and me – and not a word to my old dinosaurs – I have quite a serious financial problem. I . . . Well, the truth is, I was led to believe that the house in the cove was going to be left entirely to me and I borrowed against my expectations. I won't go into why, for the moment, but you can imagine my horror when the two old fossils turned up on the doorstep.'

'Sure.' He watched her, fascinated. 'So . . .' He hesitated. 'So how can I help?'

'Do you want to help?'

'Certainly,' he said swiftly. His heart knocked against his breast. 'Do you have any suggestions?'

'It's already occurred to you that I go to many places where there are odd items of furniture that are up for grabs. You offered me commission . . . ?'

'Certainly,' he said again. 'That would be only right and proper. But I thought that you were rather upset the last time I mentioned it.'

'I wasn't on the ball that day,' she admitted. 'I'd just got engaged and it seemed that my problems were over. Well.' She shrugged. 'He's changed his mind.'

'Must be mad,' said Adrian softly. He let her see how much she attracted him. 'Not looking for a replacement, are you?'

'Why not?' The old provocative look was back. 'I'm a firm believer in mixing business with pleasure.'

He laughed. 'I should like to apply for the post. Where do we start?'

'I'm afraid,' she said, 'that we start with the business. This commission . . .'

'Well.' He thought quickly about the least he could afford commensurate with keeping her on the hook. 'Shall we say a percentage of the profit? Ten percent?'

'You mean the real profit?'

He stared at her. 'Well, of course.'

'You see,' said Tessa, smiling, 'I could sell those pieces at the cove myself, couldn't I? I have to be sure that it's going to be worth going in with you, don't I? If I sell the things at the cove I have to split three ways. Of course, they trust me . . .'

'I'm not quite with you.' He frowned a little. 'I can understand that you may want to dispense with me as middle man but you'd have to get rid of the pieces somehow.' He hid his panic at the thought of losing the profit. 'You see what I'm getting at? Whoever sells it for you will have to take a cut.'

'True.' She nodded. 'But then *they* might offer us the real value.'

Her eyes smiled coolly into his and he felt a lurching sensation in his stomach. 'I don't . . . quite understand.'

'Don't you?' Her eyebrows lifted. 'Let me be clearer. I could sell those pieces at the cove without telling the old ducks their real value. I could give them a bit but they won't have any idea of the profit I should make. But that cuts you out and if we're going to be partners I'd want to start fair.'

He decided to bluff it out. 'I'm still not with you.'

'Pity.' She pushed her mug aside and stretched back in her chair. 'I really thought you might be up to playing it straight for a moment. You see I'm not just thinking short term. I know a lot of people we could . . . help.'

Adrian was silent. If only he could be certain that she really knew the truth; if he could trust her. The golden eyes watched him coldly; presently she began to chuckle.

'You've disappointed me,' she said. 'I thought you were in a different class.'

For some reason this stung him. 'I'm not saying I'm not prepared to deal,' he said slowly, 'but it's a big step.'

'It certainly is.' She was still smiling. 'Who wants to share a profit of five thousand pounds?'

'Five thousand . . . ?'

She pursed her lips. 'Give or take. Isn't that what you stand to make on the Regency writing table you've offered my cousin four hundred pounds for? And that nice eighteenth-century stick-back armchair? Fifty quid, was it?' She was laughing openly now. 'How much did you get for Mrs Carrington's bureau? And that little Georgian chest? Come on.' She leaned across the table and touched his hand. 'I know lots of Mrs Carringtons. You should see the Queen Anne walnut tallboy upstairs. Don't look so worried. I shan't be greedy. After all, *you* have to get rid of the stuff.'

He was still too badly shaken to respond easily and she squeezed his hand encouragingly. 'I . . . may have misjudged a few items,' he began.

'Oh, for goodness' sake,' she said impatiently. 'Look, let's forget it. I'll arrange to get rid of the pieces from home. Now you've so kindly valued them Will and Bea won't expect much. I shall make a good profit and it will go a long way to sorting me out. It just seems a bit short-sighted, that's all, but I don't blame you. And you've got your girl in your London office to square, haven't you? Myra, isn't it?' She shook her head at him. 'Who else knows that it's a dingy little room, up four flights in a back street?

All that knitting she gets through! Is it your baby she's expecting?'

'OK.' He stood up, frightened but fighting to stay in control. 'So you've checked it all out, have you?'

She smiled at him. 'What did you expect? I don't go into things blind. Myra had no idea she was being checked. She thought that I was looking for a friend who was supposedly living in the building. Look,' suddenly she was serious again. 'Let's just forget it, Adrian. I understand how you feel but I hoped we might be able to get together, in more ways than one.'

He looked down at her and she shrugged and crossed her legs. He began to smile a little, beginning to feel that he might trust her after all.

'Perhaps,' he said slowly. 'Perhaps you've got an idea.'

'Oh, I've got plenty of ideas,' she said suggestively – and hesitated, looking up at him. 'Is it your baby?' she asked.

The change of tone, some note of – what was it? Could it be jealousy? – gave him a much-needed surge of power. His confidence came back and he grinned at her. 'Not as far as I'm concerned,' he said. 'So. Where do we start this new partnership.' His eyes moved over her. 'What about this tallboy upstairs?'

She laughed at him. 'First things first. Let's talk about ways and means. I'm not as experienced as you are –' he raised his eyebrows – 'in *antiques*. Tell me how we go about it.'

He perched on the end of the table. 'You look over the things and get the lie of the land. Go for the oldies. Find out if there's a cash shortage. If there is, you bring me in when you're on your own so that I can have a good scout round. Even with the *Antiques Roadshow* on TV every Sunday it's amazing how gullible people are. I suggest that we use the ploy of the leaflet through the door so that no one suspects the connection. You leave one behind. I can cover my tracks. Not so easy for you. But don't worry. I stay well within the letter of the law.'

She stared thoughtfully at the table. 'Sounds OK. How do I know you won't cheat on me? I can't check every piece thoroughly.'

'I won't cheat. Why should I?' He hauled her to her feet. 'Why should I risk the goose who lays the golden eggs. And talking of lays . . .'

He bent to kiss her but she held him off. 'Sure it's not your baby? She spoke of you with great affection.'

'That's her problem.' He strained her towards him.

'Hang on!' He swung round sharply at the sound of the voice behind him and blinked into the flash. 'Thanks.' Giles quickly took another photograph as Adrian gaped at him and smiled as he lowered his camera. 'Nice one,' he said and frowned. 'Good God,' he said slowly. 'Andy Petersen.'

'Andy . . . ?' Tessa moved away from Adrian and folded her arms across her breast. 'Who did you say?'

'His name's Andy Petersen,' said Giles. 'We were at university together. He had a nice little line in crime going even then. Same principle. Preying on the weak and vulnerable.'

After one exclamation, Adrian Pearson stood still and watchful. 'Giles Webster,' he said scornfully. 'Always so upright and boring. You've got nothing on me. Everyone has a free choice, remember. I've never made anyone do anything against their will. I suggest things; they respond. I don't force them. I never make a valuation, I offer what I think I can get for something. They don't have to accept.'

'How can you?' asked Tessa. She looked tense and distressed. 'How can you deliberately cheat people like Mrs Carrington? Or Will and Bea? You pretended to be so kind and sympathetic.'

'You put on a pretty good act yourself,' he reminded her. 'Quite the little tart, weren't you? So what are you going to do with the photographs? Send them to *Crimewatch* and make even bigger fools of yourselves.'

'No, no.' Giles set his camera on the table. 'I'm going to write an article about you and send it with the photograph to every paper that will carry it. Plus interviews and photographs of Mrs Carrington and Bea and Will. Good human interest. I can even write up one or two little memories of our university days. Remember Johnny Staines? Did you see that he hanged himself, he was so badly in debt? Well, I think it might be worth recording. What do you think?'

'I think you're the prig you always were. You honestly think anyone will print such rubbish?'

'Oh yes,' said Giles quietly. 'And so do you. You'll have to be careful when you knock on the next door, won't you? . . . Watch out!'

His warning was too late. Adrian pushed Tessa

out of his path and made a grab for the camera. Their hands reached it together and knocked it to the floor. As Giles bent to retrieve it, Adrian seized a chair and brought it down on the back of his head. Giles gave a grunt and toppled forward, cracking his forehead on the dresser and slumping to the floor. Adrian kneeled above him, pulling the camera from Giles's slack hands whilst Tessa tried to drag him away.

'You bastard!' she shouted at him. 'You absolute bastard. You've hurt him.'

'Get off, you silly bitch,' he muttered, thrusting her violently away from him.

Caught off balance she fell heavily and Adrian made a leap for the back door and, wrenching at the handle, disappeared.

'Just here,' said Sebastian. 'Oh. Looks like she's got visitors. Never mind. I can see her car up by the garage. Come on in and say hello.'

Rob pulled in just beyond the gate and they climbed out and strolled up the drive together.

'Nice spot,' said Rob appreciatively. 'Just on the edge of the moor here and handy for the town . . . Hello!' His voice changed. 'What the . . . ? Grab him, Seb!'

The man, who had come racing round from the back of the house, hesitated and swerved away but Rob, sprinting after him across the lawn, brought him down in a rugby tackle. Sebastian bent to pick up the camera which had shot from his grasp and hauled the man to his feet.

'Inside,' he said. 'Quick. Hang on to him, Rob. I want to check that Tessa's OK.'

They frogmarched him round to the back door at a run and pushed him inside.

'Christ!' Sebastian let go of the man's arm and dropped the camera on the table. 'What the hell's going on?'

Tessa stared up at him and her gaze went beyond him to Rob who had Adrian held in a half-nelson. 'You caught him,' she cried. 'Don't let him go. He hit Giles with a chair. I think . . .' her voice wavered, 'I think he's dead.'

'Have you called an ambulance?' Sebastian was on his knees beside Giles, reaching for his heart, his eyes on the gash across his forehead. He took the tea towel with which Tessa had been attempting to staunch the flow of blood. 'For God's sake, Tessa, stop wailing and call a bloody ambulance! And then get on to the police.'

As Tessa disappeared into the hall, Adrian struggled violently, swearing at Rob, who forced him down into a chair and grappled his arms behind him. 'Got something to tie him with?' he asked breathlessly.

'Here.' Sebastian grabbed Felix's lead and together they secured Adrian firmly.

Tessa came back. 'They're on their way,' she said and went back to crouch beside Giles.

'He's not dead,' said Sebastian. 'What the hell's been happening?'

'He's a con man,' said Tessa, her eyes fixed on Giles's pale face. 'He's been cheating old people. He tried it on Will and Bea and we decided to set him up to frighten him. He admitted it to me and then Giles appeared and took a photograph of him so that he could send it to all the papers as a warning. He

362

tried to get the camera and when Giles bent to pick it up he hit him with the chair.' She swallowed. 'He hit his head on the dresser as he went down. And then Adrian . . . Andy knocked me over and made a run for it.'

'What did you call him?' asked Rob curiously.

'He calls himself Adrian Pearson but Giles recognised him from university. His name's Andy Petersen.'

'Perhaps we should have taken him down to the hospital ourselves,' said Sebastian, watching Giles. 'How long will they be?'

'I don't know. The hospital's not far away.' Tessa stared up at him, her eyes full of tears. 'Do you think he'll . . . ? Oh God. It was all my fault, you see. I couldn't bear to see him getting away with it. Conning these old people like Mrs Carrington. It was my idea to set him up. Oh, Giles.' Her lips shook and holding his limp hand tightly she pressed it to her cheek and burst into tears.

Sebastian stared down at her thoughtfully and then glanced at Rob who looked uncomfortable. Adrian, his jaw set, stared at the table and tried surreptitiously to free his hands. There was silence except for Tessa's sobbing. The peal of the front doorbell made them all jump and Tessa looked quickly at Sebastian as Rob went out into the hall.

'I'm going with him to Derriford,' she said. 'You'll deal with . . . him, won't you?'

'The police will want a statement from you,' he told her. 'You'll have to tell them what happened.'

'I know. But they'll have to wait. I'm staying with Giles.'

'Yes,' he said gently. 'Yes, love. I can see that. Don't worry. I'll sort everything out.'

She continued to look up at him, Giles's hand still clutched in her own. 'Sorry,' she said. 'I'm sorry, Sebastian.'

He smiled reassuringly at her and touched her lightly on the cheek. 'Forget it,' he said. 'Don't worry. Everything will be OK, kiddo. Just trust your Uncle Seb.'

Chapter Thirty-two

Isobel put an empty cardboard box on the kitchen table and began to fill it with carefully wrapped plates. The cottage was being gradually stripped of Isobel's character and warmth. It was beginning to look now as it had looked four years ago when she had come to see it and Mathilda had shown her round. Thanks to Will she could remember Mathilda now with love and gratitude; the guilt was gone. Isobel wandered to the window and stared out at the sea which pounded across the beach, creaming over the sand, and sending spray high over the rocks. The autumn was here and the equinoctial storms would soon be upon them. She knew how terribly she would miss this view and the cove but she had made up her mind and nothing would detract her. Through a friend with whom Helen worked, they had heard that there was a part-time vacancy for an assistant at the local crèche and Isobel had immediately made an appointment to be interviewed for the post. She had been honest about her situation hoping that, once Helen's baby was born, the child could accompany her to work and, to her delight and surprise, she had been offered the job on those terms. She was much happier now that she had something of her own to look forward to, and the money would be useful, but it would be a wrench to leave all that she had come to love, here in the cove.

Isobel glanced at her watch. She had arranged to meet Pat with the other two bookshop assistants, Laura and Louise, for a farewell lunch and, abandoning the packing, she collected her bag and hurried out. As she drove through the familiar lanes to Kingsbridge she remembered how Bea and Will had reacted to her news. She knew that Bea thought her quite mad to give up her work and her home for her daughter. She was shocked that Helen had asked it of her and had been unconvinced by Isobel's attempts to reconcile her to a different point of view. To begin with, Isobel had found it difficult to come to terms with the idea of sacrificing her own life for Helen's and, at first, it was almost wholly guilt which had persuaded her that she must support her daughter. Later she thought about it more carefully. It was no more selfish of Helen to make such a request than it had been of Isobel to leave husband and daughter to pursue her own idea of happiness.

'Like mother, like daughter,' she had muttered disconsolately to herself. 'Except that I was forty-two and Helen is only twenty-one.'

Bea's reaction had made it much more difficult to be confident about her decision and even Will, whom she had counted on for comfort and support, had been strangely reticent. She remembered that afternoon clearly. Helen had gone back to Modbury when Will and Bea arrived home from their day in Tavistock. She had given them time to get indoors and, unable to keep it to herself any longer, had gone hurrying over.

'But it's madness, my dear.' Bea had stared at her in consternation across the Georgian breakfast table. 'You can't be expected to give up everything. There are excellent crèches and nurseries now for working mothers.'

'But she needs me!' Isobel had cried. 'Can't you see that if I let her down now I shall never have a relationship with her? This is my chance to make up for abandoning her. And be fair, Bea! Surely it must be better for a baby to be with its grandmother than with strangers. It's a bit different when it's three or four years old but a new baby . . . ?'

'I should have thought a new baby would find it easier than a three-year-old,' Bea had said stubbornly. 'It knows nothing at that stage. It should be able to adapt to anything.'

Isobel had looked helplessly at Will. Even now, three months on, she remembered the look of shock on his face. She had been surprised; surely Will was too broad-minded to be so deeply affected by Helen's lapse.

'Will?' she'd said pleadingly. 'What do you think? Am I mad? She's frightened, you see. She's got no one to turn to. She *needs* me.'

'Yes,' he'd answered quietly. 'I quite understand that. It was you that I was thinking of . . .'

'I know.' She'd smiled at him gratefully. 'But I wouldn't be able to live with myself if I refuse her. I let her down badly when I went off with Mike and, now that Simon's got Sally, I think that Helen really feels that she's on her own.'

'It must be very frightening for her,' he'd said quietly.

He had sighed heavily as he turned away to feed Sidney and she'd suddenly realised that he would miss her. She had been so taken up with Helen's news and the shock of it all that, for a moment, she had completely failed to understand his sadness.

'I shan't be far away,' she'd said consolingly. 'Bristol's not far. I shall come and see you. I'll bring the baby.'

'When will you go?' asked Bea. 'As soon as the baby is born? When is it due?'

'At Christmas,' said Isobel, her eyes still on Will's back. 'But I shall go before then. She'll get dreadfully tired, working full time. I can help her then.'

'But what if the baby should . . .' Bea hesitated.

'If she loses the baby or there's a problem, she'll need me more than ever,' Isobel had said firmly. 'I've got no choice,' she'd cried at Will's back. 'Please try to understand. I don't *want* to do this. Please help me.'

He'd turned round at that, putting Sidney's bowl on the floor and smiling at her. 'Of course we understand,' he said. 'We just don't want to lose you. And I think that Bea is simply trying to make sure you've thought it all through. That's all.'

'I haven't had time to take it all in properly,' admitted Isobel. 'But I feel quite sure that I must help her.'

A few days later, Tessa had telephoned to say that their plan for unmasking Adrian Pearson had gone badly wrong and that Giles was in hospital with a split head and concussion but at least Adrian had been detained by the police and his scheme exposed. The anxiety that followed this had, to some extent, taken Isobel out of the spotlight. Bea and Will had hurried off to see Tessa and visit Giles in Derriford Hospital and, when they returned, told her that Tessa had broken her engagement with Sebastian and was now engaged to Giles. Confusion reigned for a few days and Isobel had almost welcomed the opportunity to suspend her own anxieties in lieu of Tessa's. Giles recovered, Adrian was charged with assault and serenity was restored to the cove.

Meanwhile, Isobel carefully considered her own situation and finally came to the conclusion that her first decision was the right one. Through the following months she never changed her mind and, as the days passed, a sense of excitement had grown in her. She began to look forward to the change in her life and went to Bristol to see Helen in the flat. Isobel had taken one look at Helen's tired, anxious face and set out to cheer and amuse her; she made plans for the future and rearranged the flat and presently Helen had been able to join in, becoming more positive and even excited. Encouraged, Isobel had made light of the lack of space and money, making it all seem like a delightful adventure. By the time she left she was confident that she was doing the right thing for both of them. Her own old feelings of futility were gone; she felt needed, useful, happy. The expression on Helen's face, when she told her that she'd been offered the job and would be moving to Bristol as soon as she could, was all that she needed as a reward.

The farewell lunch at Orchard's in Fore Street was a heart-wrenching business. She knew that she would miss her hours in the bookshop. Her friends were full of sympathy and encouragement but as she drove out along the embankment, slowing down on Bowcombe Bridge to stare out over the estuary, she knew a moment of terror. The boats rocked gently at their moorings and the golden light of late afternoon washed the quiet scene with a soft hazy glow. Two swans glided silently on the rippling water and, on the foreshore, someone had lit a bonfire. The sharp scent of smoke drifted in the autumn air and Isobel felt nostalgia tug at her heartstrings. How could she bear to leave this place for a small flat in a busy city?

She drove on slowly, bumping down the track, and parking as usual behind the house. She stood for some time, watching the tide sweeping in, listening to the mournful crying of a gull, remembering Mathilda. For some reason she began to feel soothed. Her fear gradually diminished and hope took its place. In her mind's eye she saw the slight figure, with her gleanings bag on her arm; remembered the keen look of the slate-blue eyes; heard the clear precise voice.

'*And did you find happiness?*'

'Oh, Mathilda,' said Isobel aloud. 'I think that this time I might just be in with a chance.'

Tessa and Giles said goodbye to the Perrymans, who had been admiring her ring whilst she and Giles drank their coffee, left the Roundhouse and drove up on to the moor. Charlie Custard lounged in the back of Tessa's car, wondering if he might be allowed a walk. He was bored by the comings and goings of Giles at Freddie's. He preferred to have Tessa's attention all to himself and none of this hugging and carrying-on generally. He sighed deeply and leaned heavily against the side window.

'Nearly there, Custard,' said Tessa cheerfully and swung into a narrow lane made brilliant by the glowing colours of the beech leaves now in full autumn splendour. The red rays of the sun slanted low through the woods and the cold wind scattered the fallen leaves across the lane. Tessa parked and she and Giles climbed out, pulling on coats. They released Charlie Custard, who jumped out and ran to sniff about. Giles held out a hand to Tessa who took it, grinning up at him. He shook his head.

'I'm still getting over it,' he said. 'If it hadn't been for Andy you'd be married to Sebastian now and far away in Washington.'

'Don't talk about it.' She shivered and held his hand tighter. 'And he was so fantastic about it, saying that he'd got cold feet himself. It's worked out so well. The Andersons have been so kind and understanding. Oh, Giles. Aren't we lucky? Look! There's a leaf falling. Quick. Catch it. It's a year's good luck if you catch a falling leaf. Damn!'

The leaf twirled gently away, eluding her frantic snatches at it. Giles laughed and began to run after her as the wind sent an eddy of leaves whirling across the lane. Charlie Custard, surprised at such behaviour, began to bark. He danced about, getting in the way, and Tessa, breathless with laughter, reached up for a leaf and fell over his back. They stumbled together, falling on to the verge, and Charlie Custard scrambled up and shook himself, shocked at such disrespect. Giles hauled Tessa to her feet and kissed her.

'I've got a ready-made family,' she told him happily. 'Kate and David, Guy and Gemma. Not to mention dear old Bea and Will. And now that Isobel's off to Bristol, we can have the cottage. I shall miss her but she's promised to come back often. I think it's a brilliant idea to convert the top of the boathouse into a darkroom for you. It's going to be such fun.'

'We'll be like Mum and David,' he said, putting an arm about her as they strolled after Charlie Custard. 'Divided between Devon and London.'

'It'll be fun,' she said again. 'I shall keep my favourites, though. Mrs Carrington and Freddie. And Kate, of course.'

He held her closer, too happy to speak, and she fell silent, remembering her terror when she thought she'd lost him for ever. Another gust of wind shuddered through the trees and she reached up towards the leaves.

'OK,' he said, resigned. 'One each and one for Custard. Come on.'

They began to run, their shouts echoing in the lane, their hands stretched upwards towards the leaves which floated down from the branches above them.

The Morris, with Isobel's hand waving madly from the window, disappeared up the track. Bea and Will stood for a moment looking after her and then glanced at each other. There was a faint feeling of constraint.

'Well,' said Bea. 'I'm sure we shall be seeing her often.'

'Yes,' said Will. He bent to pat Sidney's head and then straightened his shoulders. 'Cold wind. Think I'll go and check the fire.'

'Good idea.'

They went inside together and Will went upstairs, followed by the faithful Sidney. Bea stood silently beside the sink, aware of Will's unhappiness and wondering how to help him. She had realised, quite quickly after the meeting with Helen, that Will's feeling for Isobel was, after all, more than a paternal affection. It had come as a shock but very soon she had been able to feel compassion for him. Occasionally a burst of irritation might sweep over her at the thought of it but she was too fond of him by now to be very sharp-tongued. She knew that Isobel had never viewed Will in that light and this private certainty increased her compassion and made her kind.

She was sure that Will would come to terms with Isobel's absence; he was too positive, too cheerful a man, to allow himself to become bitter. There was something ridiculous in an elderly man falling in love with a much younger woman, and Bea knew that Will was aware of this and that the knowledge helped him to hide any emotions which might damage his self-respect. Sighing to herself, she began to assemble some tea. Toast by the fire and a game of Scrabble might help to console him.

'No fool like an old fool,' she told herself. 'But it doesn't mean that it hurts less.'

Will, standing on the balcony, staring out over the sea, would have agreed with her. He had tried to

conceal his disappointment from both Isobel and
Bea but he suspected that he had not done too well.
The shock had been too great and the thought of
losing Isobel filled him with unhappiness. It had
been a relief to concentrate on Tessa and Giles and
the court case against Adrian Pearson but the pain
had been there, gnawing away in the background.
He knew now that she would never have married
him, that it had been a moment of Indian summer
madness on his part, but the knowledge that she
was gone from the cove, that he would never hear
her voice calling from the kitchen or see her wandering on the beach, was hard to bear.

For Bea's sake he tried to pull himself together.
There was still so much to be grateful for and Bea's
companionship was very important to him. He
wondered if it were the genes they had inherited
from old John Rainbird which were responsible
for the ease they found together. He thought of
Mathilda, living peacefully here in the cove, and
wondered if she had known love. For some reason
the knowledge of her life here, the use of her
belongings, a sense of her presence, brought him
comfort and he took a deeper breath and raised his
head. She, too, had stood here, holding this balustrade, listening to the boom of the surf against the
shelving sand . . .

When Bea came into the room behind him,
carrying the tray, he was able to come in from the
balcony and smile at her with real happiness. He
looked with pleasure around the room, at the two
chairs pulled up to the hearth, the Scrabble board
on the low table between them, and at the blue and

yellow flames that danced over the bone-white salty wood. He took comfort from Mathilda's books on the bookshelves and her bureau in the alcove and the security of the house all about him. He saw that Bea was watching him and laughed a little.

'Ever feel that she's here?' he asked her. 'Old Mathilda? I get the feeling of her sometimes, d'you see? It's . . . comforting.' He chuckled at the expression on Bea's face. 'Crazy? Is that what you think?'

'Possibly.' Bea went to fasten the window and draw the curtains, concealing her delight at the genuine expression of contentment on his face. 'Probably. But for someone bordering on senile dementia you play a mean game of Scrabble. Best out of three games and the loser does the washing-up. Have you seen the toasting fork . . . ?'

Evening advanced across the darkening water. The moon rose above a ragged wrack of black cloud, pouring its cold brilliance down upon the cove where the waves rushed in over the sand and the only sound was the eternal murmurings of the restless sea.

Winning Through

Marcia Willett

It's nearly thirty years since the Chadwick siblings arrived at The Keep in Devon to live with their grandmother Freddy. And while much has altered since then, The Keep remains a sanctuary for the whole family; warm, un-changing, filled with love.

Now mistress of The Keep, Fliss finds it hard to fill the place of her beloved grandmother, especially when she has so many doubts in her life. Mole has settled into his second family, the Navy. And Susanna, always the baby, is now a wife and mother herself. But whatever challenges they face, the family know that the house and its residents will always be there, ready to welcome them home.

Following on from *Looking Forward* and *Holding On*, *Winning Through* concludes the story of the delightful and unforgettable Chadwick family.

Praise for Marcia Willett's previous novels:

'A genuine voice of our times' *The Times*

'A fascinating study of character . . . A cleverly woven story with lots of human interest' *Publishing News*

'A very readable book' *Prima*

'Rich characterisation here, and not a little humour, too' *Manchester Evening News*

'Poignantly told, with fine characterisation and a lavish sprinkling of humour' *Evening Herald*

0 7472 5998 4

headline